An easy to read and interest grabbing book! While fiction, it is easy to see something like this happening. It makes you wonder if you shouldn't start "preparing" for such a catastrophic event... Highly recommend. The last book I tried to read I could only read for half an hour before needing a break. I read this in two nights. I found it to be one of those where you want to know how it ends and cannot wait to find out.

- Dan D. Goodreads -

"2051" is a must read! It is definitely a page-turner with many twists. I would highly recommend it to anyone, and not just because the author is my father-in-law! "2051" takes a glimpse at what life in the USA would be like were it to be invaded by another country, and all the trials and tribulations that go along with that. Human nature shines through in many different ways, but you'll have to read it to see! Thanks, Dan, for an amazing story!

-Gina Peavler

I enjoyed the three books of 2051. I couldn't put them down.

The author's research was extensive, and the story is imaginative.

-Steven Sievert

Wow. This book shook me up a little. As a currently serving citizen Soldier, this hits on some fears I didn't know I had. We are now in an interwar period without a clear threat to be preparing to face. The American public has not taken the Russian chaos machine's influence on our social media and election seriously. We do not see how China is using our economic reliance on them to further its expansion. If things go wrong, the setting for this book could become real.

- Goodreads review

2051

Books 1 - 3

War on American Soil

By Dan Peavler

What would your family do
if foreign powers used gangs
to paralyze American cities
and the heartland?

What would your family do
If EMPs knocked out power
and society was on the
brink of chaos?

September 2049: Colonel Deb Lisco warns the Pentagon brass about pending threats to the security of the country from foreign enemies. They do not act on her warnings, but she does. She, along with her nephew Bill, create a safe haven in eastern Colorado where family and friends can shelter during the turbulence of the war she knows is coming.

October 2051: American cities are invaded by foreign insurgents utilizing EMPs to knock out power, while homegrown rebels, on their payroll, fight the citizens to take control.

2051 is a novel about the Lisco family, who work together with friends, as the unthinkable happens, War on American Soil. It is a tale of the strength and resolve of the family as they struggle to endure the escalating threats. It becomes apparent that everyone will need to fight as the danger grows in ferocity and magnitude from enemy forces attacking from Mexico across the southern border.

The passion and fighting spirit of Colonel Deb is illustrated as she battles to save the country from the approaching enemies, as her brother, Colonel Ted Lisco, fights the insurgents. Brothers Jon and Hank, along with the rest of the family and friends work to protect the farm and people who live there. The encounters the family have with strangers show the best and worst of the human spirit.

2051 Books 1-3 contains the three books of the trilogy.

Praise for 2051

2051 is a fast-paced and engaging read. I was immediately pulled into the story and drawn to the characters. It's an inspiring story of how people can come together to support one another during the most trying times.
~Stephanie Panion

I read all three books in the series and couldn't wait for each to come out. Dan has an amazing ability to portray people, from the young Maddie to older people in the story, all are believable. His respect for women and for family shines through, as well as his sense of humor. The books are well researched and definitely worth reading.
~Debbie Stewart

Great easy reading book. I had a hard time putting it down. Love that the book talked about cars, trucks and guns from the past. Then what the future guns, cars and trucks may look like in 2051. Book presents women advancing in future and how the love of family helps keep everyone in the family safe. You see why we need a strong community to survive in disaster. Need for people to open up their hearts to create this community. Remembering that accepting all people and forgiveness is needed for a community to be formed and this community then is more powerful than its numbers suggest.
- Mary Pint -

Books 1, 2 and 3 Copyright 2021 - 2022

Paperback ISBN: 978-1-953686-23-7
eBook ISBN: 978-1-953686-24-4

Library of Congress Control Number: 2023935918

Living Springs
Publishers

WWW.LivingSpringsPublishers.com

Dedication

This book is dedicated to my father, Henry Elmer Peavler, and my father-in-law John Milet.

You can read about these amazing World War II veterans at the end of the book.

Acknowledgements

A huge thanks to my sister Jacqueline Peavler and brother Hank Peavler for partnering with me to create Living Springs Publishers. Having their expertise and knowledge in publishing "2051" has been a blessing. Also, to my sister Debbie for her help as a sounding board for ideas.

I also wish to acknowledge the encouragement I received from my family while writing "2051". Having those you care about the most in life, being there for advice and honest critique, is priceless.

Main Character List

Lisco family
- Colonel Deb Lisco. sister
- Colonel Ted Lisco, brother
- Nicole Lisco, wife of Ted
- Bill Lisco, son of Nicole and Ted
- Maddy Lisco, daughter of Bill
- Lieutenant Colonel Jon Lisco, Retired, brother
- Gina Lisco, wife of Jon
- Hank Lisco, brother and high school coach
- Jacqueline Lisco, wife of Hank
- Bobby Lisco, son of Jacqueline and Hank

Jacoby family from Utah
- Ed and Irene, farmers from Utah.
- Aaron and Ashley, son and daughter-in-law
- Adam and Megan, son and daughter-in-law
- Seth, son of Adam and Megan
- Breanna, daughter

O'Brian family
- Jessica, mother of Emilee, Avery and Reagan
- Christian, father of Emilee, former football player of Hank, leader of homegrown rebels
- Emilee, daughter of Jessica and Christian and girlfriend of Bobby.
- Avery and Reagan, daughters of Jessica

Others

- Al Jones, dentist and his wife Linda, next door neighbors of Hank and Jacqueline
- Jason and Kori Jensen, carpenter and friends of Hank and Jacqueline
- Dave Jensen, son of Jason and Kori
- Samantha, flight attendant on plane that was forced to land in Utah.
- Travis, pilot on plane that was forced to land in Utah.
- Terrance and Jerry fled Utah with Ted
- George Saxton, assistant football coach.
- Tim, ex-football player of Hank, homegrown rebel.
- Sherry, rebel who originally came to farm with Christian.
- Caroline Sanchez, attack victim
- Julia, physician assistant and her husband Fred Hamilton.
- Harold Hamilton, bricklayer and his wife Becky.
- Captain Irving Huang, Retired, served under Jon.

Book 1 Prologue

Pentagon, Arlington County Virginia
September 2049

Colonel Deb Lisco marched quickly down the long corridor at the Pentagon, with a slight limp, a full step ahead of her older brothers, Lt Col. Jon Lisco and Colonel Ted Lisco. The two warriors struggled to keep up with her. Neither of them agreed with the assessments about the threat to the country their sister had formulated. Nevertheless, family tradition warranted their support. For the previous six months she had messaged and called the office of General Ron McClinton Chief of Staff of the Army, requesting a summit. The new generation of the army encouraged discussion from the ranks, something Colonel Lisco planned to use to the best of her abilities. To her great surprise a meeting with General McClinton was granted.

The room they entered was intimidatingly large. The table at the center was intended for use by larger audiences. Colonel Deb pulled out the chair directly across from the Chief of Staff, who was flanked by a general on each side, both brothers sat to her right.

Ted was a very handsome man with a bronze colored, tanned face. He served under General McClinton in 2037, during the conflict in East Africa. His presence alone gave Deb authentication. Jon was a smaller, more compact version of Ted, whose demeanor conveyed confidence, to the point many people considered him to be brash.

"Colonel Lisco, there have always been threats to the homeland. Why have you been inundating my office with messages that the threat has escalated?" General Ron McClinton asked, quickly, after allowing the colonel to sit in her chair.

"Sir, an accumulation of information." Deb held her prominent jaw straight out and focused her attention on the general. "I believe we are nearing an invasion from foreign enemies."

Both brothers held their breath. They knew Deb was going to make extraordinary assertions. They thought, or at least hoped, she would make a case for her beliefs first.

"There is no indication of an unusual escalation of foreign troops anywhere around the world," stated General McClinton. "Please tell us what brings you to this conclusion."

Deb hesitated for a moment to gather her thoughts. She was in full dress uniform with a chest full of medals. She had been stabbed, shot and blown up during her military tenure. She was one tough soldier who understood the horrors of war, but her success, not only surviving, but flourishing in the military system came from her tactical and strategic abilities. She was also a brilliant student, who breezed through the educational aspects required to rise to the rank of colonel.

"My father…" Deb hesitated and motioned to her brothers. "Our father, once told us that he could take America with five hundred American Special Operation Forces."

"Are you suggesting that American Special Forces are planning an attack?" interrupted General McClinton.

"No sir. Absolutely not." Deb had the full attention of everyone at the table. "These are foreign infiltrators who want to change our way of life."

"Colonel," interjected General Hodge "what intelligence do you have that we don't?" General Hodge was greatly respected by Deb, and almost every other soldier in the army. His droopy eyes, and white hair made him seem much more docile than he really was.

"Nothing, sir. I'm just putting two and two together," said Deb, using a very calm tone, an attribute she had practiced with her brothers prior to the meeting.

"I've examined much of what you have messaged over the past several months," General McClinton spoke with a firm tone. "I've agreed to hear you out this morning, but we do need you to be very specific."

"Thank you, sir." Deb stood and placed her notes on the table. "In 2047 DTRA found no significant increase in biological, radiology, chemical or nuclear dangers to the homeland, from any time over the past twenty years. But in the past three years there has been a massive increase in EMP related threats." Deb made eye contact with General McClinton. "There were five separate incidents where hand-held EMP weapons were located and seized. The weapons were found in Redding, California; Billings, Montana; Hays, Kansas; Jonesboro, Arkansas and Colorado Springs, Colorado. At the Colorado, Springs location, along with the EMP weapon, a manpad was appropriated, which according to DARPA, is smaller and more potent than any known portable air defense weapon in our arsenal. But most significant of all, found with the weapons was a dossier describing a new weapon using nanotechnology capable of destroying satellites."

"We've spent billions of dollars to shield electromagnetic threats. It might be a trillion dollars since 2025," stated General Hodge in a much louder voice than required. "Space Force has spent another trillion dollars on countering robotic weaponized satellites. For more than fifty years anti-satellite technology has stayed in lock step and countered all threats toward disabling our satellite assets."

"Yes sir. But since the inception of satellite technology there has never been an actual attack on a satellite by an enemy. Many threats, but never an attack." Deb never flinched as she shuffled through her notes. "According to the dossier found in Colorado, the weapon is capable of withstanding any counter measures by our satellites defense systems. The carrier of the weapons relies on having itself being destroyed, in order to release millions of nano robotics, used to terminate the satellite."

"Colonel, we are all aware of the threats posed by advanced robotics," stated General Hodge. "We have had many rigorous debates on this subject. Since its inception nanotechnology has been nothing but positive for this country. As well as the entire world."

"This is what concerns me so greatly. There are people who want to take the technology we use to clean the oceans and make us healthier, to destroy our way of life."

General Hodge looked at General McClinton skeptically. He shook his head.

"Continue Colonel Lisco," said General McClinton, taking in a full breath.

"According to DARPA the EMP weapons found are different from any technology we have in our arsenal. They were not made by us."

"A citizen can research the internet to find specific instructions on building an EMP gun," stated General Prost. Of the six soldiers in the room, General Prost was the only one without actual combat experience. She was very petite, but her judgement held a great amount of influence within the United States Army. Deb was warned by both Ted and Jon to be careful in her dialogue with this General.

"Not like the weapons confiscated," stated Deb. Although she had never met face to face with General Prost, she knew her beliefs were in sharp contrast with her superiors concerning the future of the military, and the country. She realized it was important to mask these disagreements and focus on the issue at hand. "These are highly technical built, military grade weapons."

"Where were they made?"

"Germany."

"Germany." The general looked surprised. "If threat reduction and research would have found these weapons to be substantial, I'm sure they would have issued warnings."

"The information is in a file cabinet somewhere. It is their decision to do with it as they deem appropriate," stated Deb sharply.

General McClinton remained silent. He was gentle and fair but was also a no-nonsense leader. He was the third African American to be the Chief of Staff of the Army. The fact that he was a soldier with actual combat experience was the main reason for the audience with Colonel Lisco. He respected her, but even more so he respected the more than a hundred years of service from the Lisco family. He believed she deserved to be heard.

"I refer to these weapons as Radical Electromagnetic Pulse Weapons." Deb inadvertently looked at her brothers, knowing they advised her not to create terminology. "Besides the five recovered weapons, there have been over seventy-five reported incidents of literature found, mostly in large cities They range from simply mentioning all the way to specific operation instructions of the REMP."

"How in the world does any of this translate to a pending attack on America?" General Prost asked skeptically.

It drove Deb crazy the way General Prost held her top teeth out, wrinkled her nose and squinted her eyes. It was a phony charade created by her to appear as though she was introspective and thoughtful. She knew coming into the meeting the lady was going to be problematic. Her contemptuous attitude was starting to rub Deb the wrong way.

"If I may continue?" Deb waited for a moment and forced a smile. "Besides the growing EMP threat found last year, there has been a nearly nine hundred percent increase, from the previous year, in arrests, not reported incidents, but arrests concerning high explosives. These…"

"Ma'am, I want to indulge you," interrupted General Prost, using a superior tone, "as noted, we have Space Force, Defense Threat Reduction, Advance Research, Logistic, Intelligence and many more agencies all working hard to protect our homeland. None of them have even mentioned, much less made any of this a high priority."

"There are large holes in our security," yelled Deb, glancing at her brothers. Her eyes were olive colored with heavy, dark eyebrows some had described as cat like.

Both Jon and Ted remained stoic. All they could do was hope their sister did not contravene the authority of her superior.

"How does having more high explosives translate into war on our soil?" General McClinton asked, noticing the growing animosity between the general and the colonel.

"Sir, they are going to do it the cowboy way."

"Pardon."

"They are going to blow up our infrastructure the old-fashioned way, with explosives." Deb felt her blood pressure rising. "We are vulnerable. There are absolutely no viable federal rules to protect our utilities."

"The discussion about the economics of protecting the infrastructure has been debated for years," said General Prost gruffly. Colonel Lisco was wasting her time with absurd information. "There have been weather related issues and a few incidents of vandalism but never an attack."

"Colonel, why are you alluding to these issues at this time?" General McClinton asked, sensing General Prost's frustration.

"Our government, along with private industry, recently finished spending twenty-five years, and several trillion dollars on the infrastructure, changing much of it to sustainable energy. But we didn't put in measures to protect it. The entire country could lose power for months from simply having 120 high voltage substations and 50 solar sites destroyed. The REMP weapons will destroy much of the civilian equipment, because for the past twenty years we have taken steps back in protecting these technologies. Most cars in America are electric and haven't enough shielding for electromagnetic overload. This all could be a prerequisite and cover for an attack by a foreign enemy." Deb shuffled her feet. "And if the dossier is true, technology exists to destroy GPS, communication and surveillance. Crippling some of our military."

The generals looked at her as though she had left reality and was now reciting a conspiracy theory.

"Who?" General McClinton asked emphatically. "Who's going to invade?"

Colonel Deb swallowed hard. "I don't know sir."

"That is a big I don't know," stated General Prost.

"It could originate from Russia, China, Middle East or possibly, with all the private space ventures, someone not part of a government, maybe all of them. The main point I want to make is of our vulnerability." Deb thought how insignificant her presentation must seem to her superiors. "We are so divided as a country that our enemies are going to use Americans to destroy America. It's a fact that foreign money is coming in to finance many criminal factions across the country."

"Good Lord," cried General Prost. "This country has always been divided."

"We have no idea who is in our country. Our father suggested five hundred special forces taking out the country, we don't know, but maybe there are five thousand enemy special forces scattered across America. Or ten thousand." Deb narrowed her eyes and looked directly at General Prost. "Whoever is preparing to attack our country has finally realized our susceptibility of divisiveness. They are funneling in billions of dollars to fund gangs of disenfranchised people, many believing they are protesters of conformity and architects of revolution."

"We've survived wars and conflicts for nearly three hundred years," exclaimed General Hodge, his face flushed a deep red. "It's the price of freedom."

"Over the last thirty years robotics, automation and artificial intelligence has taken over our culture. In the late 20s, losing jobs was the biggest fear from robotics and artificial intelligence. After realizing jobs never disappeared, but simply changed, we embraced the technology. Now we are totally reliant on cybernetics, from paying a bill at a restaurant to checking out a book at the library. Even the old dogs on our farms lost their jobs wrangling cattle to drones. We don't realize our vulnerability."

Jon and Ted both realized that their sister was struggling to make a rational argument to the generals. She was now preaching, and implied they were doing a poor job in protecting America.

"Colonel, none of us here have our heads in the sand. What are you seeing that we are not?" General Prost asked.

"I'm seeing American citizens fighting for their lives as an invading force tries to conquer this great nation."

"We all worry about that every day," shouted General Prost, rising slightly out of her seat. "We have done a damn good job in protecting this country."

"Ma'am, in no way do I question anyone's duty or commitment." Deb decided she needed to change tactics from simply relating the threats she had observed, to unfolding the cause of the problems. General Prost was at the top of the list. "When my two brothers enlisted in the army there were nearly a million four hundred thousand active troops in the military. Today we have less than eight hundred thousand."

"The days of brigade versus brigade firefights are long gone. Today's army is much different than it was thirty years ago," stated General Prost, knowing the colonel's statement was directed at her belief in a smaller military.

"Or fifty, or a hundred years ago." Deb was almost mocking the general. "The new technology has increased so quickly that most of it is not protected adequately."

"No other agency has come to the same conclusions as Colonel Lisco." General Prost addressed her statement to General McClinton.

"Colonel, you are bringing actualities with political and economic considerations already known by our entire intelligence community." General McClinton stared at the purple heart on her chest. "We understand threats are real, but we have had no significant foreign terrorist acts on our soil for nearly fifty-years."

"Sir, that's what worries me. As a nation we are too complacent. We believe there is a global economic and cultural cohesiveness that really doesn't exist." Deb swallowed. "Gangs in every city in America have become more cutting-edge in communication and technology. Now we have a national gang that is enmeshed in illicit drugs, rather than the local community gangs of the past, These gangs would never be able to take control of our largest cities police forces, but they could cause enough mayhem for citizens to fight each other. It would be much different in smaller communities like the towns where the EMPs were discovered, they could overwhelm the police."

"The end of America because of a gang problem we have had for nearly a hundred years," General Prost statement rang to be condescending.

"It is one aspect." Deb's stare was chilling. They exchanged looks before she relaxed. "Americans pitted against Americans is the fuse they are going to use. Whoever it is planning to destroy our country figured this out, not today or even yesterday. They started many years ago. They have been financing this destruction of our American fiber of life with the idea of fighting us on our own soil."

General Prost tossed her pen on the papers in front of her, leaned back in her chair, squeezed her thin lips, and shook her head. She was finished with validating her subordinate's homily.

Ted reached his hand over and placed it flat in front of his sister, a warning for her to remain calm and not say something that would jeopardize her rank in the military. Deb leaned forward and placed both hands flat on the table. Ted leaned back in his seat.

"This problem is so big we can't even see it. Thirty years ago, half of the kids in high school were aware of a gang, now nearly all of them are approached by a gang recruiter. Legalizing drugs has turned the whole mess of frying people's brains into a commodity. The industry of helping these people morphed into a massive industry that will never go away. All financed by a smaller military and fewer police forces throughout the nation, replaced with counselors and so-called mental health professionals." Deb hesitated, this was not the direction she wanted the meeting to go.

"Colonel…," General McClinton attempted to interject.

Deb interrupted, "America will always endure and eventually make the correct decisions. With a little foresight, at this moment, we can, with a little extra security, eliminate targets ripe for picking by those who want to harm our way of life. I don't believe for a second that there is an enemy on this planet that can defeat us." Deb took in a deep breath, "but with all my heart, I feel we are about to be tested."

"Colonel Lisco, duly noted. I will personally ask threat reduction to reassess any information they have on the new EMP and portable air defense weapons." General McClinton stood up from his chair, and looked at Ted, indicating to Deb her presentation was over. "We very much appreciate seeing your brothers here to support you today. The United States Army will certainly miss them, and we wish them the best in retirement."

In her mind they basically told her to get the hell out, they had much more pressing and legitimate business to take care of. In actuality, the Chief of Staff took everything she said to heart. Homeland Security was aware of the uptick of spies and sleeper cells, over the previous ten years, from both Eastern Europe and China. Most of the activity dealt with stealing weapons and technology from high profile targets such as nuclear facilities. The scenario the colonel laid out of having thousands of infiltrators hiding in plain sight, embedded in communities across the country was unnerving. The process or the system was the problem. It would take many years and billions upon billions of dollars to implement anything that could make a dent in countering the issues she raised.

PART ONE

LAX, California

October 2051

Ted Lisco made a promise to himself on the red-eye flight from Denver to Los Angeles. With his retirement now in full swing he was going to enjoy every moment he had with his granddaughter. He had spent countless hours with Maddy, prior to his son Bill's divorce. Before she left for California to spend time with her mother Cindy, their time together was becoming routine. Although they were exceptional buddies, he never recognized how fleeting the time they had together was becoming.

His flight arriving at LAX was on schedule, giving him plenty of time to meet ex daughter-in-law Cindy, and help Maddy through security. Just before boarding he called his wife Nicole to tell her everything was going well with their granddaughter, and to remind his son Bill, after landing in Denver, they were planning to catch lunch, and meet everyone at the football game. He was already somewhat fatigued, having to get up in the middle of the night in order to check in at Denver International Airport to catch the flight to California.

As the plane prepared to take off for the journey home, he reached over and took hold of Maddy's hand. She smiled and squeezed. Although she was eight years-old, she knew grandpa wanted her to be worried about flying, or at least act like she was. Much of the time they had spent together was pretending of scary situations. They both looked out the window as the engine roared and the plane sped down the runway.

"We are taking off," said Ted, hoping this time would be one they remembered forever.

As the plane reached takeoff speed, Maddy leaned over from her middle seat to get a better view out the window. Her dark eyes sparkled as she watched the landscape rush by, until the accelerating airplane lifted off, causing her to sit back.

"Oh my gosh, how fast are we going?" She knew he would know, if not, he would make up some outlandish number. She was exceptional in math and would realize immediately he was kidding.

"I would guess around 320 kilometers per hour, now, but we will be going much faster shortly." The plane engine continued to wail as they moved into a roll-out angle, causing her to look straight ahead with some dismay.

Ted stared at her blonde hair, with two braids tied neatly at the back of her head. Her square jaw was very prominent, and her high cheekbones were red, probably from time spent at the beach. She looked so mature sitting with her back perfectly straight.

"Don't worry."

She turned to him, smiling, and said, "my ears just popped."

"Air pressure," said the older lady sitting in the aisle seat next to her.

"Yawn," suggested Ted.

"That's why I chew gum at take-off," explained the lady. "Would you like a piece?"

Ted enjoyed assessing people. It wasn't going out on a limb to assume the lady was a grandmother. The crow's feet which crept from the corners of her eyes told him that she was a thinker who had a passion for reading. She recently decided to allow her hair to go grey, most likely to avoid the chemicals from hair dyes. She was a woman of nature.

"Go ahead." Ted leaned forward in his seat. "I'm Ted Lisco, Colonel US Army, retired. This is my granddaughter Maddy. We are going back to Colorado."

Maddy accepted the gum, "Thank you."

"I'm also going to Colorado with my grandson Scotty." She leaned back allowing Maddy a glimpse of the little boy, who looked to be nine or ten years old. He had a big round face with freckles and was looking around his grandma, smiling. "Do you two have big plans for the weekend?"

"We are going to watch my cousin Bobby play football this afternoon," answered Maddy.

"They are playing for the state championship," stated Ted, "my brother is the head coach, so it's a pretty big deal for our family."

"That is exciting," said the old lady genially. It was obvious she was not a football fan.

"I'm sorry. I didn't catch your name," said Ted.

"I'm Carol, professor of history, retired." She smiled, turning slightly in her seat. "Maddy are you a good athlete like your cousin?"

"Oh, not as good. But I do like to run and dance."

"She is a very good dancer," interjected Ted.

"That's a good thing to be," said Carol, holding up her cell phone. "Scotty is exceptionally good with technology. He thinks it's funny how I would rather use an I-phone from thirty years ago, rather than all the newer gadgets."

"I'm the same way," said Ted.

"Look." Maddy pointed out the window at the dark clouds.

"They are beautiful." He leaned back in his seat to allow her to look around him. "Do you want to change seats so you can see better?"

Before Maddy could answer Ted noticed a quick flash of light over the horizon in front of the plane. To the other passengers it was not perceptible, or if noticed, thought to be a reflection from the sun.

Maddy just shook her head no. She enjoyed the security of being in the middle seat, looking past her grandpa.

Ted remained uncharacteristically quiet, staring out the window.

A flight attendant handed each of them a bag of pretzels. "What would you like to drink?"

Ted was unsure if he should allow Maddy to drink a soda.

"Soda," Maddy knew he wouldn't deny her a sugar drink on their special day.

As he prepared to order the soft drinks, Ted became aware of Carol's startled expression. Her mouth was wide open as she looked out the window past his head.

The sound of a jet flying over the top of the commercial airliner was deafening. The turbulence forced the plane to drop abruptly in altitude, causing the flight attendant to fall to her knees. She held onto the side of Carol's seat until the plane leveled off.

"What in the world was that?" Ted asked, grabbing Maddy's arm.

"It looked like some sort of military plane," yelled Carol, looking toward her grandson.

Before Ted could speak two more aircraft flew over the top. The plane shook in the turbulence of the powerful jets. He got a good enough look out the window to know they were F-22 Raptors.

Maddy was nearly in tears.

"Everyone put on your seatbelts." The pilot sounded shaken as he yelled the request.

"It's ok. Don't worry it's ok," said Ted to Maddy. "Make sure your seatbelt is tight."

Maddy touched her seatbelt. She had always felt completely safe around her grandfather, but now she was very frightened. She buried her face into his bicep as Ted squeezed her hand. Murmuring and screams from some of the other passengers filled the plane.

"I want my mom." Maddy looked up with tears in her eyes.

"We are going to be ok. I won't let anything happen to us." He placed his hand on her face and pulled her close. In his entire life he never experienced anything so much out of his control. It was breaking his heart that his granddaughter was next to him in this life-threatening situation. In thirty years of service in the army he never felt so helpless.

The plane continued to slowly drop in altitude without any further word from the pilot, before he finally stated, "I'm going to have to take the plane down."

Ted looked out the window at the barren landscape below. "Where is he going to land the plane?" he asked frantically.

Littleton, Colorado

Hank Lisco cradled a cup of coffee as he stared out the picture window in his living room. The leafless branches of the small trees in their front yard were swaying in the breeze. His wife Jacqueline shook her head and smiled. He had stayed up half the night talking football strategy with George Saxton, his good friend and assistant coach.

"I've never seen you so nervous before a game," she stated.

"It's not just a game. It's the state championship, and Bobby's last high school game." He made sure to emphasize high school game.

"You'll do great."

"I know it's going to be cold. I hope the damn wind doesn't blow any harder. We have a big advantage if we can pass the football."

"I hate to break it to you, big guy, it's not going to snow until the beginning of next week, but all the weather channels predict it's going to blow like a son of a gun today. So, you might want to think about how you are going to run the ball."

Hank smirked at Jaqueline. She had just made a change to her hairstyle, making it much shorter. He thought her jet-black hair looked incredibly good with the streaks of grey.

"What time do you want to eat pre-game?" Jacqueline asked.

"We need to get to the field by one, so I'd say eleven."

"Hey Pop," Bobby stepped into the living room and threw his duffle bag onto the sofa, "I say we throw the ball every down. Central thinks we will run because of the wind. Their defensive backs are really slow."

"Oh, I guess the Lions have a new head coach now." Jacqueline placed her arm around her son's waist. His powerful frame dwarfed her.

Bobby pulled his mother close, lifted her off the ground and gave her a tight squeeze.

Hank looked at the two of them acting like best of friends. He already had ten years of coaching under his belt when Bobby was born, football was a part of their DNA. He was more than fair in coaching his son. Bobby didn't start on the varsity until he was a junior, and he did so on his merit and abilities. Hank was starting to realize that the game today was going to be more emotional than he would have ever thought.

"Did Uncle Jon and Aunt Gina make it in last night from Texas?" Bobby asked. He looked at a message on his phone from his girlfriend Emilee and quickly messaged her back.

"Yep, they got in late and they insisted on staying in a hotel. I told them to stop by before the game," said Hank. "They decided on driving instead of flying."

Bobby looked at another message from Emilee. "This is odd."

"What is it?" Jacqueline asked.

"Emilee is having some sort of problem at the apartment." He shrugged his shoulders. "How about Uncle Ted?"

"His flight left California this morning, so he's hoping to be at the game on time."

"Boy does he love his little granddaughter. There was no way he was going to let Maddy fly from California by herself," exclaimed Jacqueline. "Nicole and Bill are going to come by and ride to the game with me."

"Terrible timing, Bill tried to get Cindy to let Maddy come back on Friday, but she wanted to be difficult." Hank rolled his eyes. "At least Deb was able to shuffle her schedule. She should be at the game by kick-off."

Of his three siblings, Colonel Deb was the one most protective of her little brother. Since their parent's deaths, she called at least weekly.

The phone rang.

"Her ears must have been ringing, It's Deb," Hank picked up the phone. "Well hello Colonel Deb. I'm putting you on speaker."

"Hank, I can't tell you how important it is to listen to what I am about to say." The seriousness of her tone was alarming. "You need to pack everything you can get into your truck and head to the farm, right now!"

"Hold up Deb. What are you talking about?" Hank looked at Bobby with an incredulous look on his face. "We have the state championship to play in less than six hours."

"Listen, you are not playing football today. I don't have much time. The communication towers are being destroyed. We are under attack," Deb sounded frustrated. "For God sake, turn on your television."

"Who's under attack?" The suddenness of Deb's remarks caused Hank to look at his wife with disbelief.

"America," Deb screamed into the phone.

Hank was speechless. He used the remote to turn on the television. His phone buzzed with more calls. Caller ID showed George Saxton, and other numbers he recognized as parents of his players. He ignored the calls.

"Are they showing DIA?" Jacqueline stared at the image of destruction on the television.

"I think so," stated Bobby.

"You need to get out of the city as quickly as possible," yelled Deb.

The blood drained from Hank's face, and he looked as though he was in shock.

"Listen Deb, I know you are concerned, but…"

"Has Ted got back from California?" she interrupted.

"No, he and Maddy should arrive later this morning."

Deb was silent.

"What's going on?"

"Is Jon with you?"

"Not yet, he and Gina drove all the way through last night and should be here any minute." Hank could hear commotion over the phone.

"I couldn't get ahold of him or Ted this morning." Deb's tone softened, "Please, please Hank, pack up and go to the farm. I will connect with you in a couple days."

"Deb, are we in immediate danger here?" Jacqueline spoke loudly so she could be heard over the speaker.

"Yes Jacqueline, they are going after us in ways I didn't even perceive," shouted Deb. "You need to load up and go. Everything you need to survive is at the farm."

Hank stood with a confused look on his face. The lights began to flash, and the electricity turned off.

"When you get to the farm you are going to…."

"The phone's dead." Hank froze as he contemplated the moment.

"My cell phone doesn't have reception either," stated Jacqueline. "Check your phone Bobby."

"Nothing," Bobby looked at his phone in disbelief, "what do we do?"

"I need to get ahold of George," replied Hank. "I have no way of contacting the players and parents?"

"I'm going to run to Dave's and see what they know," said Bobby.

"I think we should sit tight and figure out what is happening."

"He's only a block away."

"Ok, but there and back." Hank watched Bobby put on his coat. "Invite the Jensen's to come back with you."

"I'm going to check and see if Al and Linda have any more information." Jacqueline put on her coat and stepped out the door toward the neighbor's home.

Cedar City, Utah

The tires on the jumbo jet squealed as the pilot applied the brakes. The plane rolled to a stop with a jolt as the front wheels fell off the end of the runway into the soft ground. Pillars of smoke could be seen from several locations surrounding their landing location.

"I'm sure everyone wants some answers as to what is going on," shouted the pilot over the intercom. "All I can tell you at this time is that I was ordered, in no uncertain terms, to land the airplane. If everyone will hang tight for a moment I will see if I can sort things out."

Ted tried calling Nicole on his cell phone. There was no signal.

After a couple hours of sitting and waiting the passengers started complaining. The flight crew did their best to keep everyone hydrated but they also began to wonder why they had not left the plane.

"What are we doing?" Maddy asked.

"I'm not sure, but we are going to have to find a different way home. This plane will never be able to take off from this runway." Ted tried to remain calm.

"Where are we?" Carol looked out the window.

"I have no idea," said Ted dubiously, "the bigger question is why did we land here."

"Grandpa, I need to go to the bathroom."

They were only three aisles from the back of the airplane. Ted followed Maddy to the rear restroom and allowed her to go first. He despised airplane restrooms because they were so small. He very seldom used them but after Maddy finished he stepped into the small compartment. As he finished a loud explosion occurred that shook the airplane. Just as he exited, another loud explosion ignited.

Some of the passengers were screaming and demanding to be let off the plane. Everyone was standing and looking out the windows; dark smoke was billowing from the control tower, and flames blazed from another area that appeared to be the terminal. Looking past the control tower toward the town were several more columns of smoke, rising into the sky.

"Please everyone, stay calm." the flight attendant at the back of the plane, nearest Ted, tried to make her way through the passengers filling the aisle. Not one person moved out of her way and it soon became a pointless endeavor. The passengers continued demanding to be let off the plane.

Maddy took hold of Ted's arm and squeezed tightly.

"It will be ok," was all he could think to say, holding her head close to his side.

"Flight attendants prepare to deplane," the captain's voice was rushed.

The door at the front of the plane was opened and the inflatable slide unfurled to the ground below. Ted took hold of Maddy by the waist and sank into a seat. He held her tight on his lap. His experience in the military had taught him to never rush into a situation he was unsure of.

Ted was surprised only one door at the front of the plane was opened for the evacuation. In a true emergency all exits would be used. Many people were pushing to get to the front. He stayed seated holding Maddy and noticed Carol and Scotty remained in their seats. After nearly twenty minutes fewer than half the passengers were on the ground.

Looking out the window he could see a column of passengers walking in the direction of a large hanger nearest the burning terminal. Two armed men, who looked like airport security, were waiting a couple hundred meters off the runway directing the passengers.

Ted tried his best to comprehend the circumstances. Maddy clenched his arm but stayed remarkably calm.

"Sir." The flight attendant was standing over him. She was very petite with blonde hair and bright red lips. "You need to deplane."

"Not yet, not until I have a little more time to think."

"What are you thinking?" Carol asked Ted. She was now standing and holding onto Scotty's hand.

"I want to talk with the captain." Ted could see that there were only a few passengers remaining at the door, along with the captain and the rest of the flight crew.

"Please move to the front." The flight attendant nudged Carol.

Carol turned sharply toward her. "What's your name?"

"Samantha," she answered, completely surprised by the aggressive nature of the older lady.

"Look Samantha, we are not moving until we know what is going on here."

Samantha showed her passive nature as she slowly moved around Carol.

Ted could see the captain speaking with his co-pilot and two flight attendants at the front of the plane. As the captain followed Samantha down the aisle to the back of the airplane, the co-pilot jumped onto the inflated ramp, followed by the two flight attendants.

"This is Travis," stated Samantha before correcting her introduction, "I mean Captain Marquardt."

The captain was a stocky man in his mid to late forties. He removed his hat and placed it into his left armpit, making eye contact with Ted, he asked, "is there a reason you're not deplaning with everyone else?"

Ted pulled Maddy tighter into his grasp. "I would like some information first."

"Any questions you have can be answered off the plane," the pilot looked irritated, "I need you to leave now."

"Not going to happen." Ted kept his head steady and stared into the pilot's eyes. "Not until I know where we are going. You see the columns of smoke. What in the hell is going on?"

"I don't know," stated Captain Marquardt, "I was told to either land or be shot out of the sky. You saw, or at least felt the fighter jets making it clear that they meant business. Las Vegas was inundated so it ended up being Cedar City."

"We are in Utah?" Carol asked.

"Yes ma'am, this is a new section of the airport not ready for an aircraft this size, but we had no alternative."

"I saw a flash of light about ten minutes before we were buzzed by the jets. Do you know what it was?" Ted asked.

Captain Marquardt hesitated before asking, "Were you in the military?" He knew the answer before asking.

"Thirty plus years, retired for nearly a year now."

"There were actually two events. The one you saw, and another about twenty minutes after take-off."

"Electromagnetic pulse." Ted wasn't asking a question.

"That's my best guess. Just last year we upgraded equipment to shield the planes from advanced technology electromagnetic weaponry threats."

"I know they did." Ted's mind wandered to Deb.

"I don't know any more about this situation than what I told you," stated the captain. "Let's exit the plane and see if we can find some answers."

Before Ted could respond all hell broke loose outside the plane.

Although the popping of the bullets was nearly a mile away, Ted knew a major battle was occurring. He figured that over a hundred rounds had been fired before the shooting stopped.

Maddy was frightened enough to be shaking in his arms. He moved her back next to Carol and joined Captain Marquardt to look out the window. Although the sun was beginning to set in the west, it was light enough to see the passengers, still outside the hanger, running toward the large structure. It was impossible to see who was fighting but it was quite apparent some of the passengers had been hit in the crossfire.

"Have you had any radio contact with the terminal at this airport?" Ted asked.

"Initially, but we lost them as we were landing."

"I was under the impression that with all the new satellites it would be impossible for the aircraft communication and navigation system to falter."

"It's not the technology. The control centers have been compromised. Even when we were communicating nobody seemed to know what was going on."

"Do your superiors know you had to ditch the plane?"

"They do," Captain Marquardt looked profoundly serious. "Having no urgent response to our landing here concerns me more than anything else."

"Do you have any weapons?" Ted asked. "I can tell you what we are hearing is not a local police response taking place."

"I have two pistols in the cockpit."

"The gunfire outside is coming from assault weapons, not pistols," stated Ted.

The captain realized all protocol and normalcy was now gone. He wanted to get off the plane and join his co-pilot and the rest of the flight crew on the ground. Hopefully, he could get some questions answered.

All the passengers and crew from the plane were now out of sight. There was an eerie silence.

Ted grasped Maddy's hands and pulled her to him. "Are you ok sweety?"

"I want to go home," she had tears streaming down her cheeks.

"So do I." He felt her little body shiver. A thought about the well-being of Bill and Nicole entered his head. He needed to clear his mind and focus on he and Maddy's safety.

Ted continued to hold Maddy close as her arms went around his neck. She hugged him as tight as she could. He was in the most difficult position of his life. What was to be a bonding adventure with his granddaughter was now turning into a soldier's role to protect her.

Littleton, Colorado

Jacqueline was talking on the sidewalk in front of their home, with her close neighbors, Al and Linda Jones. The streets in their modest, discreet neighborhood were wide, and unnervingly quiet.

Hank slipped on a jacket and wandered out into the cold breeze. He couldn't see any fires or columns of smoke, but it smelled smokey.

"Al just told me all airports across the country have been targeted," said Jacqueline, as Hank approached. "He said they heard several muffled explosions earlier this morning."

"Is it a terrorist attack?"

"Don't know," Al shrugged his shoulders, "we lost the news before they said who was doing it."

"This doesn't seem real," said Hank. "We are supposed to be playing the state championship football game in four hours. Are things really as bad as we fear?"

"Come on Hank. The country might be under attack, and you are worrying about a football game." Al's remark was disparaging, but obviously correct.

A car pulled into the driveway.

"It's Nicole and Bill," stated Jacqueline.

Nicole didn't waste any words as she approached Hank. "Have you heard from Ted? I've been trying to call him but can't get any reception."

"We haven't heard from him either," Hank answered, knowing she would have been contacted by his brother before he would have.

"He called from the airport in California. He and Maddy were getting ready to get on the plane." Nicole placed her fingertips to her forehead. "They should have landed thirty minutes ago."

"Uncle Hank, we have to go to DIA and see if we can find them," cried Bill earnestly.

Hank paused to think before responding to his nephew. Bill was fourteen years older than Bobby. Hank had coached and spent an extraordinary amount of time with him when he was a child, while Ted was deployed in different parts of the world. The bond was strong between the two of them.

"Everything is shut down. Broadway is bumper to bumper, and all the traffic lights are out," Nicole said. "It would take us all day to get there."

"I have a feeling you couldn't get within ten kilometers of DIA," attested Al.

"We have to do something," screamed Bill. "I know Dad will take care of Maddy, as well as anyone possibly could, but I can't bear thinking about the possibility of the plane crashing."

"I understand you being worried," declared Hank, "we all are, but we need to get some facts before getting too carried away."

"Gina told me she and Jon were going to get here early so they could see Bobby before the game. I wonder where they are," Jacqueline shielded her face from the breeze. "I'm going inside and throw on another pot of coffee."

"They were coming from the hotel south of 470 so they have to be stuck in traffic," said Nicole, before turning to Jacqueline. "Do you have electricity?"

"Oh, Good Lord, I guess I will go in just to get out of this wind."

"I'll fire up the generator." Hank moved to join his wife.

Before Jacqueline could take another step, several large flashes, in rapid sequence, crossed the sky. Even in the early morning light, the burst was almost blinding.

"What in the hell was that?" Hank hunched over in a defensive posture.

A slight rumble filled the air.

"It looked like lightening," said Al, "but there isn't a cloud in the sky."

"Let's get inside the house." Hank looked up hoping a bolt of lightning would race across the blue sky.

***

"Aunt Deb was planning to be here for the game. Has anyone heard from her?" Bill asked. Having run an extension cord from the generator to the television, he clicked from channel to channel. "No reception on any channels."

"She called Hank earlier this morning." Jacqueline looked at Nicole and wavered, before continuing. "She said there has been an attack and for us to go to the farm immediately."

"She won't be coming," continued Hank, "but will get in contact with us as soon as she can."

"Did she leave you a survival packet?" Bill knew full well that she had. The only ones in the family who knew he was a business partner with Aunt Deb in her holdings and investments, were his father and mother. He helped her prepare the packets for everyone else.

Hank set a binder full of notebook papers on the kitchen table and held up a large manilla envelope.

"She did put her money where her mouth was," said Jacqueline. "I'll bet she spent a hundred thousand dollars at the farm."

"Ten times that amount," professed Hank. "She has always been a little paranoid, but for the past six months she has been more than adamant about being prepared for a disaster."

Bill smiled to himself, the amount of money Aunt Deb spent at the farm was well over two million dollars. She was not only an amazing soldier but a very enterprising investor.

The sound of the generator on the back porch was annoying but it allowed for a pot of coffee to be brewed.

Bobby walked through the front door followed by the Jensen family, Dave, Jason and Kori. Dave was Bobby's best friend and one of the best football players on their team. His father Jason was a full two meters tall. But it was Dave's mom who was the most imposing figure of the family, she was nearly as tall as her husband. Being huge was their niche in life.

"Coach, this certainly isn't the way we thought this day would go," stated Kori. Hank and Jacqueline were close friends with the Jensen's since the time Dave and Bobby were in first grade. With the two families living only a block apart, their friendship blossomed to the point of having dinner together on a weekly basis.

"Come in and sit down," Hank motioned toward the living room. "All of this is mind-boggling."

"Dad," Bobby interrupted, "Uncle Jon and Aunt Gina are walking up the driveway."

Jon stormed through the front door held open by Bobby. Although he never reached the rank of full colonel in the Army, like his sister Deb and brother Ted, he always acted like he was a five-star general. "Our car went dead. We just walked four blocks," Jon announced precluding introductions.

"Isn't your car shielded?" Hank stared at his older brother, wondering how he would allow his car to be immobilized by something Deb had warned him about over and over.

"It was supposed to be. I don't think half this shit they sold us protects anything," said Jon, looking at the room full of people. "Has anyone heard from Ted?"

"He called this morning as he and Maddy were boarding the plane at LAX," stated Nicole.

"Did he take off?"

"I don't know Jon." Nicole put her elbow on the kitchen table and lowered her head into her hand.

Jon placed his hand on her shoulder. "Ted Lisco is the best soldier I have ever known. He is a problem solver. He and Maddy are going to be fine."

Nicole looked at her brother-in-law and smiled. Jon and Ted were much the same, so his positive words did make her feel better.

"Just think how we would feel, or how Dad would be feeling right now, had we let Maddy fly here by herself," said Bill. "I don't think I could live with myself."

"You're right," said Nicole. Cindy told Ted that Maddy was old enough to fly alone. But thank God he insisted she needed someone to fly with her.

"What do we want to do?" Hank addressed the entire group.

"According to Deb she's stocked enough food for a hundred people to survive for ninety days at the farm," stated Jacqueline. "We should go there."

"For those of you who don't know, we have a family farm on the eastern plains that our sister Colonel Deb Lisco has turned into a fortress," mentioned Jon, somewhat mockingly.

"She has a very meticulous outline on how to survive on the farm," said Hank, holding up the binder.

"Do you mind if I read through it Hank?" Jason asked. He and Kori had met Deb at the Fourth of July picnic that was held at the Lisco's house two years ago. Deb was very entertaining with her war stories, and she had mentioned her work at the farm.

"I'd like for everyone to check it out." Hank's voice had a tone of authority.

Jason Jensen began reading the notebook, with Kori looking over his shoulder. Jason was a successful home builder. He became particularly interested in the notes when he read Deb's vision of new buildings to be placed, for quartering up to seventy people.

"Hank, have you tried starting your car and truck?" Jon asked.

"They better start," Hank shook his head as he looked at his brother. "Last summer Deb had us install special shields for protection, they were a little pricey."

"For radical electromagnetic pulses, Deb's term," said Jon. "An electromagnetic pulse more powerful than any other."

"Bobby, could you see if the truck will start?" Hank asked.

"I think I will go home and fill the tub up with water," interjected Linda. "We will be in a real mess if the water goes off."

"Information would be helpful at this time," stated Hank. "But I agree with Linda, we should prepare for the worst."

Jaqueline began filling containers from the sink. She was joined by Nicole until the entire counter was covered with cups and bowls of water.

"The truck starts, but the car won't," stated Bobby. "I can't get anything on the GPS.

"Our car won't start now," said Bill.

"Hank, have you read this?" Jason held up the notebook. "If your sister did all she claims in this report, then we should go there immediately. There is definitely not going to be a football game today. We can always come back."

"I wish we could verify what is happening." Hank was still skeptical of the degree of danger they were facing. "Everything is happening too fast."

"This is major," declared Jon, "we should go."

Before Hank could respond another flash of light illuminated through the windows. The humming of the generator stopped.

"Ok," said Hank., "let's pack the truck."

"You guys go home and see if your cars will run," ordered Jon. He knew that the flash of light was from a handheld electromagnetic weapon, just like Deb had predicted two years earlier. "Pack everything you can, especially any medications you need."

"Al, do you have any of your dental machinery or tools at home?" Jacqueline asked.

"Some, most of it's at the office," answered Al. "I'll pack what I can."

"Let's go, back here within the hour," demanded Jon. "Who knows how long it will take us to get there, but we need to do so before dark."

"Dad," Bobby positioned himself directly in front of his father, "I have to go to Emilee's."

"Not a good time son. We need you here."

"I'm going Dad."

Jacqueline wasn't surprised by Bobby wanting to protect his girlfriend. He and Emilee had been friends since grade school and dating through high school.

"Take the truck," chimed in Jacqueline.

"No, you need to start loading. I'll ride my bike." Bobby was heading out the front door.

"I'll go with him," said Dave.

"No, you won't," bellowed Kori, "we need you to help us pack."

Because of her intimidating size Dave learned at an early age not to defy his mother. He relented without a word.

"There and back," declared Hank, thinking of the complexity and complications they were about to face. Emilee lived with her mother and two small siblings. There was no way Bobby was going to allow them to stay in the apartment unprotected. "Please Bobby, come right back. If they want to come with us, we can drive to their home and pick them up. But I need you back here within an hour."

Cedar City, Utah

Ted paused at the front door of the plane, holding Maddy's backpack, Carol and Scotty waited right behind him. The four of them with Captain Marquardt and the lone remaining flight attendant, Samantha, were the only ones on the plane.

"We have to jump Maddy. You can do that, can't you?"

Maddy wrapped her arms around his right arm. She shook her head no, as she buried her face into his bicep.

"Sure, you can," he said. He worried he was going to have to jump with her in his lap.

"I'm thirsty," stated Scotty.

"Me too," whispered Maddy.

"I'll get you a drink." Samantha maneuvered around everyone and entered the galley. She handed both a cup of water then leaned over and took hold of Maddy's hands, her red lipstick and make-up still neatly in place, and asked, "How old are you?"

"Eight."

"Oh my gosh. My niece is the same age."

Maddy smiled.

"You know what I did about a month ago?"

"No." Maddy looked at her more closely, she smelled of strawberry lotion.

"I brought my niece to training for flight attendants," she hesitated for a second, "and we jumped down the slide, off the plane."

Maddy looked up at Ted. He appreciated Samantha's approach to getting his granddaughter to jump. Before he could make the decision to jump, gunshots rang out in the distance. He moved back from the door.

"Any idea who's fighting?"

"My best guess is the local police and some sort of terrorist group," alleged Captain Marquardt, getting frustrated with Ted's hesitancy. "I don't know."

Ted looked out the door past a smoke-filled mist to the large hanger the passengers had entered after leaving the plane. There was no sign of anyone.

"What are we going to encounter when we leave the plane?" Ted looked at Carol whose face was flushed a deep red. He expected no answer. The muffled sound of an explosion caused him to turn and look back out the door. A series of gunshots could be heard coming from Cedar City, followed by another series. Even though the city was more than four kilometers away, the popping of the guns was distinctive.

"We need to get off this plane. Now!" said Captain Marquardt unhesitatingly. "We are not safe here."

"Not until I grab a few things," Ted pushed past the captain and moved to the galley.

"Good Lord," said Captain Marquardt, looking at Samantha.

Carol began filling her and Scotty's bags with granola bars and peanuts.

"Obviously, we can't go into town," said Ted. "We better be prepared. How about blankets?"

Samantha reached into a compartment and removed four small blankets.

"Maddy and Scotty will you do something for me? Will you use the restroom?"

"Grandpa it smells."

Ted filled the excess space with toilet paper, plastic utensils, aspirin, sodas and water. He placed a blanket on the ground and put three more on top of it, before folding the four corners together, then tied the corners of the blanket together.

"We're ready," Ted took in a deep breath through his nose.

"We will be right behind you," said the captain.

"Carol, would you mind going first?" Ted asked.

Carol jumped into the slide and rushed to the bottom, followed by Scotty. Maddy didn't hesitate when it was her turn. Ted tossed the supply packs next and jumped into the slide.

Ted waited at the bottom for Samantha and Captain Marquardt to jump. He wanted them to know of his anticipated destination.

Ted pointed toward a group of small hangers, isolated, nearly two kilometers to the north of their location. "We are going to the hangers over there. I would appreciate any information you come across when you go to the town."

"Scotty and I are going to go with them," Carol added hastily.

Ted nodded his approval.

"Are you sure you don't want to follow us?" Captain Marquart asked.

"I feel most comfortable staying away from the group," said Ted.

"Seems it would be safer if you follow the rest of the passengers."

A series of very loud gunshots rang out from the direction of the large hanger. Ted knew these shots were much closer to their location then the last shots he heard while waiting in the plane. A flash and then the sound of an explosion came from the entrance. He grabbed Maddy's hand and turned to Captain Marquardt.

"You need to come with us."

The captain didn't argue. The six of them moved quickly in the direction of the small hangers, away from the fighting.

Littleton, Colorado

"What time is it?" Hank asked his brother Jon. He looked down the residential street through a peculiar fog; the air smelt of smoke. It felt muggy, something unusual in the dry Colorado climate.

"Four ten, ten minutes later than you asked before," answered Jon, sitting on the tailgate of Hank's pickup truck. "I know one thing; I'm going to get you a watch the first chance I get."

"Bobby should be back by now," stated Hank.

"Give him time he'll be here." Jon was used to seeing eighteen-year-old soldiers under fire.

Al carried two suitcases to the back of the truck and sat them next to Jon before turning to Hank.

"How are we going to get everyone to your farm? Your truck is the only vehicle that runs."

"I'm not sure, we can get six or seven in the cab," stated Hank. "If everyone shows up with suitcases we won't be able to sit very many in the back."

"We can always pull a car behind us, if necessary," said Jon. "Hell, all of Gina and my stuff is at home in Texas."

"We heard sirens this morning, everything seems awfully quiet now," said Al. "By the way, I did find several drills. I have more dental tools here than I realized."

"Do you have any weapons?" Jon asked Al.

"No, I don't," he answered.

"All we have are the three pistols Deb gave you," said Jon to Hank. "At least they are old enough to not require touch verification."

Jon noticed a large group of people about a block away, walking down the middle of the street. He moved to the edge of the sidewalk as the people approached.

"Where ya'll going?" Jon used a southern accent he sometimes developed when speaking to strangers.

"The recreation center on Federal," said an older lady, continuing to walk.

"Where ya coming from?"

"Most of us live in Englewood," said a lady, crossing over from the far side of the street in front of several people so she could speak. "They chased us out."

"Who chased you out?" Al asked.

"A bunch of damn hoodlums who took over everything late last night."

"Why didn't the police stop them?"

"Because they attacked the police station," stated a tall skinny man. "The police are in a fight to protect themselves. They put on a curfew for after dark. But I don't think that means a damn thing."

"We all need to band together," said the lady, looking back as she hurried down the street. "Looks like the police will be incapacitated for a while."

"That sure changes things." Al watched the group disappear.

"I have to find Bobby," stated Hank bleakly. He recognized the situation was more dangerous then thought. He made a mistake allowing his son to leave on his own. "Jacqueline's going to freak out if he's not home by nightfall."

***

The apartment Emilee and her family lived in was only ten blocks away. It was as low rent a dwelling as could be found in Littleton. Jessica was a single mother who struggled financially but seemed to be very nurturing to her three daughters Emilee, Reagan and Avery.

"I'll go with you," broached Jon. "Let's take the truck."

"No, I'd rather you stay here." Hank moved onto his porch. "I'll walk. I don't want to take a chance of something happening to the only vehicle we have that runs. Can you back it into the garage? I'll let Jacqueline know I'm going to get Bobby."

Hank and Al entered the house to find Jacqueline, Nicole and Gina sitting at the dining room table, all wearing their winter jackets.

"Linda is at your house," Jacqueline told Al.

"Looks like we aren't going anywhere tonight," stated Hank. "Some people walking outside just told us there is a curfew."

"We filled the bathtub with water," said Jacqueline. "Is Bobby back?"

"Not yet."

He could see the dread on his wife's face.

"I'm going to walk to Emilee's apartment and see what's taking him." Hank felt slightly nauseated.

"I'll go with you," said Jacqueline.

"Have Bill go," proposed Nicole, "he's downstairs."

"No, Jon should go," interjected Gina. "He knows how to handle these situations."

Hank thought for a moment on whether to take one of the pistols, he was such an eternal optimist. Just thinking about having a gun in his possession, to travel ten blocks, in his safe neighborhood, woke him to the realization that they were under dire circumstances.

"You're right Nicole," said Hank as Jon came through the front door. "It would be best if Jon goes with me."

***

It was disturbingly quiet walking through the neighborhood. As they neared the apartment building, which was on the far side of a retail shopping complex, they could hear the loud voices of a crowd of people.

Hank initially planned to stop at the Ace hardware store to buy several rolls of duct tape, but as they neared the store, he could see men arguing outside a shattered glass door. Hanging precariously from the remaining glass in the door was a hand-written sign stating, **CASH ONLY**. Two men rammed the door open from inside and rushed out carrying several items in their arms. Looking through the door he could see people ransacking the store. The supermarket wasn't faring any better. There was total chaos with no police in sight.

"Let's go this way," Hank motioned to the center of the parking lot. "We don't need to get involved with any of this."

Two loud pops permeated the air behind them. They stopped to scrutinize the neighborhood supermarket where the gunfire originated. Several more gunshots rang out as people ran from the entrance.

"It hasn't even been a full day." Jon quickened his steps away from the danger. "Look what's taking place."

"Let's make this as quick as possible." Hank hurried to keep up with his older brother.

Hank had driven Emilee home on several occasions, before either of the kids were old enough to drive. Having escorted her to the apartment on the second floor, he was familiar with the procedure of buzzing the security door for entry. It never dawned on him, until he pushed the button with no results, that the electricity was off.

"Which apartment is she in?" Jon asked.

"I don't remember, but it's on the second floor." Hank scanned the top row of windows, trying to remember the location of the apartment. "If I get in the building, I will know right where it is."

The front door to the apartment burst open and four ominous looking men stepped outside.

"Keep on moving," ordered a middle-aged man, raising his flabby arm to point away from the apartment building.

"We are friends of Jessica O'Brian," stated Hank, as cordial as he could muster. "My son is at her apartment."

"Nobody is coming into this building," yelled a small man with shoulder length hair, holding a rifle.

Another man with long hair in a ponytail, holding a revolver in his right hand, positioned himself slightly in front of the man with the rifle.

Jon reached into the pocket of his coat and released the safety from his firearm. The four men moved further from the door, to the edge of the porch.

"We don't want to come in, we just want them to come out." Hank held his hands up. "We would really appreciate it if you would tell them we are here."

"Jessica is the hot redhead in 208," stated a man with salt and pepper hair.

"I know who she is," chimed in flabby arms. "She's safest right here."

"Hell, Toby's been trying to date her for the past two years," said the man with the ponytail, raising the pistol to chest height.

Hank figured they had made life uncomfortable for Jessica for quite some time. He turned to Jon and the first thing he noticed was his brother's hand inside the coat. He was relieved when Jon spoke.

"Would you gentlemen mind if one of us ran up to the apartment?" Jon asked in a calm, but firm voice. "It's getting dark out and we need to get home."

"We mind…"

Before the man could say another word, Jon wrested the pistol and pointed it at the man with the rifle. The man with the ponytail, standing next to him, extended and pointed his handgun. Jon fired first. The bullet went straight through the man's shoulder. He dropped to his knees with the weapon falling to his side.

"Now lower the rifle." Jon directed his pistol in the direction of the man with the rifle. He laid it at his feet.

"Hank, go get Bobby," shouted Jon.

Hank was shocked by his brother's actions but nevertheless moved quickly through the door. Residents in the hallway screamed when he pulled out his pistol and ran up the stairs to the second floor.

"Bobby, Bobby," he yelled as he pounded on the door at 208.

"Jesus, Dad," yelled Bobby, opening the door, "they wouldn't let us leave."

Hank entered the apartment. Four suitcases were sitting at the entrance.

"We have to go," Hank looked at Jessica, Emilee and the two little girls. "Come on we have to get you out of here."

Hank and Bobby grabbed the suitcases and they rushed down the staircase. Two men were assisting the wounded man. Jon hadn't moved a millimeter as he continued to point the weapon at them.

"Let's go, let's go," Jon yelled. He allowed Bobby and the O'Brian family to rush out of the building in front of him.

Jon slowly backed away from the men on the porch. How in the world had chaos taken root so quickly? In less than a full day, pandemonium had subverted the city. It wasn't supposed to happen this way.

Cedar City, Utah

The hanger was much larger on the inside than it appeared from the outside. A light in the far back area of the structure illuminated off the bright white walls and floor, giving the place a look of cleanliness. It smelled like fresh paint. The muffled sound of voices could be heard at the far end of the building.

Maddy held tightly to Ted's wrist as they cautiously walked in the direction of the voices. Samantha, Travis, Carol and Scotty lingered behind. Ted didn't try to mask the sound of his footsteps as he inched closer to the people, so as not to give any indication of being devious.

The two men sitting at a table drinking beer were not startled when the group approached. A man with a long narrow face, who appeared to be in his sixties, sat with his right leg on a chair to the side of the table, wearing a Las Vegas Raiders cap. The other man was extremely overweight, with a round, red face. Both men had AK47 rifles by their sides. Something disconcerting to Ted since the rifles had been banned nationwide twenty years earlier.

"Ya'll were on the airliner," said the man with the cap, lifting his leg off the chair and placing it on the floor.

"We were on our way to Colorado," Ted pulled Maddy close to his side. "I'm Ted Lisco and this is my granddaughter Maddy. This is Carol and her grandson Scotty, the pilot of the plane Captain Marquardt and flight attendant Samantha."

"Please call me Travis," said the captain.

"Jerry Wright," said the big man, reaching out to shake Ted's hand. He gave a quick wave to the others.

Carol turned to the man sitting on the other side of the table. He reminded her of Denzel Washington, one of her favorite actors from her younger days.

"Terrance," he said, waving his hand.

Ted felt more comfortable having made the introductions. He still wanted to proceed with caution. "Do you know what is going on?" he asked.

Terrance looked at Jerry as if to question who should reply before he answered, "we know that it's a mess in Cedar City. The police department was attacked, cell towers blown up and explosions all around town."

"Did they do it all this morning?" Carol asked.

"Late last night were the first explosions."

"When did they hit the control tower?" Travis asked.

"Maybe twenty minutes before you landed," said Jerry.

"That's when we lost contact," said Travis. "There was a lot of smoke visible, I could see it from about ten kilometers out. We didn't have any options but to land."

"The runway you landed on is still a work in progress. It wasn't supposed to be ready for use for another six months," said Jerry, standing. "Here sit down. I'll grab more chairs."

Ted and Maddy moved to the far side of the table and sat their backpacks down. Carol and Scotty sat next to them as Travis and Samantha waited for Jerry to return with chairs.

"A Cessna?" Travis noticed parts of the engine laying neatly on a blanket in front of the plane.

"It's mine and paid for." Jerry carried two chairs to the table.

Ted noticed a television monitor with a live view to the outside of the building. He pointed to the screen, but observed, before making a statement, that the lights in the building were shining brightly.

"What's the source of electricity?"

"Mostly wind and solar." Jerry pointed to a row of windows situated around the top of the building. "Every window is a panel and part of the grid."

"Have you got a radio?" Ted wondered what all the electromagnetic pulse affected.

Jerry hesitated before answering, "Not that works. Anything with an electric circuit has stopped working."

"Even my leg," said Terrance. "It locked up. I had to swap out my prosthesis to one I had nearly twenty years ago."

"It sure worked well for you Terrance," replied Jerry. "But when that electric sensory stuff goes bad it puts you in a bind."

"What's wrong with the plane?" Ted watched Terrance as he moved a chair to the table and sat down beside him.

"Waiting on parts," Jerry glanced at Terrance.

"Have you been in town today?" Ted was wondering why they were sitting in the hanger as if nothing strange had occurred.

Possibly their disposition or maybe they knew something he didn't.

"We just got here from town when you landed," stated Jerry, looking at Travis. "We heard the explosions in the control tower. We figured you was landing blind. By the way, nice job Captain, landing on that short runway."

"Why the assault rifles?" Travis knew they understood his concern. "Were you two in the military?"

"Just prepared if what's happening in town spills out here," replied Terrance crisply. "We both served."

"So, it's not safe to go to Cedar City?" Carol asked.

"I would say definitely not," Terrance looked at Jerry for agreement, "too much chaos."

Ted tried to assess the circumstances. He had much of his sister Deb's temperament when it came to optimism, they both wanted proof of trust before accepting something at face value.

"Can we use your restroom?" Ted asked.

"Right around the corner." Jerry pointed toward the back of the hanger.

He and Maddy entered the restroom. He locked the door and knelt beside her. Pulling her close, he hugged her tiny body.

"Listen sweetheart," he looked into her eyes, "I want you to stay by my side no matter what happens. I mean right next to me. Do you understand?"

"Yes," she looked so tired that she might fall asleep at any moment. "When are we going home?"

"Hopefully real soon. But we might have to stay here for the night." He thought about it for a moment. "It will be an adventure."

"Are we camping out?"

"Maybe, camping in this place."

"I have to go to the bathroom."

"Then we can brush our teeth."

"Aren't we going to eat?" Maddy's eyes were drooping to where she was almost asleep.

"How about if we sleep for just a little while and have a great big, gigantic breakfast in the morning?" Ted couldn't believe how incredibly accommodating she was being. He looked at himself in the mirror. He looked old and tired, with his hair chalk white and hollowed eyes. No longer the fighting machine he was twenty-five years ago.

Littleton, Colorado

Jacqueline was waiting with the front door wide open, as the group made their way inside from the cold night air. "Come in, come in," she said, greeting the O'Brian family.

Al, Linda, Nicole, Bill and Gina were sitting in the living room.

The first thing Hank noticed was warm air coming from a space heater with a cord running to a small orange generator. He had forgotten about the small solar packs. He went straight to Jacqueline and gave her an unexpected hug.

Jon sat down hard in a lounge chair. "I can't believe there is already so much mayhem." He lowered his head. "Every store in the shopping center has been pillaged."

"Did you run into trouble?" Gina could sense there was something wrong.

Jon shook his head in affirmation. He was still on a rush. "It's already chaos."

Hank noticed Nicole sitting in a kitchen chair to the back of the room with Bill by her side. She was silently weeping. He stepped next to her, not sure anything he said could comfort her. He put his hand to the side of her face and wiped away a tear.

"We need to make some decisions," stated Hank.

"We don't have a lot of food," said Jacqueline. "But the water is still running."

"I need to say something," announced Jon, standing from the easy chair and looking at Hank. "I shot a guy at the apartment."

"What," shrieked Gina, putting her hand to her mouth. "Oh my God. Is he dead?"

"No, I was only about ten meters from him. I shot him in the arm." Jon was a crack shot with the Beretta 85F 380. It had been his recommendation to Deb that she purchase the Beretta for Hank. It was an older weapon with less recoil than most pistols.

"What happened out there?" Jacqueline asked.

"This is way worse than we ever imagined." Hank shook his head and looked at his brother. "Jon did what he had to in order to keep us safe."

"Was the guy you shot the one sitting on the step when we left?" Bobby asked.

"Yes," said Hank, turning to Bobby. "How did you get by the men at the door when you first arrived at the apartment?"

"I yelled up to Emilee at her window. She had her mother come down and we just walked past them."

"These guys are real jerks," said Jessica with her heavy Irish accent. "They have been monitoring the front door for the past three days. We have been avoiding them for a long time. They know I won't put up with any of their shit."

"Any idea when the trouble at the King Soopers started?" Jon asked.

"We heard gunshots last night," stated Jessica, placing a hand on Reagan's head, who was sitting at her feet.

"Around ten," said Emilee. "Our window faces away from the shopping center, but we could see a lot of people mulling around outside the building, late into the night."

"We need to get out of here as fast as possible." Jon remembered back to Deb's presentation to the Army Chief of Staff where she stated that one aspect of the attack would be Americans fighting Americans.

"The sooner we can get out of the city, the better. Things are only going to get worse." Hank turned to Bill, "Could you grab the envelope next to the notebook Aunt Deb left"

Bill handed him the package. Hank tipped it to allow the contents to fall to the countertop. Ten one hundred-dollar bills, twenty-one-ounce silver eagles and a cache of maps tumbled out.

"The same as what Aunt Deb left all her siblings." Bill knew this because he helped his aunt prepare the envelopes.

"This is why I love my sister," stated Hank.

"Where in the hell did she get paper maps?" Al asked.

"She bought them at the gift shop when we visited Buffalo Bills grave last year," answered Bill.

Hank pushed the cash and coins to the side. Unfolding the Denver metro map, he laid it out on the kitchen table, allowing others to gather around.

"We need to travel through residential neighborhoods," Hank knew the paper map would be invaluable, without GPS, if they found themselves in a position of having to travel through an unfamiliar neighborhood. "When we get out of the city, we can take the backroads through the countryside."

"How far is it to your farm?" Linda asked.

"We have always been able to get there in a little less than two hours, depending on traffic in the city." Hank thought for a moment, knowing it was going to take a lot longer than two hours, "It is about a hundred sixty kilometers."

"Dad," Bobby hesitated, "should I go get Dave and his mom and dad?"

"They'll be here in the morning."

"They should be a part of this," Bobby looked at Emilee. "They are only a block away."

Jessica knew Emilee was about to offer to go with Bobby. Something she was completely comfortable with, knowing how street smart her daughter had become from living in parts much different than this safe suburban neighborhood.

"I'll go with him," Emilee jumped out of her seat.

"What time is it?" Hank directed his question to Jon.

"11:35."

"Fifteen minutes, deliver the message and straight back."

Bobby grabbed Emilee's hand and they both ran down the street.

Jacqueline looked at Jessica sitting on the folding chair with her two young daughters at her feet. She looked majestic with her bright red hair, high cheek bones and big beautiful blue eyes. Jacqueline felt somewhat guilty for never bothering to get to know her over the many years Bobby had been dating Emilee. Part of it was because they had children at different times in their lives, and there was a big disparity in age. If really being honest with herself, it was because she saw the O'Brians as being beneath the status, she was hoping Bobby would marry into.

"Jessica, I didn't get a chance to greet you properly." Jacqueline sat down in the chair Emilee had vacated. "Can I get you and the girls something to drink?"

"The girls would like to use the restroom if possible."

"Of course," Jacqueline felt even worse that she had not offered the facilities, "it's down the hall, first door on the left."

"Thank you."

"How old are the girls now?" Jacqueline asked, making it sound as if she knew their ages at an earlier time.

"Reagan's nine and Avery is ten."

"We'll figure out a place for them to rest."

"Thank you."

Jacqueline went to the linen closet. The shelves were empty. Hank had already packed the bedding into the back of the truck. She stood at the end of the hall, deep in thought. Bobby was very fond of, if not in love with Emilee, but never once had she invited Jessica, Reagan and Avery to one of the family functions. Jessica was nearly twenty years younger than her, but they were both mothers of children the same age. Now with the O'Brian family at her home, very vulnerable, her thoughts of snubbing these beautiful people for so many years almost made her sick to her stomach.

Cedar City, Utah

Terrance and Samantha were still sitting at the table while Jerry and Travis checked out the small aircraft. Carol had removed the blankets they took from the plane. Scotty was sleeping a few feet from the table on a make-shift bed and there were two blankets next to him with a pillow.

"Jerry found us a couple pillows for the kids," whispered Carol. "I told him to use the restroom first, but he fell asleep the second he laid down."

Ted helped Maddy settle into the improvised bed. Usually at home when she had a sleep over at grandma and grandpa's house, he and Nicole would tell her a story before tucking her away for the night. He laid her head on the pillow and gave her a kiss on the cheek, she smiled as she fell asleep.

"What a nightmare this has turned into," stated Ted as he pulled up a chair at the table.

"Carol was telling us you are from Littleton," said Jerry. "My brother lives in Englewood."

"Nice." Ted's focus was on how to get back home. "Are you pilots?"

"I am, Terrance is a mechanic."

"Have you ever flown to Colorado?"

"Only in a commercial airplane. I don't like the idea of flying over the Rockies," replied Jerry. "Especially without a flight plan. If that's what you're thinking. Besides the parts we need to get this plane flying are a week out."

"I'm trying to come to grips with everything right now." Having left Denver in the middle of the night Ted was now pushing twenty-four hours without any sleep.

"Is there a car rental at this airport?" Carol asked. She could see that Ted was very tired. "I know it wouldn't be open, but it might be an option."

"They moved them back into the city until the airport is completely renovated. It will be a while before they get the infrastructure built around it." Jerry leaned back in his chair. "We can't go back into the city. On our way out this morning the gas station coming out of town was under siege."

"Under siege. By whom?" Carol asked skeptically.

"Gangs."

Carol looked at everyone at the table with a confused look on her face. The long day was beginning to catch up with her too.

"This isn't just an event that happened today," stated Terrance. "It started months ago."

"What do you mean months ago?" Ted asked.

"I have many clients I fly, mostly to Vegas or Phoenix. About two years ago, I was hired by a guy I'd never seen before, by the name of Jeff, who wanted me to fly him to Salt Lake City. He became my best client. I would fly him to either Tucson, Vegas or Salt Lake at least once a month."

"The population of this part of Utah along the I-15 corridor has grown by hundreds of thousands over the past twenty years," said Terrance. "New faces aren't as noticeable as they used to be."

"Last April, Jeff hired me to pick up and fly four gentlemen from Patagonia, Arizona back here to Cedar City," said Jerry, hesitating for a moment. "I don't transport drugs if that's what you're thinking. Anyway, one of the guys was Mexican, one, the best I could tell with the accent was Eastern European and the other two Asian."

"They weren't carrying drugs either," stated Terrance, looking at Carol. "Just so you know."

"They stayed in Cedar City for two nights and I flew them back to Arizona," continued Jerry.

"Right after they arrived, the gang problem in the area increased," Terrance grimaced as he spoke. "These guys were vicious. They did have drugs, lots of drugs for sale. They chased off the local drug dealers who didn't go along with them and merged with the ones who did."

"I flew the same four guys to Salt Lake City in late July, and then again to Vegas in August," stated Jerry, clearing his throat.

"The police had so many calls concerning the gangs, over the past two weeks, that they were ready to call in the Utah National Guard," said Terrance grimly. "I wish they would have."

Jerry hesitated for a moment wondering how to proceed.

"What was Jeff's role?" Travis asked.

"I'm coming to that." Jerry looked at Terrance. "We didn't realize until this morning exactly what these men were doing."

"We told you the gas station was under siege as we left this morning," stated Terrance. "The gangsters all had AK47s strapped to their arms."

"And there was a large semi-truck with the back open, with lots of different weapons visible," said Jerry. "Jeff was standing next to it."

"Is that where you got the AKs?" Ted asked.

"Yea," answered Jerry in a very weak voice. "They were a tip of sorts. Now we find ourselves holed up here."

Jerry could sense the tension. He glanced at Terrance, who looked back at his friend with the same judgmental expression as the strangers.

"Terrance did warn me about the guy," stated Jerry conciliatorily. "I had no idea how devious Jeff was. All I did was fly him and his friends. I never did anything illegal."

"You accepted illegal weapons," mentioned Carol. She thought how, just months earlier, she had spearheaded a debate in her college class about the effect on society of decriminalizing drugs during the late 20s. It was a policy she would change if she could go back in history. The decriminalizing of drugs made a new commodity for treatment centers and distributers. Drug dealers were no longer fearful of being charged with a felony, and illegally sold drugs flourished.

Ted was glad they had the rifles, but he would like to have them under his control. This information quelled any notion he had of going into the city at daylight. He wondered how the rest of the passengers on the airplane fared.

"I need to go into town," stated Travis, glancing briefly at Samantha. He pulled his blazer tightly around his neck. "I have to see about my crew."

Samantha remained seated with a deadpan look on her face, something that surprised Ted. She was obviously not planning to volunteer to go into the cold night with the pilot.

"They could be anywhere in the city by now," stated Terrance.

"I need to check," said Travis impatiently. "I'm really shocked there hasn't been some sort of response by the airlines to our landing here. I just can't sit and wait any longer."

"Go around to the west edge of the terminal first. If your crew is not at the terminal, keep going west. There are a lot of dangerous people on the main road going into the city on the north side," warned Jerry.

"I'll either be back by daylight or send a message to let you know what is taking place." Travis looked at Samantha with a macho expression, Samantha continued to ignore him. He quickly turned and walked away.

"What's our plan?" Carol directed the question to Ted before turning to Jerry and Terrance. "We can't stay here forever, are there any cars around here that we can use?"

Ted knew that Carol was correct. He was glad Travis volunteered to go into town; the information from him would help to evaluate the entire situation. He hoped things were not as bad as they appeared to be.

"My car stopped on the way here this morning," stated Terrance. "I'm sure it had to do with the flash of light."

A gift from Jeff thought Ted.

"If the car hadn't stopped, we would have already been out of here," replied Jerry. "We do know someone who has lots of cars."

"Ed Jacoby." Terrance looked at Jerry for confirmation.

"Yeah if you have an extra hundred thousand to spend."

"I work on some old cars for a guy about twenty kilometers from here," stated Terrance. "These are antique cars. Some of them nearly a hundred years old."

"He has a 1957 Chevy with less than 10,000 miles on it," said Jerry.

"He wants an arm and a leg for that car." A slight smile crossed Terrance's lips. "He has an old 2038 pickup I worked on, along with a couple newer cars too. I think they are his and probably not for sale."

"You said his place is about twenty kilometers. Which way?" Ted asked.

"Northwest, just west of Parowan," said Terrance. "If you are thinking of walking, it's one hell of a walk."

Ted lowered his head to think for a moment.

"Ted, you can lay down and rest for a couple hours," whispered Carol. "You look like you are about to fall asleep in the chair."

"What time is it?"

Terrance glanced at his watch, "Two-ten."

"Can you wake me at daylight?"

He could remain awake for a few more hours but eventually would have to get some sleep. His only logical choice was to trust the people he had just met. He slipped off the chair and cuddled up to his granddaughter and fell asleep.

***

"Ted, wake up."

Ted jerked as he tried to get his bearings. Terrance was standing over him with the AK-47 strapped across his right shoulder. He could smell coffee.

"We have company outside." Terrance pointed to the small monitor. Several men carrying weapons were huddled together on the tarmac about two hundred meters from the hanger.

Ted placed his hand on Maddy's shoulder and shook.

"What time is it?" Ted asked.

"A little past six."

"Maddy, wake up," Ted whispered, lightly shaking his granddaughter. "Time to get up."

Maddy woke from her deep sleep and sat up straight. Her hair was a mess and the braid she had the night before was partially unraveled. Her eyes blinked to adjust to the light. She looked like she might start crying.

"It's ok," he grabbed her by the hands and lifted her to her feet.

"What are we doing Grandpa?"

"I'll get some water," said Carol. Scotty was standing, wobbling half asleep.

"We are trying to decide that right now," stated Ted, straightening out her blouse. "We are trying to find a way to get home."

"Are we going to have a big breakfast?"

Ted dug through the backpack and pulled out some granola bars. He threw one to Terrance, who caught it in midair. Then gave one to each of the kids.

"Here's water," Carol set a cup of water in front of Scotty and one in front of Maddy.

Maddy quietly ate her food. She didn't make any sort of fuss about it not being a big breakfast. Ted could see Jerry and Samantha walking in their direction.

"Are the guys outside someone you can approach?" Carol asked anxiously.

"I don't think they are the approachable type," said Jerry. "They are the type we better keep close tabs on."

A loud explosion shook the metal building, causing a flash of light to shoot through the front window.

"What the hell was that?" Terrance asked.

Terrance, Jerry and Samantha moved to the window and looked outside. Although it was nearly two kilometers away, they could see the entire front of the airliner was missing, with smoke and dust rising into the air. A crowd of men had assembled on the runway, standing fifty meters from the plane, watching the mayhem.

"It was our aircraft," Samantha looked sad. "I'm sure they are planning on looting the cargo for valuables."

"It's time we go." Ted realized it wasn't safe to be near the airport. "Who knows what these guys will do when they finish looting the plane."

"Go where?" Carol asked. "The city isn't an option."

"Terrance's friend with the cars," answered Ted.

"It's twenty kilometers," replied Terrance.

"I agree with Ted," interjected Samantha.

"Well Scotty and I are ready to go too." Carol wondered if she could walk the long distance. "But we should give Travis a little more time."

"Can you give us the address and draw us a map?" Ted asked Terrance. "We can give Travis another hour and prepare for the trip in that time."

"The address is programed in my car. I have no idea what it is," said Terrance. "I just push the button that says Ed Jacoby and it drives me there."

"And there are no other cars nearby."

"Not that I know of." Terrance looked at Jerry and shrugged his shoulders. "What ya think, should we show them how to get there?"

"I don't know Ed as well as you do," said Jerry. "But what I do know of him is that he is a fair person."

"That he is," stated Terrance.

"It's been a long time since I walked twenty kilometers, especially over some very treacherous terrain," Jerry sighed. "But leaving seems to be a better option than staying here."

"We can leave out the back door and go west to the row of trees. It's about two and a half kilometers to the hyperloop, which runs parallel with the interstate," said Terrance.

"Once we get to the hyperloop there is a trail we can follow north for several kilometers," added Jerry.

"Any idea about the weather?" Ted asked. Maddy had only a light coat and one change of clothes in her bag. She kept what she needed at both her mother and father's households so there was no need to transport many clothes when traveling back and forth.

"Next week is a slight chance of snow," answered Jerry. He was an avid weather watcher. "The temperature should be near fifty today."

"Do you have some more blankets? We have the blankets from the plane, but it would be nice to have more just in case everything doesn't go as planned." Ted glanced at Samantha.

"We only have the light blankets and pillows we gave the kids last night," stated Jerry.

"Do you have any food we can take with us?" Carol asked.

"Ha," Terrance looked at Carol, "you just asked that big man if he has any food around."

Jerry grabbed two small duffle bags from a closet on the side of the kitchen. He packed one bag with peanut butter, sandwich meats, mustard, hot sauce, apples and bread. The other he jammed full of bottled water.

"We have two extra jackets." Terrance set two light jackets on the table. "You can fight over them."

"I'm good with my coat." Carol pushed a jacket in the direction of Samantha and the other toward Ted. "You two take them."

Ted put the jacket on. It was slightly large, but he really wasn't worried about himself. All Maddy had in her bag was two sweaters, a light jacket, a tee-shirt and an extra pair of long pants. He removed a light blue sweater and placed it over her head, pulling it tight to her side. She remained quiet as he helped her put on the jacket.

Terrance disappeared into the office to the side of the kitchen. When he came back, he was carrying a pistol and a duffle bag. He walked straight to Ted and handed him the pistol.

"Thought you might feel more comfortable carrying this," Terrance raised the duffle bag for Ted to see. "We have some ammo, but not a lot."

Ted ejected the clip from the pistol, inspected it and jammed it back into place before nodding his appreciation to Terrance. He placed the weapon in the pocket of the jacket, something he would never do under normal circumstances. He had instructed many soldiers on the safety of holstering a firearm in the past. Some had shot themselves in the leg. This time he had no choice.

"Hopefully, we will never need to use any of these weapons," said Terrance.

Ted leaned down to be eye level with Maddy and zipped her light pink jacket. "Remember what we talked about you staying right by my side. Even if I don't see you, I want you to see me."

Maddy shook her head that she understood.

"We are going on a long, long hike. Are your shoes ok to walk in?"

"Yes," she said, not really comprehending the trek they were about to take.

"I'll go first," said Terrance. "I'm going to head straight for the trees. I'll wait for everyone to catch up. After we get to the tree line we will head northeast through the field."

"I'll bring up the rear." Jerry grabbed the supplies and strapped the AK47 on his shoulder.

"Go in front of us," Ted told Carol. He turned to Maddy, "We're going to run when we get outside, we'll follow Scotty."

Maddy tugged on Ted's arm. "I don't want to go," she stated, nearly crying.

Ted was surprised when Samantha reached out and took ahold of her hand.

"Let's see if we can outrun your grandpa," said Samantha, winking.

Maddy looked at the flight attendant before giving Ted a slight smile. With his bad knees, he thought they both probably could outrun him.

Jerry opened the back door of the hanger, allowing the cold breeze to flow inside. He looked to his right and quickly sprinted to the trees. Everyone else followed behind. Maddy held both Samantha and Ted's hands as they ran across the concrete. Jerry lingered behind to make sure they were not spotted or followed while the others rushed into the cover of the trees.

Littleton, Colorado

The Lisco home was full of dozing people. The logistics of the situation were much more elaborate than first thought, and discussions lasted almost until daybreak. There was the issue of communicating with parents, siblings and other loved ones. Then there was the subject of pets. The biggest issue of all was transportation. Hank's truck was the only functioning vehicle.

Everyone agreed on going to the farm and making decisions to contact others when the situation was better understood. The Jensen's owned a toy terrier and Al and Linda's dog was a Yorkshire terrier, both small dogs that would take up little room. There was never any real notion that the dogs would be left behind. Transportation was problematic.

"How about pulling Nicole's car behind us?" Jon asked. "It's not very heavy."

"It's light but too small." Ted shook his head.

"What are we going to pull the car with?" Bobby recently had his car towed. "We can't call AAA."

"I have several garden hoses," stated Al.

Dave looked at his father, Jason, with an amused look on his face. Al's suggestion sounded like something a dentist would come up with. After listening awhile, Jason spoke, "Ok, ok. We have an extremely large SUV sitting in our garage. It's one of the biggest there is, but the damn thing won't start. We already have it packed with our things. There is room for several more suitcases, and still fit six people."

"Do you have a way to tow it behind my truck?" Hank asked.

"I have several rolls of tie wire. We can cut them in eight-meter lengths and weave them together," suggested Jason. "If we wrap forty pieces of wire into a cable, it will be strong enough to pull my SUV."

"Sounds good to me," said Hank.

"If I can get some help, we can push it out of the garage and let it roll back here to your house. I'll grab the tie wire while we're at it."

Immediately after the SUV came to a stop in front of the Lisco home, Jason started an assembly line in cutting the wire. It took less than fifteen minutes to have a wire strap attached to the undercarriage at the front of the vehicle. Hank backed his truck up and attached it to his tow bar. With a few more items to pack, they would be ready to start the trip.

"Can we put Emilee's family suitcases in your vehicle?" Bobby asked Dave.

"Put them in the third seat. We can still seat five or six people."

"The O'Brians can ride in the club cab of the truck." Hank looked at Bobby, "You and Dave are going to have to ride in the bed."

"Mom and Aunt Nicole in the front of the truck with you and Aunt Gina, Uncle Jon, Al and Linda are going to have to squeeze in with the Jensens." Bobby tried his best to make the seating arrangements equitable when he noticed Bill. "Bill's going to have to ride in the back with us."

***

Hank was edgy on so many levels as he pulled out from the curb onto the wide residential street. The wire tow strap held as his truck pulled the SUV behind. Bobby, Bill and Dave wore three layers of clothing, but it was still cold as they rode in the bed of the truck. It was going to be a long trip.

Hank turned up the heat in the cab. Jacqueline was sitting next to him with Nicole by the window in the front seat. Jacqueline held a neatly folded map of the Denver metro area in her hand. They had marked the route in pen. Hank was familiar with the area around his house but knew once they got into the residential area farther to the south, without GPS, he would have to rely on a map.

The smell of smoke was more noticeable the closer they came to the shopping area near Broadway. Hank planned to stay several blocks from the area near the O'Brian's apartment complex. The first hurdle they faced was to cross Broadway.

Abandoned cars were everywhere, yet there was not a soul on the street. All the homes had blinds closed, and no one visible. When they arrived at Broadway five cars were blocking the intersection. It was obvious the cars had been intentionally situated bumper to bumper. Hank slowed the truck, finally stopping about a hundred meters from the street. He stepped from the truck into the cold wind. Jon and Jason joined him.

"I can pull up on the sidewalk and get around them," stated Hank.

"It looks like a set-up to me," said Jon. "Those cars didn't just land there."

"Where in the hell are the police?" Hank looked at both Jason and Jon. "Shouldn't there be some law enforcement around?"

Jon thought for a moment. This was such a screwed-up mess. At least in war you knew somebody was trying to kill you, and you had every right to shoot back. Urban warfare was not something he enjoyed.

"Let's have me and Jason lead the way on foot." Jon looked up at the giant man and handed him one of the pistols. "Do you know how to use this?"

"No," Jason stared blankly at the weapon. "I've only shot clay pigeons with my shotgun."

"Having the shotgun out in the open might cause some problems. Let me show you how to operate this weapon." As Jon proceeded to give him a lesson with the pistol, Bobby, Dave and Bill climbed from the back of the pickup truck, Bobby and Dave were holding shotguns. With a look from Jon, they placed the shotguns back in the bed of the truck.

"Let's keep those guns out of sight." Jon directed his statement to the high school boys, before turning to Bill. "Bill, you know how to use the Beretta don't you?"

"Yeah, I've been to the range many times with Dad."

"Dave, can you steer your dad's car while he walks ahead?" Hank asked.

"Keep the pistols concealed in your pockets as we move forward," said Jon. "I'll go down the middle, Bill you walk on the right side of the road and Jason you go on the left. Hank stay back with the vehicles until we signal."

Jon placed the pistol in his pocket and pulled his jacket tight around his neck. He began to walk on the hard pavement toward the roadblock. Jason and Bill stayed a couple paces behind him. He slowly moved to the driver side window of the first car and looked inside. It was empty. Taking a quick glance in all the cars, he progressed to the far side of the roadblock and walked to the east side of Broadway.

"I don't see anyone," he said as Jason and Bill joined him at the middle of the usually busy intersection.

He waved to Hank. Hank slowly moved to the edge of the roadblock and drove over the curb, up on the sidewalk, pulling the Jensen SUV behind. He ended up in the middle of Broadway surrounded by abandoned vehicles.

Hank opened the front door of his truck as Bobby jumped out of the back. He looked south down the once busy road at the carnage, that ran as far as his eyes could see. Everyone stepped out of the vehicles and stood with Hank, looking at the devastation.

"It's going to be difficult if not impossible to drive south," Hank stated.

"How about going east on Easter? It might be better to go down the side streets," Al interjected

Before anyone could respond a group of over twenty people appeared, about 100 meters to the north, walking quickly in their direction, maneuvering around the deserted cars and trucks, down the middle of the street. They were carrying assault rifles.

Hank moved to Jon's side as they advanced. A man and a woman walking ten meters in front of the others lowered their rifles in a threatening manner. Jon placed his hand on the pistol but left it in his pocket.

"We set those cars there for a reason," said the woman as she neared, pointing the rifle at Jon. She was a large woman with a silver ring in her nose.

"We are just trying to get out of the city." Jon held his hands to his side.

"Coach Lisco!" yelled a large, tattooed man from the middle of the oncoming pack.

Hank stared at the disheveled man, who was wearing a heavy coat and ski cap and looked to be in his mid-thirties. He couldn't identify him.

"Yes." Hank stared intently as the man moved around the large woman.

The man could tell the coach didn't recognize him.

"It's me, Christian Jeffers."

"Oh my gosh," said Hank astonishingly. Christian was a four-year starter as the center on the Lions team in the early 30s.

But after graduating from high school he became hooked on drugs. "What's going on here Christian?"

"You're caught up in a real revolution Coach," stated Christian. Coach Lisco was one of the few people in the world who had ever treated him with kindness. The four years he played football were by far the best time of his life. "You need to get as far away from here as you can."

"Dad," Bobby pointed at one of the men standing behind Christian, "there's Tim."

Hank peeked around Christian and stared at a man with an AK47 strapped to his shoulder. It was Tim Brockman, the starting wide receiver on the team with Bobby two years prior. Hank went to bat as a character witness for Tim when he was being investigated by the police department for some minor theft charges relating to drug paraphernalia.

"Tim," Hank acknowledged him, "we need to get out of town. Can you help us?"

Christian glanced at Tim and then at the other members of the gang. He had clout amongst the followers as everyone remained silent. "We can get you to the southern end of town. That's as far as we control."

"That would be great," said Hank, looking at Christian's crooked nose. He slapped him on the shoulder. "I want to give you something."

Hank went to the window of his truck. "Can you give me a piece of paper and pen?" he asked Jacqueline. He placed the paper on the hood of the truck and drew a map.

"When you get to a point where you need to leave this mess." Hank handed the paper to Christian. He looked at Tim, making it apparent he was speaking to both men. "There is enough room for you at our farm when you need to leave here."

Tim leaned over Christian's shoulder and looked at the map. He thought how typical it was of the coach to say, "when they need to leave", rather than "if".

"Coach," said Tim, "you need to stay on the south side of the reservoir."

"They are planning on blowing up the Cherry Creek reservoir," stated Christian anxiously, giving Tim a menacing look. He then turned to stare at the others in his group, taking a quick tally of their response to Tim's relinquishing the information.

Hank wasn't sure if Christian's response to Tim was because he didn't want the younger man to mention the destruction of the reservoir, or if it was that he wanted to be the one to mention it to him. He remembered Christian to be somewhat of an intellect. His intimidating size made it easy for others to underestimate his smarts.

"Who's doing all this?" Jason asked, towering over Tim. "How is all this happening so quick?"

"It's not happening quick," said Tim. He knew that the giant man was Dave's father. "I knew something like this was going to happen two years ago when I was playing football at LHS. All the talk about keeping students out of gangs should have been taken more seriously."

"That's when you were recruited, but it's been in the works before then." Christian continued to stare at Tim in a threatening manner, making it clear he was in charge. "It's been in the works for years, but we found out about a month ago that it was really happening."

"Why are there no police?" Hank noticed the tension between his former players.

"The number one priority for each sector was to take over and disable the local police," Christian answered with a bitter tone. "Within twenty-four hours from the start of the revolution all police stations were to be destroyed or at least indisposed."

"Who's in charge?" Jon stepped forward to stand next to Jason and Hank. "Who was it that recruited you?"

"When I first joined, I thought it was local drug dealers partnering with the Mexican cartel," stated Christian. "Now I know it's not the Mexicans making the decisions. Over the past three years there have been too many Chinese and Eastern Europeans supplying us with money, guns and drugs. Now they are here in force."

"How many are in this following?" Jon asked, wondering if he used the right word to describe the group.

"There are over three thousand in our sector. So, three thousand times eight. I guess at least twenty-four thousand locals and hundreds if not a thousand outsiders in the Denver metro area."

Jon couldn't believe how undeniably accurate Deb was in her cataclysmic prediction. Thank God she was never swayed by the powerful forces telling her she was wrong.

As Christian was speaking Jessica and Emilee emerged from the shadows of the crowd. Jessica held her coat jacket tightly to her neck while her bright red hair blew to the side of her face in the light breeze. Christian stopped speaking when he noticed her.

"Hello Christian," Jessica uttered as she stepped in front of him. It had been over eighteen years since they had seen each other.

"Jessica," Christian stated awkwardly. "How did you end up with the coach?"

Jessica pulled Emilee to her side. "My daughter Emilee is friends with Bobby, the coach's son."

Christian looked at the bright red hair and classical features of Emilee's face. Her high cheekbones and pert nose matched her mother, but her deep set eyes were not the same blue, they were a chocolate brown; the same as his.

Jessica could tell Christian noticed the eyes of their daughter.

Jon thought how insignificant each of these young people were in the grand scheme. Just like Deb had imagined and warned about, these were the pawns being used to help bring the country down. He knew that, even as bad as the situation was with the taking of the city, the worst was soon to come. The lack of common sense they were displaying was shocking. They never bothered to think far enough ahead to consider where the food would come from as soon as the supermarket supplies diminished. Or even more ludicrous, where the water would come from if the reservoirs were destroyed.

"We should go," Jon motioned irritably. "We need to hurry if we are going to get to the farm before dark."

"Coach, you're going to have to creep along as you follow us, but we'll get you out of town," said Christian. "We need to be with you if we come across the Europeans."

Cedar City, Utah

Ted helped Maddy maneuver past the heavy bushes, and over the rocky field, as they slowly moved away from the airport. The heavy smell of smoke lingered in the cool air, causing some throat irritation. He was worried the light pants Maddy was wearing would not give much protection from the sharp branches of the bushes. Ahead, the hyperloop stretched, like a long snake, with no end in either direction, across the countryside. The empty interstate could be seen a full kilometer to the east, on the other side of the hyperloop.

"Once we get to the hyperloop there is a trail," said Terrance, noticing the difficulty everyone was having traversing the terrain. "It will be a lot easier to walk."

A cold wind was blowing hard out of the west. There was a feeling of accomplishment as they neared the white tube, covered in solar panels, sitting on concrete pillars. It towered nearly ten meters into the air, making it worthless as a buffer from the wind. And, much more important, it was ineffectual as a shield from anyone, with devious intentions, traveling on the highway.

"Wow, that's quite a structure." Carol looked straight up at the tube towering above them. "This is what they figure will put most of the pilots out of business."

"They finished this one from Salt Lake to Vegas about two years ago," said Terrance. "The damn thing goes nearly a thousand kilometers an hour."

Ted removed a blanket from his pack and placed it around Maddy's shoulder. The small jacket she was wearing would be terribly insufficient should the weather get any colder. Scotty was wearing a ski jacket.

The trail, nearly two meters wide, going parallel with the hyperloop, was neatly built out of compacted road base. The clean smell from a plethora of plants outlining the trail, filtered the air, giving a little relief from the smoke.

"Volunteers built this hiking trail right after the hyperloop was built. The construction workers did most of the work, but the locals leveled it off for bikers and hikers," the tone of Terrance's voice giving the history of the trail was comforting.

"Are we going to be able to follow this all the way to your friend's house?" Carol asked, looking at the trail flowing as far ahead as she could see.

"No, the trail cuts west toward the canyon and makes its way back to Cedar City. Everyone says it's a beautiful hike," said Terrance. "It's called the loop trail."

Ted kneeled next to Maddy and pointed at the tube. "Look how straight it is. It took a lot of work to make it so straight."

"Grandpa, I rode on one with Mom in California." Maddy was not impressed.

"You did?"

"Yeah, we went to San Diego."

"Well, I've never rode on the train yet," said Ted.

"There's someone coming," yelled Jerry, pointing to the field they had just crossed. "It's Travis."

Travis moved quickly over the field. He was carrying his flight blazer over his arm and his shirt was distinctly soiled. Carol was the first to greet him.

"Did you find them?" she asked.

"No," he was noticeably stressed, "I think they headed toward St. George."

"You didn't see any of them?"

"I came across a group of Cedar City police officers. These guys were beat, doing all they could to protect themselves. They told me they saw several people walking from the airport south, out of town." Travis shook his head. "I don't know where you are planning to go, but I know we can't go into the city. It's not safe."

"We are going to a friend of Terrance and Jerry, at a farming community about twenty kilometers from here," stated Ted. "Hopefully, we can figure things out there."

"Let's do it," said Travis.

Ted picked up the pace with Maddy walking next to him. Samantha followed on the opposite side of Maddy. He felt some security in Samantha taking an interest in his granddaughter but could not help wondering about the coldness between the flight attendant and the pilot. The rumbling noise of vehicles in the distance brought him out of his deliberation. The reverberating roar of engines, and rattling of metal, was loud enough, to make it clear it was a convoy of heavy trucks. Grabbing Maddy's hand, they moved to the side of a concrete pillar, everyone followed into hiding.

"Is it military?" Travis asked Ted.

"We need to wait and make sure." Ted leaned away from the pillar to get a better view of the highway. It was empty, but the sound was getting nearer. "They are really moving."

"We need to get closer to the highway," said Travis.

There was no way Ted was going to take Maddy into a situation where he might have to use force to escape, but on the other hand, there was no way he could leave her behind by herself. He looked at Travis.

"I'll go," Travis could tell by the expression on Ted's face that he was not going to leave his granddaughter. He put on his blazer and moved quickly toward the highway.

Travis' dark blue jacket blended into the dark bushes. He was camouflaged enough that most of the group had trouble keeping track of his whereabouts as he zigged and zagged forward. He was about a hundred meters away when the first truck rushed past. Ted immediately took hold of Maddy's hand and began running over the rough ground. "It's US Army," he yelled.

Travis was waving his arms and yelling. He made it to the side of the freeway when the last of the vehicles passed, going south at a high rate of speed. He stepped to the middle of the highway and stared at the disappearing caravan.

"They were really moving," said Travis as Ted and Maddy came to his side.

Before Ted could reply they heard a vehicle quickly approaching. Ted held Maddy against him and hurried off into the ditch. He held up his arm motioning for the soldiers to stop. Travis took a more aggressive approach and moved to the center of the highway. The jeep stopped.

"Lieutenant, where you headed?" Ted shifted to the side of the vehicle. He was speaking to the soldier in the front passenger seat. "I'm Colonel Ted Lisco, now retired."

"The Mexican border, sir," said the soldier. "We had a little problem. Just trying to catch up with our unit."

"What's going on? Are we at war?" Ted asked.

"We have orders to go to the border. We're just following orders to get there, ASAP," said the lieutenant. "With all the ammunition we are transporting, it looks to me like we are at war."

"The cities up ahead are under attack," stated Travis, "are you going to stop and help?"

"No sir," he answered hastily. "Every city in the country has the same problems. As of now, civilian populations are under the protection of local law enforcement."

"Can you radio a message for me?" Ted asked firmly.

"Negative mister," the lieutenant shook his head. "We have direct orders not to engage in civilian affairs. Now we need to get going."

Calling him mister made it clear, in the eyes of the lieutenant, Ted was a civilian. Ted thought for a moment. "Are you from Tooele?"

"We left early this morning."

"Son, as one soldier to another, I'm asking you to do me a favor. Just radio my information to Colonel Ruiz."

"I have very, very explicit orders not to interact with civilians, repeated to the entire force just before we left this morning. And now you want me to radio Colonel Ruiz with your request. I don't think so."

"I'm in a bind here son."

The lieutenant hesitated and stared at the old man with Maddy peeking around his leg. He turned and looked at the two soldiers, in full combat gear, sitting in the back seat. He handed Ted a clipboard. "Quickly, I won't radio but I will deliver a note," he said candidly.

Ted wrote the note. "URGENT MESSAGE for Colonel Deb Lisco, 4th Infantry, Fort Carson, Colorado. Colonel Ted Lisco and Maddy stranded north of Cedar City, Utah. Both OK. Trying to figure transportation home."

"Thank you," Ted handed him the note. "Son, I'm asking you to give this to Colonel Ruiz personally."

The young soldier looked at the message and shook his head in confirmation. "If you continue north, in about ten klicks you're going to encounter a roadblock. You might want to stay clear and avoid them." He motioned to his driver and yelled, "Let's go."

They watched the jeep speed away. In the distance they could see plumes of smoke billowing high in the sky as the city burned. He picked Maddy up and gave her a huge hug. "They are going to help us Maddy."

"Grandpa I really want to go home."

"We have to keep hiking." Ted smiled, spinning around a full turn as he held her. "We are going to figure a way home."

South Central Utah

"There is the pavilion with restrooms." Terrance pointed to a concrete block structure nearly a kilometer ahead. "The trail heads west at the rest area, so we are going to lose it there."

As they walked closer to the structure the silhouettes of two people became visible. The shadows soon took the form of two men, both holding rifles. Terrance and Jerry removed their AKs from their shoulders. Surprisingly, Travis took the initiative to lead the group. Both Terrance and Jerry flanked him.

"Hello," shouted Travis, waving his left hand as he approached the men.

Ted stopped and placed his hand on the side of Maddy's face and pulled her close to his side. He watched as Travis moved closer to the two strangers. He turned to Samantha, who took hold of Maddy's hand, and without saying a word, retreated a few meters back to stand next to Carol and Scotty. He motioned for them to move further back and to the side. They stepped off the trail and took refuge behind a concrete pillar under the hyperloop.

Ted hesitated, wishing he could speak with Travis about taking a more cautious approach with encountering the strangers. He was several hundred meters behind Travis when the men ahead raised their rifles. He clicked the safety off the pistol in his coat pocket.

"Hold it," yelled Travis frantically. He was less than fifty meters from the men, holding his hands out. "We are just passing through."

Jerry and Terrance both stopped. They elevated their guns and put the two men in their sights.

As Travis moved closer, he could see from the looks on the men's faces that they were not going to negotiate. Each of the men fired one shot apiece before Terrance and Jerry opened fire. The men recoiled backwards, one with a large hole in his chest, and the other with a wound to the neck.

Travis turned around in shock. He looked at Ted running at him. "How in the hell did they miss me?" he asked incredulously. His face had turned a pale white as he fell to a knee.

Ted glanced back to make sure Carol and Samantha were not following with the kids. When sure they were going to wait, he approached the horrible scene. Having witnessed death before, he knew they were dead. The reality of the dangerous situation had unfolded.

Terrance and Jerry were disconcertingly quiet as they stared at the bodies.

"They didn't give us any choice," stated Jerry, with a morose expression on his face. "They fired without saying a word."

"Listen," said Ted, placing his hand on Terrance's shoulder. "You did what you had to do, in order to protect us."

"It's a miracle they didn't hit one of us," said Travis, still in shock. "I was being careful in approaching them. I just wanted to talk. I can't believe they were going to kill us for no reason at all."

It was the first time Travis had witnessed someone die. It would take a while for the shock of the situation to disappear.

"We need to move them," Ted spoke with urgency. "Those gunshots can be heard for a long way."

"Over there. In the bushes." Jerry was surprisingly coherent and to the point. He picked up one of the rifles. "What kind of rifle is this?"

Ted inspected the rifle as the others disposed of the bodies in the shrubbery. He was unsure of the type of weapon the men were using.

"We definitely don't want to have these weapons on us if we come across some of their friends," said Ted, tossing the rifles next to the bodies. "We need to get far away from here, as quick as we can."

Carol and Samantha were able to bring the children past the area to the far end of the trail without any mention of the terrible incident that took the lives of the two unknown assailants.

Ted understood the urgency of leaving the area quickly, but he also knew the importance of taking the time to make a prudent decision. He slowed to think, allowing everyone to use the restroom facilities. He looked under the hyperloop in the direction of the highway. Although unnoticeable, he knew the roadblock the soldier warned him about was only a few kilometers away. He supposed the two disposed men were part of the group. It would be too risky an endeavor to go forward so close to Interstate 15. Being noticed by the group could be a deadly mistake. He waited for everyone to join him on the edge of the trail.

"What is the terrain like to the west of here?" Ted directed his question to Terrance.

"How far west?"

"Far enough that we can't be spotted from the highway, maybe four or five kilometers."

"If we go fifteen kilometers or so it turns into canyons. But I would imagine within five kilometers the ground would be much the same as here, maybe a little hillier," stated Terrance.

"The soldier we spoke with told us to avoid a roadblock," said Travis anxiously. "We need to avoid them at all costs."

"Let's follow the marked trail to the west and then head north." Ted never waited for acknowledgment. He took Maddy's hand and started walking.

Terrance moved up to walk alongside Ted. "Going west now won't make a whole lot of difference, since Ed's place is about eight kilometers west of Interstate 15."

Ted quickened the pace. He could tell Terrance wanted to talk, but that would need to come later. He wanted to concentrate on getting as far away from the area, as swiftly as possible. The reality of he and Maddy's situation seemed to be worsening. He needed to find a safe place to make decisions on how to get them back home.

***

Ted was relieved everyone stayed focused on traversing the rugged landscape as they slowly shifted away from the loop trail. Having been in combat he understood the importance of reflection on coping with such a horrific incident as they had just experienced. The prolonged silence of everyone was welcomed as they came to a barb wire fence.

"We are getting close." Terrance placed the large shoe at the bottom of his prosthesis on the lower rung of the fence and pulled up on the next wire. "I'll bet we can see Ed's red barn when we get to the top of the hill over there," he said.

Ted crawled under the wire and helped the others through. The sun was rapidly setting.

"Grandpa, my foot hurts." Maddy looked at Ted with wide open eyes, trying not to cry.

Ted sat down on the cold ground and pulled Maddy onto his lap. He pulled her two light tennis shoes off and removed her dirty pink socks. There was a bright red spot on her left foot from the rubbing of her shoe. It obviously had been rubbing for quite a while. He pulled her to his chest and hugged her tightly, "I'm sorry Maddy, Grandpa should have noticed you were having trouble walking."

Ted held her for a full minute, thinking it was time for him to get in control of the situation.

"Terrance," Ted continued to hold Maddy closely as he looked up, "would you mind doing a little reconnaissance for us by going ahead and making sure we are welcome at Ed's house."

"I suppose I can," replied Terrance. "I'll wave to you if I see Ed's red barn from the top of the hill."

"We'll be right behind."

"Do you have another pair of socks in your bag?" Samantha asked, leaning over Ted and Maddy.

Ted rummaged through Maddy's bag. He shuffled through the bottles of water situated on top of the clothes and removed a clean pair of socks. He handed them to Samantha.

"Let's put these clean socks on and put the dirty ones over them. That way the shoes won't rub so hard on your feet." Samantha smiled as she came down on her knees. She placed the small foot in her hand, inspecting the bright red sore. She softly rubbed the bottom of Maddy's foot before slipping on the socks and then her shoes.

Ted regarded Samantha's tender manner, in sharp contrast to the harsh surroundings, which gave him a good feeling in the pit of his stomach. He blatantly stared at her face, taking note of her natural beauty. There was something intriguing, alluring about the way she concentrated on the simple task of changing socks.

"Thank you," Ted whispered as Maddy buried her face in his chest.

"He's waving," Jerry yelled, motioning toward his friend high on the hill. Terrance stopped waving and disappeared onto the opposite side of the mound. "He can see the Jacobys place."

"Let's walk to the top so we can get a better idea of how far we have to go," said Ted, looking at Jerry. "Maybe we can have some food while we wait to hear back from Terrance."

Carol was struggling to climb the steep embankment, with every step becoming more and more painful. "This damn ankle," she said, grimacing, "it always picks the worst time to flare up."

Ted had her place her arm over his shoulder, as he wrapped his arm around her waist. He was all but carrying her as Maddy and Scotty walked alongside them. Eventually Travis noticed the struggle and took over the duty of helping Carol climb the hill. The sun was rapidly setting, it was becoming apparent they would not make their destination that evening.

Littleton, Colorado

Christian and Tim walked next to the truck as Hank drove slowly down Broadway, often maneuvering onto the sidewalk to avoid abandoned vehicles. They were flanked in front and back by their companions. The sky was a dark grey and it was getting cold, nevertheless, Hank left the window open so he could converse with his former players. Christian, on several occasions, glanced to the backseat at Jessica and her daughters. He never spoke to them.

Hank was confident in Christian's motive in moving the group safely through town. He thought back to how much of a team player the big man was when he was on the football team. Sometimes he was overly aggressive and knocked the hell out of the opponents, but that was just his nature.

Jacqueline listened to the conversation. The idea that Christian could be Emilee's father was almost comical to her. If Bobby and Emilee continued their relationship, the thought of dinner with the in-laws was quite intriguing.

The band of young men and women, who made up Christian's pack, were all armed with automatic weapons. Three female members led the way, approximately a hundred meters ahead, with the others in the group spaced far apart, as they watched closely for any threats. The abandoned cars blocking the way thinned as they passed the hospital.

"Do you have control of the hospital?" Hank asked inquisitively, noticing the parking lot to the hospital was nearly empty.

"No, we were explicitly told to stay away from the hospital or any medical facilities," stated Christian.

"Do you know if they still have doctors working there?"

"I heard a lot of them have already left."

"Our only targets are the police and the supermarkets," replied Tim. "The foreigners have the hospitals."

"What are your plans when you use up the food from the stores?" Hank asked. Although the street was clear of debris, they were still moving at a snail's pace.

"We have a lot of food," Christian spoke with an air of confidence, "it shouldn't be a problem."

"There's not going to be anyone to supply the stores. Eventually you will run out."

"It's all been taken into consideration," Christian seemed slightly irritated he was being asked about the future.

Hank decided to press the issue. "Have you two thought about what the foreign forces are going to do with you, when they have what they want?"

"It's a big world, we'll get our piece of the pie," stated Christian. "If we don't, we'll take it."

Hank could see the bridge over Broadway less than a kilometer ahead as he continued the conversation. Speaking with his former player jogged his memory, helping him remember the difficult times the big lineman endured after high school; the encounters with law enforcement and the homelessness Christian faced at an early stage of his life were shocking to his family and friends, especially because he had so much potential. The coach was curious as to why.

"Why did you choose this path instead of a family and home?" he asked, truly hoping he would receive an answer.

Christian hesitated, the question did merit serious consideration, as it had haunted him on many occasions. "Drugs, alcohol and hopelessness. Coach, it was drugs, alcohol and hopelessness."

Hank wished there were more time to pursue the answer, but he wanted to make sure Christian and Tim realized the consequences of their actions now. "Did anyone warn you about an attack from another country? Even if you did disassemble the local police, and they can't regain immediate control, it's only a matter of time for the military and citizens to take everything back."

Christian did not answer.

"This is a revolution," stated Tim adamantly. "We will be in charge when it's finished."

"I'm telling you it's not adding up. Sooner or later our military will come storming through. You can't fight them, not even close." Hank pressed the issue hoping to get a reasonable reaction to the impossible situation they would eventually face.

"It's all been thought out," Tim stated with uncertainty in his voice. "When the military arrive, we will blend in with everyone else. They will have to leave, and we will take over again."

"You two know you are more than welcome to join us at our farm," stated Hank. "There is plenty of room."

Tim glanced at Christian for his response. He made none.

"My sister is a colonel in the Army. She predicted this over two years ago. You are being used as a disruption to pave the way for Russia and China to take over the country."

"Screw the military Coach," shouted Tim.

"Listen Coach. I like you," Christian was becoming angry. "You can come up with all the theories you want. It's not going to make any difference; we've already passed the point of no return. So, I suggest you keep quiet before I change my mind about getting you out of here."

"Just one more thing."

"What?" Christian stopped in his tracks and stared at Hank.

"I meant it from the bottom of my heart when I said you are welcome to join us at our farm," stated Hank. "That's all…."

"Stop," Christian yelled. He unshouldered his AK-47. "Wait here."

The three women in front of the group were standing about fifty meters ahead with their hands in the air signaling for the rest of the group to halt. A cluster of people in dark hoods were standing under the overpass about a hundred fifty meters away from the front group.

Christian moved quickly forward. He waited for a moment to converse with the women at the front before moving, leading the entire pack in the direction of the bridge.

Hank stepped from the truck and looked back at the Jensen's car. He waited for Jon to join him as they watched their escorts walk near the ominous looking people. Everyone emptied from the vehicles.

"I don't like this," said Jon, looking back to where they just came. "We need to make sure we have an escape route, if they start shooting."

"We can drive through the parking lot at the hospital and come out on the street on the other side." Hank looked back at the empty parking lot of the hospital.

"Hank, are you sure you can trust these guys?" Jon asked. "It would be very easy for them to lead us into a trap."

"I think I can trust them Jon, but you know me, sometimes I trust too much." Hank glanced at Jessica and her daughters. He lowered his voice, "I don't think he will betray Jessica and Emilee. He was staring at them the whole time he was talking with me."

They waited for nearly ten minutes until Tim separated from the mass of people under the bridge and waved for them to move closer. Jon decided to ride in the bed of the pickup so he could be near enough to be a part of any negotiations. He was overly concerned about going into a situation with such uncertainty. He took the safety off his pistol and told Bill to do the same. Bobby and Dave stayed close to the hidden shotguns.

There were nine people in the hooded group. They were more than daunting, they were scary, wearing matching black hoods and black long sleeve sweatshirts. Both groups were in the middle of the street.

Hank drove to within twenty meters of where they were facing off. A quick jerk by several of the people wearing the hoods caused everyone to elevate their weapons. The two groups were positioned less than ten meters apart with high powered rifles pointed toward one another. Hank slammed on the brakes.

Bobby and Dave grabbed the shotguns and Bill pulled out his pistol. Jon waved for them to lower the weapons. The situation was so volatile that any sudden action could cause many deaths.

Christian and Tim were right in the middle of the pack. Both were yelling for the hooded group to lower their weapons. Each faction was slowly moving apart, making it difficult for the band of foreign fighters to have sights on a target. Being outgunned more than two to one, the alien subversives lowered their weapons. Christian's group remained with weapons leveled at them.

Hank and Jon moved in the direction of Christian. Jon stepped between Christian and one of the collaborators. He took the weapon from the man. "I've never seen anything like this," he looked the man in the eyes peeking out from the hood, "where is this from?"

"China," he said with a distinct accent.

Jon looked at Christian and said, "I'd feel better if you secure their weapons."

Christian kept his sights on the man in front of him. He motioned with his head and said, "Take their weapons."

Hank waited until all the rifles were removed from the offenders. The subversives in hoods most likely would have murdered his family had they not met Christian and Tim when they first arrived at the Broadway intersection. He wasn't sure how to thank the big man and the rest of his group.

Jon was almost foaming at the mouth at the opportunity to question the outsiders. "Remove your hoods" he ordered, looking at the man whose gun he held.

The man looked to the person in the center of the group for affirmation, none of them removed their hoods.

This is the leader thought Jon. With such a small group under his control, he most likely was a minor cog in the whole of the greater picture. Jon stepped in front of the man and stood nose to nose. "Take off your hoods," he demanded.

The leader removed his hood, followed by the rest of the group. Jon moved back a couple of steps. He could see Gina and the rest of his family and friends were only a few meters away watching. He turned to Christian and said, "Move back and keep your weapons on them. Send a couple of your people to the top of the overpass to keep a look out for any of their associates."

Jon turned back to the leader, "Are you an American citizen?"

The man didn't say a word.

"Have you ever seen any of these guys before?" Jon asked Christian.

"I haven't."

Jon pulled his pistol from his coat pocket and stepped in front of the leader. He placed the barrel of the gun right between the man's eyes. Hank moved to Jon's side and placed his hand on his brother's shoulder. After the incident at the apartment, Hank knew his brother meant business when he pointed his weapon.

Jon looked into the man's dark eyes. "I will shoot you," he said with his head steady, not even flinching a centimeter. "After I do, I guarantee this man standing next to you will tell me everything I want to know."

"I am an Iranian citizen," answered the man with a very thick accent. He could tell the old man pointing the gun was serious about shooting him.

"How long have you been in America?" asked Jon, lowering his pistol, leaving a mark on the man's forehead.

"Maybe three months."

"How many of you are in Colorado?"

"Many, many, there are several from China, Eastern Europe and Iran. I don't know the total number." He held his hands palms up.

"Are your comrades planning to attack our country?"

The man tightened his lips and remained silent.

"I can see a group of the black hoods at the top of the hill on the highway to the west," yelled Christian's lookout from the top of the overpass. "According to the binoculars they are a little over twenty-two hundred meters out."

"Are they coming our way?" yelled Christian.

"I just noticed them, so I can't tell. I'll let you know in a minute."

"We need to get out of here," said Hank nervously. "Christian, I want you to come with us, you can bring everyone."

Christian took in a deep breath but didn't answer.

"Alright comrades take your boots off," Jon waved the pistol over the rebels heads. He watched as they all sat on the ground and removed their boots. He noticed a hidden pistol in an ankle holster of one of the men. He turned to Christian. "Now, we need to relieve them of all their weapons."

"Christian," shouted the lookout from the top of the overpass, "they aren't moving. It's a large group, probably fifty or more."

Hank was still waiting for an answer from Christian about following them to the farm. Christian was undoubtedly the leader and the others in the group would accept his decision. Christian ordered the two scouts down from the overpass. After several of his troops confiscated the hidden weapons, he answered Hank, "Coach, are you sure there is a place for us if we follow you?"

"Positive, it is set up to be staffed by as many as a hundred people. We need workers and security. Do you still have the map?"

"I have it. My dad took me quail hunting near Limon when he was still alive, so I'm sure I can find your farm," stated Christian. "We need to finalize a few obligations here, and then we will decide."

Jon looked the leader of the subversives directly in the eyes and said, "I want you and your men to walk down Broadway. I don't want you to look back." He grabbed him by the collar with his powerful left hand. "You need to know that your time is very limited here in America, now start walking."

Jessica stepped in front of Christian. She took his hand in hers and looked up at his rugged face. "Thank you," she said with a glow in her eye.

"We need to get out of here." Hank held his hand out to Tim, "I'll be expecting to see you."

Tim never replied. By the way Christian was looking at Jessica, there was a good chance they would be heading to the coach's farm.

Hank hurried everyone into the vehicles and quickly drove off. Many of the abandoned and disabled vehicles were off to the side of the road on the south side of the overpass. By navigating the empty backstreets, it took only an hour before Hank was driving on a country road. Although snowflakes were beginning to spit from the grey sky, they would make it to the farm before dark.

South Central Utah

The view from the top of the hill was spectacular. It was much rockier at the peak. The bright red barn of the Jacoby farm was hardly discernable with the naked eye. Once located, it was somewhat disheartening that it was so far away, over some very hazardous ground. Especially since the sun was rapidly setting and the temperature was beginning to drop.

Jerry sat on a large rock and placed his rifle to his side, then placed the bulging bag of food on the ground by his feet. Nobody wanted to be the first to state how they thought Jerry's food should be shared. He broke the ice, "I have peanut butter and jelly or lunch meat."

Ted thought that a peanut butter and jelly sandwich had never tasted so good. Jerry's magnanimous gesture came with complete duty to making everyone as comfortable as possible under the circumstances. He was the master when it came to food.

Carol removed her shoe and sock from her left foot. The cold wind felt good on the exposed skin. She crossed her leg and examined the swollen ankle and moaned as she applied pressure with her hand.

"We don't have a wrap," stated Ted, pulling the collar of his jacket around his neck.

"I never dreamed I would need to pack a brace for this trip," Carol stared at her naked foot.

"It will be dark in a few minutes," said Travis anxiously. He was still shaken from the near-death experience. "We will have to spend the night here."

"I agree," Jerry used a subdued tone, knowing that sleeping outdoors was something he loathed. "It will be hard enough to travel across those ravines without trying to do it at night."

"I'll get you and Scotty something to eat," Ted told Carol, grumbling to himself as he stood and stretched. "These old fifty-six-year old bones aren't going to take well to sleeping on the cold ground tonight."

"Try it when you reach seventy-four," replied Carol.

Ted stopped in his tracks and looked at Carol suspiciously. Jerry handed her and Scotty sandwiches. "You're seventy-four?"

"Closer to seventy-five," she stated, gritting her teeth.

"You are in incredible shape. It's obvious you have spent a lot of time outdoors." Ted looked at her with admiration.

"I love our Colorado mountains."

"What did you teach?" Samantha asked.

"History."

"Which college?"

"University of Colorado Denver campus," she answered as she lowered her ankle to the ground. "It's located near downtown Denver."

"I took classes at MSU downtown," stated Samantha proudly.

Maddy jerked on Ted's jacket, he leaned down.

"I need to go to the bathroom," she whispered in his ear.

"So do I," he whispered back.

Ted removed one of the blankets from the bag. He fumbled around and pulled out the roll of toilet paper.

"This way Grandpa." Maddy led him around to the far side of the rocks.

Ted used the blanket as a barrier for privacy. Although in a desolate and hidden area, he was concerned about being set upon by the fanatics who fired at them without any provocation. He felt some relief when he looked to the east, in the direction of Interstate 15. There was only darkness.

"We are one blanket short," stated Carol, as Maddy and Ted returned.

"Me and Maddy can share," said Ted, noticing that the wind had picked up.

"I'll share with you two," Samantha moved to Maddy's side.

Her statement caught Ted off balance. His expression might have given some indication to what he was thinking but he never said a word. He stepped to a flat area at the base of a house sized boulder and removed the snack bars and water from one of the travel bags. He then pulled out everything but Maddy's clothes from the other bag and put the bags on the ground.

"Cowboys used to sleep out in the wild using their saddles for a pillow." Ted removed his jacket and placed it on the ground. Maddy removed her coat and slipped a hoodie over her head, then placed the coat back over the hoodie. It was going to be uncomfortable sleeping with all the clothes, but with the temperature dropping, at least she would be warm.

"What a great idea," Samantha tossed her bag to the ground next to Maddy's make-shift bed. She left her jacket on.

Carol and Scotty made their bed only a few feet away.

"Lay on the coat." Ted allowed Maddy to get on top of the warm coat before lying down next to her on the cold exposed ground. For him, it was going to be a long cold night.

Samantha placed part of her larger blanket over the small girl.

The bright glittering stars shone a dazzling light over the rocks on the hill.

"My God look at the stars," said Ted.

"Grandpa, you can almost touch them."

"It's the most beautiful thing I have ever seen." Samantha looked over Maddy toward Ted.

"Sit up, I can show you how to find the Big Dipper, the Little Dipper and north using the stars." Ted had shown the same technique of navigation to soldiers on many occasions. Never had he seen a canvas of bright stars so visible to teach from. Sharing the experience with Maddy, from a setting that could only be experienced by the reality of their situation, was priceless.

Both Maddy and Samantha sat up with the same expression of wonder. Maddy pulled the blanket around her as she leaned back to be held by Samantha. Carol and Scotty both took notice as the stars swirled.

"We are so lucky to have an unobstructed view of the Big Dipper, or Ursa Major. It would seem almost impossible to find a single star with all these stars in the sky. What we are trying to find is the star Polaris. Polaris is always north." Ted picked up a small stick and waved it at the sky. He leaned down and touched his nose to Maddy's nose. "I have already found it."

Maddy turned her head and smiled at Samantha.

"The location of the Big Dipper will change in relation to the North Star, depending on the month. We know it will be in the north. We saw the sun go down in that direction." Ted pointed to where the sun had set. "So, we have an idea of north. During the month of October, the Big Dipper will be low on the horizon. There are seven stars in the Big Dipper, and it rotates counterclockwise throughout the year. In spring it will be on top of Polaris. Because we are so high on this hill, we can see it."

"I don't see it," said Maddy.

Ted went cheek to cheek with her and pointed the stick to the horizon. He traced the stars as if using a black board.

"I see the Big Dipper," she yelled.

"I still don't," said Samantha.

Ted put his hand on her shoulder and placed his cheek on Samantha's cheek. Using the stick, he drew the outline of the Big Dipper. After all they experienced, she still smelled like lotion. She seemed to hesitate for a long time before whispering, "I see it now."

"Do you and Scotty see it?" Ted asked Carol.

"We do."

Travis and Jerry stopped talking and were listening to his lecture, both seemed confused.

"The two stars in the cup of the dipper, Murak and Dubhe, are the important ones, because they point to Polaris. Polaris is not as bright as one would assume. Look at the distance between Murak and Dubhe, go five or six times the distance they are separated, and you will find Polaris." Ted leaned over Maddy and used the stick to draw the line to Polaris. He then leaned over Samantha to draw the same line. He couldn't see her eyes, but he sensed she was looking at him rather than the sky. A quick thought entered his mind, lingering for only a second, that Travis and Samantha were having a torrid love affair that went terribly wrong. He stepped back.

"Polaris is the farthest star on the handle of the Little Dipper. It is always north." Ted put the stick on the ground and sat down next to Maddy.

"Very nicely done," stated Carol. "I've never heard it explained so well."

"Thank you," whispered Ted, laying his head back on the travel bag. Maddy helped place part of the blanket over her grandpa. He stayed awake late into the night with conflicting thoughts about the duplicity of the situation of being in such a beautiful place at such a frightful time. He tried to clear his mind of the ghastly events of the day, by thinking about Nicole. With this being the second night away, he wondered how she and Bill were handling not knowing about the fate of he and Maddy. He dozed in and out of sleep until he could see the light of the sun rising in the east.

Jacoby Ranch

The journey was slow as they made their way to the red barn. They traveled in as straight a line as the terrain would allow. The farm was well in sight when they saw Terrance approaching from the north.

"Hey everyone," Terrance looked refreshed as he came to stand next to Jerry. "You look exhausted."

"Cold night," said Jerry. "What did you find out with Ed?"

"To be honest he's not overly enthused about having us intrude on his living space." Terrance glanced back at the farm. "Let's go down and meet him and Irene. We can play it by ear."

"Do they live alone?" Ted asked.

"His two sons and daughter live in the area, but he and Irene live on the farm by themselves." Terrance began walking without giving any more specifics.

Ed and Irene were standing on the edge of the porch, watching the group approach as Terrance opened the gate to allow everyone to walk up a long stone sidewalk. The landscaping around the home was immaculate, as was every part of the property.

Ed was a small man with a weathered face. The tautness of the skin on his tan face made it difficult to judge his age. Had Terrance not mentioned that the couple were in their nineties, nobody would have guessed it. Irene was dressed in a very plain yellow dress. Her round face and white hair gave her a pleasant appearance.

"Ed, Irene, you remember Jerry; here are the others I spoke to you about," Terrance motioned to the group behind him.

Carol was standing on one leg, leaning on Scotty. Travis, still in his uniform, was dirty and disheveled. Samantha looked exhausted. Maddy buried her face into Ted's side.

Irene hesitated for a moment, staring intently at the interlopers. After Terrance left early in the morning to fetch the group, she and Ed had discussed and decided that they would offer water before sending them on their way. But when she saw the faces of the people, all previous plans went out the window. She moved around Ed and stepped off the porch.

"Good God, what have you people been through?" Irene asked, taking Carol's arm and helping her up the steps to their porch. "Come inside and we'll get you something to eat and drink."

Ed stood with his mouth wide open as he watched his wife open the screen door.

"Well come on," said Irene sharply, "we need some water."

Ed lowered his head and marched through the door. He never said a word to dispute his wife's decision to bring the strangers into their home.

The foyer to the home opened to a large living room on the left and dining area to the right, with a large dark wood table in the middle. The kitchen was on the far side of the dining table. Irene waited at the end of the table, allowing everyone to file in.

"The restroom is around the corner on the right." She pointed at a hall on the other side of the living room.

"Thank you so much. Maddy and I appreciate cleaning up a bit," said Ted.

"How old is Maddy?"

"Eight," replied Maddy, smiling at the elderly lady.

"I have a great granddaughter who is nine."

"I'll be nine on March 9."

"That will be here before you know it," said Irene warmly.

Ted led Maddy in the direction of the restroom. The living room had a large, brick, wood burning fireplace on the wall opposite the staircase going upstairs. Although everything inside the home was pristine, the house was incredibly old. Maddy used the restroom, with orders to wash her face and hands, as Ted looked down the hall at three doors, most likely bedrooms.

When they returned to the dining area everyone was sitting with a glass of water in front of them. Maddy sat next to Carol, as Ted sat at the end of the table next to her.

"Thank you so much for your hospitality," stated Ted. "This has been an experience almost beyond imagination."

"Terrance told us you were on an airplane that crash landed," said Irene. She seemed to be in constant motion.

"It really didn't crash," stated Travis. "I simply didn't have a choice but to land it at the airport."

"What's going on?" Ed asked in a gruff voice. "Are there terrorist attacks again"

Ted was somewhat surprised by the lack of knowledge Ed held about what had happened.

"As far as we know the airports have been attacked. What's happening in Parowan?"

"There have been some problems with the electricity and our phones, but as far as we know they are taking care of it," answered Irene. "Our son, Aaron, stopped by yesterday and said there have been some problems."

"Terrance told us how bad it is in the cities," interjected Ed, "but they don't seem to have that many problems in Parowan."

"Are the supermarkets open?" Ted asked.

"As far as we know," replied Irene, looking at Ed.

"How far is it to town?"

"About five miles," Ed showed his age in that he didn't use kilometers.

"I take it your son drove here yesterday." Ted wondered what the range of the hand-held EMPs would be. "Do all your vehicles run?"

"They did yesterday," said Irene.

"There was an electromagnetic attack across the cities to the south that put most cars out of commission." Ted had discussed with Deb the range of the hand-held EMP. He wasn't sure of the direction or origination of the initial pulse fired in the Cedar City location, so he couldn't be sure of the strength of the weapon. Nonetheless he was glad to hear that the automobiles were operational.

"Ted is a colonel in the Army," interjected Terrance.

"Retired."

"Anyway, we should get to the point of why we came here," said Terrance. "Ed, do you have any cars you want to sell?"

Ed hesitated for a moment, looking at the group of people sitting at his table. "I have several cars I want to sell. But they ain't cheap."

"I'm interested in an old car or truck early 1970s," stated Ted. Over the past couple of years, he and Deb had discussed the possibility of older cars being able to survive an EMP. He wasn't sure if the coil and alternator would be affected. But after hearing that Ed's cars started, he had a better understanding of the capability of the EMP. He needed to decide whether to take a newer car and chance another electromagnetic attack or take the older vehicle.

"I have a 1970 F-250 with a 360 V8," mentioned Ed. "It's a little rusty."

"It runs pretty well," exclaimed Terrance. "I worked on it about six months ago. The tires are a little iffy."

"Well let's take a look," said Ted.

The Quonset housing the truck was huge on the inside. It was high enough to have a basketball hoop at one end. There were eleven antique cars and trucks taking up most of the space. At the far back were several shelves full of old engine and body parts. The smell of gasoline and oil was very noticeable in the building.

"That's it," Ed stood next to the pickup.

The paint on the hood and top of the truck was completely rusted away. There were still remnants of white paint on the grill. The windshield and rest of the glass was in good shape and the cab-lights were still intact. Terrance opened the hood and proudly showed the clean engine. "Start it up," he said.

Ted allowed Maddy to enter the front door to the cab, and they both sat on the hard bench seat. He twisted the key ignition. The engine turned over but didn't start.

"Pump it," Ed stood next to the driver's side window and yelled.

Ted pumped the gas pedal and the engine started with a loud roar. The smell of gasoline fumes filled the garage. Maddy smiled at her grandpa and asked, "Are we going to buy this old truck?"

"What do you think?"

"It smells kind of funny," Maddy took in a deep breath. "But I like it."

Ted turned off the ignition and stepped from the cab. He walked around to the back of the truck. He was thinking as he lingered, would the vehicle work well enough to get he and Maddy back to Colorado? What about Carol, Scotty, Travis and Samantha? At least two people would have to ride in the bed if they used the old vehicle as their form of transportation.

"How much?" Ted asked, looking at Ed.

"Well I had a fella who offered me fifteen thousand, but he backed out." Ed was scratching his chin. "I suppose I would take twelve."

"I can TAP you the money, but my phone doesn't have reception." Ted never planned to haggle over the price.

"We can take care of it at the bank in Parowan," said Ed.

"The banks are open?" Ted looked perplexed.

"As far as I know they are." Ed looked mystified at being asked the question.

Ted was all but certain that Ed held a false belief that the town of Parowan was functioning. He wanted to make sure for himself. He was going to take Maddy with him. With all the uncertainty he wasn't about to leave her out of his sight for even a few hours.

"Can we go now?" Ted asked. "I'd like to take the truck for a spin to see how it runs."

"I don't have plates for it, but I'll grab the title. There shouldn't be any problems even if we get stopped by the police," said Ed, walking toward the exit. "I'm sure Irene will want me to go by the market."

Ted drove the truck out of the Quonset. He and Maddy fidgeted with the unusual knobs on the truck as they waited for Ed.

Parowan, Utah

The sprawl leading up to Parowan was significant as Ted, Maddy and Ed drove past several new housing developments, before coming to the paved road that would take them to the small town. The old F-250 was driving extremely well. Ted was impressed with the power and acceleration capability of the truck. Ed was overly talkative.

"The supermarket is just over the hill ahead. Let's go to the bank in town first. We might want to get some ice cream on the way back." Ed enjoyed joshing with Maddy. "We don't want to have it melt on us. Do we?"

"Nope, I don't like soft ice cream." Maddy smiled at the old man sitting next to her. His gentle and kidding approach made it easy to like him.

Ted drove up the steep hill. He slammed on the brakes as he came upon a roadblock of police cars situated across the highway just over the crest of the hill. He slowly eased the truck up to the officer, who was holding his hand up signifying for them to stop and rolled down the front window.

"Do you live in Parowan?" the officer asked as he looked around Ted, noticing Ed. "Mr. Jacoby."

"What's going on here?" Ed recognized the officer but for the life of him couldn't remember his name. "We just want to get to the bank."

"Good Lord, the banks aren't open."

"How about the supermarket?" Ed asked.

"There's nothing left," answered the officer. "Nearly everything was taken off the shelves yesterday."

"Are you still in control of the town?" Ted noticed the young officer continued to look past him at Ed.

"We are doing our best." He gave Ted a condescending look. "We are aware of the problems taking place in the cities and are trying to keep them from spreading here."

"Sounds like you are aware of what's going on," said Ted.

"We understand." The officer looked around Ted and in a very contemptuous manner asked, "Mr. Jacoby is this someone you know?"

"He was on the airplane that crashed at the airport Saturday."

"It didn't crash, we were forced to land. I'm Colonel Ted Lisco, retired, from Colorado. This is my granddaughter Maddy, we are trying to buy this truck from Mr. Jacoby so we can get home."

A second police officer approached. "There are no plates on the vehicle," he said dramatically.

The officer stepped to the back of the truck, then walked around to the front. "Can I get your license, registration and proof of insurance?" he asked firmly. "I'm going to give you a citation."

Ted almost started laughing as he looked at the small-town policeman with disbelief. With all that was taking place he was going to get a ticket.

"You are not serious? Are you?"

"Of course, I'm serious," he answered belligerently. "I need your license, registration and proof of insurance."

Ted reached for his wallet. Maddy was looking at him with a big smile on her face.

"It looks like a ticket for you Grandpa."

"I guess so," said Ted, pulling out his license. He looked at Ed, "Do you have insurance on this thing?"

Ed handed him the title without saying a word.

"Here's my license and the title for the vehicle. We can't seem to find the insurance papers."

The officer took the documents and walked to his patrol car. The second officer remained a couple feet from the window in a defensive posture.

"Yep Grandpa, he's giving you a ticket." Maddy shook her head as she continued to smile. "Grandma is going to be so mad at you."

Ted chuckled; he didn't have any desire to speak to the young officer watching over them. He knew that the town was likely going to have a great deal of trouble in the foreseeable future. But these cocksure officers were so disenfranchised from reality that he wasn't going to try and convince them about anything. He waited silently until the officer approached.

"Alright sir, you are receiving a citation for no visible license plates or proof of insurance." The officer handed Ted his license and title. "I need you to sign the citation at the bottom."

Ted looked at the ticket and then at Maddy. He took the pen and shielded the ticket with his hand. He printed "and Maddy" after his name before signing the ticket. He handed it back to the officer.

"The information on paying the citation and showing proof of insurance is on the back." He handed Ted the ticket.

Ted smiled at the officer and started the truck. He backed up and turned the truck around and headed back to Ed's ranch.

"Them bastards," Ed held up his fist and shook his head. "Pardon my French, but you ought to throw that damn thing out the window."

"I can't believe he gave me and Maddy a ticket." Ted winked at Ed.

"I didn't get a ticket Grandpa, you did."

"Oh no," said Ted. "Look at the names on it."

Maddy held the ticket up. Ed pointed at the names where it said Ted Ellis Lisco and Maddy. Ed laughed and slapped his knee.

"Grandpa, am I in trouble too?"

"As much as I am with the police force at Parowan," quipped Ted, taking the ticket and holding it in his lap. "I want to save this to show everyone in Colorado when we get home."

"That was one hell of a waste of time," said Ed.

"Maybe not," replied Ted. "At least we know things are not good in Parowan. I'm thinking you should get ahold of your family and make some decisions about how to protect yourselves. Things are going to get awfully bad around here."

"What are you thinking?"

"People are going to be looking for food. The supermarket is already empty. Where better to look than at a farm or ranch. If the people from the city come looking, you better be prepared."

Before Ed could reply Ted heard a loud roar coming from the far distance. He pulled the truck to the side. They got out and stood in the middle of the dirt road as the rumbling came closer and closer. The sky was soon filled with contrails from airplanes flying over the top of them.

After watching the planes, they hopped back into the pickup and began driving. Ted was about ready to explain the massive force of aircraft when a bright flash of light filled the air.

"What in the hell was that?" Ed yelled.

"Grandpa," screamed Maddy, pushing her face into Ted's shoulder.

"Electromagnetic pulse," explained Ted. Although the airplane display was daunting, the flash of light brought a much bigger threat to their immediate safety. He was relieved that the old F-250 was still running.

"That was the damndest thing I've ever seen." Ed leaned forward and looked out the windshield into the bright blue sky. He looked at Maddy. "I've never seen nothing like that."

"Ed you need to get in touch with your family immediately. We have to fortify the ranch," Ted spoke with a noticeable quiver to his voice. He realized the use of the pulse on the rural communities could only signify one thing. The gangs and perpetrators of the rebellion were about to take control of the farms.

Colorado Farm

Hank could see lights as they pulled into the long driveway leading to the farmhouse. The topic of living quarters dominated the conversation as they neared their destination. The farmhouse had five upper bedrooms, with another four bedrooms in the basement. The bedrooms in the basement gave less privacy because they were separated by thin plywood partitions. There were also four campers on the backside of the property. Twenty-four people could comfortably live on the property, without anybody having to quarter in the garage. She had enough lumber and building material on the premises to construct an apartment type building. The plans for it, along with several other structures were drawn up and waiting on Deb's desk. The foundations, electrical and plumbing were already in place. All that was needed was a knowledgeable builder and a lot of laborers.

Heavy snow was beginning to fall as they pulled into the parking area outside the large house. Hank and Jon had spent many nights at the farm when it was owned by their grandfather. They had not been to the property in over three years, but Deb had kept them updated on many of the improvements. As they made their way around the circular drive Hank noticed four cars parked on the back side.

"Is there someone here?" Hank asked incredulously. He stepped from the truck as everyone else piled out of the vehicles.

Five men stormed out of the front door of the house. Three of them were carrying hunting rifles and the other two held revolvers. They walked quickly toward Hank.

"You people need to get off this property, now," shouted a large man with bushy blond hair. "You're trespassing."

"What?" Hank was completely caught off guard. He looked to Jacqueline and then at Jon.

"This house is owned by our sister Deb Lisco," declared Jon. "You are the ones trespassing."

"It is ours," repeated the bushy haired man.

"You need to pack up and get off the premises." Jon stepped closer to the five men. He felt the weight of the pistol in his coat pocket. He hoped that Bobby and Dave would remain calm and leave the shotguns under the tarp. He could see other people moving around behind the five men.

"You must be stupid, old man," asserted a pudgy man, pointing in the direction of several men and women surrounding them. "We ain't going nowhere."

"There must be some sort of miscommunication here," said Jon coolly, trying to de-escalate the situation.

The blond man moved closer to Jon. He took the butt of his rifle and faked like he was going to hit him in the head. Jon flinched backward; all the men started laughing.

"Now, get back in your vehicles and get off of this property," said the blond-haired man. "Believe me, we are very capable of protecting this place. So, get going before I decide not to be so nice."

Hank motioned for everyone to get back into the vehicles. They slowly drove back down the driveway and off the family farm. He needed to get his family away from the volatile situation.

Jacoby Ranch

The electric grid for the Jacoby's ranch was solar and wind, all self-sustained. The water wells had hand pumps to back up the electric pumps. Unfortunately, when Ted, Maddy and Ed returned from the trip to Parowan the electric water pump was not working, disabled by the electromagnetic pulse. Terrance and Jerry disassembled the motor and were in the process of putting it back together.

Besides six bedrooms in the main house, there were five large outbuildings with three of them having bathrooms. About twelve hundred meters deep into the property were two small homes used for hired hands. One house empty and the other occupied by long-time friend and employee, Phil Lucero, who handled the cattle business for Ed and Irene. Ravines and gullies covered much of the property with only about ten percent of the 12,000 acres being flat enough to grow crops.

Ted was in full colonel mode. He was happy Ed and Irene took the perilous situation they were facing seriously. He asked them to contact all their relatives in the area. They had many. He wanted everyone to bring their stored food and basic living items to the farm. None of the newer cars were operational, but Ed's antique cars from the1950s, 1960s and early 1970s worked. All it took was for Ed to drive to his son Aaron's home, about three kilometers away, for the entire plan to become procedural. Aaron contacted his brother Adam and sister Breanna and the word spread. Within two hours four tractors pulling wagons could be seen coming down the road toward the farmhouse.

Maddy held onto Ted's arm as the loud tractors filled the parking area in front of the main farmhouse. Ted was really impressed by Ed and Irene's ability to bring their family together so quickly. He figured they sensed the gravity of the situation and were wondering what they should do.

"Is everyone here related to you?" Ted asked, watching the people exiting the wagons.

"Yep," answered Irene. "Our youngest great granddaughter is nine."

"Not a one of their cars would start," stated Ed, "just them old tractors."

Ted took mental notes of each person as they were introduced. He could sense skepticism from some of the older family members, about the intentions of the strangers invading their parent's home. After a few interactions between Ed, Irene and their children, it became blatantly clear that the old couple was still in charge. Now, Ted needed to figure out a way to gain their family's trust.

"Let's move into the living room and out of this breeze," yelled Irene, leading the parade of people into the house. "We have a lot to talk about and we might as well be comfortable."

Ted realized this was an important moment to find a refuge for him and Maddy. His hope was that the message he gave the soldier on Interstate 15 found its way to Deb. If she received it, she would undoubtedly find them. The decision to stay or trek out to Colorado would depend on how safe he felt at Ed and Irene's farm. To protect these people was very much in his wheelhouse. He needed to find a way for them to trust enough to allow him to help. He and Maddy stood to the side of the living room with Samantha, Travis, Carol and Scotty. Ed and Irene sat on chairs in front of the large fireplace surrounded by the family. Terrance and Jerry were positioned near the front door, wiping their hands with rags, having finished repairing the electric motor to the water pump.

"We aren't sure what is happening right now," stated Irene, "but I guess that's why we're here."

"I went into town this morning," said Ed. "The entire place is shut down."

"I could have told you that," replied Breanna. Breanna was a plump woman with a round face and small chin. She was Ed and Irene's youngest child at sixty-five years of age. There was no husband with her. "We went to the market yesterday afternoon and there wasn't a thing left on the shelves, not even a can of soup."

"Does anyone really know what's going on?" Aaron asked. He was sixty-nine and the oldest child. Although all members of the family had a country flair, he was stereotypically country, dressed in bib overhauls with a John Deere cap covering his grey hair. His wife Ashley was a small woman who payed close attention to her husband as he spoke. "We heard that it's impossible to get to the cities."

Ted remained quiet and listened. There were several times where he wanted to join the conversation, but he knew that there could be nothing worse for the country folk to consider him a know-it-all. His desire was to help them defend the farm from marauders, and in the interim, find he and Maddy a place to stay until he could discover a way home. The longer he watched and listened to the interaction between the different generations, he started to believe that some members of the family were certifiably insane. Many insults and inuendoes were exchanged. The older grandchildren considered the liquor store being empty as the number one priority they faced. There were several verbal fights between cousins and aunts and uncles. Every word uttered was very telling, and it became obvious that several family members were addicted to drugs or alcohol. According to one grandson, some were addicted to both. With their supply of drugs and booze interrupted, withdrawal was something that could raise a major problem.

"Alright enough," demanded Irene. "I won't have this kind of fighting in my house."

"Dad, what do you want us to do?" shouted Adam. He was the middle child who looked more like a cowboy than a farmer. His wife Megan, sitting next to him, looked to be several years younger. "We have no idea what's happening."

"We know our cell phones, computers and televisions don't work," said Ed. Watching football and making wagers on the games were his passion. "I couldn't watch one damn football game over the weekend, I'd say something is pretty wrong around here."

"Hey Grandpa," yelled Arthur, he was Adam's son who had long stringy hair with a ring in his nose, "I forgot to tell you. I met a girl who can pick every football game. Not just the point spread, but the exact score."

"Jesus Christ," uttered Ed, looking at his grandson incredulously. "Are you stupid? Do you really believe that?"

"There ain't even any football on anymore, you moron," retorted one of Breanna's sons. "Grandpa, he thinks football is still on."

Ed shook his head and placed a hand over his eyes. "God, give me strength."

"Stop! We need to work together. Not fight like animals," shouted Irene. "To help each other."

"I was trying to help," said Arthur.

"The uncertainty of what is happening is the problem. We are all on edge," said Breanna, pouting as she looked at Irene.

"Something tells me this is worse than anything we have ever faced," said Ed. "The flash of light this morning scared the living hell out of me. It made it clear to me that we are facing a dangerous situation."

Ted wondered if Ed might bring him into the conversation. It was a perfect time for him to participate, but he still wasn't asked to share his knowledge.

"I heard none of the cars in St George and Cedar City are running," remarked Adam. "Now ours don't work."

"It was an electromagnetic pulse," explained Aaron. "Anyway, I figure that's what it was."

"Taylor Jefferson told us they couldn't get to the nursing home in Cedar City to see Tom's mother," said Breanna. "She said the gangs have taken over."

"I'll go ape shit on those gangsters if they come out here," said one of the grandkids.

"Just quit that kind of talk," yelled Irene to her tattooed grandson, with a menacing look on her face.

"I was just outside Parowan when the flash occurred, with Ted and his granddaughter Maddy. Ted is a retired colonel in the Army." Ed pointed at Ted. "He said it was electromagnetic."

"I guess I need to bring up the question of why we have these strangers here in your house?" Aaron asked. "I don't want to be mean about it, but I need to ask."

"Nothing personal," Breanna looked toward the group, "but we don't have any idea who you people are."

"I've known Terrance for quite some time." Aaron glanced at Terrance. "He is one hell of a mechanic."

Surprisingly, Ed remained quiet.

"They were stranded, by no cause of their own," Irene stated in a very stern voice. "There is no way I will ever put people in need out when I have the ability to help."

"Mom, you need to be careful," stated Breanna, looking at the intruders. "We know nothing about them."

Ted wondered how nice, moral people like Ed and Irene could have children so depraved. He took Maddy's hand and stepped to the middle of the room. He was finished waiting to be acknowledged.

"I found them to be very gracious and…." Irene stopped in midsentence as she noticed Ted.

"I understand your concern. I'm Ted Lisco and this is my granddaughter Maddy. I completely understand you questioning our intrusion on your family. I have a large family back in Colorado and undoubtedly would have the same suspicions," Ted spoke with a soothing voice. "Ed and Irene, if you don't mind, I would like to give your family some information that might not only help them understand the circumstances we are facing but might actually save their lives."

Irene nodded her head in affirmation. She was startled by Ted's straightforwardness.

"Please do," said Ed, surprised by Ted stating his information might save their lives.

Ted took in a deep breath, "First of all, I was a colonel in the United States Army, retired for less than a year. I have a wife named Nicole in Colorado. Maddy is the daughter of our son Bill. I traveled to California on Saturday to escort her home, from time she spent with her mother. I thank God, with all my heart, I made the decision to meet and fly with her on this occasion as she has traveled to California on her own. Knowing what I know now, I can't bear the thought of having her on that flight by herself."

"Oh my gosh," Irene placed her hand over her mouth. She looked at Maddy who was standing next to her grandfather surveying the room.

"I have an older brother, Lt. Col. Jon Lisco, who retired from the Army the same day I did. I also have a younger sister, Colonel Deb Lisco, who is actively serving," continued Ted. "My sister Deb has been warning and preparing for this very scenario for the past two years. Although I am unsure of the precise circumstances of what is happening around the country, I have seen and heard enough about gangs and infiltrators to believe that Deb's projections about the United States being attacked by a foreign government is a real possibility."

"Colonel, are you saying the people raising hell in Cedar City are from another country?" Adam's son Seth asked. He had served four years in the Marine Corps.

"They are mostly homegrown gang members," stated Ted, noting he now had everyone's full attention. "But there is a foreign influence. Terrance can validate everything I'm telling you."

"Are we being attacked?" Seth asked.

"It is a possibility," answered Ted. "On our trip here, we met an Army convoy traveling on Interstate 15, heading to the southern border with ammunition."

"The planes we saw today?" questioned Ed.

"I'm not sure where they were going but my guess is to protect the border."

"What should we be doing?" Aaron asked.

"The immediate threat to this ranch is from the gangs in Cedar City, not a foreign army," answered Ted. "We should prepare to protect ourselves from them."

"We can never fight off another countries army," stated Seth.

"Absolutely correct," Ted shook his head in agreement with the young man. "Hopefully, it never comes to that. So, we need to prepare to protect ourselves from the gangs at hand."

"How?" Breanna asked.

"Everyone needs to move to Ed and Irene's property."

"Leave our farms?" Aaron showed his tetchy personality. "I don't think so."

"You need to load all your food, clothes, bedding, and personal items and get them here as soon as possible. Bring weapons and ammunition because we are going to need them."

"This seems terribly over the top," said Adam, looking at Ed.

"It's not. If anyone knows of friends or even acquaintances who have weapons or were in the service, you should make every effort to convince them to come to the ranch." Ted turned to Ed and Irene. "Are you two good with this?"

Ed looked at Irene and held up his hands in wonderment. Irene folded her hands on her lap and sat silently.

"This is real," stated Ted. "I want to help you and your family. In return I want a place to stay until I can figure a way back to Colorado."

"I can't ask you to abandon your farms." Ed looked at his family. "But we will open the ranch to those of you who want to come here."

"Maybe we should be safe rather than sorry," said Irene perceptively. "Seth you and Judy have the RV you can park it out front."

"We should all head home and talk it over with our families." Aaron stood up.

"Ok, let's make noon tomorrow the time for everyone to decide," stated Ed. "We can decide living arrangements at that time."

"Before you leave." Irene held up her hand motioning to her family she wanted them to wait and hear her out. "I want everyone to know, we will be allowing all our new guests a welcoming place to stay."

Maddy looked at Ted with a look he could not identify. He wasn't sure if she was sad, scared or simply contemplating what circumstances they were facing. He had a night to figure out the best way to secure and maintain the property. There were a lot of decisions to be made. One item he must deal with was to have Ed sell him the F-250 pickup, using only a promissory note as collateral. If not, and the situation became too dangerous, he was planning to take it anyway, and leave an IOU as indemnity.

Eastern Colorado

The temperature had dropped to well below freezing. What was moderately heavy snow, only moments earlier, quickly turned into a blizzard. The swirling snow made it impossible for Hank to see more than five meters ahead. Rather than driving into the ditch he pulled the truck to the side of the narrow road. Bobby, Dave and Bill were under the tarp in the bed of the truck. Although those in the truck were warm from the heater in the cab, the people in the back vehicle were extremely cold. The arctic weather turned terrible circumstances into a potentially dangerous situation.

Jon tapped on the window of the truck. He was using the collar of his coat to shield his face from the blowing snow. Hank rolled the window down, allowing the warm air from the blaring heater to hit Jon's face.

"I can't see the road," said Hank.

"We are freezing our butt's off," Jon grimaced. "With any luck, the snow will let up enough for us to drive to Clint Brown's farm."

"It's a good eight kilometers to his place."

"We will be in real trouble if we go off the road. Jason is getting some blankets from the back of his car so I think we will survive." Jon peeked under the tarp at Bobby, Dave and Bill. They looked completely miserable, using the thin tarp as a tent to shield themselves from the wind and snow. At least there was some heat coming from the open window on the back of the cab of the truck.

"We have to tough it out," snapped Hank. "There is no way we can drive in this blizzard."

Jon walked back to the car he and Gina were sharing with Jason and Kori. He got in the back seat and cuddled under a blanket as they watched the windows of the car being covered with snow.

***

The wind had blown much of the snow off the windshield of both vehicles, allowing the welcoming sun to shine through to the weary occupants. Bobby, Dave and Bill pushed the frozen snow off the tarp as they emerged from their uncomfortable entrapment. The wind had blown so hard that there was little snow on the road. Hank had been turning the engine on and off to use the heater all through the night. Nobody slept for more than a few minutes.

Hank was becoming angry with the situation of having been chased out of the one place he thought to be a safe destination. It was somewhat humiliating for everyone to find a place to use the restroom. He knew that they could now drive to the Brown farm. Clint and his wife Peg were lifelong friends of the Lisco family. They would be more than welcoming. As he was about to tell everyone that it was time to leave, he heard the noise of approaching vehicles.

An ATV followed by two MRAP vehicles pulled up next to the pickup truck. Just as Deb was stepping out of the ATV, an RG-35 Nyala with a manned open-air 0.50 caliber heavy machine gun pulled in behind the other vehicles.

"What in the hell are you doing out here?" Deb asked, using a powerful voice. She was in full fatigues, flanked by a soldier.

"When we got here the house was occupied," answered Hank dismally. "We were totally out gunned."

"There are fifteen to twenty of them," declared Jon. "They are armed to the teeth."

"Did they have any of our weapons?" Deb addressed the question to Bill.

"No, all I saw were hunting rifles," answered Bill.

"Any idea how long they've been in the house?" Deb was worried that they were tearing up her pride and joy.

"No, only that they were there last night," Hank shrugged.

"Wait a few minutes and then follow us." She climbed back into the ATV. The convoy of army vehicles drove quickly toward the farmhouse.

Flanked by three men, Deb went to the front door and tried to open it. It was locked. She didn't want to ruin the door, which cost her nearly three thousand dollars. She returned to her vehicle and clicked on the microphone. "You in the house. You have five minutes to remove yourself from the premises. It will not bode well for you to make us come in."

"We have snipers on the roof," shouted a soldier from a position behind a truck.

"You on the roof. You are ten seconds from having your heads removed. Place your weapons down and come to the front yard," ordered Deb over the loud-speaker. "You shoot at one of my soldiers it will be the last thing you do on this earth."

Soldiers were preparing to surround the house when the front door opened. The blond, bushy haired man dressed in fatigues came out first, followed by the rest of the intruders.

"What do you want?" asked the blond-haired man. "You need a warrant to enter."

"This happens to be my home," announced Deb.

"Not anymore."

Deb ignored the statement, walking past him to enter the house, followed closely by three soldiers.

"Dammit, look at the mess," she mused. "The whole house smells like marijuana."

The soldiers followed her into the living room, making sure to secure each room.

"Oh my God." Deb picked up a cut piece of two by ten lumber sitting next to the fireplace. "They cut up some of the two by tens for firewood."

The soldiers followed close behind as Colonel Deb stormed out of the house. She stared down the group of young men and women before getting in the face of the bushy haired man.

"Are you the leader of this pack of thieves?" Even though he was a good thirty centimeters taller than her, she placed her face as close to his as she could.

"Does it look like I take orders from anyone?" he replied sarcastically.

"What makes you think you can take possession of someone else's property?" She knew the ridiculous laws that existed caused the freeloaders to believe they had rights to the property.

"Possession is ninety percent of the law."

"It's my house! While you were using your money to smoke weed, I was skimping to pay for this." She waved her hand indicating she was talking about the entire property. "For three years I used every spare dollar I made to buy these materials. Now get the hell off my property."

"Take us to court."

"What!" Deb stuck out her chin. Every one of the soldiers knew that meant trouble.

"We're not going anywhere. My dad's a lawyer and I know my rights."

Deb stepped closer to the man. She was prepared to punch him in the face, not only because he thought he was entitled to benefit from her foresight and hard work, but because he had used her framing lumber for burning. Before she could strike, he stepped back into a karate stance.

"Take your best shot."

Deb hesitated and looked, for an extraordinary amount of time, piercing into the man's eyes. She had been in many skirmishes during her time fighting for the country, but it wasn't her combat experience that made her a great leader. It was because under any circumstance she would find a way to win.

"Master Sergeant Herrera," Deb yelled, placing her hands at her side.

"Yes ma'am."

"Would you do me a personal favor?"

"Of course, ma'am."

"Would you beat the living shit out of this guy?"

"With great pleasure ma'am." Sergeant Herrera began to remove his ammunition belt.

"Son," Deb turned to the blond man. "I have thousands of soldiers in my command. It is your extreme bad luck that traveling with me today is this particular sergeant."

"Like I said before, take your best shot." He held his arms wide open.

Colonel Deb turned to a soldier behind her, "I'll give all of you one more chance to get into your vehicles and leave this property. Corporal Dobbs make a note that Sergeant Herrera is under my direct order to remove a threatening civilian from the premises. Note, I am giving the civilian another opportunity to leave."

"Noted," replied the corporal, stepping into the cab of the vehicle.

Sergeant Herrera was down to his undershirt, he was 235 pounds of muscle. Not only was this civilian overmatched but nearly everyone in the Army would have refused to fight the soldier.

A private standing next to Deb said, "This is not going to be pretty."

The blond man shot a karate kick, one that for a civilian was more than adequate, in the direction of the sergeant's head. The sergeant walked right past the kick and grabbed the man by the back of his neck, lifted him high in the air and slammed him face first into the snow-covered ground. His nose shattered on the frozen lawn, leaving a pool of red on the white snow. Had he been a true enemy he would have been dead from a knife to a vital organ. Sergeant Herrera picked up the dazed civilian and held him in front of Colonel Deb.

"Can you apologize to Colonel Lisco?" Sergeant Herrera asked in a calm voice.

"Fuck you."

Sergeant Herrera snapped his wrist, causing a loud popping noise. He kicked him in the chest sending him falling to the feet of his accomplices, screaming in pain.

The trespassers picked up their leader, placing him, bleeding, on the back seat of a 2047 Chevy Camaro. The remainder of the squatters jumped into the other vehicles. Before they drove off Jon approached the Camaro holding the pudgy man who had intimidated him earlier.

"Just so you know, if you come back to this property, we will shoot you on sight." Jon felt a sense of redemption in threatening his tormentors. "There is no reason in the world for you to come here in the future."

After they drove away, Jon turned to Deb. "I'm glad their cars started. It looks like we now know that the EMPs have a limited range."

"I found out about the tests DARPA performed with the confiscated EMPs about three months ago," replied Deb. "It gave me enough time to purchase a couple new vehicles and store them in the garage. They should run."

"Thank God you came when you did." Jacqueline noticed how calm her sister-in-law was after the confrontation. "Last night was the most miserable night I have ever had."

"I tried to warn Hank before our phones quit that the security cameras showed trespassers on the property. The little bastards covered the cameras before I could tell how many of them were here."

"Can you stay for a while?" Hank asked, looking at Sergeant Herrera standing next to Deb. "I'm going to take the sergeant behind the shed and kick his ass."

"Yeah right," Deb smiled and slapped the sergeant on the back. "I have one hell of a fighting force. I do want to stay long enough for them to show you how to operate some of the weapons. But first, let's get everyone settled in the house."

"I'm all for that," said Hank, turning to Sergeant Herrera. "By the way, thank you."

Sergeant Herrera smiled and nodded his head.

Deb turned to Nicole and told her, "I'm trying my best to find out about Ted and Maddy. It's a very confusing situation, with several of the airplanes out of LAX last Saturday being forced to land in Las Vegas and Phoenix, I'm not sure where Ted and Maddy ended up. The only good news is that none of the planes crashed."

"Are we sure they didn't make it to DIA?" Nicole asked.

"None of the planes from the west coast made it over the Rockies."

Bill asked, "Aunt Deb, wouldn't Dad be able to locate a military facility and get help?"

Deb hesitated for a moment. "Bill, we are being threatened at our borders. All military are to be utilized to protect the borders, and not assist civilians. Your dad is a civilian now. Having said that, I'm sure if he gets to a base, they will assist him. No question they will give him refuge."

Deb never mentioned that she was concerned about not hearing anything from Ted. At the very least if he ended up in Phoenix or Las Vegas he would have gotten a message to her.

"Deb, I'm exhausted from worrying. I know there is nothing I can do, but not knowing where they are has worn me out," stated Nicole.

"You have been married to Ted for more than thirty years. You know he has lived through some extremely dangerous times. He knows how to survive."

"And with Maddy being there with him, I'm sure he will do everything he can to bring her home," said Bill. He felt better hearing the words of encouragement from his aunt. He knew she would tell him the truth.

"Without question he will. Now, let's go in and get everyone situated," said Deb.

Nicole took hold of Debs hand and squeezed. She was so lucky to have such an amazing sister-in-law who could show such power on one hand and such compassion on the other. She felt much better about her husband and granddaughter as they made their way into the farmhouse.

Jacoby Ranch

Ed and Irene discussed the sleeping arrangements, and decided that Ted, Maddy, Carol, Scotty and Samantha could use the three upstairs bedrooms. Travis, Jerry and Terrance could use the bunks in the main garage. Over the years Terrance had slept in the garage on several occasions.

Ted and Samantha agreed Carol and Scotty could use the largest bedroom with an attached bathroom. The other two bedrooms shared a bathroom. He and Maddy desperately needed to shower. One of the problems was that their clothes were filthy. Irene was more than compliant in letting them use the washing machine, in fact she insisted on washing the clothes herself.

Since Maddy had two sets of clothes, Ted had her leave on her pants and a tee-shirt. He stripped down to his boxer shorts while Maddy carried the clothes downstairs to Irene.

Ted decided to take the first shower so he could determine how hot to make the water. He looked to make sure nobody was present, then slipped across the hall, into the bathroom. He desperately needed a shave, but that would have to wait. The hot water on his body felt invigorating as he washed the dirt and grime away. He turned off the spicket and pulled the shower curtain to the side. The bathroom door opened, in stepped Samantha, wearing a very revealing bright gold, geisha nighty. She froze with her mouth wide open staring at him, in all his glory, unable to grab anything to cover himself.

"Oh my gosh. I'm so sorry," she muttered, backing out the door.

***

Ted threw on his boxers, wrapped a towel around his waist, and crossed the hall to his room. He had Maddy go down the hall and knock-on Samantha's door to tell her she could take a shower next.

"What did she say?" Ted asked anxiously, as Maddy came back into the room.

"She told me to go first," answered Maddy. "Grandpa, she was laughing when she said it. She was laughing so hard I thought she was crying."

"Oh boy, she must have been thinking of something really funny," said Ted, thinking how interesting breakfast would be in the morning.

After Maddy's shower Ted tucked her into the bed. He planned to tell her a story, but she wasn't interested in hearing one. She wanted to talk about the first sleepover she had at his home when they read a book called "Big Dog Thinks he is a Doctor". They talked for about ten minutes before she fell into a deep sleep.

Ted sat in a chair looking out the bedroom window. He had a perfect view of the main road leading to the farmhouse. Eventually there was going to be a need to protect the property. He wondered how Ed and Irene's family would respond. The three children were all older than him, and the crazy grandkids would be all but useless in a skirmish. Seth, the grandson, who had been in the military, was the exception. It was important to use all the resources available in the most proficient manner. Yet after thinking of the many scenarios they might have to confront; he decided there was a good chance he and Maddy would need to flee the ranch. The problem was that all the main highways were too dangerous to travel, and there was no military base within hundreds of kilometers. There had never been a time in his life where he was so isolated and unable to communicate with his family.

After sitting and thinking for a while he realized he was not going to fall asleep. Now would be a good time to figure a way to safely carry the pistol he received back at the hangar. He noticed an ace bandage in the bathroom cabinet, something from which he could create a makeshift holster. Not perfect but better than nothing.

***

Ted woke slumped over in the chair to the smell of bacon. Maddy was sitting in the bed rubbing her eyes. He moved to her side and gave her a kiss on the forehead. She jerked away.

"Grandpa, I'm not a baby."

"I was showing you how happy I am to see you this morning."

"Ok, but I'm not a baby."

"I will make a note not to treat you like a baby." Ted moved away from the bed. "Miss lady, do you think you could go down and see if Irene has our clothes, so I don't have to spend the entire day in my skivvies."

She chuckled. Her hair was a total snarled mess as she got out of bed and went downstairs. She came back with a hairbrush on top of the neatly folded clothes.

"Irene said I can use the brush and breakfast is ready."

She wanted to brush her tangled hair, which took quite some time, making them the last to arrive for breakfast. Irene and Jerry were shuffling plates of food to the large dining room table. Everyone was busy eating like it would be their last meal.

Ted tried to push Maddy to sit in the chair next to Samantha. She jumped into the one next to Scotty. By the time they sat down there was a plate full of eggs, bacon and potatoes sitting in front of them. Irene handed him a cup of coffee without saying anything. It would not be long before a large breakfast would be a thing of the past. He figured he might as well enjoy, like everyone else.

After the meal Ted turned to look at Samantha. Her hair and make-up were impeccable. When she made eye contact with him, she closed her eyes and started laughing.

"Alright, alright, let's get this out of the way. That was so embarrassing," he whispered, bending his neck away from the others at the table. The laughing was contagious, and he began to laugh. "I should have locked the door."

"I'm so sorry I walked in on you. But you should have seen your face," she sniffled and stopped laughing.

"Your face was pretty funny too," stated Ted. "Can we forget it, and act like it never occurred?"

"I'll try, but I think it might be etched in my mind."

Ted thought about telling her that her little nighty would be etched in his mind for a long time. Not wanting to give her the wrong idea about his intentions, he remained silent.

The sound of a tractor in front of the house caused everyone to look out the large picture window. Outside was Adam pulling a trailer full of supplies. Riding on the side of the trailer were his immediate family. Another tractor could be heard coming up the driveway. It was Breanna and her family.

Ed leaned back in his chair and watched the two families mull around outside, pointing in different directions, and loudly fighting amongst themselves. He calmly sipped on his coffee, stopping only to hold the cup out so Irene could fill it from the carafe. He patiently watched as the two families continued to scream and yell at each other.

Breanna came storming through the front door. She looked at everyone at the table with a look of disgust as she stopped in front of Ed. "Dad, Adam's little brats think they are going to get the upstairs rooms for themselves. You know they were my rooms."

Ed looked at her in disbelief. Good lord he thought, it has been over forty-five years since she slept at the farmhouse. Ed looked away and shook his head.

"Mom," she turned to her mother, "don't let those little drug addicts use the upstairs."

"Enough Breanna," Irene held up her hand, "we'll make those decisions when Aaron gets here."

"He ain't coming."

"How do you know?" Ed asked skeptically.

"We stopped at his place on the way over. He said he's staying at his farm."

"There's someone coming up the drive," yelled Adam through the front door.

Two black SUVs drove onto the driveway and parked behind the tractors. A total of six men dressed in black pants and matching black leather coats stepped out of the vehicles.

Ted knew immediately this was the nightmare scenario he hoped to avoid. He looked at Terrance and asked, "Where are your AK-47s?"

"In the garage," answered Terrance.

"Go out the back and get them. Make sure to keep out of sight," commanded Ted, turning to Ed. "Ed you have to talk with these men. You need to agree with everything they say."

"Why would I do that?"

"Because they are very dangerous."

The men spoke for a moment with the grandchildren at the tractors, before walking up the sidewalk. Ed joined Adam on the porch, with Irene and Breanna standing behind the screen door. They waited for the approaching men.

Ted ran upstairs and grabbed the pistol from his jacket. He placed it in his makeshift holster, tucked it under his shirt, and hurried down the stairs. Maddy, Carol, Scotty, Travis and Samantha were in the kitchen waiting near the backdoor.

"If there is any sort of shooting, you run to the garage," he said, before moving to the door, waiting behind Breanna and Irene. He could see the others in the kitchen from his vantage point, as he looked at Ed and Adam.

"Can we help you gentlemen?" Ed asked.

One of the men came to the steps in front of the porch and stopped. The other five stayed a few meters back, separating so they were spaced apart on the lawn.

"Are you the owner?" the man asked with a very thick accent.

"Yes I am."

"I see you have cattle on this farm?"

"I prefer to call it a ranch. Nonetheless, I do have cattle."

"We are going to need your cattle."

"I suppose for the right price I can part with some of my cattle."

The man smiled and shook his head. "No, no, no, by working with us you will be allowed to continue with ranching. To show us good faith we want all the frozen meat you have already processed."

"I do a lot of good in this community. But giving my cattle or my meat away for free, well that just will never happen."

The five men behind the leader opened their coats showing Ed holstered pistols.

Ted knew that the men wanting to take the frozen meat was a game changer. He noted several of Ed's grandchildren standing by the tractors with their firearms. They were staring at the men. Behind the tractors he could see Terrance and Jerry.

"It will be better for everyone if you agree to give us the meat. We will leave you enough, so your family won't starve." The man spoke with an arrogance that really rubbed Ed the wrong way.

"Listen you commie bastards," Ed yelled loudly. "You get in your cars and get the hell off my property."

Adam placed his hand on his dad's shoulder.

When they heard their grandfather raise his voice, all the grandchildren moved toward the men, led by Seth. Terrance and

Jerry were right behind them. Ted moved around Irene and stepped on the porch.

"Look behind you, look behind you," yelled Ted. "Do not pull your guns out."

All six of the men turned to look. The grandchildren gathered at the white picket fence encircling the lawn. All rifles were raised, and the subversives were in their sights.

"Ok, we will leave for now," said the leader very calmly, turning to walk down the sidewalk. "But we will be back. When we do all of your food will be taken."

Ted stepped off the porch and followed the men as they walked past the grandchildren. He motioned for Terrance and Jerry to follow. He wasn't about to let these guys get away without getting a better feel as to who they were. He preferred that the seven grandchildren with the rifles not follow, but they pushed forward, and were in the subversives faces before they reached the cars.

"Stop for a moment." Ted blocked the leader as he neared the door to his SUV, as the others entered the cars. "Before you leave, we need some answers."

"I am a very forthright person. We need food. You have it. We will take it."

"It won't be that easy." He knew these men would be back in force. Many members of Ed's family could die, but he was confident he could defend the farm.

"Yes, it will," said the leader. "You have no idea what is about to happen."

"Enlighten me."

"You are about to be in the middle of a very strategic deployment of forces."

"Are you saying in Utah?" Ted asked incredulously.

"Right here in Utah," answered the man, opening the door to the SUV.

Ted still was not sure if he was talking about gangs, or a foreign military. "Are you saying invading forces are going to penetrate our borders and deploy here?"

"Believe me, thousands of troops will be within sight of this farm by dawn tomorrow." He sat down in the SUV. "Then we will need the food from this ranch."

"Why would you tell me this?"

"Because it's about to happen. There isn't a thing you can do about it, except comply with our wishes and have the meat ready, and at our disposal."

Ted stood back and allowed the men to leave. He waited, watching a cloud of dust disappear in the distance. What was he missing? He had discussed with Jon and Deb the many possibilities and scenarios on ways the country might be attacked. How in the world could a strategic deployment of enemy forces occur here, in southwest Utah?

Colorado Farm

Deb was on cloud nine as she sat in the living room of her home. General Lauer at Fort Carson was fully aware of her making the trip to the farm. He commanded the base with the idea that strong families make strong soldiers, so when Deb asked to make the hour and half drive to the eastern plains, it was his idea for her to take the platoon along for training. She had a couple of hours before she had to get back to soldiering. Although she was in a holding pattern waiting to see where they would be positioned, if at all. With all the posturing and sabre rattling she figured the two sides would agree that war would be a losing proposition for all sides. It would be avoided.

"I love that picture of grandpa," said Jon, pointing to a picture on the fireplace mantle of a young man standing outside a stone building with the words Dattenburg, Germany, March 1945. He knew it was Deb's favorite picture. It made her feel good to talk about it.

"March 1945," said Deb, scanning the non-family members in the room. She was holding a cup of hot tea in one hand. "It was significant because the American Army just crossed the Rhine over the Ludendorff bridge. Grandpa Henry, three months earlier, fought in the Battle of the Bulge. His division, the 99th, were preparing to clear out the Ruhr pocket in the middle of Germany and move south toward Bavaria to join General Patton for a final march to the Danube."

"It's too bad we never got to meet him," said Jon sorrowfully. "He was in his late forties when Dad was born."

"All the stories Dad told us made it seem like we knew him well," stated Deb.

"That is really awesome," Jason Jensen listened intently to the Lisco family reminiscence. "You have a lot of history."

"Yes, Colonel Lisco," said Kori, standing next to her husband. "Your home is really special. Thank you for letting us share it."

"It's exceptional," stated Al. "You even have a dental chair."

"Hopefully, everyone will come to their senses, and you can go home." Deb turned toward Reagan and Avery. "The neighbor is taking care of my horses. You can ride them when we bring them back to the farm."

Both girls smiled and looked at their mother.

"Well, tell her you would like that," said Jessica.

"We would like that," declared Avery.

"Yeah," said Reagan. "Thank you."

"You are welcome." Deb smiled at the girls. She turned to Hank. "Have you figured the sleeping arrangements?"

"Nicole, Gina and Jacqueline have it figured out," answered Hank.

"Nice." Deb noticed a soldier coming in the front door. Bobby, Bill, Dave and Emilee were in the process of being taught how to shoot all the weapons on the property.

"Colonel," the private saluted, "the civilians are now adequately proficient in the operation of the weapons on the premises."

Deb saluted. "We leave in fifteen minutes."

"Yes ma'am." He left just as Bobby and Emilee entered. Bobby noticed the look of lust the soldier gave Emilee.

Deb informed Jon, "Bill is aware of all the systems installed on the farm. They are state of the art. The Browns have been caring for my farm animals, they will bring the chickens over in the next couple of days. You can work with them to arrange delivery of the cattle. The ponds have been stocked. I've left notes and plans in my office that will help with running the farm. They detail what you can do to make it sustainable.

"I'm looking forward to starting the framing," Jason remarked.

"I'm glad we have a builder here." Having a master builder for the projects was a concern of Deb's from the beginning of her endeavor at the farm.

"Have our borders been breached?" Jon changed the subject.

"We are negotiating right now in Washington with Russia and China to try and avoid a full out war. Russia has moved a massive number of troops to their border at the Bering Strait. That is only 85 kilometers from Alaska. We know there are Chinese and Iranian troops in Mexico but are unsure how many. It's wait and see."

"Has the east coast been hit?"

"Every city has been targeted by gangs and the subversives. Some worse than others. But the government is still working."

"Do you know if we will get cell phones back?" Hank asked.

"Depends if we are able to assist in getting the electrical grid operational and cell towers functioning. If we go to the border it will be a long time before they work. The guard is clearing out the gangs in Colorado Springs and gaining back control for the police, as we speak, and then they will go to the Denver metro area. They have caused so much damage, even best-case scenario it will be months to repair our infrastructure."

"So, we best prepare to be here a while," stated Jason.

"Hopefully, it will only be days, but you should prepare as if you will be here for years," answered Deb, turning to Bobby. "Do you feel comfortable with the weapons?"

"Your guys are amazing. They were thorough in teaching us."

"We are good with everything," said Bill. "Even the fifty calibers."

"That's great," Deb hesitated for a moment. She scanned the room for the parents. "I have to bring this up. I know your kids are only seventeen right now, but there is already mention of a bill being pushed to implement the draft. With them turning eighteen sometime in the next year, it is something to keep in the back of your minds. If we are attacked, we will need troops, and we will need them in a hurry."

"It's something I hadn't thought about. Only a couple of days ago the most important thing in the world was the state championship football game. Now it's worrying about our kids going to war," stated Jacqueline remorsefully. "How quick things can change."

"I have to go." Deb moved in the direction of the front door. "I don't know when I'll be back. It might be next week, or it might be a month."

"Deb," Nicole followed her sister-in-law outside, "will you get in touch with us if you receive any information about Ted and Maddy."

"I'll do my best." Deb gave her a quick hug and hopped into the ATV.

The military vehicles drove down the wet driveway, disappearing into the distance. Nicole waited outside as the sun broke through the clouds; the warmth felt good as she looked over the vast open farmland. She thought back to the different ages of Maddy and all the wonderful times they had together. The only way she would ever be able to rid herself of the anguish was to feel the skinny little arms of her granddaughter around her neck, giving her a hug. And Ted, their relationship for the past five years had been rocky, to say the least. Now, with so much insecurity, she missed his confidence and the safety net he offered when faced with a true crisis. The pettiness of fighting over trivial matters seemed ludicrous. She wondered if he was thinking the same, wherever he might be.

***

Everyone was busy trying to find their niche at the farm. The three hundred twenty-acre homestead allowed for a lot of room to roam. Hank was taking the leadership role in organizing and administering different duties. He had a knack of making decisions on issues and making them seem like they were concepts generated by the entire group.

Hank noticed Bill seemed to want to be involved with whatever task Jessica was working on. When she decided she wanted to work with plants in the small greenhouse, Bill acted like he was a great horticulturist. It never dawned on him that his nephew was the same age as mother of his son's girlfriend. And a very pretty mother she was. They spent the entire day working with plants. By night fall they were holding hands and talking under the moon.

Hank wondered if a tactical error was made in giving Bill one of the small bedrooms in the basement, where Jessica and her girls were quartered. The more he thought about it, he was treating his nephew as though he was fifteen years old. He never heard any of the details on his dating after the divorce from Cindy. This was one of the things that would play out over time.

Jacoby Ranch

Ted followed everyone to the front door of the farmhouse and watched as they went inside. He sat on the railing of the hundred-year-old porch. The picturesque landscape of the ranch, from the red barn to the fences, had a clean fresh look. Ed and Irene put decades of work into making it so impressive. It was like many other ranches across the country, each one special in their own way. This is truly America. Safeguarding our soil was why the Liscos fought for the country.

"Grandpa, why are you out here?" Maddy opened the screen door and joined him on the deck.

Ted was having a hard time grasping the conversation he only minutes ago participated in, with the heinous insurgent. He was not one to be intimidated, but the conversation left him shaken. He placed his hand on the side of Maddy's face as she stood beside him. Her little jaw was sticking straight out. Deb's jaw was always considered to be the most pronounced of all his siblings, but Maddy's might be more prominent than his sister's. He remembered his father's jaw sticking out while telling stories of their grandfather's battles from World War II. He loved hearing the real-life stories of heroism and sacrifice.

"Grandpa," yelled Maddy, pulling on his sleeve, "you didn't even hear me."

"Tell me again."

"Did you see Samantha naked?"

"What! No, I didn't see her naked. She saw me."

"Oh my gosh." She put her hands to her mouth and giggled.

"How did you know?"

"She told Carol you saw her in the shower."

"Oh boy. I didn't see her; she saw me naked in the shower." Ted dropped his eyes to look at her. "Remember all the secrets I have kept of yours over the years? This is one we will never tell anyone. Deal."

"Ok, deal."

Ted looked at her and smiled. Being around her always made him feel good. Yet being in this situation was almost unfathomable.

Samantha came out the screen door.

"Thanks Samantha," said Ted sarcastically as she approached them.

"Carol asked why we were laughing at breakfast," she held up both hands. "I didn't think Maddy could hear us talking."

Ted shook his head. He turned to Maddy. "Could you go inside with Samantha and see if you can help Irene with some chores?"

"Why do you ask Grandpa?"

"I need a little time to think."

"Come on, I know what we can do." Samantha held Maddy's hand as they went through the door. Samantha glanced back at Ted as they went inside. "Maybe we can put some nail polish on."

Ted remained motionless for nearly half an hour, deep in thought, contemplating the different scenarios the subversives were preparing to launch against the farms and ranches in the surrounding area. He looked at the beautiful panorama in front of him. A visual of the area with planes flying overhead dropping thousands of parachutes from the sky, hit him like a ton of bricks. They were going to parachute the soldiers to this location. He always considered America's borders to be impregnable. He wasn't sure how, but he felt they were preparing for a massive drop of troops at this beautiful but void area. Giving them a foothold in the country, spreading our already depleted military away from defending the borders.

Ted turned to where he could hear the people inside the farmhouse. Less than twenty-four hours earlier he told them the immediate threat to the farm was from gangs, and not from invading forces, that he could help them defend their property. Now, he realized his assumption was completely wrong. He, Maddy and anyone else who wanted to go with them, needed to leave the area immediately. He was looking at being caught at the epicenter of war with his granddaughter at his side. It was something he refused to do. They had to flee, with as many of the people from the ranch as he could convince to go.

PART TWO

Washington DC
Situation Room, White House

"What the hell is this? There isn't even a seat for the Vice Chairman," yelled Secretary of Defense Robert Maes, looking directly at President Weller seated at the head of the long table. "We are going to have to find a bigger room."

A member of the White House council relinquished his seat and took a place next to the wall, allowing the Secretary's Adviser a chair. The President's Cabinet, the Joint Chiefs of Staff, along with Military Service Chiefs and many White House advisers crowded into the room.

"People," yelled the President. "We no longer are communicating with the Russians or the Chinese. War is imminent."

"It has started," stated the Secretary of Defense. "We are scurrying to strategically place troops within our borders."

"Bob, what is the latest on the southern border?" asked the President.

"We estimate one hundred and ten thousand Chinese and Iranian troops at the Mexican border," answered Secretary Maes. "There are some skirmishes with the Mexican forces, but for the most part they are moving unopposed into the large cities along the border on the Mexican side."

"Another two hundred thousand troops are moving up from the south, completely unopposed," added the Defense Secretary's Vice Chairman. "They could already be there."

"Have we thought about striking before they amass anymore troops?" asked Vice President John Trupp.

President Weller gave the Vice President a sharp look. He was anything but a wartime president. Never in the history of the country had there been a bigger dove elected to the highest honor in the country. Peace and antiwar sentiments were a big part of his platform during the 2048 election that he won in a landslide. For him to give the order for a preemptive strike was inconceivable.

"What about the northern border?" President Weller ignored the question brought forth by the Vice President.

"Many of Canada's cities are experiencing disruptions, but nothing like our cities are suffering. There is an extraordinary amount of activity across the Bering Strait, near Anadyr air base. It's something we have been keeping an eye on for the past six months," answered the Vice Chairman.

"We have to prepare for the worst," President Weller was emphatic. He turned to Peg Nygaard, the Secretary of Homeland Security. "Can we our cities under control?"

"Eventually," stated the Secretary. "The National Guard has been called up, but they are running thin. We will take the streets back, but the citizens are going to have to rise up and fight back."

"Prudence is not a virtue any of us can aspire to. We have to act precisely and quickly, anything else will be counterproductive." The President was standing as he used his loud booming voice to rally the multitude of advisers. "This is the time we must rally all Americans. I am being advised as to all laws and procedures this Presidency will need to invoke. Congress needs to immediately pass into law a new Military Selective Service Act to bring back the draft. They should be working on this as we speak. We are going to need soldiers. The very existence of our country is at stake."

"Sir, can we use troops to enforce law in the cities?" Secretary of Defense Maes asked. "Am I hearing you correct? Marshal Law has been invoked."

"Whatever it takes. You have the finest military minds in the world at your disposal, right here in this room. Use them," the President demanded loudly, without giving a definitive yes.

"I take that as a yes, sir," said the Secretary.

"Yes, we have to take control of our cities. Millions of Americans will die if we don't." The President remained standing but lowered his voice. "I am shocked by the precision and quickness of our enemies to cripple the country. A hundred and ten years ago Franklin D Roosevelt, who used a radio to address the nation after the attack on Pearl Harbor, was able to communicate with the citizenry. How ludicrous it is, with all the modern technology, there is no way for me to address the country. How could we not see this coming?"

Army Chief of Staff Ron McClinton sat quietly alongside the Chiefs of Staff from the other military branches. It was too late for anyone to change the past, but he could use the information he had accumulated from his short meeting with the Lisco family two years earlier. If Colonel Deb Lisco was correct, as every indication showed she was, then the President was about to make a big mistake.

"Mr. President," interjected General McClinton, getting a quizzical look from the Secretary of Defense, "if I might sir. I do believe prudence is necessary at this time. I believe the Russians and the Chinese want us to use our troops to fight the battles in our cities. And the second you invoke Marshall Law our borders will be attacked."

"Can you explain?" the President looked at Secretary of Defense Maes, who in turn looked to General McClinton.

"We should move all our infantry into strategic positions along the border first," said General McClinton. "The enemy want us to commit to clearing out the cities. I believe when we do, even though it is a slight advantage, they plan to attack."

A staff member approached the President and handed him a note.

"Camp Red Cloud is under attack," announced the President. "We are officially at war."

Jacoby Ranch

Ted entered the house unsure of how to approach the issue of fleeing the ranch. Maddy, Samantha and Carol were helping Irene with lunch. The smell of barbeque beef flowed from the kitchen. Ed was still visibly shaken, sitting at the dining room table with Breanna and Adam on each side of him. Terrance and Jerry were at the opposite end of the large table. The grandkids were in front of the house, gathered around the tractors, still holding on to their rifles.

Ted went straight to the kitchen. It was only a couple of hours earlier that Irene finished cooking breakfast, and now she was back preparing lunch. Cooking was truly her forte.

"Grandpa, I'm in charge of the biscuits," Maddy held up one finger and shook it at him. "Don't distract me."

"She's doing a wonderful job." Irene moved from one station to the next, busily preparing an extraordinary lunch.

Ted remained silent. He could not believe the vibrance and energy of the great-grandmother, as she created a parallel realm of happiness and safety away from the dangerous world that surrounded them. Although in her mid-nineties she moved like a lady in her fifties. He knew she was the one he needed to first inform of the change of heart he held about the impending danger to their ranch. He moved to her side as she scurried around.

"Irene, can I speak with you outside?" Ted asked nonchalantly. "I'd like to run something by you."

"Ok," said Irene. The earlier incident had her shaken, so she was relieved to speak with Ted. "Let's step out the back door."

Irene was a very plain-spoken woman, so he was quick and to the point. He explained how the guerillas wanting to confiscate their meat was not a surprise. What was alarming, was the leader insinuating to him there was about to be an invasion. The confidence of the insurgent was distressing because it caused him to believe the threat. If true, it would be impossible to protect their ranch. By doing so she would lose many members of the family.

"I take it that you are planning on leaving," stated Irene, after listening quietly. "That we need to figure this out for ourselves."

"No… Partly," Ted stammered. "Maddy and I are leaving. But I want you, Ed and as many others willing to leave, to go with us."

Irene looked at him with a surprised look. "You know that will never happen. We will never leave this farm. We've lived here our entire lives."

"I understand your hesitancy. But, if you do not leave, you are going to find yourself right smack in the middle of war. Believe me Irene, I'm telling you, I know from experience that many of your family will die."

"This ranch is our whole life."

"Please Irene." Ted took hold of her right hand and held it with both of his. He felt such a connection with the old lady that he was willing to beg her to leave. "This ranch won't go anywhere. Worst case scenario is they cause some damage. But if you stay here, it will be much worse. Wars always end, and you can return."

Irene took in a deep breath. She patted his hands with her left hand. "Give me a little time to think about it."

"Ok," Ted released her hand and thought for a moment. Although he had no mode of transportation he stated, "Maddy and I are leaving this afternoon."

Maddy opened the back door and leaned halfway out. "Irene, I think I burnt the bottom of my biscuits."

"Oh, my goodness," Irene lowered her head and rushed back into the kitchen. She went to work showing Maddy how to scrape the bottom off the burnt biscuits.

Ted understood her hesitancy in leaving such an ideal life. He wanted to give it one more stab at persuading her to leave the ranch, knowing she could influence the others to follow.

Ed was still at the dining room table talking to Breanna and Adam. Ted moved to the far end of the table, accepting a menacing look from Breanna.

"Here Grandpa," Maddy handed him a biscuit covered in jam, "they are so delicious."

Ted took a bite. "Wow, that really is delicious."

"Me and Irene scrapped off the bottoms. You can't even tell they got burnt."

"Is that Laney?" asked Breanna, standing to look out the window at the grandkids. Riding, at a full gallop, on a horse was a young girl. She jumped off the mount and handed the reins to one of her cousins. She screamed something to the others and sprinted to the front door of the ranch house. Seth started the tractor while the entire group jumped on the back of the trailer. They took off down the driveway.

"Grandpa, Grandma," yelled Laney as she rushed through the front door, "they shot Dad."

"What, who shot your dad?" Ed placed his hand on his granddaughter's shoulder.

"Men who came to take our meat."

"How bad is he hurt?" Irene anxiously asked. "Is he alive?"

"They shot him in the leg. Mom wants you to come and help."

"Are the men who shot him gone?" Adam asked.

"They left right before I did. Dad told me to ride as quick as I could."

"Well, let's go," Irene opened the front door.

"Wait just a moment." Ted stood next to Irene. Irene looked at him but didn't say anything. "Did you listen to the men and your dad talking before they shot him?"

"Yeah." Laney looked at Ted and then turned to Ed. "Me and Mom were standing there the whole time."

"Did your dad argue with them?" Ted asked, "or refuse to give them what they wanted?"

"No," she yelled emphatically. "He let them take all the meat. They emptied the freezers. They told Dad to round up the cattle and they would be back to follow him to the meat packing plant tomorrow. Then one of them shot him."

"Did they threaten you or your mom?" Irene asked, still blocking the front door.

"No, only Dad. They shot him because they are just mean," she began to cry. "He gave them the meat."

"Ok, ok," Ed placed his arm around his granddaughter. "We can take the Chevy. Everything will be fine."

"Edith Beck told Mom that we can't get to Parowan because they are fighting there, and some of the town is burning.

So, someone might have to go and bring a doctor to our ranch," said Laney, with tears in her eyes, directing her statement to her Uncle Adam.

Maddy was standing next to Ted, nearly in tears. He went down to a knee and grabbed her by the shoulders. "It's ok, Laney's just sad her dad got hurt."

Maddy leaned over gasping, trying not to cry, she whispered, "I want to go home. I want to see my daddy."

Ted anticipated from the moment they landed in Cedar City that Maddy would become frightened, because the dangers surrounding them were real. She had been such a trooper throughout the entire ordeal. He tried his best to mask the real peril they faced, but now he felt it necessary she understand they were in danger.

"Maddy, I need a hug from you."

She threw her arms around his neck and squeezed tight. The wetness from her eyes set on his chin. Maddy finally released her hug.

"That made me feel so much better," said Ted. "How about you?"

She shook her head up and down. "But I still want to see Daddy."

"I want you to look at me Maddy, right in my eyes."

Very seriously, she stared at him. He looked back at the little girl he, only a couple years ago, play-acted with, as she pretended to be a princess and he a prince.

"We are in a serious situation. It's not imaginary or make believe, but something that is very real and dangerous." Her big, dark eyes were staring directly at him. "I want you to help grandpa. You and I are a team. We can work together and figure out how to get home. But you need to listen and never question me when I tell you to do something, deal?"

"Deal," Maddy stood up tall.

Ted, seeing the 1957 Chevy pulling out of the Quonset, approached the vehicle, holding his hand in the air. Ed rolled down the window in the back seat.

"Irene, I know this is a stressful time with Aaron hurt, but there's no better time to tell your family about the things we discussed," said Ted, leaning into the window and speaking over Ed.

Irene looked at him with a blank look on her face. He turned to Ed, "Can I use the Ford while your away?"

"You're not planning on leaving with it are you?" Ed bent his bushy eyebrows downward.

"No, of course not. I want to do some reconnaissance to try and figure out what is really happening around here. I'm going to take your binoculars too."

"The keys are in the truck." Ed rolled up the window and they drove away.

Ted watched them leave. He had no qualms about stealing the Ford if the circumstances dictated. The shooting of Aaron, without provocation, caused him to wonder if there really was going to be an invasion. His plan was for he, Maddy and Terrance to get a firsthand account of everything transpiring in Parowan. Hopefully, the information gleaned would help determine if the insurgent's threats were real; or if they were they bluffing to make the ranchers agree to their terms of relinquishing their produce. Terrance would be able to locate the best vantage point to survey the entire area.

Parowan, Utah

Ted drove the F-250 down the main road outside Parowan. Approximately five kilometers from where he received the ticket from the city policeman. Terrance directed him to pull onto a little used road, leading them to a high hill, where they could see both Parowan and Cedar City. Several buildings were smoldering and a couple others blazing as they looked toward Parowan. He, Maddy and Terrance got out of the truck. It was a picture-perfect day with a bright blue sky.

"Good Lord," said Terrance, "they are doing a job on Parowan."

"Yeah, and Cedar City is still smoldering." Ted looked south over the rough terrain they had crossed to get to the farm.

"Look at that," Terrance pointed at the highway to the east, "cars are strewn all over the place."

Ted investigated through the binoculars in the direction of Interstate 15. Numerous tents were assembled along the ditch on both sides of the highway, with several armed men walking around. He turned to look at the fiery town of Parowan. Flames were visible in two buildings, but very few people were moving about.

"I'm not sure what I'm seeing here." Terrance stood closer to Ted and pointed at a large structure. Even with his bare eyes he was noticing something different about the town. "See the large building with the white roof? That's the new bank. About three hundred meters to the right, is something I've never seen."

Ted drew the binoculars from his eyes and located the bank. He looked to the right of the bank and brought the binoculars back up. It was a wooden structure with a platform. His heart sank as he noticed sitting on the dais was a 105 MM anti-aircraft gun. He scanned the entire town. Right in the dead center of the town was another shed type building with an anti-aircraft gun, and another on the far side of the town.

"We need to leave here, now," Ted said with alarm. "Those are anti-aircraft guns."

"Anti-aircraft guns?" Terrance asked.

"How in the hell did they get them. They are weapons from the Iraq war, or even Vietnam." Ted raised the binoculars and scanned the area toward Cedar City. He turned to Maddy and Terrance. "Let's get off this hill before someone spots us."

Ted drove off the hill as fast as he dared, making sure to avoid hitting any rocks. By the time he arrived at the blacktop of the county road, he made up his mind to go directly to Aaron's farm. He did not see any anti-aircraft weapons when he took a quick look in the direction of Cedar City, but he would bet there were several guns positioned in the inhabited regions surrounding the city. What better place to quarter an invading army than in the residential areas of a town or city? If left out in the open the American air power would destroy them in a matter of minutes. Everything he saw made it clear plans were being made for a massive influx of troops, whether they were capable of engendering the invading forces to the middle of the country was one thing, but what was for sure, they were preparing for the arrival of armed forces.

Ed and Irene were standing in the driveway next to the 1957 Chevy at Aaron's farm. Ted parked the pickup next to the car. He made up his mind that he would give the old couple ten minutes to decide to leave the area. If they decided to go with him, he would insist they depart before dark. If they decided to stay, he and Maddy would check with Carol, Scotty, Travis and Samantha to see if they wanted to leave. Any way he looked at it, he and Maddy were leaving.

Ted was surprised how much help he received from Terrance in communicating the inevitability of everyone in the community being caught in the middle of a war. He felt a great amount of compassion for the old couple as he described the devastation of the community they helped build. It was heartbreaking to see the sadness in Irene's grandmotherly face.

"We decided to go to Colorado with you," Ed slumped his shoulders in a distressing manner.

"I'm terribly sorry it has come to this." Ted placed a hand on the old man's shoulder. "But we do need to leave as quick as possible."

"Aaron has a flesh wound to his calf," said Irene. "He, Adam and Breanna are figuring out which of the grandkids are going to stay. They want to bring the Excursion RV."

"Are you saying Aaron, Adam and Breanna are planning on leaving with us?" Ted asked.

"Yes, along with Ashley and Megan," answered Irene. "As hard as it is to believe, they agreed to leave."

"Will they go now?"

"They just need time to pack."

"We don't want to be here tomorrow." Ted turned to Terrance. "How about you Terrance, are you and Jerry coming with us?"

"Oh yeah, and the sooner we leave the better."

"Can we use your antique vehicles." Ted looked at Ed.

"Better to take them than leave them here."

"We are going back to your place and prepare the others to leave," said Ted. "Could you have your family throw in extra clothes, especially your great granddaughter's clothes for Maddy?"

"We will," answered Ed. "Terrance, you can fill the vehicles with gas."

Jacoby Ranch

Samantha, sitting on the front porch, talking with Carol and Scotty, gawped at Ted as he drove swiftly by the farmhouse, straight to the side of the large Quonset. Jerry and Travis stepped out of the overhanging doors of the garage and watched the pickup pull alongside the large red gas tank, raised high in the air on four metal legs. Terrance quickly jumped out, pulled down the gas hose and began fueling the truck.

"We are going to have to leave," yelled Ted to Jerry. "Get as many gas cans as you can find."

"The keys to Ed's cars are in the locked cabinet on the west wall," yelled Terrance. "The combination is CAR."

"What's going on?" Jerry asked. "What did you find?"

"The insurgent this morning wasn't lying about there being an invasion," stated Ted, realizing with all the time he spent with Jerry and Terrance, knowing they had military experience, he never discussed it with them. "There are anti-aircraft guns in Parowan, and I'll bet there are several more, all the way to St George."

"What size guns?"

"105 MM."

"What, are you sure?" Jerry asked skeptically. "It doesn't seem possible."

"I'm not sure about anything right now Jerry."

"They would have had to take them from a war museum." Jerry shook his head. "I spent four years in field artillery."

"So, you know about anti-aircraft weapons."

"I'm not an expert on them, but I know enough that it would be very difficult to find one, much less several," said Jerry. "Are you sure they're real?"

"I think they are. But you make me wonder." Ted looked at the ground in deep thought. There were several times in history where an enemy, during wartime, would create a fake army. Right before the invasion of Normandy the Americans left General Patton on the outer reaches of England with a faux army consisting of tanks and equipment made from balloons. The Germans fell for the ruse and kept many of their weapons far away from the beaches of Normandy. But why would the insurgents use fake anti-aircraft guns? "We weren't close enough to verify if they were real or not," he finally answered.

"I don't think they are," stated Jerry. "Our missiles would knock them out in a matter of minutes, hell our guys could take out something as small as a five-gallon bucket from the comfort of their office on the east coast. There is no reason for them to go through so much trouble?"

Jerry was most likely correct in his reasoning of the anti-aircraft weapons. The manpads Deb warned about were mobile and just as effective. All the new howitzers were equipped with radar guided computer systems. One way or the other, it didn't make much difference, the only logical conclusion was that they were planning for the arrival of troops.

Ed parked the 1957 Chevy behind the Ford F-250 just as Terrance finished filling it with gas. Coming down the driveway was a 1970 GMC wheat truck. Aaron parked the truck to the side of the barn. Ten of Ed and Irene's grandchildren piled from the bed. They headed straight toward the horses in the corral.

Aaron and his wife Ashley stepped from the wheat truck. Aaron was limping noticeably.

"What did the kids decide?" Ed asked.

"They are going to take the horses and ride to our cabin in the hills," answered Aaron.

"All the kids?" Irene asked.

"Everyone's staying," said Ashley anxiously.

"Seth rode over to the Myers farm to check if any of the neighbors wanted to go with them," stated Aaron. "He found out that everyone has already left their farms."

"They can hook the wagon to the horse so they can haul supplies." Irene accepted the fact that all her grandchildren and great grandchildren were going to hide out in the hills. "We want to empty the freezers."

Samantha, Carol and Scotty walked across the crushed rock driveway to gather with the congregated group.

"Can someone tell us what is happening?" Carol asked with some indignation in her voice.

"We're preparing the cars to leave," answered Ted.

"When?"

"As soon as possible."

"Do we have a route?"

Ted looked at Ed. Ed turned to Aaron.

"We can't go near Interstate 15. We have to go east on 12," said Aaron. "It's impossible to get to 70 north of here."

"We are all familiar with the parks, but Aaron knows that area better than anyone," stated Ed.

"Irene, can we load up supplies and bedding from your house?" Ted asked.

"Go ahead, of course, take anything, it's better than leaving it here to be stolen." Irene turned to Ed. "I wonder if Breanna and Adam are having trouble starting the RV."

"They'll be along. I'm sure they are loading everything they have." Ed started walking in the direction of the barn. "I'm going to go and help the kids with the horses and grab the drones."

"Get the Suburban," yelled Terrance to Jerry, who was waiting with Travis at the door of the garage. He turned to Carol, "You and Scotty can ride with Travis, Jerry and me."

Ted drove the pickup to the gate in front of the main house. Jerry parked the Suburban next to them, Samantha followed Ted and Maddy upstairs to the bedrooms. She watched as Ted pulled the bedding apart, taking the sheets, quilt, and bedspread. He handed Maddy two pillows, they took the bedding to the pickup and placed it in the bed. Samantha followed right behind and placed her bedding on top of theirs. Ted stared at her dubiously but never said a word.

"Maddy, can you run upstairs and get our backpacks?" Ted asked. "I'm going to run to the garage and grab a tarp to cover everything."

"Ok Grandpa, I'm on it."

"I'll grab mine, come on Maddy," said Samantha. "We can get some food too."

Ted headed for the Quonset. Ed came through the gate to the corrals, driving a wagon being pulled by a single horse. Right behind him were his grandchildren riding on horses. Ed pulled the wagon in front of the door to the Quonset.

"Take all the meat from the freezers in the garage," Ed spoke to his grandchildren as they latched the horses reins to a bar on the side of the building. "You need to get as much canned food from the cellar as you can carry. Arthur you drive this wagon."

Seth, along with the remaining cousins riding on horses, trotted to the side of the wagon. There were over thirty horses standing in front of the garage. The grandchildren were busy filling the wagon and loading the pack horses with food, tents and other supplies.

"Grandpa, we need to take your ammunition," voiced Seth. "There's no way to get to Parowan to get more."

"Take it all. You need to get going. It will take you a good six hours to get to the cabin with this wagon. It's going to be pitch dark by the time you get there," said Ed, taking the rein to Seth's horse. "I want you to open the gates and scatter the cattle when you go through the pasture."

Ted stood next to Irene and Ed as they watched the restless horses being loaded with supplies. There was enough room in the wagon to empty both large freezers of meat from the garage. Aaron and Ashley helped them pack and finally stood back as everyone mounted their horses.

"Please, stay at the cabin until everything calms down," said Ashley with tears in her eyes as she watched her nine-year-old granddaughter climb into the saddle of her horse and ride up next to her son. "We will be back as soon as it's safe. Don't you come back here, for anything."

"For no reason," echoed Irene. "Seth, you watch after your family. Don't be a hero."

"We'll be ok." Seth pulled back the reins to his horse. "We need to go."

Ted watched as Seth galloped his horse to the front of the group and they slowly rode off into the hills. He felt relief that it was now time to concentrate on getting the rest of the family on the road. Aaron had his arm around Ashley as they watched them leave. He wanted to speak with Aaron about the route he was planning on taking to Colorado. Under normal circumstances they could drive to the Denver metro area in about nine hours using the highways. Going back country would take much longer. The idea of leaving for home was exhilarating.

"Aaron," Ted moved closer to the couple. He felt a little uncomfortable as he realized he had not communicated directly with the old farmer. He noticed Ed and Irene were headed for their house. "Do you feel confident about taking Highway 12."

"I do, we have to go by way of Escalante," said Aaron, very emphatically. "Others from Parowan tried leaving to the north, they already came back."

"Are you familiar with the back roads?" Ted asked.

"He's been hunting all his life in the area," said Ashley.

"I know eastern Utah and western Colorado about as well as anyone. After that you'll have to help."

"Irene told us that when we get to Colorado you have a place for all of us to stay. Is that true, and is it going to be better than here?" Ashley asked the question using a very calm voice. She realized, after the incident where the men shot her husband, that anywhere would be better than staying at their home.

"I'll be honest, I have no idea what is happening in Colorado." Ted looked her directly in the eyes. She looked old and tired. "But I will tell you my sister saw this coming. She prepared a place for all her family. I do believe it will be better."

"Adam and Breanna should be here soon with that monstrosity," said Aaron. "We need to get our stuff out of the truck and into the Chevy."

Ted took two tarps from the garage and headed back to the pickup in front of the farmhouse. Coming down the driveway was a large RV. Samantha and Maddy walked down the front walk struggling to carry a large cooler, Samantha was carrying most of the weight. They dropped it with a thud next to the tarps.

"Grandpa, we have so much food in this, you won't believe it," stated Maddy. "Irene told us to take all we want, even some cake."

"There's another cooler inside with water." Samantha was rubbing her bicep. "You will have to get it."

Ted watched the RV pull in front of the house. He reached down and picked the cooler up and placed it in the front of the truck bed. Looking to the east, over the top of the RV something caught his eye. Flying in the far distance was an aircraft, different than any he had ever seen. The sun was shining off the side of the craft as it slowly made its way down. Off to the north were many, many more, all moving silently through the blue sky. Without the roar of an ordinary airplane, the flying contraptions seemed fake. He stepped out to the middle of the driveway. Everyone gathered around and looked to the east.

"What in the hell are those?" Ed asked.

"I have never seen anything like them," answered Ted. "I'm guessing they are some sort of glider."

"I'll bet they are landing on the interstate," replied Aaron. "No wonder nobody has been able to go north."

"Can we eventually get to Interstate 70, if we go east from here?" Ted knew the United States Military would keep the east/west highway a high priority for moving equipment.

"We can go to Moab and over," answered Aaron.

"Where are Terrance and Jerry?" Carol asked, standing next to the Suburban with Scotty and Travis waiting next to her.

"I had them pull the motors from the water wells and disable the solar," said Ed. "Here they come."

"Grab the bushel basket of apples," yelled Irene.

"Just leave them," screamed Breanna. "There's not enough room in the motorhome."

"I'm not going to leave them for those men to enjoy."

"Let's take them," Adam hurried to the house. "We'll never hear the end of it if we don't."

Terrance and Jerry literally ran to their car.

"Get our water Grandpa," said Maddy. Ted followed her to the cooler and carried it to the back of the truck. Samantha took one end of the heavy cooler and helped him place it on top of the food. Ted tossed the tarps on top of their luggage and bedding.

"I'll lead," Aaron pulled the 1957 Chevy in front of Adam's RV.

Ted waited for the RV to pull in behind the Chevy for him to drive the old F-250 behind the large vehicle. Jerry drove the Suburban right behind him, as they made their way to the dirt road, leading away from the farm.

Fort Carson Army Base

Colonel Deb sat at her desk, preparing to leave for the day. She was tired from a full day of briefings but also tired of the waiting game. Who would have thought she would be held in reserve at the home base in Fort Carson? Half of the Army's divisions had already deployed within the country, most along the border with Mexico. Enemy, foreign troops infiltrated the municipalities, south of the border, from Monterrey to Tijuana. They now occupied the border cities inhabited with nearly ten million citizens of Mexico. The exact number of troops staged at the border was undetermined.

The realignment for the new generation of the military cut the population of soldiers while increasing the size of the base at Fort Carson by a full brigade. The meeting of the day was long and daunting with all indications pointing toward the certainty of war on American soil. Deb's staff kept the troops under her command busy with maintenance of equipment and drills, which consisted of firing weapons and some small unit training.

"Colonel," a soldier opened the door and knocked at the same time, "I have a message for you, that I'm sure you want to see."

Deb leaned back in her chair as the lieutenant handed her the message. She read it and quickly leaned forward in her seat.

"When did this arrive?"

"Just now."

"This came from Colonel Ruiz from Toole?" Deb asked.

"Yes ma'am," said the lieutenant "But he is concentrated in western Arizona, attached to the 1st Calvary Division. The message came from headquarters there."

Deb released the roll down map of the United States. She had driven through Utah on several occasions. She located Cedar City.

"So, he and Maddy are right here," she said to herself, pointing to southern Utah on the map.

"Ma'am, do you want me to respond to the message?"

"Just that it is received," Deb saluted. "That's all."

She sat back and stared at the map. One of the main concerns at the morning briefing was the devastation occurring in the small municipalities across the country. The police departments in the largest cities were able to maintain some control, although chaos was ensuing from the loss of electricity and the rush on stores. The small communities were under complete control of the subversives. She wished she had been wrong in her predictions, but she was correct on nearly every aspect of her warnings concerning the gang problem. If anything, the terror was worse than she anticipated. She figured the citizens and the police in small communities would fight back and keep some semblance of lawfulness.

"Where are you?" Deb moved closer to the map and looked at the area north of Cedar City. She was going to do everything in her power to find a way to assist her brother, everything but put the troops under her command at undue risk. It would take every ounce of her creativity and ingenuity to figure out how to help.

"Colonel," the lieutenant was back at the door, "General Lauer wants you back at briefing immediately."

Brigadier General Robert Schroth was the first of the brass to enter the room. He placed a folder at the podium and stepped back. Brigadier General Frank Lopez entered, followed immediately by Major General Lauer. All colonels were present except one, Colonel Tyler of the Stryker Brigade Combat Team.

"At approximately five o'clock this afternoon, American troops along the southern border received artillery fire from enemy positions on the Mexican side of the border. Concurrent with the attack our satellite assets were compromised, to what degree, at this time unknown. Concomitantly, the northern border was breached through glider aircraft transporting enemy troops to Boseman, Montana, Logan, Utah and Cedar City, Utah."

Deb's heart leaped to her throat when she heard the general mention Cedar City. The North American Aerospace Defense Command NORAD was only a stone's throw away from where she sat. How were gliders able to breach our borders? A question she was sure her superiors were in the process of correcting.

"Colonel Tyler with the Stryker Brigade Combat Team is in transport to the Salt Lake City area," continued General Lauer. "The east coast and the west coast are being threatened from the air, and from the sea. We are at war. I want every brigade, every battalion, every company, every platoon and every squad organized and ready to move at a moment's notice. Some of you will be leaving within the hour."

The General exited.

General Lopez held up his hand signaling Deb to stop as the others filtered out of the room. Deb knew plans for her brigade were already in the mix.

"Colonel, you need everyone up and ready to go. You're leaving in five hours," commanded the general.

"Where to sir?" General Lopez was an exceptional, common sense leader who Deb respected immensely.

"Grand Junction, you will stay in reserve, securing the area, until we coordinate with the 3rd Infantry in Salt Lake and the 1st Infantry in Albuquerque. You will adjust your position to meet with their plans. Colonel, we need you to move. You have a long drive."

"Yes sir," said Deb. "Sir, was Stryker air lifted?"

"They are in the air now."

Deb understood the need for 2nd Infantry Brigade to transport by land, all plans were tentative, and she needed the ability to move quickly and efficiency. There was no mention of any Division Artillery being attached to her on the mission. With the 1st Infantry already in Albuquerque; the 3rd Infantry in Salt Lake City; the 1st Calvary in Tucson; and the 82nd Airborne in Montana, Corps must be using the Army to fight for the middle of the country. If so, she deduced, the Marines and Navy must be protecting the coasts, with the Air Force supporting all branches. This was an all-out fight for survival, with all hands-on deck. She was more than ready to join the fight. Up until now, there had been a confidence the conflict would be avoided through political methods, but those optimistic assumptions were by the wayside. Her soldiers were chomping at the bit to go to combat. It would not be hard to have them prepared to leave, in fact, they would most likely be ready within the hour.

Deb knew Ted, if he were close enough to see gliders land, he would flee the area in Utah. She could now review all the intelligence on the area and make a good guess as to the whereabouts of her brother. A major problem was that she had no way, or time, to get a message to Nicole and Bill about Maddy and Ted's situation.

Colorado Farm

Hank could only do so much supervising with the small group of people at the farm. Everyone there was more than willing to pull their own weight, the problem was organizing them. The number one principle Deb made clear in her notes, was to progress, move forward, not use all the resources without replenishing them. In other words, think further ahead than the tip of your nose.

Jason Jensen was a godsend with his building abilities. He recruited every idle body to be a part of his crew to construct the apartment building Deb had dreamed about building for over two years. It was a massive building, sixty-five meters long and eleven meters wide. It consisted of eight large family sized apartments and twelve smaller rooms. Four large community bathrooms were spaced equally throughout the structure. The foundation, along with the rough plumbing and electrical service were already in place.

Everyone was surprised how fast the small crew of workers erected the outer walls. Jason came up with the idea of constructing the building in four segments. By giving part of the building a roof, it would allow inside work to continue in case of inclement weather. The design was to forego floor joists for a concrete floor, which could be poured after the shell was assembled. After one day of framing, he was ready to place the first set of trusses. He planned to work late into the night, everyone else quit for the evening.

Kori watched her husband for a moment through the two-by-four wall, before entering the shell of the building. He was standing on a ladder, setting truss marks on top of the framing. The aroma from the plate of food she was carrying filled the room, "I brought supper."

"It smells so good." Jason stepped off the ladder and sat down next to his wife.

"You are really enjoying this aren't you?"

Jason smiled, "The design is really well thought out. Framing it is simple, but finishing the plumbing is going to be tricky."

"How is your crew working out?"

"I'm really happy with Dave and Bobby, I shouldn't single them out because everyone is working hard. Even the little girls Reagan and Avery are helping." Jason ate while talking. "Bill and Jessica are hard to separate so when I ask one to do something, I usually get two for one."

"Oh, to be young and in love."

"I guess so. I just hope we can lift the trusses for the first section tomorrow without anybody getting injured."

"I'll bet you have no problem; you've only done this for thirty years." Kori took his empty plate. "Why don't you quit for the night?"

"A couple more measurements, and I'll come in."

Jason made measurements as quickly as he could, moving the ladder and stretching as far down the wall as he could reach. He was within two meters of the end of the set wall, where a small trench was open with pipes for plumbing sticking up. He placed the bottom of the ladder a few inches from the trench and reached over to mark the wall. The dirt on the side of the trench gave way, causing the ladder to fall to the side. The big man tumbled over with his left knee falling into the trench. He landed hard on his left arm and heard the bone snap. A small part of bone was sticking out of the skin and his arm was bleeding. He lay in the cold until he willed himself out of the trench. He walked toward the farmhouse cradling his arm.

Jacqueline was the first to see him coming into the house. At first, she thought he was carrying a wounded animal, when she realized he was injured, she cried for assistance. Kori rushed to his side and helped him sit at the kitchen table.

Hank quickly brought him a towel to place under the injured arm. He had seen many broken bones as a coach, but he was always able to get the player to a doctor. "Where's Al?" he yelled.

"Good God," said Al, stepping forward, "I'm a dentist. I don't know how to set a bone."

"You're as close as we have to a doctor." Hank had been afraid this situation would occur.

"Keep the arm still. It doesn't look like he has lost very much blood. Put pressure on it if it starts bleeding," ordered Al. "We need to see what's here as far as medical supplies. Can someone find the key and open the narcotics cabinet?"

Jacqueline quickly followed him into the medical clinic. Deb had stocked the room with every type of medicinal, therapeutic and remedial products and supplies she could find, taken from a list one of her army doctors prepared for her. They had everything except a doctor.

"Are you in a lot of pain?" Hank asked, placing his hand on his friend's shoulder.

"Not really," said Jason, shrugging his shoulder. "It really doesn't hurt."

"Alright, we'll get you something just in case it does." Hank knew the giant man was a tough old trooper. He removed the cloth and examined the wound. The bleeding was very minimal, and the bone was barely visible.

"Dad, are you ok?" Dave came rushing to his father's side. When he saw the tip of the bone sticking out of the side of the arm, he stepped back. "We have to get you to the hospital."

"There isn't a hospital to go to," said Jason. "We'll figure this out on our own."

"I'll drive you into town. You need a doctor."

"We can't do that son." Jason gritted his teeth, he was becoming nauseous.

"Where in the hell is Al?" Hank yelled, getting up from the table to investigate.

Jacqueline, Linda, Nicole and Al were in the back room looking at a medical book. They were scrutinizing very graphic pictures on how to set a compound fracture of the arm. Al had Linda's left arm in his hands as he practiced the process.

"Oh boy," said Hank. "Have you found the pain medication?"

"It's morphine, so it will work quickly." Linda laid a syringe and vial of medication on the table.

"Shall I bring him in?" Nicole asked.

"Yeah, let's get it over with."

"Can you do this?" Hank asked Al.

"Not correctly, it should be screwed or pinned," he answered honestly. "I'll try to put it back in place and see what happens."

Al scrubbed his hands for what seemed to be an extraordinary amount of time. He removed a pair of gloves from a box and pulled them over his hands.

"We need to remove your shirt," stated Al. "I imagine this will hurt like a son-of-a-gun. The only way I can tell if it is set will be by feel."

"I'll have to grit and bear it," responded Jason, as Linda helped him remove his shirt. Al prepared and injected the morphine into his good arm.

"I have sutures and wraps ready," declared Linda. She previously assisted with dental procedures when Al first started his practice. She had all the faith in the world her husband would successfully repair Jason's arm. He was a perfectionist with great problem-solving skills.

Jason was such a large man; he had a hard time sitting in the small chair. Nevertheless, he sat in it, placed his arm on the table and closed his eyes.

Al lifted his arm and looked at the puncture wound. The broken bone had slipped back under the skin. Using both hands to hold the massive arm, he applied force on both sides of the break to the ulna, pulling with great pressure until he heard a slight pop. He set the arm on the table and felt the bone through the soft tissue. To his surprise, the entire length of the ulna felt smooth, with only a slight bump at the break.

"Did you just set that bone?" Jason asked incredulously.

"I'm not sure." Al pushed hard through the muscle and tissue, digging deep with his fingers to feel the gap between the ulna and radius bones.

"Ouch," yelled Jason in response to Al's probing.

"It's back in place, but you broke both bones. All you need are five or six stitches and a soft cast; give it a little time and you might be as good as new."

"That was about as painless as I could have imagined." Jason looked at Al with a big smile on his face. "Thank you, Al."

"No problem."

"Morphine is one amazing pain killer," stated Linda. "But you are going to be pretty sore when it wears off."

"See if Dave and Kori want to come in while we finish," said Al.

Al was happy everything turned out ok with setting Jason's arm. He was going to have a talk with everyone about the breadth of his abilities. He wanted all to realize he was a dentist and not a physician.

Hank and Jon sat up after everyone went to bed. Deb kept the bar stocked with the finest liquor and they had no qualms about drinking it. Losing Jason to an injury was going to be hard to overcome. It would undoubtedly put the construction of the apartment building way behind schedule. What was even more disconcerting was for them to decide what to do if someone was seriously injured or became deathly sick. Just like everything else, they would have to deal with each issue as they materialized.

Central Utah

Ted tried his best to keep Maddy and Samantha engaged in conversation as they drove away from the invading troops. With so many unanswered questions, his mind was swirling. The uncertainty of the scope of the attack, not only here but across the country was worrisome. The roar of planes in the sky was frequent but locating them in the deep blue was difficult. No question, war was occurring on American soil. He had a terrible yearning to be back in the fray of fighting for the country, he missed every aspect of being a soldier. From the day he retired his longing to live in the past was having repercussions on his relationship with Nicole. Now, as he worked his way to Colorado, he wasn't sure if he wanted to get there to see his family, or to go to Fort Carson to join the fight for the nation.

Aaron's knowledge of the area was paying off. They were able to cut off several miles of highway and bypass the town of Panquitch by traveling over a logging road through the Dixie National Forest. The speedometer on the truck was in miles per hour, something seldom seen over the past ten years. Maddy and Samantha kept busy making the calculations for miles per hour to the metric scale.

The temperature cooled as the sun fell slowly. It was still warm for being October. Ted was somewhat surprised how populated the small communities were as they drove on the north side of Bryce Canyon. Irene mentioned, before leaving their farm, that under different circumstances, the drive would be extraordinary. The scenery was stunning as the setting sun brought out the beige, red and brown colors framed within the dark shadows of the rocky landscape. There were many new homes in the surrounding developments scattered around the small towns. The further east they traveled the more traffic they encountered. After passing through the town of Escalante it took nearly two hours to travel thirty-five kilometers, before they came to a complete stop. Stalled vehicles were visible for miles ahead.

"Let's get out and stretch," said Ted to Maddy and Samantha. There was a small embankment with a wooded area to the left of the road. To the right was a field chock-full of rocks and small bushes, leading to a green pasture with several horses grazing. Barely visible lights from homes flickered in the distance through the darkness.

"Grandpa, I need to use the restroom," Maddy said, pulling her jacket tight around her neck.

"You'll have to go in the trees up there," Ted looked at Samantha. Behind them Carol was already climbing the hill.

"I'll go with her." Samantha took the hint from Ted.

The Jacobys were all standing outside the RV, staring at the long line of cars.

"We're quite a way from Boulder," stated Aaron. "It looks to me like this jam goes all the way there."

"What are those lights?" Ted pointed across the fields.

"Residential development," answered Aaron, "every time we drive through that area, they are building more and more new homes."

"There is a maze of roads back there," replied Ed, stepping to the back of the RV. "We went exploring a couple years ago on our way to Lake Powell. If we can get to the houses, there's a new road that will take us back to the highway on the east side of Boulder."

"Well, do you remember, we were lost for some time on our exploring adventure," Irene reminded Ed.

Ted stepped off the highway across the shallow ditch and walked about twenty meters onto the rocky ground. Terrance, Jerry and Travis joined him in the field. It was eerily quiet as they looked at the area, but every so often they could hear the rumbling of planes flying in the distance to the north of them.

"This road is a terrible spot for us to be waiting," shouted Ted, looking back toward the RV. "We have to cut across these fields. How far away do you think the lights are?"

"I would guess seven or eight kilometers," said Terrance. "It's hard to judge, but that would be my guess."

Ted walked back to the highway and approached Adam. "How much does the Excursion weigh?"

"30,000 pounds," Ed answered. "I was just looking at the specifications in the handbook."

"The ground is hard," remarked Ted, "but that is a lot of weight, nearly thirteen and a half metric tons."

The entire group clustered between the pickup and the RV. Ed wandered off the road onto the hard ground. He agreed the field would support the weight of the RV. The pasture, past the open field, mostly hidden from sight in the darkness, could be a problem. Besides the difficulties of traversing the countryside, they needed to worry about the local resident's reaction to them crossing their property.

It was determined that Travis and Jerry would walk in front of the vehicles to look for rocks and navigate the caravan around vegetation and hidden ravines. Ted would go first, followed by the RV, then the Chevy and the caboose would be the Suburban. They would leave the lights off. The hope was that others in the traffic jam would not follow them off road.

Adam unlatched two shovels, strapped on the back of the RV and gave them to Travis and Jerry. They hiked into the darkness, walking about four meters apart, picking up loose rocks and tossing them to the side. All of the rocks were moveable, so they only needed to use the shovels for walking sticks.

Ted waited to allow Travis and Jerry time to get about thirty meters deep into the field. When he got back in, he found sandwiches and water sitting on the dashboard. He smiled at Maddy and Samantha as he started the truck. He drove it over the ditch and made a straight line toward the two men, hitting some small rocks but none big enough to cause damage. He watched through the rearview mirror as Adam pulled the large RV into the field, directly behind him. The massive vehicle rocked as it made it over the ditch and onto solid ground.

Ted drove slowly about ten meters behind Travis and Jerry. He kept a close eye on the other cars from the traffic jam, none were following. They meandered through the field avoiding the large boulders, often running over small bushes. When within fifty meters of the fence to the green pasture Travis held up his hand, indicating they needed to stop. He walked back to the pickup as Jerry proceeded to the west.

"There's a drainage ditch," proclaimed Travis bleakly. "It looks like it goes the length of the field."

"How deep is it?" Ted stepped from the pick-up and walked to the ditch.

"Maybe eighty centimeters deep and a meter across," answered Travis, following Ted as the others gathered around.

Standing in the pitch dark, in the middle of a field, Ted felt a sense of anxiousness. Maddy came to his side and held tightly to his left arm. He stared at the ravine in deep thought, there was no way the vehicles could drive over the ditch. Jerry returned from exploring.

"I can see it going all the way up into the hills," stated Jerry, pointing into the darkness. "It's dry as a bone, but there's no way to drive around it. We're stuck here."

"The hell we are." Aaron limped forward to stand at the edge of the ditch. "Fill the damn thing up. There's plenty of rocks to use for a bridge."

"Come on," yelled Breanna, grabbing a large rock and throwing it into the ravine, "let's get it done."

"If we get to the other side there's a furrowed road next to the fence," said Jerry.

All, including Ed and Irene, with a great amount of pent-up energy, went to work, in the dead of night, hurling stones into the gully. A bounty of loose rocks was scattered around the area. Although the temperature was cool, Ted removed his coat because he was sweating so hard.

"Toss them to the sides," yelled Ed. The center of the trough was filled to the top, enough to walk across to the other side.

"Don't lift any of the heavy ones," Ted told Maddy. She was carrying rocks that were too heavy for her and dropping them into the hole with her hands coming close to hitting the rocks already in the trench. "Be careful not to smash your finger."

"Grandpa," Maddy rushed past Ted to grab another stone as she said, "remember — not a baby."

"I'll keep an eye on her," decreed Samantha, carrying a large, heavy rock, cradled with both hands, between her bent knees. She shuffled her feet until arriving at the nearly full trench and let go of the rock. The weight of the stone smashed her right hand on top of a jagged rock.

"Ahhh," she screamed, jerking her hand quickly away. Using her left hand, she grabbed the fingers of her right hand and squeezed tightly.

Ted and Maddy came to her side as she sat down on the hard ground, moaning in pain.

"Let me see." Ted leaned down next to her as Maddy placed a hand on her shoulder.

Samantha held her hand out as she closed her eyes tightly and gritted her teeth. The sides of her three middle fingers were already turning purple and there was blood coming from under her well-manicured nails.

"We have to get some ice on this," stated Ted, allowing her time to adapt to the pain. He felt a great amount of compassion for the lady who had done nothing but be nice and helpful to him and Maddy. Maddy comforted her by patting her shoulder.

"Come on," said Irene, who looked completely exhausted, "let's get something cold on that."

Ted reached down with his right arm, allowing her to grasp his powerful forearm with her left hand. He pulled her to her feet. "Maddy, can you help Samantha?"

Jerry and Terrance were pitching and organizing the stones on top of the pile.

Terrance, taking long strides, stepped off the distance across the makeshift pathway. "It's nearly four meters wide. Should be enough for the RV. That is if the sides will hold the weight."

"Let's get the other vehicles across first," advised Aaron, insinuating they would leave the RV if it should sink while traversing the trench.

Maddy and Samantha came out of the RV with Samantha holding a package of meat over her wrapped fingers. They all got into the truck.

"I haven't eaten meat in fifteen years." Samantha looked at Ted with dark mascara running down the sides of both eyes. Her hair was a complete mess as she held the frozen sirloin steak to her bandaged fingers.

"Maybe we can eat that when you're done with it." Maddy looked at Samantha before turning to address Ted. "Huh, Grandpa?"

Ted shook his head and smiled. He easily drove over the ravine before parking on the furrowed road next to the fence surrounding the pasture. Aaron drove the Chevy across, followed by Terrance with the Suburban. Although the RV was of great concern, Ted noticed the clouds clearing and the stars were peeking out. The night sky was a magnificent sight.

"Hop out," he said to Maddy and Samantha. Maddy followed him out the driver's side door. Samantha stayed in the truck. The frequent sound of hidden aircraft brought him to reality, although everyone was tired, they needed to keep traveling. He reached down and picked Maddy up. She held her arms around his shoulder looking at the starlight shining on the surrounding landscape. She leaned in and gave him a hug.

"Whoa!" Jerry yelled, stepping away from the RV as it tipped far to the right before righting itself. Adam gunned the engine, racing the back wheels across the stones, just in time, as the loose rocks on the outer edge of the crossing gave way.

Ted hesitated after getting back in the truck, to allow the other vehicles to move forward, unsure which was the best way in driving down the worn path along the fence. Aaron made the decision for him by gunning the Chevy in front, driving southeast. Ted waited and allowed Adam to steer the RV in behind Aaron.

Terrance pulled alongside Ted. "Look," he pointed back toward the highway. The bright headlights of several cars were slowly meandering through the field. "They must have gotten tired of sitting there."

"Can't blame them," said Ted.

The road along the fence came to a halt at a gate, which was the back entrance to a farmhouse. The silhouettes of the homes, that had displayed the lights they saw from the highway, were now plainly visible on the far side of the farm.

Aaron walked back to the RV and said a few words to Ed. He moved to the utility compartment, opened it, and pulled out a large bolt cutter. Adam joined him at the gate, they cut the lock, opened the gate and returned to their vehicles.

They were going to have to travel right next to the farmhouse in order to get to the road on the other side. Lights began flashing inside the farmhouse. Out rushed an old farmer carrying a shotgun. He stepped right in front of the Chevy. Immediately behind the farmer were two young men, both carrying rifles. The brake lights to the Chevy lit the darkness.

"Oh boy," said Ted, looking at Maddy and Samantha.

Boom, the sound of the shotgun was resounding. The farmer shot high in the air, right over the top of Aaron and Ashley. Maddy and Samantha automatically fell to the floorboard. Before Ted could react, Terrance and Jerry were racing into the fracas, both carrying their assault rifles. Out of the RV jumped Adam with a shotgun, Megan with a shotgun and most forbidding of all, Breanna with a shotgun.

Breanna didn't hesitate. She returned fire over the top of the farmer. "You son-of-a-bitch," she yelled. "All we are trying to do is drive through."

The farmers lowered their weapons as the group approached.

Ted watched as Breanna went nose to nose with the old farmer, calling him every name in the book. It was obvious where the crazy grandchildren acquired their dispositions. Maddy and Samantha peeked over the dashboard while Breanna continued her assault on the farmers, finally ending with telling them how her brother was already shot earlier in the day.

Irene whispered something to Megan, who moved to the RV. She approached the group tendering a bag full of meat. As Terrance and Jerry returned to their vehicles, the farmers and the Jacobys talked for several minutes. Ted could see the headlights of the cars in the distant field trying to figure how to cross the drainage ditch. Finally, the farmers shook hands with Ed and Irene. Everyone returned to their vehicles and prepared to leave.

"What in the world has happened here?" Samantha asked, looking at Ted in disbelief, holding up her bandaged hand. "A week ago, I closed on a four-bedroom house in Highlands Ranch. I was on top of the world. But now, look at me. How did I end up here in the middle of nowhere? Just look at me, I am a complete and utter mess. And these fingers are throbbing."

"You don't look bad," Maddy turned to her grandpa and nodded. "Does she?"

"No, you look really good." He overtly raised his eyebrow as he stared at her. Besides all her other problems, her lipstick was now smeared across her chin from rubbing her mouth on the bandaged hand.

At least it brought a slight smile.

Ted figured she was the same age as his son Bill, but her mature ways made it hard to gauge. The reality of the fast and disastrous life changing events of the past four days finally caught up with her. He was used to dealing with complex emotional reactions to terrifying circumstances. Samantha was simply being human.

Colorado Farm

Nicole listened to the emergency broadcast radio as she sat at the kitchen table drinking coffee with Jon and Hank. It was her way of coping with the stress of not knowing about the condition of Maddy and Ted. With each tidbit of information, the hopefulness from the knowledge of Ted being an experienced and tested soldier was spiraling into worry and doubt. She was becoming an alarmist. Her doomsayer attitude was noticed by her in-laws and son.

"Congress passed a conscription act," stated Nicole, looking at Jon. "Everyone between the age of eighteen and twenty-five need to report for duty. This is going to affect a lot of our kids."

"We knew it would happen. The top age will go to thirty-five or forty as soon as the young people are processed," replied Jon. Ever since Deb left the farm, he had been contemplating the idea of re-enlisting. If the attack on the country wasn't quashed or resolved, it wouldn't only be the young fighting, it would be every citizen having to bear arms.

"Bobby won't be eighteen until April and Dave in May, but Emilee will be eighteen in about six weeks," stated Hank. "They were hoping it wouldn't be necessary to bring the draft back. I don't think Jacqueline and Kori are going to take it well."

"I just hate this," tears filled her eyes as she slammed her hands on the table. Coffee spattered from the cups. "I hate war. I always have."

"Believe me Nicole, nobody likes war, especially those of us who have witnessed it," Jon spoke with a harsh tone. "But we have to consider the things we control right now. It is a possibility that war is coming to our doorstep."

"If they get this far into the country, there's not a lot we can do about it," said Hank.

"We can always fight back, no matter how futile it might seem. We should plan and make decisions on how we react, should it happen."

"I wish Ted was here to help us," Nicole said.

"I do too," Jon used a softer tone. He never let on to Nicole, but he was terribly worried about his brother's safety. "If he was here, we could be discussing all the different scenarios that could occur."

"It's pretty much up to you to give us some ideas on how to protect the property. We can discuss it at dinner tonight," Hank spoke as he used a towel to wipe the spilt coffee from the table. "I'm going out and see how Bobby and Dave are coming along without Jason able to help them with the building."

The October sun was beating down, causing the snow to melt, creating puddles and muddy conditions around the construction site. Bobby, Kori and Gina were counterbalancing a truss on the outside of the framed wall. Bill, Jessica and Dave were on ladders inside the building slowly feeding the truss toward the opposite side. Hank stopped in his tracks when he saw Jason, on a ladder, being steadied by Emilee, using one hand to gently set the end of the truss on top of the wall.

"A little further," yelled Jason, holding the arm with the cast at his side as he held the heavy end of the wooden truss with his good arm, "another six inches."

"I can't believe it either," stated Kori, noticing Hank's expression as she stepped from a ladder. "He's an old warrior."

"I guess so," said Hank, "I can't believe he's working."

"He's always been that way Coach." Kori shrugged her shoulders. "He's one of those guys who gets things done."

"Can I help?" Hank asked, directing the question to Jason.

"Not really Coach, we have a good system going right now. We have three more to set and I'm going to have the kids start sheeting."

"What? You're not going to get on the roof?" Hank asked sarcastically.

Jason smiled, "I might have a little trouble steadying myself and hammering at the same time. I'll work on laying out the next set of walls so we can begin framing."

Hank shook his head, "I have to hand it to you, big guy, you are a trooper."

Everyone was falling into line as far as distributing the workload. The natural process of filling in the holes where necessity called for a needed service, was occurring. If something needed to be taken care of, it was, without conflict. Everyone was working together, but there was still a need for more people to handle the development of the farm. Now, with the inevitability of the draft, the lack of workers would soon become a concern.

Hank was happy to see Bill finding a partner in Jessica to help him cope with the worry about Maddy. He heard the two of them the previous night sitting and cuddling on the cold porch, discussing the importance of family. They were obviously planning a future together. He was getting ready to advise his nephew to take some time and comfort Nicole when he saw Reagan running in the direction of her mother.

"Mom, there's someone coming," yelled Reagan, sloshing through the mud, followed closely by her sister. "They are riding bikes."

The two terriers were barking at six individuals riding bicycles down the driveway. Hank moved to the front of the house, followed by all the workers. Jon and Nicole came out the front door and waited with the others for the approaching riders. Hank was the first to recognize them.

"It's Christian and Tim," said Hank. "This doesn't surprise me."

Tim was leading the group of three men and three women. He stopped the bicycle directly in front of Hank. Christian stopped next to him, with the others pausing right behind the two tired men.

"You look beat," quipped Hank, placing his hand on the handlebar of Tim's bicycle. "Are you out of shape?"

"Coach, you don't know the half of it," said Tim. "It is one hell of a long ways out here."

"I can't believe we made it." Christian climbed off, letting the bike fall onto the wet ground. He took a couple steps and leaned over to stretch. "My God, I don't know if I'll ever be able to straighten out."

"Hey Coach," said Tim, "we saw Coach Saxton on the road just outside town."

"Was he coming here?" Bobby asked.

"Yeah, he wasn't sure of the directions," answered Christian, "so we gave him a copy of the map."

"How many others were with him?" Hank asked.

"He and his wife," replied Tim, looking at Christian in a questioning manner, "with two other couples and maybe five kids. I think they were parents of kids on your team this year."

"They were from the team," stated Christian. He was blatantly staring at Jessica.

"Let's see about getting you all settled in," said Jacqueline, looking at Jon and Hank. "I suppose the best place for you to stay will be the campers. We'll have to figure where George and his group can stay when they arrive."

"With the extra help we should have some of the rooms ready to live in within a week," stated Jason confidently.

"Back to work then," said Bill louder than he intended. He stared at Jessica trying to gauge her reaction to the arrival of Christian.

Hank and Jon waited at the driveway as Nicole, Jacqueline and Gina led the new arrivals into the house to be indoctrinated into life on the farm. Everyone else went to work on the apartment.

"I don't know if you noticed how Christian was looking at Jessica," stated Jon. Although the group proved to be loyal to Hank when they stood up to the subversives, he still wasn't sure how dependable Christian and Tim would be in a crisis.

"I noticed," replied Hank. "You know Jon, Bill's a grown man. This is something he needs to handle on his own. I'm sure it will all work out."

It didn't take long before Christian, Tim and their friends were on the rafters of the building pounding nails into the plywood sheeting.

Bobby offered to help lay out the roofing. After a full hour of hard work, they all sat down for a break.

"I heard you had a hell of a team this year." Tim sat on the peak of the building next to Bobby.

"Yeah, we were loaded. Clint Kissler and Chuck Hurtado received Division I scholarships," Bobby responded with some remorse of having missed the championship game. Tim played varsity when Bobby was a freshman. "They both suited up a couple games with you guys on varsity when you were a senior. You played receiver, didn't you?"

"Yea, I was a receiver. I don't hardly remember the Kissler kid, but I do remember, for a freshman, how quick Hurtado was."

Bobby looked at Tim and Christian's friends. The man was handsome from a distance but when looked at closely he had pockmarks on his face, giving him a harsh appearance. He was about thirty years old with his hair long enough to be pulled into a ponytail. Two of the women looked to be sisters, if not twins. They were of Indian heritage with beautiful dark skin and short black hair. They wore sleeveless blouses showing off their buff arms. But it was the third woman who intrigued Bobby. She was small in stature, with long blonde hair and beautiful blue eyes. Her nose was large for her face, but still extremely attractive.

"Do you know Sherry?" Tim asked, noticing Bobby looking at the lady. "She was a cheerleader a year behind me."

"Sort of," Bobby lied. Boy did he remember her. He fantasized about her for a full year when she was a senior. He thought she was the most captivating girl he had ever laid eyes on.

"Sherry, come over here," Tim motioned with his hand. "Do you remember Bobby?"

She walked up the slope of the roof and sat down next to Bobby, whose heart was beating out of his chest. "You were a couple years younger than me. I do remember you because you were the coach's son."

"Yeah, you graduated in 49." Bobby stopped talking as she sat close enough for him to bump legs. He didn't want to let her know he remembered everything about her.

"Yep, 49," she said, showing her white teeth.

Even dirty and sweaty there was something alluring about her. It was leaving him tongue tied. He looked down and saw Emilee looking up at him.

"Bobby, do you want water?" Emilee asked. She was using her hand to shield the sun from her eyes.

"Yeah, I'm coming down." He quickly stood up and walked to the edge of the roof. "We need some more plywood."

Hank was surprised and pleased how easily the six newcomers joined in with working on the building, especially since they were exhausted when they arrived. They all seemed to be attuned to the concept of functioning on the farm and willingly accepted the rules set by the Lisco family. He called for everyone to stop working at three-thirty in order to allow Christian, Tim and their friends a chance to settle into their sleeping areas.

Nicole received the news on the emergency band radio that foreign troops breached the southern borders and were in combat with American troops. After supper, the older couples on the farm gathered in the large living room to discuss the situation concerning the chance of the war spreading to the eastern plains of Colorado. Jon filled everyone's glasses with libations before sitting down next to Gina on the sofa.

"I'm thinking I need to go to Fort Carson tomorrow," stated Jon, lifting his glass and taking a drink. "I can check to see what in the hell is really happening."

"Why don't you give it another day or so?" Jacqueline asked, looking at Gina.

"I wonder if Deb has been deployed," Nicole expressed quietly. She tried all day not to think the worst about the unthinkable prospect of Maddy being caught up in war.

"I'm sure if she hasn't, she will be," replied Jon. "I can get a lot of answers to questions we have with a few minutes talking with the right people at the base."

"Christian said there are a lot of people walking out of the city," mentioned Hank. "There's no telling what you might encounter between here and Colorado Springs."

"If Christian is correct that Coach Saxton is on his way here, why don't we send someone to find him in the morning? It will give us a gage on what's taking place," said Kori.

"That sounds sensible," replied Hank. "Are you good with that, Jon?"

"Deb's new cars in the garage hold up to eight people, so I'll take one of them."

"I'll go with you," interjected Gina.

"That's a plan. Early tomorrow morning you two can go on an expedition." Hank was happy Gina was willing to venture away from the farm with his brother. "Hopefully, we will know a whole lot more tomorrow evening than we do now."

Central Utah

Ted followed behind the Jacobys as they drove past the new homes, in the residential area, on the opposite side of the farm where a nearly disastrous conflict with the farmers was avoided. Maddy began to doze, leaning over to lay her head, uncomfortably, on the backside of his right shoulder. Driving out of the residential development, Aaron stopped his car at the intersection of a major road and got out. There was a traffic jam, with the taillights of cars, shining in the darkness, as far as the eye could see to the north. Not one car was going south. Ted lay Maddy's head gently on the seat as he left the truck and walked toward Aaron, who was speaking to Adam at the RV. It was after midnight.

"It's impossible to go north," said Aaron.

"We can go south and then east. But you'll have to get on 95 to cross the Colorado River," Ed yelled from inside the RV. Aaron looked at Ted.

"I don't see any way for us to go to Moab. I can get us to Monticello through the back country," stated Aaron. "Then we can decide which way to go, up to Moab, or east into Colorado."

By this time everyone except Maddy and Samantha were gathered by the RV.

"How far is it to Monticello?" Carol asked.

"I imagine it's around 270 kilometers," answered Aaron. "But that's deceiving, because we will have to go off road for a good part of it. Timewise, it'll take a lot longer than if we were on the highway."

"And you know the area?" asked Carol.

"Yes, very well," replied Aaron. "Dad and Mom have spent a lot of time camping here also, Lake Powell is just to the south."

"We need to stop and rest somewhere." Terrance looked miserable. "Everyone in our car is about to fall asleep."

"If we can make it another hour, I know of a safe place to rest," stated Aaron, looking at everyone. "Are we good?"

"Sounds like a plan," said Carol. She turned and walked stiffly back to the Suburban.

Ted grabbed two pillows and a comforter from the bed of the truck. Samantha was sitting up, half asleep as he opened the passenger door and placed the pillows and blanket on her lap. He moved to the driver's side and lifted Maddy's head and body to allow her to sit straight up. Her head was wobbly, but she remained in a sitting position. He got into the driver's seat and placed the pillow on the back of his shoulder, allowing her to position herself comfortably. She fell immediately into a deep sleep. Samantha placed the pillow next to the passenger window and fell back asleep.

They drove slowly south past the stop and go traffic heading north. When the northbound traffic came to a complete stop, Ted slowed down and stopped next to a car occupied by a family. They rolled down their window.

"What's happening south of here?" he asked a middle-aged man looking out the window of a brand new 2051 Cadillac CT10.

"They attacked."

"War," yelled the wife from the passenger's seat. "Why are you going south? They are shelling us from across the Mexico border."

Ted hesitated to answer as he looked at the cars both in front and in back of the couple. The cars were all new electric cars. "Where are you coming from?"

"Florence, Arizona."

"Are all the cars working in Arizona?"

"Not in the cities," yelled the wife. "Only the cars from the surrounding towns. We couldn't even drive through Phoenix because there were so many stalled cars."

"You're going to be sitting in traffic for a long time," stated Ted. "It's backed up for miles ahead."

"We hit the traffic about thirty kilometers back," said the man. "All roads going north are packed, at least we have been moving on this road. Believe us, you don't want to go south."

"Did you see actual combat?"

"We saw the explosions on the horizon. Our planes are fighting them," yelled the wife. "You can't imagine the sound and power of what we saw."

"I suppose not," replied Ted wryly. He drove forward, catching up to the Jacobys. He was glad Aaron was continuing the journey without delaying for rest.

They drove south for nearly thirty minutes, the northbound traffic continued to be jammed. He saw a bright flash of light in the rearview mirror and realized immediately that it was an electromagnetic pulse. Of course, it made complete sense to leave some of the newer cars functional, allowing them to move away from the battles, before disabling them. The center of the country would be blocked with thousands of vehicles full of people, creating human shields if the enemy forces were able to break through the front lines along the border.

Ahead of him, Aaron slowed and turned to the east on a narrow, hidden road. Ted saw the look of curiosity on the older lady driving the car that stopped to allow them to pass in front of her. He wondered if she might follow, in a way, he hoped she would, but she continued to wait on the highway. After driving about two kilometers deep into the wilderness, away from the public road, Aaron stopped and limped back from his car.

"Turn off your lights," he yelled. He waited in the dark for the others to surround him. "There are a series of back roads we can follow all the way to the canyonlands."

The sound of planes coming from the south, was loud and distinct echoing off the rocky landscape. Ted had not seen any more planes, since the ones he Maddy and Ed saw, after venturing to Parowan.

"Can you get us to Monticello?" Ted asked. "There aren't any real roads, just trails."

"Yeah, I can get us through," answered Aaron. "There's a spot about fifteen minutes away where we can stop and rest for a spell. I can show you what we are looking at in the morning."

Ted returned to the truck. He figured Aaron's fifteen minutes would amount to another hour. It was already nearly one o'clock. At least it was easy driving right behind Adam in the motorcoach. The headlights of the four vehicles penetrated the darkness, amidst what he imagined was a beautiful landscape. He reached up and felt the growth of an ever-increasing beard. With Maddy and Samantha still sleeping, it gave him a chance to contemplate. Through all the debates he had with Deb, concerning the possibilities of an invasion, he had deemed the actuality of it ever happening as being nearly impossible. Bill and Nicole must be worried out of their minds about Maddy. They had used up all their worries about him, over the years, being deployed in dangerous parts of the world.

It was about thirty minutes later that Aaron stopped his car. The lights of the vehicles shot off the sides of rock walls surrounding the caravan of vehicles. The sound of water flowing from a small stream could be heard to the side of the stone valley. Before Ted could step out of the truck, he saw Maddy looking up, with her head wedged into her pillow.

"Grandpa, where are you going?" she asked, sitting up on the hard bench seat, wrapping the heavy comforter around her body. Samantha was awake, looking at Ted over the top of Maddy.

"Nowhere, just setting us a place to sleep in the back of the truck. We can look at the stars."

"Like camping?"

"Yes, it is like camping."

Breanna emerged out of the night, shining a powerful beam of light in front her. She approached Ted and handed him a flashlight. "There are a lot of crevices around here, so you might want to be careful where you walk," she said, looking into the cab of the truck. "Mom wants to know if the girls would like to use the restroom in the RV?"

"Maddy, can you go and use the restroom with Breanna while I fix a place to sleep?"

Samantha emerged from the passenger side door, holding her bandaged hand slightly in front of her body. The two of them stayed quiet as they waited for Breanna to walk back to the Suburban to offer Carol the same invitation to use the accommodations in the motorhome.

The clouds had completely dissipated, and the temperature was cold enough for Ted to see his breath. He removed the gas containers from the far back of the bed and placed them on the side of the truck and did the same with the coolers full of food and water. He situated the remaining blankets and pillows into a make-shift bed on the hard metal surface in the back of the truck, silently praising Maddy and Samantha for requisitioning the large amount of bedding before leaving the Jacoby's farm.

"You better be careful if you take a leak around here," said Terrance, shining the beam of his flashlight thirty meters downhill toward a deep crevice. "If you fell in that hole, we might never find you."

"Whoa, thanks for the warning." Ted looked at the hazardous landscape. "Do you have enough blankets?"

"Yeah, we're good. We have sleeping bags and tents," said Terrance. "I don't think we will be here long enough to set them up."

"Aaron is taking the lead on this," stated Ted, "but I hope we leave at daylight."

"That's going to come really quick," said Jerry. "We'll use the sleeping bags and rest the best we can in the car."

Ted re-positioned the comforter, blanket and pillow on the seat in the front cab of the Ford, hoping Samantha would take the hint and not try to crowd into the back with him and Maddy. He decided to be proactive as soon as they approached.

"I fixed you a bed." He opened the passenger door. Maddy started to climb into the seat. "No, no, Maddy, that's for Samantha, we have a place in the back."

Samantha chuckled, her hair was brushed, and the smeared make-up was washed from her face. "Thank you," she said as she climbed into the cab, obviously feeling better than she did a few hours prior.

Under different circumstances the setting would be an ideal site for a bonding, camping trip with Maddy. The two of them slipped under the warm covers. She was fast asleep in a matter of minutes.

Ted stared at the sky, feeling the cold on his nose. He could hear Samantha shuffling in the front seat, trying to find a comfortable position. He wondered about the interactions she had with Travis. With both working for the same company and flying together, it seems they would have a natural bond. But they had hardly spoken since the ditching of the airplane. There was something more to the story between the two of them. He drifted off to sleep.

Grand Junction, Colorado

Colonel Deb was in an inscrutable mood as she assessed the situation on the west side of Grand Junction. The troops were busy setting tents in the parking lot and vacant field next to an almost finished, brand new Holiday Inn. Headquarters was housed in the lobby of the hotel, with her quarters being in room 101. The inexplicable occurrences that led her to set up shop, with the idea of warfare taking place, in the beautiful area of Colorado where she vacationed on several occasions, was mindboggling. The absurdity of having to wage war on American soil hit her hardest when she noticed a medic's equipment chest sitting in direct line to a hospital on the outskirts of the small city with turrets of smoke billowing into the crystal blue sky.

She was concerned at first with the idea of having the troops face combat without artillery attached for support. But after discussing her apprehension with General Lopez, it made perfect sense, with the need to deploy quickly. New age army artillery, even more so than the twentieth century artillery, needed to have a semblance of protection from enemy ground troops. The missiles themselves could strike an adversary 1500 kilometers away, and shoot incoming missiles out of the air, which made them a desired target for the enemy. The new generation of airplanes were well equipped to give close air support to troops, and, for right now, air support was readily available.

Deb's priority was to make sure her troops were safe from any subversives imbedded in the community. Company A was already working in collaboration with the Colorado National Guard and local police forces. All four platoons from the company were operational in a coordinated effort to rout out the rebels and, using any means necessary, eliminate them. Early reports from Captain Singh indicated they were meeting mild to no resistance.

Heavy fighting was occurring on the southern border. Chinese, Iranian and Russian troops followed the barrage of artillery onto American soil. They were using the small towns as shields or stepping-stones to move troops to the large cities in California, Arizona, Texas and New Mexico. The strategy was to minimize the superior air advantage held by the Americans. Substantial casualties were being taken by both sides as the infantries clashed.

1st Infantry out of Kansas was under heavy attack at Las Cruces, New Mexico. Reports indicated they were taking the major load of casualties. One of her best friends, Colonel Daniel Read, was in the midst of the fighting.

To the surprise of everyone in Fort Carson, Army Chief of Staff General McClinton made the decision to temporarily station at the command center in Colorado Springs. With the big brass at Fort Carson, decisions and plans for the brigade could change on a dime. Deb needed to keep on her toes and be ready to move quickly. With the initial reports of heavy combat south of Albuquerque Deb figured she would be moving, at any time, the six hundred kilometers to the New Mexico battle.

1st Stryker Brigade, now attached to the 3rd Infantry near Logan, Utah was being met with mild resistance. They were preparing to travel south along the Interstate 15 corridor to the Cedar City area. Keeping the interstate highways open was a priority for not only troop movement, but also munitions and supplies distribution. If elements of the 3rd Infantry and Stryker liberated the area around Interstate 15, then there would be a chance Deb would remain at Grand Junction. So, it was wait and see for the 2nd Infantry Brigade.

Deb was surprised, but pleased, her prediction of the satellites being disabled by the new age weapons was incorrect. All military technology was still operable. On the other side was the REMP weapons, used to disable the citizenry technology and the new automobiles, were more efficient and abundant than she imagined.

Colonel Deb was very hands-on in her leading style, but she commanded an exceptional group of soldiers, capable of making decisions on their own. The new Army was top-heavy with officers, which Deb had no quarrel with, especially since they were all highly professional and qualified individuals. Command Sergeant Major Talfoya was not only competent in keeping 2nd Infantry Brigade well trained and prepared, but he was a true friend and ally of Deb's. The three lieutenant colonels leading the three Battalions all reminded her of her brother Jon, no-nonsense, work hard and pay attention types of leaders. Without needing to harangue any of the staff, she knew the perimeter surrounding their location was secured and protected.

Preliminary reports were that Camp Red Cloud in Korea was under heavy attack and the loss of the base was imminent. Deb had spent nearly a year at the South Korea base. Another of her best friends, Colonel Judy Harvey, a fellow classmate at the Army War College in Pennsylvania was stationed there.

"Colonel," Command Sergeant Major Talfoya yelled at Deb, just before she went out the front door of the hotel, "I just received a message from Fort Carson."

She hurried back to the control center. New technology for the military communication structure was exceptional. By using a shedload of inexpensive satellites, both military and commercial, in low earth orbit, being replaced, when destroyed, by new comsats, immediately shot back into place, the system gave every branch of service confidence they were reliably interconnected.

"What is it Tommy?" Deb moved back to a table the Command Sergeant Major was using as a make-shift desk. On the desk was a map of the area.

"They want us to clear and secure Highway 191 through Moab down to Monticello," he said. "We have video of the area. It looks like a slew of disabled cars and many people on foot."

"How far is it to Monticello?" Deb asked, looking at the map.

"270 kilometers, Moab is 180."

"With traffic, that's three or four hours." She stepped back and placed her hand on her chin. "Let's go with F Company. Have Lt. Col. Woodworth and Captain Hendersen report immediately for a briefing. Tell them to prepare the company, they will depart within the hour."

Deb studied the map as she waited for the briefing. All communications indicated the American Army troops were holding a line 80 kilometers from the Mexican border from San Diego, California all the way to Brownsville, Texas. The heaviest fighting was occurring between Las Cruces, New Mexico and Tucson, Arizona. With the 3rd Infantry meeting mild resistance, she figured she would be heading to either Gallup, New Mexico to support the left flank of the 1st Calvary or toward the Albuquerque area to support the right flank of 1st Infantry. Her brigade would not be in Grand Junction for long.

"Colonel," Lt. Col. Woodworth entered and moved next to the map, followed by Captain Hendersen

"Josh, we need the southbound lanes cleared from here to the town of Monticello along Highway 191. Westbound I-70 looks clear, but you will need to begin moving vehicles when you turn south on 191." Deb turned to the captain, "Look at the video, it's about two hours old, but it gives you an idea of the civilians you will encounter, especially south of Moab. We need the engineers to remove any obstructions on the southbound side of the highway, and for you to keep them open for the entire sector."

"Are we there and back, or do we remain in Monticello, ma'am?" Captain Hendersen asked.

"Hopefully once you have cleared the lanes, they will stay open. From the pictures it looks like the largest problem will exist on the 90 kilometer stretch between Moab and Monticello, so patrol this area even after your initial clearing of vehicles. Prepare to stay, at least tonight in Monticello, taking all precautions to set a perimeter defense and wait for further orders. We should know more by the time you arrive," replied Deb. "Stay prepared, your orders could change at any time."

"Captain," said Command Sergeant Major Talfoya. "EMP pulses originated in Moab. Be aware there are subversives in the town and most likely they are in control. Remind your men that this is not a sight-seeing tour."

"Captain, your communication with us should be constant," Deb turned to Lt. Col. Woodworth and Command Sergeant Major Talfoya.

"I'm ninety-nine percent certain we will be redeploying in the next twenty-four hours," stated Deb boldly, turning to the lieutenant colonel. "Josh, I want you to have the entire 2nd Battalion ready to reposition at a moment's notice. Any indication of hostility directed at F Company; I want you prepared to move."

"Yes ma'am."

"Ma'am," said Command Sergeant Major Talfoya, "the entire brigade is prepared and ready."

Maybe it was her age and the fact she had witnessed first-hand the terrible devastation of war; or the fact that she foresaw and warned those in charge of the vulnerability of an attack on the country; or maybe it was the pristine beauty of the landscape surrounding her that soon could be destroyed; or it might be the news of many casualties being endured by the 1st Infantry at Las Cruces. Whatever it was, Colonel Deb Lisco was mad.

Eastern Colorado

Jon and Gina were up before sunrise but waited for the light of day to begin their journey. Jon was familiar with every road leading to and from the farm. There were several routes that Coach Saxton could utilize to get to the farm. They decided to travel the northern roads first and circle back to the south. As they traveled down a gravel county road that paralleled Interstate 70, about forty kilometers from the farm, they spotted a small group of travelers on a frontage road. On the interstate, were pockets of people, trekking down the busy concrete highway, as cars moved past them. Getting closer to the travelers they saw four people leaning over a lady. Jon drove onto the frontage road and made a U-turn. He stopped the car on the shoulder, behind a brand-new Ford Dominator.

"Can we help?" yelled Gina out the window. In the ditch, off the road was a middle-aged woman on both knees holding a cloth to the head of a younger woman, as two men and a woman watched over her. One of the men walked up the ditch to the road.

"We are not sure what happened," replied the man. "We were traveling on the highway and when the traffic slowed my wife noticed her in the ditch."

"Is she ill?" Gina asked.

"She said she was attacked."

"How badly is she hurt?"

"Julia, my wife is checking," said the man. "She's a physician assistant."

Jon walked into the wet ditch. He could see several lacerations on the injured girls face and forehead. She looked to be in her late teens or early twenties. He bent down next to the two women nestled in mud.

"What's her name?"

"I'm not sure," answered Julia, holding a cloth to her forehead. "She's been struggling to breathe; she has some broken ribs. I'm trying to get her to calm down so I can check for other injuries."

Jon took hold of her hand, listening to her wheeze with each breath. "Can you tell me your name?"

"Caroline," she took in air through her nose, "Sanchez."

"Where are the rest of your family?"

She took in a shallow breath and answered, "Savanna."

"You mean Georgia?"

She closed her eyes and nodded.

"Were you traveling alone?" Jon noticed she was wearing a UNC sweater. "Did you come from Greeley?"

She nodded and answered, "caught a ride."

"Caroline Sanchez, you relax, so we can help you," said Jon, calmly, patting her hand and looking into her dark eyes. "Let Julia here probe around so she can see what all is wrong. Can you do that?"

"Yes."

Jon stood up as Julia laid Caroline's head onto the ground. Gina was waiting by Julia's husband and the other couple. Jon moved next to them.

"Where are you all heading?" Jon asked. "By the way, I'm Jon Lisco and this is my wife, Gina."

"I'm Fred Hamilton, this is my brother Harold and his wife Becky. We were on our way to our son's home in a small town north of St Louis. If there is a war, like everyone is saying, we wanted to be close to him and our new grandson."

"Are you from Denver?" Gina asked.

"No, we live in Nederland, Harold and Becky are from Westminster," answered Fred. "When we couldn't reach them on the phone, we drove down, off the mountain to see what was going on. Their cars wouldn't start. With all the chaos, and the talk of war, we decided to get out of the city."

"Look up there," Harold pointed to the elevated interstate about four hundred meters to the north, "it's almost at a complete stop."

"I can do only so much down here," yelled Julia. "She is so beat up. She could have a punctured lung. It will be really uncomfortable for her to ride in a car."

"What are you planning?" Jon asked. "I mean, are you taking her with you?"

"We can't leave her here," replied Julia.

"That's not what he meant," interjected Gina. "We might have another option for you. That is if you are interested."

"We have a farm, about forty kilometers from here, where you can stay and see what happens with the traffic," said Jon. "It would be a good place for Caroline to recover."

"Do you two live there alone?" Fred asked.

"No, it's a long story. But to make it brief, it is my sister's farm. She made it a place for our family to go during a disaster. There are around twenty people there, but it can sustain many more."

"Jon is retired from the Army, his sister, Deb, is an active colonel. She prepared her property as a place for her family," stated Gina. "I know it sounds crazy, after all the years of people writing off the survivalists as extremists, but now we are in the midst of war happening here, in our country, I thank my sister-in-law for being so insightful."

"It's entirely up to you," said Jon. "If you want to, you can follow us. If not, we understand."

"We should keep going toward St Louis." Fred stared at his brother with a concerned look on his face. Jon and Gina seemed harmless, but he wasn't sure he could trust them.

"I agree," said Harold anxiously. "This may be our only opportunity to travel east. The highway could close for good."

"It looks to me like they are already closed." Julia pointed at Interstate 70 where people were outside their vehicles. Some were staring down at them. "We should either turn around and head back home or take this invitation."

"I don't feel comfortable here," Gina placed her hand on Jon's shoulder, "we need to leave."

"Julia, what do you want to do?" Jon listened for her response as he stepped out of the ditch. He reached his hand down to help Gina up the slippery slope.

"I vote we go to the farm," answered Julia, looking at her husband and in-laws. She had blood splattered on the front of her blouse. She glanced at Jon and Gina standing by their car. "We can't go back, and we can't go forward. Things around here could turn ugly at any time."

"I agree," said Becky. "People are already taking the back roads. We don't want to get stranded in the middle of nowhere without water or food."

"Let's carry the girl to the car," said Harold, "and get the hell out of here."

"Ok," Fred turned toward Gina, realizing the choice of going to the farm was already made. "Thank you for the offer. It sounds like a great option for us."

South Central Utah

Ted could smell coffee and bacon, even before he opened his eyes, the mixed aroma filled the pristine air. The sun reflecting off the colorful rocks was magnificent. He was correct imagining the area as being beautiful. They were surrounded by unusual rock formations with a meadow off in the distance. He looked at Maddy's peaceful face as she slept. The make-shift bed in the back of the pickup, with the heavy blankets giving them plenty of warmth throughout the cold night, had been surprisingly comfortable. He looked over the cab of the truck to see who else was awake.

Terrance, Travis and Jerry were drinking coffee outside the RV, talking with Ed, Aaron and Adam.

Ted shook Maddy's shoulder, her big eyes opened. He allowed her a moment to adjust to being awake.

"Maddy," he said. "I smell a big breakfast being made."

She pulled the blanket tight around her neck.

"I'll grab our coats and we can see if Irene needs some help." He pulled her jacket out of the luggage. "Shall we go?" He climbed out of the bed of the truck.

"Irene's going to have to fix a lot of eggs." Samantha woke with a stiff back after hearing the two of them mulling around in the back. She waited by the cab of the pickup.

Maddy pushed the blankets to the side and climbed toward Ted. He lifted her from the back of the pickup, even in the cold her body was warm. He was surprised she allowed him to hug her, as he placed her feet on the ground, without telling him she wasn't a baby. She put her coat on and took hold of his hand as they headed toward the RV.

"Coffee cup is inside," said Adam.

Ted opened the door to the RV and stepped up. Irene was cooking bacon on the stove with Breanna standing at her side, talking her ear off. Megan and Ashley were sitting on the sofa drinking coffee.

"There's my helper," said Irene, smiling when she saw Maddy. "Use the restroom and wash your hands. I need some help beating the eggs."

Maddy went straight to the restroom. Ted looked at the back of the motorhome to the chests full of meat stacked all the way to the ceiling. Several boxes of food were stored on the washer and dryer. The refrigerator was large, and when Breanna opened it to get eggs, he noticed it was full to the brim.

"Are you good with Maddy helping?" Ted asked.

"Of course, she's a good helper," said Irene, pouring a cup of coffee and handing it to Ted. "Tell Samantha and Carol that they can come in out of the cold."

"It's good for us to have little Maddy around," said Breanna. "We are all worried sick over leaving our kids."

"They are going to be just fine," replied Irene. "Seth will make sure of that."

Samantha and Carol were glad to get out of the frigid morning air.

"Where's Scotty?" Ted asked as Carol opened the RV door.

"He's still sleeping."

Ted wanted to discuss with Aaron the route being considered once they arrived at Monticello. There needed to be an alternative if the highway to Moab was impassable. As he approached the men, who were looking past the meadow, he could hear the rumble of planes to the east.

"I was just showing everyone the route out of here," Aaron told him, pointing to the northeast. "We go between the buttes just north of the mesa. We travel through the mountains, with you coming from Colorado you might consider them hills, but we have always called them mountains. Anyway, we pass over them and down into the valley. We should be to Monticello by mid-to-late-afternoon."

"Once we get there, I'm wondering if we should go toward Montrose." Ted looked to the sky as a roar came closer and closer and five planes flashed by them about four kilometers to the east, followed by five more planes about six kilometers away.

"Whoa," yelled Adam. "How fast can those planes go? I've never seen anything like that."

"Those in the front were F-22 Raptors. They can top out a little over Mach 2 or about 2400 kilometers an hour," said Ted. "Those in the back were F-35s. They just brought them to Petersen Air Base in Colorado Springs two years ago."

Ted felt an anxiousness, an uneasy feeling more powerful than any he had felt since the landing of the airplane in Cedar City. Knowing the planes were on actual combat missions was unnerving. He was fully aware of the capabilities of the F-22 Raptor and especially of the F-35, to wreak havoc on an enemy. The new 6th generation of the F-35 had the ability to hit an enemy without them even realizing they were under attack. It was a flying computer, first used by the navy, but recently being linked directly to the Army network. The planes were able to supply data, with not only other aircraft, but with foot soldiers on the ground. He hoped he would never have to witness the power of the new, realigned military in action.

Maddy came out of the RV, balancing two paper plates full of scrambled eggs, topped with two pieces of bacon. Samantha followed her out carrying two plates, one in her left and the other flat on the palm of her injured hand. She moved past Travis and handed one plate to Terrance, then moved next to Ted and Maddy and began eating.

"Me and Samantha made the eggs," Maddy whispered.

"They are delicious," Ted, looked at Samantha, who was smiling at him. He wondered why she gave Terrance the extra plate of eggs instead of Travis. He couldn't help but wonder what happened between the two of them.

"Irene showed me how to put cream in the eggs it gives them texture."

"Irene is really nice, isn't she?" Ted asked. "I'll bet when we get home Grandma Nicole will like her."

"She'll really like her. I mean really like her a lot," Maddy replied, lowering her voice. "I think she will like Samantha too."

Ted didn't answer Maddy, he was hoping they would get on the road. The sight of the military planes reminded him of the dangers that lurked. He had no idea of how close the war could be to them. The traveler on the highway stated that there was fighting on the southern border, but he was unsure if it had flowed into the states. The unknown was something he tried to avoid his entire career, now he was faced with total uncertainty, and it was troublesome. He was ready to move.

"It's six-thirty," yelled Aaron, placing his plate in a plastic bag being held by Breanna. His limp was profound as he made his way toward the 1957 Chevy. "Let's get going."

Driving over the backcountry trails, obviously not made for cars, much less a large motorcoach, was slow and monotonous. Even the beautiful scenery was becoming repetitious. Ted found the conversation with Maddy and Samantha to be enlivening. The little girl who used to play with fairies and other creatures, was quickly disappearing. He could see glimpses of her as a young woman. It was a perfect time to find out about the flight attendant Samantha.

"Samantha," Ted looked over Maddy. Maddy turned and looked at her too. "Did you grow up in Colorado?"

"Yeah, we lived in west Littleton. My parents worked for Lockheed-Martin. I know they are worried sick about me."

"Nicole and I raised our son Bill in south Littleton. He went to Littleton High School, where my brother Hank is the head football coach."

"I went to Chatfield."

"When did you become a flight attendant?" Ted thought in the back of his mind, and why do you hate Travis.

"I have worked with the airlines for twelve years. I started a couple years after college." She looked away from Ted and Maddy, "I wonder what's happening in Denver. We know DIA was out of commission because we couldn't land there."

"I really don't know," replied Ted. "I think there are going to be problems, how bad, I don't know."

"If we get to Denver on I-70 you can drop me off at my parents. They live right off 470."

"If there are problems, your parents can come with us to our farm."

"My dad's very stubborn. I doubt he will stray far from home."

Ted was sure there would be chaos at home in Colorado but didn't want to frighten Maddy with any guesses about details of bedlam taking place. He also decided to stop the conversation short of asking Samantha about Travis. That would be for another day. He continued driving slowly behind the motorhome, just like an old pack mule following a wagon train two hundred years ago.

Grand Junction, Colorado

Colonel Deb set her computer on a table in room 101 at the Holiday Inn. Blank pieces of typing paper were scattered to the side of the computer, brand new carpet gave the room a distinct smell. The curtain was pulled open, the window looking outside to the mass of soldiers and equipment dispersed across the parking lot and countryside, as far as she could see. Being away from the hustle and bustle of the command center operating out of the lobby, gave her sanctuary and quiet to plan and prepare for going into battle.

The visual outside the window, of the tremendous power of men and machines, all at Deb's disposal was encouraging. From the time she was a little girl her father prepared her for this moment. He hammered home the importance of preparation. "A natural leader is someone who quietly outworks everyone else. Orders should be precise and clearly understood. Indecision should be a consideration of your enemies, not yours," he would tell her. He was a caring man who wanted her to succeed. The hardest thing for her to fathom was that some of the soldiers were soon to be casualties of war. Some would die. A knock on the door pulled her out of thought.

"Colonel," Command Sergeant Major Talfoya yelled from outside the door.

"Come in Tommy."

"F Company encountered sniper fire on the south side of Moab." The Command Sergeant Major opened the door but stayed in the hallway. "They sustained two wounded."

"How bad?"

"Private Risk was hit in the foot and Private Williams injured her arm."

"How in the hell did she hurt her arm?" Deb asked flabbergasted.

"I'm not sure. Captain Hendersen is speaking with Josh right now."

Deb followed the Command Sergeant Major to the communication area in the center of the lobby. Lt. Col. Woodworth was being briefed by Captain Hendersen on the situation in Moab. Lt. Col. Lloyd Barnet from 1st Battalion and Teresa Wilson of 3rd Battalion, were listening.

"Colonel," said Lt. Col. Woodworth, "Captain Hendersen reported they have encountered subversives in Moab."

"Captain," asked Deb, looking at Captain Hendersen on the monitor, "is the threat dispersed?"

"Sort of ma'am. The sniper was eliminated, but there is chaos in the streets and on the highway. A highway patrol officer told us there was an electromagnetic pulse earlier this morning."

"How bad are Risk and Williams?"

"A ricochet bullet made a mess of Risk's ankle. Corporal Williams fell out of the Humvee and landed wrong on her arm; it sounds like a torn rotator cuff."

"Captain," said Lt. Col. Woodworth, "Lieutenant Martin with 3rd platoon, G Company is en route to evacuate Risk and Williams." He turned to Deb and Command Sergeant Major Talfoya. "Shall they remain in Moab?"

"How long until they arrive?" Deb asked.

"Within two hours."

"Captain," said Deb, "what is your situation, do you have a platoon in a forward position?"

"Yes ma'am, 1st Platoon is south on Highway 119, approximately 1500 meters from our location."

"Have you any contact with the Moab authorities?"

"Only with the highway patrol. There are only four of them and they have their hands full keeping people from fighting with each other."

"I want you to send up Hermitage," said Deb. "We need a visual of the area."

Deb and her staff waited as the non-weaponized drone was released. It relayed a clear picture of the town.

"Start west of your location and go north, then go east over the town and back to the south." Deb watched the monitor.

"The population is denser than projected." Command Sergeant Major Talfoya looked at the images of a multitude of people congregated around incapacitated cars on the highway. "The number of people stranded is much greater than anticipated."

"Captain, send the drone 2000 meters east," ordered Deb.

The pictures showed the town to be almost empty. There were a few pockets of people gathered near streets giving access to higher-end neighborhoods, most likely for protection. All vehicles were idle except for an atypical vehicle moving slowly to the south. The car traveled to a warehouse on the far edge of town. Two men dressed in black left the warehouse and came out to meet the car. Three men dressed in the same dark colored clothing emerged from the vehicle. Approximately 500 meters to the west of the warehouse, the Humvees from 1st Platoon could be seen making their way down Highway 119.

"Captain, have 1st Platoon redirect to the warehouse."

"Yes ma'am."

"Move 4th Platoon through town to the north side of the warehouse. Pull the drone back to the north end of town and slowly move back to the warehouse area."

"Hold it Colonel," ordered Lt. Col. Woodworth. "Zoom in onto the roof of the house just east of the warehouse.

"It's a sniper and behind him is someone with a handheld weapon," stated Lt. Col. Barnet.

"Give me a tighter view," said Deb.

"Take Hermitage back," commanded Lt. Col. Barnet. "It's a manpad."

"Captain, did you get a good look at the rooftop?" Deb asked.

"Yes ma'am."

"Colonel," said Command Sergeant Major Talfoya, "we can have air support in about twenty minutes."

"We don't know if there are civilians in either of the structures," stated Deb, knowing the tactic of using citizens for shields was going to become a major factor in fighting this war.

"1st Platoon is within range of the sniper," said Lt. Col. Woodworth.

"Captain, have you advised 1st Platoon of the sniper?" Deb knew that Captain Hendersen was an excellent leader, but also realized it was her job to make sure he was aware of the danger.

"Affirmative ma'am." Captain Hendersen hesitated for a moment. "Both the sniper and subversive on the roof have been eliminated."

"That was quick," said Lt. Col. Woodworth. "Does 1st Platoon see any activity at the warehouse?"

"Negative sir, 4th Platoon is five minutes from the north side of the building."

"Captain put Hermitage…," Deb was interrupted before she could finish the order.

"The people inside the warehouse have exited with their hands in the air. We have them retained," said Captain Hendersen. "What do you want us to do with them?"

"Are they prisoners of war?" Lt. Col. Wilson directed her question to Command Sergeant Major Talfoya.

"As far as I know, they are," stated the Command Sergeant Major. "We can see what they say at Fort Carson."

"Captain secure the warehouse. Turn the prisoners over to 4th Platoon, send them back here with Risk and Williams," ordered Lt. Col. Woodworth.

"Yes sir," Captain Hendersen hesitated for a moment. "The prisoners say they are American citizens."

"Tell the little bastards I just revoked their citizenship," replied Colonel Deb, to the startled looks from her staff. It only took a moment for their surprise to turn to smiles.

"Yes ma'am. When they arrive, I will gladly tell them," said the captain, with a grin. "Do we proceed to Monticello?"

"Yes," answered Deb, "you should make it by night fall."

Colonel Deb stared at the map of the United States on the table in the lobby. Reports from the southern states were encouraging in that the enemy had not advanced past the eighty-kilometer line north of the United States border. It was early in the war and already an extraordinary amount of military power was being expended to hold the region. As she looked at the map, she hoped the President and those in Washington were working to find more soldiers and more munitions. If the enemy persisted, there was a real possibility of being overwhelmed.

Colorado Farm

Hank was happy that Jon and Gina were back at the farm, but a little disappointed they had not found Coach Saxton. He understood them cutting the journey short, with the urgency of getting Caroline to the infirmary. They quickly moved the young lady into the house. Julia was amazed at the modern medical equipment and facility found in the back room of the old farmhouse. Al was ecstatic when he found out that Julia was a physician assistant.

"It's beginning to turn into a mess out there," said Jon, standing in the parking area, talking to Jacqueline, Nicole and Hank. Fred, Harold and Becky waited behind him. "We found the Hamiltons giving assistance to the young girl off the frontage road of Interstate 70 about six kilometers from Limon. Traffic was at a standstill when we left."

After the introductions, Hank wasn't quite sure what to think of the two brothers. Fred was balding and very frail, while Harold was tan and muscular. He would have never guessed them to be brothers.

"Fred and Julia are from Nederland," stated Jon, "and Harold and Becky are from Westminster, they were on their way to St Louis."

"I know Julia is a physician assistant." Jacqueline looked at Fred. "What line of work are you in?"

"Bookkeeping," answered Fred.

Jacqueline looked at Harold and Becky.

"I work in food services at Westminster High School," Becky told them.

"I'm a, um, I'm in construction," Harold mumbled. "I'm a bricklayer."

"Quit acting like you're a bank robber or something," snapped Becky, turning toward Hank. "He's a very talented man and possibly the best bricklayer alive today."

"That's a very honest living," Nicole responded.

"A very good living too," replied Becky. "All the high-end homes have brick again. After years of prefab and faux material being used to veneer their homes, people have come back to wanting brick."

A cold gust of wind blew across the parking lot, raising a cloud of debris.

"Come around to the back of the house and see our projects." Hank pulled the collar of his light jacket around his neck. "I hope another storm isn't coming in."

Jason was standing to the side of the structure, with his back to the wind, waiting for the workers sheeting the roof to climb down and out of the heavy wind. He was cradling his injured arm.

Half of the apartment was now framed with trusses, making the structure look massive. The plywood on the roof and outside walls of the first quarter of the building was complete, giving the crew a place to huddle out of the howling wind. The thin plywood wall blocked much of the weather, but it was cold inside the partially built apartment.

Jason was overjoyed to find that Harold was a bricklayer. He was getting ready to go into the cold wind and show the new bricklayer the foundation for the block tower when Kori entered the crowded structure, followed by Julia.

"Jason, this is Julia," said Kori, towering over Julia. "She's a doctor and wants to look at your arm."

"Hello, Jason." Julia never bothered to correct the introduction as a doctor. "I hear you broke the arm two days ago."

"Yes, I did," he crossed his arms and held the injured arm at the elbow.

"I can tell you are uncomfortable with it. May I take a look?"

"Let's go inside to the clinic." Kori grabbed her husband by the good arm. "This wind is brutal."

Jason followed the two women into the house.

"It looks like we are done building for the day," said Bobby. "The wind won't quit blowing anytime soon."

Bobby lingered behind as all the young people left the apartment. He stopped his dad and uncle before they could walk outside. "We had an incident just a little bit ago. Bill and Christian almost came to blows."

"Let me guess," said Hank, "it was over Jessica?"

"It ended up that was the issue, but it started when Bill asked Christian to give him a handful of nails. When Christian handed him five nails, Bill told him he wanted a full handful of nails. They started fighting over the meaning of a handful." Bobby shook his head. "Then Christian made a remark about Jessica never making good decisions in her life."

"It didn't get physical, did it?" Hank asked.

"Close, but neither threw any punches."

"When you throw a group of people together, these things will happen. Let um figure it out themselves," Jon advised. "I'm ready to go inside and have a sip of something to warm me up."

"I agree, but we should keep an eye on any conflicts and make sure it doesn't get out of hand. I've seen a change in Christian's demeanor." Hank noticed Emilee and Sherry standing at the edge of the building, waiting for Bobby. "We can discuss this later."

Hank and Jon made their way past the two girls and headed toward the house. The girls moved inside as the wind shook the frame of the new apartment.

"Bobby, did you know that Sherry went to LHS?" Emilee asked.

"Yeah," stammered Bobby. "She mentioned it yesterday while we were working on the roof."

"We were just talking about how we had some of the same teachers," Emilee enthused, standing close enough to Bobby to rub shoulders.

Sherry had a presence that manifested a sensuality that was intriguing. The two girls were the same size, but where Emilee was a classic beauty, Sherry was animalistic and captivating. Emilee wore a tight blouse with the bra straps showing on the shoulders, Sherry wore a loose-fitting top with no bra, allowing her nipples to be seen through the fabric. They were two street smart, tough women who survived rough childhoods. Bobby made a conscious decision, right then and there, that he would not do anything that could give Sherry the idea he was interested in a relationship.

"Oops, there's a nail," said Sherry, leaning over to pick up a nail off the dirt floor. Bobby looked down her shirt. Even with Emilee holding tightly to his arm, he had no choice but to look.

"Emilee, um, uh…. What middle school did you go to Sherry?" Bobby asked.

"Emilee what, what were you going to say about Emilee," Emilee asked, letting go of his arm.

"I was going to say…" he tried to think quickly. "I was going to say we went to the same middle school."

Dave entered the structure, wearing a heavy coat. The wind died to the point where it was only a breeze, but the temperature dropped significantly, small snowflakes were beginning to fall.

"Everyone is meeting in the house," stated Dave, noticing the strange look on Bobby's face. "Nicole heard on the band radio that there is a good chance for heavy snow tonight."

"It's freezing now," said Emilee, "I'm ready to head in."

"I'm ready too." Sherry looked seductively at Dave. "Unless we can figure a way to keep warm out here."

Dave stared at Bobby with a look of panic on his face. No matter how much they had talked about girls and acted worldly with the subject of sex, they were still a couple of inexperienced high school boys.

"I think we better go." Dave stared wide eyed at Sherry. "They are planning a meeting tonight before supper."

"We have a couple of hours before supper. I can't believe how big these guys are." Sherry smiled at Emilee as she walked over and placed both hands around the bicep of Dave's right arm. "A lot of the guys in the revolt were football players, but you two seem so much stronger. Or should I say more robust?"

Dave looked at Bobby for help. He flexed his muscle in his bicep and muttered, "I work out."

Bobby held back from bursting out in laughter at his friend's awkwardness. He decided to help him by asking Sherry a question. "Are you and the others happy here?"

Sherry let go of Dave's bicep and got serious. "I'm glad to be here. I'm not so sure about the others."

"What makes you say that?" Bobby asked.

"Christian seems to be getting antsy. He doesn't seem to do well with structure."

"Do you think he is going to leave?"

"They are going to leave." Sherry looked troubled, "Christian mentioned last night he wants to see what's happening back in the city. He seemed kind of scared with all the talk about being drafted into the military."

"Do you know where they are now," Bobby asked.

"They went to the campers after work."

"I'll let Dad know that Christian has some concerns about being here. He can discuss the issue with him. We're the ones who should be worried about having to be drafted. It sounds like the age group they will target is eighteen to twenty-five." Bobby noticed Sherry's distress and moved closer to her. "Will you serve in the military?"

"Yes. I made up my mind. I told Christian last night that I'm finished with his group. I plan on speaking with your Uncle Jon at the meeting tonight. He can tell me how to go about enlisting." Sherry stood up straight as she spoke.

Bobby looked at Sherry much differently than he had only moments earlier. The spell he found himself having to dispel, whenever he was in her presence, was becoming entrancing. Having scruples, gave this alluring woman a vigor, a dynamism he found extremely appealing. His emotional reaction to Sherry was very much noticed by Emilee.

Monticello, Utah

Ted could see dim lights flickering in Monticello as they approached from the west. The sight of chaos and devastation came into view. Columns of smoke from the cell towers and electrical substations billowed high toward the sky. They stopped on a hill, next to a wheat field, about three kilometers from the main highway going through the town. They could hear screaming from the people stranded below, pulsating through the cool early evening air. Everyone left their vehicles and stared at the horrible scene.

"I can't believe it," said Irene, "those are Americans."

Breanna placed a hand on her mother's shoulder, noticing many more people in a long line of cars to the south. "There are thousands of them."

"Looks like the cars are incapacitated and they aren't letting people enter the town." Aaron glanced at Ted. "If those people get a chance, they will take our vehicles."

"Most likely, I know I would in their position," said Ted. "Especially if they knew of all the food in the RV."

"We have to figure a way to help. Just think if that was our family down there." Irene shook her head. "There are a lot of kids."

"We can't help them all," said Ed.

"We don't have to help all of them, we can help some."

"Mom, you have to be realistic," replied Breanna. "Your good heart is going to get us stranded. Those people down there wouldn't hesitate to cut our throats in order to take the RV."

"We can cook a big stew and put it in the five-gallon buckets and take it to them." Irene continued to shake her head as she brought her hand to her mouth. "I'll take it down myself."

"Good Lord Mom. Quit talking like that," said Aaron, pulling the binoculars away from his eyes. He handed them to Ted. "I don't see any route we can take to get us around this clutter. Do you see a way around it?"

"I see a couple of police cars, but not a single policeman," answered Ted, looking through the field glasses. "I don't see any breaks in the cars on the highway large enough for us to drive through."

"Can I look?" Carol held her hand out toward Ted.

He handed her the binoculars. Everyone was quiet as she looked down to the town.

"Why don't we use some food to bribe our way through. If we can get some help with moving about ten of the cars at the intersection, we can get to the other side and the street going east past the highway looks passable."

"Who can we get to help?" Ted asked. "Everyone down there would notice us moving the cars."

"I don't think so," replied Carol. "There is so much chaos that most people wouldn't notice."

"We need to do it tonight," said Aaron.

"No, most of those people won't sleep very well at night," countered Carol. "They would be more likely to be watching during the night, it would be better during the day."

Ted was not sure if he agreed with Carol's notion, but he was surprised with her bravado, something he had not seen from her since their meeting, he did not say a thing. Having everyone aware of the dangers, and on their toes, could only be positive.

"We need to find a secure place to park," said Aaron.

"The wheat trucks left us a road in the stubble, straight to those trees." Jerry pointed across the wheat field to a grove of trees.

"I can't understand how anyone in their right minds would plant wheat in these rocky fields," stated Aaron, "but it looks like a good spot to stay tonight."

There was no way to escape from the field if a problem should confront them, but Ted had no better options, so he followed the procession over the wheat stubble toward the trees.

"How far is Moab from here?" Samantha asked, as they drove slowly behind the RV, over the dusty field.

"I'm not positive," answered Ted, "maybe a hundred kilometers."

"About five years ago I went camping there with a girlfriend," remembered Samantha. "We left early afternoon and were back in Denver before midnight. I was just thinking how close we are, yet so far away."

"We are getting closer." Ted tried not to alarm Maddy. "We will be home before we know it."

There was a large, grassy meadow on the opposite side of the trees which made for a serene place to camp for the evening. Everyone parked their vehicles beside the RV. As Ted got out of the pickup Maddy tugged on his shirt.

"Grandpa, can Samantha sleep with us tonight?"

"Well," the question caught him completely off guard. "There's not a lot of room in the bed of the truck."

"We can make a bed on the ground," said Maddy. "Huh Samantha."

"We did a few nights ago." Samantha did not want to sleep in the cab.

"Remember how good we slept on the rocks?" Maddy asked. "We can look at the stars again."

"What do you mean how good we slept. I about froze my tush off."

"What's a tush?"

"My butt," he laughed.

Maddy put her hands to her mouth and laughed.

"Come on Maddy," said Samantha, beginning to pull the blankets from the back of the truck. "We can make a good place to sleep where none of us will freeze our tushes off."

Ted stepped toward the group that was gathering in front of the RV when he heard gunshots reverberating from the town. He stopped and listened. He knew they were high caliber weapons. Everyone froze in place, waiting to hear if the shots would continue.

"Those weren't hand-guns," said Jerry, looking at Ted.

"They were military." Ted looked at Aaron, "I'm going to walk to the hill at the end of the field and do some more surveillance. Can I get the binoculars?"

Ted waited as Maddy and Samantha placed the bedding on the ground. He was tempted to have Maddy stay with the group while he investigated the situation in town. A feeling in the pit of his stomach warned him to take his granddaughter.

"Maddy," he yelled, "come with me."

Maddy looked at Samantha.

"I'll come too," replied Samantha.

Walking over the stubble field was relatively easy. They came to a barbwire fence near the crest of the hill overlooking the town. Ted held the bottom wire and pulled hard on the top one, allowing Maddy and Samantha to crawl between the strands. After they crossed over Samantha pulled up on the wire for him. He noticed she had removed the bandage for her smashed fingers, but the three middle fingers were discolored.

They made their way to a stand of several small bushes covered with maroon colored leaves. The reverberations coming from the town below was louder than before. The size of the crowd flocking around the cars was increasing as travelers moved, from their stalled cars on the highway toward town, seeking refuge and food.

Ted surveyed the area along the highway, then directed his binoculars toward the heart of the town. His heart jumped when he spotted an army Humvee moving on the far outskirts of the small municipality. He moved the field glasses farther to the north and found the encampment of what looked to be a full company of soldiers. He lowered the binoculars and looked at the campsite with his naked eye.

"Look over there," he said to Maddy and Samantha, pointing toward the hardly noticeable army vehicles in the far distance. "Those are American Soldiers." He raised the binoculars to look closer to see if there might happen to be more forces in the area.

"Let me look," said Maddy, holding her hand out.

Ted allowed her to gaze through the field glasses. He surveyed the highway into the town. Cars were stacked for miles to the south. None of them were moving so he figured they were disabled, most likely by an EMP. To make a better assessment they would need to get closer. Before he could ask Maddy for the binoculars he heard a rapid succession of gunfire in the far distance.

"Maddy let me have the binoculars," he said.

"I see some kids." Maddy handed the glasses to her grandfather as the sound of several more shots rang out.

"Are those gunshots?" Samantha asked.

"Yeah, I think they came from the area near the army Humvee."

"Could they hit us?"

"No, we are out of their range." He estimated they were at least five kilometers away. "I do want to get a little closer."

The three of them walked slowly over small bushes and cactus for nearly four hundred meters, in the direction of town, to a flat spot on the side of the hill. The sun was setting quickly but there was still enough light to see past a golden haze. Ted looked through the binoculars. There were two Humvees moving slowly on the east side of town with several soldiers spread out flanking the vehicles. They were in a firefight with a group of about ten subversives, who were moving quickly in the direction of residential homes.

"What's that Grandpa?" yelled Maddy, pointing at a drone flying directly over the town between them and the soldiers.

Ted directed the binoculars toward the drone. He dropped them from his eyes and quickly raised them again.

"It has the 2nd Infantry logo from Fort Carson. Oh my gosh, Maddy. Those are Colonel Deb's soldiers." Ted looked at Samantha. "My sister Deb has to be close by."

"Will she be able to help us?"

"She will help us," said Ted, picking Maddy up in his arms. "We just need to get to their camp."

"Can we walk there, now?" Samantha asked.

"No, we need to let the others know. I want Terrance and Jerry along when we go across the town."

"Wonder if they leave?"

Ted hesitated for a moment, contemplating that maybe they should head straight to the army base. He thought better of it. "We need to hurry back and then go tonight."

Ted wasn't sure how he would proceed once he let the others know about his finding a company from Colonel Deb's brigade. He made a promise to himself that he would never let Maddy out of his sight, but now with the need to travel quickly at night, and the possibility of confronting danger, he wasn't sure it was feasible to take her with him.

By the time they reached the barbed wire fence surrounding the wheat field, the sun was setting, and the air cooled. Although they were a kilometer away from the caravan a dim glow from the lights in the RV could be seen reflecting through the grove of trees. The closer they got, the aroma of fresh bread filled the air, and the sounds of voices could be heard. Ted noticed movement to the right of the trees. Three men dressed in black were slowly approaching the camp. He held his arms out to stop Maddy and Samantha.

"Crouch down," he said, going down on one knee. He reached into his homemade holster and pulled out his pistol. Being caught out in the open limited his options. If he fired a warning shot it could cause them to come under fire. Something he was not willing to do. He motioned to Samantha and Maddy, "Lay down flat."

Ted watched as the subversives crept forward, only twenty meters from the camp. He was nearly four hundred meters away as he contemplated the scenario. He moved thirty meters closer and raised the pistol. Almost simultaneous with him shooting into the air came a flash and a loud blast from the campsite. His friends were alert to the danger. Traces of bullets streaked through the early dawn light from the approaching assailants. The sounds of the repeated shots from Jerry and Terrance's high-powered rifles were distinct over the sounds of the shotguns from the Jacobys. The gunfire lasted a little less than a minute, before quietness, soon to be overtaken with screams from within the campsite. The assailants were lying motionless.

"Come on," Ted motioned for Maddy and Samantha to follow him. Moving forward he kept an eye on the downed attackers. "I want you to get flat on your stomachs if shooting starts again."

The sound from Breanna screaming was distressing. Lights from the RV were turned off, but Ted could make out the forms of two different groups huddled over injured victims.

"Grandpa," Maddy held tightly to Ted's arm.

"We have to help." There was nowhere to hide his granddaughter from the disaster. He drew her closer to his side as he approached the campsite.

Ashley was laying on the ground with the Jacoby family tending her wound. Further back toward the Suburban were Jerry and Travis leaning over Carol, who was lying flat on the ground. Scotty was standing behind Jerry. Outside the camp Terrance was in the area of the three motionless subversives, checking each one for any sign of life.

Ted could see a life-threatening wound to the right side of Carol's midsection. He went to where the Jacobys were huddled over Ashley. She was sitting up when he first arrived but fell prone on her back. She had a bullet wound to the right side of her head. In order to survive both women needed immediate medical attention.

"Oh my God," yelled Breanna, standing over Aaron as he worked to limit the bleeding to the side of his wife's head.

"They came on us so quickly," said Ed, standing next to Breanna.

"We have to get her to a doctor," muttered Irene, who looked to be in shock.

"Breanna," yelled Ted, noticing Samantha staying as close to him as Maddy, "make a spot in the RV where we can put both Carol and Ashley."

"We need to hurry," screamed Aaron, looking up from his wife with blood covering his hands. "she's losing a lot of blood."

"Let's go, load them in the RV." Ted shouldered his way past Aaron and lifted Ashley in his arms. She was semi-conscious, taking in deep breaths. Adam made a half-hearted attempt to help him carry her to the RV. Travis and Jerry transported Carol into the motorhome and laid her on the floor. Aaron, Megan, Irene and Ed stayed with the two women, as Adam prepared to drive the motorhome.

"Travis, will you drive the Chevy?" Ted asked as he got out of the RV. Samantha and Maddy were waiting by the pickup, having thrown the bedding into the back. Terrance was waiting next to the Suburban.

"Do you want me to go first?"

"No, you follow last, but keep close." Ted noticed Scotty next to him with tears in his eyes. "Scotty, will you ride with us in the pickup?"

Scotty shook his head to affirm he would change vehicles. He walked over and joined Maddy and Samantha in the cab.

Ted waved to Terrance and Jerry in the Suburban to move forward. He motioned to Adam to open the door to the RV. "I'm going first, and then Jerry and then you," he said to Adam loud enough for Jerry to hear. He held no qualms about taking charge and making the decisions to get the two ladies to some sort of medical assistance. He hurried to the pickup.

Although it was dark, they drove much faster across the stubble then they did when they arrived at the wheat field. Once they reached the dirt path, they were able to make good time to

Highway 191. They came to the highway and drove north in the southbound lane, ignoring several peoples attempts to put their arms out to stop them. They came to a halt at a roadblock across the highway on the outskirts of town, four cars deep, spanning from one building on the west to another on the east. The caravan pulled in front of all the cars within a few meters of the blockade. The town was inaccessible.

A crowd of about fifty people on the town side of the roadblock made it apparent that they were aware of the new arrivals. Ted got out of the pickup. He placed his hand up, indicating to Jerry and Terrance to remain in the car.

"We need help," Ted yelled over the vehicles to the people on the other side of the roadblock. "We have two women hurt very badly."

"Nobody can enter," yelled a lady.

"It's life and death," screamed Ted, "they need help now."

"We can't help you," the lady shouted. "Our medical facilities are overwhelmed. They can't take care of the people already in town."

"Please, I'm begging you. We need help."

No reply. People with rifles were visible on the rooftops of every building, as far as he could see, on both ends of the barricade.

"Would one of you do me a favor?" Ted asked. He tried to calm his voice. "Could you deliver a note to the soldiers?"

There was complete silence. The people were looking at him, but no one was speaking. Ted turned to look back at the others in the RV. Ed and Irene were standing outside the motorhome. Several stranded travelers were approaching from the south. Travis pulled the Chevy next to Terrance and Jerry in the Suburban. A faint answer came from amongst the tongue-tied collection of town protectors, "I will."

A young woman about sixteen years old came toward Ted, walking across the hoods of the cars. She had a tear drop tattooed under her right eye. "I'll get it to them," she said, sitting down on the hood of the car closest to Ted.

"Get me a pen and paper," Ted yelled back at Jerry. Jerry rushed to the RV where Ed met him at the door with a pad and pen.

Ted quickly wrote his message on the paper and handed it to the young woman. "Please hurry and thank you."

The woman rushed into the night.

Grand Junction, Colorado

Colonel Deb finished dinner and was preparing to meet with Lt. Col. Woodworth to discuss the transportation of the subversives captured at Moab, who were now considered prisoners of war, to the base in Fort Carson. It had been a long day. Nearly every report she received during the day concerning fighting along the southern border was positive. The small contingent of Colorado National Guard in Grand Junction were requesting more assistance in helping rout out the collaborators who raised havoc in the small city over the past few days. It would be another item to discuss with Lt. Col. Woodworth. She sat comfortably in a cushioned chair in the lobby of the hotel, sipping on a glass of iced tea, as she waited. The computer whiz kids of the brigade were quickly mulling around the room with the new Pulsenet strapped to their wrists, keeping them ahead of all the needs of the troops, from food to toothpaste. It was the first time during the entire day she was able to relax.

Captain Hendersen with F Company finished clearing Highway 191 from Moab to Monticello and set camp for the evening. He reported no casualties from minor fighting in Monticello. After several skirmishes with the rebels, local authorities were back in control of the small town. They were scheduled to return to headquarters in Grand Junction early the next morning.

Lt. Col. Woodworth entered through the double glass doors and made his way to the colonel. He was exceptionally alert even after experiencing the long day.

"Deb," he greeted her, taking a seat on the soft chair next to her.

"What's the latest with the men captured in Moab?"

"They are housed in a utility shed behind the hotel. It sounds like General Lauer wants to treat them as POWs," said the lieutenant colonel, getting up from the chair to grab a bottle of water from a cooler in the middle of the lobby.

"Have you set transportation for tomorrow?" Deb asked.

"I want to make sure Captain Hendersen doesn't incur any more casualties before I make definite plans. Private Risk's foot is worse than we first assumed, so we plan to send him back to

Fort Carson with the POWs," answered Josh, noticing Command Sergeant Major Talfoya moving in their direction from the control center.

"Tommy, what's going on?" Deb asked, noticing a concerned look on his face.

"We received notice that the 3rd Armored Brigade will pass through here tomorrow. They should arrive around noon."

"What's going on Tommy? I was under the impression from all reports today that the fighting on the border was well under control."

"Everyone felt the same way, four hours ago, we thought the enemy was going to retreat back into Mexico," Tommy explained. "New intelligence shows that the initial penetration of attacks was only a feeler. There are hundreds of thousands of Chinese and Russian soldiers preparing to make a major advancement across the southern front."

"Are we going to be traffic cops, here in Grand Junction?"

"I'm not sure where we will end up. We need to make sure the 3rd Armored have a clear shot to Monticello. A company from the 1st infantry Division will clear the way from there."

"I'm starting to get a little antsy here," stated Deb testily. "I don't like sitting and waiting."

"Something tells me we won't be doing that very long." Tommy turned to go back to the control center.

"Josh, I want to talk with the guys we captured today." She stood up and removed a bottle of water from the cooler.

"They might be sleeping."

"Then let's wake them up."

"Alright, if you say so." Lt. Col. Woodworth was a little conflicted about interviewing the prisoners so late at night. He followed the colonel to the utility shed and ordered the guards to open the door.

"Just bring one at a time," ordered Deb.

Deb was surprised at the grey-haired man who stood before her. He looked to be in his late forties or early fifties. She handed him a bottle of water and asked, "How in the hell old are you?"

The man looked confused with the abruptness of the question. He answered anyway. "I'm fifty-one."

"How long have you been in the United States?"

"Since 2036," he said with a deep accent.

"What's your name?"

"Alec."

"Are the rest as old as you?" Deb inquired, somewhat surprised at how freely he spoke.

"No, I'm the oldest."

"You told the soldiers who captured you that you are a citizen of the United States."

"Yes, since 2036, I came legally."

"What is your occupation?"

"On paper, I'm a graphic designer." Alec took a drink of the cold water. He looked at Deb with a crooked grin. "In reality I'm an anarchist, an antagonist."

"You mean an enemy of the United States?"

"No, I like the country. I'm an enemy of the people of the United States."

"Why?" Deb asked. "Did this country treat you that badly?"

"Ha, you don't get it," he laughed. "I was trained to come here. Every cent I've made over the past fifteen years came from either the Chinese or Russian governments, not from America."

Deb was momentarily dissuaded by his remarks but quickly gained her composure. She glanced at Lt. Col. Woodworth to see his reaction to the dialogue. He stood by silently.

"How many anarchists like you did the Chinese and Russians send?"

"Over the past fifteen years," he answered, stopping to calculate in his head, "probably forty thousand. The majority came within the past three years."

Deb looked at him in disbelief. "How much did they pay you?"

"I averaged over a hundred thousand American dollars," he answered matter-of-factly, flipping his left hand in the air, "a year."

"So, you are saying the Chinese and Russian governments paid billions of dollars to keep subversives in America over the past fifteen years."

"Try trillions," countered Alec. "You forgot about paying the Americans we recruited into the gang scene. They came much cheaper though."

"When we take you back to our base in Colorado, will you tell them everything you told me?" Deb asked cautiously.

"Why not, everything is past keeping it a secret." Alec looked into Deb's eyes. "It is to the point now where one of us will win and one will lose."

Deb motioned to the guard. The guard placed him back into the utility shed and locked the door. She hesitated momentarily contemplating the conversation as a corporal approached. She saluted.

"Colonel, Captain Hendersen needs to speak to you on intercom."

Deb rushed to the communication control center in the lobby. She could see the tired face of Captain Hendersen on the screen.

"Yes Captain," Deb sat down in front of the monitor.

"Colonel, we received a note from a civilian who came to our camp. It's from your brother Colonel Ted Lisco." Captain Hendersen held the note so Deb could see the writing, but she couldn't quite read it. "It says that he and Maddy are on the southern edge of town. They urgently need medical assistance for members of his traveling party. It ends with Merry 1225."

Deb knew the note was from Ted. Merry 1225 was the code they used when children, while playing spy, to acknowledge a message was authentic.

"Are you secure in your position?" she asked the captain.

"Yes ma'am."

"Get Sergeant Sessions so I can speak with her." Deb wavered for a moment. "Captain. I want more than reconnaissance and recovery on this. Send out a full platoon with the sergeant. Bring Ted and his party back to the camp for the evening."

"Of course," Captain Hendersen was fully aware of the close relationship Colonel Lisco held with her brothers, "do you want me to go personally?"

"No, you stay at the camp. But I want to make sure Sergeant Sessions is fully protected."

"Ma'am." Sergeant Sessions came into view on the screen. Condoleezza Session began her career under Colonel Ted. She had an enchanting smile, made more noticeable by a large gap in her front teeth. From the moment Ted met her, they had an immediate connection. He was the one who insisted she transfer to the 2nd Infantry Brigade to serve under Deb, something not so easy in the new Army. But after finding the medic was only a couple semesters away from becoming a doctor, Deb used her clout in getting the transfer.

"Sergeant, I want you to look at the message," Deb stated, "and tell me if you are willing to go and help Ted."

"Of course, I will. I'd do anything to help him." The sergeant turned to look at Captain Hendersen. "I only need time to grab my medic kit."

"1st platoon has had a long day, so I'll send 3rd platoon," said the captain.

"I want this monitored very closely," Deb sighed. "I'll be here the entire time."

Deb knew the timing of Ted's discovery was extraordinary. If she had orders to move into the fray of the evolving war, there was no way she would have been able to help her brother. All three lieutenant colonels under her command were by her side as she waited for the platoon to leave.

Monticello, Utah

Ted moved past Ed and Irene, who were waiting at the entrance to the motorhome and stepped up and into the now makeshift hospital. It continued to smell like fresh baked bread on the inside, but there were bloody towels scattered across the room. Aaron was sitting on the floor with Ashley's head in his lap. She was lying motionless. Adam was kneeling next to Carol as Breanna tended her wound. Without medical help there was a high probability of losing both women.

"Is Scotty ok?" Carol asked, very weakly when she noticed Ted.

"He's outside with Samantha and Maddy," answered Ted.

"Are you sure?" Please tell me the truth." Her breathing was labored.

Ted stepped to the door and looked outside. He motioned to her grandson, "Scotty, come inside."

Scotty hesitantly stepped inside the motor home.

"Just tell your grandma that you are alright." Ted moved him past Ashley to where Carol was laying.

"I'm ok Grandma," he said timidly, standing with his feet at her side.

She raised her left hand. As he took it in his hand, she closed her eyes tightly and cried.

"I sent a note to the army camp." Ted looked down at Ashley. Her eyes were glazed but responsive. "I'm certain they will come to help us just as soon as they receive it."

Ted moved outside next to Ed and Irene. Irene's eyes were hollowed, and her cheeks seemed to sag. But as poorly as Irene looked, Ed looked even more haggard. They were both exhausted.

Ted opened the utility chest on the side of the RV and pulled out two chairs. Irene and Ed fell into them.

"We should have stayed at the farm," Irene clutched Ed's hand. "If Ashley lives, she will never be the same."

"Irene," Ted kneeled in front of her, "most of you, if not all of you would have been killed by the soldiers we saw flying onto the interstate before we left. You saw how vicious they were when they shot Aaron."

"We are just too old to go through this," she patted Ed's hand.

"You're not that old Irene," said Maddy, placing her arm on Ted's shoulder. "You are the best cook in the world."

"Oh Maddy, will you give me a hug?" Maddy placed her skinny arms around Irene's neck and hugged her tightly. "That makes me feel so much better."

Maddy relinquished the hug and smiled uncertainly at Irene. She followed her grandpa to the back of the RV, where Terrance, Travis and Jerry were surveying the mass of people. "Why did Irene say she wanted to go back to her home?" she asked.

"She misses her home and is worried, she needed to get it off her chest."

Maddy stared at Ted contemplating the meaning of what he told her. "What does get it off her chest mean?"

"It's being honest. It's saying something that might be bothering you, so you feel better."

Maddy nodded her head to show Ted she understood.

More and more of the stranded motorists were gathering at the back side of the RV. Terrance, Jerry and Travis were leaning on the hood of the Suburban watching the crowd as they assembled. A cold breeze came from the northwest, causing many of the people gathering to pull their coats tight around their necks.

"Have we checked with the group back here to see if there is a doctor?" Ted asked.

"They told us that the townspeople took all the doctors and nurses earlier," replied Terrance.

"They don't look very threatening right now," said Ted, "but we should move the Chevy tight to the back of the motorhome and pull the Suburban tight to the pickup."

"I haven't seen any weapons." Jerry held his rifle in his right hand. "We're keeping a close eye on everyone."

"Samantha," Irene waved for her to move closer. "There's a whole bushel of apples inside, toward the back. Why don't you and Maddy take them and give them to the people."

"I don't think that's a good idea right now," said Ted hastily. "There are too many people. We don't want to give only some of them food."

The reality of the situation was that if the war escalated, many of the people along the highway were going to die. The town was overwhelmed, and no help was on the way.

"They are just going to go bad," said Irene, "and these people are suffering."

Ted thought for a moment. He looked at Samantha. He didn't want Maddy to witness the bloody mess inside the RV. "I'll get them."

"I think they will appreciate them." Irene nodded her head to Maddy and Samantha.

Ted carried the basket of apples and sat them next to Terrance and Jerry. He walked around the Suburban, the bright moon cast a light on an incredible scene. Families scattered as far as his eyes could see, waiting to be rescued by a nonexistent entity. Children were perched on the hoods of cars, like vultures. He thought back to Irene's statement that maybe they couldn't save them all, but they could save some. The first vehicle in line behind the RV was occupied by a young couple with two children. They were standing at the front of their car.

"How are you?" Ted asked as he stood a couple meters from them.

"Could be better," said the young man, waving his arm behind him. "Our car won't run, just like everyone else's."

"I have something for you if you want to follow me," said Ted.

The man followed Ted around to the RV. Several stranded people moved closer.

"You can take as many of the apples as you want, or you can give away as many as you want." Ted pointed at the basket. "You have to take the whole bushel with you."

The man took the apples. Ted moved next to Terrance, Jerry and Travis to watch to see if he kept them or shared. He placed about a dozen apples in his car and took the rest and handed them to the people behind him. Several people pushed and shoved but eventually the bushel basket was moved back until all the apples were taken, leaving many people further back in the traffic jam to wonder why they were excluded. There was a tsunami of travelers moving forward as the news of food reverberated through the crowd. The man who originally took the apples was punched and beaten by several assailants.

Jerry and Terrance raised their rifles. Ted hustled around the Suburban and motioned to the wife of the man who was fighting for his life.

"Bring your kids and come here," Ted yelled to the frightened woman. "Hurry, come on."

The woman placed a child under each arm. She ran around the Suburban and waited behind Jerry and Terrance. Ted pulled out his pistol and aimed it at a large man with a potbelly, grappling with the woman's husband.

"Let him go," yelled Ted. His demand was not heard. He yelled louder, "let him go."

The brute fighting with the man would have been considered an ordinary citizen a week earlier, but now he was desperate enough to assault and harm an innocent man for apples. He stopped the beating and looked toward Ted. The beaten man, bleeding from his nose, ran around to join his wife and children.

"Go ahead and shoot me," yelled the brute.

"I don't want to shoot you." Ted lowered his pistol. "I only wanted you to stop beating this man."

"We are starving here."

"I'm sorry," It was all Ted could say as he looked at the mass of people. In the darkness, their faces were veiled, something he was content with. He knew that the misery was not going away.

"Ted," yelled Samantha, standing next to Maddy and Irene. She pointed to the roadblock. On the opposite side were soldiers talking with the townspeople. The cars making up the roadblock were being slowly pushed apart to make a path.

Irene and Ed quickly placed the chairs back in the utility cabinet and rushed inside the motorhome. Everyone was in their vehicles waiting for the opening, except Ted. He looked at the young couple and their children.

"What's your names," Ted asked the man.

"Victor Hernandez."

"I'm Glenda and our children Jaime and Jairo."

"Hop in the Suburban." Ted pointed in the direction of Jerry and Terrance who were entering the vehicle.

"Can we get our luggage?" Victor asked.

"Sorry, those people would never allow you to get your belongings. We have to go now."

The last car at the barricade was moved to make a clear path to the other side of the roadblock. The Hernandez family hesitantly climbed into the back of the old vehicle, not fully understanding that they were just given a chance to survive.

Two Humvees with several soldiers forming a perimeter were waiting for the group on the town side of the roadblock. Three other vehicles were waiting about two hundred meters further down the road. Ted drove about ten meters past the Humvees to allow the motorhome to pull up alongside the military vehicles. He was unsure as to whether a medic would be with the rescue party. He stepped out of the pickup, with Maddy at his side.

Soldiers were manning the protected gun turrets on top of the Humvees. The soldiers situated at the perimeter were decked out in the new Rind Impulse Operator Suit. The protective suits were placed into service right as Ted was retiring. The gear was light weight and easily removed, they had thermostats that kept the inside temperature constant, no matter the temperature on the outside. The pneumatic ankles and knees reduced the stress on their joints. But it was the helmet that made the suit exceptional, with the heads-up display that provided a 3D audio system. It was the first time Ted had seen the attire.

"Colonel Lisco," someone yelled.

"Grandpa," Maddy pointed in the direction of the Humvees.

He looked forward to a bright light beaming from the top of the vehicles, creating an unnatural glare. Several soldiers were standing in a grey darkness.

"Colonel Lisco, it's Condoleezza Session."

Maddy was holding tight to Ted's right arm as he moved next to the sergeant. He was beyond surprised. He reached out with his right arm and pulled her in to give her a hug. Something noticed by the surrounding soldiers but didn't bother the sergeant in the least.

"I was wondering if you might have forgotten who I was," she said, with a large smile on her face.

"You are someone I will never forget." Ted released his hug. "Is Deb…Colonel Lisco here in Monticello?"

"She's in Grand Junction," replied the sergeant. "I'm here with F Company. We leave for headquarters in Grand Junction early in the morning."

He released her and quickly opened the door to the motorhome. "We have two injured."

Condoleezza, along with two other medics, followed Ted into the RV. Samantha stayed outside with Maddy and Scotty. Carol was talking but Ashley was quiet.

"She's still breathing," Aaron said, looking at Condoleezza through bloodshot eyes as he continued to hold her head.

Ted placed his hand on Aaron's shoulder. "Let her help Ashley."

Ed and Irene leaned against the countertop as they watched the two younger medics start to work on Carol. Aaron stood next to his mother and father as Condoleezza took control of taking care of his wife.

"God just sent us an angel," whispered Irene, looking down at Condoleezza as she tilted Ashley's head to the side in her hands. The bullet wound extended from her right temple, over her ear, to the back edge of her skull. She moved Ashley's head to where she was looking directly into her eyes and asked, "What's your name?"

"Ashley," she answered very faintly.

"We need to go back to camp where we can work in the medical unit." The medic gave no assessment of the damage. "We'll ride in the motorhome, if you'll follow the Humvees."

Ted left the RV and prepared the others to follow the soldiers back to their camp. He looked at the mass of townspeople still guarding the barricade. The young girl with the teardrop tattoo was watching them prepare to leave. Ted approached her.

"I can't tell you how much I appreciate you delivering the note."

"No problem," she said. "Hopefully, the Army will stay and help get things under control."

"I wouldn't count on it." Ted stared at her frail figure. He did not want to disclose the information about them leaving in the morning. "You better make sure you have protection and supplies. Don't expect help to come this way for quite some time."

"We are prepared," said the young woman.

"Well thank you for helping."

Smoke filled the air and it was deathly quiet as the caravan followed the army vehicles to the camp on the north side of town. The Humvees drove quickly through the residential streets.

Ted had never officially met Captain Hendersen. The captain on the other hand was well aware of Ted's relationship to Colonel Deb.

"Colonel," Captain Hendersen searched out and greeted Ted the moment the vehicles came to a halt in the center of the encampment. "Colonel Lisco is waiting to speak with you. She asked that I take you to communications the moment you arrived."

Ted was pleased he used his former title, rather than mister, his prescribed title, since his retirement. He was extremely impressed with the composed, yet firm demeanor of the officer.

"This is my granddaughter, Maddy." She was hanging onto his right arm.

"I failed to mention Colonel Lisco did say she wanted to speak with Maddy too," replied the captain, with a smile.

Deb was ecstatic when she first saw Ted and Maddy's faces on the monitor. Behind her, were the three lieutenant colonels and Command Sergeant Major Talfoya.

"You have the whole crew up tonight," said Ted.

"We have a lot on our plates right now." Deb felt a twinge of happiness in her heart at seeing her older brother with Maddy clinging to his arm. "Maddy, we are so excited to see you."

Maddy buried her face in Ted's side. Ted placed his hand on the side of her face.

"It seems like an eternity since we took off from Los Angeles," stated Ted. "I've met some very incredible people on our trek here."

"Do you have reliable transportation?" Deb asked.

"I'm driving an eighty-year-old pickup truck that is very reliable."

"Tomorrow morning you can follow F Company back to Grand Junction and we can figure out how to get you to the farm," said Deb. "Nicole and Bill have been worried sick over you two."

"Did you speak with them since all this has taken place?"

"They are at the farm with Hank, Jon and their families, along with several others. The metro area is in total chaos."

"I spoke with a motorist yesterday who said the southern border is being attacked." Ted thought for a moment. "Outside of Cedar City Utah there were several aircraft, I can only describe as gliders, bringing in troops to the area. We fled the area before I could get any more information."

"Stryker is moving down from the Salt Lake City area tomorrow and will be engaging the forces in that region," said Deb. "I will let you get some sleep. You will be leaving the area in about five hours, so we will catch up in the morning."

Although they were in the middle of the army encampment Ted wanted to make sure to keep his guard up. He was able to keep Maddy safely by his side through a very harrowing period. He wasn't about to let anything happen to his granddaughter now.

Colorado Farm

It was a classic eastern Colorado blizzard with the wind howling from the east, and then changing to hammer them from the north. The wailing wind blew the snow to the point that the north facing windows were darkened. Hank called for everyone to meet in the large living room of the main house. His intentions were to organize and make sure the farm would be habitable for a long period of time. Deb gave them a four-month head start in surviving, now he wanted to make sure they thought beyond the four months. With the weather taking a turn for the worse he was becoming increasingly worried about his good friend George Saxton and his family being caught outside in the blizzard.

Although the building of the apartment was going exceptionally well, there were several duties that were being placed on the shoulders of a few and ignored by many. Such things as laundry, feeding of the chickens, food preparation and minor maintenance were items Hank planned to address with the group.

Jon was going to speak about security for the farm. Also, Clint Brown, the neighbor to the west who held nearly forty head of cattle that belonged to Deb, wanted the cattle moved from his ranch to the farm.

"My God, that wind is really howling." Jon sat down, next to Gina, on the fireplace hearth as many of the others settled into seats in the large family room. "Looks like we are missing most of the young people."

Bobby, Emilee, Dave and Sherry walked through the front door.

"Did anyone let Christian and the others know we are meeting?" Hank asked, looking at Sherry as they moved into the living room.

"They knew," said Sherry timidly, lowering her head.

"I think we might have a problem here," stated Bobby.

"Let me guess," interrupted Bill, stepping to the center of the room. "Christian, Tim and their friends left."

"Umm, as far as I know they haven't left yet." Bobby looked at Sherry. "Have they?"

Sherry shrugged her shoulders. "All I know is they said they planned to go back to the city."

"I'll check and see if they are in the campers." Bobby pulled his coat tight to his neck. He hurried to the back campers. They were empty. He went to the large garage. They were nowhere to be seen. Bobby returned to the house.

"They are gone," he said with a bewildered look on his face.

"They'll freeze to death," worried Hank. He hesitated, realizing how naïve and trusting he was concerning his former football players. "They stole a car, didn't they?"

"There is only one car in the garage."

"I left the damn thing open." Jon shook his head. "I didn't even consider they would steal from us."

"We can't do anything about it tonight," stated Jacqueline. She noticed Jessica had not arrived at the meeting. She turned toward Emilee. "Where are your mother and sisters?"

"I would imagine they are downstairs. I'll go get them." Emilee's face showed a twinge of concern as she left to go to the family quarters in the basement. Bobby noticed and followed his girlfriend.

Bobby was the first to come up the stairs, followed by Reagan, Avery and then Emilee. Emilee's eyes looked hollow, and her lips quivered, as she said, "the girls just told me, Mom left with Christian."

Grand Junction, Colorado

Deb woke from a restless night of sleep at 0500 She strolled out of her room to the communication center in the lobby of the hotel and poured herself a cup of coffee. Time seemed to be at a standstill as she monitored the activity taking place on the front lines of the southern border. 3rd Armored Brigade was due to move through Grand Junction by late morning, a couple hours after Ted and Maddy were expected with F Company.

"Colonel," said a soldier, approaching Deb. "F company has moved through Moab. They should arrive in two hours."

"Thank you corporal. Where is 3rd Armored?"

"They are leaving metro Denver, just heading up Floyd Hill."

Deb would be able to have some time with Ted before dealing with the 3rd Brigade. She decided to have a quick breakfast. The brand-new hotel restaurant was used for feeding the troops, with a chow line established in the parking lot outside the front door. Officers dined inside the small restaurant. Staff Sergeant Major Talfoya was eating by himself at a table in the back corner of the dining area. Deb grabbed a bowl of oatmeal and joined him. She sensed something was bothering the Command Sergeant Major.

"What's going on Tommy?" Deb looked at him as he looked at the center of the table. "What's bothering you?"

"Ok, I was going to tell you right after breakfast." He looked down at the table. "General Lopez informed me last night they received a complaint from a civilian about you having his son beaten at your farm. The civilian is a lawyer and wants article 133 leveled against you."

"Conduct unbecoming an Officer." Deb smiled at him. "Hell, I could be charged with that nearly every day."

"It's not a laughing matter. It could make it impossible for you to go any further with your career."

"Tommy, I'm happy right here where I'm at, being a colonel."

"General Lauer wants you on conference call at 0700."

Deb looked at him, smiled and shook her head.

General Lauer was on the monitor at precisely 0700. His worn face and sunken eyeballs told her he was up most the night, and it wasn't her implied charges that kept him awake.

"Colonel Lisco, we need you to immediately send out reconnaissance on Highway 139 toward Rangely, in preparation for displacement of both 2nd Brigade and 3rd Armored Brigade to Great Falls, Montana. Last night after Russian planes entered the Alaskan Air Defense Identification Zone our planes encountered a superior force of Russian aircraft. We lost six aircraft," the general hesitated for a moment. "Nine Divisions of Russian troops have come ashore in western Alaska and are moving toward the Canadian and American border."

"Are the Canadians in this fight?"

"They are being threatened from the east, so we will know more in the next twenty-four hours of the strength of forces they can commit to the west," said General Lauer. "You'll attach to the 10th Mountain Infantry in Great Falls. They are being redirected west as we speak."

"Will Stryker move up to join us?" Deb asked. She was astounded how quickly everything was changing.

"Yes, they are moving now," said the general.

Plans changed quick as a wink. She just told Ted last night that Stryker would be moving to the Cedar City area. The urgency of the situation with the Russians was quite apparent, but she wondered about the threat of the enemy soldiers in Utah.

"Sir," Deb said, "Ted told me the gliders landing near Cedar City the other night carried several enemy soldiers."

"We are fully aware of the situation," said General Lauer. "You prepare to depart."

"Are we to leave this afternoon?"

"As soon as armored arrives."

"Yes sir," Deb looked at Tommy. He immediately moved out the door toward the troops.

"Colonel Lisco," General McClinton moved in front of the camera so he could be seen by Deb, "I hear that Ted is on his way to your location."

"Yes sir, he is following F Company. They should be here within the hour." Deb was surprised about the general knowing she was helping Ted. "He is with a group of civilians who have been assisting him, after the plane he was flying on with his granddaughter, went down in Cedar City, Utah."

"We need Ted Lisco back in uniform." General McClinton wasn't about to waste time with pleasantries. "Have him contact us as soon as he arrives."

"Yes sir, I cannot speak for my brother, but I will give him the message." Deb realized the problems Ted would face with Nicole if the general talked him into re-enlisting.

"Colonel," General McClinton hesitated for a moment, "you give um hell. You have my full support."

"I will do that sir." Deb felt a little dumbfounded as the dispatch ended abruptly. No mention of misconduct. But it did make her feel good about having the full support of the Army Chief of Staff. All efforts and decisions could be done under the aegis of the upper command.

Deb was unaware that, prior to the communication, her conduct was an issue discussed by General Lauer and General McClinton. General McClinton was unyielding in his support for her. He admitted that her behavior was flamboyant, sometimes impetuous and often controversial. But the most important attribute she held was that of a leader, not a follower. At this fraught time, the United States Army, more so the country, desperately needed leaders.

***

Ted was concerned when he saw the army vehicles lined along Interstate 70, pointing west, as they followed members from F Company into the west side of Grand Junction. It meant only one thing, that the war was escalating. Deb was about to venture into combat.

The Humvee carrying Ashley and Carol drove directly toward the section, where only a day earlier a large medical tent existed. It was now an empty field. Ted thought about following Condoleezza to the area but decided to follow the jeep leading them to headquarters.

Deb was waiting as the caravan moved in front of the hotel. She was decked out in fatigues as she watched Ted drive up to the front door in the old F-250 pickup. The 1957 Chevy, the Suburban and the RV followed behind as they all parked in the circular drive to the entrance of the hotel.

"Glad to see you, big brother." Deb approached Ted and Maddy as they got out of the pickup. In the past, she was never the one to give her brothers a hug, but this time she went to Ted and gave him a quick embrace. She leaned down to Maddy. "Hi Maddy, your dad and grandma are going to be incredibly happy to see you."

"Hi," said Maddy. She continued holding tight to Ted. She knew Deb was Ted's sister, but having seen her on only a few occasions, she never got to know her.

"Does Nicole know we are ok?" Ted asked.

"No, I haven't been able to contact them, they obviously have no idea about the capabilities of the communication center at the farm. I saw them on Monday but didn't tell them that it is more than just a radio. I'm surprised Bill isn't more familiar with the communication system. It's something you will have to sort out when you get there."

"It'll be interesting when we just show up."

"Looks like you two have been put through the ringer."

"It's been a tough few days," Ted sighed. "When are you leaving?"

Maddy glanced around her grandfather, as Samantha and Scotty moved next to Ted. Ed and Irene were walking slowly from the RV, being shadowed by Breanna.

"In about two hours. Just as soon as 3rd Armored arrives." Deb was intrigued by the beautiful woman Ted had arrived with. Although she was completely disheveled, with her hair in tangles and make-up unkempt, she was a very striking woman. Ted noticed Deb's fascination with Samantha.

"This is Samantha," said Ted. "She was a flight attendant on the plane we were flying on from Los Angeles. She helped me with Maddy over the past few days. And this is Scotty."

Scotty was standing back, unsure of the situation. Ed, Irene and Breanna moved to Ted's side. The rest of the group waited in the vehicles.

"This is Ed, Irene and their daughter Breanna. They helped us out at their farm after we fled from Cedar City."

"Glad to meet you," said Deb.

"Thank you for helping us." Irene felt an instant connection with the colonel. "Are we in full out war?"

"It looks like we are ma'am."

"God help us," Irene grimaced.

The Humvee carrying Ashley and Carol pulled in behind the Chevy. Condoleezza stepped from the vehicle.

"Ma'am," she saluted Deb, then handed Ted a set of papers. "Both women are stable now, but in need of attention I can't provide them at this time. Here is a printout of medical care and medications I have given."

"Are we going to be able to get Ashley to a hospital?" Breanna asked, noticing Scotty, she added to her question. "And Carol."

"The hospitals here are beyond overflowing," stated Deb sharply. "Your best bet will be to try and find a hospital in the Denver area."

"Is the interstate safe to travel to Denver?" Ted asked, handing the paperwork to Breanna.

"It's been a high priority to keep the route open, so there should be no problems with the insurgents. You are going to be surprised by the devastation in the city. There was a blizzard yesterday on the plains, but the interstate west of Denver has been clear of snow," answered Deb. "We are sending the prisoners back to Carson. You can follow them if you want."

"When are they leaving?" Ted asked.

"Immediately," answered Deb, "but before you go, General Lauer and General McClinton want you to contact them. We are just finishing with packing the communication center."

"Is General McClinton at Fort Carson?" Ted knew why the generals wanted to talk with him. He was curious as to how they were planning on bringing him back into the fold.

"He arrived at the base yesterday. Let's go inside and contact them."

Ted and Maddy followed Deb into the lobby of the hotel. Everyone else waited outside. There was only a single table, with a monitor, left in the large lobby. It took a few minutes of waiting before the image of General McClinton appeared on the screen.

"Ted," said the general, "I'll get straight to the point. We are facing some real problems here. I need you back in uniform. We are in the process of building several new divisions. Besides needing new recruits, I need experienced soldiers to lead them."

"Has Congress passed a new law for conscription."

"Yes, it has already passed, for every citizen between the age of eighteen and twenty-five, but we are having a hell of a time coordinating the draft."

"General," Ted realized he needed to be careful what he promised, "I have to speak with Nicole before I can give you an answer."

"Ted, I have to tell you how dire our circumstances are at this time." The general's face was distraught. "The Russians, Chinese and Iranians are about to throw everything they have at us. There is a real possibility the United States could be conquered."

"What about weapons and ammunition?" Ted asked. "I've been hearing the F-22s and F-35s constantly flying for the past three days. Do we have enough missiles in the arsenal?"

"Although the cities east of us are still in chaos the factories are being re-structured to produce missiles and ammunition, but to be honest, it is going to be a real issue." Ted's knowledge of the problem made General McClinton even more determined to have him back in his command. "I understand your need to speak with Nicole before deciding, but this is a situation where we could lose all our families if we don't respond with everything we have."

"I should be at the farm on the eastern plains by dusk tonight." Ted looked down at Maddy. She looked back at him with her eyes wide open. He knew he would never sit back and watch while enemies fought to take away his family. "I'll meet with you tomorrow afternoon at the base."

"Security is tight around here, but I'll leave a pass at the west gate," stated the general. "We need you back Ted."

Ted watched the monitor go blank. He and Maddy followed Deb to the parking area as the technicians quickly broke down the final parts of the communication center behind them. Condoleezza was speaking with Ed and Irene in front of the RV as they approached.

"Both ladies are in the RV. Ashley's wound looks much worse than it really is. Carol is very seriously injured and needs to be careful not to jostle around too much," said Condoleezza, standing next to Colonel Deb. "Hopefully you'll have better luck with the hospitals when you get to the city."

"Scotty is going to ride with his grandma in the RV," stated Irene as she prepared to climb into the motorhome.

Ed walked over to Deb and held out his hand. "Check on our family for us if you happen to get to southwest Utah. They are in a cabin northeast of Cedar City."

"Sir, we are going north. But things change on a dime for us, so if we happen to end up in Utah I'll do what I can," stated Deb, taking hold of his knobby, knuckled hand, unsure how to reply to his request. "You take care of my cattle when you get to the farm."

"We will definitely do that." Ed followed Irene into the RV.

Ted looked at Condoleezza, and then back to Deb. An urge to join them rushed through his body. He felt a twinge of guilt before he looked at Maddy. He had one obligation, and that was getting his granddaughter home safely. His farewell was quick. He was planning on being back as soon as humanly possible to help fight for the country.

The Humvee with the prisoners was waiting on the highway. The convoy pulled in behind the soldiers and they began the final leg of their journey toward the farm in eastern Colorado. After moving at a snail's pace for the past couple days over rugged terrain, it was exhilarating to be traveling at a high rate of speed over the smooth highway.

About an hour out of Grand Junction they met the column from the 3rd Brigade, driving quickly past them down Interstate 70. It was an impressive display of modern military technology. Every truck they passed gave Ted a sense of reassurance that the country could be protected. From the old patriot batteries to the new Sentinel Blaze Radar, now connected to all service branches. Ted knew America could sustain attacks from the long-range, precision guided missiles from Russia and China. It was the large, odd-shaped trucks that caught Maddy's eye.

"What are those?" Maddy placed her arms on the dashboard of the old truck and looked out the window.

"That is the new Arrow defense system. It replaced a thing called THAAD."

"What does it do?" Samantha asked.

"Armies a long time ago used archers to shoot arrows at their enemies. In order to win a battle, the other side would try to kill the archers. These big trucks fire missiles and lasers to shoot the other sides missiles out of the air, but better than the old THAAD, they will identify the enemy launchers and command posts and destroy them too."

They watched the long convoy of trucks and machines, with helicopters occasionally flying above, until the last remnants of the column passed.

Maddy laid her head on Ted's upper arm as she prepared to fall asleep. Although it was only mid-morning, she had been awake for over eight hours. It was less than a week since Ted met her at the Los Angeles airport, but it seemed much longer. In contrast, he thought, how quickly the previous year had disappeared. Day to day living was tiring when there was no purpose in existing.

"Can you drop me off at my parent's home when we get to Denver?" Samantha asked quietly, bringing Ted out of his thoughts. "Their home is right off Kipling and 470."

"I'll inform everyone about the detour, when we stop for a break."

"That will be wonderful." Samantha looked at him with weary eyes, "I can't tell you how safe you have made me feel since we landed the airplane."

"Well, you were terrific with helping Maddy." He held his jaw straight forward as he stared at the highway.

"What do you think we will find when we get to Denver?"

"I'm sure it will be turmoil. I have no idea how much." Ted glanced at her. His thoughts went to the entire group of disparate strangers, he had chanced upon during the journey. He felt a twinge in his heart, a pang that made him want to protect them through the trying times they were undoubtedly destined to experience.

"My parents are very resourceful. I'm sure they will be fine."

"Like I told you before. You and your parents are welcome to follow us to the farm."

"Do you think everyone in our group will follow you there?"

"Jerry and Terrance know people in the area, so I suppose it will depend on how bad the chaos is when we arrive." He could see that the corners of her mouth were cracking but her lips were still bright red. "I don't know about Travis. What's going on with him?"

"I don't know." She turned and looked out the side window.

"Is there a problem between you two?" Ted asked boldly.

"Somewhat," she turned her head slowly and looked back at him.

He waited for her to elaborate. When she didn't, he asked, "Was he your boyfriend? Was there a love connection?"

Samantha looked at him for a long second, and then burst out laughing. "Oh my gosh." She wiped the tears of laughter from her eyes.

"What?" Ted asked, looking straight forward.

"You men," she squinted her eyes as she tried to stifle her laugh so as not to wake Maddy. "What have you been thinking about me all this time?"

Ted realized he better not answer that question, at least not honestly. He still had a vivid memory of her in the genie nighty.

"I'm sorry to say it has nothing to do with sex." She sniffled and flicked her finger under her eye, wiping the final tear drop away. "About six months ago, I was falsely accused of drinking on the job. Travis was able to exonerate me, but he refused to speak on my behalf. Of course, looking back on it now I understand, with him having a family to support, not wanting to take a chance of placing his job in jeopardy. It was a difficult time for me because I was trying to buy a place of my own. Anyway, I was completely vindicated, and everything worked out. The flight out of LA was the first time I flew with him since the incident."

Ted looked at her and smiled. "You could have spiced the story up a bit."

"Oh, I forgot to mention, I was drinking while working at the local strip club." She could see a somewhat confused look on his face. "I'm kidding."

Ted smiled at her. The Humvee pulled into a rest stop on top of Vail pass. He let them know they would no longer be following them when they arrived in the Denver metro area.

Colorado, Farm

After the news of Christian and his friends stealing the car, compounded with the discovery of Jessica leaving with them, Hank decided to forgo the meeting and allow everyone to get a good nights sleep. The morning greeted them with sunshine. Although the wind howled late into the night, the blizzard produced a minimal amount of snowfall, drifting next to the buildings, but leaving the roads mostly clear.

No surprise that Jacqueline was the one who came down the hardest on Jessica. She was a mother who, under no circumstances could find a reason for another mother to leave her children. Especially in a time of such uncertainty. Nicole and Gina were a supportive audience, listening to her tirade over a hot cup of coffee at the kitchen table.

"How in the world could she leave those little girls?" Jacqueline shook her head. "Emilee is almost an adult. But Reagan and Avery…it's unimaginable."

"It's something none of us will ever be able to figure out." Gina looked at Nicole. "What does Bill think about her leaving?"

"He didn't say anything last night. He's struggling, with worrying about Maddy. This just compounded his distress. Hank made a good decision having us sleep on it before we said too much in front of Emilee and the girls," said Nicole. "It's bizarre, with being so worried about Maddy, hoping she's safe, yet, at the same time, Jessica could leave her children. It's a different generation."

"Yes it is," replied Gina, noticing Bill coming up from the basement.

Bill poured a cup of coffee and sat down at the table. He remained quiet.

"I respect Hank so much for how he handled the different personalities and beliefs of the young men he coached," said Jacqueline. "He had diverse, different kids each year, but was always able to meld them into a team."

"We should have been more careful with trusting Christian and his friends," stated Gina, looking at Bill. "They have been planning to take over the country for quite some time. People don't change overnight."

Nicole noticed Gina looking at Bill. She sensed a lot of despair from her son as he stared at his cup of coffee.

"Bill, what do you think about Jessica leaving?" Nicole asked in as calm a voice as she could muster.

"She had deeper problems than any of us could see." He glanced at his mother. He wasn't sure how, or even if he wanted to explain to her, and his aunts, how hard it was for Christian and Tim to buy into the possibilities on the farm. No matter how it was interpreted, the farm was representative of creating the American dream, where opportunity comes from ability and achievement. Christian and his friends were anarchists, being paid for their existence by other anarchists, for too long to ever change. And Jessica was a free spirit who was captured by motherhood at an early age. "Christian gave her a way out."

"With everything over the last week happening so quickly, it never really dawned on me," stated Jacqueline, "things are not going back to the same as they were. We are going to be here for a long time."

Hank entered the kitchen. He removed his light jacket and sat down at the table.

"Jon and I are going to the Brown farm to see what he has in mind for us bringing Deb's cattle back to the farm."

"Do any of us know how to handle cattle?" Nicole asked.

Everyone momentarily looked at her with blank faces.

"All I know, there is a hell of a lot of hay in the barn," stated Hank.

"Are we going to let them treat it like a buffet?" Jacqueline chuckled as she looked at her husband.

"No, as a matter-of-fact I am going to make a list of feeding chores," Hank said smiling, "and Jacqueline is going to be at the top."

"I don't think so. I'm not going to be bucking any bales of hay as long as we have strong, young people around."

Hank laughed as he noticed Caroline standing at the kitchen door. The young woman moved very gingerly toward the table.

"Here, come sit down." Hank pulled the chair next to Bill away from the table.

Caroline's large dark eyes surveyed the room as she sat in the chair. There was heavy bruising on her high cheek bones and on both sides of her face. She held her left hand at her side.

"Would you like something to drink?" Jacqueline asked.

"Water please."

"Are you feeling better?" Gina asked sympathetically.

"Yes, much better but I'm still pretty sore," she forced a smile.

"You told us that you are from Savanna, Georgia," stated Gina. "Are your parents there?"

"Yes, I attend the University of Northern Colorado. When things started getting out of hand, I caught a ride with three guys who said they were heading to the east coast."

"Why did they attack you?"

"I knew I had made a mistake with them immediately." She took in a couple deep breaths. "I kept fighting them off. When the cars slowed down and came to a stop, I was screaming so loud they pulled off at the exit. They beat me and threw me into the field."

"I am so sorry," said Jacqueline sympathetically, setting a glass of water in front of the young lady. "You are welcome and safe here. We can figure how to get you home as soon as things settle."

"You don't know how much that means to me." She squared her shoulders and raised her chin. "When I was laying in that cold field, I was thinking how awful humanity had become. I hurt so bad that I couldn't stay conscious, but I knew I wanted to live, so I could see my family again."

"That is as good a goal as you can have," said Nicole, knowing that everyone else at the table understood the significance of her statement. She was sure her husband was feeling just the same as Caroline.

Denver metro area

Smoke was visible on the horizon for as far as the eye could see, as the caravan proceeded down Floyd Hill into the western edge of the Denver metro area. There were cars lined along the side of the highway, but none were moving. The city was unnervingly silent.

Ted felt a sickness in his stomach as he looked over the haze and smoke that blanketed the valley. The smell was rich and humid, something completely alien to the area. He could only imagine the problems they would face trying to get medical help for Ashley and Carol. Added to the immediate problems, he had the hidden stress of realizing he would have to tell Nicole he was going to reenlist. Telling her he was leaving within twenty-four hours was going to be challenging.

"Grandpa, why is there so much smoke?" Maddy asked, tugging on his shirt sleeve.

"There are bad guys blowing up parts of the city."

"Where are they?"

"They are still out there." Ted had a surge of adrenaline rush through his body from his granddaughter's question. "Hiding, but we will get them."

"Are they the same bad guys who tried to get us at Irene's farm?"

"Yep, the same ones."

"I hope they're not at Daddy's house."

Ted realized he never discussed with Maddy that she was not going home to her father's house, but out to the farm on the plains. "Do you remember about three years ago, when we went to a farm for the Fourth of July?"

"Yes."

"We are going to that farm. Your dad and grandma are already there."

"All the exits are blocked," interrupted Samantha. "Every one we passed has a barrier."

"I noticed they have police cars too. We will pull off at the Kipling exit, and find out what is going on," said Ted. "Do you have your driver's license?"

Samantha clinched her fists. "Yes, but it has my new address in Highlands Ranch."

"We'll have to play it by ear." Ted pulled off the highway, and down the off ramp for Kipling. Concrete barriers were placed across the street at the end of the exit ramp. Two police cars were on the opposite side of the barriers. The others in the caravan followed him as he pulled up to the barricade and got out of the truck. Maddy and Samantha followed him as he approached the patrolmen.

"Are we able to get through?" Ted realized after asking the question that the large concrete barriers could never be moved without a crane.

"No sir," answered an older officer. "We can't let anyone pass."

"My parents live off Remington," said Samantha, noticing the man was very unkempt for a police officer, with a heavy beard and long flowing hair under his hat. "I want to check to make sure they are ok."

"I'm sorry. It's been a difficult few days here, and now that we have some control, the people don't want anyone entering the area. There are several roadblocks on the side streets, staffed mostly by ex-military members from the community."

Three police officers, behind the initial officer, were holding long rifles. About a thousand meters further north were several more patrol cars. "Are the rebels still active?" Ted asked.

"Very much so," replied the officer. "The streets at night are uninhabitable in many parts of the city, especially to the east and south. You shouldn't be on the highway after dark."

"Are there grocery stores selling food?" Ted noticed there were a few cars moving on the street in the far distance. "Are the cars running?"

"The store shelves are all empty, and if we don't get help restocking them, people are going to start running out of food. Mechanics are in high demand. They are slowly getting some of the cars working." The officer looked at Ted with a confused look, wondering how he could be so uninformed about the dangers of the area. He turned to Samantha. "Your parents probably are at a church or high school. Most people have left their homes, and congregated en masse, for protection."

"Would one of you drive me to their house, so I can look?"

The officer looked at the men behind him. He waved one of them forward. "Tony, she needs a ride to her parent's home off Remington."

"It's literally two minutes from here," she pointed to the east.

"Come on," the officer gave her a hand to use in climbing over the barrier.

She stopped before climbing into the police car and yelled, "I'll come back and let you know, even if I find my parents." She scrambled into the patrol car and they drove off.

Ted stepped next to the Suburban and spoke to Jerry through the driver's side window. "It looks like the city is inaccessible. Are you good with following us to the farm or do you want to try and find your family?"

"I have no address for them," said Jerry, "so I'm good with getting out of the city as soon as possible."

Ted turned to Travis who remained seated in the 1957 Chevy. "How about you Travis? Do you want to follow us or try and get home?"

"I'm going to pull off when we get to Quebec. I need to get to my family." He handed Ted a pencil and old envelope. "If you can draw me a map to your farm, I would appreciate it."

"I can do that." Ted drew the map and handed it through the window. He wondered if Travis was going to talk with the Jacobys before taking the car. He decided to leave it up to the pilot.

Irene stepped out of the motorhome and stood next to Maddy. Ted turned back to the officer. "What about the hospitals?" he asked the older officer. "We have two people seriously injured who need immediate medical treatment."

"Not a chance, most of the doctors and nurses have fled the hospitals for their own safety," said the officer, shaking his head. "It's a tragedy. There are so many people needing medical attention that they are camping, some dying, in the parking lots. Many of the smaller urgent care facilities and medical clinics were burned and destroyed."

Ted was glad Irene was standing next to him to hear the exchange about the hospitals being inaccessible. She ignored the policeman and looked to Maddy.

"Ed found something in the bottom of the freezer he wanted me to share with you." Irene held out an ice cream bar.

Maddy looked at Ted, then back toward Irene, and smiled. She reached out and took the ice cream and said," thank you."

"You are welcome, sweetheart."

"How are Ashley and Carol?" Ted asked.

"Ashley is much better than I would have ever anticipated. She rests some, but Breanna won't shut-up and let her sleep. She has it in her mind that if she falls asleep, she won't wake up. Carol, not so good."

"Deb has an infirmary at the farm that is state of the art," stated Ted. "There most likely won't be a doctor."

"We don't have much of a choice, do we?"

"None that I can think of."

Maddy noticed a look of sadness on Irene's face. Irene was becoming fatigued from all the uncertainty.

"Don't be sad Irene," she had ice cream on the side of her mouth.

"I won't be," Irene placed her hand on top of Maddy's head, "because you always make me happy."

"Here comes Samantha," yelled Ted.

Samantha got out of the patrol car. By the look on her face it was obvious she was unable to locate her parents. She thanked the policeman and climbed over the barrier.

"They weren't there," she said, pouting her lips. "The neighborhood is virtually empty."

"Let's head to the farm." Ted moved toward the pickup. He realized Carol and Scotty's family would be worried to death about their welfare. The critical condition of Carol made it easy for him to make the decision, for them, to continue to the farm. When Carol recovers, they can worry about finding their family.

Colorado, Farm

Jon felt some culpability in having the car stolen by Christian. Besides being the one to leave the car open, making it possible for the young thieves to create fingerprint access, and subsequently dismantle the remote vehicle shutdown, he was the one being relied upon for security at the farm. He was relieved they didn't take any of the weapons. He planned to discuss with Hank a security strategy to protect the farm.

By midmorning Jason was back at framing the apartment. He was ordered by Kori and Julia to take a few days off from building, but he compromised by telling them he would avoid lifting anything over ten pounds. Although several of his laborers were gone, he found the new bricklayer, Harold, to be an exceptional carpenter. On the other hand, Harold's brother-in-law Fred was almost useless as a builder. He was frightened of climbing on the roof and was too weak to lift the plywood from the ground into the bucket of the tractor. Bobby and Dave took turns climbing off the roof to help him load the wood sheeting. One of them would have to operate the tractor to raise the wood to the roof.

Sherry would pull the plywood into position and tack it in place. She moved quickly in front of Bobby and Dave, securing the plywood sheeting in position, so they could nail it to the trusses. After getting three or four sheets ahead, she would join them in nailing. She was tireless.

Emilee found it extremely awkward having to deal with her mother leaving. She had an obstinate knot of anger in her belly, but in a strange way, she didn't feel any less safe. The three sisters spent the morning in the basement. It was early afternoon by the time they came out into the bright sunshine.

Emilee stepped next to the tractor and shielded her eyes. She watched her friends working on the roof for several minutes before asking, "Shall I come up and help you?"

"Can you help Fred put the plywood into the bucket? We only need six more sheets."

Emilee helped Fred lift two pieces of wood into the bucket of the tractor. Fred looked up toward Bobby who was concentrating on nailing. He decided Bobby was not going to come down, so jumped into the driver's seat of the tractor.

"I'll get down and drive the tractor," yelled Bobby anxiously, when he noticed Fred getting ready to operate it.

"I've got it." Fred revved the motor and quickly elevated the bucket. He was so close to the building that the top piece of plywood caught the soffit. The plywood flew into the air. Avery and Reagan both scrambled when they saw the sheet of wood falling. They almost avoided the injurious projectile, but the pointed corner of the plywood caught Avery square on the right hand, and she screamed in pain.

Jacqueline and Kori were on the porch in front of the house when they heard the screams. They rushed toward the apartment building. Emilee was sitting on the ground holding Avery, who was clutching her hand. Blood was visible on both girl's clothes.

"Fred, could you find Julia?" Jacqueline screamed as she leaned down next to the girls.

Avery was crying hard enough that she was having a hard time catching her breath.

"Can I see your hand?" Jacqueline asked.

She continued to cry, turning her head to press against Emilee's forehead. She squeezed her good hand tight around the wrist. A deep gash was visible at the base of her thumb.

Jacqueline placed the palm of her hand on the side of her face. "Rest for a second and then we will look at it." She felt a deep sense of motherly compassion for the young girl. Reagan was holding tightly to Bobby's arm.

"What do we have?" Julia asked, leaning down to take hold of the child's hand.

Avery relaxed, her tears evaporated, and she sat up straight. Jacqueline noticed how quickly she changed, from a crying little girl, to a strong young woman.

"It's on the meaty part of your hand," Julia said calmly. "We need to get it cleaned and then a few stitches. You will be fine."

Jacqueline followed the sisters into the clinic, trying to suppress her anger toward Jessica, by rationalizing that the girl's mother was smarter than she gave her credit for. She must have known her daughters would be well taken care of by the Liscos. Even if she left for her own selfish reasons, Jacqueline was going to make sure Avery, Reagan and Emilee were given a chance to blossom during their stay at the farm.

Eastern Colorado

The stress of worrying about subversives, and imminent danger was lifted as soon as Ted hit the dirt roads outside the city. Several snowdrifts were visible in the bar ditch, but the road was only wet.

"We are within twenty minutes of seeing your daddy," Ted tapped Maddy with his elbow.

"Do you think he will be surprised?" Maddy asked, leaning against his shoulder.

His iron will momentarily wilted as he thought about how his time with his granddaughter was coming to an end. "They are going to be so happy."

"I'm going to give Dad a big hug."

Ted thought about how hard it must have been on Nicole and Bill when he and Maddy never showed up on Saturday. "You better get ready for a lot of hugs and kisses."

"I bet your daddy won't let you out of his sight, for a long time," Samantha said.

"Everyone is going to like you too Samantha." Maddy was smiling, as she lowered her voice, "I won't tell them you saw Grandpa naked."

"Maddy," Ted looked at her incredulously, "we made a deal you weren't going to tell."

"I'm not going to tell everybody, Grandpa."

"No, the deal was you weren't going to tell anyone."

"I haven't told anybody yet," Maddy smiled at Samantha.

"Yeah, we haven't told anyone… yet," Samantha laughed.

"I can tell you two are going to cause problems." Ted could see a group of people walking on the hill about a kilometer in front of them. He slowed to a crawl as he assessed the situation. "I wonder who they are?"

"There are some kids," said Maddy, leaning on the dash.

Ted eased forward until he was within ten meters of the group. Walking at the back of the travelers was a couple with a teenage son and two younger daughters. In front of them was a man and woman with two teenage boys. When the man at the front of the group turned to acknowledge the approaching vehicles, Ted immediately recognized the large, beaked nose of

George Saxton, Hank's friend and assistant coach. His wife Toby, who looked exhausted, was the first to recognize Ted.

"It's Ted," yelled Toby.

"Good Lord, are we glad to see you." George stepped up to the window of the F-250. "I was starting to wonder if we made a terrible mistake in coming all this way."

"No mistake, you are really close to the farm," Ted forewent introductions, tales and explanations. He was too close to his family to tarry. He quickly squeezed the three families into the RV, Suburban and bed of the pickup. George and Toby were placed in the RV. They would get a slanted account of Ted and Maddy's adventures from Breanna, as they traveled the final five kilometers to the farm.

*** Colorado Farm ***

Clint Brown made it clear to Hank that he expected Deb's cattle to be removed from his land, and moved to the Lisco's pasture, immediately. The ultimatum was delivered in a very thoughtful manner, by giving the city dweller some pointers on taking care of the livestock. The first piece of advice was to make sure the fence around the property was in good shape.

Hank was surprised, when he returned to the farm from the meeting, how willing Jacqueline and Nicole were to walk with him, over the wet field, to inspect the fence. They were about fifteen hundred meters from the farmhouse when they noticed three peculiar vehicles moving down the driveway.

"Do we know anyone with a motorhome?" Jacqueline asked.

"No one I know of," answered Hank, taking several full strides in the direction of the farmhouse. "We better head back."

The farm was alive, with workers visible on the roof of the new building and some strangers sitting on the large front porch. People started to move toward them as Ted parked the pickup. Everyone from the convoy amassed out of the vehicles onto the driveway, creating a large asymmetrical crowd of people.

Hank and Jacqueline were about seven hundred meters from the group of newcomers, with Nicole lingering behind, when they recognized members of the high school football team. With the excitement of knowing Coach Saxton found the farm, they picked up their pace.

Bobby also noticed the football players and hurried off the roof, followed a few paces back by Bill.

Maddy held tight to Ted, unsure of the massive group of strangers mulling aimlessly. Ted saw Bill slowly walking with his head hanging low.

"Look Maddy, there's your dad."

Maddy took off in a full sprint. "Daddy," she yelled, with Ted following behind her.

Bill stopped in his tracks when he saw her sprinting his way. He was in a momentary state of disbelief as he dropped to a knee. She dashed past Bobby and straight into his arms. He held her frail body and hugged her tightly for several seconds.

"Oh Lord, thank you. I have been so worried about you Maddy."

"Me and Grandpa had an adventure."

"I'll bet you did." Bill looked up at the tan face of his father. "You always have been able to find your way home."

"I had a major incentive to get back," said Ted, looking at the crowd of people. "Where's Nicole?"

Hank and Jaqueline were unsure of the identities of the older strangers as they greeted the members of the football team, completely oblivious of Ted and Maddy's presence.

"Dad look who's here," yelled Bobby to Hank, pointing in the direction of Ted.

Hank stopped in his tracks. Seeing Coach Saxton gave him a feeling of relief. Seeing Ted and Maddy provided him with indescribable bliss, the kind of happiness that made him want to cry. He turned to locate Nicole. She was walking about twenty meters from the crowd, scanning the strangers, when she looked to the left, Ted was running straight at her.

"Oh!" was all she could utter. He seemed to be moving in slow motion, transitorily giving her an opportunity to relish the sight of the man she had worried about every moment of every day for the past week, pressing closer to her. Opening her arms, she latched ahold of his neck.

The two of them experienced many reunions over the entirety of their marriage, but with all the doubt and uncertainty of conflict taking place so close to home, this one was more intense and meaningful. Nicole felt an instant sense of security knowing Ted was there to help navigate through the vagueness which existed in all aspects of the new life on the farm.

Feeling her tears leaking from her eyes, onto his cheek, was heartbreaking to Ted. Each tear helped him understand the intensity of pain she experienced not knowing about his and Maddy's safety. He picked her petite body up and spun her around.

"I was so worried," she moaned, as Ted released her from the embrace.

"We had quite a time." He noticed Nicole never specified it was him she was worried about.

"Where's Maddy?" she asked, maybe a little quicker than he thought she would.

"She found her dad," he motioned toward Bill, still holding Maddy. "She's going to have many stories to tell you."

"I can't wait to sit down with her and hear them." She noticed both Hank and Jon waiting off to the side, obviously giving space for the reunion between her and Ted, before approaching to embrace their brother. "I'll give you a chance to catch up with Jon and Hank." She kissed him on the cheek and darted to her granddaughter.

"Where in the world have you been?" Hank asked, slapping his older brother on the shoulder.

"I was even starting to worry about you." Jon shook his head as he stared at Ted.

"We were forced to land in southern Utah, near Cedar City. It's a story best told over a drink tonight." Ted was starting to feel the fatigue of the long day. "I did see Deb this morning in Grand Junction, she helped us out of a jam last night."

"In Grand Junction," Jon seemed stymied from hearing she was in western Colorado.

"She was preparing to leave for the northern border."

"It sounds like the conflict is going to escalate," stated Hank.

"It's going to Hank. Things are going to get much worse." Ted decided not to mention his appointment with General McClinton, scheduled in less than twenty-four hours. There was a good chance he would be right in the middle of the war in the near future. "But right now, I want you to meet the people who helped me and Maddy over the past week."

Jacqueline engaged the Jacobys outside the RV. When learning of the injuries to Carol and Ashley, she quickly summoned Julia to their side. Ed and Irene were receiving most of the attention from Gina and Jacqueline as they waited outside the motorhome, standing next to Samantha. The Hernandez family were waiting patiently at the side of Jerry and Terrance.

"You don't need to tell us Ted," stated Irene as the brothers approached, "these are your brothers."

"Yes, they are," Ted turned toward Jon and Hank. "This group here saved Maddy and me from what could have been a very bad fate."

"Grandpa," Maddy ran at him holding Nicole's hand.

"Maddy, hold up," Nicole pulled back to slow her down. "Grandma is too old to run that fast."

"I want you to meet Irene," she continued to pull on her hand, "and Samantha too."

Bill followed behind his mother and daughter, stopping to stand next to his father. He blatantly stared at Samantha. Although she had a head full of elflocks and smeared make-up, he still found her to be intriguing.

"Maddy, is this your dad?" Samantha asked, noticing the attention she was receiving from Bill.

"I am Maddy's father, Bill," he stepped next to her and held out his hand.

"Samantha," she felt a spark from his fingers as they touched hands. "I can't believe how much you look like your father."

"Grandma," Maddy yelled, interrupting the conversation between Bill and Samantha, "Irene is the greatest cook in the world."

"Oh, thank you sweetheart," said Irene.

"Let's get you inside out of the wind," Nicole placed a hand on Irene's shoulder. She recognized how special and beneficial the old couple would be on the farm. "We'll get you something warm to drink and allow you to relax."

"Do you have any space in your freezers?" Ed asked, looking at Hank. "We have quite a bit of meat."

"We have a little room."

"Most of it in the middle is frozen solid and will last for quite a while, but we better use some of the steaks on top in the next couple days," said Ed.

"Ed is a rancher," stated Ted.

"I own the ranch, but Adam and Aaron are the ranchers," replied Ed.

"We will have a lot to discuss," said Hank, as Breanna stepped out of the RV, "but I know one thing, you couldn't have come at a better time."

"This is Ed and Irene's daughter, Breanna," announced Ted.

"Julia wants to move Ashley and Carol inside." Breanna surveyed the crowd of people as she stepped down next to her mother and father. "She needs a few minutes but will need some help moving them."

"What did the doctor say?" Irene asked.

"She thinks Ashley will be fine with time," she pursed her lips and nodded her head. "Carol's not doing so well."

"Come on Samantha," Maddy took hold of Samantha's hand. "Samantha helped me and Grandpa, sooo much."

"Everyone should come inside, we can all get acquainted," said Nicole, staring at the group of strangers.

"Ok," said Maddy. "But there is something I need to get off my chest."

"Oh God no," Ted uttered under his breath. He stared agonizingly at his granddaughter.

"Samantha," she was speaking in slow motion. "saw…. Grandpa….naked."

Samantha burst out laughing, throwing her hands to her mouth, she eyed Ted for his response. Bill looked at her with a mortified expression on his face.

Maddy was destined to tell her grandmother of the incident, because they always told each other secrets. Ted never anticipated the secret would be divulged so quickly, and at such an inopportune time. Nicole was smiling, so he realized it was more of a foofaraw that was slightly embarrassing, which his wife considered meaningless. Now, with everyone's eyes on him, his reply needed to be swift and precise. "I was in the shower and Samantha thought the bathroom was empty."

Nicole chuckled. She never doubted her husband's loyalty. It would be hard for anything to quell her elation. With all the confusion of having so many strangers at the farm, she needed to be assertive in finding alone time with him.

"I'll show you our room," Nicole said, placing her arm around Ted's waist.

"I need a shower," he smiled as they began walking toward the farmhouse.

"Do you think I might see you naked," she whispered.

Ted chuckled as they entered the house. Deb had added several rooms since his last visit to the property. He followed Nicole to the far back bedroom on the main level. She disappeared into the bathroom as he removed his shirt and sat down on the bed. She was gone for only a few moments before stepping into the bedroom wearing a tee-shirt.

"Nicole, I have to tell…."

"Not now," she straddled his lap and placed her arms around his neck. She sensed that the news he was going to give her was not going to be good, "I just want to enjoy this moment."

Ted held her for a moment before rolling over onto the bed, pulling her beneath him. He could see the whites of her eyes as he stared into her beautiful face. She was a classy lady who only wanted to love him. He quickly removed the remainder of his clothes. They both forgot about the chaos and uncertainty, as they made love.

For the first time since speaking with General McClinton Ted questioned whether he would join the fight for the country. The tenderness he felt, lying in bed, holding his wife, woke him to the reality that he had done enough for the safety of the country. Tomorrow he would meet with the generals and disclose his decision to stay with his family. To protect the farm from the certain dangers that would come their way.

Great Falls, Montana

Deb never expected a ticker tape parade from the citizens of Great Falls, but under no circumstances anticipated they would renounce the great force of military might that stormed to the outskirts of the city. There were no civilians anywhere to be seen, only military vehicles lined in a massive traffic jam. The area around the north central Montana city had grown exponentially since the pandemics of the 20s, causing the population to spread over many square miles of once agricultural land.

The entire area was buzzing with activity. Deb felt like she was the only element in the entire military complex that was not on the move. Flight activity from the air base was constant. Truckload after truckload of soldiers and supplies continued to travel through the small city on their way to Alaska.

General Maes, of the 10th Mountain Infantry, instructed Deb to keep 2nd Battalion close at hand, and to station the command center just west of Malmstrom Air Force base. 3rd Battalion would proceed 135 kilometers to the north and set up operations in Shelby, Montana, with 1st Battalion moving 200 kilometers to the northwest, establishing a base outside Browning, Montana. She was finished with accompanying the 3rd Armored Brigade as they made their way through the congestion toward Calgary, Canada.

The temperature was below freezing, and the wind was blowing. Deb grabbed a cup of coffee and watched the last aspects of the communication center come together at the temporary headquarters located in a vacant warehouse. She noticed Tommy approaching with a tall man, in a cowboy hat, walking next to him.

"Colonel, this is Walt Blake who has some information he thought we might find relevant. He has a farm about ten kilometers east of the city."

"Yes sir," said Deb, cradling her cup of coffee. "What is it you want to tell us?"

"Ma'am, I have nearly eight thousand acres outside of town. About ten years ago I sold nearly two sections of my land to a group of fellows who wanted to build some sort of warehouse.

They built and built on the place until the damn thing covered nearly five acres of land. It didn't seem quite right to me that such a large place would be so far from town. I asked them what they were building but they never gave me an answer. About two years ago I noticed a whole lot of people coming and going from the place, mostly coming."

"Is it a factory?" Deb asked.

"Supposedly they make custom wheels. That's what the sign on the outside of the building states."

"I guess I'm not following you."

"My wife said the people who worked there looked like soldiers," replied the cowboy, removing his hat and running his hand through his grey hair. "But that's not all. Last week we saw some of the damndest types of airplanes fly over our property."

Deb just stared at the man. His weathered face was one only a man who worked outside for many years in the sun and wind could acquire. His demeanor was calm and self-assured.

"All our drones are up and running," said Tommy. "Why don't we send one to the warehouse while Walt is here to help us find the place."

"Go ahead," said Deb to Tommy.

The drone was launched, and Walt helped direct it to the warehouse. First pass over of the property showed little activity around the massive structure. The only thing out of the ordinary were the amount of tire imprints running for several hundred meters in the field behind the structure, something which could be rationalized as heavy truck tracks; nothing seemed odious about the warehouse, except its size.

"It looks pretty mundane," said Tommy.

"Take the drone to the front of the building," said Deb.

The view of the front showed a sign in large red letters, "Jeff's Wheel and Rim Works"

"I don't think so," said the lieutenant operating the drone.

"What don't you think lieutenant?" Tommy asked.

"My uncle owns one of the largest custom wheel shops in the Kansas City area. You could put a hundred of his buildings into this warehouse."

"What did the aircraft look like that flew over your place?" Deb asked Walt, knowing that the building was more than a wheel factory.

"They looked like big brown boxes, really long boxes."

"Colonel," yelled one of the technicians from the back of the communication center, "General Maes wants you online. You'll have to use headphones until we finish setting the cables."

Deb walked over, sat down in a chair in front of the monitor and allowed the sergeant to place headphones over her ears. She noticed the enlarged pupils of the sergeant. Looking away from the soldier she engaged in conversation with General Maes.

"Colonel Lisco, as we proceed north, I want you to stay in the Great Falls area until further directives are given," ordered the general.

Until her brigade was attached to the 10th Mountain, Deb knew little about General Maes, only that he was the cousin of the Secretary of Defense. She was finding him to be routine at best.

"Should I keep 1st and 3rd Battalions in the forward positions?"

"Everything is to stay the same until we state otherwise," quantified General Maes. "You can assist the authorities in the surrounding towns to make sure they are in charge and there are no threats from domestic sources."

Deb wasn't overly enthused by her superior's rigid method of communicating his orders without any discussion of strategy or purpose. She figured with the changing scenarios, and uncertainty with the attacks on the country, she could be attached to another division at any time. So, she remained complacent. "Yes sir," she waited for a reply as the monitor went blank.

Deb pulled the headphones off her head and looked at the sergeant with the large pupils. She heard Walt's cell phone ring as she examined the soldier.

"Come here son," she looked closely into his eyes, as he stood uncomfortably close. "Why are your eyes so dilated?"

All the technicians in the center stopped and watched the confrontation. Tommy stepped next to the soldier as he remained silent.

"Command Sergeant Major, can you look into this soldier's eyes and tell me if we have a problem?"

"Are you on drugs?" Tommy asked. "Your pupils are about five times the size they should be."

"I have no reply, sir," said the sergeant.

"Where did you get the drugs?" Deb asked.

"No reply ma'am."

She stared at him for a moment before turning to the others in the room. "Does anyone here know where the sergeant received drugs?"

"Ma'am, the sergeant was missing for over an hour immediately after we arrived," stated a corporal.

"Command Sergeant Major, check all his personal items?" Deb stepped back and watched the removal of the sergeant. She thought how dangerous it was for a soldier in communications to be compromised.

The entire situation in the small city seemed out of whack. She wanted to investigate the large warehouse near Walt's land. She summoned Lt. Col. Woodworth to get his take on who to send.

Upon learning all the details of the large warehouse he recommended sending I Company, led by Captain Ivan Malkova. The captain was fluent in Russian.

"Josh, I want Captain Malkova to take his full company to this location. Nobody is to travel into the city until we have a better understanding of what is taking place here. It's just too damn quiet, something doesn't seem right."

"Walt," Colonel Deb turned to the civilian, "is your phone working?"

"It rings but I can't really call anyone."

"Do all the cars in Great Falls run?"

"As far as I know they do," he replied.

"Have there been any flashes of light?"

"No ma'am, none that I've seen."

"Thank you, sir. We'll see what we can find out about the warehouse."

Deb was certain there was something terribly wrong with not only the warehouse, but with the entire city. How could this small city be left unscathed by the attacks on the country. She waited for I Company to reach the location before joining Command Sergeant Major Talfoya and Lt. Col. Woodworth in observing Captain Malkova and his patrol as they entered the front of the building.

The front entrance was nonthreatening as would be expected of any legitimate business. The foyer had tile floors with a few pictures of mountain scenes hanging on the walls. Several displays with custom wheels and rims lined the side of the lobby. A kiosk was situated fifteen meters back of the front door with an attractive woman standing at the counter.

Images from the captain's camera were the ones being watched on the closest monitor at the base. Other screens showed the pictures from the drone continuing to observe the outside of the massive building. The lady at the front desk smiled as the soldiers approached, with no display of concern on her face.

"Ma'am," said Captain Malkova, "we would like to have a look at this facility."

"The entire factory is shut down right now. All my bosses are off today. I have no idea when we will be open."

"Why are you here?"

"I'm finalizing some paperwork."

It sounded as though she spoke perfect English, but Captain Malkova could hear a distinct accent.

"What part of Russia did you grow up in?" asked the captain in perfect Russian.

"I'm sorry, I don't understand." her demeanor remained pleasant.

"Colonel," said a corporal, looking at the screen from the drone, "I see activity on the roof. And the heat images are showing a lot of activity behind the doors, only about thirty meters from the captain."

Deb stepped over and looked at the imagery. "Captain, tell her you will have your superiors make an appointment," Deb said into the radio, "get out of there immediately."

Deb was unnervingly quiet as she remained seated for an inordinate amount of time. Whoever was behind the doors at the warehouse had been forewarned about the arrival of I Company. There was a traitor somewhere with her in the communication facility.

Colorado Farm

Ted was awake and outdoors at daybreak. It was cold enough for him to see his breath as he strolled the property. The farm seemed so much different than he remembered. Deb had improved almost every aspect of the ranch, from building a large garage and adding on to the barn. The large cone shaped wind turbines caught his eyes as he surveyed the estate. Looking at the concrete foundation, with several pieces of rebar protruding high into the air, and many pallets of eight-inch concrete block surrounding the perimeter, had him wondering how high the tower was projected to be built. If high enough, it would be a perfect place for a sentry. He wanted to evaluate the best way to protect the farmstead, in order to make recommendations to Jon.

He stayed up late into the evening shooting the breeze with Hank and Jon. The stories Ted told about the subversives and enemy soldiers taking over the area near Cedar City were especially foreboding to Jon, who was worried about the ability of the people at the farm to protect their new home. He was deep in thought when he noticed Bill walking toward him carrying two cups of coffee.

"What are you doing up so early?" Ted asked, accepting a steaming cup from his son.

"I usually get up early, you were walking out the door as I was coming up stairs."

"Did Maddy crash the second her head hit the pillow?"

"She couldn't stop talking. Her mouth was still moving as she fell asleep." Bill took a sip of coffee. "Dad, I can't believe how much has happened in a week."

"I know, I know," he said, taking in a deep breath. He was happy his sister and son worked so well as business partners. Bill was well off financially because of his association with Colonel Deb. "You two did an amazing job with this place."

"Thank God she thought the way she did. There were a lot of times I thought she was out of her mind for spending so much money out here."

"A lot of people, without her foresight, are going to try and take it from us," said Ted sternly. "The situation we are facing is very real, and dangerous. We need to be prepared."

"You and Jon are the only soldiers we have."

"Terrance and Jerry have military experience, and can be relied on if threatened," replied Ted, thinking back to the altercation on the trail in Cedar City, and then their quick action when attacked outside Monticello. "We will have to train everyone else."

"The Jacobys will be invaluable with farming," said Bill. "Maddy sure likes Irene."

"You won't believe how much energy she has, and she's an amazing cook." Ted thought for a moment about his son's facial expression from the previous night when he first met Samantha. "What do you think about Samantha."

Bill looked at him and smiled.

"Maddy sure likes her," said Ted.

"Yes, she does, I think I might like her a little bit too," said Bill cavalierly. "We talked late into the night."

"Her parents are in Littleton."

"Yeah, she's really worried about them," stated Bill, "and her sister and niece are in Omaha."

"She helped me a lot with Maddy." Ted remembered her stating she had a niece.

"I heard all about the trip, from smashing her fingers, to seeing you in the shower. I really like the way she laughs at herself." Bill pulled his jacket tight around his neck. "It sounds like you had a pretty harrowing experience."

"We did, I think the people I brought back with me are really special." Ted took a drink of his coffee. He was surprised his son learned more about the flight attendant in one night than he did in nearly a week of traveling with her.

"It sounds like Carol took a turn for the worse last night. Aunt Jacqueline told me when I was getting coffee that they might try and see if they can get her to a hospital in the city."

"I didn't hear that this morning." Ted thought for a moment, "If she is that serious, I suppose we should try to get her to a hospital. I don't think we will have much luck."

Having a conversation with his son helped Ted realize how much he desired, more than ever before, to be with his family. He dreaded having to trek to Fort Carson. He noticed Nicole walking quickly in their direction, she wasn't wearing a coat.

"Ted, I have some terrible news to tell you," she said anxiously. "Carol just passed."

"My God," he uttered, visualizing the first time he spoke with her when she offered Maddy some gum on the airplane. Although they were acquainted for such a short period of time, he felt a terrible sense of loss. To compound his sorrow was the thought of how Scotty would react to losing his grandmother, especially surrounded by strangers. "Is Scotty awake?"

"Yes, the Jacobys are with him."

Nicole held tight to Ted's arm as he walked into the farmhouse. She could tell her husband was moved by the loss of Carol. She sensed an aura of strength he always projected, wherever or whenever a wrong needed to be righted.

Scotty was sitting on the sofa with Breanna draping her arm around his shoulder. It broke Ted's heart to see the tears flowing from his eyes, as he looked up at him with a bewildered look on his bright red face.

"It's a terrible thing," said Breanna, patting Scotty on his shoulder. "We'll all have to work to help little Scotty."

Irene was sitting next to Ashley, who had a large white bandage wrapped around the top of her head at an angle covering the injury. Irene was holding her hand as they mourned the loss of the woman, they had known for a short time but experienced so much with. The rest of the Jacobys, along with Jerry and Terrance were sitting with their heads hanging low. Samantha came over and stood next to Bill. There was no doubt Scotty would be well taken care of.

The loss of Carol brought about a terrible confusion on Ted's part, whether his presence was more valuable with protecting the farm, or if he could better defend everyone by fighting for the entire country. It was a dilemma he never faced during his military career. He always knew his family was safe at home. He looked directly into Nicole's eyes as he thought.

"I have to go," he whispered.

"I'm going with you Ted Lisco," Nicole said bluntly, sensing her husband had a change of heart about fighting. "This is a time where we are going to make a decision with both of us thinking out every aspect of it."

Ted made no attempt to dissuade his wife from traveling to Fort Carson. Her presence would give credence, for the health, even survival, of their relationship, to any decision he would formulate in dealing with the pressure from the generals.

South Denver metro area

Christian found little resistance from the authorities, or anyone else, as he, with Jessica sitting at his side, along with Tim and the others, drove the stolen car, from the farm, down Lincoln Avenue, turning into an area of luxurious homes. The rebels, he abandoned only a few days earlier, still reigned over the area. Since his absence, the group misappropriated living quarters in a development of high-end residences, abandoned by the wealthy homeowners when the mob of insurgents stormed the neighborhood. There were still towers of smoke billowing into the bright blue sky across the city, and the dull sound of sirens could be heard in the far distance.

"Take your pick," said a bulky woman with several metal rings protruding from her forehead, and an AK47 strapped to her shoulder, acting as though she was a real estate agent. "I have a four thousand square foot home, with four bedrooms and three baths. Or if you would like something a little larger, I have a six bedroom with four baths, right across the street. They both come with solar energy and a partially stocked pantry."

"Have the police tried to enter this area?" Christian asked, standing in a beautifully landscaped yard with a picture-perfect view of the mountains.

"Not even once. There have been a few drones flying over but we shoot at them and they go away," said one of the revolutionists, holding an unopened 1945 Chateau Mouton Rothschild bottle of wine. "There are too many of us. We have people living in every house as far as you can see."

"In fact, the Europeans are still on the offense against the police," said a thin man with a grungy beard.

"Wow," said Christian, looking at Jessica. Could it be they were going to own one of the million-dollar homes, which only a couple weeks earlier seemed completely out of their reach? "We want the one with six bedrooms."

Jessica scanned down the wide street in front of the house. The trees and shrubs were neatly trimmed with the sun reflecting off the high, natural stone walls surrounding many of the homes, giving them a unique, rough look, which could only come from a mason's talent and hard work. It was the type of home she had always dreamed about living in.

As word spread throughout the community, more and more of the dissidents gathered to reconnect with Christian. Within an hour there were over a hundred revolutionists assembled in the street outside the large home Jessica and Christian were about to claim as their own.

"This is why we took the initiative to start this revolution," Christian's voice roared loud enough to bring others to the area, causing the crowd to more than double. "This is our time; we deserve to own the nice parts of this country."

"Are you going to stay with us?" a mousey lady wearing an Italian designer jacket asked. "We thought you left for good."

From his perch, high on the lawn, Christian could see the mass of people standing shoulder to shoulder. In his wildest of dreams, he never imagined having the opportunity to lead so many disenfranchised souls. This was the time to cement his position as the head of the group.

"Yeah Christian, you left. Are you going to stay?" yelled a random voice.

"I'm going to stay," hollered Christian emphatically. He never felt so confident and powerful.

"We need some IDs," said a baby-faced woman standing in the street. "If the National Guard comes through, we should have driver's licenses with these addresses."

"We can do that," said Christian, figuring, with all the chaos being caused by the Europeans, the police would not take the offensive against them. If the National Guard did try to take back the cities, then they would need to be prepared. There were several people in the immediate crowd capable of making a fake ID. "Let's start the process of everyone having a driver's license with the address you live in." Christian raised his voice to an even higher level, "Stop shooting at the drones. A good citizen from this neighborhood would never shoot at a drone."

"We are nearly out of food," a voice cried from the middle of the assemblage.

"We better start thinking about getting more food," stated another.

Christian's heart was pumping, and he took in several deep breaths. He glanced at Jessica and Tim. Maybe the trip to the farm was subliminally a trek he made in order to better equip his true friends with the supplies they would need to take over the country, and rightfully claim it as their own.

"I know where there is plenty of food. All we have to do is take it."

Fort Carson Army Base

With Nicole in tow, Ted figured it could take up to an hour for the guards at the front gate, to grant permission to allow them to proceed to the meeting with General McClinton. There was a good chance they would deny his wife access to the base. He was surprised, and happy he didn't have to deal with the scenario, as the guards immediately gave him directions, and waved him past the checkpoint.

They followed Captain Anna Silver, who Ted deduced to be General McClinton's personal aide. The captain offered water and told them the generals would be with them shortly. Nicole felt a sense of gratitude as she surveyed the large screens on a stage that dominated the room. She could only imagine the intensity of all the decisions made in the area during moments of conflict.

General McClinton rushed into the room followed by General Lopez. Having Nicole arrive with Ted changed the manner which they planned to present the offer of reenlistment to him. Not an ideal situation, but they were well versed in changing scenarios.

With Ted serving under General McClinton for many of his early years in the service, Nicole was well acquainted with the current Army Chief of Staff. She recognized him to be reasonable, and a man who cared deeply about everyone he commanded. She knew nothing about General Lopez. She sat with a straight back as the generals pulled chairs to sit uncomfortably close, directly in front of the man and wife.

"Thank you both for being here," said General McClinton, looking directly at Nicole. "I'm sure you have had a nice discussion on the trip here. But before you make any solid decisions, I want you to hear me out."

Nicole sat silently, giving the general a stone, cold stare.

"We need soldiers," he turned to address Ted. He wanted to disclose sensitive and classified material but knew it needed to be disclosed in a different setting. It would make his case much easier to convince Ted how much they needed him back in uniform if he could divulge a few bits of information. Among the facts were the horrific number of casualties from the previous week of fighting inflicted on the American Soldiers at the southern border. "We need a massive number of citizens to turn into soldiers, which we are in the process of receiving, but we need seasoned and tested soldiers to lead them."

"Ted has done his part in defending the country," said Nicole adamantly.

Ted looked at his wife, surprised how unwavering she was in making the statement. He noticed that General McClinton placed his fist under his chin.

"Nicole," stated General McClinton. He was going to be quick and to the point. "I don't know if you understand how dangerously close we are to losing our country?"

"I know that every time my husband removes his shirt, he has a large hole from a bullet in his lower right back, and a long scar under his belly button from God only knows what. He's done enough."

"Ok," General McClinton decided to speak to Ted with the knowledge Nicole would be taking in every word he spoke. "Ted, by request of the War Department, the 99th readiness division has been ordered into active service. Basic training will begin here at Fort Carson as soon as all staffing details are completed. General Lopez has been selected to command the Division. We are looking for an Assistant Division Commander."

Ted's heart sank to his stomach. The idea of him wearing the same checkerboard patch that his grandfather wore during World War II was humbling. He looked at Nicole, unsure if she understood the significance of becoming a part of the 99th Infantry Division. "Are you offering me the opportunity to be the Assistant Division Commander of the 99th?"

"Yes," stated General McClinton emphatically. "All new divisions being formed across the country will be on fast track to transitioning the civilians into soldiers, and the 99th will be no different. They will adapt their civil occupations into army functions, knowing full well technical capabilities will be overly represented. After two weeks of training, mostly on the rifle range, maneuvers will take place in sweeping the cities from coast to coast, to rid them of dissidents. The reserves have already been called forward and utilized. Our cities are in turmoil and we have no better option than to create new soldiers, as quickly as possible to fight the turmoil within, before going into combat. We are looking at a six-week turnover."

"That is asking a lot," stated Ted, looking at General Lopez.

"No doubt it will be difficult, and we will have to hammer out a lot of details," said General Lopez. "We have already brought in a lot of good soldiers to form the nucleus of the division. I would love to work with you to pull everything together."

"I'm taking it that you want me to come back immediately.

"Ted, we have a small window of opportunity to right our ship." General McClinton glanced at Nicole. "We are at a standstill with our missile defenses protecting the perimeter, the iron dome is secure. But the Chinese and Russians are ebbing slowly toward our borders. Thousands of enemy troops are moving into the border cities in Mexico. Western Alaska is now a focal point of the war. We have to keep the Russians from placing their missile defense systems on our soil."

Ted looked at Nicole, although he was fully on board with the offer, he would not sacrifice his marriage for it.

"Would it be possible for Ted to live on the farm during basic training?" Nicole asked. She fully understood the significance of the 99th Division to her husband. It would be unbelievably selfish of her to try to deny the country of his abilities.

"How far away is the farm?" asked General McClinton. He admired Nicole priming the pump of ideas.

"Drive time is an hour and a half," said Ted. He appreciated his wife having the gumption to negotiate with the powerful man. He could only imagine that twenty years ago the general would have laughed at having the question posed to him.

"I take it there is enough room for a helicopter to land."

"There definitely is."

"If it is agreed to with General Lopez, you can work here at the base three days, and work from a mobile command at your farm the other four. You need to understand that this will be for a noticeably short time, with the real possibility of being in combat within a few weeks."

"If a compromise can't be reached by our leaders with the Russians and Chinese, we will be joining the conflict in six weeks," stated General Lopez. "I have no problem with you being here three days and working from an office the other four. I'm sure together we can figure how to drum these civilians into shape."

"I'm confident we can," said Ted. He looked at Nicole.

She stared into his eyes and shook her head in the affirmative. "I would never deny you this."

"I'll sign the papers before we leave."

General McClinton slapped Ted on the shoulder and said, "I'm glad your back Ted." He marched out of the room.

Colorado farm

Carol's funeral was held in a field, high on a hill in the northeast pasture of the farm, with the sound of the wind blowing through weeds. It was a meaningful moment, in that the interment of an innocent lady, to a location unknown to her, signified the end of ordinary life; the situation was real, and dangerous.

The Jacobys took over the duties of running the agricultural components of the farm, or the ranch according to Ed. They took the initiative to introduce themselves to the neighboring ranchers. Plans were in the makings to add many more head of cattle to Deb's herd. It took Ed a short amount of time to figure out that Bill controlled the purse strings and was very willing to spend money for any improvements to the property, including the purchase of a high-priced bull being offered by Clint Brown. Ashley's injury to her head was healing well enough for her to take a short ride on one of the horses.

Ted had Jason, and the other workers, stop construction on the apartment in order to partition off the back twenty feet of the garage, and cut in a door at the west wall. They placed a door into the bathroom in the garage, which would be shared by Terrance and Jerry. A small bedroom was erected to be utilized by Ted's aide, Sergeant Willow, who followed and remained at the farm with Ted. Several technicians from the base, were able to set up a secure communication center. Being able to communicate with Deb, along with keeping tabs on the latest developments concerning the war, was a bonus to having the ability to work remotely with the staff from the 99th. Ted and Sergeant Willow were sitting at their prospective desks as the door opened and the aroma of fresh bread filtered into the room, Sherry and Caroline stepped inside.

"Mr. Lisco," Sherry said, hesitating at the door, "can we speak with you?"

"Certainly, come in."

"We wonder how we enlist," said Caroline with a slight southern drawl, moving in front of the desk.

"Sergeant Willow can help you with the process." Having spoken with Jon and Hank about the young people at the farm, he knew they were the only ones who were within the age parameters for conscription. He was happy they came forward on their own.

"Sergeant, can you help the ladies with registration?"

Sergeant Willow was a young man of twenty-five, with jet black hair, and what could only be described as an obtuse face. He stared at the two beautiful women in front of him with a dumbfounded expression.

"Sergeant," prodded Ted.

"Yes sir," said the sergeant, breaking out of his stupor. He grabbed two folding chairs and placed them in front of his desk. "Sit here, I need your identification."

"I don't have anything," said Sherry, glad she didn't bring her fake ID.

"Neither do I," stated Caroline, looking toward Ted, who raised his head to listen in on the conversation, "they took my purse when I was attacked."

"Colonel, how do I proceed?" asked the sergeant.

"Put their information in, and contact Carson to see how they want you to handle it."

Preparing the civilians for duty was proving to be more difficult than any of the brass thought possible. The time frame of six weeks was woefully short to produce a soldier Ted would consider to be safe to send into combat and protect the back of fellow combatants. He spent most of his time in the office when he was on the base, so working from the remote location on the farm was proving to be a viable alternative.

After Sergeant Willow finished with the registration of Sherry and Caroline, he was free to roam the farm property. He enjoyed walking through the spacious fields and conversing with everyone. Ted asked him to seek out and inform Hank and Jon they could come to the office to listen in on the call with Deb. At the last call she requested having the other family members present.

Late afternoon was a time when Ted could chat with Deb. It was almost therapeutic for them to discuss issues that affected them personally, but also subjects and concerns that helped them better lead. Deb's in-your-face, common-sense form of leadership often jogged Ted's mind to help him come up with ideas to use in training the new recruits to better understand the issues they would face in combat.

"Grandpa," Maddy yelled, storming through the door. She was under strict orders not to barge in on Ted. "We have something for you."

"Of course, come in."

Maddy entered, carrying a plate with two cinnamon rolls, followed by Irene and Scotty.

"Oh my gosh, what have you made?" the smell made his mouth water.

"Me and Irene are back to baking." Maddy sat the plate on top of papers on his desk. "Scotty helped too."

"She is becoming a really good baker," said Irene with a big smile on her face. Scotty stood next to her also smiling. "So is Scotty."

"Go ahead and take a bite," said Maddy. "You won't believe how good they are."

Ted took a bite of the cinnamon roll. He figured it would be good but in truth it was the best tasting pastry he had ever tasted.

"Grandpa, me and Scotty need you to take us back to California."

Ted stared at his granddaughter with a large mouthful of cinnamon roll. Irene looked at him with a serious expression.

"Scotty's mom and dad are in California, and so is my mom. We want you to go there and bring them to the farm."

For a split-second Ted considered the request as something feasible but that thought evaporated quickly, he swallowed.

"Come here Maddy." He placed his hands in front of him, she placed her small hands in his. "I can't go back to California at this time. But I will go there just as soon as I can."

"We were talking," Maddy whispered into his ear. "Scotty is really lonely."

"I understand." He pulled her closer and hugged her. Hugging was something he was going to do as often as possible.

"We are having stew tonight," said Irene. "Jerry is in charge of cooking."

"I'll bet it will be good," replied Ted, releasing Maddy from the hug. "Are you doing ok?"

"We are worried about our kids back home, but we are adapting. Aaron and Adam are always busy." Irene placed her hand over the side of Maddy's face as she moved next to her. "Breanna is whining a great deal of the time but in her own way she is staying helpful."

"How about Ed?"

"He's been a little under the weather."

"I'm glad you are here," Ted looked her directly in the eyes. The situation in southern Utah remained volatile. He didn't go into any detail. "You made the right choice."

"We couldn't feel any more accepted. Ed and I were just talking about how fortunate we were to have you stumble upon us."

"Me and Maddy were the fortunate ones."

Scotty was hovering to the side of Irene with a sad look on his face. He was staring at the floor.

Ted motioned for him to come closer. The thought of Maddy being stranded with strangers, had he decided not to make the trip to California, entered his mind

"Can I get a hug from you too?" Ted asked Scotty.

Scotty never hesitated to throw his arms around Ted's neck and hug him firmly. Although in a vulnerable state his well-being was secure with the people on the farm. The depth of his parent's misery in not knowing the fate of their son must be overwhelming.

Hank stepped through the door, followed by Jacqueline, Jon, Gina and Nicole.

"Grandma," yelled Maddy, moving away from Irene to run into Nicole's arms, "did you get a cinnamon roll?"

"No, but they sure smell good."

"We'll get you one," Maddy placed her mouth next to Nicole's ear and whispered loud enough for the others to hear, "don't tell Grandpa. Me and Irene put butter on ours before we ate them."

"I won't tell," Nicole smiled at Irene. "Are you taking some to the workers. Bill and Bobby would probably love to have a break."

"Yep, come on Scotty," she grabbed Irene's arm and pulled. "We have a whole plate full for them."

"Don't pull so hard on Irene's arm," shouted Nicole as she watched them leave.

"Pull the chairs around," said Ted. "I'll get us connected."

The monitor was large enough for everyone to see as they crowded around Ted. Deb was sitting where the backdrop of soldiers working feverishly behind her was visible.

"How is the building coming along?" Deb asked, looking through the monitor at her family.

"It's coming right along," said Hank. "They poured the floor for the first half."

"Is the electrical in?"

"They should have it for the first couple bedrooms today."

"Did you get the cattle from Clint?"

"The Jacobys brought them back a couple of days ago," replied Hank, unsure if he should be the one to tell his sister about buying the bull.

"They bought a bull from him too," said Jon.

Deb laughed. "I'm sure it was a fine choice if Bill wrote them a check."

"Is everything going good with you?" Jacqueline asked.

"I'm doing ok. I do have some sensitive issues I need to discuss with Ted after we finish. There is just so much uncertainty." Deb turned her head to acknowledge commotion taking place from outside the range of the monitor. "What's going on," she yelled.

A bright flash of light came across the screen, and a muffled explosion occurred causing dust to spread across the back of the room. Command Sergeant Major Talfoya came onto the screen and aggressively clutched Deb's shoulders. "We have to get out," he screamed. A much louder sound of a detonation could be heard before an explosion hit directly on the monitor. Ted's monitor showed only black.

Everyone was standing looking at the terrible black image. Ted stared at his family wondering if they just witnessed the death of their sister. The monitor came back to life with an urgent message for Ted to return to the base in Fort Carson. The sound of a helicopter quickly approaching could be heard from outside the office.

2051

Book 2

War on American Soil

Book 2 Prologue

Washington DC
White House war room

More than a million enemy troops from China, Russia, Iran and their allies were playing cat and mouse with the American troops along the United States southern border by crossing over and striking before returning to the protection of the largest cities on the Mexican side. They were biding their time while stockpiling weapons and allowing insurgents planted years earlier to disrupt and cause chaos across America. Russian armed forces crossed over the Bering Strait into Alaska and were being held in check by United States troops. The enemies next phase in the master plan to take over the world came in the form of a message to Washington warning of an impending missile attack.

The lights in the situation room were bright enough to reflect off the large table, where top advisors sat with the President of the United States. The brighter lights were installed so the older members, which included most of them, could read the memorandums and documents.

"So, they warned us," a bead of sweat dampened President Weller's forehead. "Both Beijing and Moscow have sent messages that our country is about to be hit with thousands of missiles. After all the deception and underhandedness, they want us to believe they are now following Marquess of Queensberry rules."

"They claim the missiles are not nuclear. Can we really be sure?" Vice President John Trupp was amazed he would be asking the question about world annihilation to the President, who only months earlier was so proud of his record on promoting world peace.

"They emphasized the missiles are not nuclear," the President swallowed hard. His face was noticeably pale as he thought of the geopolitical and budgetary discussions over the years about the ideas of shielding the country from the treats of intercontinental missiles. He was fully on the side of not spending money on expensive missiles to shoot down cheap missiles. "Bob, do we have an estimate on the damage we can expect from these strikes?"

"We cannot counter advancing Russian and Chinese ICBM threats. When it comes to missiles, we are at a terrible numerical disadvantage. The Ground Based Midcourse system recently was reduced from 44 to 40 interceptors and two-thirds of the Naval fleets with Aegis are too far away to supply interceptors for short range and intermediate defense. So, we can defend against some of the missiles, but ultimately many will find their way to our soil." Secretary of Defense Maes tried his best to speak professionally and remain non-adversarial. He had passionately and vigorously debated with the President and congress on many occasions about funding collaborative technologies, hypersonic and direct energy solutions for missile defense. He also knew the President to be an honorable man who, just like all Presidents before him, had to consider many different aspects to détente.

"They gave us a warning. Now we must consider our response," interjected Secretary of State Aida Mahorn.

"I just left the meeting with the Chiefs of Staff," said the Secretary of Defense. "Our first inclination was that we should respond directly to the Russian and Chinese homelands with our own missiles. That would be a political reaction, with many rockets being intercepted and a great waste of our arsenal. We are beyond politics. It is the Chief of Staff's recommendation that we hit the Russian forces in Alaska with as many missiles as needed to eradicate the threat. Then to focus on destroying the Chinese ships capable of hitting our land with mid-range missiles. We can strategically hit targets in the Mexican cities along the border with minimal civilian casualties. For the most part we are going to have to use ground forces to fight these battles."

"How many missiles do we have stockpiled?" Vice President Trupp asked.

"That is the problem. If used correctly, we have enough to fulfill our immediate objectives. But before we can escalate an all-out offensive assault on the enemy, we first need to start the process of changing our factories into weapon plants."

"Aida," President Weller was bending over slightly from the effects of his ulcer acting up. "What allies will give us immediate assistance."

"Australia, for sure. They have several hundred air breathing hypersonic missiles ready to go. Canada and Mexico are in the mix and will help to the extent they are capable." The Secretary of State turned to Director of National Intelligence Barbara Stone, "Who else can we really rely on for immediate support, Barbara?"

"The honest answer, we don't know." She stopped the statement there, rather than going into the past couple of decades where the Chinese and Russians had foiled American alliances by creating economic and diplomatic partners with many of the United States traditional allies.

A singular figure sat in the shadows directly behind the Director of National Intelligence, completely discounted by the powerful assembly of decision makers. He breathed silently through his nose as he candidly listened.

"How do we respond to Beijing and Moscow?" President Weller measured the reaction of his assembly. "At least they have started a dialogue."

"Sir, with all due respect," The Secretary of Defense leaned forward in his seat at the center of the long table. "The message we received from Beijing is not for negotiating. They only want more data to use for better understanding our mind set. We should be wary of our response, if any."

"It may not be a communication stating they are willing to negotiate, but the message in itself is an implication of discourse," stated the Secretary of State, turning her attention back in the direction of the Director of National Intelligence. "Barbara, what do you make of the correspondence?"

"Actions around the world are not suggesting compromise. Make no mistake here, Russia and China are not our only adversaries." She squinted, bringing her heavy grey eyebrows down over her eyes, "Troop movement is significant in central Asia, India and parts of Africa."

"Eventually we are going to have to deal with the cartels and stop the enemy from advancing through Mexico," stated

Vice President Trupp. "We should go on the offense immediately in Mexico."

President Weller gave him an ominous look. Not because he disagreed with the assumption, but because the Vice President's statement implied that he was asleep at the wheel when the enemy first moved into the northern cities in Mexico. He understood that as Commander and Chief he needed to make the ultimate decisions for the response from the American Forces. The attack occurred so quickly and unexpectedly that his retort to the enemy was woefully slow.

Unnoticed by several at the table, the clandestine figure came to his feet and brushed the back of the Director of National Intelligence, who rose from her seat and pulled the chair back, allowing him to move around. He placed both hands on the long table. Even with the bright lights pounding down, his eyes and the cheeks on his face were sunken, giving him an undistinguishable, shadowy appearance.

"Hard to kill," the man yelled extremely loud. He moved his dark eyes from one person at the table to another. "We have allowed our enemies to become pre-positioned throughout every region in the world, and within the boundaries of our own country. They have strategically placed multi-domain forces capable of engaging our military establishment in our own backyard. These inside forces are mobile, hidden and resilient, making them…hard to kill. And you all sit here debating procedure."

"Who is this man?" President Weller's voice boomed across the table.

"He's someone we must listen to," stated Stone, the Director of National Intelligence. "His acumen is why we are now in serious discussion about the evacuation of American citizens from nearly two million square kilometers of our homeland."

The President slowly fell back into his chair with his heart beating rapidly. He continued to intently measure the man. He allowed him to speak.

"Survival…our enemies have studied our strengths for many decades and have calculated models and concepts to exploit our weaknesses. Their geostrategic alliances with our traditional allies have isolated us to fight them alone. It is too late for us to deem our homeland a sanctuary with the same benefits of safety and projection of power we once enjoyed. Our aspiration now is to survive." The lines meandering from the sides of his eyes seemed to deepen when he emphasized the word survive. "Rather than bickering about decree and rapprochement, you must immediately start the vital process of creating weapons and food supplies. You, as leaders must have the mettle to do what is necessary, no matter how odious, to make sure we survive. With time we can figure a way to defeat this scourge."

The man stepped back into the shadow as the Director of National Intelligence brought her chair to the table. There was some chatter and grumbling from the council as President Weller sucked in a deep breath and prepared to speak. He took a double take at the wall behind the Director's chair. There was nobody there.

PART ONE

Great Falls, Montana

Colonel Deb Lisco gasped for air as she fell on the seat of her pants into six inches of snow, a good two hundred meters from a cloud of smoke curling from the warehouse used as headquarters for the 2nd Brigade. Command Sergeant Major Tommy Talfoya stood above her with dark smudges of ash covering his face. He had pulled her to safety moments earlier.

She rose from the slush and coughed. Blood was dripping from her nose as she used the back side of her left hand to remove some of the moistness. Soldiers from the command post continued to exit the building as their comrades rushed to help.

"Tommy," Deb's eyes were red and watering. She struggled to speak as she hacked up soot. "What hit us?"

Tommy was unsure. He waved to a medic to render aid to the colonel. He then addressed a soldier with a pulsnet radio on her wrist. "Corporal, is your radio functional?"

"Yes sir," she answered.

"We need F Company's mobile command center on site immediately."

Colonel Deb's ears were ringing as she tried to focus on the rescue efforts. Her vision was blurred, and the upper right part of her head was throbbing. She held both hands to her ears to try and stop the drumming noise pounding in her head.

"Colonel," Medic Sergeant Condoleezza Sessions approached. She steadied Deb and stared into her eyes. "I need you to come with me."

"I have to stay and help."

"No ma'am. You need to allow me to help you."

Deb felt nauseous as she coughed into her arm while Condoleezza struggled to hold her weight. Two privates rushed to relieve the medic from the burden of carrying the colonel. They sat her on one of ten beds in the dimly lit, air supported medical tent.

She lay back on the hard bed and closed her eyes, allowing some relief from the sledgehammer pounding on the temple above her right eye. She took in several shallow breaths as she waited for Condoleezza to return. Lieutenant Bridges was placed in the bed next to her, with blood covering his left hand. Only a couple hours before he was the soldier who manned the monitor supplying pictures from a drone as Captain Malkova entered the large warehouse allegedly used to manufacture custom wheels on the outskirt of town.

Inside the tent it was cold enough to see the breath of the people speaking. Deb sat up, placed her feet flat on the ground and rose from the bed. She took two steps, staggered and passed out, landing with a thud on the floor.

Soft voices from the end of the bed brought her back to consciousness. Although it took a moment for her to focus, she knew it was commander of 2nd Battalion, Lt. Col. Woodworth, speaking with Command Sergeant Major Talfoya.

"How long have I been out?" she asked with a soft voice. It was now warmer in the tent, and she had an OD wool blanket tucked around her neck.

"About thirty minutes," the command sergeant major moved to the edge of the bed. He stared into her dark eyes which were wide open and fixed with a large, reddish bruise just to the right of her eye, going all the way down to her earlobe.

"What in the hell hit us, Tommy?" she looked at a bandage on her wrist and felt the hospital gown hanging loosely over her upper body.

"It was some sort of Dewy. Not sure exactly what type of direct energy weapon."

"Were there any fatalities?" she swung her feet to the floor, lowered her head and gently rubbed her temple. She felt nauseas.

"Three," answered Lt. Col. Woodworth, looking away in distress, before turning back to the colonel. "Five with severe injuries have been airlifted."

"Josh, I'm sure you have everyone on high alert and prepared should there be another attack." She swallowed hard, stood up and steadied herself while checking out her surroundings. Injured soldiers were crammed into all the beds inside the tent.

"Everyone is aware and prepared." Josh looked at Tommy, "General Maes is fully informed on our situation."

"Is command center operational?" Deb pulled the hospital gown straight out from her belly. "Where in the hell are my clothes?"

"Yes ma'am, the mobile units are all functional." The Command Sergeant Major was unsure how to handle the colonel's unwillingness to rest.

"Colonel," Sergeant Session yelled from the far end of the medical tent, "you need to lay back down."

"Tommy, find me my clothes. We don't have time to waste." She could see the medic moving toward her.

"Ma'am, please, you have a severe concussion." Sergeant Session placed her hand on the colonel's shoulder. "Resting for a little now will allow you to get back to full steam much quicker."

Before Colonel Deb could respond, a corporal entered the tent and approached Lt. Col. Woodworth.

"Sir, F Company has engaged insurgents. They are at the outskirts of the city and Captain Hendersen is requesting clarification on how far they should pursue." The corporal stared at Colonel Deb dressed in the hospital gown.

"Are the drones up?" Lt. Col. Woodworth asked.

"Yes sir, we have limited visibility, but the forward platoon's cameras are sending vivid images." The corporal remained at attention.

"Josh, see where they go. I'll bet you money they are heading to the factory outside of town." Deb pulled the gown over her head and tossed it on the bed, leaving her standing only in a bra and pants from her combat uniform. "I need my clothes."

Sergeant Session scoffed, "Give me a moment and I will get you a clean shirt."

"Deb, you should rest." Lt. Col. Woodworth momentarily stared at her, even as hard as he tried not too, his eyes lowered to her taut abdomen and large breasts bulging out of the side of her bra. Her biceps were as big as his.

"Something is about to happen. Respond to Captain Hendersen," said Deb. "I'll be there in a moment."

Lt. Col. Woodworth and Command Sergeant Major Talfoya followed the corporal out of the medical tent as Sergeant Session handed her a clean shirt before continuing to aid the wounded.

Her head was still aching. She either needed to lay down and give her body a chance to heal or bear the brunt of the pain and get back to work. Tommy rushed back into the tent.

"Colonel," his face had a look of pure fear, "missiles have been launched toward the United States."

She followed Tommy out of the medic tent while still tucking in her shirt. Both ends of the large command center tent were open, but heaters kept it warm and comfortable on the inside.

"What do we know?" Deb directed her question to Lt. Col. Woodworth.

The lieutenant colonel looked at Captain Laura Dodson who was standing in the middle of a group of communication tech specialists. Captain Dodson motioned toward the monitor, "Ma'am, thirty minutes ago, we received a message that a missile attack was eminent. Missiles have been launched from platforms in mainland Russia, mainland China and their naval ships."

"Are we talking nuclear?" Deb placed her fingers to her forehead and tried to focus. She considered the captain to be one of the brightest officers under her command, whose husband worked with the Missile Defense Agency. The information she held would be accurate.

"Ma'am, all indications are they are not nuclear. But we are finding several aspects of the Chinese technology are not what we thought they were. We have to wait and see just what they have launched," answered Captain Dodson. "All branches have responded in kind with our own missiles."

"What's the speed and range of the missiles?"

"Theoretically, the Chinese have hypersonic missiles that can travel up to eight thousand kilometers per hour and travel a distance of twelve thousand kilometers." Everyone in the tent seemed to be frozen in place as they listened to the captain. "We have the ability to identify the incoming missiles, but with the number airborne and the rate they are being fired, there is no way we will destroy all of them.

"Malmstrom is the most likely target in our proximity," stated Tommy. "We should secure our perimeter, but also stay prepared to assist the air base if they are hit."

The roar of aircraft flying overhead was deafening as the airbase scattered planes from the runways. Deb looked to the floor, and took in several deep breaths, before rushing out the open end of the tent. She leaned over and vomited. Tommy came to her side and placed a hand on her back. She continued to bend over and spit on the frozen ground.

"You must be a hell of a lot tougher than me, Tommy," she sniffled and looked up. "How did you come out without a scratch? You were standing right next to me."

"You blocked the explosion. I happened to be on the back side." He took his handkerchief and handed it to her.

Looking up into his deep-set green eyes she detected something she had never seen before in the way he was observing her. Or perhaps, in the past she had not noticed the intensity of his gaze. She stood up straight as the ground shook from planes soaring overhead.

"Whatever happens when the missiles hit, we are going to give it right back to them. Most of those fighter jets have the scram jet powered missiles onboard," she wiped her mouth with the handkerchief.

"Colonel, we have incoming on Malmstrom. They are about to be hit." Captain Dodson moved out of the tent and positioned to the side of Tommy and looked toward the airbase.

They heard the whistling sound of the missile approaching before a thud. The missile was intercepted before it hit the base. The lack of an explosion surprised everyone.

"Is that it?" Tommy directed the question to Captain Dodson."

"Yes sir, I have no idea why but, obviously, that was not an armed missile." There are hundreds of missiles on radar that are designated for central or southern United States. The ones heading north already struck or have been taken out. The power-scaling lasers seem to be performing very well."

Deb moved back inside the communication tent and addressed Lt. Col. Woodworth, "It's time to find out what is at the custom wheel factory east of town."

"I'll arrange air support." Lt. Col. Woodworth felt a rush of adrenaline flash through his body. "I'm going to go with Company I."

"If this place is what I think it is, it is about to be wiped from the face of the earth." Colonel Deb was tired of taking a flailing without a response, it was completely against her nature. "I want all companies ready to go within the hour. Let's find out once and for all what is happening in this city."

Colorado Farm

Hank Lisco stared to the west, across the vast open field as he sat on the porch of the farmhouse. It was too noisy for his liking inside the house, where several people were crammed into the living room. The stars were eerily bright, causing the water in the creek to sparkle as it meandered through the pasture. Life on the farm appeared to be slowing down, which gave him time to think of the predicament he, his family and friends were facing. Being such an optimistic person, he was still having trouble accepting that war was taking place on American soil. As a football coach, he always planned and strategized to prepare for an opponent.

Ted's quick departure to the army base in Colorado Springs, and unsure if Deb was seriously injured or even killed in the blast, caused even more angst. He could see lights flickering in the corrals as the Jacobys handled the chores of taking care of the animals. Terrance was outside the garage piddling with the tractor. The temperature was rapidly falling. A cold breeze blew into his face. He pulled his coat tight around his neck as Bill, Maddy and Samantha came out the front door.

"Do you mind if we join you Coach?" Bill moved to Hank's side. He started addressing his uncle as coach when he played football for the Lions, in order to keep the other players from thinking he was getting preferential treatment. The terming carried over to when they were alone.

"Of course, I don't. It's actually a good time to have some company."

"I hope we hear something from Dad," said Bill. Maddy was holding on to his arm looking at Hank with her mouth slightly open. Samantha crossed her arms to keep warm.

"Bobby, Emilee, Caroline and Sherry are in the garage waiting by the computer. I'm sure Ted will contact us as soon as he can." Hank placed his hand on the side of Maddy's face.

"Where is Grandpa?" Maddy stared at Hank's chiseled chin.

"He is at the army base," Bill squatted down and picked her up, easily holding her in his right arm. She turned and put her arms around his neck, hugging him tightly. "Grandpa is ok," he whispered in her ear.

"I want to help him," she sniffled.

"Your grandpa will be back to help us when we need him," Samantha said, reaching up to rub her arm.

Bill could feel Maddy's cold nose on the side of his face as she shook her head in agreement. He turned to Samantha. "Do you two want to go back inside?"

"No, not really," she said, taking hold of Maddy's hand as he sat her down. "It's really beautiful out here, huh Maddy?"

"It's like when we camped out on the rocks." Maddy looked at Samantha with her big eyes, "Remember you slept by Grandpa."

Bill laughed and looked at Samantha's reaction. She just smiled.

"I don't believe I have ever seen a clearer night," said Jon, stepping out the front door and moving to the edge of the porch next to Hank. He pointed to the west where the glare of lights radiated into the cold night air. "All the lights from the farms sure shine bright on a night like this."

"That has to be good sign," said Hank to his brother. "Jon, I'm really having a hard time dealing with all the uncertainty."

"Dammit Hank, it's uncertain for everyone. We just have to take it one day at a time," stated Jon.

"Did you just see that?" Bill stepped off the porch and onto the driveway. He pointed to the horizon. "There was a flash of light."

Hank and Jon joined him on the driveway. A small, but noticeable flash appeared again, followed quickly by another. A low humming sound came from the south and several greyish black contrails lined the darkened sky.

"Missiles," Jon spoke with a lump in his throat. "They are attacking us with missiles. The explosions we just saw were warheads we intercepted. They never hit ground."

Adam and Aaron walked from the barn to join them. Irene and Breanna exited the motorhome and before long most of the people on the farm were standing in the driveway looking at the dark contrails decorating the bright night sky.

"Are we looking at the end of the world?" Gina asked anxiously, staring at Jon with her lips quivering.

"The ones that exploded weren't nuclear," Jon said in a clear voice. "But this is an escalation of war that there is no returning from."

"Jon, how did these missiles reach all the way to Colorado?" Jacqueline took hold of Hank's arm as they all looked to the western sky.

"It's because they just sent a hell of a lot of them our way." Jon noticed that everyone was looking at him for answers. He turned to Nicole and then Bill before continuing, "What they are doing, is measuring our abilities."

Bobby, Sherry, Emilee and Caroline crossed the driveway to gather with the others as they watched the attack unfolding in the night sky. Terrance and Jerry followed closely behind them, both carrying AK-47s. A bright flash of light, followed by a loud boom made them stop and look to the west.

"That just came from the Brown's farm." Bill stared across the pasture and listened. The low muffled sound of gunshots could be heard. He turned to his uncle Jon. "That explosion wasn't from a missile, was it?"

"No. It was probably a propane tank," replied Jon.

The distinct sound of gunshots continued.

"Someone is attacking them. We have to help." Hank took a couple steps in the direction of the farm to the west.

"We have to secure and protect this place first," Jon went into full lieutenant colonel mode.

"I'm going to his farm and see if I can help Clint Brown," said Hank emphatically.

"No, you are not. You and Bill need to prepare everyone with weapons and then work to set a perimeter around this farm," Jon stated adamantly.

Hank folded his arms at his chest and continued looking to the west.

"Hank, I'm going to go check on the Browns. But I really want you to focus on our families." Jon placed his hand on his brother's shoulder before turning to the crowd, "I need two volunteers to come with me."

"I'll go," said Terrance quickly.

"I will go," Sherry moved right in front of Jon.

Jon glanced back and forth between the two of them. His team was to be a young girl, who only weeks earlier was a member of the insurgents trying to take over the city, and the other, an older man with one leg.

Jon turned to Bill, "Can you get Sherry and me a couple of rifles?"

"I'd prefer a pistol, or an AK. They are the only weapons I have fired." Sherry pulled out a black stocking cap and stuffed her thick, blonde hair inside before pulling it over her ears.

"We should prepare to be out the entire night." Jon noticed some dark clouds on the horizon. "It's clear now, but it looks like clouds are building so we will probably be dealing with cold and snowy conditions."

"Uncle Jon, do you want me to go with you?" Bobby glanced quickly at Sherry before bringing his gaze back to his uncle. Emilee was standing next to Sherry and noticed the look.

"No, you stay here and help your father." Jon motioned to Nicole and Samantha who were standing on each side of Maddy, "Have all the kids sleep in the basement supply room this evening."

The three made their way across the pasture in the direction of the neighbor's farm.

Brown Farm

There was a distinct smell of smoke in the bitterly cold air as Jon, Sherry and Terrance advanced forward on their reconnaissance journey. Light from the three-quarter-moon peeking through the ever-increasing clouds made travel over the rough pasture easier than if the night were pitch black, it also created a greater risk of them being spotted as they moved to the Brown's farm. They were within three kilometers of the neighbor's barn where they approached the narrow, live water creek that signified the western edge of the Lisco property.

"There is no way around it. We are going to have to get wet." Jon's face was bright red as he moved to the edge of the icy water. He took four long steps with the water rising to slightly below knee level before making it to the opposite shore. Sherry hesitated before crossing the stream. She was wearing jeans which immediately froze to the lower half of her legs. Terrance's artificial leg worked commendably as he stepped through the water. They waited in the cold wind, listening to the loud voices coming from the farm.

"When we get to the wire fence on the backside of the barn, Terrance, I want you to go about twenty-five meters to the north and hold your location on this side of the fence. Sherry, you go twenty-five meters to the south and hold that spot. I will advance through the fence and find a position to observe on the north side of the barn. Hopefully, I'll have a vantage point where I can see what is taking place without being detected."

Flashes of light from flames billowing into the air past the barn were noticeable near the farmhouse. When they arrived at the barbed wire fence Jon pointed to the north and then to the south. Terrance and Sherry split off, without uttering a word.

Jon crawled through the strands of sharp wire and ran to the back of the red barn. He looked back to see if he could see Sherry or Terrance. No sign of either of them. He scurried along the edge to the northwest corner of the barn and gazed toward the farmhouse. The house itself was nearly three hundred meters away with a throng of boisterous people gathered in the driveway and front yard, grouped around campfires. Several of the intruders had hunting rifles strapped to their shoulders, with no military weapons visible.

All Jon could see amidst the fog of smoke, past the horde in the driveway, were several people mulling around the front door of the home. He pulled in a deep breath and leaned against the back side of the barn, hidden from anyone who should look his way. The bottom part of his pant legs was frozen solid. He could not tell if the crowd was travelers who found a place to dwell or if they were marauders who overtook the homestead. The wood they were burning must have come from a shed or outhouse on the farm, something Clint Brown would never allow. He thought, for a moment, debating if he should advance to the farmhouse. With the unruly nature of the raiders, he decided to be prudent in his approach and have Terrance back him up.

He returned to the barbed wire fence line and motioned for Sherry and Terrance. A slight wind was blowing, and large snowflakes tumbled from the sky. It was much darker now with heavy clouds blocking the moonlight.

"I'm about to freeze my ass off out here Jon," said Terrance. His white frosted eyebrows were pronounced on his black face. "What is happening up there?"

"I can't tell if they are friendly or not."

"I've never been so cold in my life." Sherry held her frozen gloves in front of her bright red face, "My gloves are frozen solid, and so are my pants."

"Pull your gloves off, you can use mine." Jon removed his waterproof fleece gloves and handed them to her. "There ain't nothing I can do about your pants."

"Something tells me these people aren't friendly," stated Terrance.

Jon stuck his jaw straight out. With his teeth clenched his jaw was more prominent than ever before. His thoughts were with Clint and Peg. They were both in their seventies and the type of people who went out of their way to help others. They were decade long friends of the Lisco family.

"I need to find out the situation here before we go back. Terrance, you and I can slip through the corral on the south and enter the barn through the utility door. Sherry, you wait here on this side of the fence. If you see us coming with people on our tail, fire five shots in the direction of our pursuers, then turn and run back to the farm as quickly as you can." Jon's breath created a heavy fog out of his mouth, "You will still have bullets in your weapon but make damn sure you don't shoot us."

"How long do I wait?" Sherry felt much better with the warm gloves. The frozen lower half of her pants was causing a tingling sensation with her legs.

"Until you hear gunfire, or we return." Jon motioned to Terrance. They crawled through the barbed wire fence.

The corral was in full sight of the intruders at the driveway, but the wood fence, along with the increasing snow, shielded them enough to reach the door on the side of the barn without being detected. The inside was cold and dark with a musky smell of wet manure. The large overhanging doors at the west end were wide open, giving an unobstructed view to the farmhouse. They inched toward the light of the pendulous doors, staying close to the horse stalls. The ability to see the Brown's home from the front of the barn was better than the vantage point Jon had on the side, but still not sufficient to observe anything but the mass of people in the driveway and front yard.

"All I see is smoke and a hell of a lot of people," said Terrance. "They sure in hell don't look very friendly to me."

"There are so many of them, I wonder if they would even notice me if I walked up to the house."

Terrance gave him a dubious look and shook his head. "I wouldn't take that chance."

"I don't see any other way. I can't leave without knowing they are safe."

"If I go with you, I'll be the only one with an AK." Terrance was kneeling on his right knee with the rifle pointing toward the barn floor.

The snowfall intensified to where the house could no longer be seen from the barn.

"You can give me cover from here. I'll move along the corral to the south and make my way to the house. This snow will give me some cover in order to get close enough to blend in with the crowd."

"Let's get it over with." Terrance lifted the AK-47 and pointed it out the overhanging door. He remained far enough back to be concealed in the shadow of darkness.

Jon shouldered his rifle and stepped into the heavy snow. He took three steps to the south and yelled, "Oh God."

Terrance leaned out the door and looked at Jon hunched over three frozen bodies. Two were face down but Clint Brown was face up, with snow covering much of his face.

"Is it the Browns? Terrance stepped from the barn.

"Yeah, and their hired hand," Jon's voice cracked.

"There's someone at the barn," a low voice shouted from the driveway, followed by indiscernible chatter.

"We have to get out of here," said Terrance, moving back into the darkness of the barn.

Jon hesitated. When he saw several of the invaders rushing in his direction, he receded inside the barn, raised his rifle and fired three shots into the snow in front of the approaching group. He allowed Terrance time to exit out the utility door, before withdrawing back and firing three more shots out the large opening of the overhanging doors.

Terrance climbed through the wooden fence at the back of the corral and leveled his rifle on the wood railing. The loud popping of gunshots filled the air. The thud of bullets hitting the fence forced him to fall to the wet ground. As Jon climbed under the lower rung of the wood fence, he fired several rounds toward the utility door, hitting at least one of the pursuers, before retreating to the barbed wire fence.

Sherry jumped when she heard the gunfire. She could see the shadowy forms of Jon and Terrance running directly at her. She pulled the glove off her right hand and pointed the pistol in the direction of a cluster of people at the north edge of the barn. She fired five shots in quick succession, holstered her pistol, then turned and ran. She sprinted right through the water of the creek before turning around to check to see who was following. The visibility had deteriorated to the point she could no longer see more than twenty meters. Out of the heavy snow the forms of Terrance and Jon appeared. The three of them jogged together through ankle deep snow across the wet pasture.

Great Falls, Montana

"See if we can get in touch with General Maes." Colonel Deb dreaded having to brief the general. She knew exactly what needed to happen.

"We have a drone ready for support," stated Command Sergeant Major Talfoya, "it is launched and readily available."

Deb gave him a dubious look. She was unconvinced that weaponized drones were reliable. With the unknown capabilities of the Chinese in hacking and reprogramming the intent of our Nonhuman Aerial Vehicle (NAV), she felt better with having an actual pilot in control of firing a missile, rather than a robot. She was appreciative that the F-35 was brought back into the fold after being shelved for several years.

"Ma'am, we have General Maes."

Deb stepped in front of the monitor, "Sir we have a situation occurring here."

"I heard," the general was blunt, "are you capable of continuing command?"

"Yes sir." Deb could not stand this man. To protect herself, she wanted to make sure she informed him of everything taking place within her command. "We were hit by a group sheltered at a warehouse on the outskirts of town. We have I, G and F Companies positioned and ready to deal with the source of the attack. Also, I would like to request 1st and 3rd Battalions withdraw back to Great Falls."

"With missiles being launched in our direction, you want to congregate troops in one place. 1st and 3rd Battalions are to remain in place." General Maes waited for affirmation. With no reply, he asked, "Anything else?"

"Yes sir, are we going to go on the offensive here at any time, or are we going to sit and let the enemy take pot shots at us?" Deb's head was throbbing.

"All that is in the works." The general accepted her question much better than she thought he would. "Right now, you sustain and secure your location."

"Yes sir."

The monitor went blank. Deb looked at Tommy and shook her head.

"You should take a look at this, Colonel," stated a technician.

She looked over the shoulder of the specialist controlling the monitor. A large group of people were in the streets, about seventy-five meters in front of I Company's forward weapons platoon.

"Are they protestors? I don't see any firearms." Deb stepped back and looked at the images transmitting over the area around F and G Companies. "Lt. Col. Woodworth is with I Company, isn't he?" Deb asked.

"Yes ma'am."

"Get him online," Deb turned to the Command Sergeant Major, "this doesn't feel right Tommy."

"Give us some different vantage angles on the crowd," said Tommy. "I want a 360-degree view around I Company.

Deb noticed one of the technicians standing to the side of the room, typing into the monitor of a four-inch screen strapped to his wrist. She moved two steps closer to him. He quickly looked up, startled and placed his arms to his side.

"Who are you contacting?" She looked at his name tag. "Corporal Turner, who are you messaging?"

"Ma'am, I am just programming my Pulsenet."

"Captain Dodson, can you appease me and check Corporal Turner's computer?"

The corporal looked frantically at his approaching superior. He pulled the screen close to his mouth and said, "Delete last three messages."

Colonel Deb grabbed his wrist as Captain Dodson took hold of his other arm. Tommy grabbed him from behind, into a bear hug, and pulled him to the ground. The corporal continued trying to speak into the monitor.

"Gag him," yelled Captain Dodson emphatically. "Don't let him talk."

Deb pulled out the handkerchief Tommy had given her after vomiting. She pinched his jaw open and stuck it in his mouth.

"Give me his monitor," Captain Dodson moved back as a group of soldiers held the corporal on his back.

Deb looked at the group of technicians sitting at their stations scrutinizing the information displayed on the screens. All the information needed for her to make life and death decisions were relayed to her from these specialists. Her stomach sank as she wondered how many of the operators were enemy operatives.

"Colonel," yelled a technician, "I Company's forward platoon is under attack."

Deb stepped to the monitor. Tommy moved next to her. The platoon was being hit with a massive amount of large and small caliber fire. The high-resolution camera took a moment to normalize through the smoke and cold fog. When it did, the vivid image showed many soldiers from the platoon laying in the street. Traces of gunfire filled the air as the heavy armored vehicles from I Company approached the fallen soldiers.

"Ma'am, I have Lt. Col Woodworth on my screen," stated a technician.

"Josh, F Company and G Company are redirecting to your location. Are you secure?"

There was no reply. The views from the cameras projected on the different monitors showed an eerie scene. There was smoke and fog rising into the dark sky, but not a person visible.

"Josh," Deb yelled.

"It's like they disappeared into thin air." Lt. Col. Woodworth had a blank expression on his face. "We need helicopters to evacuate the wounded."

"They are almost there," stated Tommy. "The NAV is overhead if needed."

"Tommy, have all three companies return to base."

"Colonel," Captain Dodson stepped next to Deb, "Corporal Turner was communicating with the enemy we just encountered. He gave them the position, times of departure and number of troops for the deployment."

Deb swallowed hard as she watched the corporal being led from the communication tent. She thought for a moment and asked, "Does he incriminate any other members of the communication team?"

Captain Dodson blinked several times before answering, "Ma'am, the answer might be yes. We need to examine all computers. I do have three soldiers I want to remove from their duties until we know for sure."

"Ok." Deb was feeling sick to her stomach and her head was pounding. She began to wobble as Captain Dodson moved to her side and steadied her.

"I need some assistance here," yelled Captain Dodson. Several soldiers came to her side.

"Take her to her tent," ordered Command Sergeant Major Talfoya, pointing to a soldier.

Colorado Farm

The temperature was well below freezing with snow falling, even so Hank and Jaqueline remained on the porch looking across the pasture toward the Brown farm. Others would come out to join them but would quickly retreat inside the farmhouse. Jon, Terrance and Sherry were taking much longer to check on the Browns than anyone had anticipated.

"Hopefully, Clint brought out some of his good Scotch, and they are all sitting around the fireplace hashing over old times." Hank forced a smile to his wife.

"The weather is getting really bad," Jacqueline straightened her shoulders. "Only a few hours ago it was the clearest night I had ever seen. Now, the snow is coming down so hard we can't see across the driveway."

"Bobby and the others are guarding the perimeter of the farm. It seems almost futile now with the visibility so poor."

Hank thought how different the situation was with his high school football players now guarding the farm with military grade weapons, rather than celebrating the state championship.

Breanna stepped out of the motor home carrying two cups with steam rising from them. Snow accumulated on the top of her hair by the time she stepped under the overhang of the porch.

"Mom made you some hot chocolate."

"How are your mom and dad doing?" Hank asked. It felt good to take his mind off Jon, if only for a second.

"Mom is doing good. Dad is kind of struggling."

"Ed hasn't been out very much lately." Jacqueline smacked her lips, "My God this hot chocolate is delicious."

"Mom has a knack that everything she makes is tasty." Breanna was much less talkative than usual. "Have you heard anything from Jon, Terrance and the girl?"

"Not yet."

"I'm sure they found shelter somewhere. If the wind picks up this storm is going to turn into a blizzard." She turned her back to the breeze, "I'm going to go back and get out of the cold."

"Tell Irene thank you," Jacqueline watched Breanna leave. She wanted to go inside too but felt an obligation to stand in the cold with her husband as he waited for his brother.

The wind picked up speed. Just before Jacqueline gave up, to go inside, she noticed Hank move to the furthest edge of the porch. Out of the white blanket of snow came three figures moving in unison, side by side. He stepped off the porch.

"Good Lord," Hank moved out of their way as they rushed by.

Jacqueline opened the door to allow them entry. Inside, they stood silently, unable to speak, with the snow slowly melting from their bodies.

Jon pulled out a chair at the kitchen table and helped Sherry into it. He looked at her intently, clicked his tongue, and shook his head up and down. Terrance moved slowly to take a seat. They pulled off their frozen gloves and placed them on the table.

"It's not good," said Jon hoarsely. He lowered his eyes. A crowd of people was now in the kitchen. "We need to make sure nobody followed us."

Bobby, Dave, Emilee and Caroline were at the front entrance to the door, all carrying weapons.

"Bobby," Jon ran his hand through his hair wringing away the wetness, "take your friends down to the fence and make sure nobody is coming across the pasture. If someone is coming across the grassland, they are not friendly."

"What happened?" Gina placed a hand on the side of her husband's face, "Are the Browns, ok?"

"They're dead."

"Bobby," Terrance looked at the youngsters standing with their weapons, "have Jerry go with you."

"There were probably a hundred people at the Brown's farm," Jon sighed, then continued, "many of them had weapons."

"Are you sure Clint and Peg are dead?" Hank asked in as delicate voice as he could muster.

Jon nodded his head at his brother.

"Their bodies were placed outside the doors of the barn," said Terrance. "There was another body next to them."

"It was Hector the hired hand," stated Jon softly.

"We need everyone aware of the danger we are facing." Hank looked in the direction of his assistant coach and football players, "If they do come our way, we need them to know we can protect ourselves."

"I'll go to the RV and inform the Jacobys," stated Coach Saxton, putting on his coat. He had never seen Coach Lisco so serious, or so uneasy.

Bobby moved close to the kitchen table and watched as Sherry removed her stocking cap, allowing her hair to flow free. Her face was flushed red. He glanced at Emilee before walking out the front door.

"You all need to get out of those wet clothes," said Gina. A puddle of water was forming on the kitchen floor under each of their feet.

"I'll go to my room in the garage," said Terrance. He stood up and stiffly took a couple steps.

"Terrance," Jon's voice was much stronger now, "thank you."

Terrance grabbed his rifle, nodded his head and walked out the door.

"Can I grab a change of clothes for you from the camper?" Jacqueline asked Sherry. "You should go downstairs and get a warm shower."

"I can get them myself. But I do think I will take a warm shower."

"Ok." Jacqueline stared at Sherry, observing the dynamic of beauty and animalism that enveloped the young lady. The skin around her eyes was taut, giving them a depth that generated a depiction of potency as she innocently observed the surroundings in the kitchen.

"Mrs. Lisco," Sherry stood up, "I think I will sleep in the basement tonight. I don't feel good about sleeping in the camper alone."

"All the kids are sleeping in the storage area downstairs. I would think there would be no problem with you sleeping in Avery and Reagans bed tonight."

She pulled her cap back over her hair and stepped out the front door without replying to Jacqueline's confirmation of sleeping in the main farmhouse.

"We need to keep a close watch tonight," said Jon.

"Uncle Jon, we'll take care of it," stated Bill.

"Why don't you get some rest. It will be light in about five hours." Hank placed his hand on his brother's shoulder.

Jon was exhausted. He had just finished an eight-kilometer run in dreadful conditions. He wondered whether he had sufficiently described the horror he witnessed at the Brown farm for the others to realize the danger of the situation. His once frozen pants were now wet and sticking to his leg. He felt a twinge in his back as he made his way to the bedroom.

***

The bright morning sun shimmered on the pastel papered wall of the kitchen. The smell of freshly grilled pancakes mixed with the aroma of coffee and bacon filled the rooms of the house. Irene and Jerry took turns between hovering over the stove and cooking the food. The living room was full to the brim with people. Terrance, Bobby, Emilee, Caroline and Dave were outside keeping an eye on the pasture and the road to the farm. Bill and Samantha were in Ted's office at the garage monitoring his computer.

"Everyone, can I say a few words?" Hank anxiously pranced back and forth in front of the fireplace. "I know the events last night were alarming. At the same time, it should be a wakeup call for us. Clint and Peg were good people who never should have lost their lives in this manner."

"It is very important that we understand the danger surrounding us." Jon moved next to Hank, "We have to be prepared to fight if we are confronted with the same people who took over the Brown's farm."

"Do you think they are still there?" Al made a point of looking at each person in the room. "I'm a dentist, not a fighter."

"I presume they haven't left," said Jon. "Believe me these people will not hesitate to harm us."

"With the sun out, I was hoping to build some more on the apartment," said Jason, holding the tattered cast on his arm out in front of him. He was standing to the side of the sofa where his wife Kori was sitting next to Harold and Becky. "I know Harold would like to lay more block on the tower."

"It would be great to get back to building and improving our living conditions on the farm, but we do need to address the security issue first," Hank looked at Jon.

"We would like for everyone to, at the very least, learn how to load and fire a weapon safely," said Jon. "It would be best to instruct only three people at a time."

"So, we can do both," stated Hank, looking at Jason.

"Um, I have something to say," Coach Saxton stood to the side of the room. "Toby and I, along with the Piersons and Smiths have decided we are going back to the city. It seems to be a safer alternative for us at this time."

"Why?" Jacqueline moved next to Hank. "You know how bad it is in the city."

"I have never been so scared in my life as I was last night, not knowing if people were coming out of the night to kill us," said Toby frantically.

"I'm sorry Hank, we spent our whole life talking about being a team and going into battle with one another. The big difference with a football game is that the other team was not shooting at us," Coach Saxton lowered his head.

"And losing did not mean being killed," said Toby.

"I really don't know what to say here George." Hank moved to the side of the room and stared at the members of his football team. "You are making a huge mistake. At least you know we have food here."

"We made our decision," said Toby.

"How are you going to get to the city?" Jon asked.

"We are hoping to use the old pickup Ted arrived in."

"That ain't going to happen," said Aaron Jacoby sharply.

"Oh boy," Hank didn't want his friend's decision to cause conflict with everyone. "Let's make these decisions after we've eaten breakfast."

Nicole came up from the basement followed by Maddy, Scotty and the other children. They all looked wide awake after sleeping in the food storage area in the basement. Maddy went directly to Irene's side.

She stood with her back straight and her hair neatly brushed as she asked, "Can I help you cook Irene?"

"Maddy we are just finishing with the pancakes." She put her hand on the side of the little girl's face. "But you know what we can do a little later?"

"Make some more cinnamon rolls?"

"Nope, don't tell anybody," Irene leaned down and whispered, "I have a special way of making angel food cake with chocolate fudge icing. Maybe we can have you and Grandma Nicole help."

"And Samantha."

"It will be a girls cooking party."

Hank forced a smile as he poured himself a cup of coffee. He remained silent as he walked out the front door. Although it was a brisk morning, the bright sun felt good on his face as he sloshed through the snow on the driveway in the direction of the corrals.

Bobby leaned on a wooden picket. "Well Dad, have you got things figured out?"

Emilee and Caroline stood on each side of Bobby.

Hank smiled wryly and shook his head. "I think our situation is even more confusing than it was last night. George, the Piersons and Smiths all want to go back to the city."

"What, Jesus, it's a terrible time for them to do that."

Terrance, carrying a telescope and Dave holding binoculars came closer to listen to the conversation.

"I can't believe Coach Saxton would want to leave us here," stated Dave, towering over Caroline as he moved behind her.

"Can you see anything at the Brown's farm with that telescope?" Hank asked Terrance.

"Not really," he answered candidly.

"What about the drone?" Hank asked. "Doesn't it have the range to go that far?"

"Bill and Samantha are working on it. It launches but they can't get a signal on the computer monitor," said Bobby, shaking his head.

"Why don't you all go in and get something to eat. I'll keep an eye out here." Hank was looking at Emilee and Caroline as he spoke," there are a lot of pancakes ready to eat."

"I'll stay with you Dad," said Bobby.

"I thought I smelled pancakes," said Terrance, moving in the direction of the farmhouse. "You don't have to ask me twice."

"You sure Bobby that you don't want to get out of the cold?" Emilee asked.

"I'll be there shortly. You go ahead."

The father and son waited silently for a moment as they watched Jason and Harold begin to shovel snow off the construction sites. The temperature was rising quickly.

"I needed to get out of the house before I said something to George that I would regret," Hank lamented.

"Did you get into an argument?"

"No," Hank took a sip of his cold coffee, then looked into Bobby's eyes. "Having him tell me he was leaving at a time when we all should be working together, really hit me wrong. But neither of us said anything we might regret."

"Dad, he's your best friend."

"Yes, he is," Hank swallowed hard. The confusion and uncertainty of everything was making it difficult for him to make good decisions. Bobby was correct. If George and Toby wanted to leave, then he would help them in any way he could.

Lone Tree, Colorado

Christian was awake well before daylight. He walked through the foyer of the large home they had confiscated in the ritzy neighborhood. He traipsed into the family room and looked out the picture window. A perfect view of the Rocky Mountains with their snow-covered peaks bathed in sunlight was ruined by several pockets of smoke billowing into the sky from buildings burning across the city.

"Couldn't sleep either?" Jessica, with a heavy wool blanket wrapped around her was sitting in a chair with her knees pulled up to her chest. "It was really cold last night."

"Cold doesn't bother me at all."

"This is beautiful, but…"

"I know, it's not ours and never will be." He was shirtless and the belt buckle was open at the front of his pants.

Jessica stared at his crooked nose and protruding forehead as he stood over her. When they were in high school, she made fun of his caveman head. He was never handsome by any imagination but had a strength to him that always attracted girls.

"What are we going to do?" she asked.

He grimaced. A loud knock came from the front door.

"Christian, open up."

A cold rush of air filled the room as he opened the door. Standing on the porch was Shira and two more of his followers. She pointed across the lawn where hundreds of insurgents dressed in black covered the street.

"They want to talk with you," Shira said. She looked past him into the living room at Jessica.

"What do they want?" he pulled his pants tight and latched his belt buckle.

"They want us to take out the police station on Colorado Boulevard." She stepped back and glanced over her shoulder to the street. "The leader of this group is not very compromising. She wants to speak to you face to face to make sure you are fully aware of their expectations."

Although unofficially so, Christian considered Shira to be second in command of the rebels dedicated to following him. He remained shirtless as he stepped into the cold and marched down the sidewalk to the curb at the street. A group of about twenty of the people dressed in black, some with their faces covered with masks, waited for him. They all held weapons.

"How can I help you?" he asked.

"We are beginning the execution of the next phase of disruption and now have the directives for you to follow," said a man at the front of the group before stepping to the side, allowing a small woman to move in front of him.

"What kind of directives?" Christian felt his heartrate quicken when he heard the word directive. He was smart enough to know it was another word for orders.

Insurgents at the back of the crowd leveled their weapons in his direction. It made no sense why they would show such a blatant display of power to those they considered confederates. He glanced at Tim standing at the door holding an AK-47 with Jessica still wearing only a tee-shirt at his side. Shira stood close to him.

"The police have taken command of the station on Colorado Boulevard. Early tomorrow morning you are to take control back." The lady speaking sounded more like a robot than a person. "Prepare to leave for Colorado Springs immediately after you have control. Get dressed and we will give you the details."

Christian felt the cold wind on his bare chest while he watched her step back and disappear in the group. He was surprised how unbending and rigid her demands were being relayed to him.

"Are we going to follow their orders?" Tim asked as he followed him into the vestibule.

"I don't know," Christian hesitated for a moment. "I guess I'll get dressed and see what they expect of us."

Jessica followed him to the bedroom. "We should take off and get as far away from these people as possible. They are not our friends and never will be. We should all leave now."

"That will be pretty hard to do Jessica with hundreds of them outside the door." He stopped to stare at her for a moment.

"Christian, I'm telling you, this will end very bad for us if you allow these people to make all the decisions." She stared at him while he ignored her musing.

He dressed and put on a light jacket before joining Tim in the foyer.

"They never moved an inch," said Tim. "Aren't we supposed to be on the same side?"

"Theoretically we are," said Christian. "Stay inside the house. I'll agree with everything they say. We can hash it all out after they leave."

Christian pulled the collar of his jacket around his neck as he approached the lady at the curb. He towered over her as he stepped into the street.

"You are to leave at six am and take your soldiers west to Colorado Boulevard where the police have established a substation. You will take control and eliminate their ability to operate."

"Ok," he shook his head in affirmation. He despised the way she used the phrase "you will". "What do we do then?"

"We have transportation for you and five of your top command to transport to a base we have at a ranch just outside of Colorado Springs, south of the small town of Peyton. The rest of your assemblage will transfer to the location over the following two days."

"Why are we going to Colorado Springs?"

He was surprised at how long she hesitated. She was so used to others taking her orders without query that his question caught her off guard. He waited silently for her response as she continued to stare, never diverting her eyes.

"We are going to strike the North American Aerospace Defense Command," she answered.

Christian could not believe the objective was NORAD.

"I understand," Christian replied as calmly as he could.

"Six am tomorrow morning," she turned and disappeared into the crowd.

He watched the large group peel away in perfect unison.

Inside the house Christian took in a deep breath. He looked at Tim and Jessica, "We have a big problem here."

"We have to take the police station," said Tim. "Then we should leave. NORAD is inside the damn mountain near the army base. If we try to take it, we will all be killed."

"This is a mess. Attacking NORAD makes absolutely no sense," Christian scoffed. He stared at the floor and shook his head.

"We should leave the city, right now," Jessica pleaded.

"Where Jessica, back to the Lisco farm?" Christian spoke with a rage she had never witnessed with him before, not even in high school. "We stole their car. And by the way you are a real, great mom. You left all three of your children. I don't think they will throw a parade for our return."

She glared at him with a mist forming in her eyes.

Christian turned away and stared out the picture window. About fifty of the rebels in black were visible at the end of the street.

"What are we going to do?" Tim asked. "They are watching us."

"We don't have much choice," Christian moved closer to Jessica. As he tried to make eye contact, she blatantly turned to look away. The mist in her eyes had turned to anger.

Great Falls, Montana

"Colonel."

Deb felt a slight tap on her chin.

"Colonel, can you wake up?" Condoleezza was standing over the top of her.

"What time is it?" Deb noticed she was only half covered with a blanket.

"0900, ma'am." The medic placed her hand behind the colonel's head and helped her sit up. "I need you to drink some water."

Deb placed her feet on the floor. She held the cup of water and took a sip.

"You were nearly airlifted out of here last night. You almost found yourself in Minot, North Dakota this morning. If it weren't for the number of casualties, you would have been," she waited for Deb to finish drinking and lifted her legs back onto the bed. "Command Sergeant Major Talfoya wants me to notify him now that you are awake."

"I have to use the restroom."

"Go ahead, but then right back in bed."

Deb felt nauseous. Her whole body ached as she crawled back into the bed. She was nearly asleep when Tommy entered her tent.

"Colonel, how are you feeling?"

"I'm tired."

"You can rest. I know you don't want to but maybe a little patience at this time is the best thing."

"I have to ask you Tommy," she raised her head slightly, "did I make a mistake last night?"

"No," the Command Sergeant Major moved to the edge of her bed. "The mission was in response to a low collateral damage threat. We responded prudently, with more than adequate firepower required to take care of the problem."

"How did we not see them before they hit us?"

"Everyone blended in. It looked like townspeople protesting, but they attacked without any warning. In reviewing the images from the camera on the Stryker vehicle we are lucky the damage was not worse. The forward platoon had no chance to counter.”

“How bad was it?” Deb held her breath.

“Five KIA.”

“Oh my God.” She put her left hand to her temple. “We haven’t done a damn thing and we have already lost eight soldiers.”

“We have eyes on every square inch of this city. The threat just disappeared into the woodwork. We have all the intelligence system maintainers working to find a link to the enemy that attacked. All we can do is sit and wait.”

“Colonel,” a private placed a tray of food and a pitcher of water on the night table next to the bed. “They want you to drink a lot of water.”

“Tommy,” Deb waited for the private to leave. “We have a bigger problem within our ranks than we thought. Can you get ahold of General Lauer at Fort Carson and see if others have been infiltrated?”

“I think you are correct on this. We need to bypass General Maes and see if General Lauer will give us some help with rooting out the subversives.” Tommy took in a deep breath, “I’m also going to place guards at the front entrance to your tent.”

“Do you think that is necessary?” she glanced up at him. The way he was looking at her was probably no different than the way he had stared at her a hundred times before. Maybe it was the knock to the head that made her think he was looking at her more as a woman and not as a commander.

“Condoleezza is not going to allow you to go back to work today. I know resting like this is totally against your character but a day or two of rest and you will be back at full strength.” He placed a hand on the side of her bare bicep. He tried to capture her gaze as he looked indiscreetly into her eyes. She cocked her head slightly away. “I’ll keep you fully informed on any developments.”

Deb didn’t feel like eating. She did drink a full cup of water before crawling into the bed and pulling the covers tight around her neck. Her mind wandered to the times she saw the Command Sergeant Major without a shirt. His chest was massive and solid. She visualized him with only a towel wrapped around his waist. She took in a deep breath and whispered, “What am I thinking? The guy is a career soldier just like me. Besides his damn head is way too big for his body." She chuckled before letting out a deep breath and falling asleep.

Lone Tree, Colorado

The street was full of homegrown rebels friendly to Christian. Walking to the police substation on Colorado Boulevard would take at least two hours. With the element of surprise gone, it would be more difficult to overwhelm the forces protecting the city than when they first started the insurrection.

Jessica felt a pang of anger, verging on loathing, as she watched Christian address the crowd. She hadn't said a word to him since his attack on her character. His statement about her being a bad mother stung much worse than she would have ever thought it would.

"I'm going to stay here. I'm not going to fight the police," she declared with a heavier Irish accent than usual while she waited next to Tim only a couple meters behind Christian.

"Christian will never let you stay behind."

"I don't give a shit what he thinks." She turned and walked back inside the mansion. She went to the back bedroom and emptied her duffel on the bed. After pulling a sweater over her shirt she entered a large walk-in closet and rummaged through the homeowner's clothes. She found a ski jacket, ski gloves and stocking cap. She placed a hairbrush and toothpaste in the bag and hurried to the kitchen where she filled it with fruit, lunchmeat and water.

As she entered the living room she saw outside the large picture window, Christian and Tim charging up the sidewalk. She grabbed the duffle bag and rushed out the back door. The frozen grass made a crunching noise as she rushed across the neighbor's lawn and climbed over a stone wall. She hit the street running, sprinting until she was at the outskirts of the wealthy neighborhood.

She ran until her body begged her to rest as she came to a hiking trail adjacent to a park. Following the concrete trail to an area with several soccer fields, she made the decision to exit the trail and walk across the open area. Although it would be easier to be spotted, she felt a sense of security in having the ability to see anyone approaching. At the far end of the playing fields was a large building with a brick sign in front of the structure with the words, "Douglas County Library".

The front of the library was mostly glass with a high gable entry made from brick. After shaking the locked front door, she walked around to the back and looked through a small window. A platform to a staircase going into the basement was visible about a meter down from the bottom of the window.

She went to the front of the building and picked up a large rock from the landscaped entry. She smashed in the window. It would be a perfect place for her to take refuge for at least a day.

Colorado Farm

It was unusual for all the Jacobys to be inside the house at one time. They were usually working relentlessly taking care of the farm animals. Mingling with the rest of the people on the farm was low priority on their list of things to do.

"We should check on the other ranches around the area. We could all benefit with working together," stated Aaron.

"How can we safely do that?" Hank asked, knowing the Jacobys were a prototypical farm family who would take a chance to support a neighbor.

"There had to be at least a hundred people at the Brown's farm last night," stated Jon. "Once we get the drone up and running, we can use it to get a visual of the different farms. Until then it would be a great risk to travel to these places without knowing who occupies them.

"We need to take care of the Brown's livestock." Aaron looked at his father, "Bring his cattle here and deal with the logistics of ownership later."

"It would be best to notify the sheriff in Limon," stated Ed, reaching down to massage his knee. It was the first time he felt strong enough to venture from the bedroom in the RV. "Limon is on Interstate 70, so there has to be some military passing through from time to time."

"My guess is that it is overrun with people by now," replied Jon. "Traveling there would be dangerous too."

"If there are a lot of people, they need food," Ed spoke very clearly. "The military has to keep the Interstate open, so I'm sure they have some sort of presence in the town. How about if we offer them food for some sort of protection?"

"Like Jon said, traveling anywhere seems to be risky." Hank thought of the discussion he was going to have with George Saxton about them leaving the farm.

Nicole and Jacqueline entered the room. Aaron and Ashley moved to the end of the sofa so they could sit.

"Has anyone heard from Ted?" Ashley asked softly. She held her head cocked slightly to the right, a condition she was trying to correct from the gunshot wound she received outside Monticello.

"Bill has monitored the computer in his office, trying to contact him," stated Nicole.

"He will get in touch with us as soon as he can." Jon stood in front of everyone with his arms crossed.

"I agree with Aaron. We should take care of the Brown's livestock," Hank stood up.

"We can't do it if the people from last night are still there," said Jon adamantly.

"Can you drive to their entrance and look?" Jacqueline asked.

"Well…" Jon placed his hand to his chin.

"I'd rather saddle up the horses and go across the pasture," Adam spoke for the first time. He moved next to Hank. He was dressed in his western button-down shirt and jeans. "If the farm is vacant, we can herd the cattle back here. If the people are still there, we come back."

"We have eight saddles, but can we find eight riders?" Aaron asked.

"Jon, it would be good if you went with them. Do you feel comfortable on a horse?" Hank asked.

"You know Hank, I haven't ridden a horse since I was ten years old. But I suppose I can."

"Breanna can ride," Ed glanced at his daughter.

"I have no problem going," she stated.

"Bill has been riding with Deb on many occasions." Nicole hesitated for a moment, wondering if she should be volunteering her son, "You can ask him if he is willing to go."

"That would be five. I'm sure we can find three more out of this group. They need only be able to ride along the cattle and push them here to our pasture." Aaron stood up and walked behind the sofa. "We should get this done immediately before someone else does."

"Being able to ride a horse hasn't come up since we arrived here." Hank held his hands out, "I guess we'll find out who can."

"There is one more thing," Jon stuck his jaw out, "if Peg and Clint are still laying in front of the barn, we have to bring them back and give them a proper burial."

"We still haven't found those damn radios," stated Hank. "You'll have to signal that it's safe at the Brown farm and I'll drive there."

"You can use the Ford pick-up Ted drove here," said Ed.

"Ok. Let's get everything underway," said Hank.

Nicole watched the group leave the living room. She was going to increase her effort to contact Ted. Fort Carson was a major target for the missiles, but she never doubted her husband was safe and out of harms way.

"Grandma, are you ready to make a cake?" Maddy yelled across the living room from the kitchen. "Irene and Samantha are already here."

Irene was busy laying out the ingredients on the counter. Both Maddy and Samantha had their blonde hair pulled back into matching ponytails.

"So, what are we making here?" Nicole moved next to the table.

"Angel food cake." Maddy looked at her grandma with dark eyes wide in anticipation.

"It's angel food cake with chocolate fudge icing." Irene gave them a tender smile, "It's a little different from a traditional angel food cake. This one is in a flat pan and will only be about three inches high."

"It sounds delicious." Nicole's heart was pounding as she thought about Bill and the others traveling to the Brown farm, but she didn't want to frighten Maddy. She placed the palm of her hand on the side of a large glass bowl full of fixings and stated, "Them are the biggest bowls I have ever seen."

"What do you want us to do?" Samantha asked enthusiastically. It would be the first time for her to spend a meaningful amount of time with Nicole. She had formed a deep connection with Nicole's husband and granddaughter and was in the process of doing the same with her son. It was time she put her best foot forward and make a good impression.

"This is a team effort." Irene shook both fists out in front of her before pointing in the direction of two large bowls. "I have prepared the egg whites in one bowl and sifted the powdered sugar and flour together in the other. But with all the gadgets we have in this kitchen, I cannot find a mixer. So, we have to beat it by hand."

"We can do it," said Nicole enthusiastically.

"Nicole you can hold the bowl while Maddy and Samantha beat the ingredients. I'll slowly put everything in as you whip it together."

Nicole held the bowl of eggs tightly as Irene used a tablespoon to add the light ingredients of salt and extract while Maddy and Samantha easily beat it all together. It became much harder to stir when Irene began adding half cups of flour and sugar into the vessel with the egg mixture.

"It's getting thicker," said Samantha, "my wrists are getting a little tired."

"Mine too," said Maddy, stirring lightly.

"It's almost ready." Irene placed three flat baking pans on the table. "Most people use a ten-inch table pan for angel food cake. This will make more pieces."

"How long will it take to bake?" Samantha asked.

"About thirty-five minutes on a low heat, or until it's golden brown." Irene smiled at Maddy. "But we do have frosting to make. No hurry though. We'll have to let it cool for about an hour after we pull it from the oven."

Nicole was sitting at the table where she could see outside the kitchen window. There was a flurry of activity as all eight horses waited at the railing of the corral. Hank and Jacqueline were sitting in the old Ford F-250 talking to Bill who strapped a rifle to his back and took the reins of a horse.

Her breathing increased as she changed her perspective from the tense scene outside back to the kitchen. It was obvious by the way Irene had moments of staring blankly into space that the tension of the situation of her sons and daughter facing danger was weighing heavily on her. With true country fortitude she was trusting that everything would work out, leaving her to do what she enjoyed most, cooking.

"Irene and Samantha, would you drink a glass of wine while we wait?" Nicole asked.

"Absolutely," said Samantha quickly.

"Maybe a small one," Irene smiled and clasped her hands together.

"And I have some sparkling water for you," Nicole touched Maddy on the nose.

Nicole took one drink of wine and let out a large sigh and said, "What a wonderful idea this has been."

Samantha held the glass close to her bright red lips before taking a sip.

"Ladies, I haven't had a drink in quite some time. But here goes," Irene took a large swallow.

Maddy sat back and watched. The atmosphere was contagious. She enjoyed seeing her grandma so relaxed, something she had not seen since they arrived at the farm. And having Samantha laughing again, like she had many times on their trip with Grandpa Ted, made her happy.

"Bill said you grew up in the Littleton area," Nicole stared into Samantha's green eyes. Although they had been together for a short time, she knew Bill was becoming infatuated with the beautiful flight attendant.

"Yes. I recently bought a home in Highlands Ranch." She held her wine close to her chest. "God only knows what is going on with that place now."

"And your parents are in Littleton?"

"We stopped on our way through, but they weren't at their home," she took a drink of wine. "I have been discussing with Bill how I might be able to check on them. It would be wonderful to bring them here. We just don't know how we are going to do it."

They all sat quietly for a moment and sipped their wine. Maddy broke the silence.

"I heard Bobby talking with Emilee." Maddy narrowed her eyes and looked at Samantha. "I heard him say that he's pretty sure you and Dad are doing it."

Samantha gritted her teeth. She chuckled and brought her right hand to her forehead, reflexively shielding her face from Nicole.

Irene giggled and turned her head slightly away from the others. She took a sip of her wine.

"Doing what dear?" Nicole innocently looked at her granddaughter. Then it dawned on her what she had just heard. "Oh my gosh. Maybe we should start making the icing."

"We all went through a heck of a lot in the last few weeks." Irene looked at little Maddy. "We have all become good friends. Huh?"

"Yeah," Maddy leaned toward Irene and shielded her mouth. She whispered, "We are best friends."

Irene leaned back and smiled. The warm sensation in her chest from drinking the wine made her feel better than she had felt in a long time. It engendered hope she would live long enough to see her own grandchildren again.

"Ok." Samantha took in a deep breath and finished the last of her wine. Lipstick was noticeable on the rim of the glass as she sat it down. She gave a welcoming smile toward Nicole, and said, "I'm ready to see how to make this fudge frosting."

Irene was able to make everyone feel as though they were the ones making the delicious dessert. She placed everything together and had the others simply beat the mixture.

Nicole, Samantha and Maddy took turns stirring the fudge frosting while Irene removed the pans of cake and inverted them on the countertop.

Brown Farm

Bill made every effort to coax his horse to take the lead after they crossed the creek whilst Bobby, Dave and Emilee cantered alongside of him. But Breanna would have none of it. She rode ahead, making it evident how well versed she was in the art of horseback riding. A pistol was visible in a side holster above the waistline of her jeans.

Jon was extremely uncomfortable riding the horse. He wanted to be in the front, but his mount was a follower and no matter how hard he tried to make it pass the other horses, it would refuse. He stayed at the back riding behind Adam.

"There is a gate in the wire fence about two hundred meters south of the corral where we brought our cattle through," said Aaron. He felt remorse, remembering, only a couple days earlier, negotiating the purchase of a bull with Clint Brown.

"We need to make sure there is nobody in the farmhouse," stated Bill.

When they arrived at the fence line Breanna stopped and allowed her older brother, Aaron, to move in front of her. He pulled open the gate to the barbwire fence and allowed everyone to ride through. He pulled the gate to the side and left it open. The sky was bright blue, and the sun was beating down on the snow, creating rivers of slush along the beaten path leading up to the farmhouse.

Bill reined his horse to a stop and stood tall in his saddle. He used his binoculars to check for any movement around and inside the farmhouse. He saw nothing. Breanna was already at the picket fence surrounding the vacant lawn in front of the home.

Jon looked in the direction of the barn, then slowly began to ride toward the large overhanging doors. The Browns were laying in the same spot as when he saw them the night before. They were almost unrecognizable with remnants of snow slowly dripping off their clothes. The others gathered next to him.

"I'll see if there are some blankets in the barn." Aaron's cheeks hung loosely from his face and his nostrils widened. He climbed off his horse and hooked the reins to a wooden rail on the corral.

"Good God, who could possibly do this?" Breanna clambered from her horse and continued to hold the reins while she leaned down to the three bodies. She said a silent prayer.

Aaron returned from the barn carrying three horse blankets. He took his time draping the bodies of Peg, Clint and Hector. He neatly tucked the blanket on all sides, then removed his hat and ran his fingers through his thin hair. He turned to Jon.

"We have to go to the west pasture to herd the cattle, so we better get started. The less time we spend here the better."

"I'll wait for Hank and Jacqueline to show up with the truck." Jon looked in the direction of the farmhouse. "We should check the house."

"I'll look with you Jon." Breanna watched the others ride off, without making a move to mount her horse.

Jon kept his rifle at the ready as he opened the front door to the farmhouse. Breanna was close enough behind to brush into him every time he stopped. A large hole at the door of the coat closet in the foyer gave an indication as to what the rest of the house might have endured. After taking two steps into the living room, Jon held up his hand for Breanna to stop.

They waited for a moment as he studied the situation with his rifle at full ready. The living room furniture was all tidily in place and the carpet was vacuumed. He stepped into the kitchen. The refrigerator was humming without a dirty dish to be seen. The distinct smell of cleaning products filled the room.

"Somethings wrong here," he whispered, slowly backing into the living room. Breanna held her right hand on his back as she matched his steps in retreat.

"Is someone living here?" Breanna mouthed the words while placing both hands on her pistol and holding it out in front of her.

"I don't know," he whispered, pointing at the back bedrooms.

They walked slowly to the hall leading to the bedrooms. The sound of her breathing loudly caused him to turn around and say, "Don't shoot me."

She nodded and followed him down the hall to the first bedroom with the door open. Stuffed animals were scattered on top of a neatly made bed. Jon stepped inside the bathroom on the opposite side of the hall. Toothbrushes were in a glass on the sink.

"Someone's here," he whispered.

Breanna's usually beady eyes were the size of saucers as he moved past her in the direction of the closed door at the end of the hall. She walked sideways close enough behind Jon to be touching him. She held her gun aimed at the floor as she rotated her eyes in looking down the hall behind them and then forward again.

Jon held the rifle in his right hand while he leaned ahead and pushed the bedroom door open with his left hand. He stuck his head inside the room. It took a second for his eyes to adjust to the dark conditions.

"Jesus," he yelled, jumping back and leaning next to the wall of the hall.

"What is it?" Breanna kept her back flat to the wall.

"Put the gun down," Jon yelled into the room with his back next to the wall. "We aren't going to hurt you."

Inside the bedroom, at the end of the bed, was a woman pointing a gun in the direction of the door.

"Go away," the woman yelled. A small child began to cry.

"The others are going to be back at any time," shouted a different woman.

"You have a child in there. Just aim the gun somewhere but at us." Jon peeked around the corner. The lady was pointing the pistol off to the side. He stepped into the room. Breanna moved next to him with her gun pointed in the air.

"What are you doing in this house?"

"We are waiting for my boyfriend and his friend to return." The lady looked at two older women crouching behind the bed. "They went to a farmhouse, we passed yesterday on our way here, to see if they have any food to spare."

"So, you murdered the owners and took over their home?" Breanna took a step closer to the lady. One of the older women stood up and placed her body in front of a toddler aged boy.

"There was nobody in the house when we arrived yesterday," said the old lady shielding the child.

"Who were all the people here last night?" Jon sensed they were telling the truth.

"We came with a large group we met at a camp in Limon. They told us about a commune outside the little town of Kiowa, so we hitched a ride with them in the back of a U-Haul truck," stated the young woman. "There was an explosion and lots of shooting last night so we locked ourselves in this room."

"We decided not to leave with the people we came with this morning," the old lady spoke. "They seemed dangerous, and I didn't want to take the chance of something happening with my grandson."

"Ok, come out here." Jon walked into the living room as they followed.

"We cleaned up the best we could this morning," said the young lady. "We figured it was the least we could do, since they took all the food."

"Well, your friends killed the people who own this ranch," Breanna looked at them with animosity.

"If that's true, we knew nothing about it." The young lady looked as if she was going to cry. "Mom told us we shouldn't go with them when we were in Limon.

"They were definitely not our friends," insisted the mother, looking out the picture window to the driveway.

Hank and Jacqueline were in the old F-250 at the front of the house. Jon quickly exited out the front door.

"They are over here," Jon pointed as he walked around the pick-up in the direction of the barn. Breanna followed him outside with the mother and young woman lingering behind her. The other lady and child remained at the door to the farmhouse.

Hank backed the pick-up next to the bodies.

Jacqueline gasped when she saw the Browns and their hired hand.

The mother and daughter following Breanna looked on in horror as the bodies were lifted into the bed of the truck. By the time the three bodies were placed in the back of the truck the young lady was crying. She held her hand over the bodies with her eyes closed, saying a silent prayer. She looked at Breanna and said, "God knows we had no idea this happened."

"I believe you," said Breanna solemnly.

"What are your names?" Jacqueline was standing next to the door of the pickup.

"I'm Trenda," the young woman sniffled, "my mother is Alice."

"Alice, how long were you at the camp in Limon?" Jon asked.

"We got there real early yesterday morning just as the others were preparing to depart for the commune. The camp was unbelievably packed, and everyone was complaining about not having enough food. There was room in the U-Haul, so we decided to leave with them," she shook her head.

Hank looked at the lady. Her face was as ordinary as any he had ever seen. She was the type of person who would disappear into a crowd. "Did you come from Denver yesterday?"

"Aurora," she moved a finger across a red crack at the center of her lower lip. "We were staying at the high school, but the situation was unbearable. They kept telling us there would be a shipment of food coming at any time, but it never came."

"How did you get to Limon?" Hank asked.

"Sam, my boyfriend and his brother Timothy, are good with cars, actually good with electrical," said Trenda. "They were able to get a van they owned running, but it only got us to Limon before it quit."

Hank wondered if George Saxton would be influenced about returning to the city after hearing the lady's stories. Both ladies were thin as rails, obviously in need of a good meal. He looked at Jacqueline before saying, "We have a place for you to stay."

Fort Carson Army Base

Ted held a black marker in his right hand while he slouched over a large paper map of the Denver metro area. The map covered a large table in the situation room, just two doors down from his office. Neither General Lopez nor Colonel Bonney Myer, having come from the east coast, were familiar with the city, so they were relying on Ted to give them the layout of the main streets and location of schools, hospitals and other significant locations of interest, which would be relevant to them helping the local government take back the urban area.

Colonel Myer's 3rd Brigade was made up of inexperienced soldiers on most levels, many with only a few months of training, but the sergeants and first lieutenants at the squad and platoon level were seasoned veterans. Every indication was pointing to the war being one of urban warfare, something the United States forces were well versed at. Training for the 3rd Brigade was about to become real.

"Reconnaissance indicates the area of turmoil is predominantly south of Hampden Avenue." Ted marked from east to west across the entire map. He then moved to the bottom of the map and placed an arrow. "By coming up through the town of Parker, we can allow the local governments to take back control as we move to the west."

"How dense is the population from Parker into the metro," Colonel Myer asked.

"It's wall to wall people Bonney," Ted circled the area from Parker to Lone Tree. "The threat from subversives in the city of Parker is low, but still there. The last report from reconnaissance indicates that much of the populace are still in their homes. With the availability of food being the biggest issue."

"We are in contact with local law enforcement, and they are aware of our arrival," stated General Lopez.

"What are we going to encounter when we move to the west?" Bonney pointed to the west side of Interstate 25.

"We estimate there are up to 8000 rebels in the urban area, with over sixty percent of them on the south side." Ted stood up straight, "This is why we want you to utilize the full brigade."

"Colonel, we will keep you posted on new intel. You can prepare your soldiers to leave at daybreak." General Lopez turned to Ted, "We have about fifteen minutes before we meet with General Lauer."

Ted was having a difficult time adjusting to his new position as assistant division commander. The new Army was focused on utilizing specialized units of brigade and battalion sized forces. Artificial intelligence was utilized far too often by the upper echelon of the Military in making decisions. The commanders at the brigade level still had some semblance of decree in creating strategy and control over their commands. He would trade places with Colonel Myer in a heartbeat.

"I don't know what kind of resistance they are going to encounter tomorrow," said Ted, "she sure has a lot of green soldiers to deal with."

"I'm afraid they are going to have to learn under fire." General Lopez shook his head. "I just received orders that the 99th Division is about to join the fight. 1st and 2nd Brigades are to leave for the southern border on Wednesday. It is my understanding that several Brigades from the 4th Infantry Division will do the same."

"Part of the 4th Infantry is located near San Antonio," Ted stated. "Do you know if Deb's 2nd Brigade are going to join them."

"Right now, she is still outside Great Falls, Montana, but things are going to change very quickly. We are about to find out what is planned." He opened the door and allowed Ted to go out first. Ted sensed there was something on the general's mind as they began walking toward the command center.

"Ted, I want you to stay here in Fort Carson with 3rd Brigade." The general stopped walking and looked earnestly at Ted. "If Bonney is successful with the mission in the Denver metro area, we want to keep her group in reserve and prepared to relocate to other cities to clear out the rebels. I want to be honest with you. We are hoping you will be willing to help with this part of the war."

Ted remained silent as he walked along side General Lopez down the narrow hallway. They were the last to arrive at the briefing. Major General Lauer was at a podium, ready to begin. He and General Lopez took a seat at the back of the room.

"The chiefs of staff and the department of defense has drafted a specific plan of action to respond to the threats this nation is facing. I will break down into two parts where we stand as a military at this time. First will be the greater world-wide threat and second is the capacity this military base will have in answering that threat." General Lauer spoke clearly and with authority, "We did receive minimal injury from the missile attack to both military and civilian targets on the mainland, but Guam, the Philippines and Japan all received significant damage. Keeping these allies from falling into the enemies hands is vital to the security of the west coast."

Ted glanced at General Lopez who was listening intently to the commanding general. He then looked at the room full of soldiers. In all his years of service he had never seen so many combatants fixed and absorbed while being informed during a briefing.

"We underestimated the support the Chinese military was receiving from the Mexican cartels. The current estimated number of enemy troops at and near the southern border has been updated to be over two million. They have been able to establish launch sites and take-off points for cruise missiles, nonhuman ariel vehicles, rockets and artillery. It is a stalemate of sorts at the border. We have transported and emplaced PAC-10 and PAC-11 interceptors adjacent to the border. These are vital in keeping the balance of power in missile defense." The general hesitated for a moment and looked out across the darkened room. "Our immediate objective is to protect the interceptors. 1st and 2nd Brigades from the 99th Infantry Division are to collect in Phoenix and redirect to positions in support of the missile interceptors. 1st Stryker Brigade Combat from Fourth Infantry Division will move to San Antonio. Fourth Infantry Division's 2nd Brigade will move to an assembly area in the vicinity of St George, Utah. All Battalion commanders must stay mobile and be ready to adjust their position to meet with plans and alterations as deemed necessary."

Ted knew Deb would be happy to be attached with the 4th Infantry again. After the missile attack the base placed a seventy-two-hour moratorium on nonessential radio use. He tried several times under the appearance of military necessity, unsuccessfully, to communicate with his sister. His staff had assured him her name was not on the list of casualties.

"The final objective coming from the Department of Defense and Homeland Security with the directive of the President of the United States is the deployment of the Army to help establish order in our cities. As we have done in Colorado Springs, we will have all units in reserve being utilized to help local law enforcement gain control over their domain."

Ted felt a terrible sense of irrelevance as he sat back in the cushy stadium seat listening to the Major General finish. He made a mistake in accepting the job of Assistant Division Commander. When he and Nicole met with Army Chief of Staff McClinton to discuss his re-enlisting, the general made it sound like he was going to play a significant role in helping to protect the country. He should have remembered the words of his father, "Cemeteries are full of indispensable people."

"Ted," General Lopez brought him out of his thoughts. "I am leaving this evening for Texas. I want to arrive ahead of 1st and 2nd Brigades to help set up command."

"Is there anything specific you want me to do?" Ted asked.

"I think Colonel Myer is prepared for the sweep of the Denver metro area, but you can advise and assist her with any logistics in the morning."

Ted simply shook his head. He continued to sit as everyone exited the room. He dreaded going back to his quarters. It made things worse as he thought of Nicole, Bill and Maddy. He wished he were back at the farm with them.

Great Falls, Montana

A sharp pain in Deb's lower left hip caused her to roll off the bed. The good thing was that the throbbing in her head had disappeared. She was dressed in a white cotton nightgown as she stretched before moving to the door of the tent. The two guards stationed at the front acknowledged her while consciously ignoring her scanty attire.

"Can we assist you, ma'am? I can procure you a jacket." A heavy fog appeared out of the private's mouth as he asked the question.

"That's not necessary." She could see several people inside the command tent with the lights from monitors flickering in the cold night air. "I need you to find Lt. Col. Woodworth and have him join me in my tent."

"Yes ma'am." The private rushed off as Deb moved back inside her tent out of the frigid air.

She sat in a chair and silently waited for Lt. Col Woodworth. She had been out of the loop for nearly twenty-four hours and needed to be informed of any new developments. She felt weak, but for the first time since the explosion she sensed she was recuperating.

"Colonel," Lt. Col. Woodworth stuck his head through the door. When he noticed Deb sitting in a chair dressed in her night clothes he hesitated. He looked away as he asked, "Did you call for me?"

"Come in Josh, have a seat," she pointed to a chair, "I want to be updated."

"I take it you haven't spoken with Tommy this afternoon." He tried to keep his eyes away from her large breasts with the nipples poking out of the thin material of the nightgown.

"Not since this morning," she poured a cup of water and held it up. "Would you like some?"

"No thanks," he hesitated for a moment and then shifted straight to the point. "General Lauer has reattached us to the 4th and we have orders to leave for southern Utah on Thursday. Tommy has contacted 1st and 3rd Battalions and they should be back here sometime tomorrow afternoon."

"Wow," she shook her head, "that happened quickly."

"Another thing, the drones we launched this morning have encountered a significant amount of interference with returning signals. Captain Dodson is trying to figure out how they are blocking our images."

"What about the warehouse?" Deb asked. "We used the drone when I Company investigated the wheel factory and had no problems."

"We only used the drones over the city. With your permission I would like to send them to the warehouse tonight." Josh stood up, "If we leave without some sort of response to the attacks, we may never know what is taking place here."

"You have my permission. But no matter what you find, I don't want any action until we discuss the scope and nature of the mission." She rolled her eyes down toward the floor in thought. "Contact the Air Force Base and have them place a squadron of armed NAVs on standby. If we get verification that this warehouse is an enemy stronghold, I want it completely destroyed."

"Colonel," the private standing guard in front of the tent yelled, "permission for Sergeant Sessions to enter?"

"Granted."

Condoleezza stepped into the tent carrying a covered plate. She was pleased to find Colonel Lisco still dressed in her nightgown. "Ma'am, I brought your dinner."

Lt. Col. Woodworth moved to the side allowing the medic to set the food on a small wooden table being used as a nightstand.

"Sergeant," he acknowledged the medic, then put on his cap and moved to the door. "I will keep you informed colonel."

Condoleezza watched him leave before moving uncomfortably close to Deb. "Can you look up and open your eyes wide?"

Deb took in a couple deep breaths and looked up.

"Have you been having any headaches?" the medic looked into her eyes.

"None, as much as I slept this afternoon, I'm hoping I can sleep tonight."

"If you can sleep tonight," Condoleezza thought about telling her to limit the workload for a couple of days, but knew that would not happen, "you'll be back too normal in no time."

"Thank-you Condoleezza."

The medic smiled and left the tent.

Deb did plan to rest but knew, come morning, she was going to be back stronger than ever.

Colorado Farm

"I would be calling for a framing inspection today if I were building this apartment under normal circumstances." Jason sat across the kitchen table from Hank, cradling a cup of coffee. "I'm going to frame the rooms inside and start running the electrical wires."

"You are doing everything by the book anyway," stated Hank.

"Your sister had the foundation and rough plumbing inspected before all this took place. The permit card was signed off for both the apartment and block tower foundations, as well as the rough plumbing." Jason placed the dirty and battered cast on his arm onto the table. "As long as the foundations are sound, especially with the block tower, we should be ok."

"Harold seems to know what he is doing with laying the block," Hank leaned back in his chair.

"I thought I was going to have to help him with placing the wood joists for the first floor, but he already has them on. He plans to place the floors as he builds each level. He then can lay the block over the wall, using one section of scaffolding to lay the high part, then do the same for the next floor. If he had enough block, he could lay the damn thing a hundred meters high." Jason shook his head, "He has been mixing cement and grout, plus carrying his own block. The guy is amazingly efficient."

"Bobby told me he, Emilee and Sherry are going to start helping him," stated Hank. "They are about to learn what work is all about."

"You're right about that. The higher he gets with the tower, the harder it will be to get him material." Jason slammed the coffee cup onto the table, "I need to get out and go to work."

"Jon placed some concrete blankets and the solar heater up by Carol's grave site last night. He left the three bodies there," Hank spoke in a woeful tone. "We need to have some of your helpers go up and dig the graves. They are going to have to use a pick to get past the frost line."

"I'll have Dave get some help and do it." The giant man stood up from his chair. "Jerry and Terrance are going to help me pull electrical wiring today, so it is a good time to take care of that.”

Hank sat at the table contemplating having a bowl of oatmeal when he heard the front door open. George and Toby walked into the kitchen. For the first time in his life, he felt uneasiness in the presence of his best friend.

“Hank,” Toby’s voice was strained as she moved right next to him. “We are going to leave this morning. Even if we must walk, we are going.”

“Sit down and have some coffee.” Hank could feel the cold radiating from their clothes, “We can figure this out.”

“We don’t want to figure anything out,” yelled Toby. “We want to go home.”

“Ok, ok.” Hank held up his right hand. He looked at George. “Let’s figure how to get you home. It’s much too dangerous for you to walk.”

“Have you heard from Ted?” George asked. He pulled out a chair and sat down.

“Bill and Samantha have been trying to contact him, but no luck.”

“Can we take one of your cars?” Toby asked sharply.

“No. you can’t,” Hank licked his lips as he stared at her. “The Jacobys made it clear that you cannot take either of their vehicles and you sure as hell can’t take our only mode of transportation.”

“Can someone drive us part way?” George asked in a much more confrontational manner than Hank would have expected him to. “Take us to the edge of the city.”

Hank took in a deep breath through his nose. He placed his hand on the handle to the coffee cup but never brought it to his mouth.

“I don’t think our request is unreasonable,” stated Toby still standing behind her husband.

“There are eleven of you. It will take two vehicles.”

“Using the pick-up and another vehicle will allow us to take all our stuff,” Toby’s tone was still foreboding.

“We need to run this by the others, especially the Jacobys.” Hank looked directly at George and tried to relieve the tension. “I’m sorry everything has worked out this way.”

"Hank it's not anyone's fault. We are city people who would be frightened out here even if there weren't a threat from some gang trying to kill people." George wrinkled his nose.

"I hope you are not making a big mistake here," said Hank. "We have no idea what is going to happen with this war."

"We will take that chance." Toby looked away from the two men.

Hank took a sip of coffee and looked at Toby, "It may come down to you having to walk if you want to leave."

"It will be easier to get back than it was to get here." She stood up tall and folded her arms across her chest.

Great Falls, Montana

Even with the heater in her tent on high, Deb was chilled to the bone as she put on her fatigues.

"Colonel," Lt. Col. Woodworth yelled from outside, "are you decent?"

"Yeah, come on in," Deb looked at her watch, it showed 6:15.

"Jesus, it's twenty-eight below." He entered the tent wearing a heavy coat with a hood, "I told the guards to go to the mess tent."

"I should have dismissed them last night."

"I don't think we can be too careful," he continued to stand at the door. "Have you eaten?"

"Not yet."

"Tommy wants to meet us in fifteen minutes at the communication tent."

"I can wait to eat. I could use a coffee though." She pulled on her coat, "Did you deploy the drones last night?"

"We did. We couldn't get closer than four hundred meters to the warehouse without them being jammed," said Josh. "Captain Dodson will be at communications with Tommy. She can better define how she thinks they are blocking the images."

Command Sergeant Major Talfoya was watching a fuzzy picture on a monitor as Captain Dodson pointed to the image. Each monitor in the center had a soldier actively scrutinizing the screen.

"Colonel," Tommy leaned back from the monitor. "We were just looking at the video from last night's surveillance by the drones."

"What are you finding?"

"There is a lot of activity on the north side of the warehouse. But when we get within 380 meters of the center of the building, we lose the picture. It is the same with all the drones," stated Tommy.

"We thought we were keeping up with the Chinese technology with jamming our pictures, but obviously we weren't."

"Have we tried a larger NAV?"

"No ma'am." Captain Dodson looked at Lt. Col. Woodworth, "If they have the PS-4 tracker scout available it will eliminate our guess work about having a drone that will get past their jamming technology.

"I'll request they do so immediately," Tommy replied.

Deb looked across the room. There were unfamiliar faces amongst the crew of soldiers sitting in front of the many screens. If there were dissidents among the soldiers, she was confident they would be spotted.

A private handed her a cup of coffee. She turned to the Command Sergeant Major. He took several steps back, and she followed, to where they were out of earshot of the others. "1st and 3rd Battalions should be here by late afternoon. General Lauer has instructed us to leave early Thursday morning. He'll direct us as to the route we are to take."

"Any idea where we will end up?"

"Southern Utah." He squinted his eyes, "I'm so ready for some warm weather."

"Colonel," Josh yelled across the room. "They launched the NAV for surveillance of the warehouse."

"Is it armed?" Deb moved next to Captain Dodson.

"No ma'am, all armed NAVs are unavailable." Captain Dodson checked the monitor as the images cleared up on the largest monitor in the room."

The drone made the first pass over the warehouse with pictures being transmitted back without any type of interference. It made two more passes before one of the communication technicians said, "Malmstrom is requesting clarification of how many more passes they should make."

"Inform them we are good with what we have," said Deb. "We can slow it down and look at the footage."

They replayed, in slow motion, the pictures without seeing the slightest movement from anywhere around the warehouse. As they scrutinized the last set of images from the north side of the building, one of the technicians yelled, "Hold it, look at the far window."

Captain Dodson focused her eyes as she tried to identify the protrusion located in the window. She rubbed her chin and shook her head. "I can't see enough of it to tell what it is."

"Look at all the tire marks and footprints in the snow," said a corporal manning one of the monitors. "There has been a lot of recent activity at the site."

"Colonel," Josh motioned to both Tommy and Deb. He stepped to the far opening of the tent as they followed. "With all the troop movement through this area we have to find out if this structure is a direct threat to our armed forces. It would be a dereliction of our duty to leave without knowing its purpose."

"I completely agree. The mission needs to take place immediately," stated Deb.

"Josh, can you have them ready to go in two hours?" Tommy asked, looking over his shoulder to make sure nobody at the monitors could hear him. "I will notify Fort Carson of the operation."

"Captain Dodson," Deb motioned for her to join them, "we are going to shut down this command center. Not another message is to leave this tent. Everything from here on will be communicated through G Company mobile. I want you, and you alone, to observe all messages at this location."

Captain Dodson rushed to the middle of the room. "Everything off, now! Turn off anything that can transmit a signal, including your Pulsenet."

"Ma'am, I'm in the middle of ordering supplies, I'll lose the order if I shut down," said a corporal innocuously.

"Turn it off!" Captain Dodson shouted. Having someone in her command as a traitor made her sick to her stomach. "Everyone is to look at the soldier next to you and verify their devices are completely shut down."

"Tommy, you and I will go with G Company to the farm owned by the rancher who told us about the warehouse," said Deb.

"Walt Blake."

"Yes," she turned to LT. Col. Woodworth. "Are you coming with us?"

"No, I'll go with H Company."

"Is two hours enough time?" Tommy asked Josh.

"I can have fire squads up and ready within thirty minutes."

"We'll release the drones after everyone is in place," stated Deb. "We leave in two hours."

Blake Farm

The low hanging fog allowed for a visibility of six kilometers. The driveway and part of the adjacent field to Walt Blake's farmhouse was covered with army vehicles. The old rancher slowly moved from the front door of his small home, wearing a large, hooded winter coat, and proceeded down the sidewalk in the direction of the massive force of military weaponry. His wife waited at the open door while he made his way toward Colonel Lisco and Command Sergeant Major Talfoya, standing at the side of a light tactical vehicle.

"What in God's name are you people doing out in this cold weather?" Walt asked as he approached.

"We are going to find out exactly who you sold your land too," answered Tommy. He could feel the hairs in his nose freezing.

"You told us when you came to Great Falls to report suspicious activity at the warehouse that you were the one who initially sold the land to the people who built it," stated Deb. "Where is the property line."

"That's their fence line, right across the road." Walt pointed at the dirt road they arrived on, then lifted his arm and pointed over the grassland. "If you look close enough you can see the top of the warehouse. But whenever I get curious about the place, I go to the hill over there and watch them." He pointed to a hill about a kilometer further down the road past his home. "The fog is already starting to burn off so you should have a birds eye view of the place."

"Have you noticed activity lately?" Tommy asked.

"Hell yes, they have lots of people shuffling around down there." Walt placed his right thumb to his nostril, leaned his head back toward his house and blew his nose onto the ground. "Excuse me, but I told you all about that the other day."

"Do you and your wife have some place you can go for the afternoon?" Deb stared at his bright red nose.

"I suppose we can go into town," Walt looked at them suspiciously.

"You need to go immediately," Deb stated.

"Sir," Captain Jensen yelled to Tommy, "F Company is twenty kilometers from the site."

"Captain," Deb pointed to the east, "we will follow you with 1st Platoon and mobile command to the top of that hill."

"Yes ma'am," Captain Jensen stepped back into the mobile command center. The cumbersome vehicle moved down the frozen driveway to the dirt road.

"Thank you, sir." Deb waved to Walt as she hurried to the tactical vehicle. Tommy was already inside and ready to move. The old man never moved an inch as he watched them leave his property.

They drove through an open gate to the pasture on top of the knoll and parked on the frozen grass. The command center vehicle was fifteen meters long and looked like a cross between a tan fire truck and a recreational vehicle. The inside was HVAC climate controlled, making it comfortable to work in shirt sleeves. There were four large monitors situated on the walls.

"Colonel, Lieutenant Murphy will be in charge of images for the monitors." Captain Jensen stood to the side of the lieutenant who sat in a chair in front of the largest monitor.

"Ma'am," said the lieutenant, "we have contact with Captain Hendersen with F Company on screen 2. Images from the drones just released from H Company's position are on both 3 and 4 screens. As soon as we get pictures from F Company forward fireteams and squads we will alternatively display on screen 1."

"We can connect visual with H Company at any time," stated Captain Jensen.

"Put Captain Hendersen on speaker." Deb stared at Captain Jensen's hand grasping the back of Lieutenant Murphy's chair. She always considered the captain to be one of the biggest women she ever met, but never really noticed her enormous hands.

The pictures from the drones were crystal clear as they hovered over the rooftop of the colossal building. Just as they started to go to the side of the warehouse the picture turned white.

"They jammed them," Lieutenant Murphy turned to Colonel Lisco.

"Captain Hendersen, what is your position?" Deb rubbed her chin as she looked at the monitor.

"We are on a dirt road approximately two klicks north of the warehouse. We are on the backside of a hill in the grove of trees, so we do not have a visual of the building from our location."

"Do you have direct access to the site?"

"Affirmative, there is a utility road that goes through the trees to the back of the building. It's well used and wide enough for all our equipment." Captain Hendersen looked away from the monitor with indistinct chattering being heard behind him. He directed back to the screen. "Do you want us to proceed to the parking lot of the warehouse?"

Deb hesitated, she looked out the windshield of the command vehicle down in the valley. The fog had dissipated, and she had a clear view of the structure. The tree covered hill the captain mentioned hid the entire company from her sight. She studied the area while contemplating where best to place the soldiers. The parking lot and entrance to the warehouse was on the opposite side of his position. It might be advantageous to surround the area to limit the ability of the force inside to escape.

"Ma'am?" the captain broke the silence.

"No, stay where you are," she answered decisively. "Are your men in forward positions close enough to give us a visual."

"Fireteam four is located at a gulley about sixty meters northeast of the structure." He hesitated for a moment, "We will relay as soon as they have their camera fixed on the site."

Deb stepped back and stared blankly at the monitors, then stepped out of the vehicle into the ice-cold air. She looked through her binoculars at the warehouse. Tommy followed outside and stood next to her.

"What do you see?" he asked.

"Look at the fields around the warehouse. Those aren't natural hills. Someone dug out thousands of yards of dirt." She lowered the binoculars to her side. "Walt told us there might be hundreds of soldiers living there. I'll bet there is a whole city under that building."

"Ma'am," Captain Jensen's body took up the entire door as she leaned outside. "We have images from F Company's forward squad."

Deb and Tommy hurried back inside the command vehicle. They scrutinized the pictures of the side of the warehouse. There were large casks protruding approximately fifty centimeters out from eight different windows.

"Anyone have any idea what we are looking at," Deb asked.

"No idea," said Lieutenant Murphy. "Could it be part of their ventilation?"

"Put Lt. Col. Woodworth on this monitor," Deb pointed to the first screen. She waited until his face appeared. "Josh, bring up the platoon of MT-3 Bradleys to Captain Hendersen's location."

"Just the tanks?" he asked.

"Yes," she turned to the screen with Captain Hendersen. "Captain, pull all your men back to your present location."

"Ma'am, the image of the roof captured from the drone before it was jammed shows more barrels on the rooftop." Lieutenant Murphy leaned back from screen 3.

"Get the images to Captain Dodson back at base and see if she can get us an answer to what in the hell they are." Deb spoke directly to Lieutenant Murphy and then turned to Tommy. "Check on the availability of immediate air support."

Deb pivoted to the screen with Lt. Col. Woodworth. "Josh. As soon as you arrive, have the tanks locate to where they have visual on the windows."

"We have to assume people inside this place are American citizens," Josh stated, but never asked about rules of engagement.

"Captain Hendersen, are your forward teams back?" Deb did not reply to the lieutenant colonel.

"Yes ma'am," the captain answered.

"Begin broadcasting over the loudspeakers the message that identifies us as the United States Army, and we require all people inside the building to exit immediately. Have Sergeant Chen repeat it in Chinese and then have Specialist Ivanov do the same in Russian. Keep broadcasting until they respond, or you receive further orders."

"Yes ma'am, also, Colonel, we have visual on H Company's tanks, they are arriving at our location," stated Captain Hendersen.

"Ma'am, we have an artillery battery that was on their way to Sunburst, Montana preparing to give us support. The air base can't guarantee immediate support," said Tommy.

"Where in the hell is Sunburst?" Deb looked at him with frustration.

"It's about one hundred and seventy kilometers to the north," stated Tommy. "The battery of long-range cannons are about twenty kilometers away."

"Colonel," Captain Jensen moved next to Deb, "Captain Dodson just responded that Research and Development could not identify the barrels as weapons."

"Damn, that is not the answer to the RFI I was hoping for." Deb looked at Tommy. The sound of the message in the distance could be heard being broadcast by F Company. "It just complicates the hell out of everything. That's all I need on my record is to attack a custom wheel factory in the middle of America because I thought the ventilation system was a new age weapon."

"We are going to have to send a team to investigate," stated Tommy.

"I don't know how they can get much better pictures than we already have," Deb declared. "Call it intuition or whatever, but I don't like the idea of sending anyone inside this place. They have already surprised us twice."

Before the command sergeant major could reply, a blinding flash of light shot through the windows of the command center. The screens on the monitors all flashed off and then came back on.

"What in the world," Lieutenant Murphy leaned back in his chair holding both arms over his head. "What in the hell was that?"

"Was that an explosion?" Captain Jensen asked anxiously, thinking for a moment a nuclear weapon detonated.

Deb looked through the front window of the command vehicle in the direction of the warehouse and answered, "No, it was an electromagnetic pulse."

"Lt. Col. Woodworth is on screen one," said Lieutenant Murphy.

"I have never experienced anything like that," stated the lieutenant colonel. "With that blinding light we are bound to have some casualties here."

"Do the tanks have the targets in sight?"

"Yes ma'am.

Before she could reply, glaring flashes of light filled the air. She moved next to Tommy at the front window of the vehicle where they could see bright lasers pulsing out of every opening of the building. "We need artillery support," Deb yelled as she took a couple steps back from the window. Fragments of light from the lasers reflected off the walls of the command center. "Have them level the place."

Every five seconds a surge of light would burst from the roof top, compounding the effect of the constant light pulsating from the sides of the building. Flashes from the Bradley tanks could be seen responding to the attack.

Several intense flashes dashed through the air above the command center.

"They are shooting at us." Captain Jensen looked astounded as a beam hit the back top of the vehicle, creating a baseball size hole in the roof. "Should we move from this location?"

Rocket boosted shells exploded loudly as they ripped into the warehouse. The intensity of the explosions shook the vehicle. Within the melee of bursting shells, the blinding lights from the lasers curtailed as parts of the building disseminated into the air. The bombardment lasted for little more than a minute, culminating with smoke and dust soaring from the rubble. The areas visible through the debris of the smoldering building showed that much of the roof had collapsed and the walls imploded.

"Josh, are you still there?" Deb moved in front of the screens.

There was silence before he replied, "Yeah we are still here."

"Captain Hendersen."

"Yes ma'am.

"What is your status?"

"Nothing here was hit directly," the captain's voice was rushed.

"Josh, what about you?"

"The crews are still responding in the Bradleys. We are going to have some damage. We'll wait for the dust to settle and then assess the situation on getting the crew back to this command post."

"Are the tanks still operational?" Deb asked.

"I'll get back to you on that," Josh wavered. "The rest of H Company is moving to this location."

"Colonel, do you want me to direct 2nd and 3rd Platoons to the site?" Captain Jensen asked.

"No, use the drones to give us a view of the inside of the warehouse. Have everybody remain in place."

"Colonel, 3rd Battalion is thirty minutes north of the city," said Tommy. "Do you want them to come here or continue on to headquarters?"

"Have them go to headquarters in Great Falls." Deb grabbed her coat and stepped out of the command vehicle. She stared down at the devastation. "Good God," she said to herself. Tommy came to her side.

"Colonel, are you ok?"

She stared straight ahead and took in a deep breath. The smoke filled her lungs.

"It's freezing out here. Are you sure you don't want to come back inside?" He continued to stand next to her as she remained fixated on the wreckage.

"Is this what war has turned into?" she looked at him with her dark eyes narrowed. "Look at all the damage. It took less than ten minutes."

"Colonel, we need to contain the location."

"Use the drones and nonhuman vehicles. Observe it from a distance but no soldier goes near it until we are positive what we are dealing with." She cleared her throat, "Tommy, contact Fort Carson and see if we can get some assistance with excavating the site. We need combat engineers to work through this mess."

Deb continued to stare at the columns of smoke rising from the valley below. The smell in the air was brackish, like what a person might experience near a volcano in Hawaii. The trees around the premises were all demolished, knocked down like a tornado had rumbled over the site. She was briefed on the massive power of the high energy lasers but never imagined the magnitude of their destruction. One mistake by her, one wrong move and a complete Battalion or even her entire Brigade could have been obliterated in the blink of an eye.

"Ma'am," Tommy yelled from the door of the command vehicle. "A team is on its way from Fort Drum to help with extracting the site. They will be here before nightfall."

"Have all units remain in place until they arrive." Deb looked back toward Walt's farmhouse. The old rancher and his wife were standing in their driveway watching the smoke rise. She turned in the direction of Tommy and said, "Let's go back to headquarters."

Lone Tree, Colorado

Jessica spent a restless and worrisome night sleeping on the carpet inside the library. At first light she poked her head out the broken window. She tossed her duffle bag outside before climbing through the opening, being extra careful not to cut herself on the jagged glass. Once in the wide-open parking lot she checked in all directions. She felt exposed and vulnerable while considering which way to go. Knowing the Lisco farm was east, she began to run eastwardly.

The cold air saturated her lungs as she sprinted until her legs begged her to stop. The tip of her nose was ice cold, but the sides of her breasts were wet with sweat underneath the winter coat. Although she had a night away from the rebels, she constantly looked back to make sure Christian, or his henchmen were not following. She stopped and bent at the waist and rested.

Her decision to leave Christian was completely unexpected, without any thought of consequence, or a plan. She was familiar with the area on the south side of town to the extent of knowing where she was, but none of the side streets were recognizable.

She began to jog until she came to a major thoroughfare that she recognized as Lincoln Avenue. The remnants of a supermarket and other shops were visible on the opposite side of the street. Her heart pounded in her chest as she sprinted across the wide road and paused at a tavern on the edge of the shopping center. The entire area was eerily quiet.

A bright green sign at the top of a bar, with its front door knocked off the hinges, identified the establishment as Mulligans. She waited at the entrance while her eyes adjusted to the darkness. With the first step inside her nostrils were filled with the smell of stale beer. The place was completely ransacked, picked to the bone with only a blackboard laying to the side with the words, daily special mulligan stew, written in white chalk. She moved further inside and found a partition wall where she had a view looking out a large picture window at Lincoln Avenue. She kneeled on her left knee and pulled out a bottle of water from her pack.

For a brief second, she wondered what happened with Christian when he attacked the police station. Then the images of

Emilee, Reagan and Avery appeared in her mind. It felt as though her heart was about to come up through her throat as she visualized them. It was strange that the contemplation about her three daughters centered on Avery and Reagan. Emilee was older and was such a devoted daughter that she would be willing to forgive her mother for abandoning the family. The younger girls were loyal to one another. It would take more effort to gain their forgiveness and understanding. No matter what had transpired in the past she was going to find a way to be with them once again.

She stared out the window lost in thought. Facing the people at the farm, especially Jacqueline Lisco, would be difficult, but something she was willing to endure. The problem was she had no idea where the farm was located. She never paid attention to the roads while riding with the girls in the back of Hank's truck or when she left with Christian in the Lisco's stolen car.

It was still early morning and there wasn't a cloud in the bright blue sky. Even in the shade of the bar she could feel the temperature rising. In her haste she packed water, food and warm clothing, yet she terribly regretted not taking a weapon. She was completely vulnerable in so many ways, yet she felt some contentment in knowing a solid decision was made to travel to the farm and see her girls.

The loud thumping of helicopter blades brought her out of her deep thought. The noise increased until several of the choppers rushed over her location causing the building to shake. She stepped outside the tavern to witness the massive display of military might filling the air above the city. Two bright flashes of light caused her to lower her head and move back inside the shelter. The sound of muffled explosions could be heard in the distance.

Her knees were trembling as she listened to the helicopters scouring the sky above. Two more bright flashes reflected off the walls of the dark room. She stayed frozen in position as the sounds of explosions followed. In the distance she could hear the roar of engines as a convoy of trucks headed her way.

Fort Carson Army Base

By the time Ted made his way to the base command, control and communication facility, Colonel Myer was already nearing the town of Parker. He felt oddly strange that he was not making any decisions about strategy or maneuverability and was present only to offer advice, guidance or recommendations. He watched images being sent from a camera attached to a forward tactical vehicle. Several screens in the room relayed pictures from the Denver metro area. The conversation between troops could be heard chattering back and forth throughout the large room.

Colonel Myer was in contact with the specialists and technicians at the monitors, relaying the local officials' requests for food and drinking water. Her mission so far appeared to be one of a humanitarian relief effort.

Ted moved to the screens displaying the area to the north and west of the colonel's location. The drones were displaying columns of smoke where explosions had occurred at the newly constructed emergency power stations and temporary police bases. Helicopters were flying in a grid pattern over the area trying to capture pictures of rebels on the ground. There was not one face-to-face encounter between the United States Army and the rebels.

Colonel Myer paused with a platoon of soldiers from B Company at a location west of Interstate 25 on Lincoln Avenue to evaluate the circumstances and process the information of the massive force covering the city. The chatter over the communication channels continued to be constant with many reports of sightings of insurgents who seemed to disappear before their eyes.

Ted moved from monitor to monitor trying to discern the information so he could help Colonel Myer make sense of the hidden enemy. As he was contemplating, a technician summoned him to a screen where Colonel Myer waited.

"Ted, we have a young lady who just approached our convoy." Colonel Myer was sitting in a cramped position in the mobile communication unit. "She has information to give about the rebels but first wants directions to the Lisco farm on the eastern plains. She says her daughters are there."

"Is her name Jessica?" Ted never met her but heard all about how enamored Bill was with the lady before she up and left the farm without her children. He also knew his nephew Bobby was still very much attached to Jessica's daughter Emilee.

"Affirmative, her name is Jessica."

"Tell her that I am Colonel Ted Lisco, Bill's father."

"She is speaking with Captain O'Brian and seems to be cooperative. We will see how much she can help us with pinpointing the location of the rebels she has been working with. Then we will transport her to the base later this evening."

Ted noticed a corporal approaching.

"Sir, General Lopez wants to speak with you," said the corporal.

Ted followed him to a monitor toward the back of the facility where he found some privacy to speak with the general.

"Ted, I want to let you know I will be back on base Monday morning."

"Are preparations for advancing to the southern border going as planned?"

"I can't communicate anything more until I arrive in person," stated General Lopez.

Ted hesitated for a moment, surprised the general couldn't further the discussion.

"General, I would like to take a platoon and travel to my office at the farm tomorrow after Colonel Myer arrives back to base."

"Remind me Ted, it is about two hours away?"

"It's less than that from here." He was surprised the general would waver in giving permission.

"Ted, go ahead and make plans to travel to your farm. We have been having issues with security on our open communications so I will speak with you after I return to Fort Carson." The general disappeared from the screen.

Ted took in a deep breath and let it out slowly. He wondered what the general had in mind for him. When he first joined the Army, he was enamored with the magnitude of the massive, powerful force that gained its strength from everyone working together. The interoperability of all branches made the military stronger. Now he felt it would not matter if he were a part of it, or not. He hated the idea of being ineffectual.

Colorado Farm

Bobby and Emilee carried eight-inch concrete blocks up the stairway to the second level of the masonry tower. Every third trip they each would lug a five-gallon bucket of mortar to the work area and dump it on a mortar board. Although the temperature was cool, they were working up a sweat.

After placing a five-gallon bucket of water into a mortar mixer, and ten shovels of sand, Sherry hoisted a thirty-two-kilogram bag of cement on to the grate of the powerful machine. After stepping back and allowing the dust to settle she shoveled in ten more scoops of sand. The loud machine would spit out wet globs of cement as it mixed the mortar. She had smudges of cement smeared across her forehead.

Jon and Hank watched the masonry crew as they worked. Harold was visible through the openings being left for windows on each side of the structure as he worked at a frantic pace. He already had the bolts sticking out of the bond beam at the top course of block signifying the second story of the tower was almost to full height.

"I haven't had a time to talk with Sherry since we returned from the Brown's farm," said Jon. "I need to let her know I appreciate the job she did that night.

"Bobby told me she wants to talk with you about the next step she and Caroline need to take with their enlistment." Hank cleared his throat, "Apparently Ted helped them with the paperwork before he left."

"Hell Hank, I'm not sure what the process would be. I doubt anyone could get into Fort Carson now." Jon noticed Dave approaching.

"Coach," the young man towered over Hank. "We dug the three graves."

"How deep did you get?"

"Close to six feet. Once we got through the frozen part it was easy digging." Dave stared at Sherry while she worked.

"Ask your dad if he will have time this afternoon to make the caskets," said Hank.

"Will do coach." Dave never took his eyes off Sherry as he walked away.

"I am going to check with Bill to see if he has had any luck contacting Ted. I see Maddy and Scotty playing outside the garage, so he and Samantha are probably at the computer." Hank took one step toward the garage when he noticed George and Toby Saxton coming his way.

"Hank," George set a large backpack at his feet. "I need to apologize to you."

Toby remained slightly behind her husband.

"With all we've been through I can't let it end this way," George extended his hand.

"George, this never would have ended our friendship," Hank took George's hand and looked at their belongings. "Looks like you have made a decision?"

"Now that we know where we are going, we figure it will take us a day and a half to reach Franktown south of Parker."

"We are not going to find a warmer day then this," said Toby.

"I wish we had more information on what is happening in the city before you leave. It might be total chaos by now." Hank was genuinely concerned about his friend.

"I'll be honest. I'm a little worried why Ted hasn't contacted us with some sort of update," Jon interjected.

"The young lady we spoke with at the Browns told us her family found it dangerous enough in Aurora to make the journey east." Hank knew his connotation about the people who left the city was meaningless. George and the others were planning to leave and had already disassociated themselves with everyone at the farm. "I know you are dead set on leaving, so let me see if we can't figure a way to get you at least part of the way there."

"No, Hank, I'm not putting you in a situation where you could lose one of the vehicles here at the farm. We are completely prepared for the journey and want to make amends with you before we go."

"We want to part ways as friends," said Toby.

Hank looked at George's big, hook nose and felt a terrible sense of loss. "We will always be friends. You can come back if things don't work out. I'm serious about that George. You can always come back," he reached over and gave Toby a hug. The others in George's group gathered behind them.

"Hopefully, we will see you back in Littleton." George picked up his backpack and led the group away.

Hank and Jon watched them as they walked briskly down the driveway to the county road.

"There goes a quarter of our people," said Jon.

"Jacqueline and I were talking about that last night. That leaves us with thirty-one adults and the six kids," Hank replied. "The good thing is that we have a group of people who are efficient and know how to get things done."

"Case in point," Jon stared at the masonry crew. "How high are they taking that tower?"

"I guess they are going three stories." Hank turned as he heard horses approaching. Breanna on a beautiful Bay with a white blaze running down his face rode up next to the two men. Avery on a dappled white horse with a dark mane and tail came next, followed by Reagan on a large chestnut horse. Both girls looked small on their giant steeds.

"How far does our property go to the east?" Breanna asked as she pulled back exceedingly hard on the rein to her horse.

"I have no idea Breanna," stated Hank. He looked. His brother shrugged his shoulders.

"I rode out there yesterday. There was no fence," Brenna patted the side of her horse's neck. "I guess me, and the girls will go on an adventure and see if we can find the property line."

"Are you enjoying riding the horses?" Hank looked at Avery and Reagan as they smiled while steadying their mounts.

"Yes," said Avery, holding the reins with her bandaged hand.

"Breanna is a good teacher," stated Reagan. "We are going to gallop the horses today."

Hank thought how odd Breanna had seemed the first time they met. Her constant talking and opinionated views were just her exterior. On the inside she was a caring person who would be there during bad circumstances.

"I agree with you, she is definitely an accomplished horse woman." Jon smiled at Breanna, "I sure couldn't keep up with her on a horse."

"You did pretty good for a city guy," said Breanna smiling.

"How long are you going to be gone? Jon asked.

"We will be back within the hour."

"I want to have everyone meet right after lunch."

"I'll let Mom and Dad know." Breanna looked at Avery and Reagan than nudged the side of her horse. "We couldn't have asked for better weather for a ride. Come on girls."

***

Hank and Jon decided to have the meeting, with the remaining occupants of the farm, on the driveway in front of the Jacoby's motorhome. Ed was having more and more difficulty walking. Although Irene was as mobile as ever, she found herself spending an exorbitant amount of time playing cards with her husband in the confines of the RV.

Bill, Samantha, Maddy and Scotty carried folding chairs to the location. It was nearly one o'clock when the final group of Harold, Bobby, Emilee and Sherry made their way to the gathering.

"Sorry for taking so long. We had to finish using the mortar," stated Harold, taking a seat next to Becky.

"It is really impressive how fast the tower is being built." Jacqueline looked at Harold and then fixed her eyes on her son and his two friends. Their clothes were covered in cement and all three had blotches of cement on their faces.

"The apartment progress is amazing too." Gina glanced at Kori to make sure she knew how much everyone appreciated Jason's carpentry skills.

"Thanks to Terrance and Jerry we only need a couple more hours to have the rough electrical wiring pulled for the first half of the building," stated Jason proudly. "Tomorrow, while we still have good weather, we are going to start roofing the final half of the structure."

"I guess everyone knows by now that Coach Saxton and his group left earlier this morning." Hank took a position in front of the crowd.

"Why did he leave?" Al asked apprehensively. "Linda and I were discussing their going. Do they know something we don't?"

"No, they don't. Actually, they have no idea what sort of situation they are returning to in the city." Hank was a bit put off by Al trying to create conflict.

"Could it be that they are correct that things are not so bad in the city?" Al looked at the others. "I know the country is being threatened at the borders, but it might not be as treacherous back home in Littleton."

"Ever since Ted left, Bill and Samantha have been at the radio trying to get information. The news we have received over the radio doesn't give us an accurate description of what is happening in the city. We know it is bad. To what degree we don't know," stated Nicole.

"I guess what I'm saying," Al hesitated for a moment. "Before we put so much into creating a place to live here it would be helpful to know the condition back home."

Hank looked at Jon in search for a reply. Before Jon could respond Ed stood up.

"I know we are not going back to Utah for quite some time," Ed spoke softly, almost too low for everyone to hear. "Why not work to make this place better. It doesn't matter if we leave tomorrow, or we are here a year from now. Colonel Lisco created this place to help others, not for herself. We should all respect that."

"We need to get the hay from the Brown's ranch." Aaron wasn't about to deal with the frivolity of whether to make the farm a better place. "If we can take the backhoe to the creek and make a dirt bridge so we can cross with the tractor and trailer, it will save us about ten kilometers a trip."

"Do you need help with that?" Jon asked.

"No, me and Adam can take care of it."

"I agree with what everybody is saying," said Al emphatically, ignoring the Jacobys thoughts on making the farm more efficient. "We should still find a way to stay informed. To keep abreast of what is happening."

"How do you suggest we do that Al?" Jon asked.

"We could go to Limon and speak with the people who recently arrived from the city. With the apartment progressing so well it might be a good time to find more people." Al glanced at the others.

"I volunteer to go," Bill stepped forward. He looked at Samantha.

"I'll go with him," said Samantha.

"I'll go too," yelled Terrance.

"Me too," Linda surprised everyone, including her husband. Al stared at her with his mouth wide open.

"Is everyone good with going tomorrow morning?" Hank asked.

Everyone answered in the affirmative.

"One last thing," said Jacqueline. "We are going to bury the Browns this afternoon for anyone who wants to attend."

Great Falls, Montana

With the clouds completely dissipated, the sunset glittering over the Montana landscape was stunning. Deb hesitated outside the mess tent to take in the beauty. She hadn't had a bite to eat the entire day, so the aroma of freshly baked bread was invigorating.

After retrieving her food, she joined Lieutenant Colonels Barnet and Wilson at the back of the pavilion.

"Colonel, it's good to see you all in one piece." Lt. Col. Wilson smiled at Deb as she took a seat. "I guess our information about you being on your death bed was a bit exaggerated. You just missed Tommy. He was summoned to the communication tent."

"I'm still kicking," Deb looked back and forth between her two friends.

"What happened out there today?" Teresa looked at the colonel with wide, saggy eyes.

"We shook a hornet's nest." Deb lowered her eyes and continued eating. She could feel her heart racing.

"Colonel," Tommy took two steps into the tent. "General Lauer wants to speak with you."

"Looks like a change of plans." She stood up and tossed her napkin on her food and followed Tommy out of the mess tent toward communications.

General Lauer was standing to the side, with only a part of his back visible on the screen. When his face did come into view Deb was surprised at how tired and haggard he looked.

"Colonel, you are to move with 1st and 3rd Battalions for southern Utah tomorrow morning via Interstate 15."

"What about 2nd Battalion?"

"They are to stay in Great Falls and assist General Prost with the warehouse situation."

"General Prost?" Deb looked at Tommy. He shrugged his shoulders. "Is she part of the combat engineer team working on the extraction?"

"No, she will be supervising cyber. She arrived in Fort Carson last night with General McClinton and left this afternoon after hearing about the incident at the warehouse." The general's voice was almost monotonous as he gave her the surprising news, "She should be there now."

"Anything else?"

"Specific orders will be relayed on your journey in the morning." She was preparing to ask about Ted when the general disappeared from the screen.

Deb took a couple steps away from the monitor and stared at the Command Sergeant Major. "What is that mousey little bitch doing here?"

"I take it you have a past with her?" Tommy lowered his chin and stared at the colonel.

"She was at a meeting I, along with Ted and Jon, had with General McClinton a couple of years ago. She was a total pain in the ass."

"Colonel Lisco," a tech specialist interrupted. "General Prost wants to speak with you."

Deb forced a smile as she followed the specialist to his monitor.

"Colonel Lisco," the general's face seemed different from two years earlier. It seemed fuller. "I'm hoping I can meet with you, in person, this evening."

"Yes, certainly ma'am." Deb tried not to flounder with the unexpected request. She turned to Tommy and rolled her eyes, trying to convey her desire for him to make an excuse. "Command Sergeant Major is this a good time, I mean, are we all caught up with preparation for departure tomorrow?"

"Right now, is as good a time as any," Tommy smiled at Deb.

"I'm ten minutes from your location," stated the general.

"Have the sentry direct you to the officer's tent. I'll meet you there," Deb said. As soon as the general went off the screen she chuckled, "This will be interesting, and by the way thanks a lot."

The lighting at the center of the empty officer's tent was bright, with a darkness around the outer edges, closer to the walls. Of the four tables, Deb chose the one farthest away from the door. She sat and waited in utter confusion for the arrival of General Prost, remembering how different their personalities and viewpoints were during their first face to face meeting over two years earlier.

General Prost entered the tent and looked Deb directly in the eyes, and continued to do so, as she quickly walked across the room. She held out her hand and said, "Colonel Lisco, I'm glad you are available this evening."

Deb stood up and took her hand. "Would you like something to drink ma'am?"

"No thank-you," before sitting down the general removed her coat and placed it on an empty chair. After sitting she leaned forward and confidently engaged Deb with her eyes. "I'm sure you wonder why I want to meet this evening."

"Yes ma'am. I guess I do wonder," Deb fidgeted in her seat. She was intimidated by the general continuing to stare directly into her eyes.

"I was scheduled to be in Calgary tonight, but I flew from Virginia to Fort Carson this morning with General McClinton. We had a good talk on the trip that, amongst other things, included recollecting the meeting we had with you and your brothers nearly two years ago."

Deb felt somewhat unsettled in the presence of her diminutive superior. She sat straight in the chair, placed her prominent chin out and listened intently as the general continued.

"When we heard about the warehouse, General McClinton asked me to head the team from cyber command during the excavation."

"Something tells me you are going to find a hell of a lot of information at the bottom of that building."

"We believe so too," the general declared. "But that is not the only reason I wanted to take this opportunity to meet with you in person."

Deb cocked her head, "What might that be ma'am?"

"You were right Colonel. You were correct in almost every aspect that you warned us about in the meeting at the Pentagon. We blew it off," General Prost raised her voice. "The situation the country is facing wouldn't be nearly as dire if we had listened to you. I want to let you know how much I regret not investigating more deeply into your concerns."

"General, I misjudged you too. I wasn't entirely correct at that meeting. When you told me that the days of brigade versus brigade warfare were over, I miscalculated the value of your knowledge and experience." She swallowed hard. "Today when I witnessed the high-speed lasers and the power of our own rockets, I realized this war will be much different than any before."

"This is a war that will have decisions made by machines far away from the battlefield. I hope we, as a country, can counter the technological aspects of our enemies. The entire scenario we are facing at this time has come about from models they created from hundreds of thousands of simulations. Artificial intelligence has morphed into not only making the decisions but enforcing them. It's really frightening." The general wrinkled her nose and squinted her eyes, "But Colonel Lisco, the one calculation I think they are missing is that all great leaders have an instinct unavailable to a machine."

"What do you expect to find at the warehouse, ma'am?"

"I expect there to be a cache of information," General Prost inhaled deeply. "Since the place has been there for years, we should find not only information about weapons, but plenty of hard data on the embedded forces throughout the country."

"More information for the machines to create more models," Deb smiled.

"Exactly," she smiled back.

Having someone as knowledgeable as the general discuss strategy and tactics was uplifting to Deb. It was something she relished doing with her father when he was still alive. General Prost was able to give her a better perspective on not only the danger they were to face in the combat zones but also from the ones within the ranks. The compelling discussion covered nearly all topics Deb could think of that might help make her a better leader.

As the conversation ran its course Deb's opinion of the lady was completely changed. She took a moment to think how fortunate she was to converse on equal terms with such a brilliant trail blazer as General Prost. She took in a deep breath and asked, "Can I get you something to drink now, ma'am?"

The general placed her small hands flat on the table. "How about a scotch? On the rocks."

Deb cocked her head back. She knew exactly where the scotch was located. "Two scotches it is."

"I didn't see him. But I know your brother is back at Fort Carson," the general remained seated and spoke loudly as Deb fussed around the bar.

"I'm going to try and contact him sometime tomorrow while we are moving." She placed two large glasses of scotch over ice cubes on the table. "Would you like something to eat ma'am?"

"No, I'm good," she took a drink. "Please, call me Ann. We don't need to be so formal while we are having a drink."

"Certainly, feel free to call me Deb." She took a drink of the scotch whisky. The warm sensation of the liquor flowing down her throat and caused her shoulders to relax. "That is so good."

"The Lisco family has such an interesting history with the Army," Ann stated congenially, obviously feeling the same calming sensation. "Was it your great grandfather who fought in the Battle of the Bulge?"

"Actually, it was my grandfather. He and my father both had children later in life."

Both women were drinking their libations at a quickened pace. As soon as their glasses were empty, Deb went to the bar and returned with the bottle and filled them to the top.

"Ann, umm where did you grow up?" Deb opened and closed her mouth. Her jaw felt a little numb.

"Massachusetts."

"Were your family in the military?"

"My aunt was."

They both drank and told stories neither would remember, not to outdo one another, but to be amiable. Both women were feeling no pain as Deb filled the general's glass and then poured the remainder of the bottle of scotch into hers.

"Looks like we drank the whole damn bottle," Deb laughed loudly, slamming the bottle to the table.

"I am delighted we had a chance to spend this time together." Ann was speaking loudly as she lifted the glass to her thin lips and swallowed the last of her drink. Her head was moving in a circular motion. "But now that we know each other so well, I have to come completely clean. I made some disparaging remarks about you a couple of days after your meeting with General McClinton. I want to make amends, right now." She put her right hand up by her ear, then slammed it down hard on the table as she stood up.

"What did you say?" Deb was slumping and leaning in her chair.

Ann stared blankly through blood-shot eyes, then stuck her chin way out in front of her and said, "Look at me. Look at me, I'm colonel know-it-all." She relaxed back in her chair and said, "I'm sorry."

Deb started laughing. Pretty soon they were both laughing loudly.

"Ok, ok I have to admit that I have said disparaging words about you too, Ann." Deb tried to focus her eyes.

"What did you shay?" Ann slurred.

Deb tried to open her eyes wide as she moved forward in her chair and pronounced her words slowly and clearly, "Well, I called you a mousey, little bitch."

"When did you do that?"

Deb's head was bobbling slightly as she answered, "This afternoon."

They both burst out laughing.

Tommy rushed into the tent, followed closely by another soldier.

"Colonel, the entire encampment can hear you."

Deb's upper body felt numb as she stared vacantly at the command sergeant major.

"Let me help you to your quarters. The corporal can assist General Prost." The command sergeant major lifted her out of the chair.

"Tommy, that is Ann," she pointed her left index finger in the direction of the ceiling.

"Please ma'am," Tommy whispered. "You really can't afford being charged with another conduct unbecoming an officer."

"General Prost, it was a pleasure meeting with you this evening." Deb wobbled. "Tommy, this is what happens when you stay up all night drinking."

"Come on," he directed her to the door, "it's not even 2100 yet."

"I would appreciate it if you can assist me to my quarters," she spoke softly as she leaned on Tommy's arm. "I don't want another officer unbecoming the conduct charge."

In all the years serving with Colonel Lisco it was the first time Tommy had seen her totally intoxicated. He knew she was aware of the consequences of being drunk and disorderly on base. There was much more to her making the decision to get plastered with General Prost than was on the surface.

Limon, Colorado

Bill steered cautiously over the wet dirt roads in the new car he helped Deb pick out less than a year earlier. Terrance was sitting shotgun with Samantha and Linda riding in the back seat of the spacious automobile. When they reached the frontage road that ran parallel to Interstate 70, he stopped the vehicle. There were several abandoned cars and trucks visible on the highway. They arrived at an exit ramp that would allow them to enter onto the freeway but chose to travel along the frontage road.

Approaching the small town, they crested a large hill where they could see a massive amount of people confined to an area that spanned the road. Orange colored, sand filled, fifty-gallon barrels traversed the pavement in front of a tall fence where people could be seen beyond the enclosure. They stopped the car about four hundred meters from the barricade.

"Any ideas how to approach this?" Bill continued to look in the direction of the compound.

"For one thing I want to make damn sure nobody takes this car," stated Terrance. "I don't want to have to walk all the way back."

"How about if Samantha and I go and check," Linda smiled and nodded at Samantha. "What do you think?"

"Well…," Samantha wavered.

"We go in and ask some questions and come back out," said Linda, opening the door.

"Why not," Samantha chuckled nervously and stepped out without any more discussion.

"Just a second," Bill hurried out the door and moved close to Samantha. "If something seems wrong, don't take any chances, come back and we can re-evaluate."

"Do either of you want to take a weapon?" Terrance held a pistol out in front of him.

"This is why it will be better for us to go rather than either of you," said Linda confidently. "We are not threatening to anyone."

A cool breeze blew at their back while the two women walked down the black-top. When they were within twenty meters of the sand barrels four figures became visible. They stopped ten meters short of the barricade and spoke with the guards for nearly five minutes before advancing into the community.

Terrance opened the trunk of the car and retrieved his AK 47. He hid it in a coat so as not to take a chance of provoking someone into thinking he was a threat. Both men waited anxiously as the women remained out of sight for over three hours.

"Did we make a mistake here?" Bill asked. "We should have been more specific about having them check back within a certain amount of time."

"You would think they would have figured we would be worried," said Terrance.

"I don't see any place where we could get a better vantage point to look inside the encampment."

"Hell Bill, that wouldn't do us any good. There are thousands of people scattered for God knows how far," Terrance rubbed his chin.

"None of this makes any sense," said Bill. "The people we found inside the Brown's farmhouse never did show up at the farm. I would sure like to talk with them about this place."

"The guards here don't look like police or National Guard," stated Terrance.

"I'm going to go and talk with them."

Terrance wavered for a moment as he stared at Bill's facial features. His high cheek bones and pronounced chin were the same as his father. He remembered Ted's intensity when faced with duress. He could see the same strength now in the son. He responded, "Sounds better than just sitting around."

Bill walked quickly. A man and three women greeted him as he approached the roadblock. All four were slight of build and dressed in matching shirts.

One of the women held up her hand indicating for Bill to stop.

"We have some questions you need to answer before going any further."

"I only want to find out about the two women who came through here about three hours ago." Bill tried to be as amicable as possible. He could see a two-meter-high wire fence about fifty meters past the roadblock.

"Have you been sick or around anyone who is sick within the last thirty days?"

"No, I'm healthy and I haven't been around any sick people." Bill decided it would be better to answer the questions than to cause a fuss.

"Do you have any weapons?"

"No," he felt the holster rub the back of his upper hip. "I don't want to enter your communal, or whatever it is. I just want to find out about the safety of the two women who just entered."

"Is that your car on the top of the hill?"

"Yes ma'am." He noticed all four of them had holstered pistols. "What does that have to do with me wanting to find out about my friends?"

"Both women went to registration," said one of the sentries.

"How long would it take them to register?" Bill noticed a small, red insignia at the upper left of each of the guard's shirts that read FEMA.

"They are backed up, so I would guess most of the afternoon."

"Well," Bill scoffed. He placed his hands up in the air in frustration and looked back in the direction of Terrance. "Could you have someone go and get them for me?"

"You can follow us."

"I don't want to enter," Bill glanced at the gate in the distance behind the sentries. Samantha was tossing her hands and yelling as she pushed the gate open. She walked quickly toward him.

Bill watched her stomp his way until she was five meters away. "Where's Linda?" he yelled.

"They placed her in quarantine," Samantha could not stop prancing as she inhaled deeply. "They literally drug her away."

"We need you to go inside and find our friend, right now." Bill looked deeply into the eyes of the woman guard closest to him.

"If she went to quarantine, she can't come out for seven days."

"Here comes Terrance," Samantha had her back to the guards as she looked down the highway.

Terrance was driving slowly toward them. Three guards from the fenced area moved through the gate and jogged toward the roadblock.

"Sir," said the first guard to arrive, "we are going to confiscate your automobile. By executive order signed by the President of the United States we have the right to take and use any item necessary for the betterment and advancement of the common good of society. Your car falls into the realm of this order."

"The hell you are," said Bill with exasperation.

"We have the full power of the United States government to seize your vehicle."

"I don't care who you are, you sure as hell can't have this car." Bill reached around and grabbed his pistol. He pointed at the head of the closest guard. Terrance leaped from the driver's seat and moved to the front of the car with his AK 47 at the ready. Samantha quickly climbed into the back seat. Terrance waited for Bill to be in the driver's seat before jumping inside. They sped about two kilometers up the frontage road before stopping to contemplate their options in rescuing Linda.

None of the guards had unholstered their weapons. When they saw the weapons aimed at them, they placed their arms over their heads and retreated behind the sand filled barrels.

Colorado Farm

Bill slowly maneuvered the car down the driveway to the farm. After much calculation and some debate, they made the decision to return without Linda. Explaining to Al that his wife was in quarantine at the camp was not something any of them were looking forward to.

It was a beautiful day with the temperature well above freezing. It was the warmest day since arriving at the farm. Hank and Jacqueline, sitting on the front porch, were the first to notice the car coming down the driveway. Nicole and Maddy were the first to arrive to greet Bill. Soon the car was surrounded by a crowd.

"Where's Linda?" Jacqueline asked quizzically as the three vacated the car.

"She is still at the compound," Bill looked at Hank. "It's a FEMA run camp and they quarantined her."

Hank looked over his shoulder toward the house. Al was hurrying down the driveway, where he stopped about three meters from the main body of people.

"Where's Linda?" he took in several deep breaths with his mouth partially open.

"Al, she was quarantined at the camp in Limon," said Bill. "They wouldn't release her."

"So, you left her there?" Al's upper lip was twisted. "Why would they quarantine her?"

"Her temperature was over a hundred," Samantha took one step in the direction of Al. "And she had a bad rash on the inside of her right arm."

"She had a rash on her arm from cleaning things around here with cheap soap." Al puffed his chest out and pointed to the car. "Now get back in and let's go get her."

"I argued with them for an hour trying to get her discharged," said Samantha.

"Maybe you should have argued for two hours, or three."

"I went to find Bill to help, but the guards at the gate threatened to take the car." Samantha looked at Bill, "So, we took off before they could take it."

"You left her behind so you could save the car." Al slapped his hand hard on the hood. "Of all the stupid things I have done in my life, coming to this place has to top them all."

"Let's figure this out," said Hank. "Just calm down for a second Al."

"Fuck you Hank. If that were Jacqueline they left behind, I'm sure you wouldn't be so condescending. Now get in the car. I'm not leaving her there all night."

"If you drive there in the dark, they will see the lights of this car and seize it," stated Terrance firmly.

"I don't give a shit if they take every vehicle here. Did you two try to stop them from taking her?" Al was breathing heavily as he looked back and forth between Bill and Terrance.

"Samantha and Linda went inside the compound while we waited outside," Bill inhaled deeply. "Like Samantha said she tried her best to get them to release her."

"So, you two big brave guys sent my wife into a dangerous situation with this bimbo." Al licked his lips and shook his head up and down.

There was complete silence. Bill's heart was pounding the walls of his chest as he moved his nose a couple of centimeters from Al's nose. Hank moved closer to the two of them.

"You have one chance and one chance only to apologize to her," Bill towered over the dentist. He held his finger right under Al's chin. "I mean right now."

Al didn't say a word, as he stood his ground. Hank placed a hand between the two men.

"It's alright Bill, calm down here."

"It was Linda's idea for the two of them to go alone. Samantha was the brave one in this whole ordeal," said Bill angrily, pointing at Al. "I won't sit back and allow you to call her names."

"Did you say it was a government compound?" Ed asked, limping forward to the center of the crowd. "I'm sure they have strict rules but at least they are responding to this mess. Why don't we sleep on it tonight and go back in the morning?"

"Terrance was right about them taking the car." Bill glanced at Samantha as he moved next to her. "The guards told us that the President signed an executive order stating they can take anything that is necessary for the betterment of society."

"That's all the more reason we should go talk with them before they come here and take all our livestock," said Jon. "I'm willing to go in the morning and speak with whoever is in charge to see about them releasing Linda. Also, to see if we can make a deal with us supplying beef for protection."

"That was exactly my thought too," said Ed.

Al looked menacingly at the entire crowd before stomping in the direction of the house.

Hank thought how his good friend and neighbor's Napoleon Complex was brought out into the open for all to see. He chuckled to himself when he thought about Linda being held in quarantine at the FEMA compound. The only time in her entire life that she took a chance and now she was missing. He knew her well enough to know she was happy to have a change of pace. As far as Al calling Samantha a bimbo, that would take some mending for the relationship between the dentist and Bill to ever become amicable. Samantha did not seem to be distraught in the least from the remark.

Fort Carson Army Base

Ted reached the departure location on the western edge of the base just as Lieutenant Hanson of Company E, 2nd Platoon arrived. He had a large smile on his face as he escorted Jessica.

"Sir," he saluted, "Colonel Murphy requested I personally escort Ms. Jessica O'Brian to your location."

Ted saluted the lieutenant, "I'm ready to leave immediately." Jessica remained silent as she stepped in front of Ted.

"Did you arrive last night?" Ted noticed Jessica's hair, pulled back in a ponytail, looked freshly washed. All she was carrying was a small duffle bag.

"Yes, I slept in a guest apartment," she spoke with an Irish accent while staring at Ted for several seconds with her bright blue eyes. "Thank-you, it was more than adequate."

"Is this all your gear?" he sensed she was nervous as he stared at the duffle bag.

"That's it, I didn't take much when I left." Ted's easy disposition gave her cause to relax. She looked at the vehicle Ted was standing nearby. "Are we riding in this truck?"

"This is a XM 4400 Electric Survivable Combat Tactical Vehicle." Ted smiled warmly as he looked closely at Jessica's face. With her hair pulled back she looked young. Nicole told him how enamored Bill was with her, now he could see why. With her high cheek bones and bright red hair, she was a beautiful woman. His wife also told him about her leaving behind her children, so he planned on finding out all about Jessica O'Brian on the trip to the farm.

"Sir, we are ready to go when you are," said Lieutenant Hanson.

"Let's go," Ted opened the door to the tactical vehicle and allowed Jessica to enter the back seat. He followed her inside.

After several minutes of small talk as the platoon made its way into the countryside Ted decided to break the ice about Jessica's children.

"Are you worried about how your children are going to react to you going back to the farm?"

She stared at him for a moment, then lowered her gaze. There was wetness in the corner of her eyes.

"Have you thought about what you are going to tell everyone?" Ted continued without receiving an answer.

"Not really," she whispered. "I just want to be with my girls again."

"Why did you leave?"

"I guess because for all my life I have been strapped down with something or another. I had a chance to leave and be free," she sighed, "I took it."

"I take it, you now regret the decision?" Ted stared at her as she continued to look away. Colonel Murphy told him that she was helpful in giving information about the movement of Christian's rebels, and now he wanted to help her. "Can I give you some advice?"

"Of course."

"Don't be the victim."

"I don't think I am."

"Your daughters deserve to have a mother who can admit a mistake." Ted thought for a moment, "The others at the farm will be more likely to accept you if you don't make excuses."

Jessica stared at him for a moment. It was completely against her nature to submit. But Emilee's relationship with Bobby complicated the need to be accepted by the Lisco family.

"What I'm trying to tell you, is that at this time, there is less tolerance being given for bad decisions. With all the unknowns with the war, everyone is scared and confused."

"I've been that way my entire life." Jessica raised her eyebrow and slanted her head toward the colonel.

"I don't doubt you have gotten the short end of the stick on many occasions." He could see why his son had become so enamored with the woman. She had a toughness that could easily be taken for confidence. "I hope you will take my advice and show vulnerability without complaining. Take responsibility for your actions."

"I'm tired," she took in a deep breath and relinquished it. "When we get to the farm, I will try my best to not blame others for my mistakes."

"I know my family," Ted gave her a reassuring smile. "They are willing to forgive."

"I hope they will," she smiled softly as she lowered her chin.

Ted knew he had reached the point where any more advice would be counterproductive. He wondered how Bill and Samantha's relationship was developing. Before duty required him to leave so quickly the flight attendant and his son seemed to be getting along quite well. But, according to Nicole, before Jessica left the farm, Bill was under the assumption that he and the beautiful Irish lady were a couple. It would all be an interesting scene when Jessica showed up unannounced.

"Sir," said the private driving the vehicle. "There are cars blocking the road ahead."

Ted leaned forward to look out the windshield. "Wait for the lieutenant to handle the situation."

Lieutenant Hanson had the infantry soldiers exit the vehicles and fan out on both sides of the convoy, as he and two privates approached the roadblock. A Humvee was blocking the view to the area, so Ted stepped outside the safe confines of his tactical vehicle. "Stay here," he said to Jessica before closing the door. He advanced to the area nearly twenty meters from the cars blocking the road where the lieutenant was speaking to a group of five people. Behind the cars of the barricade there were between thirty and forty more people pointing their weapons in his direction. The soldiers of the platoon were spaced on both sides of the road.

"Sir, they say they are members of the farming community," said the lieutenant. "I asked them to move the cars so we can proceed."

The three men and two women speaking with the lieutenant were all dressed in black. Ted looked past them to the others standing behind the cars. They all wore the same black clothing.

"Lieutenant, bring the Nyalas up to this location." Ted looked directly at the people the lieutenant was speaking with. He didn't say a word to them as Lieutenant Hanson spoke into his radio. Two RG-35 Nyalas with manned open-air 0.50 caliber heavy machine guns pulled within two meters on each side of the group.

"Now," Ted looked directly at the rebels in front of him. "Tell us who you really are."

"We are farmers."

"I don't think so.'

"We work for the farmers."

"Who hired you," Ted realized they were within thirty kilometers of Deb's farm, and he might recognize the name of a farmer.

"All of them did," said one of the women.

"Right," Ted scoffed. "I don't know who you are, but I want this roadblock out of our way."

A powerful gust of wind blew into the agitator's face before they turned and walked back to the roadblock. Within a minute the cars pulled to the side of the road. It was disconcerting to Ted as he looked out the window of the tactical vehicle. The rebels brazenly stared at the convoy of soldiers as they quickly passed through their blockade.

Limon, Colorado

Hank drove the Jacoby's antique, Ford F-250 right up to the sand filled barrels blocking the entrance to the FEMA camp. It was predetermined that they would let Jon and Jacqueline out at the outpost and Hank would drive the truck back a kilometer to the west and wait for them to take care of business inside the compound.

The air was crisp, and the morning sun was peeking over the top of the wire fencing on the back side of the barricade. Jacqueline pulled the wide lapel of her pea coat tightly around her neck and followed slightly behind her brother-in-law as he confidently gauged the lone sentry waiting at the roadblock. Jon wore a trench coat which gave him an aura of intrigue.

"Can you tell the head of the incident management assistance team that Lieutenant Colonel Jon Lisco requests a meeting," Jon spoke first. He was cleanly shaven, and his hair was neatly combed.

"FEMA headquarters is located on the northern edge of the compound in the town." The guard was an older lady, "You can get there through the compound."

"Are you with FEMA?" Jon asked authoritatively.

"Since Monday," her approach was good-natured. "Last week I was the town librarian. FEMA hired several people from the area to help with all the travelers stranded here, so I guess you could say I am with them."

"I need to speak with whoever is in charge. Could you please call ahead and inform them we are on our way?"

She spoke into a radio as Jon and Jacqueline waited patiently. She finally lowered the radio.

"Go to the gate and one of the guards there will take you to the operations center." She pointed to the gate at the tall fence about fifty meters to the east.

The people inside the compound were wandering around the grounds like a flock of ducks trying to find a morsel of food in a large lake. Jon and Jacqueline walked briskly through the mass of lost souls for nearly twenty minutes before arriving at a gate on the northern fence line separating the throng of travelers from the citizens of the town of Limon. They continued past the guards at the gate and walked to a dilapidated hotel about a hundred meters south of Interstate 70.

After entering the atrium of the hotel, the guard stopped and pointed in the direction of an old man with chalk white hair.

"That's Deputy Director Garrett. He should be able to help you." The guard quickly turned and exited.

"Sir," Jon said loudly as he approached the deputy. "Can I have a moment of your time?"

"What do you want?" The deputy director asked curtly without looking at Jon. He continued shuffling papers on a desk.

"My name is Lieutenant Colonel Jon Lisco." Jon could tell the guy was a real hard ass. "I would like to speak about a proposition I can offer that will get some beef to this location."

"Retired?" The deputy raised an eyebrow and glanced at Jon. "I take it you are retired. Anyway, we have a team already appropriating cattle from the area ranches."

Jon stared at the man for a moment. He knew immediately he should discontinue speaking about the situation at the farm with the man who was obviously former military. Appropriating meant he was seizing the property of others.

"Where is the ranch you are speaking of?" the deputy stood up tall. He was several centimeters taller than Jon. When Jon failed to respond he said, "Sir."

"Several ranches north of here, by Last Chance." Jon looked at Jacqueline to see how she would respond to his blatant lie.

"We are overwhelmed right now and would appreciate any help we can get." The man sniffled and wiped his nose with the back of his left hand. It was almost as cold inside the lobby as it was outside. "We have never experienced a disaster of this magnitude. The only way to survive here is for local people to step up and help."

"Are you going to be able to keep up with feeding all these people?"

"We probably can here but it will affect the others in the Denver area." The man-made eye contact with Jon. "This is the eastern border of FEMA's region 8. More than seventy-five percent of deliveries to the region by truck from the east come through here, so we have first chance to replenish our supplies. To be honest, transportation is a bigger issue right now.

Although the cities east of the Mississippi are disrupted it is not the same degree of chaos we are experiencing in our metropolitan zones."

"Transportation?" Jon looked at him skeptically. He thought about it for a moment. "Of course, there wouldn't be a problem if the people weren't here."

"Exactly, we have had five different electromagnetic pulse incidents in the last week. Most of the people are stranded because their vehicles have been disabled. Some have walked over eighty kilometers to get here. The town of Limon had a population of six thousand three weeks ago, now there are four times that amount."

"Have you been briefed on the EMP weapon that is being used by the insurgents?"

"No, but we know it is small enough to hide quickly after it's employed. You would think it would be easy to catch the people responsible in a town this size, but local law enforcement has no idea who they are. The flash of light is so intense that it is hard to find the exact location it was fired from. The sheriff here calls them magicians because they disappear into thin air immediately after discharging the weapon."

Jon glanced at Jacqueline, "Linda," she mouthed. He nodded that he had not forgotten.

"I would like to come back in a couple of days and assist you with finding these rebels," Jon spoke convincingly. "I have some familiarity with the EMP weapon."

"I'm sure the sheriff would accept any help he can get. Mechanics are ready to work on the cars as soon as we stop the EMPs."

"Also, we have a friend of ours quarantined at your medical facility who we would like to have released to us."

"Are you taking her out of the facility?"

"Yes sir."

"Inform the sentry at the gate that Deputy Director Garrett gave permission to release your friend. If there is any problem, have them radio me," the deputy looked sternly at Jon.

"Thank you, sir," Jon motioned to Jacqueline that it was time to go retrieve Linda.

Upon hearing the deputy director gave verbal permission for releasing Linda, the guard at the gate to the quarantine area was more than willing to set her free. It took less than ten minutes before Jacqueline and Jon saw her hurrying in their direction. Her hair was disheveled, and there were bags under her eyes, but she smiled when she noticed Jacqueline.

"Hello neighbor," Jacqueline gave her a hug as she exited the gate.

"Oh my God," Linda chuckled, "what an experience."

"Well, you are out now," stated Jacqueline.

"Thank God," Linda seemed in good spirits. "I take it Samantha made it back?"

"Yes, Al didn't take it very well when they showed up without you last night."

"I can only imagine," Linda scoffed.

"You'll hear all about it when we get back to the farm," Jacqueline glanced at Jon.

"Samantha was so good when they took me into quarantine. She screamed and yelled at them, and she actually slugged one of the guards," Linda laughed out loud.

"You'll have to give her a hug and thank her when you get back," said Jon knowingly.

"I will do that," replied Linda.

"Hank is waiting in the Jacoby's pick-up, so it's going to be a little crowded on the way back." Jacqueline grinned, "We are going to have a lot to discuss."

"Lieutenant Colonel Lisco," a voice resonated from the crowd.

All three turned to locate the person yelling at Jon.

"Sir, it's Captain Huang," A short, stocky middle-aged man yelled from about ten meters away. He was wearing a short-sleeved khaki shirt that embellished his large biceps.

"I'll be damn. Irving Huang," Jon said. The captain was a soldier he had thought about on several occasions since his retirement. "What are you doing here?"

"My parents and I left Arvada for my aunt's home in Nashville. We were about three kilometers east of here on Interstate 70 when we were hit by an EMP. It completely fried the engine." He shook his head, "I thought you were in Texas?"

"It's a long story. We came here to watch a football game and were stranded too." Jon motioned with his arm toward the two women. "Irving, this is my sister-in-law Jacqueline Lisco and a neighbor of hers, Linda Jones."

The captain was a small man in stature but the confidence he exhumed gave him a large presence. Both women could tell that Jon considered him to be someone special.

"Irving was captain of Company K, which was part of my battalion before I retired," stated Jon.

"How long have you been at this compound?" Irving asked.

"We aren't staying here. We are at a farm about forty kilometers to the south." Jon thought for a moment, "There is plenty of room if you and your parents would like to come with us."

"My mom would definitely like to get out of this place." The captain clenched his jaw, "But our car is still on Interstate 70. I wouldn't want to leave it."

"The rebels responsible for firing the EMP weapon have to be found before the mechanics, here in town, can even begin to work on the cars. With the availability of parts and time to repair them, most vehicles will never be fixed," Jon declared. "You might be stranded here for quite some time."

"Can we pull their car to the farm with the pick-up?" Jacqueline asked. "Jerry and Terrance might be able to fix it."

"I think this would be a very good choice for you Irving." Jon turned his head as a gust of wind hit him square in the face. "I have met your parents, but I can't remember their names."

"Mom is Li Na and my dad's name is Shen." The captain took a moment to glance at trash swirling around the compound. "Why not, if you are sure there is room for us."

"There are already more than thirty people at the farm, and room for many more," said Jacqueline.

"You know my sister, Colonel Deb Lisco. The farm is her place."

"Of course, I do. I will pack up my parents and meet you back here in thirty minutes," he walked quickly away.

"We should use the restroom," said Linda to Jacqueline, pointing at a line of port-a-potty toilets. "You have to see just how disgusting it is. I promise, I won't complain about the conditions on the farm again."

***

The wind was blowing at a constant rate of over thirty kilometers an hour as Hank pulled the pick-up to the Huang's car on Interstate 70. Jacqueline, Jon and Irving were riding in the bed of the truck.

As soon as the truck stopped Irving jumped out and Jon handed him the chain. He quickly shimmied on his back under the car and attached one end to the chassis and the other to the tow bar on the bumper of the truck.

Linda rode with the Huangs in the towed car as Hank turned around on the wide Interstate and drove west for nearly fifteen hundred meters in the east bound lane. When they found an emergency vehicle road between the two lanes he crossed over to the west bound side of the highway. They were on a level which gave them a perfect view of the small town and the FEMA compound. Jon asked Hank to stop the vehicle. There was no traffic in either direction as Jon contemplated the panorama.

"This would be a perfect spot to do reconnaissance to see if we can locate the magicians who are firing the EMP weapons." He looked at both Jacqueline and Hank. "I wonder if Captain Huang will be willing to take a little hiatus from his retirement to help me do some more soldiering. If we can get the Interstate flowing again and free up most of the people at the compound, it would certainly help us at the farm."

"At the very least, keep the mass of people from increasing in size," stated Hank. "If the supply chain is cut off to this location, there will be a terrible humanitarian disaster."

Colorado Farm

Hank drove past the Jacoby's RV and parked near the garage. The warm wind of the day melted most of the snow, leaving shallow puddles of water throughout the hardened gravel of the farm grounds.

Bobby, Sherry, Emilee and Harold were just cleaning up around the site of the block tower, while Dave and his crew continued roofing the final half of the apartment. Jerry and Terrance stepped out of the door to the apartment, after a long day of working on the final phase of the electrical wiring for the first half of the large building. The Huang family stood outside their disabled car surprised at the amount of activity occurring on the farm.

"I'll get that," said Irving when he noticed Jon getting ready to climb under the car to release the chain.

Jon stepped back as Gina approached.

"You remember Captain Huang," Jon said to Gina before looking at the captain. "This is my wife, Gina."

"Of course," Gina acknowledged the captain as he bounced up from under the car. She had met the captain at several army functions over the years, as well as his parents on a couple of occasions. "And I remember your parents too."

Li Na and Shen were both smiling as they witnessed the flurry of activity happening at the rural location, in what they would have considered the middle of nowhere.

"If I remember right, you were a school principal," said Gina. "I can't recall your name."

"Yes, I was an elementary school principal." The small lady turned to her husband, "I'm Li Na and this is my husband Shen."

"I remember now, Shen is a cabinet maker," stated Gina.

"Yes," Li Na smiled, appreciating the tranquil nature of their welcome.

Bill, Maddy and Samantha came out of the office in the garage and approached Linda.

"It looks like you survived your ordeal," Samantha gave Linda a quick hug. "I figured you would be ok, but they sure made me mad how they took you."

"I could tell," Linda chuckled, "I think you might have given the one guard a black eye."

"He deserved it," Samantha showed her white teeth as she smiled.

"Where's Al?" Linda looked in the direction of the farmhouse. Riding with the Huangs on the trip to the farm, Linda remained unaware of the disagreement between Al and the others at the farm.

"Umm," Maddy moved next to Samantha and looked up at Linda, "Al has been hiding, because he called Samantha a bad name."

"Maddy," yelled Bill.

"What happened?" Linda raised her eyes from Maddy as she turned to Samantha. "What did he call you?"

"Al was upset with you not coming back with us." Samantha turned to the others for support. "Let's let bygones be bygones."

Linda leaned down to Maddy, "What did he call her?"

Maddy glanced up to Bill with both eyes wide open and whispered, "He called her a bongo."

Linda jerked her head to look at the others. Samantha burst out laughing.

"A what?" Linda shrugged her shoulders and looked directly at Samantha.

Samantha closed her eyes and sniffled, "A bimbo," she breathed out hard as she said the word.

"Oh my God, what in the world was he thinking?" Linda sighed and placed a hand on Samantha's arm. "I am so sorry."

Jacqueline came over to stand next to her neighbor. "You and Al can discuss all this in private. I'm sure we can work everything out." She gave Bill a quick glance.

"There are some army vehicles coming," yelled Jason from the roof of the apartment.

Jon stepped to the side of the garage and looked down the driveway. The convoy was not visible. "How many?" he yelled to Jason.

"Six."

"Platoon size," he turned to Nicole, "it has to be Ted."

Nicole followed Jon as he moved to the front of the crowd to watch the convoy come to a halt in front of the farmhouse. A tactical vehicle drove around and parked next to Jon. Bill, Maddy and Samantha moved closer to see if Ted would emerge.

"Grandpa," Maddy yelled as soon as Ted opened the door. "You're back."

Ted did not have a chance to get out of the seat before Maddy ran into his arms. She hugged him for several seconds.

"Let me get out so I can give Grandma a hug too." Ted held her so he could see her tiny face. "I really missed you," he said.

"I missed you too." Maddy grabbed his hands to help him out of the vehicle.

Nicole threw her arms around his neck. They embraced as Jon and Bill moved next to them. Bill was the first to notice Jessica sitting in the back of the tactical vehicle. He watched her as she opened the door on the opposite side of the crowd. There was a hush as she made her way around to stand next to Ted.

Jacqueline stared a hole through her as she stood with her mouth open in disbelief. Jessica turned her head to scan the property in search of her daughters.

"I understand there are going to be some problems here with the return of Jessica. But I want everyone to know she has been very cooperative in providing information about the rebel's movements." Ted was going to do all he could to help the young mother.

"What are your plans?" Jacqueline asked tersely, slighting Ted's remarks. "Reagan, Avery and Emilee are doing very well."

"They are my children," Jessica said much more aggressively than she would have liked.

"They are your children who you left," Jacqueline yelled with her face turning a bright red. Hank moved to his wife's side.

"I made a mistake, ok." She turned her head to the side.

"A mistake is when you spill a gallon of milk or burn some cookies." Jacqueline was breathing hard as she tried to make eye contact. "Leaving your children at such a dangerous time is not a mistake."

"I knew immediately after leaving that I was wrong." Jessica bit her upper lip as she tried to hold back the tears. She saw Emilee and Bobby walking in her direction. She took several steps, around Jacqueline, in their direction. Emilee stopped and folded her arms.

"I'm sorry," Jessica mouthed the words as she approached her daughter. "I missed you so much."

"Why, Mom?" Emilee looked at Bobby and then back at her mother. "How could you take off and leave us without saying anything?"

"Where are your sisters?" she ignored the question.

Emilee squinted her eyes as she stared at her mother. She was breathing from a barely open mouth as she folded her arms even tighter.

"They are coming now," Bobby pointed to the barn as he answered Jessica's inquiry. Avery and Reagan were walking with Breanna. "They must have finished with riding the horses."

The two girls walked to Emilee and stood next to their sister. They looked vacantly at Jessica.

"Can we find somewhere to talk?" Jessica glanced quickly over her shoulder at the group behind her.

"There's a table in the back yard," Emilee replied. She turned to Bobby. "Come with us?"

"No, you should talk alone." Bobby was surprised Emilee would ask him. She looked tired and was still dirty from working with the masonry. "I'm going to get cleaned up and we can talk at supper."

She gave him a kiss on the cheek before turning and walking in the direction of the farmhouse without saying a word to her mother. Jessica followed her three daughters.

"What about Deb?" Hank asked Ted. "We haven't heard anything from her."

"She sustained a concussion in the explosion we saw on the monitor before I left, but it is my understanding she is doing ok." Ted turned toward Irene and Ed. Ed was slumping much more than when he last saw him. "Her Brigade is relocating to southern Utah. They might even be there already."

"Can we get her to check on the kids?" Ed asked anxiously.

"If our technicians can get communication up and running in the next hour, I'll try and contact her from here." Ted noticed Captain Huang. "My God, is that Irving Huang?" Ted walked quickly to where the Huang family were waiting patiently. "How in the world did you end up here?"

"We were stranded, and Jon helped us out." Irving shook Ted's hand. "I thought you retired."

"I did, but I believed I was needed back in the fold. But I'm not so sure about that now." Ted gritted his teeth as Jon and Hank came to his side. "Irving, it really makes me feel better that you are here at the farm."

"How long can you stay?" Jon asked Ted.

"Another two hours," Ted looked toward Nicole, and then at Bill. "I have to be back at the base this evening."

"You probably want to get caught up with Bill and Nicole," said Jon. "We can get the Huang's situated and talk with you in a bit."

Ted listened to Maddy explain all that happened since he left, while Bill, Samantha and Nicole listened and corrected her when she was blatantly wrong. It was obvious that Bill and Samantha had grown much closer over the past few days. He stared into Nicole's beautiful eyes as everyone spoke. He was about to grab her and break away when he saw Lieutenant Hanson approach.

"Colonel, the communication center is now operational."

Ted moved to the garage and waited at the office for everyone else to catch up. Irene and Ed were especially interested in seeing if he could contact Colonel Deb.

"Dad," Bill stepped in front of his father. "I forgot to tell you. We found the Browns murdered at their farm."

"When?"

"The night of the missile attacks," answered Nicole. She could see the distress in his face. "It was absolutely horrible."

The technician from his platoon who revived the system was still sitting at the desk in front of the screen. When the specialist noticed Ted approaching, he stood up and saluted. "The problem was the setting was wrong for the satellite position. Everything else is functional, it was really a very minor glitch."

"Sit back down," said Ted. "I want you to locate and connect with Colonel Deb Lisco with 4th Infantry, 2nd Brigade."

"Yes sir."

"This news about the Browns, really worries me." Ted's left eye twitched and his charmed expression faded. "We ran into a roadblock on the way here this afternoon. There were nearly forty rebels."

"There were another thirty to forty of the insurgents hiding about five hundred meters off the road in the field," said Lieutenant Hanson emphatically.

"They were well armed," Ted shook his head. "We need to have a meeting with everyone before I leave."

"Sir, I have Colonel Lisco on the radio. We won't be able to bring her up on the monitor," said the specialist as he relinquished the seat at the radio.

"Ted," Deb's voice was loud and clear. "Where are you?"

"I'm at the farm." Ted hesitated, then looked at Samantha, "Could you run and get Jon and Hank?"

"Is everything ok?" Deb asked.

"Everything is good here." Ted wanted to wait to discuss the issue of the murder of the Browns. "Where are you?"

"We are just south of Richfield, Utah on Interstate 15. Trying to get around a blown bridge. It is the second one we have had to deal with today."

"I'm glad to hear you sounding so good," said Ted, noticing Jon and Hank at his side.

"You had us worried to death," said Hank.

"Is Jon there?" Deb asked.

"I'm here."

"You need to continue to fortify the farm. This war is not going to be over for a long time." Deb's voice cracked. "This is just the beginning."

"Everything is coming along well," Hank assured her. "Did they tell you about the Browns?"

"No," Deb said softly.

"We found them murdered at their farm."

"Oh, good Lord," Deb yelled before lowering her voice. "Jon and Ted, you need to make sure to set up adequate security measures."

"Colonel, this is Ed Jacoby," Ed leaned closer to the radio. "You are close to our farm outside of Parowan. If I can have Ted send you a map with the location of our grandchildren, will you check on them for us?"

"Ed, send the map, but there is no guarantee I will have the time to find them," Deb's voice was forceful. "Most of the citizens have already departed from the towns we passed through. I'm hearing more and more rumblings that all civilians will be ordered to relocate."

"We are worried sick about them," said Irene pleadingly. "Please check on them."

"Get me the map." Clamoring filled the radio and Colonel Deb could be heard shouting to others in the distance.

"Deb," Ted yelled into the receiver, "are you there?"

"I'll get back in touch as soon as I can." The radio went silent.

It was quiet enough in the garage to hear the battery-operated clock on the wall ticking. After a few seconds of silence Hank locked eyes with Ted. "Things are about to get a lot worse, aren't they?" he asked.

Ted rubbed the grey hair at his right temple. His mind was churning as he reached around Nicole's waist and pulled her close. Most of the people important to his existence were in the cold garage, staring at him like a group of Sunday morning parishioners waiting to hear a positive message of hope and salvation. He smiled at Maddy.

"Grandpa," Maddy moved next to him, "can you stay here tonight?"

Ted reached down and picked her up in his arms. He stared at her as she leaned in and placed her forehead on his.

"We can play some games," she said.

He hankered for a moment with her head gently pressing on his. It all hit him like a ton of bricks, for the first time he realized he was better situated at the base in Fort Carson where he held the power of the United States Army at his calling. He was going to make sure his son, his wife and his brothers had a direct line to him twenty-four hours a day. The farm was going to be protected by the full force of the Army.

"I'm sorry Maddy. I have to go back to the base tonight."

Parowan, Utah

A cold November wind blew into Tommy's face as he walked nearly four hundred meters past the convoy of 1st Battalion's vehicles to where Colonel Deb was riding, with twelve soldiers, in an Oshkosh R-ATV assault vehicle. It had already been a strenuous fifteen-hour journey from Great Falls, and they were still nearly a hundred kilometers north of their destination of St. George, Utah. Deb stepped out of the vehicle onto the concrete of Interstate 15 to address the command sergeant major.

"Colonel, I just received a message from Corps that they want us to secure Interstate 15 between Cedar City and Interstate 70 for a shipment that will be passing through at approximately 2200. They want us to inspect all bridges," stated Tommy. "I already dispatched Company B forward to Cedar City and Company A about ten kilometers south of here between Parowan and Cedar City. 3rd Battalion will have to backtrack about thirty kilometers to the Interstate 70 interchange."

"Are we removing nuclear warheads?"

"That's my assumption."

"It's real nice of them to give us some warning," Deb looked at Tommy with concern. "Make sure all search and reconnaissance is conducted by platoon sized units. This is where Ted said he witnessed the landing of several odd aircraft. I have a bad feeling about this place."

"They were going to move the nukes north of Las Vegas through the countryside but changed routes at the last moment."

"Where's Lieutenant Colonel Barnet?"

"He is with Company D at Parowan."

The humming of the MQ-30T Reaper broke the silence as it flew quietly over the top of the convoy. The drumming of chopper blades became louder and louder as helicopters approached from the south. Five M200 Guardian vehicles passed swiftly by, traveling north bound in the south bound lanes, causing Deb and Tommy to reconsider standing so close to the highway. Several more assault and fighter vehicles passed by before fifteen large semi-trucks slowly threaded their way down the freeway. It took nearly thirty minutes for the entire convoy of military might to pass.

"What is going on here Tommy? Where are they moving these weapons?"

"I have no idea where they are going," Tommy wrung his hands. "They must feel they are unsafe here."

"Colonel," a specialist approached and saluted. "General Lauer wants to speak with you."

"Jesus, it's almost midnight at Fort Carson." Deb shot Tommy a look of unease, "This can't be good."

Tommy followed her into the back of the command vehicle. The full face of General Lauer was visible on the largest screen.

"Sir," Deb said as she sat down in the seat at the monitor.

"Colonel, there will be a helicopter arriving for you in St George for a departure of 0500 to deliver you back to the base here at Fort Carson."

"What is this all about General?"

"It is all I am at liberty to disclose at this time. Just be ready to leave," stated General Lauer.

Fort Carson Army Base

After arriving on base, Colonel Deb rushed to the briefing room. She was one of the last to arrive. Besides General McClinton and General Lauer all the big brass for the 4th and 99th Divisions were present, as were all the Colonels from within the Divisions. She acknowledged Colonel Tyler from Stryker as she sat down a couple of seats to the right of him. She noticed Ted walking up the incline toward her. He took the seats next to her as General McClinton began to speak at the podium.

"The reason we summoned everyone here today can be explained in one word, security." General McClinton looked over the large group of soldiers. "It is a terrible state-of-affairs that we cannot be confident in the refuge of our own communication system from the Chinese and Russian hacking technologies. What we know for certain is that we are in a fight for our lives. The enemy is vicious, they are shrewd, and they are not going to negotiate. With information we have gleaned from our operatives entrenched with the enemy forces along the Mexican border, and with prisoners we have captured on our own soil, we have been able to better understand their tactics and possibly their blueprint for defeating us. We now have a strategy with which each soldier in this room will have a specific part in implementing. General Lauer at your leisure, sir."

General McClinton stepped back from the podium, and General Lauer moved to the microphone. He turned toward a large map of the United States on a screen behind him.

"As you can see on this map there is a dark line from Corpus Christi, Texas to the Continental Divide of the Rocky Mountains, that proceeds to northern Montana. On the western portion of the map is a line from Los Angeles, California to Reno, Nevada proceeding to the Oregon and Washington state borders. It is our intention to evacuate all American citizens from this area between the Sierra Nevada's all the way to the Rocky Mountains. Civilians from Phoenix on a line north to Las Vegas and northward to Washington state will migrate to the west coast, with everyone east of this line moving east. Sixteen bridges on the Interstate system have been destroyed and many others have been compromised." General Lauer turned from the map as another map became visible. The map displayed four areas with the names of brigades of the 4th Infantry, and two areas designated for brigades of the 99th Infantry.

Deb could see an area shaded in blue designated for the 2nd Infantry Brigade, 4th Division, which included the entire state of Utah, the eastern third of Idaho, the western half of Wyoming and the eastern third of Colorado. Of the six shaded areas, hers was by far the largest.

"Aircraft will be used from the Salt Lake City and Albuquerque locations. Otherwise, evacuation will be through land transport. FEMA has halted all deliveries of food and supplies to these areas and will now assist in the transporting of civilians." General McClinton stepped next to General Lauer, indicating he wanted to address the troops.

"It must be made perfectly clear that the enemy entrenched in the cities and small towns are just that, enemies. The rebels are engrained deep within the fabric of the neighborhoods. Some will remain imbedded, and others will leave with the citizens. The process to vet them will take place after they have evacuated. By executive order just signed by President Weller, leaving the area is not a request and anyone staying behind will be considered a combatant." General Lauer took a deep breath, "We have a short time period, so, it is imperative that you do your jobs quickly and efficiently. Each of you have general orders in your secure systems. The timetable for the evacuation is three days, so get back to your soldiers and take care of business."

"Sir," Colonel Taylor of 1st Stryker Brigade yelled from the center of the auditorium.

"Yes, Colonel," General Lauer pointed at him.

"Why, sir, can you tell us why we are evacuating all these civilians?"

General Lauer glanced at Chief of Staff McClinton. General McClinton motioned to a man dressed in a suit coat to take the podium. He was the same undetectable man who warned President Weller and his Cabinet of the dangers the country faced.

"Every model we have run with us committing hundreds of thousands of soldiers to protect our soil north of the Mexico border, indicates us losing more than two hundred thousand soldiers and a million civilians. Every one of these models shows us eventually losing the war. By removing the noncombatants and using nonhuman forces we can reposition troops that the enemy supposes us to use to protect this sector."

"Sir, do your models show us winning the war if we do this?" Colonel Tyler yelled.

"Not in all scenarios." The man breathed through his nose before continuing, "But we don't lose in all circumstances."

"So, we are going to have pimple faced technicians on the east coast fighting the invading forces across an area from San Antonio to Phoenix using their computers to control weaponized robots."

"I will allow the brass to answer that question for you." The man moved away from the podium.

"Colonel," Chief of Staff McClinton stepped to the podium, "our land-based forces will be involved with all the combat we can handle as the enemy adjusts to the situation. We will leave it there."

After the generals stepped away from the platform and others began to clamor about the room, Colonel Taylor edged his way to stand in the aisle next to Ted and Deb as they remained seated. Tyler was the type of soldier who was serious as hell, who could never possibly look at something from the sunny side. Yet there was something soothing about his cocky smile that always intrigued Deb.

"Three days to move millions of people." Colonel Tyler gave an acknowledging glance to Ted as he spoke directly to Deb.

"We just traveled south on Interstate 15, and most of the citizens have already fled," Deb remained seated. There had always been an unofficial competition between the two commanders to be the most knowledgeable about any circumstance they encountered.

"Stryker is going to be to the west of your location, and it might suit us both if we coordinate missions." The colonel moved back from Deb so she could better look him in the eyes. "Have you thought about how you are going to direct your battalions to cover the area?"

Deb glanced up at him and took in a deep breath. His eyes were flat with no cheek bones visible on his round face. "I have some ideas but will hash it over with my commanders before making any solid decisions," she said.

"Keep me informed, I'm out of here in about an hour." He surveyed the room before turning and walking quickly out the door.

Deb shot Ted a smile.

"When are you scheduled to leave?" Ted asked.

"1300 mountain time. I have about thirty minutes before I should go."

"You need to be careful with the area around Cedar City. I know for a fact; insurgents are there in great force." The muscles in Ted's jaw clenched, "I'm sure you realize the danger."

"After what I witnessed in Great Falls, I will never underestimate the threat. In order to cover the entire sector, I will have to spread the troops pretty thin."

"The main threat you will face will be along the Interstate 15 corridor." Ted leaned back in his chair. "Captain Hendersen has full knowledge of the area of eastern Utah. There are a lot of stranded people in that section, but I have a feeling the locals have taken care of the resistance from the insurgents. I don't know how they expect you to move everyone in three days, not just because of the number of people, but because it will be difficult to locate them over the vast area."

"I'll do the best I can."

Ted leaned forward and removed his wallet. He pulled out a piece of paper and handed it to his sister. "Here is the map Irene made showing the location of her grandkids."

"I'll find them," Deb said firmly, using a tone he knew she used only when she meant something. "It's as good a place as any to start."

"The Jacobys will be happy to hear that."

"What about you Ted?" Deb checked her watch. "Have they told you anything about where you will be during all of this?"

"Nothing," Ted hated the feeling of uselessness. He also despised the portrayal of selfishness he was showing to Deb by complaining about his situation. Their father would not approve of moaning about oneself, especially during a time of crisis. It was against everything the Army embodied. "I'm going to suggest to General Lopez that I take over a company sized unit to work on getting rid of the insurgents along the front range."

She looked at him for a long moment with a quizzical expression on her face. He was a terrific soldier, yet his strategic and analytical talents would never be used from a desk in Fort Carson. The Department of Defense made all the decisions and most likely any of his suggestions would be taken with a grain of salt.

"I need to go," said Deb, taking a step toward the door before turning back and stating, "You are absolutely correct in wanting to take care of the problems here. Make sure to speak with the general in private. Too many ears might help him find reasons to deny the request."

Colorado Farm

The view from the third floor of the concrete block tower was stunning as the sun began to set over the wide-open landscape. The farm was located on top of a hill which provided a vantage to see for many kilometers in all directions. The tower provided a perfect perch for surveillance. Harold planned to set the trusses for the roof in the morning and then place the plywood sheeting later in the afternoon. He made it clear he would be doing the dangerous job by himself. Bobby, Emilee and Sherry made room for Dave and Caroline to join them in the small room at the top of the structure. No more carrying concrete blocks and buckets of mortar up the stairs.

Deep down in his soul Bobby was sad that working with the two beautiful ladies was over. Being covered in cement and so exhausted he could hardly move seemed like an odd thing to pine for, yet the hard work brought a sense of allegiance between the three of them that could never be emulated.

Sherry stared out the open-air window with the breeze blowing her blonde hair onto her neck, shutting out the entire surroundings inside, as she viewed the world below. She moved closer and placed her hands on the concrete filled block that made the sill of the window and looked straight down to the ground below. A sense of vertigo caused her to lean back. It seemed much higher inside the tower than it looked from below.

Emilee locked her arms around Bobby's waist, feeling the hidden pistol holstered on his hip, as they moved next to Sherry at the edge of the window and scanned the farm. Dave and Caroline tried to acclimate being in the structure and remained back from the openings.

"I can't believe we helped build this tower. I did learn that this is a bond beam." Sherry showed her bright smile as she tapped her index finger on the block.

"The tips of my fingers are so cracked; I don't know if they will ever heal." Emilee held her hands palms up out the window in front of her.

"You'll be just fine." Bobby playfully nudged her with his elbow. He had not discussed with her about how the meeting with her mother had gone earlier. A heavy smell of dinner being cooked filled his nostrils as the wind blew lightly from the southwest, he noticed his mother and father gathering with a group of people by the garage.

"There's a van coming down the driveway." Dave leaned between Bobby and Sherry and pointed in the direction of a light blue van entering the parking area in front of the farmhouse. There was a blind spot for observation from the tower directly in front of the house, so as the van moved closer, they lost sight of it. The vehicle came back into sight as it slowly moved past the house, in front of the Jacoby's RV, toward the group at the garage. Hank and Jon moved forward to receive the vehicle as it approached.

Four young men stepped out of the van, and from their actions seemed very cordial as they were greeted by Hank and Jon.

"Look over there," Emilee's voice was rushed as she held her hand out the window in the direction of the county road about three kilometers to the south. "Are those people?"

The tiny silhouettes of people were visible, spread out on a hill nearly eight hundred meters south of the gravel road. A large box truck was parked on the road in front of the threatening figures.

Caroline brushed Bobby as she stuck her head out the window. Her large almond shaped eyes squinted as she scrutinized the four strangers talking below, where Jon and Hank were now joined by Jacqueline, Nicole and Gina. She ground her teeth and raised her hand to her mouth. She lurched back from the window."

"Two of those guys are the ones who attacked me." She thought back to lying, barely conscious, in the bar ditch before she was found by the Hamiltons.

"Are you sure?" Bobby jerked his head to look at her.

"The one with the blond hair and the guy with the gray cap." She swallowed hard and leaned her head back on the cold block wall. She never thought she would have to relive the horrible experience. "They attacked me. They are both bad, but the guy with the cap is… he's cruel."

Bobby glanced quickly at the massive assemblage of people to the south and then gazed toward the garage where Terrance and Jerry were standing next to Breanna, Irene and Ed. Samantha and Maddy lingered at the utility door to the garage.

"I'll go down and warn them. With Maddy and Samantha at the door Bill must be inside with the radio," Bobby spoke quickly, when he noticed the man in the cap glance toward the tower. Although Caroline was away from the window, he used the back of his arm to nudge her deeper into the corner, further away from the openings. "Don't let them see you."

Bobby leaped down the stairs but slowed when he exited the door of the tower. He gave a wider than usual swath as he made his way to the garage. He used his peripheral vision to keep an eye on the perpetrators as he approached Terrance and Jerry. Ed, Irene and Breanna were slowly making their way to the RV.

"Can I speak with you two inside?" Bobby asked softly, giving Terrance a serious look as he moved to the garage door and prodded Samantha and Maddy to step inside. Bill's voice could be heard in the distance from the back office. Bobby shut the door and turned to Terrance.

"We have a problem. The guys outside are not friendly." Bobby grabbed Maddy's hand and rushed to the office where Bill was talking to Scotty and Irving Huang. Bill stopped in mid-sentence as Bobby quickly moved to his side.

"Caroline just identified two of the guys outside as her attackers," Bobby spoke rapidly.

"What guys?" Bill looked at his cousin confusedly.

"Listen," he slowed and gained his breath. "Four guys just arrived outside. Mom and Dad, along with Uncle Jon, Aunt Gina and Aunt Nicole are speaking with them right now. There are a massive group of people on the road to the south, who are obviously with them. It's a set up."

Terrance glanced at Jerry. He took a step toward the exit.

"Terrance, wait a minute," yelled Bill. "We need to make sure we are all armed before you confront them."

"Where do you keep the weapons?" Irving asked.

"They are in a safe room in the basement of the main house." Bill looked directly at Bobby, "Only seven of us have our eyes scanned for access."

"And five of them are talking to the guys outside," stated Bobby.

"And you are the remaining two." Irving brought his right hand to his chin and looked directly at Bobby.

"I take it that if Colonel Lisco stockpiled the arms, they will be military quality. How proficient are you and your friends with firing the weapons?"

"Aunt Deb's soldiers gave us a crash course. We know how to load and fire them." Bobby did not seem overly confident in the abilities of his friends with handling the guns.

"Terrance and I both have AK-47s here in the garage," stated Jerry. "There are five .50 Caliber rifles in the gun vault."

Irving shot Jerry a surprised look before asking the general question, "Do all of you know how to fire the fifty?"

"Dave, Sherry, Emilee and I all know how," said Bobby. "There are a lot of other weapons in the vault besides those."

"These are your friends who are in the tower?" Captain Huang inquired.

"Yeah."

"Besides the two AKs, what do we have for weapons here?"

"Bill and I both have pistols." Bobby hesitated for a moment, "Uncle Jon always carries his handgun."

"We both have pistols, too," stated Jerry.

"Can I use one of your weapons?"

"Of course, but what is the plan? It is going to be dark before long."

"We have to surprise them, before they do it to us." Irving looked out the window. He could see Ed, Irene and Breanna, in the distance, walking slowly toward the RV past the car, which was a good fifty meters from the garage. Everyone at the car seemed to be talking amiably. Sherry and Emilee were noticeable in the window of the block tower. "I can't tell if the strangers have any weapons on them."

"Samantha, I want you to take Maddy and Scotty to the farmhouse." Bill rose from his chair.

"Bill," Irving stepped away from the window and placed his left hand on his shoulder. "I want you to go with them."

"Irving are you sure that's what you want me to do?" he scoffed.

"As soon as we see you are safely in the house, I will go out and join the conversation at the car. I can warn Lieutenant Colonel Lisco about the danger without being detected. When you get to the house, open the gun safe and arm everyone capable of firing a weapon."

"What about us?" Jerry asked, glancing at Terrance.

"Give me thirty seconds after I engage the group, and then quickly come to my side."

"And me?" Bobby asked.

"Are any of your friends in the tower armed?"

"Sherry still has the pistol she used when she went to the Brown's farm."

"Walk back to the tower as if nothing has happened." The captain's tone was calm and confident.

"Watch to make sure none of the people on the road are advancing. As soon as you see me unholster my weapon, then, and only then do you and Sherry come to our side."

"Ok," Bobby was not about to question the captain's judgement.

"You can leave now." He looked at Bill, Samantha, Maddy and Scotty, "I won't go until I see you safely in the house."

Although the temperature was rapidly falling and the sun was beginning to set, Jon continued talking with the four strangers. They were making such a good impression, that all five of the Liscos considered asking them to stay at the farm. The two youngest strangers were leaning on the hood of their van while the other two stood in the center of the group, laughing and joking, as Irving entered the assemblage and paused at the back side of Jon.

"This is Irving Huang," Jon said, stepping to the side to allow Irving a chance to advance closer. "He was a captain in the Army, who I served with."

The men smiled and acknowledged him. The man with the cap blatantly stared at the concrete tower, although quite a distance away, Sherry and Emilee were still perched in the window. Hank, Jacqueline, Nicole and Gina were all calm and completely unsuspecting of any danger from the four intruders.

"Hello," Irving nodded, glancing at the strangers, before turning to Jon and giving him a serious look. "I was just telling Terrance a great story about the time Sergeant Spencer met the group outside the bar in Bamako."

Jon momentarily let Irving's comment pass as general conversation before suddenly taking in a deep breath. His heart flipped in his chest as he twisted his neck in the direction of the retired captain, hard enough for it to pop. Nearly ten years earlier, a good friend of theirs, Sergeant Spencer, was murdered by acquaintances he thought were friendly, in a trap set by a group in Mali.

"Are you telling me these guys remind you of the ones in Bamako?"

Irving clapped Jon on his muscular shoulder and said, "It's about to happen here."

Jon slid in front of Gina, reached to his back and flipped the latch to his holster. Irving drew his pistol out and leveled it in the direction of the two men leaning on the hood of the car. Hank jerked back as his brother moved in front of him and aimed his weapon at the two closest perpetrators. Terrance and Jerry rushed past Gina, Jacqueline and Nicole with their AKs at the ready. Bobby and Sherry were running across the gravel driveway, with Caroline right behind them.

"What is going on?" Jacqueline yelled, shuffling her feet as she moved back quick enough to bump into Nicole.

"Place your hands straight up," ordered Irving. "Now."

All four men remained frozen in place with their arms slightly raised. Bill hurried from the house carrying a M16 A2 battle rifle with Breanna and Aaron Jacoby joining him as he passed their RV.

"Why are you doing this?" asked the blond man, holding his muscular arms barely over his head.

"Uncle Jon, there is a large group assembled at our driveway on the dirt road south of here," Bobby yelled.

"Ok," Jon swallowed hard. "Let's sort this all out."

"We are just trying to find a place to stay." The guy with the cap had a long, skinny nose and an oblong face. He put his hands out in a questioning manner and raised his upper lip. "You seem like nice people."

"Like everyone else, we have been having a hard time over the past few weeks," said the man with blond hair. His head was on a swivel as he checked out the growing crowd of people. He gasped when he noticed Caroline step next to Jon.

"Do you remember me? My name is Caroline Sanchez." Her dark eyes raged, and her high cheek bones quivered as she untucked her blouse and pulled it up high enough to show half her bra. Both sides of her ribcage were dark black and blue, and there was a small cut under her left breast. She turned so they could see the large welts on her back. "I am still having a hard time breathing after you beat and raped me."

"It wasn't us," the man with the cap lowered his eyes.

"It was you. I remember every little detail about you. You are an animal." Her nostrils flared as she stared at him. "There were four of you, but you were the most vicious."

"They will pay for this." Jon put his left hand on Caroline's shoulder and patted her gently. He licked his lips as he remembered her lying in the ditch, like garbage discarded to the side of the road. The more he thought about it, the more furious he became. "All right, all four of you face down. Put your noses in the gravel."

The four men slowly fell to their knees and folded over onto their stomachs. Hank reached down to the man with blond hair and removed a pistol from the back of his pants. He lifted the shirt of the man with the cap and removed his concealed firearm. Neither of the two younger men were armed.

"Check their pant legs," said Jon.

Both armed men had ankle holsters. Hank removed their weapons.

Caroline leaped at the man with the cap and kicked, she aimed for his head but missed and booted him on his right shoulder. The man swiped at her foot with his right hand. Jon smacked him hard on the side of his ear with the butt of his Beretta.

"Jon," Hank moved between his brother and the perpetrator on the ground, just as Jon was about to kick him. "Let the sheriff handle this."

Jon backed away to stand next to Gina, trying to catch his breath. "I can't stand bullies who use their strength to abuse people." He smacked his lips and shook his head. "I never could stand them."

"What about the people on the road?" asked Bobby.

"Who are they?" Hank realized he was standing less than a meter away from the men, so he took a large step in the direction of Terrance. He continued to look down at them. "Are they a threat to us?"

"You are going to find out how big of a threat they are to you." The man with the blond hair raised his chin off the cold ground and smirked.

"Can I take a look inside the gun safe?" Irving took the man's warning seriously. "I'd feel a hell of a lot better with a M16 in my hand right now."

"I'll show you," Bobby was shoulder to shoulder with Sherry with his pistol directed at the men on the ground. He holstered his weapon and looked to the tower where Emilee and Dave were watching from the window. Irving followed as he headed to the farmhouse.

"Where are we going to put these guys?" Jacqueline asked.

Jon moved to the two younger men who were not privy to Caroline's attack. He nudged the young man closest to him with the side of his foot. "Stand up," he ordered.

He pushed himself from the ground. Terrance and Jerry continued to aim their weapons. Bill held his rifle pointed down away from the intruders. Jon holstered his pistol and motioned for Sherry to do the same. He turned to the frightened young man.

"How do you know these men?" Jon was calm, while breathing through his nose as he moved directly in front of the frightened man and looked him directly in the eyes. He looked to be about sixteen years old.

"My brother, father and I came across them the day before yesterday." He lowered his eyes to the other boy still prone on the ground at his feet. "We left the city on Thursday with the idea of walking to Kansas City."

"Who are the people on the road?" Jon asked.

"Mostly friends of theirs."

"Are these men the leaders of the group?" Jon glanced toward the man in the cap.

"Ummm, I don't think so."

"Do they have weapons."

"A lot of them do."

"What's your name?"

"Tyrone."

"Can I trust you, Tyrone?" Jon put his chin straight out in front of the young man. "Don't tell me I can, if I can't."

Irving and Bobby returned to the group, both carrying heavy rifles. Bobby took a double take at the boy on the ground as he moved next to his dad.

"You can," he stated barely loud enough to hear. He pointed to Bobby and spoke louder, "Von played football against you this fall."

"Von is your brother?" Jon prodded the boy on the ground with the toe of his shoe. "You can get up."

"I thought I recognized you. You were a linebacker for Arvada." Bobby watched the young man pull himself from the ground, then turned to Hank. "Remember him Dad? He's the guy who intercepted me in the endzone during the last game of the regular season."

"I remember," Hank looked at Jon. "I think we can trust these kids."

"I want you two to take a message from us to the people at the road. Tell them that this farm is a place they should leave alone. We are very capable of protecting ourselves and we want them at least ten kilometers away from this area." Jon took in a deep breath. "We want them gone immediately. If they stay, we will consider it an act of hostility."

"Are they coming with us?" Tyrone looked toward the two on the ground.

"They are going to stay here. They will have to answer to the sheriff in Limon for attacking Caroline." Jon glanced at Caroline. He opened the front door of the van. "You can go now."

"I'll have Dave take some plywood and board up a horse stall to hold these guys." Hank stepped next to Jacqueline. "It looks like it will be a long night."

Hank, Bill, Terrance and Jerry marched the two attackers to the barn. The van drove down the driveway and disappeared into the darkness. Caroline made eye contact with Sherry before staring at the backside of her attackers. Her chest heaved as she remembered the monstrous things the men did to her.

PART TWO

Jacoby Ranch

The area was much more rugged than Colonel Deb anticipated as she stood outside her Humvee parked on the side of the county road, nearly five kilometers from the Jacoby ranch in central Utah. A steady wind of thirty kilometers an hour blew from the north as she inspected the overwhelming vastness of the desolate area.

Captain Hendersen with F Company spent most of the morning executing the tedious task of directing the troops to check for civilians occupying farmhouses. Drones sped up the process but many of the inhabitants refused to leave and hid out until the armed forces passed by their homes. FEMA vehicles transported the few civilians willing to leave to a staging area at the I-70 and I-15 junction near Beaver, Utah. Larger modes of transportation were ready to convey the citizens eastward across the Rockies and beyond.

Deb scrutinized the handwritten map Ted gave her for the location of the Jacoby's farm before opening the door of the Humvee and placing it on the seat to keep it from blowing away. After examining the diagram, she stepped into the middle of the road and looked to the east, attempting to locate a red barn. It was not in sight.

Lt. Col. Woodworth was planning to take G Company and H Company to Parowan to vacate the tiny municipality of any remaining civilians and dispatch all the residual subversives. Having lingered behind to finish cleaning up the attack at the warehouse in Great Falls, the convoy of the 2nd Battalion traveled south on Interstate 15, past the little town less than twelve hours prior without encountering any sign of the enemy. Colonel Deb made the decision to bring Josh to the Southern Utah location and send Lt. Col Barnet north. She felt more comfortable around Josh, so, it was a personal decision with little strategic value.

"Colonel," Captain Hendersen joined her at the side of the Humvee. Dirt was blowing across the road. "We located the farm with the red barn. First squad with 2nd Platoon are on the outskirts of the location."

"Is there anyone on the premises."

"It is occupied."

"Have 2nd platoon wait to engage with the occupants until we arrive." Deb hesitated for a moment before asking, "Is the rest of the Company close?"

"All but 3rd Platoon." Captain Hendersen always portrayed a sense of being under control. "They are about twenty kilometers to the north."

"Dispatch them to our location." During the past two days the small city of St. George was overtaken by United States Military Forces, as was most of Cedar City. Ted warned her that enemy soldiers were in the area before he fled with the Jacobys. So, they had to be somewhere. The whole damn ordeal felt like a large sudoku puzzle, where, finding one aspect of the dilemma would lead to the next step in solving the problem.

Deb's Humvee was at the back of the convoy as they drove down the long driveway to the ranch where they parked behind the tactical vehicles in front of the farmhouse. The Jacoby ranch was immaculate. From the white fence around the front yard to the perfectly laid stone sidewalk going in a straight line to the porch in front of the farmhouse.

A dark-haired man, holding a cup of coffee, watched from the porch while soldiers flooded the farm grounds. He was soon joined by a small lady who walked down the sidewalk to the gate. Sergeant Collins of 2nd Platoon was the first to approach her with his entire platoon spread out across the fence line.

Colonel Deb observed the encounter from the front seat of her Humvee, nearly fifty meters away. The small lady turned toward the man on the porch and yelled indiscernibly. He opened the screen door and spoke to others inside. Soon several men and women were standing on the porch. Deb exited and made her way toward the sergeant at the gate.

"Ma'am," said Sergeant Collins, "she says they are friends of the rancher." The sergeant nodded toward the small lady. There were four men and three women on the porch.

"Where are the Jacobys now?" Deb kept her eyes on the group at the entryway as she spoke.

"They left a couple of weeks ago. We came by to check on them and decided to watch over their home until they return."

"Are any of their kids or grandchildren here?"

"No, we haven't seen any of them."

Had Deb not known better, the woman aired a confidence and calmness in her mannerisms that radiated a sense of honesty. That all passed in an instant when Deb noticed she was wearing Giveh shoes, footwear common in rural and mountainous parts of Iran. Besides being durable, the shoes were soft and comfortable, perfect for the Utah terrain. Deb brought her eyes back up to gaze into the woman's emerald-green eyes. A corporal from the communication vehicle approached.

"Ma'am, Command Sergeant Major Talfoya wants to speak with you." The corporal seemed confused about his task. "He wants you to come to communication but not to speak or appear on screen."

"I'm not following you here." Deb abruptly turned from the woman and began walking in the direction of the communication vehicle.

"Captain Hendersen will explain, ma'am," the corporal hurried to walk by her side.

Captain Hendersen stopped them at the door to the large communication truck. Standing next to him, speaking into her Pulsnet wrist radio, was Specialist Sophia Grant.

"Colonel, this may seem out of the ordinary, but we have a specialist who is communicating for Command Sergeant Major Talfoya. They are requesting that you personally cease all forms of exchange transmitted by way of our communication system." Captain Hendersen looked directly at the colonel before turning to Specialist Grant. "Tell Command Sergeant Major Talfoya that Colonel Lisco is here."

"Ma'am, the Command Sergeant Major, via the specialist, wants me to repeat verbatim his words to you." Specialist Grant's voice was clear and steady as she repeated the message. "Colonel, cyber security has sent a warning that the enemy has figured a way to intercept and encrypt data, using voice and visual acknowledgement of all commanding officers, colonel and higher. They are homing in on radio-frequency emissions to track targets.

The identifying information is being used to locate and eliminate our upper command, whether they are moving or not."

Deb listened with her heart rate increasing, letting the information soak in. "Ask if the enemy has been successful."

Specialist Grant grimaced as she replied, "They have been very successful."

"Let him know I understand and will reveal further directives as our situation mandates."

"Yes ma'am." The specialist relayed the message and turned toward Captain Hendersen. "Is that all, sir?"

"That's all." The captain turned to Colonel Deb, "Ma'am, something doesn't feel right about this place."

Deb breathed through her nose as she stared at the white sideburns poking out from beneath the captain's cap. His once salt and pepper hair was now almost all white. She concurred with his observation and was about to acknowledge her agreement when Sergeant Chamberland 2nd Platoon approached from the north.

"Captain," the sergeant was out of breath. "We came across two civilians about three klicks north of here who say they are members of the family from this ranch. They claim the people in the farmhouse are not who they claim to be."

"Where are they now?" Captain Hendersen asked.

"On the other side of the barn. I didn't want to bring them into this setting."

"Sergeant, load the two civilians into your Humvee and follow us out of here." Captain Hendersen turned to Deb. "I'm going to pull everyone back and re-evaluate this location."

"Let's go," the captain stepped in front of her. "Ma'am. Command advised that you transport in the Cougar XR MRAP. It's best you travel with 1st Platoon."

Master Sergeant Herrera was waiting at the side of the combat vehicle. It was the first time she came face to face with him since the incident at her farm in Colorado where she asked the Master Sergeant to beat the living hell out of a squatter. There was no soldier she would rather have by her side. She took a couple steps in the direction of the combat vehicle before turning to look back at the Jacoby's home. The woman was still at the fence calmly watching.

Colorado Farm

Bill felt more invigorated than he would have imagined after catching only two hours of sleep for the entire night. The kitchen table was already surrounded by people having coffee. He pulled out a chair for Samantha and retrieved one from the living room for himself. They spent the night, along with Bobby, Emilee, Terrance and Jerry, watching over the two attackers being held in the horse stall at the barn. Nicole poured two cups of coffee and placed them in front her son and Samantha.

"Is Maddy still asleep?" Bill asked his mother.

"She was just getting around a few minutes ago." Nicole took a seat at the table. "She's in the basement playing with Avery and Reagan. I told her to come up for breakfast."

"I'll go down and check on her." Bill placed his left hand on Samantha's right shoulder as he stood up. She patted his hand and smiled.

He could hear the girls talking as he walked past the first bedroom toward the room the girls used as a play area at the far back of the large basement. It was dark and the musky smell of steam from a shower filled his nostrils. He could feel the moisture as he came closer to the second bedroom where Avery, Reagan, Emilee and now Jessica slept. When he reached the open door to the bedroom, he hesitated and looked through the mist. Standing at the edge of the bed was Jessica wrapped in a large white towel, wringing her wet hair to the side of her head with both hands. Dark circles were apparent under her eyes as she straightened her head and gazed in his direction.

"I'm sorry," Bill turned quickly and began to walk away.

"Wait," she yelled loudly, then lowered her voice, "please, can we talk."

Bill grimaced before taking a full step inside the room. Blood rushed to his head as he remembered the intimacy, he and the beautiful mother experienced only a short time ago.

The previous night had been spent cuddling and holding Samantha, who he now had a promising connection, which he hoped would lead to a meaningful relationship. If being honest with himself, he had the same feelings for Jessica only days earlier.

"I'm not sure we have anything to talk about," he sighed.

"I know I screwed up," she spoke softly. "I made a split-second decision to leave with Christian that I wish I could take back. I truly regret losing what we had together."

He took in a sharp breath when he smelled the mixture of shampoo and lotion as she moved around the bed to stand in front of him. The top half of her breasts were exposed.

"But I'm sure I can make it up to you," she said with an exaggerated accent.

He gasped when she dropped the towel and reached over with her right hand and placed it on his elbow. She held her head steady and stared into his eyes with her lower lip pushing out as if she were pouting.

"It's not going to be that easy Jessica. I have to get Maddy and get her some breakfast." Bill felt a sense of redemption as he turned and walked out the bedroom.

"Here comes Maddy," said Irene when she saw Bill and Maddy coming up the stairs. She hurried to the kitchen counter and filled a small bowl half full of oatmeal.

Maddy went to her side and placed an open hand to her mouth and whispered," do we have our secret ingredient?"

"Shhh…" Irene placed a finger to her mouth and reached into the cabinet and pulled out a plastic bag from behind the boxes. She scooped a tablespoon full of brown sugar and put it on top of the oatmeal, before pouring in the hot water. "Our secret."

Samantha was cradling her cup of coffee as Bill sat back down. He blatantly stared at her sun beaten face and frazzled hair. He had held her close only hours earlier while she told him how worried she was for the safety of her parents. With wetness filling her eyes, she reiterated how worried they must feel not knowing of her wellbeing.

"Do I have something on my face?" Samantha placed a hand to the side of her face as she stared at Bill.

"No, no, just like looking at you," he said before turning toward Maddy. "Do you want to sit here with us?"

"I'll sit with Grandma," Nicole moved to the edge of her seat as Maddy sat on a corner of her chair.

Nicole looked directly across the table to where Shen and Li Na were sitting between Gina and Jacqueline and asked, "Is Irving your only child?"

"Yes," said Li Na, "we had him a little later in life."

"Jon and Irving have known each other for over twenty years." Gina looked sideways at Shen. "I met you two a couple nights before they were deployed to Africa."

"Yes, in Texas," said Li Na. "That was a scary time. Having loved one's in the military teaches us priorities in worrying."

"It certainly does," stated Gina, noticing Bobby and Emilee entering the kitchen.

"There has been a lot of chatter taking place on the radio about activity on the southern border," Bobby said, looking directly at Bill. "We lost the signal and wonder if you might see if you can help."

"Where's your dad and Uncle Jon?" Bill rose from his chair.

"They took off with Irving in the car about thirty minutes ago to check and see where the group of people from last night went." Bobby took in a deep breath. "I think they want to try and take the two guys who attacked Caroline into Limon this afternoon."

"Why didn't they use the drone to follow the group?"

"They sent it in a three-kilometer radius but didn't see anything. They were worried about it getting shot out of the air."

"What are you hearing on the radio?" Nicole asked.

"It sounds like there is a lot of fighting taking place at the border," Bobby hesitated. "Al and Linda are there with Kori trying to get the radio back to working."

"Have you tried to contact Ted?" Nicole moved off her chair to give Maddy the full seat.

"Not this morning."

Nicole took in a heavy breath and looked at Bill. She never mentioned how hard Ted tried to get her to go back with him to stay on the base at Fort Carson before he left. When she told him that she would rather stay at the farm with her son and granddaughter he never tried to pressure her to change her mind. "Let's go and see if we can get in touch with him."

"Are you finished?" Bill asked Maddy.

"Yes," Maddy walked to the sink and washed her bowl and placed it in the drainer. She walked to Samantha and took her hand as they all walked out the door.

Although it was still cold outside, activity throughout the farm was bustling. Harold and Jason were high on top of the tower, precariously building the hip roof. Dave and Sherry were visible at the second-floor window with the .50 Caliber rifle perched on the ledge pointed to the bright blue sky, safe from any falling debris by the floor of the third tier of the structure above them. The Jacobys were busy at the barn and corrals taking care of the cattle.

Linda and Kori were seated at Ted's desk in the garage fidgeting with the instruments of the radio, as Al watched, standing slightly to the side of his wife. Al had avoided Bill and Samantha since the incident where Samantha was called a bimbo. Bill tried to make eye contact with the dentist but was unsuccessful as Al continued to ogle the radio.

"We lost the connection," said Linda, twisting her head to look at both Bill and Nicole. "There was a major push north across the Mexican border by the enemy early this morning."

"We've been following it since about five, but now we can't get access or a signal," stated Kori.

"Can I try and see if I can contact Ted?" Nicole leaned against the back of Linda's chair. Kori pushed back and stepped out to let Nicole slide into the seat.

Nicole typed in the entrance information given to her by the communication specialist and waited to be connected. In small red letters at the bottom of the screen appeared the words "access denied". She tried again with the same results, this time with a small FBI icon visible at the lower righthand corner of the screen.

"Something major has happened," said Nicole. "If they are stopping all communication, then there must be a reason."

"Let's keep trying," replied Bill, noticing Al finally making eye contact with him. "Maybe it is only a temporary glitch."

"Bill and Samantha," Al moved next to them with Linda watching closely, "can I have a word with you two?" He took a couple steps back.

Bill stared at Al for a moment before looking at Samantha, who was standing with both hands on Maddy's shoulders.

Samantha removed her hands and shifted toward Bill. They followed Al out the side door of the office to the west side of the garage. The wind was blowing from the northwest, directly through the corrals, bringing about a pungent smell of manure.

"I've been meaning to speak with you." Al shuffled his feet as he resisted looking either of them in the eyes. "I've lost a lot of sleep over my behavior."

Neither Bill nor Samantha replied.

"I'm sorry Samantha. Sometimes I speak before I think. I'm one of those guys who thinks out loud," Bill looked her directly in the eye. "I am such an idiot. I hope you will accept my apology."

"Of course, I will," Samantha laughed softly. "I was hoping we could talk. It would have been really uncomfortable having to come to you if I would have had a toothache."

"Believe me I would take good care of you," Al stated. He reached his hand out in the direction of Bill. "Are we good?"

"We are good Al," Bill took the smaller hand in his large hand and firmly shook. He knew Al was sincere in the apology and now they could move beyond the entire incident.

"Here comes Hank," said Al, pointing in the direction of the driveway.

The three of them moved to the front of the garage as the car sped down the driveway. Bobby, Emilee, Sherry and Caroline joined them just as the vehicle came to a stop. Jon, Hank and Irving quickly hopped out.

"Did you find the people?" Bobby asked.

"Yep," Jon nodded his head. "They are about forty-five kilometers south of here."

"We believe they took our threat seriously," said Hank.

"Can we take the guys to the sheriff now?" Caroline came to stand close enough to Jon that she brushed his shoulder.

"Yes," he never faltered in his answer. "If you and Sherry want to go with me, we can take them there as soon as I get back from taking a break.

Bobby was caught completely by surprise that his Uncle Jon requested the two women to assist him in transporting the dangerous men to Limon. He knew Jon respected Sherry's ability to come through in a hostile situation, but still, there was a chance that the two men might overpower them.

"Do you want me to come with you?" Bobby asked.

"No," Jon answered emphatically. "Caroline can drive, and Sherry and I will watch them."

"We need to make sure they are restrained tight enough that they can't get loose," said Hank, looking with concern at his brother.

"Take care of it. We'll leave in fifteen minutes."

Limon, Colorado

The concrete blockade on the road to the FEMA camp was nearly two kilometers further west than it was when Jon was there only a few days before. It was his understanding, at that time, the camp was expected to have fewer inhabitants, not expand in such a drastic manner.

Jon decided to have Caroline take the entrance ramp to Interstate 70 and drive eastward toward the town. It would be difficult to walk through the camp dragging the criminals. The hands of both men were bound tightly behind their backs, and neither caused any problems during the ride from the farm. Having Caroline drive was a thoughtful strategy in that she didn't have an opportunity to shoot the men. Sherry kept a keen eye to the back seat and retained her pistol at the ready, but at no time pointed it directly at the prisoners as she rode in the front seat between Caroline and Jon.

The hotel which housed the FEMA director was visible from the highway but at the bottom of the exit ramp was a roadblock with several guards visible. They parked on the Interstate nearly a kilometer from the blockade.

"Wait here, I'll see if one of these guards will find the sheriff for us," Jon spoke through the door before closing it. He walked down the exit ramp to the sentries, who seemed indifferent to his arrival.

"Can we help you?" asked a muscular man.

"Yes sir, I believe you can. I'm Lieutenant Colonel Jon Lisco." Jon stood as straight as his arthritic back would allow him. "I was wondering if one of you could retrieve the sheriff for me. I have two men who attacked a young lady that I would like for him to take into custody."

"Are you serious?" the man looked at him with his forehead crinkled. "We've had, like eight murders in the area over the past week."

"Bob is still sitting in his cruiser by the Holiday Inn." An older lady joined the conversation as she moved next to the muscular man. "I can run over and see if he will talk to this gentleman."

"I would appreciate that," said Jon. As the lady scurried off, he noticed a massive amount of people in the FEMA camp. "Why are there so many people in the camp?"

"There are going to be a hell of a lot more real soon," said a young kid who looked to be about sixteen years old. "They are going to bring a whole lot of people from the west side of the mountains now that the Russians and Chinese have attacked from Mexico."

"When did all this happen?" Jon looked away from the kid toward the muscular man.

"They started evacuating a couple of days ago. They attacked across the border last night."

Jon swallowed hard. He could see the sheriff pulling up to the backside of the roadblock. He looked like a character out of the old west as he exited his cruiser. The old lawman rubbed his right knee as he struggled to walk to the concrete barricade.

"What can I help you with?" his cowboy hat was tipped as he spoke slowly.

"I have two men who attacked a young lady that I would like to place in your custody." Jon noticed the sheriff's worn blue jeans and cowboy boots as he stood bow-legged in front of him.

"I told him about all the murders we've had," stated the muscular man.

"Honestly, what do you want me to do with these guys?" the sheriff scoffed. He rubbed the white stubble on his chin. "There is no place to put them. We expect another twenty thousand people to arrive here over the next week. The whole damn town is overwhelmed. I would have to set them free the second you left."

"We are just trying to do the right thing here," said Jon.

"Listen, if you haven't noticed, it's the wild west out there. If you don't believe me, take a look at the bullet holes in my cruiser over there." He pointed at the police vehicle.

"We know times are dangerous. Our neighbor Clint Brown was murdered a few days ago." Jon looked at the ground and shook his head.

"Oh, good Lord," the sheriff sighed. "I know the Browns. What about Peg?"

"Her too, and the hired hand."

"God have mercy on all of us. We are doing all we can, but things are going to get worse." His eyes were puffy as he shook his head. "Are you one of the Liscos?"

"Lieutenant Colonel Jon Lisco, retired."

"I've met your sister," the sheriff grimaced. "She is one of the few people I would never cross."

"We are all staying at her farm." Jon glanced up the hill. Caroline was staring out the open window of the car. "Now, I have to figure out what to do with these two men."

"You look like a moral man. Do whatever you think is just and right." He removed his hat, swallowed hard, then turned around and limped back to his cruiser.

Jon thought for a moment as he watched the sheriff leave. He planned to speak to him about helping find the infiltrators in the little town who fired the EMP weapon. But now with all the chaos and the massive invasion of people to the location, it really didn't matter. Both men had more pressing issues to deal with.

Southern Utah

Sergeant Chamberland was standing outside a Humvee with his back to the howling wind. Next to him were Adam and Megan Jacoby's sons, Seth and Arthur. Colonel Deb stepped down from the Cougar into the menacing wind.

"Are you Irene Jacoby's grandsons?" she spoke loudly as she moved right in front of the disheveled boys.

"Yes ma'am. I'm Seth and this is my brother Arthur." Seth noticed the name tag on Deb's uniform. "Are you Ted's sister."

"Yes, he gave me the map to find your grandma's house." Deb held her hand to the side of her face to block some of the wind. "Where is the rest of your family?"

"They are outside a mountain resort about thirty kilometers from here."

"I'm going to send a squad with you to locate them and we will get you transportation east to Colorado." Deb looked at the tattoos and ring in Arthur's nose. He was completely different from his clean-cut brother. "I'll give you a map to find my farm on the plains. It's where your family is now."

"They made it to Colorado without any problems?" Seth asked.

"They had a few problems." Deb did not want to get into the details about his Aunt Ashley's head injury. "But they are all safe at the farm now."

"Colonel, this place is full of enemy troops." Seth looked at the convoy that made up most of F Company, strung out along the dirt road. "They are hidden in the hills and farms all across this area."

"Do you have any idea how many there are?"

"Thousands," stated Seth. "it seems like they are everywhere."

"How have you been able to keep from being detected? Were you in the military?"

"Marines," Seth adjusted his rifle at his shoulder. "I know every valley and canyon in this area."

"So, you can help the squad we send with you to find your family?"

"The enemy are located almost entirely along the ridge lines. There are several routes we can use to get back."

"Are there still civilians in the farms around this area?" Captain Hendersen asked.

"There are some, but you will never convince them to leave. The people willing to leave already took off around the same time our parents left."

"We don't have time to search for those unwilling to leave," stated Deb.

"Let's get going," said Captain Hendersen.

Deb clutched tightly to the piece of paper with the map to the farm to keep the whistling wind from blowing it away. She handed it to Seth. Captain Hendersen was briefing the squad from 2nd Platoon on the mission of having the Jacoby brothers help with identifying locals in the area as they escorted them to their hidden family, when Corporal Dobbs rushed between the captain and the colonel.

"Colonel Lisco, Corp is sending a helicopter to extradite you from this location." Corporal Dobbs hesitated in front of Deb and then turned to Captain Hendersen. "The transport is twenty mikes out."

"Did they say what location I will be transported too?"

"No, ma'am."

Deb watched as Seth and Arthur entered the Humvee and the platoon drove north on the county road.

Eastern Colorado

Caroline and Sherry were as baffled as Jon was by the dilemma of deciding what to do with the two men, created when the sheriff refused to take them into custody. They drove west bound in the east bound lanes of Interstate 70, then back down the entrance ramp to the county road. Both women were surprised when Jon told Caroline to turn north, rather than south at the junction under the overpass of the highway.

"What are you planning?" Sherry focused her eyes on the back seat where the two prisoners were both slumped, one to the right door and the other to the left.

"We can't take them back to the farm," Jon spoke forcefully with an ominous tone.

They quietly drove for more than twenty minutes down a desolate dirt road, when Jon pointed at a tree on the left side of the road. "Turn around and pull over next to that cottonwood."

Caroline slowed the car and made a U-turn and parked on the side of the road. Jon exited and opened the door to the back seat. He grabbed the man still wearing the cap and yanked him out onto the ground. His hands remained bound as he rolled a couple meters into the ditch. He pulled the blond man out from the opposite side, dragged him on his butt behind the car and pushed him into the bar ditch, next to his friend.

Sherry stood about ten meters behind the car with her pistol directed at the men. Caroline slowly walked around to the back edge of the vehicle and leaned on the trunk.

"Caroline," Jon aimed his revolver at the two men. "This is going to be your call."

Both men were laying in a fetal position in the moist dirt and weeds, gritting their teeth so hard that the muscles of their jaws were protruding out. They looked down and away so as not to make eye contact with their once victim.

"What are you saying?" Caroline asked.

"We have two options. We let them go." Jon smacked his lips and looked into her dark eyes. "Or we don't."

The vivid memory of the brutality of the attack pounded in Caroline's head as she took a step into the ditch with her shoe sinking about two centimeters into the semi-frozen dirt. Jon followed behind her. She held out her hand. He gave her the pistol.

"Why did you hit me so many times? All I wanted was a ride to see my family." She knelt over the man wearing the cap, remembering the pain of her ribs cracking as he continued to pound her with his fists. "Tell me why."

"I'm sorry," he murmured, closing his eyes. A smell of wet dirt rose into his nose as he breathed into the ground.

"Why?" She pointed the pistol only a centimeter from his head. Her hand was shaking.

"I don't know."

"Open your eyes."

He opened his eyes and looked at her twisted face. The cheeks on his oblong face were white and drooping as if they were melting off the bone. Dirt surrounded his nostrils.

"What you did to me wasn't human. You are an evil, evil person." The gun continued to quiver in her hand. "You are lucky that I am not. God will take care of you."

She handed the firearm back to Jon and stepped out of the ditch, back onto the gravel road. Sherry came to Jon's side.

"We can't let them go," Sherry yelled. "We will be watching over our shoulders from now on. They are going to come back in the dead of night and kill us."

"Do you want to be the one to finish them?" Jon asked. He was sure she would back away.

"Hell, yes I will." She moved over the top of the man wearing the cap and pointed the pistol. He rolled onto his back. His eyes were the size of saucers as he leaned back into the dirt.

"Hold it. Hold it." Jon stepped between the man and Sherry. He placed his hand on her muscular shoulder. "I think they know not to come anywhere near the farm again."

Sherry lowered the handgun and backed away. Jon breathed through his open mouth as he watched her stride up the embankment. In all his years as a soldier he never met a person as perplexing as the innocent looking young lady. He rotated to the men.

"You know we will fire first and ask questions later if you come near our home again? You need to point your asses that way." He kicked the man wearing the cap with the point of his shoe, then pointed northwest. "Right."

"We won't be back," the blond man said loudly, spinning his head to look at Jon.

Sherry moved next to Caroline by the car.

"Lean forward," Jon looked up to Sherry as the men slumped forward. "Keep your pistol on them."

Sherry stood with both hands on the weapon as he proceeded to unwind the tie wire from around each of their wrists. He purposefully showed his back to the men as he scrambled out of the ditch, onto the road. He had complete confidence Sherry would not hesitate to fire on the men should they try to overtake him. His trust was something he as a military man gave to very few people.

"Get in ladies." Jon walked to the driver's side and entered the car. Caroline never looked at the men as she climbed into the back seat. Sherry on the other hand stared at them as she backed to the car door. They understood, she wanted them to give her a chance to finish the situation.

Jon could see the men clambering out of the ditch in the rearview mirror as they sped away.

South Central Utah

The clapping blades of the helicopter could be heard coming in from the east as the sun rapidly set, bringing about a stinging chill to the diminishing wind. Captain Hendersen waited next to Deb as her ride came closer. Out of the corner of her eye she saw a flash race across the sky. A rocket hit the tail rotor of the low flying aircraft, causing it to flail about in the sky and finally hit hard into a field about five hundred meters north of their location.

Before anyone from F Company could react to the downing of the helicopter, rockets began to strike all around them, destroying several vehicles. Chaos ensued as small arms fire swept the area. Master Sergeant Herrera rushed to Colonel Deb's side and returned fire at the clearly identifiable enemy on the eastern edge of the convoy. He shielded the colonel as they backed out of the opening between trucks to cover next to the Cougar. The clanging of shells hitting the metal of the combat vehicles and the sound of the weapons being fired in response to the attack was almost deafening. The attack lasted only a couple minutes.

"Are you ok, ma'am?" Sergeant Herrera asked.

"Yes," Deb looked at smoke rising from many vehicles along the skirmish line. She moved out from the side of the Cougar. "I need to procure a rifle."

"Yes ma'am," he moved quickly as Captain Hendersen came to the colonel's side in a crouched position.

"Colonel, you need to stay as concealed as possible." The captain remained slumped over. "We have to move from this location.

"Are you able to assist the crew in the helicopter?" With darkness setting in, she could see dust rising from the area of the helicopter crash.

"3rd Squad is at the scene."

Before Deb could reply, an explosion from a rocket shook the ground. Sergeant Herrera with a large ammunition bag on his shoulder ran to her side carrying a M-16 and a Barrett M210 50 Caliber rifle, another rocket hit the Cougar behind them. Several small splinters from the shell hit Deb squarely on the right calf of her leg. She grimaced as she accepted the M-16 from the sergeant.

"Are you ok Colonel?" Sergeant Herrera asked.

"I'll live," she answered just as she saw a soldier in front of her hit by a bullet directly in the chest. She saw the form of the enemy who claimed the lieutenant's life retreating from the eastern edge of the convoy. She leveled the M-16 and fired.

"We have to move off the road," yelled Captain Hendersen, turning to Specialist Grant. "Redirect everyone to the ravine." He pointed to the south.

"Sir, they jammed communication," yelled the specialist frantically. "Everything is dead."

Captain Hendersen did a double take at the soldier before yelling, "Let's move out."

Deb limped noticeably as she followed closely behind the captain. Sergeant Herrera, carrying the heavy rifle and ammunition bag, grabbed her under the right arm and all but carried her away from the dirt road. Soldiers abandoned their vehicles and jumped into the deep ravine.

Captain Hendersen noticed the blood soaking the back of her pant leg while they leaned into the red clay on the side of the gully. Soldiers all along the line popped out and set their weapons, checking for the enemy with the veil of darkness quickly covering the area.

"Do you need medical?" The captain crawled up the bank of dirt as he spoke. He looked at the burning vehicles on the road.

"I don't know." Deb placed the M-16 to her side and pulled the torn pant leg up and twisted her leg to look at the back of her calf. She began pulling out small shards of metal.

"I'll send for a medic," said Captain Hendersen, glancing back down at her.

"No, I'm good." She picked at the bloody wound, took her handkerchief and poured a small portion of water on it. She wiped away much of the blood, then looked up at the captain. "What do you think our best options are?"

"Even if we can't drive out, we need to obtain our supplies and ammunition from the trucks," stated the captain. "Hopefully, we can get communication up."

"Captain," Sergeant Herrera was looking through the telescope of his rifle, "there is a hell of a lot of activity taking place on the hill northeast of here."

"How far out are they?"

"A little more than a kilometer."

"Within range then."

"Yes sir. Even in the dark." The sergeant worked on adjusting the sights as he looked through the telescope. "There are manpads visible."

"Let us bring in more snipers before you fire. We might as well take out as many as we can before they go into hiding."

"Sir," a private shuffled next to the captain. "3rd squad extracted the helicopter crew and have taken them to medical."

"Is medical west of here?"

"Yes sir," the private stood up with half his body out of the ravine.

Captain Hendersen grabbed his shirt at the back of the neck and pulled him down. "You can't expose yourself like that son. There are people out there that want you dead."

"Yes sir."

"Private, I want you to escort me to medical." Deb slid about a meter deeper to a level spot at the bottom of the chasm. She limped behind the private down the wash line.

Medical was situated at the end of the ravine where the steep walls flared out into a meadow. 2nd Platoon was located at the area with two M6 Bradley fighting vehicles positioned safely in the pasture. Condoleezza was busy rendering aid to one of the pilots when she observed Colonel Lisco limping her way.

"How are the pilots?" Deb noticed several soldiers with severe injuries receiving medical aid from the other medics. All the medics were functioning under dim light as they worked at a hectic pace to care for the wounded.

"The pilots suffered bumps and bruises." Condoleezza had an excessive amount of blood on her blouse as she stepped closer to the colonel. "What's wrong with your leg?"

Deb pulled up her trouser leg and turned around. She could feel the blood running down to her ankle.

"It will need to be cleaned and wrapped."

Condoleezza supported Deb's right arm as she led her to sit next to the pilot. The sound of intermittent gunfire could be heard. An RG 75 NYLA and a Humvee appeared nearly 400 meters past the other combat vehicles in the fallow pasture. All the vehicles moved north in the direction of the attacking forces.

"Private," Deb motioned to the soldier who arrived with her at the medical area. She pointed to the pasture. "Go to where the Bradley just left and ask 1st Lieutenant James if any of the drones are operational."

"Yes ma'am," the private took off in a full sprint.

"Turn over on your stomach." Condoleezza placed a small mat on the dirt.

Deb felt the back of her pant leg being cut as she placed her nose into a hard, plastic mat. The temperature dropped below freezing, making the frosty fluid being poured over her leg seem even colder. She shivered as the medic worked quickly on the lacerations. Her thoughts were on Tommy and the other soldiers in the 2nd Brigade.

"Ma'am," the private was breathing hard as he lowered his face to be only a couple centimeters from Colonel Deb's nose. "Lieutenant James said the drone is up and working. We also have communication back."

"Dammit private, move back a bit." Deb shifted her chin on the hard mat, to give some relief to her neck, before turning back to the side. The private was now on one knee. "Find Specialist Grant in communications and have her come here."

"Yes ma'am," the private hopped up and left in a full sprint.

"Lucky you didn't have further orders for him," Condoleezza chuckled. "I just need to wrap this, and I'll be done."

The humming sound of a squadron of MQ 7T Reapers could be heard flying overhead to the north. Soon the sound of explosions filled the air. Flashes of light lit up the horizon through the cloud covered darkness.

"Ok," Condoleezza finished the wrap and released her leg. "Just keep an eye on it."

Deb turned to sit on her butt, before standing. She was surprised how far away the blasts were taking place. F Company had pushed the enemy back.

"Colonel," Specialist Grant stood at full attention, "your new ride should be here by 2200." She turned to Condoleezza. "Helicopters are in route to evacuate the wounded."

"What is their ETA?" Condoleezza asked.

"Within fifteen mikes, ma'am." The specialist turned back to Deb. "We received a message from Command Sergeant Major Talfoya that G Company is in route to this location. The remainder of 2nd Battalion is moving headquarters to the civilian conveyance location north of Beaver."

"Did he say why they are moving?"

"No, ma'am, but that is where you are scheduled to be transported." Specialist Grant hesitated for a moment, before continuing, "Command Sergeant Major Talfoya didn't specify, ma'am, but the enemy has broken through and there is continuous fighting about a hundred and fifty klicks south of our location. It's quickly moving northward."

***

Deb was whisked away in the new generation AH-102 long range attack helicopter which allowed for the crew of two plus room for two passengers. Perfect for the scenario where the colonel found herself in need of a ride in the war zone.

As the helicopter ascended rapidly, she could see fires filling the valley. A column of lights making up G Company was momentarily visible snaking along a dirt road rushing toward F Company's position. Her head was aching, and her leg hurt as she looked out the window at the dark landscape. She gasped when she saw the Jacoby home burning and several big holes blown into the side of the red barn.

"How long to my destination?" Deb asked with a humming noise in her ear, causing her discomfort.

"About fifty minutes, ma'am."

She leaned back in the seat and closed her eyes. The battle happened so quickly she was glad to have a moment to reflect on how she handled her duties, and the performance of the soldiers under her command. The distinct, unwavering commands shouted by Captain Hendersen filled her thoughts. One of her dad's oft used quotes was "If you cannot do great things, do small things in a great way". The captain processed situations quickly and made solid decisions while under distress. He handled all the small details greatly. She dozed off.

"Ma'am, we are here," said the pilot, waking her from the light sleep.

Her stomach rose to her throat as the chopper plummeted quickly to the ground. Once she was out of the helicopter and standing next to Tommy, it ascended and sped away, causing her to turn away from the wind caused by the blades.

"We have your quarters all set." Tommy had his arm around her waist, pulling her close to shield her from the force of the wind.

"I need an update," she leaned back, slipping out of his arms.

"We can do it in your tent." He noticed she was limping. "What happened to your leg?"

"Shrapnel." She was surprised at the amount of activity happening in the middle of the night. There were hundreds of large buses lined for kilometers along the Interstate highway. Crowds of people were in lines, roped off, leading them to tables where each would stop and speak to a soldier before climbing on to a bus.

"Do you want to go to the medical tent?"

"No," she allowed him to place his hand around her back to help her walk. "How well are we vetting these people before they are transported?"

"We don't have anything to say about the process. Families are taken on certain buses and individuals are on others. They will be evaluated by Homeland Security when they reach the FEMA encampments."

"Where are Lloyd and Teresa?" she was still chilled by the cold breeze. Tommy released her waist. She held his arm to keep the weight off her leg.

"3rd Battalion is at Salt Lake City and 1st has made it to Grand Junction."

"Did they encounter any problems?"

"Nothing significant. Here are your quarters."

Tommy held open the canvas door to the tent. Deb stepped inside and he followed. She sat on the bed.

"What is going on with communication?" she asked, placing her injured leg onto the bed, but keeping the other on the floor while continuing to sit upright.

"They are using voice patterns to identify and locate our commanding officers. They have been successful in eliminating some of our upper command."

"Who?" Her eyes widened in anticipation of the update.

Tommy hesitated and swallowed. "Colonel Tyler with Stryker. Among others."

"Is he KIA?" she asked.

"Yes." Tommy knew Deb's relationship with Colonel Tyler was tight. "You and I are scheduled to leave here tomorrow morning at 1100."

"Where are we going?"

"Catch a chopper to Toole, then fly to Peterson, and onto Fort Carson." Tommy stared at her, obviously wanting to talk.

Deb brought up her hanging leg and leaned her head back, stretching the skin under her chin. She took in a deep breath and asked, "Can you give me a little time? If I'm not out by 0500 have someone wake me."

Colorado Farm

Bill rubbed the three-day old stubble on his chin, watching the clouds overhead accumulate from the third floor of the concrete tower, knowing snow would be flying soon. Although everyone was trying to work together to make the place better, there was still an underlying sentiment that everything would soon change, and everyone would be able to go home to their normal lives. The progress, especially the building of the block tower and apartment was spectacular. His mind wandered to when he and Aunt Deb deliberated on the best ways to supply and organize the farm, how everything was more a fantasy, a game they played to prepare for the worse, without real human emotions.

Finding someone like Samantha amongst the chaos and confusion was another thing he never envisioned. She was becoming more than just a girlfriend; she was the one he wanted to spend the rest of his life with. Seeing Harold and Jason carrying pieces of plywood from the garage in his direction brought him from his thoughts.

"We are coming up to place the folding windows," Harold set the plywood down as he yelled to Bill. "I'd like to get them built today to keep snow out."

"Do you need me to help carry the plywood up," Bill yelled down.

"No, I measure and cut it down here." Jason pulled the collar of his coat tight around his neck to block the cold wind.

"We will need help getting the flat iron pieces up," said Harold. "It's going to take more than two of us to carry them."

Deb insisted on having the one-inch-thick pieces of iron placed at the bottom of the windows in the tower. She realized many bullets could pierce the grout filled concrete blocks, but not through both the reinforced concrete block and the iron. The problem was the iron was two meters long by a hundred and ten centimeters high, making them extremely heavy.

"The front-end loader on the tractor can lift them high enough to get to the second-floor window," stated Bill.

"We can figure all that out later. I need to get the window shuttered," yelled Harold as a gust of wind blew hard enough to lift the plywood in his grasp. Jason grabbed hold and helped push the wood level to the ground.

Bill looked to the southwest, over the top of the house. An old car, a 1957 Chevy was slowly coming down the driveway. He watched until they were no longer visible behind the house. Breanna and Irene scurried out of the RV and made their way in the direction of the new vehicle.

"Looks like we have a visitor," Bill yelled down.

Jason took several steps backwards to find a vantage point to look in front of the house. "It's a family," he yelled. "Irene must know them."

By the time Bill found his way to the car, some of the Jacobys and most of the people from inside were greeting the people. Maddy was holding onto Irene's hand, with Scotty standing next to her.

"Daddy," Maddy rushed to his side and pulled him in front of the man. "This is Travis, he was the pilot who wrecked our airplane."

"He didn't wreck it Maddy," Irene scoffed, laughing softly. "He landed it."

"It wasn't wrecked?" Maddy turned to Irene and pulled on the neckline of her sweater. "Then why did we have to walk to your house?"

"She has a point there Irene." Travis chuckled before motioning toward his family. "This is my wife Sue and our two girls Willow and Aubrey."

"Nice to meet you," said Bill, noticing how handsome the pilot was as he stood next to his petite wife with their two children holding onto his legs. The younger girl looked to be about Maddy's age and the other slightly older.

"I was becoming a little concerned I wasn't going to be able to find this place. Ted's map was good, but the dirt roads aren't marked very well." Travis looked at Irene. "I figured Ed would like his car back."

"Believe me he will." Irene looked to the RV where Megan and Ashley were sauntering in their direction.

"Thank God," Travis looked to Ashley, "how is Carol?"

"She passed," Breanna answered quickly, glancing at Scotty with her lower lip covering her upper. "We couldn't save her."

"Ummm," Travis looked directly at Scotty, "I'm terribly sorry to hear that."

Scotty's big round face turned bright red. Maddy went to his side. "Grandpa is going to take us to California to find Scotty's mom. And then we are going to get my mom and bring them back to the farm."

Irene moved closer to the two children, smiling she reinforced Maddy's thoughts. "It may take a while, but we have confidence Ted is going to do all he can to help us."

"We are adapting to the changes we have to face each day." Breanna redirected the conversation, "Our family, Terrance, Jerry and of course Samantha seem to be getting along better each day."

Bill noticed Samantha remained at the edge of the crowd, making no attempt to interact with the pilot. She was looking off into space. Her mind was on something besides greeting Travis and his family.

"Is everything alright?" Bill stepped to her side.

"Fine," her smile tried to portray her feelings as being content, but her drooping eyes told him otherwise.

Bill was sure there was something major bothering Samantha concerning the arrival of Travis. Remembering how Jessica disappeared unexpectedly with Christian after creating a union with him, caused him to question his ability to understand the new woman in his life. He had a strange feeling he was being set up to be betrayed again.

He could hear Travis telling Hank and Jon how much they looked like Ted. Jacqueline and Gina were gushing over how cute the little girls were. Samantha slowly turned and walked into the house.

Littleton, Colorado

Christian and Tim could see their breath as they waited in the morning cold for the food line to move forward so they could receive breakfast. It was easier than expected for the entire group of insurgents to blend in with the locals at the encampment located at the Denver Seminary off Santa Fe Drive in Littleton. The military sweep of the area was successful in that it kept them from overtaking the new police station and pushed them into hiding. Food was now an issue. They left their large weapons at a small house in old town Littleton that they used for a rendezvous spot. Several of the rebels slipped handguns through the minimally secure checkpoint at the entry gate.

After receiving their plate of food, eight confederates joined Christian and Tim at a table. The rest of the rebels scattered across the large open space park where more than a hundred tables covered the frigid landscape. Armed security patrolled the grounds, keeping an eye on the crowd partaking in breakfast. Most looked like police but several were armed civilians.

"I don't feel very good about this place," Christian surveyed the surroundings. "We better locate some other areas for food."

"All the other camps in the Denver area are north or east of here. We have to go way east, or way north, to find them." Tim placed a frayed map of Colorado, with several areas circled in red pen, on the table before taking in a large mouthful of powdered eggs. "Yuk. This is awful."

"You better eat a lot; it might be a while before we eat again." Christian ate quickly. He took note of an older man in a khaki shirt who seemed to be keeping close tabs on the group.

"There are a lot of police around here." Tim sensed there was something bothering Christian. "What's wrong?"

"This guy," he said lightly, smiling at the man in the khaki shirt positioning himself next to their table. He stopped and stood right behind Tim's chair.

"How are ya all doing? I'm the director of the camp," the man spoke pleasantly. His face was freshly shaven with noticeable blood marks from nicks on his sunken chin. "I haven't seen you here before."

"We literally arrived an hour ago." Christian noticed several of the security personnel assembling closer to the table. "We left the encampment near Red Rocks this morning."

"Why here?" the man rested his hand on the back of Tim's metal chair.

"Just stopping to get something to eat as we pass through." Christian took a large bite of food.

"And where are you heading?"

"We are going to Fort Carson to enlist."

"Are you walking there? We are expecting cold temperatures and snow." The man was surprised and a little confused with the response of enlisting. He was not sure if he was dealing with rebels or patriots. All FEMA personnel were required to report large, unknown groups who suddenly arrive at a camp without previous notification or approval from regional headquarters. It was obvious some of the people at separate tables were part of Christian's group, making them fit the criteria to be reported. "It's nearly a hundred kilometers to the base."

"That's the plan." Christian leaned back in his chair. "Unless you want to give us a ride."

"All of you planning to enlist?" He measured the looks from the five women eating at the table.

"All of us," stated a large woman with a scar on her forehead. "I'll probably be infantry."

"I want to drive a tank," said the woman next to her, smiling with crooked, yellow teeth.

The man sensed they were having fun with him. There was no way the group of misfits were planning to travel to the army base. "I'll tell you what. I will contact the base and have them send a truck to transport you." He took a step away from the back of Tim's chair and enjoyed the surprised expressions.

"That would be great," said Christian confidently, smiling at the others.

"I'll do it now."

The man stopped to talk with the security personnel before disappearing into one of the buildings on the edge of the field. Several more armed members joined the others to watch over the group.

"Here is the exit strategy. There is a wooded area to the south of here." Christian leaned over the table and spoke quietly.

He nodded his head to the south. "If we have to leave in a hurry, run through the crowd toward the woods."

"That won't work Christian," said the large woman sitting next to him.

"What do you mean, Shira, it won't work?" Christian scoffed.

"I walked around the perimeter when we first arrived. There is a chain length fence surrounding the entire property. It is about three meters high."

Placing his right hand to his chin, Christian stared at Shira Rosenfeld. She was an acquaintance from high school, where he thought of her as quite odd. She was an intellectual with a tendency to question everything, just like him, which caused them to draw to one another. She had a sand texture on both cheeks of her face that easily turned a bright red in the cold or when she got excited. Although she and Jessica were quasi friends, she quickly moved to take Jessica's place with him the same afternoon Jessica left.

"Nix that then." Christian felt anxious as he watched the director of the camp approach, flanked by four armed police officers in uniform. Another twenty members of the security team lined up about ten meters away. Christian looked in the direction of the other insurrectionists at the surrounding tables, who were all closely watching the actions at their leader's table.

"Ok, here is the deal. I don't believe for a second that you are going to Fort Carson to enlist." The director stood at the far end of the table away from Christian. "But…the base will send transportation here in the morning."

"What time should we be back in the morning?" Christian asked in a calm manner.

"No, no. You need to stay here tonight."

Christian folded his arms. He was sure the man informed the Army that there were rebels at the government camp. More than likely forces were on their way to the location as they spoke.

"I don't want to stay here. Half these people look diseased," said Shira.

"Everyone has had their temperature monitored and we have members keeping an eye out for sickness," stated the director.

"It will be alright." Christian squinted his eyes, giving her a cold stare.

"Here's the rules. No weapons of any kind. No political speech. No words or statements that can be perceived as disrespectful. No..."

"What the hell," Shira shouted, interrupting him. "What is wrong with you people. Why are we fighting so hard to defeat the Russians and Chinese? You are suppressing our freedoms more than they will. This is the reason the cities are burning, you authoritarian asshole."

Christian rose from his chair with his head on a swivel, looking at the rebels at the other tables." It's time for us to go," he shouted.

Director Westmoreland motioned to the security team. The four police officers pulled their weapons and leveled them in the direction of the people at Christian's table.

"I wouldn't do that if I were you." Christian signaled to the rebels eating at the other tables. More than a hundred of them popped up from their chairs and advanced toward him and the director. "You give us no other option. If you want a blood bath at your camp, you will be one of the first to go."

The multitude of armed insurrectionists swarmed to surround the security detail.

"Just go." The director stepped back next to the police officers and motioned with his right arm in the direction of the gated entrance. His hand was shaking. "Lower your weapons please, we won't try to stop you."

Christian was the first out of the gate, followed by the throng of dissidents. He jogged across an open field, over some railroad tracks and did not stop until arriving at the nearly vacant residential area of old town Littleton. Locating food in the city was going to be much harder than anticipated. His militia was recognizable and the camps that offered food were on high alert.

He had not crossed paths with the foreigners since they were thwarted by the presence of the Army after being ordered to take the police station on Colorado Boulevard. He came to the realization, after the confrontation at the FEMA camp, that the foreign rebels were the supreme threat to him and his friends. They faced being arrested by the government people, whereas confrontation with the foreign rebels would be much more deadly. Eventually either the rebels or the authorities were bound to catch up with them if they stayed in any one place for a long period of time. There was no place to hide in the city.

Beaver, Utah

Deb was up and pulling on her boots when she heard Tommy yell her name from outside the tent. She looked at her watch. It was exactly 0500. What the hell she thought, did he sit outside the entire night waiting to wake her.

"Come in Tommy."

He backed through the entrance carrying two steaming cups of coffee. He handed her a cup.

"Fighting has moved all the way to the St. George area and Corp wants us to expedite our schedule," Tommy stated.

"Are all the people evacuated?"

"FEMA ran out of buses last night, so they transferred ten bus loads to Grand Junction and let the civilians off before heading back this way. They should be finishing up with loading the final group of passengers."

"When are we leaving?"

"0700."

Deb cradled the warm cup of coffee. "This is absolutely ridiculous that I can't communicate directly with upper brass.

"Hopefully the issues with communication will be resolved by the time we get to Fort Carson," stated Tommy.

"Ma'am," a soldier yelled from outside the tent.

Tommy opened the flap to the tent and stuck his head outside. "What is it private?"

"There is a civilian who wants the colonel to come to the extradition site to help resolve a conflict."

He turned to Deb, "Did you hear."

Give me more information," Deb yelled loud enough for the soldier to hear. "What is the conflict?"

"It's a family, ma'am. They all want to ride in one bus and not split up. The civilian asked for you personally. Sergeant Bishop told me to see if you could come and help resolve the problem."

"Do we have time?" Deb asked Tommy.

"We can take our gear and stop there on the way to our expulsion area. It's the same location you were dropped off last night."

"Tell Sergeant Bishop we will be there in ten minutes," Deb shook her head. "If it's not one thing, it's another."

Tommy carried both his and the colonel's duffle bags while Deb limped alongside to the area where two lone buses were waiting to depart. The Jacobys were standing at the open door yelling at several of the personnel from FEMA."

"Colonel Lisco," Josh stepped toward Deb, "these people want to have us split-up. They say that some of our family need to get on the other bus that is going to Casper Wyoming."

Deb looked at a man of about forty dressed in a light blue button-down shirt with FEMA written on the pocket at his breast. His eyes were drooping and there was no hint of a smile on his face.

"Are there people on the Colorado bus willing to go to the Wyoming bus?" Deb asked.

"Obviously, Colonel, I am not so incompetent to have not already tried to coax people off," the FEMA official scoffed. "Now, I have about had it with these people. Either they get on the buses, or I will arrest them, and they can ride to their destinations in handcuffs."

"Arrest them?" Deb glanced at Seth before turning to the man. "For what?"

"Failure to obey my orders," he screamed.

Deb stared at him with her nose curled and her hands palms up.

Tommy sat the bags at his feet, grabbed ahold of Deb's arm and led her back about ten meters before speaking softly, "Since Martial Law has been implemented, he most likely has the authority to arrest and detain civilians without a warrant."

"So, it is possible he has the power to arrest them?" Deb squinted her eyes as she twisted her neck to look back at the FEMA group.

"Not only possible but most likely. Executive orders go back before FEMA existed to President Kennedy where he gave powers to the government when the threat of a nuclear attack was a real possibility. Over the years the orders have been revoked and shuffled to other departments within the United States government," stated Tommy. "I don't know the specifics of the scope of his power. One thing I know is that Homeland Security has complete authority over this situation."

Deb limped in the direction of the director, knowing it would take all she had to be civil.

"Can we use some common sense here?" Deb forced a smile. Her head was beginning to throb. "These are all young people who would have no problem sitting in the aisle of the bus or doubling up on the seats."

"These buses have a capacity for fifty people. We stretched the rule to allow for a sixty person maximum, which we have followed all night long." He held his right hand in the palm of his left hand. "If this entire group goes on the Colorado bus there will be sixty-nine passengers. I won't allow the bus to be that overloaded when we have another bus leaving the area that is only half full."

Deb swallowed hard. She looked at his colleagues glaring at her with smug expressions. "What is your name?"

"I am Theodore Sutherland, Deputy Assistant of response for region 8."

"I truly sympathize with the task you have had to deal with. You have done an outstanding job." Deb smiled at him and motioned out with her left hand. "But can we be reasonable here? Use a little foresight? In this time of complete chaos none of us would want to separate from our families. Having an afternoon of being crowded on a bus would save a lot of suffering and worry for this family down the road."

"Not going to happen." The deputy shook his head. He turned his back on Deb and stepped nearer to Seth. "Pick nine to ride on the other bus."

"Ok, listen here Deputy Sutherland. We are going to put this entire family on the Colorado bound bus." Deb positioned next to Seth. "All of you, go ahead and get on."

"Hold it," the deputy moved closer to the bus as the Jacobys boarded.

Deb hobbled forward and put the index finger of her left hand about a centimeter from his nose, stopping him in his tracks.

"Oh Jesus," Tommy shuffled next to her. "Colonel, please."

The entire Jacoby family climbed on the bus. The door closed.

"If you," she shook her finger, "or anyone else from FEMA detains this family, I will take it as a personal affront to me."

"Are you crazy? I have complete authority of this base, given to me by the Department of Homeland Security." The deputy jerked his head straight back and stared at the tip of her finger with his mouth wide open. "Are you threatening me?"

"Sergeant Bishop," Deb never floundered as she yelled, "see these buses off."

"Colonel, your career in the Army is over." He recoiled back to the safety of the other personnel from FEMA.

"Just shut up," Deb's dark eyebrows folded over her eyes. She started to walk away before stopping and pointing at the cowering man. "Just remember what I told you Deputy Sutherland. Leave that family alone or I'll knock the living hell out of you."

"Oh, Lord," Tommy shuddered while placing his left hand to the top of his head. He stared at the startled group from FEMA.

Deb waited patiently as the bus made its way to the Interstate. She turned quickly and walked away.

"Oh my God, Colonel, I wish you had handled that differently." Tommy ran to keep up with her, bouncing both duffle bags on his knees. "This is awful. I mean this is really awful."

They hurried to the open field. The hacking sound of the blades of the chopper became louder and louder as it neared. She turned to the command sergeant major.

"Tommy, I am who I am. I told Irene and Ed Jacoby I would watch out for their family. I will never stand by and allow stupidity to stand in the way of veracity and common sense."

They watched the helicopter land.

Colorado Farm

Maddy ran downstairs and grabbed her heavier coat while Scotty waited for her in the front yard. He was already wearing a winter jacket, albeit a size too large for his little body, but one that protected him from the dropping temperature and spitting snow.

She ran out the front door on the kitchen side, quickly past Scotty and out the side gate of the yard. She was halfway across the courtyard by the time he caught her. They both ran past the garage and around the barn to an area they discovered the day before, about five hundred meters further from the corrals on the north side of the barn. A dusty concrete foundation from the remnants of an old farmhouse poked from the ground covered with dirt and weeds. Deteriorated wood siding and two by fours were scattered on top and to the side of the structure.

"Be careful," Maddy removed her heavy mitten from her right hand and pulled a rusty nail from a piece of wood. She held it out for Scotty to see with her dark eyes wide open. "This could go right through your shoes."

"Look at this." He held up an old mason jar with a small band of metal around the threaded neck of the container. "We should keep this."

"Look at this," Maddy kicked a wasp nest off a pile of red brick from the chimney laying at the side of the structure. The nest turned to powder in the cold wind.

Scotty stepped onto a floor of eight pieces of wood with an opening of about two centimeters between each of them. He went to a knee and tried to look through a gap.

"Look," he yelled, raising onto his feet, allowing Maddy to get closer.

Maddy stepped onto the sagging structure. Just as she was preparing to go to her knees to look through the cracks, the wood floor collapsed. They fell straight down with Maddy landing feet first before falling backwards into the brick wall, partially breaking the fall with her arm. Scotty landed on his feet and fell backward onto his butt.

"Ohh…," Scotty moaned loudly as he lay on the cold dirt floor. He could see up sheer walls of brick to a circular opening about four meters above.

Maddy gasped for air as she struggled to gain her breath. She grabbed her left wrist with her right hand and continued struggling to breath.

"Are you ok Maddy?" Scotty moved to her side, scattering fragments of the wood floor which followed them down into the old well. He put a hand on her shoulder.

Maddy caught a deep breath and tears flowed from her eyes.

"I hurt my arm," she gasped.

Scotty placed a hand on the cold brick and stretched upward. His reach was not even close to the opening. His big round face was rosy.

"We can't get out of here Maddy." He could feel a sharp pain at his left hip. "We're trapped."

"I want my daddy," Maddy sniffled, "and mommy."

Scotty sat down next to her and placed his arm around her. His lower lip pushed out and he cried.

Maddy quieted and stared at Scotty through wet eyes. She leaned her head to the cold fabric of the coat on his shoulder. She looked up at small snowflakes floating above, evaporating before they reached her.

***

Immediately after lunch, Nicole sat down at the kitchen table with Jacqueline and Gina to contemplate a list of food items still left in the large pantry in the basement. It was becoming ever apparent they would be living at the farm for an extended period. The three women were taking it upon themselves to organize and delegate different tasks important to keeping the farm operational.

One concern Nicole confronted was the consideration of taking care of the children that were arriving. As a grandmother she feared that Maddy and the other children were unsupervised on too many occasions while adults tended to other tasks. She wanted to bring some structure to their lives by organizing care for the children. Bill, along with Travis' wife Sue and Glenda Hernandez were all more than willing to take their turns tending to the kids. Travis and Victor were recruited to help drywall the southern rooms at the apartment in anticipation of having them ready for occupancy within a day, so they were going to be too busy hanging drywall to help care for the kids.

Nicole was hesitant to ask Jessica if she was willing to spend time with the children. It was an awful thing to think, but she was not sure she could trust her. Avery and Reagan were probably old enough to wander on their own. Since she arrived back at the farm Jessica was either working in the greenhouse or hiding in the basement, with Emilee keeping track of her little sisters most of the time.

Irene was around Maddy on many occasions during the day and Nicole wanted to leave it to the discretion of her on how often she wanted to be involved. Samantha on the other hand was someone who should be offered the opportunity to be immersed with the kids.

Nicole rose from her chair and walked to the kitchen window and looked outside. Maddy and Scotty were nowhere in sight.

"I'm going to go check on Maddy." Nicole put on her coat and walked outside. Light snow dampened her hair before she pulled the hood up and tightened the draw strings tight around her chin. She walked through the yard, across the driveway to the Jacoby's RV. She knocked and Breanna opened the door.

"Are Maddy or Scotty here?"

"No, I'll ask Mom if she has seen them." She turned but Irene had heard the inquiry and was already nudging her way to the door.

"We are planning on baking some cornbread this afternoon. I will help you look," Irene grabbed her coat from the hanger.

"No, that's okay. Let me check with Bill and Samantha. I'm sure they are with them." Nicole stepped back from the RV.

Bill and Samantha were at the apartment watching Jason and his crew place electrical switch plates and finish wiring for the electrical heat on the first set of apartments. The room smelled of caulking and fresh paint. Samantha decided she wanted the single bedroom on the southeast corner of the structure. It would still be a couple of days before the first of three community bathrooms would be ready to use, but she was still excited to have a room for herself. Finding themselves alone in the room, Bill decided it would be a good time to find out why she was so distant around Travis.

"Can I ask you a personal question?" Bill asked.

She twisted her mouth which signaled to him she was waiting to have the inevitable conversation.

"What's going on with Travis?" he waited for an answer as she peered out the window at the back pasture. He continued when she didn't answer, "I'm surprised you never acknowledged him or his family when they arrived."

Bill was wondering if maybe they were lovers. The more she remained silent the more he conjectured.

"I spoke with your dad about part of this on our way back to Colorado," she remembered Ted asking if Travis was her lover. She imagined Bill was pondering the same visions in his mind. She looked him directly in the eyes. "Travis and I were friends who worked together for the same airline."

"Why are you so distant?"

"His wife Sue thinks we were having an affair. She still does." Her breathing was increasing as she positioned herself directly in front of him. "I was about to lose my job for an alcohol related issue, that was false. Travis and I were in a compromising situation at a hotel in Los Angeles that Sue found out about. I lied to her about certain things that she was able to confirm as being a lie. She and Travis have been working through the issues ever since. She thinks of me, not only as a liar, but someone who was sleeping with her husband."

Bill was having trouble following her conversation. Her whole explanation was vague and so unclear, he didn't know how to reply. He struggled with understanding what she meant by both a compromising situation and an alcohol related issue? He decided not to pursue the questions because she was vulnerable to believing everyone would consider her a liar.

"Is it something that might be resolved by sitting down with Travis and his wife?" Bill heard his mother yelling for him outside the apartment, but he waited to hear Samantha's reply.

"I don't want to face her just quite yet." Samantha raised her eyebrow over her right eye and then looked away.

He tried to look her in the eyes, but she refused to make eye contact. He could hear his mother continue to call his name from outside. He stepped out of the apartment into the cold.

"Have you seen Maddy or Scotty?" Nicole was holding the collar of her coat tight around her neck.

"Not for a while. Did you check with Irene?"

"Yes, she hasn't seen her."

"Maddy, Scotty," Bill yelled loudly. He walked nearer the garage and yelled again. Jon and Hank, followed by Irving, Terrance and Jerry stepped out the door of the garage.

"What's wrong, Bill?" Hank yelled.

"We are trying to locate Maddy and Scotty."

"Well, they can't be very far." Jon walked to the west edge of the garage and yelled in the direction of the barn, "Maddy."

Soon, the sound of people yelling the kids names could be heard from all directions. After nearly thirty minutes of searching everyone on the farm gathered in front of the Jacoby's RV.

"Oh God, where could they be?" Nicole inhaled deeply.

"This is not like her," Irene claimed, folding her arms in front of her.

The door to the RV opened and Breanna helped her dad down the steps. Ed was wearing a patched coat with an original Kromer cap. He hobbled to the middle of the pack of anxious people.

"When was the last time anyone saw them?" Ed asked.

"It was around lunch time," stated Nicole.

"We have to open and check all the freezers and refrigerators. Look in all the corrals and under all the machinery," Ed's eyes were watery. "Look in all the closets and rooms in the house. Check any old wells or cellars on the property."

"Mom, would you, Aunt Gina and Aunt Jacqueline organize a group to search the house?" Bill felt nauseous.

Heavy snow began to cover the ground. The sun was barely visible as it sat low on the horizon.

"Oh Lord, I hope the snow doesn't get any worse," Nicole covered her mouth with her hand.

"The snow might not be bad. If they are outside the cloud cover will keep the temperature from falling," stated Ed. "But darkness will be a problem with the sun setting so early this time of year."

"We will check all the farm equipment and around the barn," said Aaron, motioning to Adam, Ashley and Megan.

"Maddy is afraid of the horses, but I'll check the stalls." Breanna walked quickly toward the barn.

"Let's set this up systematically. Break into four equal groups." Jon pointed at Hank, Irving and Terrance. "I'll go north, Hank west, Terrance east and Irving south."

Bill wandered aimlessly from farm building to farm building. Everything imaginable, from being attacked by a wild animal, to someone coming to the farm and taking Maddy, began to cram his mind. It was nearly time to eat supper and darkness covered the landscape. He sat down in the snow outside the garage and grabbed tightly to the hair on top of his head.

"Come on Bill," Bobby placed his hand on his cousin's shoulder. "Let's keep looking. We are going to find them."

Fort Carson Army Base

Operation Lumberjack was grounded on three independent movements. First was the placement of forces in Northern Africa; Second was American Special Forces, along with the Mexican Army, to systematically begin taking back the occupied cities of northern Mexico; Third was to use mostly nonhuman weaponry to engage the enemy moving through the area of the western United States from the Rockies west to the Sierra Nevada mountains.

Army Chief of Staff General Ron McClinton, General Lopez and General Prost sat at a table in the army base mess hall. They were taking a lunch break after a long morning of coordinating the movements and strategic placement of the nonhuman weaponry. They were preparing for the attack on embedded insurrectionists and advancing enemy troops in the evacuation area.

According to the information formulated over the past several days, everything the enemy was doing was predicted within the models. The process of putting into motion the United States military machine was slow, but, cutting off the supply chains to the embedded enemy and giving them no options but to move northward into the non-human forces of the United States was already beginning to develop. The massive size of the enemy forces at the border would eventually be their undoing. General Lauer was summoned to a call immediately after leaving the strategy session. He rejoined them at the table.

"I just got off the horn with the Chief Security Officer from Homeland Security," General Lauer sat his plate of food on the table. "He was all up in arms. Apparently, Colonel Lisco threatened the FEMA Director for Section 8 this morning at the civilian dispersion site in Utah."

"Ha, ha, does that surprise any of us?" General McClinton laughed while leaning back in his chair.

"He was genuinely upset," General Lauer scoffed. "I told him I would discipline her appropriately."

"Ted met her this morning at Peterson, and they went straight to the base hospital," stated General Lopez. "She has a wound to her leg."

"Is it serious?" General Prost asked.

"Ted indicated it was for precaution," General Lopez looked at General Lauer. "Looks like you might be pinning a medal on her at the same time you are chastening her."

"I have to respond to her behavior." General Lauer took a bite of mashed potatoes. His right eye twitched as he swallowed.

General Prost glanced at Chief of Staff General McClinton. He was still smiling while General Lauer grimaced.

"Did Colonel Lisco physically strike the man?" General McClinton asked. He tossed a napkin onto his half empty plate.

"No, it never reached that point."

"We all know who Colonel Lisco is," stated General McClinton. "Let's get her version of what happened before we make any decisions."

"Without structure and discipline, mostly from our commanding officers, our whole chain of command will collapse." General Lauer placed his fork down. "I have to address her conduct."

"I agree, we could not exist without discipline within the ranks. But Colonel Deb Lisco is a whole different animal," stated General Prost.

"Ann," General McClinton pushed out his barrel chest, "as contentious as the encounter was between you and the colonel a couple of years ago, I am surprised you would come to her defense."

"I understand her better after our meeting in Great Falls. Besides, she was correct in almost all aspects she raised at our conference two years ago." General Prost decided not to mention the bonding over a bottle of scotch. "The information we collected at the warehouse outside Great Falls gave me a different perspective on the colonel. Besides being incredibly discerning, she is someone we need on our side."

"We have an Army full of hardnosed leaders who are perceptive and dedicated. How is Colonel Lisco different?" General Lauer looked at the determined eyes of the petite general staring at him across the table. He took a sip of coffee.

"The warehouse in Great Falls has been a location used by enemy insurgents for over fifteen years. Since the structure was built, there have been twenty-six different inspections by county officials, and sixteen calls handled by the local sheriff at the location. Last year there was a walk through by an FBI agent in response to complaints from local farmers, claiming they witnessed flying objects traveling from the location into Canada," stated General Prost. "Not one thing was found to be out of the ordinary during any of these visits. It was simply a store providing jobs for the community. A factory and warehouse for building and selling custom wheels, much like thousands of others in the United States."

"It was a warehouse," General Lauer held his cup out in front of him. "I'm not following your point about Colonel Lisco."

"She blew the damn thing to smithereens," shouted General Prost, motioning across the table with her hand. "What other commander in our forces would have the gumption to take the initiative to use the power of the United States Army to blow up a factory, in a city, in the middle of America?"

"I'm pretty sure none," stated General McClinton.

"I can guarantee the Chinese and Russian models never predicted it either," stated General Prost. "There was a crater thirty meters deep in the center of the building, and we had to excavate down another twenty meters to find the fuel and weapons. It was a massive structure. The information and documents we found made it clear our enemies were confident none of it would ever be discovered. It is so significant. Being a World War II buff, it reminds me of the secret bunkers Hitler built so the German Army could hide fuel and weapons from the Americans and their allies. If the supplies would have been above ground, they would have been noticed and easily destroyed by American forces."

"With information from that factory alone we have been able to locate and destroy five other strongholds across the country. This all should be taken into consideration with handling Colonel Lisco," stated General McClinton, turning to look at General Lauer.

"I have a meeting with staff this afternoon. I'll have her and Command Sergeant Major Talfoya come to my office before the briefing," said General Lauer.

"Would you mind if Ted and I also attend?" General Lopez asked. "Maybe I can clear some of the air with him at the same time."

"Did you discuss with Ted about the possibility of him leading the effort to search and destroy the local rebels?" General McClinton asked.

"Actually, it was his idea," General Lopez grinned. "It is almost uncanny how accurate the behavior model has been in-regards-to his duty and commitment.

"It is absolutely imperative we diminish the threat of the imbedded rebels along the front range," stated General McClinton. "This will be a topic discussed at the Chief of Staff meeting this afternoon. Ted Lisco is the perfect soldier to figure out the complexities of separating the external threats from the domestic revolutionary fighters and dealing with them accordingly. When this is all over, we, as well as our enemies will find these two groups to be total opposites."

"I am thinking Ted could take a platoon size force and work from his base at Colonel Lisco's farm. Most new data suggest the majority of rebels moving eastward." General Lopez looked to General Lauer, "We had no problems when he worked remotely during training."

"Let's meet at 1400."

"Everything else is on schedule," stated General McClinton. "Ann and I are leaving for Virginia in two hours."

"I wish I was going to be here to speak with Colonel Lisco," said General Prost.

"Why don't you send Colonel Lisco to her farm with Ted for a week?" General McClinton pushed his chair back. "With the missions planned and scheduled for next week it would be a good time and place for her to recuperate and take leave. Knowing Colonel Lisco, she will consider it punitive."

***

Colonel Deb waited with Command Sergeant Major Talfoya to be summoned into General Lauer's office. The command sergeant major was constantly shuffling his feet, having a hard time sitting still.

"Jesus, Tommy, why are you so nervous?" Deb chuckled. "You would think we are about to go on trial for murdering someone."

"This isn't a laughing matter colonel. It really could be the end of your career."

"If this is the end of my career for putting an overreaching bureaucrat in his place, then so be it." Deb relaxed back in her chair.

"Was there anything new with Ted?" Tommy asked.

"He had just talked with Nicole at the farm, so he was in a good mood."

"Colonel, the general will see you and the command sergeant major." A soldier stepped in front of her and pointed to the open door.

"I thought Ted was going to be here." Tommy waited to let Deb go in first.

"He is supposed to be," she glanced toward the entrance to the waiting area before stepping through the door into General Lauer's office.

"Sit," General Lauer said gruffly, pointing to two chairs opposite his desk.

The skin on his face was sagging, with light gray patches under both eyes. He stared at Deb and Tommy as they parked themselves into the cushy chairs.

"Colonel," he yelled, "do you understand that military discipline applies to you, as well as others?"

"Yes sir," she sat with her back washer board straight. "I do understand it does apply to me."

"So, you do recognize your actions are a reflection on every other member of the United States Army and every other branch of service."

"Yes sir."

"Members of 2nd Brigade were called upon to assist the Department of Homeland Security in transporting civilians out of central Utah. You were supporting them, not in charge of the movements," stated General Lauer.

"Yes sir, I understood our role."

"Do you disagree with the functions Homeland Security was performing?"

"No sir, I wish the situation in our country would never have reached this point, but I understand the purpose of FEMA is necessary and honorable. I have absolutely no problem with the agency."

"Then why in hell did you threaten the administrator from FEMA?" General Lauer spoke loudly and pronounced his words clearly.

"Sir, he was acting in an un-American manner."

"An un-American manner." The general curled his lip. He almost burst out laughing, wishing General McClinton were there to listen in on the interview. "An un-American manner," he repeated.

"Yes sir," Deb's head never moved as she continued, "I often ask soldiers within our ranks to recite the Articles of the Code of Conduct."

"Explain how you were following the Code of Conduct when you threatened the FEMA official?" General Lauer remained calm as he stared at the bruise above the Colonel's eye, to the side of her thick eyebrow.

"The deputy was being unreasonable in his actions to the Americans he was charged with helping. We, in the military, are fighting for the rights of our citizens to live in a free country where officials use common sense when making decisions that affect their lives. I understand the Code of Conduct is for members of the Armed Forces to fulfill their responsibilities and survive captivity with honor. But Article 6 of the Code is a way I justify my role in the Army with the idea of eventually becoming a citizen." She could see Tommy peripherally staring at her with squinted eyes while she prepared to recite the Article. "I will never forget I am an American, fighting for freedom, responsible for my actions, and dedicated to the principles which made my Country free. I will trust in my God and the United States of America."

General Lauer inhaled deeply. He stared at her for a few seconds and then let the breath out loudly.

Tommy opened his mouth as though he were going to speak, before leaning back in the chair. He thought that this meeting must have been like the same one where General Patton was brought before the brass for slapping a soldier more than a hundred years earlier.

"Sir, I take full responsibility for my actions. I will always stand for what makes this country great." Deb held her head high with her chin straight out.

"Well Colonel, you have some very powerful people in your corner," he scoffed. He looked at Tommy and shook his head before looking back at her. "What did the doctor tell you about your physical condition?"

"I'm a little beat up. Nothing that will affect me long term."

"Here's what is going to happen. Tomorrow you will go to your farm on the eastern plains and take leave, for a week."

"Sir, with the enemy advancing I can't leave 2nd Brigade." She glanced at Tommy.

"Not only can you, but you will. The commanders for all three battalions of 2nd Brigade are capable soldiers." General Lauer smiled, remembering General McClinton stating she would consider the leave as punishment. "The battalions are repositioning eastward while nonhuman infantry Divisions and aerial squadrons are preparing to confront the enemy."

"Sir, please, with communications being unreliable, I can't be disconnected from them." Deb was sitting on the edge of her chair.

"All communications to this facility are secure. You will have a secure system to communicate with the battalion headquarters from your farm."

"Sir, am I to travel with the colonel?" Tommy was trying to figure out the strategy of casting Colonel Lisco away from the action.

"Yes," the general moved to the side of his desk and sat on the edge. "Also, Ted is going to join you with a platoon of soldiers from the 99th.

Deb's mouth was partly open. She licked her lips while staring at the general's name plaque on the desk. She folded her arms and sat back in the chair.

The general's aide opened the door and announced, "General Lopez and Colonel Lisco have arrived."

Colorado Farm

"It's past midnight." Nicole leaned back into the cushions of the sofa, rubbing her temples. "Oh Lord. I don't know what to do with myself right now."

Jacqueline sat on the edge of the couch, unsure of what to say to comfort her sister-in-law. She glanced at Gina who was sitting in a lounge chair. They were exhausted from looking through every nook and cranny in the house. She could only imagine how tired the others were as they searched in the dark and cold.

"I think I will go back out and look," said Irene, barely able to stand.

"No, please Irene, stay here with us." Nicole put up her hand. "Everyone is looking as hard as they can."

"Maybe we should say a prayer." Irene took hold of Nicole's hand and sat down beside her. She prayed for the two children.

Nicole smiled and then sniffled. She did feel better after listening to the plea from the country woman to God to help her granddaughter and Scotty. Jon burst through the door causing her heart to jump. She looked in anticipation for good news.

"Nothing," Jon looked at them and shook his head. "We have looked everywhere."

There was a collective moan from the women.

"Are there any old water wells around here?" Irene gritted her teeth. It was something Ed brought up earlier, but everyone seemed to dismiss. "A lot of old farmsteads have hand dug wells that were never filled after the new water wells were drilled."

"I don't know enough about the property to know," Jon swallowed hard.

"Ted told me this morning that he was planning to take Deb to the hospital on base at Fort Carson." Nicole jumped from the sofa. "We have to get in touch with her and see if there is something we are missing."

"Wait here, I'll try and get hold of her."

Jon was out the door, running to the communication area in the garage before Nicole could say another word.

Nicole's heart was pounding in her chest as she looked at the clock on the kitchen wall. It showed 12:20. She tried to make small talk with the other women. When the clock showed 12:30 she grabbed her coat and rushed out the door.

The utility door to the garage burst open and Jon, Hank, Irving, Bobby and Bill rushed out and sprinted to the south, past the garage. Terrance, Jerry and Breanna dashed through the door behind them before it had a chance to close.

"What happened?" Nicole screamed.

"Colonel Deb said there was an old house south of the property that was torn down before the Liscos owned the property. If there is an abandoned well it would be there," Jerry stopped to inform her. He was carrying a rope. "Come on."

Nicole and Breanna followed Jerry as he shined the flashlight ahead of them. The frozen grass under the snow crackled as they walked in the direction of the voices in the distance. Beams of light were shooting into the frozen air from the rescuers frantically searching. Nicole turned and saw the form of Samantha following behind them in the pitch darkness.

"Here," Bobby yelled, "it's a concrete footer of some sort."

Jon shined his flashlight on the remains of the old house. Plywood on the floor joists was rotted to the point that the dirt below them was visible. "The place didn't have a cellar," he said.

"Be careful," yelled Hank, "it's so dark out here it's impossible to see without a light."

Bobby noticed some pieces of one-by-six wood sticking in the air. He shined his light on a piece of jagged lumber sticking up about twenty centimeters above the snow on the ground. He heard a noise he thought might be from an animal as his light caught the top of the brick well, nearly concealed by dirt, weeds and snow. He leaned precariously over the opening and shined the light down. "They're here," he yelled. The light flickered off the wall of the well where Maddy and Scotty were holding on to each other. "It's ok we are here."

Bill rushed to the edge and looked down. "Are you hurt," he yelled.

"Yes," Maddy's voice was hardly audible.

"Secure the end of the rope and I'll go down." Irving's muscles were noticeable through the down jacket he was wearing. "You will have to pull me up."

Irving tied the rope around his waist and easily shimmied down the side of the brick well while the others held tight to the opposite end. When he reached the bottom, he straddled the two children. He reached down and easily picked Scotty up.

"Grab ahold of my neck, real tight."

Scotty held tight as Irving rappelled up the wall as the others pulled. When he was at the top, he allowed Scotty to place his feet on the ground at the edge of the well, Breanna stepped forward and grabbed him. As soon as he was out of his arms Irving hurried back down. He placed his feet in the soft dirt on each side of Maddy. He easily picked her up.

"Grab my neck."

"I hurted my arm," Maddy sobbed, letting her arm fall limp.

"Ok, I'm going to grab tight, and you lean over my shoulder."

Maddy leaned over his shoulder as he climbed out of the well. Bill reached down and lifted her off his shoulder.

"Let's get them to the house," yelled Hank.

***

Maddy was so tired she could barely keep her eyes open while Julia wrapped her arm. She sat on Bill's lap covered with a blanket with her face buried in his chest. Scotty sat on the exam table with Breanna standing next to him.

"You are going to be ok," Julia secured the wrap and patted her gently on the shoulder. "Nothing broke."

Maddy closed her eyes and dug her head deeper into her dad's chest.

"Keep an eye on them tonight. Tomorrow we can check to make sure I haven't missed anything." Julia wiped her hand with a towel.

"Ok, let's get you two to bed," Nicole placed her hand onto Scotty's shoulder.

Maddy sat forward in Bill's lap. She looked past Nicole.

"Irene," she was so tired her head was wobbling.

"Yes Maddy," Irene moved closer and placed her hand out. Maddy took hold of it.

"Did you make cornbread without me?"

"No, I waited," Irene smiled, her face was pale. "We can make it another time."

"Come on Mom. The sun is going to come up in a couple hours, we might as well try and get some sleep." Breanna placed her hand on the back of Irene's arm. They slowly walked out of the clinic.

"All right you two," Bill scooted Maddy off his lap. He reached for Scotty's hand, "Let's go to bed."

Nicole followed them to the basement. Samantha hesitated at the top of the stairs before proceeding after them.

Jon, Gina, Jacqueline and Hank were so wound up from the activities they decided to remain awake and talk. Jon waited for Nicole to come back upstairs before mentioning that Deb told him, in the hectic call, she was going to arrive that afternoon to spend a week at the farm. Also, Ted and a platoon of soldiers would be arriving with her.

Nicole was taken by surprise of the news that her husband would be coming back to the farm. He must have just found out or he would have told her so in their conversation earlier the previous morning. She sensed the news might mean Ted would be at the farm much more often than they anticipated.

Samantha waited by Maddy's bed, with her hand on Bill's shoulder, as they both watched the little girl fall asleep.

"Can we talk?" Samantha moved back away from the bed.

"Let's go to my room," Bill moved off the bed.

The door to Jessica and her daughter's room was slightly open with a light shining from a table lamp. Bill placed his hand on Samantha's lower back and nudged her quickly past and into his small room. He quietly closed his door.

He collapsed into the soft bed and fell back with his legs dangling over the end. Samantha slithered onto the bed and turned toward him on her side. She placed a hand on his stomach and rested her head on his chest, breathing in the smell of his musky shirt.

"I'm sorry Bill," she whispered, "I never expected Travis to come here."

He remained still as he felt his heart beating next to her head. The warmth of her breath could be felt through his shirt.

"All I want you to do is tell me the truth," he whispered. The walls between his room and Jessica's were thin.

”Ok,” she lifted her head slightly and swallowed. “I did sleep with Travis in Los Angeles. But it was a one-time thing, that I regretted immediately after it happened.”

He moved up, readjusting his position to cause her to sit on the end of the bed. They turned toward each other. “Was it really just a one-time thing?”

“Yes, I have lied about this incident on so many occasions that I sometimes think it never happened. I was about to lie to you yesterday in the apartment.”

He heard the toilet flush, through the thin wall, in Jessica’s room.

“Are you in love with Travis?” he lowered his voice.

“No,” she noticed he was speaking softly and followed suit by whispering, “it was never love. I was intrigued with him being a pilot.”

“Travis said there is a lot of chaos still in town, but the police are gaining more and more control. If you had a chance to go to Littleton to be with your parents, would you go?” Bill asked.

She waited to answer while they listened to Jessica’s muffled voice conversing with her daughters on the other side of the wall.

“I don’t know,” she answered, before turning her head away. “I care for you and Maddy, but with Travis and Sue arriving here, it might make it unbearable for me to stay.”

“You are strong enough to handle these circumstances.” He placed his hand onto her lap. “If you stay you will have to be straightforward with Travis and his wife.”

“I don’t want to ruin his marriage. I don’t know if he ever told Sue the truth about what happened that night.”

“Then ask him,” he swallowed hard. “Decide how to handle it from there.”

He felt her stop breathing and swallow. She placed her lips to the side of his mouth and asked, “Do you trust me, Bill?”

He flinched, thinking how odd a question to ask at that point of their conversation. He was glad her head was not still positioned over his heart as it thumped his chest. He leaned in and kissed her, keeping his lip next to her as he whispered, “Of course I do.”

Watkins, Colorado

Christian hunched his shoulders, trying to avert the piercing wind from drumming the back of his naked neck. After a night of walking, they arrived at a hill west of the small town of Watkins on the eastern plains. Tim and Shira looked over his shoulder as he deliberated over a tattered paper map of Colorado. Waiting nearly two hundred meters to the east, the remnants of his rebels who agreed to leave the city with him, clustered together along a stone wall in a grove of Colorado blue spruce, unnaturally placed as part of the landscape entrance to a housing development.

"It shows the government camp to be right around here." Tim looked to the east in the direction of the small town. "These places are supposed to have thousands of people. How can we not see it?"

"The map shows it being east of the little town," stated Shira, "just north of Interstate 70."

"Let's follow the highway and cross over on the other side of the town." Christian wiped his nose with his fingers and sniffled. "If a camp is there, we have to run into it sooner or later."

"Wonder if it isn't? We can't go on without food." Tim looked to the north at several high-end homes. He pointed. "I think we should check some of those houses for food."

"Take five people with you and check it out."

Tim ran down the hill to the group in the trees. Soon he and five others were advancing in the direction of the large houses. Christian and Shira continued to study the map for the locations of the other encampments. According to the markings on the map, the next camp was nearly 90 kilometers further east in Limon.

A column of eight large buses appeared on the interstate and zipped by them at a high rate of speed. The buses turned off at the interchange from Interstate 70 and Watkins. They continued through the small town and turned onto highway 40 east bound. They disappeared over a hill, before reappearing on a ridge traveling north several kilometers away.

"Those buses have to be taking people to the camp," stated Christian. "This map can't be correct. It's not next to the Interstate."

"We are going to be in trouble if we stay here much longer." Shira thought how small the big man seemed as he slouched in the wind. "You have to make a decision."

Christian shielded his face from the blowing snow while considering the circumstances. There was no sign of human activity in the small town. The area to the east, where the buses traveled, seemed to be rolling hills of fallow fields, with kilometers of emptiness. The homes to the north where Tim was scouting were the best option for the group in the immediate future.

"Christian," Shira yelled from nearly three meters away with large flakes of snow falling between them. "What are we doing? Without food and water, we can't stay here any longer."

"We are going to that house." He pointed at the first house in the development.

The group of insurrectionists covered the entire gravel road as they walked up a slight incline in the direction of the large home. The front door flew open and a man of about fifty stepped out onto the small porch. He held his hand up in a greeting manner.

"Hello, can I help you?" his voice was high pitched and soft.

"We are trying to find the government camp," Christian spoke with a non-threatening tone. He stepped closer to the porch.

"It's at the old airport northeast of here." The man looked at the large mass of rebels gathered across his driveway and on his snow-covered lawn, all shouldering rifles.

"How far away is that?" asked Shira, moving next to Christian.

"Oh gosh, I'd say between ten and fifteen kilometers." He was forcing a smile.

Christian let out a heavy breath. He could see movement through the partially opened door inside the house. "Here comes Tim," resonated a voice, causing Christian to turn and step away. The man moved back inside his house and shut the door.

Christian rambled down the driveway, past his group, in the direction of Tim who was jogging, all alone.

"You aren't going to believe this." Tim bent his neck to look up at Christian as he leaned over at his waist to catch his breath. "There is a farm on the outskirts of this development being used by Anastasia Wolf as her base. She said she will give us a place to stay."

"Anastasia, her area is Aurora and eastern Denver," stated Christian. "I'm surprised she would be out this far.

"She has had this base for a long time," said Tim. "It's just over the crest of this hill.

Christian was not overly enthused about interacting with Anastasia. Of all the rebels in the Denver metropolitan area, she was by far the most radicalized. She was the offspring of long enduring anarchists who came from California about five years earlier to organize and stabilize the homegrown groups in Colorado.

***

Smoke was rising from the chimney sitting on the sharply pitched roof of the small farmhouse. Snow catching on the rooftop gave the place a serene aura. The round roof of a barn was visible over the top of three large Quonset buildings, spaced about thirty meters apart from one another, north of the house.

Several people watched from a vantage point at the first Quonset as the mass of new rebels arrived at the property. A small woman with very thick hips, who Christian recognized as Anastasia Wolf, was waiting on the small concrete porch, right outside the door of the main house. She motioned with her arm when she saw him.

"Christian, come inside, Tim can help your people get settled," she yelled loudly.

Shira followed behind, through a small hall and into the kitchen. Sitting at a table were two men wearing black biker jackets and a woman dressed in a green synthetically made parka jacket. There were four empty coffee cups on the table.

"This is Christian and…." Anastasia pointed at Shira.

"Shira." Shira scrutinized the lady who was dressed in a dark blue blazer over a tan turtleneck sweater. She had shoulder length sandy colored hair that was receding at the hairline. Her tan pants were stretched to the limit by her large legs which were out of proportion to her small upper body. The image she portrayed was far more retro than any of the other women rebels she had come across.

"Why are you here?" Anastasia remained standing, not offering a place for the two to sit.

"We need food."

"Is it why you left the city?"

"For the most part." Christian looked past the table to the small living room. There was an old piano resting on worn carpet, but no indication of others in the house.

"Why didn't you blend in at the shelters?"

"We tried, we stuck out like a sore thumb, and they called the authorities on us." Christian noticed the three sitting at the table were much older than Anastasia.

"You have to go in small groups?" Anastasia placed her hand on the back of a chair but continued to stand. "None of this is anything we didn't anticipate. You were forewarned that the authorities in the cities would fight us."

"I never realized how much of a danger the foreign fighters would be." Melting water was dripping from his shoulders onto the linoleum floor. "They seem more threatening than the police or military."

Anastasia twisted to look at her three friends. She turned back to make eye contact with Christian, intertwined her fingers and lowered her hands. One of the men rose from his chair, towering over her.

"What in the hell do you think this is?" Anastasia scoffed. "Without the foreign revolutionaries we would still be whining and complaining to a group of hypocritical politicians and elite managers of corporations. Blindly following them while they grew richer, and we simply tried to exist."

"What's our place going to be when everything is settled?" Christian raised his voice, "What do you think your place will be in a new world."

"To build a place where we all count and have an opportunity to reach our full potential," she never faltered in her reply.

"I'm not seeing any cooperation with the foreigners. They don't have any inclination of working together with us." Christian felt water drip on the back of his hand from the sleeve of his coat. "What will be the difference when all of this is over. Will they expect us to follow their orders?"

"The Army chased us out of the houses we were staying in," interjected Shira, crowding closer to Christian.

"I know you, Christian, you are bright." Anastasia disregarded Shira. "This is not just disruption of life in Colorado. Chaos is taking place over the entire world. When we win there will be a place for all of us at the table."

"I want to ask you straight out Anastasia. Have you got an agreement with the foreign insurgents that will sell all of us out?"

"Christian," she swallowed hard and glanced at the large man at her shoulder. "I don't have to discuss this with you right now."

The second large man pushed his chair back and stood. He was nearly as large as the man standing.

Christian pressed his lips together, wetting them as he took in a deep breath through his nose. He stared at a Howard Miller wrought-iron pendulum clock with black Roman numerals hanging on the wall next to the door going into the living room. The house had the same furnishings from forty years ago. He was tired and hungry and needed time to think before making any more decisions.

"Can we stay here," he asked.

"One night," Anastasia turned her back and sat in the chair. She looked across the table to the old lady who seemed completely detached from the conversation. "Then you need to prepare to go to Colorado Springs and complete the duties you agreed to when you began receiving money from the foreigners."

"They plan to attack NORAD. You know as well as we do it is an underground fortress. There is no way we can invade the place successfully." He could see the old lady breathing easy as she listened while he spoke to the back of Anastasia's head. "We are going east from here tomorrow."

After a moment of silence with no discussion from Anastasia, Christian and Shira turned and were out the door into the darkness.

Colorado Farm

Tommy and Deb caught a ride to the farm with Ted and the platoon from the 99th. Ted had met Command Sergeant Major Talfoya on several occasions, but never really got to know him. The short ride from Fort Carson made it apparent to Ted that his sister and Tommy were more than soldiers to one another. It gave him a peaceful feeling knowing Deb had someone completely devoted to her well-being. Jon radioed earlier, before they left the base, to inform them that Maddy had been found.

Nicole and Bill were up by ten o'clock, but Maddy slept until noon. Although Maddy's arm was sore, she was managing ordinary tasks without any problems. She sat with Nicole on the porch watching the road in anticipation of the convoy. The sun was falling quickly when the rumble of trucks emanated from the distance.

"Here they come," yelled Nicole, pointing to the six vehicles moving quickly down the driveway. They rushed to the front gate where Nicole placed her hand over Maddy's chest to keep her from running in front of the procession.

The moment the Humvee transporting Deb came to a stop, she was out the door. "That is just spectacular." She motioned toward the tower before turning to the apartment where the large silhouettes of Jason and Dave Jensen were visible placing outdoor lights next to an entry door. "They have almost finished the outside of the apartments."

"Wow, I never imagined your farm would be like this." Tommy inspected the surroundings as he joined her on the wet driveway.

Ted scanned the property for Nicole as everyone began to gather around the convoy. Out of nowhere Maddy sprinted at full speed right toward him. He leaned down and she ran into his arms. He held her at arms-length and surveyed the wrap on her arm.

"What is this?" he put her tiny wrist in his hand.

She bobbed her head up and down and declared, "I fell into a well."

"I heard about that, but I didn't know you hurt your arm." Ted felt Nicole's hand on his shoulder. He rose and placed a hand around her waist and lifted her. He gave her a quick kiss on the lips. "You will have to catch me up on all the action that happened here yesterday."

"It was something I hope we never have to go through again," stated Bill, picking Maddy up so she was eye level with Ted. Samantha moved next to him.

Ted noticed the 57 Chevy sitting in front of the garage with frosted windows and a layer of snow on the roof. "Is Travis here?"

"Yeah, he along with his wife and two children." Bill left it there. "How long will you be here?"

"My duties keep changing, so I suppose it all depends on what happens over the next week," stated Ted. "With the foreign insurgents creating more strongholds east of the city, there is a possibility of using the farm as a base."

Deb took in a deep breath when she noticed Breanna and Irene walking slowly in her direction. By the time Irene arrived at her side, the entire Jacoby family were standing next to her.

"Were you able to find the kids?" Irene asked with a raspy voice. She had her hands clasped together as if in prayer.

"I did," Deb glanced at Tommy. "They were placed on a bus the night before last outside of Beaver, headed to the Denver area."

"Do they know we are here?" Breanna asked with moistness showing in her eyes.

"Seth has a map with directions to the farm." Deb felt blood rushing to her head.

"Are you hurt?" Irene noticed she was dragging her leg.

"I took some shrapnel in my calf during fighting west of Parowan." She glanced at Jon and Hank, "It's a superficial wound."

"Is there a lot of destruction around our place?" Aaron asked.

"I don't know if you heard but the citizens of Utah have been relocated," Deb turned to Irene and stared directly into her eyes. "Irene, I need to be straightforward with you. Your farmhouse was destroyed. I witnessed it myself as I was being evacuated from the area."

"Oh God," yelled Breanna.

Irene clenched her teeth, then sighed. She reached over and placed a hand on Ed's shoulder.

"We have to look on the bright side Mom." Breanna rubbed the back of Irene's neck. "The kids are safe."

"I know this news is devastating," Deb stepped closer to Tommy. "But war is occurring in the region around your ranch and the combat is only going to escalate. I'm glad you and your family fled the area when you did."

Irene looked at Ted.

"Is there a way we can go to the camp in the city and pick up the kids?" Breanna asked.

"We aren't sure where they ended up." Deb twisted her neck to look at Tommy. "Do you know?

"All I heard was that Homeland Security was opening several encampments at golf courses and shopping malls from Denver, north to Casper. The people evacuated from the Beaver location were transported to one of those camps," Tommy answered. "Most will be vetted and sent east."

"Do you know what is happening in the cities east of here?" Irving asked.

"There is chaos, with different amounts of severity, occurring in most cities across the country. But there are some localities that have experienced little or no affect from the insurgents. Northern Ohio, much of the area around the Shenandoah Valley, most of Missouri and Arkansas have hardly been impacted." Tommy answered, glancing at Deb. "I learned most of this before you arrived at the transfer location in Beaver."

"Ted, is there anything you can do to find out where they transported the kids?" Irene asked. "Can you get in touch with the FEMA people?"

"I'll see what I can do tomorrow. I can speak with Colonel Myer and see if she has any suggestions about locating Seth and the others. With the large number of people being processed, it will take time to have updated records," Ted answered.

"I want to get settled in," said Deb. "Is there an empty room ready for Tommy in the apartment."

"There is, but we will need to move a bed," stated Bill. "The restroom isn't finished yet so he will have to use one in the main house or garage."

"You can use the one in my room," Deb looked at Tommy.

"Everyone looks so tired," stated Nicole. "Why don't we all get settled and meet in the living room later."

***

With the three battalions from 2nd Brigade located on the western slope of the Rocky Mountains it was a high priority for Deb to keep in contact and follow their movements in real time. Tommy was the one who communicated almost hourly with the commanders, and then relayed all activities to her. His diligence allowed her to relax and enjoy the farm and her family.

Imagining people together talking and having fun was a huge part in her aspirations when she first decided to build the haven. It was meant to be much more than a fortification for protection during the war she hoped would never happen. She remembered telling her father, nearly two months before he passed, about her ambitions of turning the farm into a special place to survive an attack or disaster should it ever occur. He told her that if anyone could find paradise amidst the chaos, it would be her.

She was in front of the fireplace mantle staring at the picture of her grandfather standing outside a stone building in Dattenburg, Germany. She took a sip of scotch as she felt Tommy brush her shoulder.

"You look like you are lost in thought," Tommy moved right in front of her. The living room was packed with people.

"Just thinking," Deb smiled at him. "I really like seeing my family safe and together."

"If you don't mind, I'm going to take a quick shower in your room and then retire for the night."

"Of course," she placed her hand on the side of his arm. "I'm going to go to bed early too."

She had an extraordinary amount of saliva build up in her mouth as she watched him walk away. Just as she was taking the final swallow from her drink, Jacqueline moved to her side.

"Are you doing ok?" Jacqueline noticed the dark bruising around the raspberry to the side of her head.

"I'm doing great," Deb assured her.

"Thank you, Deb."

"You know Jacqueline, this is everything I envisioned when I began preparing the farm."

"I wish we were back home with our boring lives," Jacqueline took in a deep breath. "But, since we can't, I thank God, you gave us this place."

"Thank you for saying that," Deb gazed into her eyes and smiled. "I am really tired. I think I will go to bed early."

"Of course, let me take your glass." Jacqueline took the glass and watched as Deb limped her way through the crowd and down the hallway to her bedroom.

The door to the bathroom was open with steam filling the bedroom. Tommy's clothes were neatly folded and placed on the chair in the corner of the room. His shoes were sitting together, tucked under the chair.

Deb went to her dresser and opened a drawer. A white, satin negligee sat on top of her warmer nightgowns. She hesitated for a moment before removing her clothes and slipping on the negligee. The water in the shower quieted as she pulled the comforter from the bed.

Tommy was momentarily startled when he came to the door of the bathroom with a white towel wrapped around his waist. A large smile filled his bronze face when he saw Deb slinking at the edge of the bed dressed in the short nighty with her large breasts barely concealed by the fabric.

She paused before moving closer, never bringing her eyes above his muscular chest. He placed his thumbs to the edge of the towel and released it. She tried to catch her breath as he moved his left arm to allow her to embrace him. His muscular back felt hard as steel as he slowly walked her back to the bed.

Once on the bed she rolled over on top of him and sat up. She reached down and pulled the negligee over her head. Tommy completely relaxed as they made love.

Watkins, Colorado

The inside of the Quonset was ice cold with no heat source, making for a restless night. Dinner the previous night was a bowl of rice with cinnamon and sugar. Breakfast was a small bowl of oatmeal. There were only twenty-five rebels from Anastasia's force housed at the farm, far fewer than anticipated when they arrived the night before.

Anastasia saying she expected he and his rebels to honor their duties because they had been paid by the insurrectionists over the past several years, triggered Christian to contemplate his role in the revolution. The further he analyzed the future of his rebels, in the scheme of things, at the end of the war, no matter who won, he could configure no other outcome than his fighters being discarded, arrested or killed. Something Coach Lisco tried to beat into his head when he helped the teacher and his family escape from the city.

"I was talking to Anastasia's people last night," said Tim. "There were hundreds of foreign fighters at this location yesterday. Apparently with all the military activity in the city they are moving eastward."

"Just like we are," Shira shivered as she took a bite of oatmeal. She noticed Christian turn away after hearing Tim mention that many foreign fighters were recently at the location.

"Apparently, there are hundreds of thousands of new people being evacuated from the west." Tim put the empty bowl of rolled oats on the concrete floor. He wanted to share all the information he gleaned from the other rebels. "All the golf courses in the city are being used as camps for the evacuees."

"It seems the military is more focused on the south side of the city. Maybe it's because Fort Carson is closer." Shira focused on Christian standing in a trance, staring out the open door of the building, paying no attention to the conversation. She moved next to him and asked, "What's wrong?"

"I'm thinking we are a bunch of fools," Christian spoke loudly. "What in the world are we thinking, letting someone like Anastasia Wolf decide our destiny?"

"She's been a leader of the movement for years. What's different now?" Shira asked.

"She has made a different deal with these people than we have. I'm not exactly sure what, but she has a much better relationship with them than we do."

"Most everything that has happened so far is what we were told would occur," Shira spoke confidently. "She isn't coming up with anything new."

"You and I are always implying how intelligent we are." Christian looked at her choppy bob haircut. "But if we are so damn smart, why are we freezing our asses off, eating stale oatmeal and being commanded to follow orders as if we haven't a living brain cell in our heads?"

"You are overthinking all of this."

"The hell I am, we are pawns in this insurgency." The skin on his large forehead creased as he stood up tall and narrowed his eyes. "We have been betrayed."

"Christian, what are we planning to do?" Tim's hands were shaking as he spoke.

"Shira, are you with me?" Christian yelled, aggressively placing his face close enough in front of hers for his breath to hit her eyes.

"One hundred percent," she yelled.

"We are taking all the food, water and clothing we can carry, and getting as far away from these people as possible." Christian let out a breath of relief. "Tim, start packing the supplies. Let everyone know that the plan is to leave in an hour."

"What if Anastasia's rebels try to stop us?" Tim asked.

"We outnumber them. Make it clear to them not to interfere." He stepped out the Quonset door into the snow and glanced back. "Shira, let's have another talk with Anastasia and that big son of a bitch who tried to intimidate us last night."

They marched through the snow, onto the concrete porch and opened the unlocked door. Christian rushed in first, past the hall and into the kitchen. The large man who stood up and the woman from the previous night, along with Anastasia were sitting at the table. All three of them jerked their heads and watched as Christian moved right over the top of Anastasia.

"What is wrong with you?" Anastasia yelled, reaching her arm up to put pressure on the rifle as Christian pinned her head.

The big man rose from his chair. Christian popped him on the nose with the butt of the rifle. He dropped like a fly to the floor. The old woman pulled her hands up and held them slightly above the table. She sat calmly and watched, making no attempt to help Anastasia.

"Alright, alright," moaned Anastasia, unable to move as Christian used his knee to push her chair tight to the table. "Why are you doing this?"

"Keep an eye on the living room." Christian eased up on the pressure from his knee as he motioned to Shira with his head. "The other guy is somewhere in there."

The man on the linoleum gasped but remained on the floor.

"You are double crossing us," Christian nudged the chair with his thigh. "There is no way all the revolutionaries are part of the grand scheme when the war is over. I think we will be disposed of at the end."

"That's not true," her voice cracked.

"I don't care what kind of deal you made with the foreigners. But I want you to know we are on to you and will never be used as your pawns again."

"Christian," Shira motioned toward the door to the living room. "There is someone in there."

"Move back," Christian leveled his AK-47 toward the door as Shira stepped back, shielding herself behind Christian's large body just as a shirtless man, holding a pistol with both hands, rushed into the room. He positioned himself right under the kitchen clock.

Anastasia raised up from the chair with her powerful legs, pushing Christian's rifle into the air. The shirtless man fired his pistol trying to pick off Christian over the top of Anastasia. The bullet flew well over their heads. Shira fired four rapid shots into his chest. Christian pushed Anastasia hard to the opposite side of the table.

"We are going to leave now." He leveled his rifle squarely at the head of Anastasia. "If you take a shot at any of my people when we leave, we will burn this place to the ground."

"Wait Christian, I have to know this for my own sanity." Shira pointed her pistol at the lady sitting at the table. The woman's pale face was smooth with deep wrinkles meandering from the corners of her eyes. "Tell us what the plans are for all the homegrown rebels if the Americans lose this war?"

The woman took in several shallow breaths and folded her arms across her chest. "None of you will survive," she answered matter-of-factly, staring straight at Shira.

"Is she your daughter?" Shira motioned with the pistol in the direction of Anastasia as she focused her eyes on the older woman.

She shrugged her skinny shoulders, leaned back in the chair and said, "You are making the correct decision. Let's just leave it at that."

They backed out of front door. Tim and the others were waiting. The sky was bright blue as they began to walk through the snow down the driveway.

Colorado Farm

The forty-person platoon positioned tents in the field northeast of the apartment. Bivouacs used for living quarters were placed the night before but there was still work for the mess tent and communications.

Corporal Mary Pint took a liking to the colonel's granddaughter and offered to have Maddy work with her to supervise the digging of a trench from the garage to the communication tent. Having the platoon at the farm was a perfect time to give Maddy a chance to learn the discipline and work ethic of the soldiers.

"Just remember you have an eight-year-old in your presence." Ted stood alongside Corporal Pint, addressing Private Tiger and Private Sinclair while they stood at attention with picks in their hands, preparing to break the frozen dirt.

"Yes sir," both men barked at the same time, holding their chests out in front of them.

"Corporal, are you good with having Maddy follow you?" Ted stared at the corporal's chubby cheeks with strands of brown hair escaping from under her cap while she stood at attention. She didn't look to be a day over fourteen.

"Yes sir, it will be a pleasure having her help," she showed her large front teeth as she smiled.

"You need to listen to everything the corporal tells you." Ted placed a hand on Maddy's shoulder. She pulled away while glancing at Corporal Pint.

"Grandpa," she tipped her head. "Remember…."

"You are not a baby," Ted smiled and looked at the corporal. "If you need me to take her at any time I will understand.

"I'm sure that won't be necessary, sir. Come on Maddy let's make sure this trench is being dug correctly."

Ted observed for a moment while Maddy joined the soldiers as they began digging. He spotted Deb and Tommy wandering from the concrete tower in the direction of Hank and Jon, who were talking to Jason Jensen at the far end of the apartment.

Jason was towering over the others as Deb commended him on his work with the apartment. Tommy seemed to be getting along exceptionally well with Hank and Jon.

"Ted, we were just discussing what we think should be the next project as soon as Jason finishes the apartment," Deb was relaxed and smiling.

"You are thinking of building more?" Ted grinned at Jon and Hank.

"A community building to meet, where we could watch films and play games. It would relieve all the congestion at the main house. We could build it in the opening on the east side of the house." Deb turned to Tommy, "I want the farm to be more than just a place to survive. As long as people live here it should be treated as a home."

"We have some lumber left but not nearly enough to build the kind of structure you are talking about," stated Jason. "I can come up with a design and then do some figuring on how much more we will need."

"We also need to check how much cement would be needed to pour the foundation. I'll run this by Bill this evening," said Deb.

"Where would you get the lumber?" Hank asked.

"We could go into Limon. I bought so much lumber from Ben Stewart at the lumber yard over the years, I'm sure if he has it, he will sell it to us. The guy is a go getter, who drilled the water wells, put in the septic tank and helped with the wind cones on the farm."

"I ran into the sheriff the other day," stated Jon.

"Old Bob Wilkins, he's a pretty good fella. Did you tell him about Clint and Peg?"

"He seemed pretty upset."

"Bob and his wife Judy played cards with the Browns, so I imagine it was hard news to take."

"I would think all the lumber and other supplies would be gone by now. What are you thinking Deb?" Jon asked. "Are you planning on going to Limon and check?"

"Yeah, even if the lumber is gone, it won't hurt to keep in touch with the locals. I know these people well enough that they will give me straight answers about what is happening around here." Deb looked at Tommy, who was looking back at her with a smile on his face. "Let's go in the morning."

Nicole walked up and placed her hand on Ted's lower back and said, "We are going to have the kids do some art projects. Could you have Maddy come inside in about thirty minutes?"

"I'll go get her now."

Private Tiger leaned on the pick as Corporal Pint, with Maddy at her side, secured a string line pulled from the electrical box at the garage. Private Sinclair was helping a sergeant near the communication tent.

"How is everything going?" Ted asked, moving between Maddy and Corporal Pint.

"Fine sir," stated the corporal, smiling hard enough to have her pink cheeks puff out. "Maddy and I have kept things going pretty well and we are almost ready to start pulling lines."

"If the f-ing sergeant over there would get his head out of his a-s-s, we'd have had this thing done a long time ago," Maddy took in a deep breath and nodded toward the men digging near the tents.

Ted's jaw dropped. Corporal Pint rose to full attention with her smile turning into clenched teeth. Private Tiger began to slowly walk away.

"Grandpa, this ground is hard as h-e-l-l."

"Private Tiger," Ted yelled. "Have you been using inappropriate language in front of my granddaughter?"

"Sir," Private Tiger stopped and did an about-face. He stood at attention, slightly hunched over, with his shirt half out from his pants. "I might have inadvertently said some words I now regret to have used. I never realized your granddaughter was such a good speller."

"The latrines are now your responsibility," Ted yelled. "If I go inside one of them at any time during our stay, they better smell like a fresh pine tree blowing in the breeze. Do you understand me soldier?"

"Yes sir."

"Maddy," he motioned to her, then turned to Corporal Pint. "As you were Corporal, continue with your work.

"Yes sir," she ran in the direction of the sergeant.

Maddy came to him as he knelt on one knee. He held out his hand. She put her small hand in his.

"Those words you used are really, really bad." He thought for a moment with her looking at him with tears developing in her eyes. "I'm not mad at you. You didn't know they were bad. If your grandma heard you say them, she would be so mad at you, and even more mad at me."

"I'm sorry."

"We have to be careful using words we don't know, even if we are spelling them."

"Ok."

Ted placed his hand on her cheek.

"Grandpa, is the latrine a bathroom?"

"Yes."

"Don't make Private Tiger clean the latrine," she lowered her chin. "He and Corporal Pint are really nice."

"He'll only have to clean them his share of the time," Ted winked at her. "I just wanted to let him know not to use bad words around you."

Maddy smiled and placed her arms around his neck.

"Your grandma wants you to go inside to work on art projects." Ted let her slide off his chest and rose to his feet. "We'll forget about using the bad words. Deal?"

"Deal."

***

One of Deb's objectives was becoming better acquainted with Bobby. Being partners with Bill in the farm, as well as other businesses, created a special bond with her oldest nephew. Before the war started, she made plans to spend an extra week in Colorado, after attending the state championship football game, to discuss with Bobby some business opportunities for him during his time in college. Although Bill was partners with her on certain endeavors, making him wealthy in his own right, her two nephews were equal beneficiaries of all her possessions.

Bobby spent much of his time on the highest floor of the tower with Emilee, Sherry, Caroline and Dave. They furnished the observation area with several chairs. A solar heater kept the room warm enough to keep the shutters open during the coldest night.

"We have hot cocoa," Bobby held up two thermoses.

Caroline and Sherry placed two chairs about a meter from the window and situated the remaining chairs in a semi-circle around the two.

Tommy glanced out the window onto the moon covered landscape. He noticed two grooves about five centimeters deep in the block at the bottom of the window to be used to rest the barrel of a rifle. The warmth radiating from the heater was comfortable, countering the cold air blowing lightly through the window. He sat down in the chair next to Deb.

Deb watched Emilee as she held the two cups for Bobby to pour the hot chocolate. Her beautiful facial features blossomed as she smiled at her nephew and giggled while he poured the hot chocolate. Her approach was one of appreciating the small things in life that could have only come from experiencing the hardest of times.

"We helped build this," Emilee stated, handing the steaming cups of cocoa to Tommy and Deb. "I have never worked so hard in my life."

"You did?" Deb was surprised. Jon bragged endlessly about Harold's hard work but never mentioned his helpers.

"Oh yeah, Bobby and I carried block, mortar and grout while Sherry mixed the cement," stated Emilee.

"I actually miss the workout from lifting the bags of cement." Sherry showed her white teeth as she smiled.

"I'll admit it was much harder than lifting weights during football," stated Bobby, smiling. "How are you doing Aunt Deb. Everyone around here was really worried about you when the explosion happened during your conference call."

"I'm doing good," she glanced at Tommy.

"Do you two work together?" Sherry leaned forward as she asked. "What is a Command Sergeant?"

Deb looked at Sherry with her blonde hair ruffled, giving her a wild appearance. Jon was impressed with the young woman who he said was a true soldier at heart. Her hardened character was different from Emilee, although it was obvious, she too never had an easy life. She was ready to fight.

"I'm a Command Sergeant Major. I give Colonel Lisco feedback and perspective on issues and concerns she faces while commanding the 2nd Brigade." Tommy also noticed the fighting spirit in the young woman.

"Colonel Lisco is going to help me and Caroline get to basic training." Sherry remarked, "We have already joined but are having difficulty finding out where to go."

"Everything is in total chaos right now with everyone displaced. It's hard to locate individuals to give them specific orders." Tommy looked at Deb, "I'll speak with Ted. I'm sure we can have you an order to report and transportation before we leave."

"Why are you so adamant about joining the Army?" Deb had been briefed by Hank about the past Sherry had with the homegrown rebel group.

"They lied."

"Who lied?" Deb asked.

"The foreigners who paid us," Sherry glanced at Bobby. "They recruited us hard in high school and I fell for their lies. These people are beyond ruthless."

"How much did they pay you?"

"I got $2400.00 a month."

"Right out of high school?"

"Payments actually started during the spring of my senior year."

"Bobby, did they try to recruit you too?" Deb asked.

"Our sophomore year, and a little bit our junior year, we were aware of the gangs offering kids money." Bobby glanced at Emilee and then at Dave. "We never heard of anyone this year being contacted. There was a buzz about the FBI cracking down on the gangs."

"There were a few kids approached," Emilee swallowed as she stared at Bobby.

"Coach Lisco talked a lot about not being influenced by the recruiters," stated Dave. "He and his assistants did a good job of warning about the danger."

"I wish I would have listened to the counselors at school," said Sherry. "We were trained with weapons but never expected we would need to use them. When the war started to take over the city, we were asked to kill people in our neighborhoods."

"Did you?" Deb asked.

"Never, I didn't fire my weapon." Tears were welling up in her eyes. "I stayed back and tried to find a way to escape the situation while the others fought the police. The foreigners who paid us were in total control of our orders. I am positive if we didn't follow their commands, we would all be dead."

Emilee was sitting on the edge of her chair. She was having a hard time catching her breath as she listened to Sherry speak about the group of pawns her father was leading, something they had kept out of previous conversations.

"Did my dad shoot at the police?" Emilee asked.

"No, none of the six of us who rode the bikes to the farm shot anyone," Sherry declared. "It was something we discussed on our way here."

"Why did he leave to go back?" Emilee was asking the question to not only understand Christian, but her mother also.

"Probably because his mantra has always been live free or die. He couldn't fathom conforming to working with everyone at the farm." Sherry twisted her head to look into Emilee's eyes. "He's not an evil person."

Although having all of Bobby's friends present was stifling her getting to speak with him about the future, Deb found the conversation intriguing. After the discussion with the foreign rebel in Grand Junction she was well-aware of the tactics employed by the insurgents against the homegrown revolutionaries. Sherry's rendition of her experience with the enemy was heartening in that it gave hope for the many young people already caught up in the trap set by them to fight against their own country.

"Bobby," Deb changed the subject, "how are you adapting?"

"Everything is different, especially not having electronics. But when I really think about it, most of the time was communicating with Emilee. Now we are always together." Bobby looked to Dave, "Not having football is a bummer."

"We only had one game left anyway," stated Dave.

"Aunt Deb, is this war going to last a long time?"

Deb turned to Tommy.

"It's not going to be resolved quickly," answered Tommy. "There is constant fighting at the southern border but neither side is advancing or retreating. We are waiting to figure the best way to root them out of the cities in Mexico. I believe they are biding their time while the entrenched warriors within our borders continue to disrupt."

"We are going to be eighteen here shortly," Dave looked at Bobby and Emilee, "so, we most likely will be in the fight."

"Yes," Deb replied. Captain Jensen in communication came to her mind as she looked at Dave dwarfing the small chair, he was sitting in. "It's not going to be over quickly."

"What about supplies and food?" Bobby was worried about the others on the farm. "There isn't enough to last past spring."

"It is why everyone needs to realize they have to adapt and replenish," stated Deb. "I plan to go into Limon tomorrow morning and see about getting more supplies to help with the greenhouse. It was the one part of the farm I was still working on."

"Dad said you are going to get some more lumber so we can build a recreational building," said Dave.

"I'm going the first thing in the morning to check if there is any to buy."

"Thank you, Colonel, for doing all this," said Dave.

"Yes, thanks. I would be dead right now if your place wasn't here," Caroline professed.

Deb felt blood rush to her head as she listened to Bobby's friends take turns in thanking her for creating the farm. Their acknowledgement of her vision was much more significant to her than anyone of them would have imagined. They were young and supposedly naïve to the ways of the world, but they were all intelligent enough to recognize opportunity. Not only identify it but were willing to fight for it.

Deb realized she would need to find a different time and place to speak with Bobby about his inheritance. She decided to sit back and relax while enjoying the company of the young people and Tommy. Sitting in the block tower that she dreamt about building for many years, now allotted her the chance to witness the farm as she imagined it would be. All the hard decisions and expenditures she made over the years were well worth the effort.

Agate, Colorado

Christian and his rebel followers were exhausted from the long, cold march across the plains to Limon. They traveled all day and through the night, taking only short pauses to sleep as they walked parallel with Interstate 70. They made a large swath around the small towns on the journey in order to avoid any form of conflict. Each hill they crested brought disappointment of only more pasture and unplanted fields as far as the eye could see. The morning sun was shining into their eyes as they came upon a small town.

The settlement was smaller than the others they passed, yet it was bustling with people. Christian directed the group to move in a southernly direction away from the town.

After traveling for about fifteen minutes Tim noticed people on the rim of a hill hardly noticeable in the bright sun. He looked through the binoculars at the figures.

"Oh crap," he handed the binoculars to Christian, "look."

Christian viewed the group of approximately fifteen fighters, all dressed in black, carrying rifles. He directed the field glasses slightly to the right and further back where he focused in on an accumulation of enough soldiers to cover a field. Three Jeep Wranglers were positioned on the backside of the militia of insurgents.

"We have to move quickly," Christian lowered the binoculars. "They have an army."

"Who are they?" Shira asked.

"Foreign rebels," Christian stated. "I bet Anastasia informed them of our decision to leave. I never should have mentioned we were going east."

"I'll go talk with them," Shira took a step.

"No, let's go around and see if they follow." Christian waved for everyone to start walking.

As they trekked in a south easterly direction, the group of dissidents stalked, moving parallel with them. After traveling nearly three kilometers, they were edging closer to the three Jeep Wranglers slowly moving along the road with the large army following behind.

"Stop," Christian held up his hand. They were in a flat snow-covered field with no gullies or hills. He gazed at the insurgents. "There must be three hundred of them. They aren't going to let us pass without a confrontation."

"Now do you want me to go and talk with them?" Shira asked.

"I'll go," Tim took two steps in the direction of the road.

"Wait," Christian yelled. "Maybe we should move west, out of this area, where they can't use the road to follow. We need to be in a better location for cover should this escalate."

"If we run now, they will attack us." Tim was moving as he spoke. "I'll get a feel as to what they want."

"Tell them we are still on the same side."

Tim nodded and began jogging over the crusted snow.

Christian moved back to his assemblage, who were huddled together.

"Spread out," he motioned with his hands to direct some of them to move to the south. He pulled his AK-47 off his shoulder, knowing they were too far away for their weapons to be efficient. "Prepare your weapons."

"Don't be confrontational," Shira held up a hand. "Give Tim a chance to let them know we are not a threat."

The sun was high enough to no longer be a factor in watching the movements of the large army of foreign insurgents as they formed a line, shoulder to shoulder, along the road, stretching out on both sides of the Jeeps. All of them held their weapons leveled toward the field of homegrown rebels.

Tim was about fifty meters from the Jeeps when he stopped jogging and began walking with his right hand up in the air. Several loud pops materialized simultaneously with Tim jerking to the left and then falling face first into the field.

Christian grabbed the collar of Shira's coat and pulled her back. They fell into the snow with the sound of bullets whizzing all around them. He turned on his stomach and began returning fire until the magazine was emptied. Bullets were hitting close enough in front of him to have pellets of frozen ground and snow splatter his face. Whatever weapons they were using had a better range than those of the AK-47.

"We can't stay here," he yelled. The sound from the weapons firing behind him drowned out his warning.

"There is no place to go," screamed Shira.

"We have to run," he yelled.

They crawled to the edge of the skirmish line his followers were fighting from. He hesitated as he looked down the long row where many of them were slumped over dead, with only about a quarter of his people still shooting. Shira's mouth was wide open while she stared at their friends. He grabbed her coat at the shoulder and pulled.

"Run, get out of here," he yelled as loud as he could.

With no cover to fight from, he dashed past the decimated fighters from his group. Bullets struck the ground with a zing and hit his friends with a thud as they tried to retreat with him.

Shira sprinted step for step with him as they ran more than two kilometers before stopping and looking back. None of his rebels were following.

Still breathing heavily, she removed the binoculars from her backpack and raised them to her eyes. In the distance a lone person was jogging across the field.

"Someone's coming," she yelled.

Christian was slightly bent at the waist as he caught his breath. He ejected the magazine to his AK and replaced it with a full one.

"We have to keep moving." He glanced to the west where the sun was reflecting off the hard snow covering the flat prairie land. To the south, he could see hilly terrain with bushes popping out of the landscape. "This way," he said.

Jogging until they came to a ravine where they stopped next to a Four wing Saltbush shrub sticking nearly a meter up from the ground. Several more shrubs dotted the area surrounding the small gulley. The man behind them in chase was still nearly seven hundred meters away, relentlessly following their tracks. He was slowly catching up.

Christian slid into the gully with Shira jumping in behind him. It was less than a meter deep but low enough to shield them from the man.

"I'm going to try and surprise him." He pointed to a bush nearly twenty meters nearer to the pursuer. "When he gets close enough don't show yourself until you hear me fire."

Shira nodded her head in agreement as she set the rifle and aimed. Christian belly crawled to the shrub and hid with his rifle leveled at the rebel. The man stopped when he was two hundred meters out and surveyed the area.

When the pursuer hesitated, Shira slid into the ditch, completely out of sight. Christian watched him through the branches of the dense plant. The man waited for about thirty seconds before leveling his weapon directly at him. He fell to his stomach at the base of the shrub as three bullets shattered the small limbs exiting only centimeters over the top of him.

He kept his head level with the ground and looked around the base of the plant. The man, dressed in black with a kerchief around his neck, was cautiously treading on their footprints, crouching as he held his rifle straight out in front, meticulously checking left and right as he walked.

When he was within thirty meters, and fifty meters away from Shira, Christian adjusted his position to the side of the bush. The hunter was looking past his location in the direction of the gulley shielding Shira.

Christian was laying at an awkward angle as he leaned around the backside of the bush and aimed the rifle. He fired two shots. The first bullet hit high and right, causing the stuffing from the tracker's jacket to fly into the air. The second one caught him in the right hip.

Shira raised up as the assailant turned in the direction of Christian. She opened fire, striking him twice in the right side of his lower torso. He dropped his rifle as he fell into the snow.

"We have to keep moving," yelled Christian, standing up on the back side of the shrub.

Shira scrambled out of the ditch and ran toward him. They scurried across the prairie for nearly two hours, stopping only long enough to catch their breath and check the massive fields behind them for any pursuers. When they came to a dirt road going east and west, they contemplated for a moment, before jogging on the wet road to the east.

Limon, Colorado

Ted insisted on taking two squads for security to escort himself along with Jon, Hank, Deb and Tommy to Limon. They arrived in two Oshkosh R-ATV assault vehicles at the outskirts, which was now a good four kilometers from the original downtown. Traffic was bumper to bumper with large buses and military vehicles bottlenecking as they made their way past the town on the way to destinations east of the Mississippi. After moving at a snail's pace for nearly forty-five minutes they turned off the exit ramp from the Interstate and were waved through the barricade blocking the entrance to the town.

Hardly a soul was to be seen anywhere on the main streets within the city limits. On the outskirts, a constant chatter could be heard from the encampment as thousands of people endured the discomfiture of being crammed together like cattle in a corral. The sheriff was standing outside his vehicle parked in front of the hotel utilized as headquarters for the FEMA team. He watched as the assault vehicle pulled up and stopped next to the high metal fencing separating the town from the government encampment. Deb climbed down from the vehicle, followed by her brothers and Tommy. Deb, Tommy and Ted were dressed in army fatigues.

"Colonel Deb Lisco," the sheriff's cowboy hat was cocked back on his head. He smiled as he limped across the wet pavement. "Did you come to pay your tickets?"

"Hell no, I tossed them damn things away a long time ago." Deb smiled while extending her hand. "How are you doing Bob."

"I'm trying to figure out this upside-down world we are living in." He slapped his hand into hers and squeezed before letting go. "It gets worse by the day."

"Things aren't going to get better anytime soon."

"I guess your brother told you about Clint and Peg." The Sheriff grimaced as he looked at Jon.

"It was terrible what happened to them, Bob," stated Deb.

"They are not the only ones. We have had so much crime and killings over the last two weeks that half the time I can only keep myself and Judy safe." He turned his head and spit on the ground. "They opened the doors to the prison and let all the prisoners walk out scot-free."

"When did they do that?"

"It was right after your brother came to town with the guys who attacked the girl." He turned to Jon, "What did you decide to do with them?"

Jon sighed, "We let them go."

"I figured so." The sheriff lifted his hat and ran his fingers through his thin white hair before placing it forward on his head. "Like I told you, this place is now the wild west."

"Well, you can always come out to our farm."

"Are you serious?" he asked with his mouth partially open.

"Of course, I am. Pack your stuff up and you can follow us out."

"By God, I believe I'll take you up on that. Judy is scared to death being home by herself." Bob sniffled and ran the sleeve of his coat over his nose. "This whole damn place seems to be closing in all around us."

"Do you know if Ben Stewart has any material left at the lumber yard?" Deb asked, noticing Jon quickly move to the chain length fence.

"The inside of his store has been ransacked but I think there is still lumber. Nobody has been building anything. The FEMA people are using our offices and hotels or have canvas tents for the people they are housing."

"We'll head over to the lumber yard."

"No, you'll have to go to his house. He and Paula have locked themselves inside, like everyone else in town."

"I'll be damned," Jon yelled from the compound fence. "Hank, come here and tell me if I'm seeing things."

Hank went to the fence and looked through the wire, trying to locate whoever Jon was pointing at. He looked for a moment and then turned to Jon with his eyebrows raised.

"I don't see what you are looking at."

"Isn't that your football player?" Jon moved closer to his brother and pointed to a table in the dining area nearly two hundred meters away.

Christian was walking away from a table with Shira at his side. Hank got a glimpse of the big man before he disappeared into the crowd.

"That was Christian," said Hank. "I wonder why he came here?"

"They were chased out of the city." Jon turned to Ted. "Wouldn't you imagine so Ted."

"Most likely. I wonder if we can get inside the camp." Ted looked to the sheriff. "He has a lot of information that would be valuable to our mission of clearing out the cities."

"I don't have a damn bit of pull in this place," stated the sheriff. "I bet with you being a colonel in the United States Army they won't have a problem with allowing you inside."

"Why don't you three go and see if you can find him. Tommy and I will see if we can talk with Ben Stewart." Deb turned to the sheriff. "Bob, would you mind helping us track down Ben.

"I'm pretty sure he is at his house. I will drive over with you and check."

***

The camp was longer from east to west than it was wide from north to south. The congestion and pandemonium inside the fence were worse than it appeared to be from the outside. The brothers decided to syphon through the mass of people in a systematic manner by starting the search at the east border and walking to the west.

They spread out with Ted going on the south edge and Jon on the north while Hank walked down the middle. Ted never met face to face with Christian, but he was given a good enough description, from Hank, of the large man to feel confident in identifying him, should he make first contact.

The smell from the toilets and food cooking was almost unbearable as they made their way past the dining area where Christian was seen from outside the fence. The inhabitants of the camp seemed angry and defeated. Although there were times when Hank lost sight of his brothers, for the most part he was able to keep tabs on them.

They walked the entire length of the camp without a glimpse of Christian. They came together at the far west edge of the encampment.

"There are so many people in this place we could have walked right by him without noticing it was him," stated Jon.

"He might have spotted us first and hid while we walked past," replied Hank.

"This place is like a viper pit," stated Ted. "Let's head back to where we entered and get the hell out of here."

"This camp is much worse now than when we came to get Linda out," said Jon.

Hank kept a keen eye out for Christian as he continued to walk for nearly twenty minutes when he noticed a group of men about twenty meters in front of him. The oblong face of a man wearing a cap was vaguely familiar, but it did not dawn on him who he was looking at until the blond man he was talking with turned to offer his profile.

Hank tried to locate Jon but could only see a crowd of people. He focused his attention to the south in the direction of Ted. Ted was closer and noticed him waving.

Hank pointed at the two men as Ted approached. "Those are the two men who attacked Caroline."

The man in the cap glanced toward Hank and Ted. When he saw Hank with his attention fixed on him, he tapped the blond man on the shoulder. They slid into the crowd of humanity and disappeared.

Hank and Ted walked to the location. It would be futile to try and follow the two men. Jon was walking back toward them.

"We just saw the two guys who attacked Caroline." Hank swept his arm toward the swarm of people. "They're gone now."

"I can't believe they would come back. I made it clear to them that we would shoot first and ask questions later."

"They know the location of the farm," stated Hank still staring in the direction of where they ran off.

"It's another thing we have to worry about." The vision of Sherry standing over the men with her pistol zeroed in on the men entered his mind.

"Coach," an indistinct voice yelled.

Hank stopped and listened. When he didn't find anyone, he turned to his brothers to ask if either of them heard the word.

"Coach," Christian with Shira at his side emerged from the multitude of people. Dark lines were winding from the corners of his eyes. His face was pale white, making him appear to be an old man.

"Christian," Hank went to his side. "What are you doing here?"

"They killed Tim," he swallowed hard and grimaced. "We didn't have a chance."

"My God, are you sure he's dead?" Hank asked.

"He's gone. They killed everyone in our group."

"Who?" Ted stepped right next to Hank.

"The foreign rebels," The skin on his face was dark red.

"Where did you fight them?" Ted asked.

"About twenty kilometers west of here," Christian looked at Shira for verification.

"It was in a field southeast of the little town of Agate," Shira's eyes were sagging from the lack of sleep.

"How many rebels were there?" Ted stood tall as he asked the question.

"At least three hundred," answered Shira.

"Their weapons were far superior to our AKs," Christian sniffled.

"Will you come and give Ted all the information you have on the rebels?" Hank still believed in his former player and wanted to make sure he would be given a chance to atone for the many mistakes he made throughout his life.

"We'll go with you coach." Christian straightened his shoulders and looked into Ted's eyes, "They are going after NORAD."

Ted returned the gaze but did not reply. The base for the North American Aerospace Defense Command is deep inside Cheyenne Mountain just a stone's throw away from Fort Carson, west of Colorado Springs. It is built inside solid granite and able to survive a nuclear attack.

"I know it sounds crazy. The place is a fortress." Christian took in a deep breath, noticing Ted's skepticism. "Don't underestimate these people."

"Let's go find Deb and get back to the farm." Ted took a step toward Jon, "We can sort things out there."

***

Ben Stewart opened the front door after seeing the sheriff cruiser, followed by the army attack vehicle, stop in front of his home. He waited inside the door while Deb and the sheriff approached.

"Did you finally capture her?" Ben yelled, chuckling, as the two stepped onto the small porch of his two-story cottage.

"More like she finally caught me," Bob chuckled.

"What in the hell happened to you Colonel?" Ben asked. "You're walking like you have a wooden leg."

"Just protecting your crinkled old ass from some of the nastiest people in the world." Deb could see Paula standing back and to the side of him inside the door as she stepped up to their entry.

"And I do thank-you for that," he clicked his tongue and nodded his head. "What is it that I have the pleasure of your visit for this morning."

"I need some lumber."

"Why in the hell would anyone need lumber during these times?"

Deb looked over to the sheriff and then back at Ben. "What in the hell difference does it make to you what I want it for."

"Ok, ok," Ben chuckled, holding up his hands. Paula moved around him and stepped onto the porch. "How much do you need?"

"I have a list." Deb handed him a paper with the inventory calculated by Jason Jensen.

Ben looked at the piece of paper. He rubbed his chin and stated, "I haven't been to the yard in nearly a week. But there was enough there to fill your order before we left."

"What are you building Deb?" Paula asked.

"It's an extra room for people to meet and socialize in order to free up space in the main house."

"How many people do you have at the farm now?"

"You know Paula, I'm not really sure of the number. I would guess maybe a few less than fifty."

"I'm going to see if Judy wants to go out there," Bob adjusted his hat. "It's just not safe to stay here. I feel like I have a target on my back every morning when I leave the house."

"Ben." Deb knew all she had to do was ask and Paula would jump at the chance of going to the farm. With the knowledge Ben had with the solar grid and septic system he would be invaluable to have on the premises. "You two are more than welcome to come with us."

"We've been talking about leaving for the past two days," Paula sighed. "We were thinking of going east but we don't have any family we are close enough with to show up on their doorstep."

"Do you have a car that runs?" asked Bob.

"The delivery truck starts," stated Ben. He gazed at Deb, "We can load it up and take all the lumber you need."

"We stored a lot of goods from the store when we realized we were going to have problems. We have most of it in the garage," stated Paula. "We have more coffee than we could drink in a lifetime."

Deb stared at them for a moment. She could not think of a better outcome to the visit to Limon.

"Let's load everything up and go

***

Ben and Paula Stewart, driving the lumber yards twelve-ton deliver truck, overloaded with lumber and supplies, followed closely behind the two Oshkosh R-ATV assault vehicles, with Sheriff Bob and his wife Judy close behind in their brand new 2051 Chevy Sombrero. Deb, Tommy, Ted, Jon, Hank, Christian and Shira were riding in the second assault vehicle.

Nearly halfway to the farm the convoy crested a hill on the wet gravel road. The front vehicle eased to a stop. Lieutenant Rod Millet stepped out of the front vehicle and walked to the trailing assault vehicle.

"Colonel," Lieutenant Millet looked up into the open door at Ted. "There is a roadblock, about two klicks ahead. The field on both sides are full of people."

Ted stepped out, followed by Tommy and Deb. He took the lieutenant's field glasses and viewed the vehicles blocking the road. He handed them to Tommy. The Command Sergeant Major carefully observed the location.

"Sir," Lieutenant Millet stood shoulder to shoulder with Tommy and pointed to a ridge west of the roadblock. "Irregulars are accumulating to the west."

"We will need support from Fort Carson if we are going to confront them," Tommy glanced at Ted.

"We are overmatched, and I don't want to put the civilians in the middle of a battle." Ted looked at Lieutenant Millet. "Lieutenant, have the base send out a NAV to follow the rebels."

Before anyone responded several shots rang out and bullets pinged off the front assault vehicle.

"Back up," Ted motioned with his arms to Ben and Bob. Both vehicles quickly backed-up while he jumped inside the door being held open by Deb. The assault vehicles backed down the dirt road, following the civilians, until they were a safe enough distance away to turn around.

Colorado Farm

Emilee and Bobby were in the concrete tower when they saw the convoy returning down the driveway. Both the large truck carrying lumber and the brand-new car stopped between the Jacoby's RV and the garage. The military vehicles zoomed past and parked at the far end of the apartment.

Jacqueline and Nicole approached the newcomers while Bobby and Emilee continued to watch out the window on the third floor of the tower. Emilee focused on Jacqueline and Nicole greeting the strangers, with several others, including Irene and Breanna, joining to make them welcome, when she glanced in the direction of the soldiers exiting the military vehicles. She gasped, causing Bobby to jerk toward her.

"What is it?" Bobby asked.

"Christian," she responded, "my dad."

Bobby placed his hand on her shoulder. She never discussed, with him, her feelings about learning that Christian is her father. He remained quiet and looked at her.

"Mom guaranteed me that he is my father," she swallowed hard. "I told her, the first chance I get, I will have a paternity test. She still assured me that she is one-hundred percent certain he is my dad."

They looked out the window while Ted escorted Christian and Shira in the direction of the offices in the garage. Deb and Tommy went to the vehicles with the lumber while Jason and Harold wandered toward them.

Bobby and Emilee watched from their perch as everyone became acquainted. Jon was busy speaking with Irving, Terrance and Jerry. Deb and Tommy were back at the lumber truck with the group talking to Bob and Ben.

Out of the corner of his eye Bobby caught sight of three men running down the driveway. He leaned out the window and raised his binoculars. Tyrone and Von, the two young men who came to the farm with the men who attacked Caroline were jogging past the farmhouse with a larger man between them.

"Aunt Deb," Bobby yelled out the window. He flailed his hands. "Uncle Jon, there are men coming up the drive."

Jon and Irving walked to the side of the Jacoby RV and waited as the men jogged past the house. Deb and Tommy joined them as the men stopped next to them and leaned over to catch their breath.

"Are you running away from someone?" Jon asked.

"Yeah," the older man raised up and took in a deep breath and released it. He opened his eyes wide and said, "A lot of people."

"Are they the foreign fighters dressed in black?" Tommy moved in front of the man.

"Yeah, them plus a number of young people." The man noticed Deb and Tommy dressed in fatigues.

"We ran into the group about twenty klicks northwest of here," Tommy interjected, speaking directly to Irving. "We had to divert back north and then east to go around them."

"Not the same group, the one we were with is south of here," the man stated adamantly to Tommy. "They have a base at a ranch southeast of Colorado Springs."

"When did you last have contact with them?" Tommy asked.

"This morning, about six hours ago."

"How large a group are they?"

"I don't know." He held his hands up. "Maybe five hundred."

Tommy glanced at Deb.

"We need ariel surveillance," said Deb, pulling the collar of her jacket tight. "But it's going to be hard with this low cloud cover."

"I'll let Ted know about the additional enemy to the south. Maybe he can get a company from the 3rd Battalion of the 99th to assist us," Tommy hesitated to see if Deb wanted to reply. She stood with her hand on her chin, so he turned and jogged in the direction of the garage.

Hank, Bobby and Emilee walked next to the young brothers.

"Where did you go after you left here?" Hank asked.

"We all went back to the original group we arrived with, but they met up with the militants," said Von.

"It sounds crazy, but we thought they were going to somewhere we would be safe to wait out this conflict. We never made it to their ranch but apparently it is a place used as the main base for several dissident groups," stated the older man. "Since we joined the militants, they have ransacked two ranches."

"Did you hear anything about why they are so far from the city?" Deb asked. "It doesn't seem worth their while to destroy farms."

"It's really confusing what is taking place." Leroy glanced at his sons. "To the best of our understanding they came to the country to establish a place to go when the authorities put too much pressure on them in the city."

"When we were here the other day, before you detained the two guys we were with, the plan was to attack this farm. After we told them how well armed you are, they decided to leave," stated Von.

"The foreign group has better weapons and is a whole lot more organized than the American rebels," Leroy said. "Even with the military presence here, they won't back down."

"The younger boy played football against Bobby," Hank told Deb. "I trust what they tell us is what they believe to be true."

"Actually Coach, I played against your team too, in 2030," stated the older man.

"What is your name?" Hank asked.

"Leroy Roberts."

Hank nodded, there were so many different players his teams competed against over the years that it was impossible to remember all of them.

"The foreign fighters are placing Americans in their ranks thinking it will protect them from being destroyed from the air," stated Deb.

"That is a pretty large force. If there are five hundred rebels south, along with the three hundred or so we came across to the north," said Hank.

"It's an army," stated Deb. "They are soldiers who eventually will have to be eliminated."

"About a third of the force are regular people like us," stated Leroy. "Some of the Americans are buying into the foreign rebel's beliefs, but there are only a few."

"Hank, you should make sure all the kids are close. Give everyone else a heads up to stay on the alert," said Deb.

"I want to take the M82 .50 Caliber rifle and set up in the tower," said Irving.

"We'll go with you." Bobby glanced at Emilee, thinking he should not have spoken for her. "Do you want to come with me or check with your mom and sisters?"

"I'll make sure Avery and Reagan are inside the house."

"Can you help me carry ammunition and supplies to the tower?" Irving asked Bobby. "Find Dave, Sherry and Caroline and have them bring the spotter scopes to the top."

"Irving, why don't you get the sensors and set them on the perimeter," said Deb. "If the snow comes in it will be difficult to get a visual."

He looked at the colonel with his mouth open. "This is the first I have heard about any sensors."

There is a box of ten Trinity 180 camera sensors in the weapons cabinet."

"If I had known that I would have had them set."

***

Jessica was watering plants inside the greenhouse when Samantha opened the sliding door and entered. She continued to spray water with her eyes transfixed on the plants while Samantha approached.

"Bill wanted me to let you know that Ted brought Christian back with him from Limon." She moved close enough to feel the mist of the water being squirted. It was comfortably warm and humid inside the glasshouse.

Jessica swallowed hard as she tightened her grip on the hose. Her eyes never left the plants.

Samantha turned away. She had given the message and it was apparent Jessica did not want to discuss the situation with her. She took a step in the direction of the door.

"How many people are with him?" Jessica asked.

Samantha stopped and turned around.

"Just one," Samantha spoke with a soft tone, "a girl."

"Do you know where they are at now?" She finally made eye contact with Samantha.

"In the garage."

"Is Bill with them?"

"No, we have been at the barn helping the Jacobys with the cattle. Now he's with Hank and the others at the farmhouse discussing how to prepare for a threat."

"Does he want me to go to the garage?" Jessica asked lethargically. She was moving slowly and seemed to be completely distracted as she turned off the water and set the hose to the side. Her hair was in a hastily placed ponytail.

"He didn't say. He only wanted me to let you know that Christian had returned to the farm." Samantha sensed the distress the lady was experiencing. "Are you ok Jessica?"

She held her mouth closed and breathed through her nose as she stared at Samantha. She picked up a towel and dried her hands.

"I know this whole situation can't be easy for you." Samantha offered.

"God knows everything seems to be falling apart," Jessica stated. "I never thought things could get worse in my life. It's almost unbearable."

"Something tells me you are a fighter," Samantha swallowed hard. "Maybe it's time for you to start fighting."

A hint of a smile came across Jessica's lips. Samantha was the last person she would have considered to become an ally, to offer encouragement.

"It is time to fight back." She tossed the towel, "I will confront Christian right now."

Samantha followed Jessica out of the greenhouse and watched as she sauntered in the direction of the garage. She felt good about handling the conversation with the feisty mother in a cordial manner. The two of them may never be friends but coexisting at the farm would now be much easier.

***

The outer part of the garage was cold compared to the toasty room partitioned off for Ted's office. Christian and Shira sat next to the wall with Jon standing over them. Ted was at the monitor speaking with Colonel Myers at Fort Carson while Tommy looked over his shoulder.

"The snow and thick cloud cover will hinder the use of drones. It all should change shortly." Tommy took a step away from the back of Ted's chair. "I just checked the weather with Fort Carson. A squall of snow is about thirty kilometers to the west. It's going to pass over us quickly, leaving partly cloudy skies. Tomorrow it will be bitterly cold and remain so for the next several days."

"Then, visibility here will be no problem in a couple of hours." Deb noticed Tommy had changed into his olive drab softshell tactical M-102 field jacket. She moved closer to listen in on the conversation between Ted and Colonel Myer. The more she listened the more she realized that Colonel Myer was overwhelmed with the destruction taking place in the city. There was a huge uptick in attacks against utilities with reliable intel that Cherry Creek Dam was to be targeted. She waited patiently as Ted terminated the call.

"I can understand Bonny's wanting to keep her troops close at hand. With significant threats against the reservoirs, she is making the correct decision. General Lopez is fully occupied at the border and is not going to deal with our problem," Ted informed them. He rose from the chair and faced Deb. "I have 2nd and 3rd squads out now to see if they can locate and track the two groups of rebels."

"Tommy, can you try and get through to Lauer. Emphasize to the general that the rebels are highly trained soldiers, not just a bunch of civilians." Deb could feel the soreness in her calf from the shrapnel she had received in Utah.

Christian was listening to the conversation when he noticed Jessica enter the room. He kept his eyes on her as she moved next to Ted.

Jessica made eye contact with Shira momentarily avoiding Christian's gaze. Although she was not friends with Shira, she was aware of the headstrong woman's fascination for Christian.

"Why did you come back?" Jessica asked.

Neither of them replied.

"Jessica," Ted stepped in front of her, "they told us their entire group has been killed."

Jessica felt her heartbeat quicken. She looked closer at Christian. His face was expressionless as if he had lost his soul. He leaned his head back and held his mouth wide open, trying to capture air. She turned to stare at Shira who was rail thin, with a redness around her neck that was rough and wrinkled.

"All of them? Tim too?" she inquired.

Shira nodded; her hands were shaking.

"You two are disgusting." Jessica leaned closer with her upper lip clenched, showing her teeth. Ted caught her with his arm while Christian never budged. "It was so obvious that you should have left when you had a chance. You are pathetic."

"We did leave," Shira shouted. "The foreigners are everywhere."

"You could have escaped if you would have left when I did. How could you be so stupid to go along with them."

"I agree," Shira rubbed the corners of her eyes where crust had accumulated, "but we didn't."

"Everything you have done is so pointless," spit shot out of Jessica's mouth. She thought how stupid it was on her part for falling for the false opportunity of being free when she joined them. She gnashed her teeth, shook her head, turned and walked out the door.

"Deb, General Lauer is unavailable. Lieutenant Delk told me that there is major enemy movement at the southern border, with a surge in rockets being fired at the troops in Texas and New Mexico. There is a major escalation taking place," Tommy cleared his throat, "all of 4th Division is heading to the Albuquerque sector."

"Including 2nd Brigade?"

"Yes."

If it wasn't for the immediate crisis at the farm Deb would be loading her gear and driving to Fort Carson.

Corporal Pint entered the garage. Her cheeks were red with snow accumulated on the top of her cap as she stood at attention in front of Ted and saluted.

"Sir, 3rd Squad has encountered the enemy force about eleven kilometers north of our location." The corporal held her arm with a Pulsenet processor out in front of her and looked at the computer on Ted's desk. "I can redirect communication to this site if you wish."

"Do it."

The corporal sat in the chair and within a minute was finished. "I have Sergeant Phillips."

"What's the situation?" Ted asked, looking at the image of the sergeant on the monitor. He was near the location where earlier in the day they encountered the insurgents.

"The force just left a farmhouse on county road 53 and is moving to the south at about four kilometers an hour." Sergeant Phillips was dressed in the Rind Impulse Operator Suit, standing on a gravel road with light snow falling. "We are eight kilometers northwest of your location, preparing to move back to a hill approximately two kilometers to the south."

"Fall back to the hill. When you get there transmit pictures of the force and gauge their speed. Then return to the base."

"Yes sir."

"Corporal Pint connect with 2nd Squad." Ted moved back from the chair in front of the monitor and glanced at Deb. "If these two forces merge and come this way we are going to have a real problem."

"If they combine, they will be a battalion size army," Deb declared.

"Sir, Sergeant Fakharzedeh is linked," Corporal Pint rose from the chair, allowing Ted to sit.

"Sergeant, have you located the rebel forces?" Ted could see the sergeant peeking out from his helmet.

"It is not one centralized army. There are eight groups of about fifty soldiers in each, spread out over a ten kilometer stretch of the road," stated the sergeant. "They are moving in a concerted manner to the north."

"How far south of our base are you now?"

"About fifteen kilometers. We are a good four kilometers north of the closest group of insurgents. It's beginning to snow hard, and visibility is becoming difficult."

"Are they on county road 53?"

"They are moving parallel with 53."

"Return to base," Ted took in a deep breath. "Make sure they don't flank you."

"They are coming our way," said Deb. "We have about four hours before they merge and hit our location."

Tommy looked back and forth between Ted and Deb. "The request made for air support has been granted. Petersen Air Base should be coordinating with your communication center for the precise location and time needed for the NAV."

"Hopefully the weather will clear off like predicted so we can use the drone effectively," stated Ted.

"I'm going to check with Jon to make sure everyone here is prepared," Deb turned to Tommy. "I'll be in the house."

***

Jon was standing on the hearth of the fireplace, holding his hand up, trying to quiet the multitude crammed into the living room. Hank stepped onto the hearth next to his brother. Jacqueline and Gina were standing to the side of their husbands.

Deb waited in the kitchen as her brothers struggled to secure control. She heard the roar of one of the assault vehicles returning from the surveillance mission as it hurried past the farmhouse. She looked out the window at the light snow falling. A rush of blood surged to her brain as she visualized enemy forces attacking the farmhouse. Her thoughts went to the children and their safety should the house be destroyed.

Bill came to her side.

"What can I do Aunt Deb?" Bill asked.

"There are several five-gallon buckets in the supply shed. I want you to get some help and bring them inside the house. Then hook the hoses up outside and pull them through the windows and fill the buckets. Grab some insulation to wrap around the hoses and sill cocks, so they don't freeze. "

"Do you think there will be an attack, even with Dad's platoon here?"

"I don't know for sure," Deb swallowed hard. "If this army attacks, they will do so only if they think they can win."

"Is the army base going to send help?" Bill could feel his heart beating hard.

"If the situation warrants us needing help, they will definitely get us help. Right now, we are unsure of the scope of the danger."

"I know we discussed the possibility of a threat to the farm but now that it's taking place it seems unreal." Bill shook his head, "I am really glad you and Dad are here."

"Your dad knows better than anyone how to strategically situate his soldiers. I'll direct the civilians at the farm to best support him. I want you to coordinate the effort in the house, especially the children. The safest place for them will be in the weapons closet, but we need an escape route should the house start on fire," Deb clasped her hands. "I will move the frontend loader to the east side of the house, as close to the egress window from the downstairs bedroom as possible to shield the children should they have to be moved."

"Where will we take them?"

"Bill, that will be determined by the situation. We have to be prepared to escape whether it be to the bottom of the tower or the garage," Deb cleared her throat. "All the parents need to stay either inside the house or right on the outside."

"I take that includes me also?"

"Yes, we need to make sure the house is protected. The fewer civilians outside the less chance of someone being shot accidentally by your dad's soldiers."

"Makes sense," Bill moved toward the door. "I'll get on the bucket detail."

Deb stepped outside and moved next to the Jacoby's RV. Irving was visible through the window at the top level of the tower with Bobby and Emilee. The sound of the second assault vehicle returning with Sergeant Fakharzedeh's squad could be heard coming down the driveway. She waited for it to pass before walking to the tower and jogging up the stairs.

"Colonel Lisco," Irving rested the .50 Caliber rifle below the window before moving to the middle of the room. Bobby, holding a radio, and Emilee were working on a computer situated on a chair. "We are setting the Trinity sensors, loading them to the computer. Dave, Caroline and Sherry are finishing the positioning to give us a full 360 view."

Deb moved to the window and looked across the landscape. The sun was setting low in the southwest, shining through the haze and light snow. Several head of cattle were visible in the corrals with Breanna leading a horse inside the barn. She contemplated quietly until Irving broke her train of thought.

"Colonel do you think the rebels will attack?" Irving stepped next to her.

"Even with Ted's forty soldier platoon, the forces advancing our way outnumber us about ten to one," she declared. "With the exception of the FEMA camp in Limon we are the only threat to them on the eastern plains. I'm almost sure they want to eliminate us."

"We will be prepared if they do launch an attack."

Deb turned to Bobby. "Could you go to the garage and ask Tommy to join us?"

Bobby ran down the stairs just as Dave and Sherry were coming up.

"We should have the Jacobys move the RV from in front of the house," said Irving.

"They can park it on the side of the garage," stated Deb.

"Dave, will you go down and ask Aaron Jacoby to move the RV to the side of the garage."

"Ok."

"Ask Jon and Hank to come back with you. Also, grab some paper and a pen." Deb slapped Irving on the shoulder and walked to the head of the stairs. "I'll be right back. I'll check with Ted to see if he can give us about ten minutes of his time to go over where we can best assist his troops."

***

"Everybody should grab a flashlight and a bottle of water before we go to the basement." Nicole took over Hank and Jon's position standing on the fireplace hearth. Maddy was holding tight to her left arm with Scotty standing next to her. "I don't want to scare the children, but we have to be prepared if the lights or water go off."

"Are we all going to spend the night in the basement?" Travis asked, sitting next to his wife in a metal chair with his daughters standing next to them.

"We want all the parents to stay in the house and all the children in the basement." Nicole glanced at Sheriff Bob who was helping Bill fill buckets of water in the kitchen. "Bill is in communication with his father to coordinate the effort to protect the farmhouse. I know Ted wants to make sure we don't place any of his soldiers at risk by shooting randomly from this position."

"Have you talked with Ted in the last couple hours," Al asked. "Is there a legitimate threat?"

"Yes, we are facing real danger Al," Nicole squinted her eyes at the dentist, "an immediate threat.

"Is Bill filling buckets in the kitchen with water because they are worried this place might burn down." Al looked around the room while holding both hands up before turning back to face Nicole. "Are you sure we want to be in the basement if there is a fire?"

Samantha opened the window in the living room and pulled out the screen causing a rush of cold air to enter. Jacqueline standing on a brick flower planter on the outside, handed her a garden hose with a thumb-controlled nozzle. Samantha pulled the twenty-five-meter hose inside before closing the window onto it, allowing for a small gap. Cold air continued to flow into the living room.

"Where do you suggest we go?" Nicole stared at the dentist.

"Not the basement."

"The weapons closet is the most secure place on the farm." Nicole pulled her arm away from Maddy and stepped off the hearth, "It's the best place for the kids."

Maddy moved next to Irene and took her hand.

"Al, this is a scary situation for all of us." Linda placed her hand on the back of her husband's arm and squeezed.

"Everything here is so ill planned. All this should have been predetermined," Al scoffed. "Why isn't there a bunker away from the house for everyone to go into?"

"My God, why are you always complaining?" Ed asked, sitting between Breanna and Ashley on the edge of the sofa. "Complaining never makes anything better."

"Oh, shut-up," Al yelled. He leered at Ed. "There's a difference between com...."

Breanna jumped out of her seat and was nose to nose with Al before he could finish his sentence.

"You shut the fuck up," she yelled, poking him in his chest with her eyes bulging. "Don't you ever talk to my dad that way. I'll knock the living hell out of you."

Al cowered to Linda's side with his mouth wide open.

"Ok, ok, I know everyone is on edge, but we can't fight amongst ourselves." Nicole placed her hand on Breanna's shoulder. "All the children are going to the basement. We will have a plan in place for everyone else. Whether you follow it is up to you."

Maddy pulled on Irene's arm. Irene leaned down so the little girl could whisper in her ear, "Tell Breanna not to use those words in front of Grandpa. He'll make her clean the bathrooms."

"I will tell her," Irene smiled. She wasn't the least bit surprised at her daughter's reaction in protecting Ed. "I'm going to the kitchen to see if I can find some snacks for all of us while we are downstairs. You and Scotty go with your grandma and find a good place to make a bed."

Nicole's head was throbbing as she took in a deep breath. There was going to be combat taking place at the farm and everyone seemed to be unaware of the magnitude of danger they were about to face. She realized Ted was busy figuring out how to keep everyone alive, but she wished he would take a moment to come inside the house to give them an idea of what to expect.

Julia was standing in the clinic door listening to the chatter. Hopefully not, but it could end up being a busy night for the physician assistant.

***

Deb scurried up the steps to the tower with Ted dressed in full combat gear right behind her. He was carrying headsets. Hank and Jon were standing at the north window while Irving looked through a spotter scope out the large south window. Bobby, Emilee, Dave and Sherry were huddled around the computer placed on the floor in the corner of the crowded room.

"We have visibility of nearly two kilometers," stated Irving.

"I have five headsets for the people who have the .50 Caliber rifles," Ted held up the receivers.

"That will be me, Tommy, Jon, Terrance and Irving," said Deb.

"I want Irving and Terrance in the tower with the main focus on the east flank." Ted turned to Bobby and his friends, "You four will be the spotters. You can give information of troop movement, as well as range, to either Irving or Terrance. They can relay the message to the platoon communication, or to Deb, Jon or Tommy."

"We moved a tractor to the area about two hundred meters northeast of the corner of the apartment." Deb made eye contact with Jon. "Jon, Hank, Christian, Shira, and Jerry are to locate at this position."

"It's a good location at high ground. Your main objective is to protect the four-person mortar squad on the north sector of our base." Ted could see that Jon was concerned about something.

"Are we sure Christian and Shira want to engage in combat?" Jon asked.

"They assured me they very much want to fight," Ted answered.

"Tommy and I will go to the southeast corner of the house. The front-end loader is positioned near the back window on the east side." Deb glanced at Tommy, "Is there anything you can think of we are missing."

"Just make sure to have plenty of ammunition. Keep communication lines open so we can work as a team," said Tommy. "We should make sure everyone has night goggles."

"Another thing for the civilians," Deb looked at Bobby and his friends, "do not shoot at shadows. Make sure you identify what you are firing at before you pull the trigger."

"What weapons should we use?" Bobby asked.

"Everyone not carrying a .50 Caliber should have an M-16. We have plenty of ammunition on hand," stated Deb. "Make sure you have ear protection."

"Colonel Lisco," yelled a private from down below. "We are receiving pictures from Vocaro of a large group approaching from the southwest, about four klicks out."

"Are you sure of the distance?" Ted yelled down from the window.

"Yes sir."

"Private have communication begin calibrating the assault vehicles for remote. I will be right down."

"Look at the ridge." Irving was looking through the scope of his .50 Caliber rifle at a group of ten rebels. "They are eighteen hundred and fifty meters out."

Deb, Tommy and Ted looked through the spotter scope. Jon and Hank tried to see with their bare eyes but could not make out any people on the hill in the distance.

"Look at the two soldiers kneeling on the right side," said Tommy. "They are setting a mortar system."

"Irving, can you make that shot?" Deb looked at Ted for his approval. "We can't let them set up that close.

"I can make it." He had the rebel holding a shell in his cross hairs.

"Do it," said Ted.

"Cover your ears."

The loud crack of the .50 Caliber reverberated across the landscape. The rebel holding the shell flew to the ground with the others scattering.

"It's started," stated Deb. "We better get in position."

***

Bill stood outside the front door of the farmhouse intently surveying the countryside while Samantha remained at the threshold of the open door. He handed her his rifle and leveled his binoculars to the hills to the south and west. An assault vehicle sped in front of the house and down the driveway. It stopped about fifty meters from the county road. Every ten seconds or so the vehicle would move twenty meters in various directions.

"Do you see anything?" Samantha tried to look around his body.

"I see some people on the ridgeline, but they disappear as soon as they become visible." He lowered the field glasses and let out a deep breath. "They must be gathering on the other side of the hill."

Inside the living room the Jacobys, Sheriff Bob and Ben Stewart were staring out the picture window, with each of their rifles directed toward the carpeted floor. Jacqueline, Gina, Travis and Julia were in the kitchen.

"It's been quiet since we heard the one gunshot," stated the sheriff. "With the sun setting, things are going to get interesting."

"Look back on the hill," yelled Aaron Jacoby, pointing out the window. "Jesus, there are hundreds of people."

The side of the knoll looked like a swarm of ants moving along the landscape from west to east. Soldiers dressed in black were running along the ridge about twelve hundred meters south of the farmhouse, parallel with the county road.

A squad of ten American Soldiers dressed in combat gear sprinted up the driveway and fanned out to the west of the assault vehicle. They disappeared into the pasture. The assault vehicle raced the final few meters down the driveway to the county road and stopped. The machine gun on the turret rotated to the south and began firing. The rebels on the hillside scattered and vanished as the 32 mm shells shrouded the landscape.

Bill stepped inside the house and instinctively locked the door. Within thirty seconds of coming inside a large flash of light illuminated the area, followed by two loud explosions coming from the area near the barn. Samantha crunched down and gasped. A large blast from the back of the house, nearly shattered their eardrums, causing the entire structure to shake. The lights flickered and turned off.

Jason and Harold came running up from the downstairs and moved to the back of the house to assess the damage from the explosion. Fred lingered behind them but did not follow to the back bedrooms, instead he stepped into the kitchen and went to Travis' side to look out the window.

"Move away from the windows." Bill grabbed hold of Samantha's arm and pulled her to the enclosed area of the clinic, several of the others crowded in behind them. Travis and Fred remained in the kitchen, both holding their hands over their ears to muffle the deafening sound of gunfire being returned from the farm area.

A mortar blast hit the front door of the kitchen, causing a loud boom, followed by a whooshing sound. The detonation tossed both Travis and Fred into the air, sending bits of broken wood and tile into the living room all the way to the fireplace. Bill and Samantha were the first to reach the two men as the others lingered behind. Fred laid twisted and disfigured.

Travis was motionless on top of buckets of spilt water while bitterly cold air rushed in from the gaping hole where the kitchen door once existed. Samantha knelt at his side and listened to his labored breathing. His arm was mangled and a hole in the side of his shirt revealed a deep gash at his lower abdomen. She placed her hand under his head and lifted hard enough to straighten his body off the buckets and onto the floor.

"Let's get him into the clinic," yelled Bill, moving to his side while the others came to his aide.

"Oh my God," Julia yelled when she noticed her husband's mangled body. She fell to the floor and placed her hand on his neck.

"Oh Lord," Harold yelled as he went to his knees next to his brother and sister-in-law.

"He's dead Harold," Julia held her bloody hand next to her pale face.

"We can't leave him like this," Harold sniffled, standing and pulling Julia to her feet.

"We'll help," said Adam Jacoby, turning to Breanna and Aaron. "Let's take him into the living room."

Jacqueline and Gina cut off Travis' tattered shirt immediately after he was placed on the hospital bed in the clinic, while he lay unconscious, taking in short, labored breaths. Without the help of the physician assistant, who just lost her husband, they were lost in their effort to save the young pilot.

"We are going to need some lights in here," yelled Gina.

Bill joined his aunts in the clinic and initiated the emergency battery-operated lights and heating system, bringing bright lights to the room.

Julia watched the Jacobys move her husband to the hard tile on the foyer and cover his body with a sheet.

"I'm going to get Becky," Harold gazed at Julia as she stood rigid as a statue with her eyes fixed on the covered body of Fred. He turned and hurried down the stairs to the basement to find his wife.

Jacqueline crept away from the hospital bed and lingered back into the living room. Lights from the clinic illuminated into the kitchen, revealing blood splattered across the kitchen cabinet. She moved to Julia's side and placed a hand on her shoulder. She knew that the only chance Travis had for survival was for the devastated physician assistant to render immediate medical aid.

"Julia, I'm so sorry," Jacqueline said softly as the newly widowed wife turned her head and stared blankly. She could see the Jacobys standing near the hall with their heads hanging low.

"I need to help the others." Julia took a small step backwards and looked in the direction of the clinic.

Jacqueline nodded; she was relieved Julia made the decision to help Travis.

Gina came to Jacqueline's side while Julia walked to the clinic.

"I would never have imagined the devastation." Jacqueline was breathing hard, trying to catch her breath. "Bobby and Hank are in the middle of all this."

"Believe me Jacqueline, it is something you can't dwell on. In real war reality is bad enough without imagining bad situations," stated Gina.

Becky and Sue dashed up the basement steps with Harold following slowly behind. Sue rushed to Travis' side while Becky lingered toward Julia.

Bill instinctively began to pick pieces of splintered wood and glass off the carpet in the living room. Samantha retrieved two buckets from the kitchen to use as containers for the rubble while Breanna squirted water around the edges of the blast sight, calming some of the dust. Soon, everyone upstairs was working to clear the debris.

***

Deb realized immediately after the explosions that the house was hit. She rested her rifle and glanced at Tommy. His rifle was placed on the blade of the front-end loader leveled in the direction of the southern fields. His undivided focus was on making sure no rebel soldier would get close enough to threaten him or the colonel.

"I'm going to check on damage." Deb moved toward the back door, "I'll be right back."

A metallic smell mixed with dust greeted her as she entered the kitchen. She walked past Breanna, who was wetting the opening where the kitchen door once existed, and into the living room. She hesitated to look at the body covered with the sheet.

"Who is it?"

"It's Fred, Julia's husband and Harold the bricklayer's brother," Bill uttered, moving closer to his aunt.

"Who else?" Deb was looking into the clinic where she could see the back of Julia as she worked on her patient.

"Travis," stated Bill.

Jacqueline moved next to Bill and Deb.

"Have you heard from the others?" Jacqueline asked, holding a shaking finger to her lip.

"Yes, we are all in contact."

"Are Bobby and Hank…?" she swallowed hard as she tried to find the words. "They aren't hurt, are they?"

"Bobby is in the tower and Hank is with Jon on the north side. I haven't heard anything to suggest they are injured in any way."

Jacqueline took in a deep breath and let it out. "Deb are you and Ted going to be able to stop these people?"

"We will stop them," Deb looked into her sister-in-law's eyes. "The foreign insurgent forces are not nearly as structured as I thought they would be."

Jacqueline swallowed hard. She could not believe how anyone could be so calm under the duress of war. The sound echoing from the living room of Becky crying as she clutched Harold's arm while they looked down at Fred's body, fortified her perspective.

"Colonel," Jason Jensen towered over her as he interrupted. "The blast on the front of the house didn't cause as much damage as the one in the kitchen. We were lucky it didn't break the water line."

"We will deal with all the structural damage later. Right now, we need to make sure people stay away from the windows," she acknowledged the carpenter's assessment before turning to Bill. "It might be best if everyone, not helping with the wounded, goes to the basement. There shouldn't be any more mortar attacks, but there are active enemy troops still located close enough to take a shot at someone in the window."

"I will put some of the rifles back into the gun closet," stated Bill.

"That will be a wise choice," Deb looked at Jacqueline. "Be diligent a little while longer. This will be over shortly."

"Aunt Deb are we getting support from the base?" Bill asked. "They won't leave us here to die without helping, will they?"

"Your dad is in touch with Fort Carson, and they have already given him air support," Deb affirmed. "This enemy is sneaky and much different from an organized army. They are a resistance army, that makes them hard to find."

"I am going to stay upstairs and help." Jacqueline stared inside the clinic at Julia working on Travis, while Sue stayed to the side of the room. She knew that Julia was in shock from just learning of the death of her husband and was working on autopilot.

***

Bobby and Emilee remained on the third floor of the tower with Terrance and Irving while Dave, Sherry and Caroline went to the second floor to keep watch out the windows.

Sherry held her rifle out the small window to the east as she looked through the night goggles. Adjusting her eyes to the yellow light emitted by the goggles was giving her a headache. She would remove them every two minutes to allow her eyes to rest.

"I wonder if I should go back to the top and keep an eye to the north," said Caroline. "I could see over the greenhouse from above."

"No, Irving will let us know if he wants us up there," Dave removed his goggles. "Even though we can't see them, I'm sure Bobby is keeping an eye on Coach and Jon on the other side of the garage."

"They are about three hundred meters out with Christian, Shira and Jerry." Sherry flinched as a shot rang out from the room up above.

"Terrance must see someone," said Caroline. "That shot came from the east window."

"They keep shooting but I haven't seen one person yet." Sherry squinted and pulled the back of her hair into a ponytail and slipped on the goggles. She was beginning to wonder if she was looking too quickly over the dark field and missing the enemy. She knew they were out there. Just as she was about to speak, a bullet exploded into the side of the window, creating fragments of jagged concrete block that slammed into the right side her face. She flew back hard onto the floor and screamed loudly.

Dave and Caroline fell to their knees beside her while she clutched the side of her face. Blood was covering the plywood flooring as she rolled over onto her stomach and continued to scream.

"Sherry, let us see," Dave placed his hand on her back.

She remained hunched over as Irving came running down the stairs. He stepped on the rubble from the concrete block as he reached down and lifted, spinning her in his arms. She was limp with blood flowing from the right side of her face. After removing her night goggles, he pulled her hair away from a large gash on her cheek. There were several smaller knicks toward the top of her head that were producing much of the bleeding.

"This was caused by chips from the concrete, not a bullet," Irving hoisted her to her feet. "One of you needs to take her inside the house and have Julia dress the wounds."

"I'll do it," Dave moved next to Sherry and placed his arm around her waist. She clutched his upper back as he all but carried her down the stairs, across the courtyard, to the back door of the house.

***

The smell of gunpowder and the wailing from the farm animals was nearly too much for Hank to handle. Never in his life had he felt so vulnerable. If not for Jon's persistence in explaining how important it was for them to protect the northeast flank of the farm, he would have abandoned the area and dashed back to check on the safety of Jacqueline and Bobby.

"Should I go and check on the farmhouse?" Hank seemed like a fish out of water as he held a M-16 rifle pointed straight up in the air.

"Hank, you keep your damn head down and watch for anyone coming across the pasture." Jon took time to shake a finger at his brother before focusing on the murky landscape.

"They are bound to come this way eventually. If it gets much darker, we won't see them until they are right up on us." Jerry glanced at Jon as he aimed his rifle into the abyss of pastureland.

"It sounds to me like they are blowing the shit out of the farm." Christian laid on his belly in the cold snow aiming his rifle. Shira kneeled on one knee with her rifle pointed at the ground.

"Keep the chatter down and concentrate on any movement," said Jon, watching through tactical night vision infrared goggles past the remains of the old house where Maddy fell into the well. He adjusted his radio head gear with his left hand.

"Have you heard anything from Deb or Ted?" Hank spoke in a hushed voice. He leaned onto the large wheel of the tractor, looking back in the direction of the farmhouse. The garage, greenhouse and apartment blocked his view of the house, but he could see the top of the tower. "It looks like the electricity has been knocked out."

"Nothing," Jon decided on leaving it there, without telling his younger brother to turn around and help guard for approaching soldiers. The popping of the mortar squad shooting shells toward the enemy in the south and west fields was becoming less and less frequent. The few blasts from enemy mortar shells hitting within the confines of the farm caused him to grit his teeth with each loud explosion. It would take only one well-placed projectile to kill members of his family. He leveled his .50 Caliber rifle on the back hitch of the John Deer Tractor while scanning the flat pasture.

"You need to either get behind the tractor or get on your stomach," scoffed Christian to Shira, who continued to kneel on her knee.

"I'd just as soon not lay in the snow," she replied.

"Then go behind the tractor." He shook his head in the direction of Hank who remained staring toward the farmhouse.

She glared at him for a moment before leaning at the waist and scrambling to the tractor. She knelt next to Hank.

"I see movement," said Jon, "five-hundred and thirty meters out."

"How many?" Jerry asked, laying on his belly, aiming his AK-47 into the blackness. He had cleared the snow and was positioned on top of frozen prairie grass.

Jon pulled the night goggles off and tossed them to Jerry. He then searched the sector using the night scope on his rifle. He waited for Jerry to survey the pasture, before replying, "I'm seeing close to thirty."

"I'm only locating about ten." Jerry remained flat on his belly as he examined the enemy's position. "The pasture is flat as a pancake, so if they want to come this way, they will have to expose themselves."

Christian lifted onto his forearms to look over the prairie grass with his naked eyes. A bullet hit him squarely in the right temple of his head, causing his body to fly a meter to the side. The sound of the single shot lingered before reaching everybody's ears. Shira screamed out as Jon tried to locate where the shot originated.

"Jesus," Jerry yelled. He rolled twice before scrambling to the back of the tractor. He gazed at Christian's still body.

"Keep your heads down," Jon screamed, diligently probing the area through his scope.

"Can you see the shooter?" Jerry scrambled to the front of the tractor, hearing Shira's gasping as he moved around her.

"No," Jon continued to explore through his scope as he spoke into the radio. "Irving or Terrance?"

"Yeah, Jon." Irving was looking out the small window on the south side of the tower. His view was directly over Tommy and Deb who were situated outside the egress window on the east side of the farmhouse.

"We have a sniper. From the angle of his shot, he has to be almost directly north of our location."

"I'll check," Irving moved across the tower to the window at the north. "I'm seeing a force assembled north of your location and another group of six, forty meters east of them. I'm not finding a sniper."

"I have visual on the larger force but can only locate two targets east of them." The heads of two insurgents would pop up into the sight of his tactical night vision scope and then quickly disappear. As he brought his scope back to the west in the direction of the larger cluster, he caught the image of a rifle with an oversized scope, one larger than any he had seen in his military career, aimed directly at him. He rolled quickly to the right.

"I found the sniper." He took in two quick breaths. "He's about ten meters to the east of the larger force."

"I see him," stated Irving, "and I have a shot."

"Take him out," Jon yelled into the radio.

The sound from the .50 Caliber rang out from the tower.

Jon glanced at Shira, Hank and Jerry. He knew the rebels were too far away for the M-16 and AK to be effectual. He wanted them to be ready should the enemy advance, but also wanted them to remain hidden. He rolled over, leveled his rifle in the direction of the large group and zeroed in on one target. He pulled the trigger.

Hank jerked from the blast. He was wearing ear protection, but the intensity of the large rifle made him shudder. He remained frozen in place with fog from his breath shooting out from his mouth. The detonation from Jon discharging another round, with the shell casing ricocheting off the side of the tractor, prompted him to let go of his M-16, letting it fall in the snow. The dull sound of Irving shooting from the tower behind them coincided almost precisely with Jon's firing. Jerry was also returning fire with the pinging sound of bullets from the enemy force hitting the metal on the front of the tractor.

"Hank," Jon nodded in the direction of Shira, "get behind the tire."

"Jon," slobber was on the side of Hanks mouth. "There are too many, we can't win here."

"This isn't a damn football game we are trying to win. We just need for them to know that coming this way is not an option," Jon spoke into the side of his rifle as he continued to look through his scope. "Now move, get behind the tractor wheel."

Shira rested her head on the tire. Her rifle laid in the snow at her feet. Hank leaned his head into the hard, cold rubber of the tractor tire, next to her, and listened as shots rang out from Jerry and Jon. They remained shoulder to shoulder until the barrage of gunshots stopped. Never again would he diminish the bravery of his brothers and sister, or the ferocity of war.

Jerry stared through his goggles but saw only a darkened mist. He crawled to the back side of the tractor, still wearing the night goggles and moved past Shira and Hank. He remained shielded by the tractor.

"I don't see them anymore," he yelled to Jon. "Did they move out?"

"Irving, are they retreating?" Jon spoke into the radio while continuing to skim the horizon.

"They are running to the west," replied Irving. "Did you suffer casualties?"

"Christian is KIA," Jon glanced over the top of his rifle at Hank and Shira. "We are going to keep our heads down for a bit. I'll let you know when we come your way."

"Roger that, I'll have Bobby and Emilee keep eyes on the area should they try to circle back."

***

Maddy leaned into Nicole's lap holding a flashlight, with Scotty sitting cross-legged on the floor in front of her. All the other children were sleeping in the gun closet as a slight hum resonated from battery charged heaters.

Irene tucked a blanket around Ed's neck while he slept in the single recliner located in the basement. She plopped down on a metal chair and stared at her husband, wondering how he could have slept through the entire episode of blasts that shook the entire house. Although it had been hours since Sue and Becky were summoned upstairs, her heart continued to beat rapidly. She wished she could fall asleep like her husband.

"Irene," Maddy whispered, looking at her with wide open eyes. "Do you think the kitchen was blown up?"

"If it was, we will build it back." She felt her blood pressure lower from the welcoming sound of Maddy's voice.

"We can make some cupcakes with your special fudge frosting." Maddy moved from Nicole's lap to stand next to Irene. She took hold of her cold, rough hand.

"Aren't you tired?" Irene spoke softly.

"No."

"Me neither," said Scotty, rising to stand next to Maddy.

"I'm going to have to lay down pretty soon and try and get some sleep," Irene sighed. She squeezed Maddy's hand.

"You can lay down in my bed," Maddy tugged on her arm. "It's really comfortable."

"I might take you up on that," Irene answered.

Nicole rose from her chair as someone approached down the hall. Ted and Corporal Pint dressed in full combat attire entered the room.

Nicole rushed to Ted and threw her arms around his neck.

"Grandpa," Maddy ran into his leg and latched hold.

"Everything is ok now." Ted stared into Nicole's eyes while placing his hand on Maddy's head.

"Sir, 3rd Platoon is fifteen mikes out." Corporal Pint pulled the handless radio down to her chin and smiled at Maddy. "1st and 2nd Platoons are proceeding to Limon."

"When 3rd Platoon arrives have them come all the way down the driveway to the farm," stated Ted.

"Yes sir," Corporal Pint moved back to the hall.

"Why aren't you sleeping young lady?" Ted bent down to one knee as Maddy put her arms around his neck.

"We were too scared to sleep. A bomb hit the house." She leaned back and looked at him, "Weren't you scared Grandpa?"

"Not even a little bit." Ted tightened his eyes and took a breath through his nose, "Maybe a little scared something would happen to you and Grandma."

Maddy placed her arm around Scotty and pulled him to her side, "Scotty and I still want you to take us to California."

"We have to get things under control before we can get to California. In the meantime, you two need to get to bed." He glanced up at Nicole, "I wanted to check in and let you know the worst is over."

"General Lopez will be available for a briefing in about two hours at 0600," stated Corporal Pint.

"A lot has happened over night on the southern border and in the metro area." Ted rose and looked at Irene, "The FEMA camp in Limon was attacked."

"Were the camps in the city affected too?" Irene was so tired she could hardly stand.

"Yes."

"What does this mean for you?" Nicole licked her lips as she stared at her husband's rugged face.

"I'm going to request a full battalion to go after the local rebels."

Nicole swallowed hard. She pulled Maddy in close.

"Try to get some sleep, you are safe." He placed a hand on the side of Maddy's face and leaned in and kissed Nicole. "I'll know a whole lot more about what is happening after I talk with General Lopez."

Irene moved next to Nicole as Ted hurried up the stairs. "That man is cool as a cucumber," she said, "he's acting like he's taking a stroll in a park."

Nicole exhaled as she turned to look in the direction of the gun closet. The reality of the day in observing firsthand the devastating magnitude of war changed life at the farm. Hearing the force of the explosions and witnessing the savagery of weapons being fired allowed her to recognize, more than she ever realized in all the years of being married to a soldier, that her husband was a warrior. A fighter who the enemy feared, and it would never be the other way around.

***

Travis lay, covered with a white sheet, on the hospital bed, while Julia used all the medical supplies at her disposal, to tend to his life-threatening wounds. His wife Sue, standing next to Jacqueline, stood to the side. Under different circumstances, in a modern hospital, he would have already been in surgery.

When Dave rushed Sherry into the clinic, Jacqueline hurried to the basement to summon Al and Linda to assist Julia with tending to Sherry's wounds. Al scoffed and bantered about being a dentist and not a medical doctor, but nevertheless followed her up and immediately went to work on the young girl's mangled face. He meticulously removed bits of concrete from the side of her head as she lay on a hospital cot at the back of the small room.

"I think all the pieces have been removed." Al handed Linda the tweezers before leaning in to take a final look at the pellet wounds. He pulled back, "I'm going to let Julia stitch your cheek."

Linda lifted the gauze bandage hanging loosely on her cheek. "It's a pretty nasty cut. You are lucky none of the concrete hit directly on your eye."

"Mrs. Jones," Sherry sat up with her legs dangling and stated, "I'm pregnant."

"You're pregnant," Linda glanced at Al.

"This won't hurt the baby, will it?"

"No, it shouldn't affect the baby." Linda took a quick look at Julia to see if she was listening in on the conversation.

"Have you taken a pregnancy test?" Al asked.

"Yes, I came in here two nights ago and used one of the tests."

"Do you know who the father is?" Linda asked.

"Does it really matter?" she swallowed.

"It does," Al answered categorically, "he has responsibility for the child too."

Sherry squeezed her cracked lips and momentarily glared at Al. She pulled on the back of her hair and turned her head to look away.

Sherry was unaware of the death of Julia's husband but sensed there was something troubling the doctor as she came to her side, placed a thumb on her chin and pushed her face sideways.

"First, I'm going to spray some antiseptic numbing solution on the cut," Julia was breathing hard as she spoke.

Sherry closed her eyes as the spray hit the side of her face. She kept her eyes closed as Julia placed the sutures.

"There we go," said Julia. Bags under her eyes were drooping as she placed a large bandage over the cut. "I'll give you a packet with antibiotic ointment to place over the wound. Unfortunately, I am not a plastic surgeon, so there will be a scar."

"That's no problem. Thank you for fixing my face." Sherry hopped off the cot. Having a scar on her face was something she could care less about.

Julia stared into the living room while she watched Sherry move past the body of her husband on her way back outside. She remained frozen in place with tears dripping from her eyes.

***

Hank entered the front door of the farmhouse to the humming of a vacuum working to remove fragments of debris from the carpet. He briefly stopped to watch Jason framing the damaged area to the kitchen before continuing into the living room. He moved quickly to his wife's side.

The first thing that hit Jacqueline was that the cheeks on his pale face were sagging. Never had she seen his face so strained. She tossed her arms around his neck. He tensed, so she quickly relinquished the hug.

"Have you seen Bobby?" she tried to look him in the eyes.

"Yeah, he is outside speaking with Jon. He and Emilee will be in shortly," he sniffled and looked away.

"Are you alright?"

"No, I'm really not," he sighed. He ran his thumb and index finger over his eyes.

Jacqueline placed a hand on each of his shoulders and turned him towards her. She leaned back to better look him in the eyes. He shook his head.

"Was it that bad?"

"Yes, I saw Christian lose his life." He swallowed hard, "I learned that I can never be a soldier like my brothers and sister."

"Nobody ever expected you to be."

Hank twisted his head to look in the direction of the kitchen. Bobby and Emilee could be heard speaking with Jason and Dave.

"I know, but…" Hank turned back toward Jacqueline. "I never would have thought that I would completely freeze during a time when my friends and family were facing such a dangerous threat. Jacqueline, I was numb with fear."

"Hank, you are a football coach, not a trained soldier," stated Jacqueline.

Bobby and Emilee walked into the room.

"We just found out about Christian," Bobby held Emilee's left hand in his. He pulled her closer.

"I'm so sorry Emilee," said Hank. He recalled the loud crack of the bullet as it hit his former football player squarely in the head. Then, the vision of him lying in the blood covered snow. He shuffled his feet as he struggled to speak, "He was trying to make some amends and protect all of us."

"I will never know who he really was," Emilee cleared her throat. There was a noticeable wetness around her eyes. "If he had to die so young, I'm glad he came here to do it."

"We saw that Fred lost his life too," stated Bobby.

"Did you see where they took the bodies?" Jacqueline clenched her teeth, wondering if her question was insensitive to Emilee.

"They are in the warehouse," Emilee took hold of Bobby's right bicep.

"I'm sure the plan is to bury them on the hill in the northeast pasture." Bobby noticed Hank looking off in a daze. "Are you okay Dad?"

"I never dreamt we would witness anything like this," Hank wrenched his hands. "I was literally shaking out there today."

"Everyone was scared," Bobby's eyes narrowed as he replied adamantly to his father. "Dad, you told us we have the power to be in control of our own destiny."

Hank turned toward his son but looked at the floor rather than directly in his eyes. It didn't go unnoticed by Bobby.

"Dad, your positive speeches were always accurate." He pulled away from Emilee and placed a hand on his father's shoulder. "You always preached that it takes hard work and practice to become great at anything. We will all handle the threats better next time."

Bill entered through the front door into the living room and yelled from the foyer, "Aunt Deb and Dad want everyone to

meet on the south side of the garage. Make sure to dress warm."
He turned and exited out the door.

Rural Colorado

After being stymied in their attempt to defeat the Liscos at their farm, the foreign insurgents retreated to a ranch forty kilometers to the south. They were joined at the location by a small group of thirty dissenters from the FEMA compound in Limon, which was destroyed less than twenty hours earlier.

The thirty malcontents waited in the cold on the farm grounds, separated from the foreign insurgents, while the foreign leader spoke to his assemblage. The superior spoke directly to his troops before addressing the homegrown fighters. His message was that the taking of America was almost certain, and that those who helped at this time would be rewarded greatly after the victory.

Two men standing with the domestic group were especially interested when the foreign leader spoke about a new strategy in seizing the farms on the eastern plains of Colorado. Surprise and ambush tactics were going to be utilized, rather than all out force. When the foreign insurgent finished speaking a man with a baseball cap turned to his blond-haired friend.

"It's payback time," said the blond man, looking at his friend.

"I don't know who I am going to enjoy killing more, the old man Jon, or that gorgeous blonde Sherry," stated the man with a baseball cap. As the cold wind gusted, the skinny nose on his oblong face turned bright red. "She would have put a bullet in my head if the old man hadn't stepped in. Now we will see just how brave she is when my hands aren't tied behind my back."

"And Caroline Sanchez, I'm taking her with us when we finish."

A group of ten foreign insurgents, dressed in black with scarfs covering their faces approached the group of renegades. A small woman walked slightly ahead of the others as they all marched in unison.

"Ten of you are to come with us. Those without weapons will be supplied arms," the woman spoke loudly with perfect English.

"Are you going to the farm with the tower?" the man with the baseball cap stepped forward.

The woman stared at him with her big, brown eyes the only part visible from her covered face. She remained silent, surprised someone would ask a question.

"If you are, we want to go with you," said the blond man."

"If you go with us, you must follow orders and fight where you are commanded. The massive region we are directed with securing takes us just east of the Denver metro area all the way east to Hays. Kansas. It goes from Clayton, New Mexico on the south to Fort Morgan, Colorado on the north." The tone in her voice was empathetic, with a willingness to clarify, unlike the leader who spoke to the group before her. "We have more pressing issues to take care of first, but the answer to your question is yes, eventually we will strike the farm with the tower."

The woman was glad to have the eager young pawns in her fold. They could easily be manipulated to be used as decoys. She too had personal reasons to go back to the farm. Three of her close friends were killed during the assault on the stronghold.

Colorado Farm

The morning sky was bright blue with the sun sparkling off the snow. All the occupants of the farm, except for Julia, Sue and Travis gathered in front of the garage. Ted, flanked by four soldiers, stood silently next to Deb while they waited for everyone to assemble. The tents used for housing the platoon were all disassembled, and the combat vehicles lined the driveway.

"Are you leaving Ted?" Al yelled from the front of the group.

"Yes," he looked to the side at Nicole, Bill and Maddy. There was a seriousness about his face which only his wife had seen before. "I am meeting this evening with an FBI counter terrorism task force to work on plans to stop the insurgents."

"Are you gong to be close by if we are attacked again?" Sheriff Bob asked.

"I will communicate with you daily, but my task in fighting the insurgents will take me to different locations which will make it difficult to respond to immediate danger. You have to set security and prepare to protect this farm."

"We want to be as transparent about what is happening as we can," stated Deb. She was dressed in combat fatigues. Tommy remained behind her next to the soldiers. "The war at the border has escalated. Enemy troops have moved northward all the way to northern New Mexico and eastward into central Texas. Yesterday and last night there was a large offensive push coordinated by the embedded rebels."

"Major efforts to create chaos were made by the insurgents in all major cities across the country. None more apparent than that in the Denver metro area where the Cherry Creek reservoir was breached. We don't know the severity of the damage yet," said Ted, glancing at Samantha who was standing next to Jessica with her hand at her mouth, obviously concerned about the safety of her parents. He knew there was major flooding on the south side of the city, but no more than that.

"Colonel, is there a chance the enemy forces could advance here?" Ben Stewart yelled, looking directly at Deb.

"Yeah, Colonel, could we lose this war?" Al asked while turning to face the others.

Deb contemplated the question for a moment. Tommy stood at full attention ready to support any answer she gave to the civilians.

"I won't lie, the challenges are great. The enemy has advanced faster than I believed possible only a week ago, but I believe with all my heart that the United States Military will not be defeated," Deb answered before taking two steps forward. She looked at Jon and Hank. "Tommy and I have been ordered back to Fort Carson and are leaving at 1400 this afternoon. But before we leave, I want to make sure everyone understands that nothing has changed at this farm. Autonomy and freedom come through hard work and responsibility. It's up to each of you to make this a better place for everyone and fight to protect what you have."

Hank felt a sense of pride in listening to both Ted and Deb as they addressed the people with uncompromising confidence. They were true warriors, willing to put their lives on the line to protect America and their loved ones. He made a vow to himself to never make the mistake of quitting or giving up because of fear.

A low humming sound caused all to stop and listen. The sound soon turned into a roar of aircraft flying in the southern sky. Everyone turned to look at the massive force of planes filling the skyline with the sound of explosions causing flashes as enemy missiles intercepted the squadrons of aircraft flying in formation. The planes disappeared into the horizon, leaving the once magnificent blue sky now littered with contrails and smoke.

"War is happening on our soil; it is real, and it is right over the horizon." Ted's loud voice brought the focus of attention back to him. "Deb, Tommy and I will do everything in our power to stop the enemy from advancing. It is up to each of you to secure and make this farm a place to survive until we finish the task. This is not a war for land or freedom. It is a war for our very souls.

2051

Book 3

War on American Soil

Book 3 Prologue

White House Solarium

After spending a combative, late-night meeting with members of Congress, President Weller finally found a tranquil moment to devote to First Lady Elizabeth and White House Chief of Staff Thomas Alexander. He wore a pair of silk pajamas covered with a knee length robe as he sprawled back in his favorite recliner chair, sipping a small glass of vegetable juice.

"What would have happened during World War Two had the Japanese not attacked Pearl Harbor? How long would have the United States remained neutral before going to Europe's defense?" The President held the juice in his right hand while rubbing the white stubble on his chin with his left. "I understand that dwelling over events that happened more than a century ago is something I should not be contemplating at this time, but can we imagine what the world would be like had Hitler won?"

"Pauley, that is something nobody will ever know." The First Lady looked at the clock and rose from her chair. "It's almost midnight. You need to get some sleep."

"It's the damn ambiguity of those we consider our allies." The President lowered the legs of the recliner and sat with his feet flat on the floor. "I spoke with the Prime Minister of England this afternoon. He scoffed at the idea of sending us weaponry, and when I mentioned troops, there was mumbling and muttering for a full minute before he told me he couldn't commit any more British troops than those already here with NATO. Apparently, the people of England don't have the stomach for full out war."

"Eventually the war will come to Europe. More and more Russian troops are accumulating at their western border by the minute." The White House Chief of Staff was a thin man with white hair and bulging hazel eyes. He slumped slightly as he readjusted, trying to become comfortable in the soft cushion of his chair. "We really can't blame our NATO allies for keeping their troops close to home."

"I understand the threat they are facing, but if America falls, God help them." The President slammed his nearly empty glass on a side table. "Today was the first time I actually thought that we can lose this war."

"Remaining positive is a must. Our Navy and Air Force are more than holding their own." Chief of Staff Alexander stated with an encouraging tone. "Weapons production has increased twenty-fold from a month ago. And we are in the process of adding six new Army Divisions."

"I agree, we need to remain as optimistic as reasonably possible. America has always been able to answer the bell when challenged. We only had five Army Divisions before we entered World War Two, and by the end we had a hundred." The President unconsciously stared at the curtains covering the windows on which Elizabeth had spent so much time deciding the color. He turned to gaze incredulously at his Chief of Staff. "But this war is much different than any others in the past. Technology has changed that."

"Should the enemy launch Intercontinental Ballistic Missiles again, we have been able to more than double the laser systems that destroy them. We are working twenty-four hours a day creating more. Defense feels confident we will be able to thwart any future missile attacks. Also, we have pushed the enemy back in several locations at south central Texas." Chief of Staff Alexander was trying his best to give the President some promising news.

"Yeah Tom, but they embedded deeper to the east, along the southern border, like a tick digging into our skin. If they break through the front lines in eastern Texas, the NATO forces in Louisiana will incur many casualties. Once the wounded begin returning home, our allies resolve to send more of their young soldiers to our soil will completely diminish."

"Have you thought anymore about Congressman Morgan's proposal of arming our civilians." The Chief of Staff hopped out of the uncomfortable chair.

"There are so many insurrectionists in our midst that we wouldn't know who we would be giving the weapons to. I tried explaining to the congressperson that randomly supplying weapons to the public would ultimately end with many of them being used against us."

"What a mess." The Chief of Staff's voice quavered.

"I received a daunting memorandum this afternoon from a professor at Harvard, stating that every model he has ran, concerning the war, shows us losing. He wants me to immediately start negotiating a resolution with the Chinese and Russians. He all but told me that we should surrender." The President's eyes showed a flash of repulsion as he recoiled from the thought.

"It's easy for that fellow to make predictions from the comfort of the ivory halls of a university. You should under no circumstance begin negotiations with our enemy while they have us under their thumb." Elizabeth stared at the President with a look of tenacity that he had seen many times before in their forty-three years of marriage. She was a small woman, with penetrating brown eyes, but she had the resolve of a giant. "Promise me that you will remain steadfast and never convey a message to the enemy that might be considered a sign of weakness."

"Liz, I would rather die than lose this country." He held out his hand to his wife. "Now help me up so I can get at least a couple hours of sleep."

"One other thing Paul." Chief of Staff Alexander was to the door of the solarium when he turned back to the President. "We should address the people. There are millions of citizens we can reach by television in the north and northeastern parts of the country who have been minimally affected, so far, by this war. We can contact the remaining people online or by radio."

"I agree. Why don't you make the arrangements?" The President tried to steady himself as blood rushed from his head. "Let's discuss the details in the morning."

"Yes sir." The Chief of Staff left the room.

"The message you give must be one of strength and truth. Straight to the point, nothing wishy-washy." Elizabeth reached up and placed her hand on the side of his flushed face. "You have to trust the American people to fight for their freedoms, but they need to know the truth."

The truth, the President thought, what a nice change it would be to tell the truth to the people without even the remotest thoughts of politics. He knew that it was going to be a restless night. He now would be thinking about the message he needed to get to the citizenry. In a calming way, it gave him faith that, although everything seemed hopeless, there was a solution, and an avenue for ridding the enemy from American soil. The United States Military was the most competent in the world. He must trust them to find a road to victory.

PART ONE

Colorado Farm

The muffled sound of shovels hitting the concrete at the front porch echoed inside the farmhouse as Bill, holding a cup of coffee, stared out the kitchen window. His mother Nicole, Aunt Jacqueline and Irene Jacoby sat at the kitchen table. The bright snow sparkled as it contrasted against the deep blue sky, with the only clue of disturbance to the pristine scene being footprints heading to the barn, made by the early rising Jacobys. He wondered if his father would find his way back to the farm before Christmas, which loomed only a week away. He never had a chance to talk with Ted when he and Colonel Deb were hurriedly called back to Fort Carson after the terrible attack on the farm, which left Christian and Fred dead, and Travis severely injured.

The assault created a new awareness amongst everyone that life could change on a dime. It was ever apparent that they were going to be at the farm for a long time, and although the food pantry was still well stocked, if left unchecked, it would deplete very quickly.

"Being without food is one of my greatest fears." Nicole sat at the end of the kitchen table. "I can't imagine having to make decisions about who survives and who doesn't because of the lack of food."

"You're right Mom." Bill turned back to address the women at the table. Both his mother and Aunt Jacqueline's hair had turned a whiter shade of grey over the past two months. "We aren't using the greenhouse to its full capacity. We have enough meat to last for quite some time, but there are many items that are going to be used up in the immediate future."

"On a positive note, we found about ninety packages of frozen vegetables and fruit hidden under the meat in the freezer at the warehouse." Jacqueline ran her hand over the bangs of her matted hair. "Also, Hank and Jon are working with Ben and Sheriff Bob to see if there are other avenues available in Limon to help bring in more food."

"The pantry and refrigerators in the basement still have quite a bit of food, but the freezers with the vegetables are both more than half empty. With the supply from the Stewarts, coffee is the one item we still have plenty of." Nicole held up her cup of coffee.

"Christmas has always been a special time for our family," said Irene with a mollifying tone. "There are a lot of treats we can make with a minimal amount of ingredients. I know that worrying about treats for Christmas is the least of our worries, but the shortage of sugar and flour are good examples of how fast the food will disappear."

"Hank woke up at four this morning. He has become more focused than ever, working to make sure everyone is prepared if we are attacked again," stated Jacqueline.

"I'm surprised people haven't started congregating in the living room yet." Bill looked at his watch. "According to what Uncle Hank told me, he is supposed to begin the meeting in about fifteen minutes."

Jacqueline lowered her voice. "Travis doesn't seem to be getting any better, and Julia is struggling with grief from losing Fred."

"Julia seems to be at her wits end. I'm worried she is going to say the hell with everything, and just give up," said Bill with an expression of apprehension.

"We need to make sure we help her with taking care of Travis. She needs some time to rest," stated Nicole.

"Sheriff Bob mentioned that there is a hospital in the small town of Hugo, northeast of here." Bill stood up from his chair and moved to where he could glance across the living room to the closed door of the medical clinic to make sure Julia and Sue were not listening to their conversation. "He has no idea if it is still functional but threw it out as an option to help save Travis. I'm afraid if we don't take him there, he is not going to make it."

Terrance was the first to enter the living room, and soon the area was crowded with people. Jon insisted that twenty-four-hour surveillance be kept at the tower, and that the office in the garage was always staffed. Irving, Caroline, and Sherry stayed in the tower, while Bobby and Emilee remained at Ted's office. Samantha and Jessica were the only others not present.

"Any idea where Samantha might be?" Bill whispered to Linda, who was standing next to him at the back of the room.

"She and Jessica are in the greenhouse." Linda raised her eyebrows.

Hank and Jon moved to their typical spot next to the fireplace hearth. They were about ready to begin the meeting when the front door swung open, bringing a rush of wind into the house. Caroline stepped inside and went straight to Jon.

"There are a whole bunch of people on the road about a kilometer west of us," she yelled frantically.

Hank felt his heart leap to his throat. He looked at Jon.

"Can you tell if they are friendly?" Jon barked to Caroline, as he darted past her to the front door.

"Not sure. Irving just told me to hurry and let you know," she continued speaking as she shadowed him out the door into the cold. They stopped at the gate to the yard and looked down the driveway in the direction of the county road. Two antique pickup trucks pulled into the entrance to the farm. They moseyed down the snow-covered driveway with a large crowd of people strung out behind them.

Jon waited in the yard, gauging the approaching throng before stepping through the ankle-deep snow in the direction of the tower. He yelled up to Irving, "are they armed?"

"I don't see any weapons," Irving shouted down, taking his eye away from the scope of his rifle, and leaning out the window at the top level of the tower. "There are several women and children."

A 1949 Ford F-1, followed closely by a 1955 Chevy 3100 short bed pick-up truck, came to stop next to the Jacoby's RV. The beds of both vehicles were filled to the brim with suitcases and various items. A huge man, with great difficulty, lumbered his long body out the door of the Ford and moaned as he stretched, trying to stand upright.

"Is this the Lisco farm?" He asked gruffly with a distinct British accent.

"It is. I'm Lieutenant Colonel Jon Lisco." Jon answered brusquely. He looked past the massive man in the direction of the throng of people. They were strung out all the way to the county road, slowly trudging down the icy driveway. He returned his gaze to the new arrival. "I take it you are arriving from the Denver area?"

"Yes sir, most of us are residents of the city, with some from the FEMA camps. It's been a long trip, and everyone is knackered." The man placed both hands on his lower back, he pushed, causing his hefty stomach to budge forward. He took in a deep breath through his enormous nostrils and pointed to the passenger seat of the antique Ford pick-up. "I'm Patrick Montgomery and the lady continuing to sit is my wife, Odette."

Ed Jacoby walked over to stand next to the pickup. He knew an old truck in such prime shape was worth an extraordinary amount of money. He used his index finger to wipe some mud off the hood. He was about to ask Patrick about the antique vehicles when he heard someone yell, "grandpa."

Seth and the rest of the Jacoby kids separated from the approaching group and ran forward to surround Ed. Irene could hardly control her breathing as she hurried from the yard. She turned to look for Breanna, Adam, Megan, Aaron and Ashley. When she didn't see them, she folded her arms with tears welling in her eyes. Several of the grandkids rushed to her side. The smallest great-granddaughter latched onto her leg.

"We made it," said Seth energetically. "It's a terrible mess in Denver."

"People are actually starving to death." Arthur still had a gold ring in his nose, and his stringy hair was as greasy as ever. He looked carefully at the crowd of people. "Where are Mom and Dad?"

"They are working the cattle." Ed had a big smile on his weathered face as he took his tattooed grandson into a headlock. "I didn't figure I would ever see you again."

"Ah, you are too ornery to ever go anywhere." Arthur pulled out of the headlock and placed his hand on his grandfather's shoulder.

Bill scrutinized the multitude of haggard strangers bundled in coats, some with blankets wrapped over their shoulders, as they gathered at the farm grounds. He made a quick estimation that the throng of people numbered around seventy-five.

"They look starved," Nicole approached Bill, with an expression of concern.

"I guess the first thing to do is feed them and find a warm place for everyone to sleep." Bill scratched his head. "Then we can deal with everything else."

Nicole didn't offer any sort of counsel as she watched the fog from her son's breath disappear into the cold air. Although it generated many problems, gaining more people at the farm created a sense of security of knowing there was safety in numbers.

"I am going to check on Maddy." She rubbed Bill's arm before walking back into the house.

South Santa Fe, New Mexico

The visual, from the helicopter, of Assault Vehicles smoldering on the side of Interstate 25 north of Santa Fe, New Mexico prepared Colonel Deb Lisco and Command Sergeant Major Talfoya for the devastation of the capital city of New Mexico. As they hurried across the skyline of the urban area, they could see pockets of damaged adobe buildings with no sight of human life on the streets. A battle raged only two days earlier where American forces pushed the enemy back to nearly thirty kilometers south of Albuquerque.

The helicopter descended rapidly to a vacant field immediately south of Santa Fe, where tents covered the countryside. They had arrived at 4th Division Infantry's newly established headquarters. The thunderous sound of helicopters landing and quickly taking off, rang loudly. Colonel Lisco and Command Sergeant Major Talfoya hurried to a waiting jeep as soon as they exited the chopper. The soldier driving the all-terrain vehicle concentrated on the new dirt road winding through the prairie land as he whisked them to the command center, where they were shuffled inside a large air supported tent. General Lauer was busy marking positions on a table size map. Deb and Tommy waited to be noticed. Two other Colonels were at his side, examining the drawings, with their aides remaining behind the commanders.

"Come around." The General motioned to Deb. He had not seen her since he chastised her in his office, and sent her to the family farm, a little over a week prior. He gazed at her bronzed face and stout chin as though he had never seen her before. She moved to his side and immediately engaged her full attention into studying the map.

Tommy remained at the back side of the map near the entrance of the tent. General Lauer was flanked on each side by Colonel Blake, who replaced deceased Colonel Taylor in command of 1st Stryker Brigade Combat team, and Colonel McDonald the commander of 4th Infantry field artillery Brigade.

Deb nodded to the two Colonels. She stared particularly long at Colonel Blake's deeply tanned face, while reconsidering the loss of her friend Colonel Taylor. An expression of attentiveness flashed across her face, and her thick, dark eyebrows folded over her eyes when she returned her attention to the map in front of General Lauer.

"Colonel Lisco, I assume you have had a chance to review the field order I sent you? The reason for the vagueness of the directive is that this mission is vitally important. So much so, that I could not risk a breach in communications." The General pointed to an area just east of Albuquerque on the map sprawled across the table. "This is the Sandia Mountain Wilderness area. The enemy has three midrange hypersonic missile launch vehicles embedded within the confines of this area."

The General hesitated for a moment.

"You want us to find and destroy these launchers?" Colonel Deb stared intently at the map.

"No, that is not your primary mission. American interceptors and jammers are in place at ten different locations from west Texas all the way to the Oklahoma panhandle. We have the capability to seek and destroy the enemies' missiles immediately after they are fired. The problem is that the enemy have ground based jammers and laser interceptors in this strategic location, with the likes of which are unknown to our research agencies. Our missiles or aircraft cannot penetrate the laser interceptors to destroy the embedded launchers. We already have lost an F-35 attempting to pierce this highly mobile system."

"The mission is to find and destroy the interceptors." Colonel Deb looked fervently at General Lauer.

"Yes, before the enemy destroys ours."

"Do we know the number of their forces in the wilderness area?"

"Estimated to be 20,000."

"Are they PLA?"

"No, they are not Chinese Army." General Lauer sniffled. "According to Intelligence they are almost entirely North Korean Special-Operations."

Deb raised an eyebrow and glanced in the direction of Tommy. They had spent time at Camp Red Cloud in South Korea and were very aware of the difficulties associated with fighting the methodical and highly trained North Korean troops. The Korean special ops were organized in standard formations of brigades, battalions and companies, creating a very disciplined army that utilized unconventional warfare, with an emphasis of attacking from the flanks.

"Sir, do you know who is commanding their forces?" She asked knowingly.

"We believe it to be General Kim Il Song," stated General Lauer, noticing Colonel Lisco stare again in the direction of Command Sergeant Major Talfoya. "Have you dealt with him before?"

"Yes sir. He is someone whose military mind should be respected."

"Colonel Blake, 1st Stryker will approach from the northeast side of the wilderness area and maneuver to the south from this point." General Lauer indicated a junction at state highway 41 and state highway 285.

"What are the boundaries of their jamming capabilities?" Colonel Blake asked.

"Drones are useless within a ten-kilometer radius from the middle of the enemy area, and their interceptors are proficient up to a fifty-kilometer radius."

"How far out are we going to encounter hostile troops?" Colonel Blake asked.

"Without having to worry about air strikes their troops have bulged out to the east nearly to the small town of Moriarty. You will find resistance from highway 41 all the way south to Interstate 40."

"Without air support?" Colonel Blake's words were more of a statement than a question.

"For the most part. Our extended range cannons should be effective." General Lauer turned to Colonel McDonald. "4th Infantry Division Artillery will supply surveillance. We know that the enemy has armaments we have never encountered. All brigade movement will have to coordinate with artillery. I want to emphasize that under no circumstances should troops move forward without short range artillery support, and protection from the Arrow mobile laser interceptors. Do I make myself clear on this?"

"Yes sir," all answered.

"Colonel Lisco, 2nd Brigade will work from Interstate 25 and highway 14. You will move south into the wilderness area from this location." He pointed to the map. "It is rugged terrain."

"How in the world did they move that many troops and equipment so quickly to establish a stronghold this far north?" Deb stuck her prominent chin straight out. Albuquerque was only about six hours away from her farm.

"They stored and embedded much of the machinery years ago. This has been part of their overall plan all along," stated General Lauer. "Make no mistake, the enemy soldiers have the capability to move lightning fast. They are willing to forfeit their resources and troops to win any battle because this area is crucial for their plans to systematically move the war eastwardly. They will gladly sacrifice three soldiers for every one of ours, and they have the numbers to win by doing so."

"Is there anything else we need to know?" Deb asked. The General stared at her with sagging eyes, squinting to the point they were only slits. She sensed there was something very much troubling him.

"There is a tramway on the Albuquerque side of the mountain. The enemy controls the mountainous area at the top. We have Army Special Forces working their way to secure the top of the tramway." His shoulders slumped while he pointed to the location on the map. "The area to the south and southwest is somewhat of a dead zone with our Nonhuman Battalions having a semblance of control, but the PLA continue to find ways to supply the Korean Special Operation forces at Sandia."

"Should we try and stop the flow of supplies?" Deb asked.

"Colonel, time is of essence, you will need all your troops available at the wilderness area. Your mission is to destroy the new generation jammers and interceptors in the area as quickly as possible. Once you do that, our air power will end this threat in short order."

Colonel Deb folded her arms, and looked at the two Colonels, and then at the General. She was being allowed plenty of leeway in formatting her attack, somewhat of a two-edged sword in that there were few specifics about the threat, but at the same time she had full authority to use her own judgement in the life and death decisions that would face her soldiers. She moved around the table to stand next to Tommy. She was excited to get to 2nd Brigades headquarters to begin briefing her commanders.

Her heart pounded hard against her chest. In a short time, they would be heading into combat.

General Lauer let out a deep breath as he watched the three commanders leave the briefing room. He understood better now what General Prost was talking about when she told him that Colonel Lisco was a one-of-a-kind soldier. The second she stepped into the briefing, a sense of strength and confidence filled the room. She was about to rattle a hornet's nest, but he knew she was the best leader he could send to successfully accomplish the vitally important mission.

Colorado Farm

Bill watched from a seat on the front porch of the farmhouse, with Maddy sitting on his lap, as his two uncles, Hank and Jon, took complete control in acclimating the new arrivals to the farm. Jon was back to his Lieutenant Colonel mode of being a leader, enlisting the help of Nicole, Gina, Linda, and Jacqueline to categorize each new individual into groups according to occupation, military experience, medical skills, and other special talents, that would help keep the farm operating.

Jon emphasized repeatedly the importance of checking the identities of the new arrivals, along with having them declare any weapons. The problem he found was that many of the people left their homes without proper identification, or so they claimed.

Terrance used the tractor to clear the melting snow from the driveway before Bobby and his friends placed a long table with four chairs next to the Jacoby's RV. It was no longer bitterly cold with the temperature rising rapidly.

"Dad, I have something I want you to do." Maddy reached up and grabbed Bill's chin with her right hand. She twisted his face so she could look him directly in the eyes. She squeezed the edges of his mouth tightly before lowering her hand down to his jaw.

"What do you want me to do?" Bill felt her breath hit his face as she tugged his prominent chin to where they were nose to nose.

"I want you to marry Samantha." She let go and placed her hand in front of him with her index finger pointing in the air. "Then I want you and her to adopt me and Scotty."

Bill leaned back. He hesitated with a smile forming on his lips, before replying, "you are already my daughter. I don't need to adopt you."

"Me and Scotty need a mom." Her dark eyes dropped, and she placed her lower lip over her upper.

"You both have moms. And if I married Samantha, she would be your stepmother."

"She wouldn't be Scotty's stepmom."

"That's right, she wouldn't."

"Well then you have to adopt him." She reached up and placed her finger on his chin and tapped. "It's too dangerous out here not to have a mom."

Bill chuckled before pulling her face into his chest. He wrapped the folds of his coat around her, and held tight, with his heart noticeably beating on the side of her face. He looked down at the haphazard braid in the back of her blonde hair as she cuddled with him. He wondered about the fate of Maddy's mom Cindy, in California. Their separation and eventual divorce were amicable, with both mutually realizing that they were distinctly different. She was a California surfer girl with an easy-going disposition, and he was a future oriented person with a business temperament, who would never leave Colorado. He was worried about his ex-wife's wellbeing but avoided burdening his daughter with his concern for her mother.

"You should ask Samantha to marry you, right now." Maddy kept her face buried in his chest as she persisted with her request.

"I don't think Samantha wants to marry me."

She sat up in his lap. "Do you want me to ask her for you?"

"Good God, no."

The front door to the house opened, allowing the smell of stew and baked bread to escape from the kitchen. Irene stepped onto the porch with her great-granddaughter holding onto her arm.

"Maddy, do you want to help Bella and me take some homemade bread and jam to the new people?" Irene asked.

Although the girl was smaller than her, Maddy surmised they must be close to the same age. They stared at each other before the little girl relinquished her hold on Irene's arm and took a half step in her direction. She had a pudge nose with freckled, sunburnt cheeks. Her dark hair was short and unevenly cut.

"Jerry is slicing the bread now." Irene held out her right hand. Maddy crawled off Bill's lap and latched hold of the soft, blue veined hand, while keeping both eyes on Bella.

"I'll help carry the bread. I'm going to go to the garage office and see if Bobby and Emilee have had any communication with Dad." Bill rose from the chair and placed his hand on top of Maddy's head. "Boy does that bread smell good."

"We still have flour, but it is going fast." Irene gave Bill a concerned look. "I thought I should mention it."

"Uncle Hank is going to have a meeting with everyone this afternoon. Food is one of the issues we plan to address." Bill smiled at the two little girls. "I'm sure we will figure it all out."

****

The inside of the garage office was wall to wall with people. After finding out that Bobby had not been able to contact Ted, Bill decided to take two pieces of bread to the greenhouse where Samantha and Jessica were working. Both women were sitting in chairs talking when he entered the hot and humid building.

"I thought you might like some fresh bread." Bill set the bread on the table. For the past two days Samantha became distant, avoiding him, while spending much more time with Jessica.

"We were just comparing notes," stated Jessica, crinkling her nose and scrutinizing him with her dazzling blue eyes. Her bright red hair was uncombed and frazzled, giving her the appearance of a wild tiger ready to spring on its prey.

From the feral looks he was receiving, he realized that the notes they were comparing were not complimentary toward him, and he most likely was going to have some explaining to do. Subconsciously he was glad to have everything put on the line. He especially missed talking with Samantha, but the amorous memories of Jessica were also fresh on his mind.

"The similarities of our experiences here at your farm are quite remarkable," Samantha gazed at him. "Was it always your intention to bed all the available women who came here?"

"Come on Samantha, that is really unfair." She wasn't wearing any lipstick on her dry, cracked lips, and her blonde hair was brushed straight down, eliminating the normal wave. Bill wondered if she might have run out of make-up, because rough and red blotched areas of skin were visible on her face.

"It took you a total of two days, for each of us, before you lured us into your bedroom." Samantha dipped her chin, "That is only forty-eight hours."

"What do you want me to say?" Bill thought about stating that having them in his bed revealed as much about them as it did about him. He decided to wiggle his way out of the situation without causing strife.

"How about saying, I made a mistake and I'm sorry?"

"I'm not sorry." He swallowed, noticing both women's eyes narrow.

"Are we the only ones who have been blessed in your chambers?" Jessica's question was malicious in tone. "How about Sherry, are you the father of her baby?"

"Okay, you are being spiteful now."

He took two steps in the direction of the door before it swung open. Bobby stuck his head inside the greenhouse and yelled, "Another group of people just turned off the county road and are coming down the driveway."

Bill hurried outside, following his cousin, with Samantha tagging close behind. The temperature had risen dramatically, creating slushy conditions around the farm grounds.

Hank and Jacqueline hurried out to meet the group after realizing the Saxton's and several members of the Lions football team were part of the assemblage. George Saxton looked to be fifty pounds lighter than when he previously left the farm, and Toby's face was thin as a rail. Many of the parents of the football players appeared to be in a great amount of discomfort. Bobby began giving aid to his former teammates families as some of them sat down onto the wet driveway, unable to walk any further.

The group parted slightly and directly in the center of the misery was a woman with a large smile on her bronzed face. She looked like a princess amidst paupers. Bill stared at her until they finally made eye contact.

"Oh my God. You have this down to a science, don't you?" Samantha watched him while he stared at the beautiful new arrival, with the goddess unmistakably returning his gaze. "Something tells me this one isn't even going to take a day."

"Come on, quit Samantha." He turned and took a step closer to her. "You know my feelings toward you are real."

She didn't reply but he could see moisture surfacing in her eyes. He sensed she wanted him to comfort her, for him to let her know he understood her turmoil, and that he would stand by her even if she feigned disappointment in him. He noticed out of the corner of his eye Maddy holding Irene's hand walking slowly toward them.

"Did you get some bread?" Irene directed her question to Samantha.

"Yes, thank you, it was delicious." Samantha smiled, not wanting to disclose that she hadn't tasted the bread. She changed her focus to Maddy. "Did you help make it?"

"No, I just carried it."

"You can help when we bake tomorrow," said Irene.

"Dad, did you ask her?" Maddy looked up at her father with wide open eyes.

"This is not a good time Maddy." He faked a smile before putting his arm around her neck. He pulled her in tight to his chest.

"Ask me what Maddy?" Samantha leaned down.

Bill realized there was nothing he could do to stop his daughter from speaking. He relaxed as Maddy withdrew from his grasp and took hold of Samantha's hand.

"We were thinking that you should marry Dad." Maddy didn't stipulate that we in her statement was her and Scotty, not Bill and her. "Then you two can adopt Scotty."

Samantha rolled back on her feet. She closed her eyes tightly, twisted her head back and forth, and chuckled. She leaned back down to eye level with Maddy, and replied, "This is something we will have to talk about when things are a little more normal."

"Ok, that was something I needed to get off of my chest." Maddy let her arms slump to her side.

"Let's go to the house and see what Jerry has planned to feed all these people." Irene smiled at Bill.

"Things are not going to go back to normal. Not for a long time, if ever." Bill watched Maddy and Irene stroll away. "Samantha, what is normal with us?"

Samantha didn't answer. She turned and walked in the direction of the green house.

Bill could see Julia standing alone on the front porch of the farmhouse, as Irene and Maddy made their way past her. His mind wandered to how awful the situation was for the physician assistant after losing Fred. Life is short and fragile with no guarantees of more tomorrows. With all the destruction that had taken place over the past few days, he realized his approach to everyone needed to be one of understanding and gentleness.

Fort Carson Army Base

When General Lopez informed Ted that he was going to work in lockstep with the Federal Bureau of Investigation to create a strategy to defeat the foreign insurgents, he wasn't overly enthused. On one hand, the FBI could offer many resources in finding the insurgents, but on the other, they were very controlling.

It took him nearly twenty minutes to proceed through the three tiers of security protecting the location of the clandestine meeting at the center of Fort Carson Army Base. The gathering was already forty-five minutes behind schedule by the time everyone settled into the conference room.

A man standing near the front of the large room, waved for Ted to come forward the moment he entered the door. He surmised it was the FBI Special Agent he held a long conversation with the night before. The tiny body and ferret like features on the face of the G-man created a much different image from what he perceived when he spoke with him over the phone.

Special Agent Elder moved forward to meet the Colonel in front of a wooden podium so he could make quick introductions with others from the task force. He pointed out associates from the Drug Enforcement Administration, from Immigration and Customs Enforcement and two from Alcohol, Tobacco, Firearms and Explosives Division.

Ted made no effort to try and remember the names of the people from each agency. He did make note of two men sitting to the side of the room, who were left out of the initial introduction. Both men, sporting unkempt beards, wore tee-shirts and khaki pants.

"Let's proceed to get this meeting underway," Agent Elder spoke as he stepped in the direction of the podium. He moved to the back of the stage and hesitated for a moment. He could barely see over the top of the lectern, so he moved to the side and stated, "Colonel Lisco informs me that he will have two companies from the 99th Infantry at the disposal of this task force. Am I correct Colonel?"

"Yes sir, we have Companies D and E from 3rd Battalion." Ted looked to the others, still standing. He wasn't sure if he should go to the front to address them or join the others sitting in metal chairs lined in front of the stage. The meeting was beginning in a chaotic manner.

"How many soldiers?" A lady from Immigration and Customs Enforcement asked.

"Three hundred twenty total," Ted answered.

"That's not very many when we consider the entire front range of Colorado," stated the lady.

"In terms of personnel available for this sector we have around eighty people," a member from Alcohol, Tobacco, Firearms and Explosives Division chimed in. "So, 320 sounds like quite a few."

"Isn't that fewer than you had two weeks ago?" Agent Elder looked sideways at the man.

"Yes, the threat on the east coast has worsened, and staff has been shuffled away from us."

"How about Customs and Drug Enforcement. Has your work force been minimized?"

"We still have a large staff, but most of our employees are software engineers and general office workers," stated a woman from Immigration and Customs.

"Colonel, it looks like you are going to be the muscle of this outfit." The special agent glanced at Ted with an encouraging look on his face.

Ted appreciated the cordiality of the agent. He had already decided after their initial conversation, the night before, he would wait and see what the government people brought to the table in terms of activeness and procedure before committing his soldiers to anything specific. So, he simply nodded at the FBI man.

"The four parts that are vital to the success of this task force are, one, to define and pursue the objectives crucial to the success of stopping the insurgents responsible for the unrest in Colorado, especially along the front range. Second, to prioritize all resources available. Third, to track our progress. Forth, to deliver constant results." Agent Elder stood at the forefront with his hand showing four fingers.

Ted held his mouth wide open as he watched and listened. The man looking back at him from the side of the podium seemed like someone waiting for a bus on a quiet street. He was flabbergasted that with the turmoil and disorder threatening to destroy the country the agent was giving a standard bureaucratic summary of FBI modus operandi.

"The three agencies here can supply Colonel Lisco and his team with all pertinent data, everything from information concerning blown transformers and water treatment plants, to known locations of individuals and groups relevant to the gangs creating social disorder."

"Do we have a liaison we can coordinate with?" A voice asked from the back of the room.

"A central command center for communication has been established here on base. We will need someone from each agency at the site twenty-four, seven," answered Agent Elder. "Colonel Lisco will have complete directive over the center."

"Lieutenant Siegman will be in command of the site," stated Ted. "She will be the liaison."

"We should address the one concern that has come up during the many conversations I have had with several of you, the elephant in the room shall we say, about the rules of engagement in dealing with the insurgency. All the homegrown rebels and nearly seventy percent of what we are referring to as the foreign insurgents are American citizens."

"Are we not required by law to arrest American citizens if they are breaking the law? They then should have the right to a trial," a member of Immigration and Custom Enforcement stated dramatically.

"I agree. Congress can change legislation, or the President can create an executive order stating otherwise," added a member from Drug Enforcement.

"America has fought many urban wars and always used the same rules of engagement. If someone points a weapon at one of Colonel Lisco's soldiers, then that soldier should respond in kind, without worrying if the perpetrator is a citizen or not," indicated a member from the Alcohol, Tobacco, Firearms and Explosives Division.

"What about if they are setting explosives at an electrical tower or water treatment site? Or how about shooting off the

EMP weapon that has been raging hell on us since this war began? Should they be fair game to be fired upon without due process?" yelled a voice.

"Those waging war on us are no longer citizens."

"Who are you to decide who is an American citizen?" A shrill voice responded.

Ted leaned back, wishing that his sister Colonel Deb was present to hear the exchange between the government officials. They would be getting an earful from her. He decided he would let them hash everything out between themselves. As far as he was concerned the rules of engagement would be determined at another time, with General Lopez. No matter what anyone thought, he would never jeopardize his soldier's safety.

"Colonel Lisco, let me explain what is happening here. Having spoken with the other members of the task force during the past two days, the discussion about what will happen with the homegrown rebels, when the war is over, has become a very heated topic. Several people here are concerned we will never be able to assimilate them back into society if we treat them as if they are not American citizens. What are your thoughts?"

"I understand the concern, and this is an issue that at some time will need to be resolved. It might be an undertaking of this task force to establish ideas on how to turn the tables on the foreign insurgents by bringing over the homegrown rebels to our side." Ted's thoughts went to Shira and Christian. "For the immediate future, those under my command will always follow the Law of Armed Conflict."

"Colonel, what do you consider the laws of war?" One of the unintroduced men from the side of the room scathingly asked.

"Military necessity, distinction, proportionality, humanity and chivalry," Ted turned toward the men and ended his answer in a matter-of-fact manner, without elaborating further. He continued to look in their direction, with his jaw held high, while they both sat with their legs crossed. Their shoes looked like bedroom slippers that might be worn by a retired person while lounging around the house on a Saturday morning. The older grey-haired man who asked the question was not wearing any socks. Although he knew they would never admit it, he figured them to be with CIA Special Activities Division, a paramilitary operations unit, who, under most circumstances, would be working alongside Delta or Special Forces performing a covert or clandestine operation in a foreign country, not part of an FBI task force on American soil.

"The best way for the Agencies from this task force to help my Soldier's," Ted hesitated for a moment and turned back to look at Special Agent Elder, "is to re-establish the local police forces and hospitals in the metro area. Create citizen units throughout the city to fight the insurgents."

"I agree with you Colonel. Having local control by the police should be of the highest priority. There is a mass exodus of people out of the Denver area taking place right now," stated Agent Elder.

"There are still estimated to be more than a million, five hundred thousand citizens left in the Denver metro area," replied a member of Immigration and Customs. "With many of the cities to the east having problems of their own, it will be best if we can stop the migration."

Ted took a seat while the other members talked over the specifics of each of their responsibilities to help fight the insurgency. With the war rapidly progressing to the south and east he realized there was a real possibility of the enemy advancing all the way to Denver. The two operatives from the side of the room approached. They sat down in the chairs on each side of him.

"Colonel, can we talk with you in private?" The grey-haired man asked softly, almost whispering.

"We can speak at my office." He slowly rose from his chair. Agent Elder acknowledged Colonel Lisco with his eyes, and nodded before Ted exited from the room, followed closely behind by the two men.

****

Ted took a seat at his chair behind his desk.

"Have a seat," Ted pointed to the chairs on the opposite side of the desk. "Can I offer you something to drink?"

"No, Colonel. We'd like to get to the point," stated the grey-haired man.

"Okay, how can we help each other?" Ted thought about asking them their names, but figured that most likely this meeting would be the last time they would ever meet face-to-face.

"Colonel, we have information that will better help you understand who you are pursuing."

"Do you have names and locations of the leaders of the foreign insurgents?"

"Mike Chen, Troy Vasilyeva and his sister Anastasia Vasilyeva."

"Do you know where they are?"

"Fourteen months ago, the three of them traveled to Wuhan, China before journeying to Moscow. Five months ago, they returned to the United States. After returning, they disappeared, but we have confirmed information that the Vasilyeva's are in Colorado."

"How much control do they have over the insurgency?" Ted was completely intrigued with the information, but somewhat confused. "If we find them, do we stop the threats?"

"Over the past five years they coordinated everything from supplying the EMP weapons to identifying and synchronizing the destruction of cell towers, electrical power stations and water treatment plants," stated the younger man. "They are in control at the top of the chain of command of the foreign insurgents."

"Who are they?"

"In 2014 the Chinese initiated a covert operation named "Fox Hunt", where Chinese Nationals who disagreed with their government were hunted down. Many of those considered dissidents were American citizens. One citizen, Xi Chen, his wife and small child named Mike, were given protection by the American government. Chen was an operative of the Chinese Intelligence Agency. While protected in the United States Chen became associated with Oscar Vasilyeva, another American citizen who had two young children named Anastasia and Troy. Of course, their connection was not by happenstance."

"At this time Russia and China began working more closely with one another, and were becoming strong strategic partners," interrupted the younger man. "Also, the Chinese Intelligence philosophy was that of a thousand grains of sand concept, in which they used amateurs, civilians and academics for clandestine operations, rather than professional spies."

"The plan to defeat us started many years ago, but within the past five years Mike Chen, Troy and Anastasia Vasilyeva took over the leadership of the foreign insurgency in recruiting disenfranchised Americans, mostly younger people. They took an already well-organized plan, that began years earlier, to the next level. Having been raised in America they were able to understand the fears and problems facing the homegrown youth."

Ted remembered some of the information that Shira gave him during the brief time he spent with her and Christian at the farm. "Have you any information about an attack on NORAD?" he asked.

Both men stared at one another for a moment before the grey-haired man replied, "There is a threat that has been echoed by some of the insurgents we captured. We believe some type of weapon has been developed, which according to our sources is a credible danger to NORAD. But to be honest with you Colonel, it all doesn't add up. We think it might be a deception to hide something even bigger. It is another reason we need to quickly find the three dissidents."

"I do have someone we should speak with." Ted took in a heavy breath. "I believe she was recently in contact with Anastasia."

"When can we speak with her?"

Taking a helicopter to the farm to pick up Shira would be a perfect opportunity for Ted to check on the family. He didn't know enough about the background of the young woman who arrived at the farm with Christian, so he decided he wouldn't take a chance of her fleeing, by giving her prior notice. "I'll have her here this evening."

Colorado Farm

Although it was only three in the afternoon the bright sun lying low in the southern sky was almost blinding to the crowd gathered at the center of the courtyard. The once pristine snow was now scattered puddles of water. People were visible from the front yard all the way to the garage. Hank and Jon were standing next to the front gate preparing to address the group, which had tripled the population of the farm. The two brothers didn't need to start the proceedings, because Al began speaking first.

"What happens if more people show up? We can't sustain everyone at this farm. Food is going to quickly become a problem." Al swept his arms at the crowd behind him. He could hear coughing and moaning.

"We can only do the best we can. Many of these people need medical attention," Hank yelled to his dentist friend, noticing several of the new arrivals wearing makeshift cloth masks.

"Only a couple of people had the sickness when we left the city, but now all of us have it," a middle-aged lady with red rings around her eyes stated, before lowering her head and coughing into her arm through a tee-shirt she was using as a mask.

"We understand that you have several automobiles that are operational. We need to take them and leave as quickly as possible," a husky man yelled, while sliding forward past several people, in the direction of Hank and Jon. "We know that there are parts of the country where life is going on normally."

"We should load up and leave before it is too late," said a thin woman standing next to the man.

"Yeah, we agree," several voices echoed across the farm grounds, affirming the idea of taking the vehicles.

A low roar could be heard coming from the east. A squadron of airplanes soared in a westerly direction, passing through the southern sky past the farm. With the steadily increasing rumble from the jets becoming too loud to speak over, everyone turned to look at the aircraft which were soon hidden by the glare of the sun, giving Jon a chance to gather his thoughts. He waited until the noise ebbed before turning back to address the crowd. Bill moved to stand next to his uncles. His movement to take a position next to Jon and Hank didn't go unnoticed by the rest of the original members of the farm. They came forward, with many of them moving inside the fenced yard.

"Let me make one thing perfectly clear to everyone. You people are guests here. If you want to work with us, then we will be very accommodating, but if not, there is the road," Jon's voice bellowed. He held his arm out, pointing down the driveway to the county road.

Patrick Montgomery, towering over the rest of the people, lumbered his way forward through the group outside the fence. He stood between Hank and Jon, with his gigantic body dwarfing the two men.

"Over the past couple hours, since we arrived, I have had a chance to inspect the premises of this farm. I can tell you that the electrical network with the solar grid, and the high-capacity wind cones, are state-of-the-art. All of it is of a higher quality than found in most modern buildings anywhere in the world. This alone tells me that we have arrived at a place where much thought and reasoning has taken place prior to our arrival." The large man stopped to nod toward Jon and Hank.

"How can you make such a judgement so quickly?" asked the same man who led the charge to take the cars from the farm. The sun reflected off his bald head while he continued his diatribe, "who are you to judge? This place doesn't look different from any farm I have seen."

"I am an electrical engineer."

"He's the main reason we can all drive around in our electric cars without having to wait to use a cord to charge the damn things, mate," yelled a man from the front of the crowd, using the same distinct British accent as Patrick.

"We heard that war has already spilled over the southern border of Colorado," yelled a man with wire rimmed glasses. He crinkled his nose and rotated his head to measure the response to his information. "It's only a matter of time before it arrives here. We should leave immediately."

"Hold it, I don't know where you are getting your information." Hank turned to Jon, expecting his brother to respond to the information about the enemy at the Colorado border, when he heard the low thumping of a helicopter in the distance. Everyone turned to watch a UH-211 Blackhawk

Helicopter approaching from the south. It looped around on the west side of the farm, landing north of the apartments.

"I'm taking that you know who this is?" Patrick looked directly at Jon.

"It is most likely my brother Colonel Ted Lisco." Jon swallowed hard. "I have no idea why he would arrive at this time unannounced."

Jon followed Bill, walking quickly in the direction of the helicopter. Ted, still in his Army Dress Blues uniform, met them at the base of the tower.

"My God, when did all these people arrive?" Ted asked Bill in amazement.

"Just this afternoon." Bill could tell that there was a sense of urgency with his father. "Why didn't you let us know you were coming?"

"I need for Shira to come with me back to the base." Ted scanned the area for the young woman. When he couldn't locate her, he turned to Jon. "Jon, can you find Shira and bring her here."

"What's going on Dad?" Bill watched as Jon, along with Terrance and Irving moved around the crowd, and proceeded in the direction of the garage.

"I have two Companies under my command as part of an FBI task force to go after the insurgents." Ted could hear the crowd of people speaking loudly in an unruly manner. "Are you having problems here?"

"We are about to have a lot of problems with the new arrivals wanting to take our vehicles and leave," said Bill. "One of them just told us that the enemy has arrived at the Colorado border, and the war is coming our way. Is that true?"

"That's not true. They did push all the way to Santa Fe, where we drove them back south of Albuquerque. Deb's Brigade is there now." Ted could see Maddy running in his direction, the wet slop from the melted snow splashing with each step. Nicole walked quickly behind, trying to keep up with her granddaughter.

"Grandpa." Maddy ran full force into his leg.

Nicole placed her hand on the side of his face. Ted leaned down and kissed her quickly on the lips.

"I'm only here for a moment," he answered the unasked question, as he looked into his wife's eyes. "I'm going to take Shira back to the base for questioning.

"Are we going to be able to communicate with you?" Bill asked his father.

"I'll make it a point to radio on a daily basis."

"You know it's almost Christmas, Grandpa." Maddy leaned back. She took hold of the fingers on his left hand and squeezed tight.

"I know, but this Christmas might have to be a time where I'm not here." He pulled his hand away and placed it on top of her head. Rather than looking at Maddy, he continued to gaze at Nicole. "I promise I will make it all up to you for the time I miss."

Nicole knowingly smiled.

"I'll have you a gift for when you do make it back." Maddy shifted to stand next to Bill.

"That's a deal." Ted could see Shira standing with Jon and Irving at the end of the apartment. He placed his hand on the side of Nicole's arm and looked at Bill. "I have to go."

Bill reached down and picked up Maddy in his right arm, while placing his left arm over his mother's shoulder. They all watched as Ted led Shira to the helicopter. They hurriedly lifted off with a roar into the western sky.

****

The living room was nearly full to the brim with many of the original members of the farm. The only ones who weren't part of the initial group were Patrick Montgomery, his wife Odette and the friend who drove the 1955 Chevy 3100 pickup when they arrived earlier. Patrick's thunderous voice, and his large body towering over everyone, including Jason Jensen, made him the center of attention in the packed room. The giant's nonstop speaking about how he helped design the cordless electric car started out being intriguing to everyone. As he persisted with the explanation on how he came to America to help with the design, his description of his work became too technical for most to understand, and his yakking soon became exasperating.

Jon poured a shot of whiskey as Bill held his glass in both hands. After he poured the double shot, he held the bottle out, tempting Hank to enjoy a taste. Hank shook his head no.

"Do you think I could have a nip, mate?" Patrick bulldozed his way through the crowd in the direction of Jon. He was smiling, revealing his crooked, but white teeth.

Jon looked up at the massive man. His head was as round as a basketball, causing him to slump forward. He hesitated with the bottle, wondering if alcohol might make Patrick even more talkative. Nevertheless, he poured a negligible snort into his glass.

"Ahh, this will ease the pain. There have been times in my life where I have drank myself sober." He tipped his head up and threw the whiskey into his mouth.

"You referred to the optimal amount of energy produced to allow for a longer life of the battery," Al was standing behind Patrick as he made the statement. "How in the world did you get all this figured out while making the wind turbines viable, even in inclement weather?"

"Oh now, that was a jigger of a problem." Patrick turned his red face in the direction of Al.

Jon rolled his eyes to the ceiling and motioned with his head. Bill, Hank, Jason Jensen and Harold, the bricklayer, followed him through the crowd into the kitchen.

"My God, that man is going to drive us all crazy by the time he's done talking." Jon could still hear Patrick's loud voice blaring as he took a seat at the kitchen table.

"Coach, I'm glad we could get you alone for a moment," said Jason, looking at Hank. "Harold and I have been discussing the construction of the large building Colonel Deb spoke about before she left."

"We have checked the amount of lumber and concrete bags. We figure there are enough supplies to erect a building around twenty meters by thirty-five meters." Harold's eyes narrowed as he looked seriously at the others. "We might need to find some more electrical wire and fixtures, along with a few other items to complete the project."

"We were thinking of getting the additional supplies from one of the abandoned farms." Jason continued to direct his words toward Hank. "Also, I made a general inquiry of the number of new arrivals who had previous construction experience. With the people already here, who helped with the apartment and tower, we have an additional forty, giving us a solid workforce of nearly sixty."

"What do you think Bill?" Hank focused on his nephew. He realized from the time Jason and Harold first started talking, it was Bill they should be addressing.

"We have an awful lot on our plate right now. If all the people stay, we are going to have a hard time feeding everyone." Bill took in a deep breath. "Our meat source is obviously good, but everything else is going to disappear very quickly."

"This afternoon I had a talk with Sheriff Bob and Ben about the local farmers who live nearest us on the south side of the Interstate." Jon leaned back in his chair. "They think we might be able to find some food sources at these farms."

"Some of the new people are already complaining about not wanting to eat meat." Hank could see that Jason and Harold were wanting to get back to discussing the possibility of the building. "Maybe we could make a trip to a couple of neighboring farms and check for construction supplies and food."

"For the electrical wire and fixtures, we can take them from the Blake farm. I want to make sure we document all the wood and fixtures we remove from any of the neighbors' buildings," Bill stated.

"Bill, I take it that is a yes for us to start the construction." Jason made eye contact with Bill before turning toward Harold.

"It's better than having everyone standing around doing nothing. It is a yes." Bill nodded to the two men, understanding that hard work was something both the bricklayer and carpenter lived for. He hoped the new undertaking would take Harold's mind off the loss of his brother Fred.

"Why don't we go first thing in the morning and check the two farms immediately west of the Brown's place?" Jon addressed his question to Hank and Bill.

"Wouldn't you imagine that the rebels have already ransacked them?" Hank placed his hand at his chin.

"There is only one way to find out."

"Who are you going to take with you?" Bill asked Jon, knowing that if his uncle wanted to go on the mission, discussing the pros and cons of it would be futile.

"Irving, Terrance, Sheriff Bob and Ben."

"Just the five of you?" Hank held his hand out toward his brother.

"We'll have the drone surveille ahead and stay in radio contact with Hank and Bobby at the monitor in the garage. After we arrive at the farm and find out if there is anything of value, we can assess the situation from there." Jon folded his hands.

"We plan to start immediately with the building. I'll begin organizing a workforce." Jason rose from his chair.

"I'm going to place concrete blankets on the frozen ground where we plan to build so we can begin excavating early in the morning." Harold also stood up and hurried to the door.

Bill understood his two uncles were giving him respect for making decisions concerning the permanent transformation of the farm. He greatly appreciated their foresight and understanding of his relationship with Aunt Deb. The thought entered his mind of whether he should involve Bobby with making choices concerning the inheritance that would be shared equally between the two at some point. His prior business dealings with Deb, along with time and money he spent over the past years in improving the property, would make the transaction tricky. He had faith that everything would work out fairly.

Fort Carson Army Base

The two CIA operatives were waiting for Ted in his outer office when he entered with Shira. Both men had changed clothes, giving them a much more professional presence. They eye-balled the young woman clinging closely to Ted's side.

Ted pulled a chair around to the back side of his desk. He motioned for Shira to sit. The two CIA men sat in chairs on the opposite side of the desk.

"Gentlemen, this is Shira…," Ted hesitated.

"Rosenfeld."

"Where are you from Shira?" the younger man asked.

"I grew up in Littleton." She glanced back and forth between the two men. "A suburb just south of Denver."

"Were you part of the insurgency?"

"Yes."

"How did you get involved with this group?" The younger man continued the line of questions.

"They recruited several of my friends in high school. Christian and I, along with a few others at the time had been following politics and cultural issues. We fell for the opportunity the insurgents offered us to take control of our future. Everything they told us sounded logical."

"Was your decision made mainly to follow your friends, or were there other reasons?"

"We didn't just blindly join. A lot of thought and discussion preceded our decision to follow the group. It was the tipping point when they told us about getting paid once a month." Red blotches were becoming more pronounced on the cheeks of her face as she spoke.

"What were the reasons? Why would so many young people try to end America?" The younger man held the palm of his right hand out. Blood rushing to the face of the young woman did not go unnoticed.

"Politics corrupted by money, along with concentrated wealth making certain individuals too powerful." She paused to stare at the older grey-haired man who was listening to her with his arms folded, leaning back in his chair. "Do you want me to continue?"

"Please do," said the younger man.

"The lack of trust, and overreach of unelected administrators."

"Or maybe it all could have been for a paycheck without working." The younger agent tipped his head toward her.

"Okay, okay, basically I could give a shit about your problems with society." The older man interrupted, as he leaned forward in his seat. "What I want to know is how familiar you are with Anastasia Vasilyeva?"

Shira turned to Ted, making a conscious effort not to look either of the CIA men in their eyes. "I don't know Anastasia Vasilyeva."

"You told me that you and Christian met with an Anastasia at a farmhouse the night before your group was attacked," Ted stated.

"It was Anastasia Wolf."

"What did she look like?" asked the older man.

"She had shoulder length sandy blonde hair." Shira momentarily turned her dark eyes to the ceiling, before looking directly into the CIA man's eyes.

"Did she have extraordinarily big legs, and thick hips?" the younger man asked.

"Yeah, she had a huge ass." Shira hesitated, realizing she needed to be very careful how she answered the two operatives' questions.

"That is Anastasia Vasilyeva. Was there anyone else with her?"

"Two older men, one extremely large, and the other a slightly smaller man who had square shoulders without a neck. Also, an older lady." Shira's deep, dark eyes flickered as she spoke. She knew that Christian had given Ted much of the information about their dealings with the group of insurgents, and she wanted her remembrance of the events to be consistent with those of her dead friend.

"The older woman is Anastasia's stepmother. The large man is Boris Drago, and the smaller man is Ivan Lundgren." The older operative looked at Ted.

"Was." Shira glanced at the older man.

"What do you mean by was?"

"The smaller man was, Ivan Lundgren. Unless he survived the four bullets I put in his chest."

There was complete silence in the room as Shira turned to Ted. She took in a deep breath and let it out quickly. The two CIA men stared, reassessing her. This information was completely unexpected.

"Where is the farmhouse located where you last saw Anastasia?" Ted asked.

"I can't tell you, but I can probably find it if I go back to the location. I know it's north of Interstate 70 near the little town of Watkins."

"How many people did Anastasia have with her at the farm?" Ted asked.

"It was a very small group, maybe twenty-five."

"Shira, when we first met at our farm, Christian told me that there was going to be an attack on NORAD. What do you know about the plan?" Ted set forward in his seat.

"Only that they expected Christian and five of us to go to Colorado Springs, with the idea that the others would join us later. This is the main reason that we decided to leave the city."

"Did they give you an exact location where you were to meet in Colorado Springs?" asked the younger CIA man.

"No."

"We need to go to the farmhouse where she last saw Anastasia," stated the older man. "Colonel, can you have your force ready immediately?"

"It's going to take about two hours to mobilize. It will take us another hour and half to get there, so it will be the middle of the night when we arrive." Ted leaned forward in his chair. "Do you have reconnoiter capabilities that we can tie into, or do we need the drone?

"We need to use your drone." The older man rubbed the center of his forehead.

Watkins, Colorado

Ted along with three Platoons remained at the Interstate 70 exit ramp. A reconnaissance patrol along with the two CIA operators, escorted Shira forward to locate the farm where she last encountered Anastasia. There were so many side roads leading to the newly constructed homes and condominium complexes that nothing in the maze of streets and thoroughfares looked familiar to her. After several attempts of jogging her memory, the patrol returned to the location on I-70.

It was a moonless night with the stars shining bright in the darkness, absent of any streetlights or residual illumination from homes, the heavenly sight was stunning. The drone was launched while Ted, Shira and the two CIA men watched on a monitor inside the communication vehicle. The drone made many passes over ranches and farmsteads before Shira finally yelled, "stop".

She moved closer to the monitor as the drone lingered. There were three Quonsets and a dim light apparent in a small house with smoke visibly billowing from the chimney.

"That's it. We spent the night in the Quonset closest to the house."

"It looks like there is only one road leading to the location." Ted looked at the CIA men, "I will send in a sniper squad to cover all exits from the buildings. They can continue surveillance while we move into position."

"Colonel Lisco, we would like to have as many of the rebels alive as possible. And under no circumstance should Anastasia be killed."

"I will give that directive." Ted took in a deep breath and released it. "But gentlemen, you must know that if any of my soldier's face imminent harm, they are going to protect themselves and their fellow combatants. I want to make it clear that using this type of force might end up with many casualties. If you would like to take a different approach, we will give you all the support necessary."

The older man clasped his hands together and looked at the monitor for about twenty seconds. He brought his left hand up and pinched his lower lip, while continuing to look at the screen.

A light came on from the front of the farmhouse where a large man stepped out of the door onto the porch. He lit a cigarette.

"That is the man who was with Anastasia when we were there," stated Shira.

"That is Drago. Move the drone back," said the older CIA operative.

Ted gave the order. The drone slowly moved away from the farm. He turned to the CIA man, sensing that he was not over enthused about assuming the task of breaching the house.

"How do you want to handle this?"

"If you can give us the squad of snipers, we will take the house. After we make the penetration, you can bring in your Soldiers to make sure any other forces on the premises are neutralized. I want to obtain constant communication with your troops with the understanding that none of them fire unless I give the order. It is vitally important that we take certain people inside the house alive." The older man ran his hand through the grey hair above his left temple. "You can send the reconnaissance team immediately to the location while we change into our gear. Let's get it over with."

The pictures being transmitted to the communication vehicle by the cameras from the scouting squad were clear and vivid. With Ted's soldiers in position, covering the out buildings, the two CIA men slipped onto the porch, and within a minute blasted the front door. Flashes from stun grenades were visible through the windows of the old farmhouse. After a couple minutes of silence, the two CIA men exited onto the porch, each leading a person in front of them. The younger man had Drago in cuffs, but there was no sign of Anastasia.

"Colonel, there are only two rebels here at this site." The older man was breathing heavily as he broke the silence. "I have a team that will arrive here within the hour. You and your men can return to the base in Fort Carson. I would like for Shira to remain here on location."

"I will bring her to you." Ted stared at Shira, who appeared to be holding her breath. She crossed her arms as though she was attempting to warm her body. She let out a deep breath and relaxed.

Colorado Farm

The December weather was nippy but uncommonly warm for the plains of Colorado at five in the morning. Harold stood next to Jason at the desk in Ted's office scribbling on a piece of typing paper. The building they planned to construct would be about twenty meters wide by thirty-five meters long. It was as big a building as they could build in the space between the main farmhouse and the tower.

"Even with all the lumber we can scrounge up, we will still be short," stated Jason Jensen.

"We have about nine hundred concrete blocks left. That is enough to build the wall on one end of the building and then frame the rest," said Harold. "We can place a fireplace in the block wall."

"We should let the Liscos know how long it will take." Jason rubbed the bandage on his wrist.

"With so many workers we can have it done by New Year." Harold stepped back and looked at the carpenter, knowing that he would be flabbergasted.

"Twelve days, that seems impossible." Jason was positive the bricklayer was joshing him. "You are kidding, right?"

"With all the people we have here now, we can organize the building process to have it done in twelve days, but we must start immediately. We need to dig out for a monolithic pour. You can begin framing the walls and building the trusses in the field to the east today while I have a crew begin to pour the concrete. With the outer perimeter poured, your crew can start setting the walls tomorrow." Harold made some marks on the paper in front of them, splashing coffee on the desk. "I figure we will need about eighty yards of concrete for the pour. There are still about twelve yards of sand left over from the tower, and still over four hundred bags of cement in the warehouse. Hauling sand from the pit will be the top priority. We can begin pouring from the south. I know it is against all building practices, but I will begin laying the block wall in the wet concrete. By pouring the deeper outer edge of the monolithic concrete pour, with an expansion joint a meter toward the inside, it will allow us to work on constructing the wall while the concrete crew pours the inside."

Jason stared at the mason knowing that he was not in any way kidding about having the building up by New Year. He realized that Harold was the type of person who didn't just talk about things, but when he set his mind to it, he got things done.

"We will need to have all the rough plumbing in place before we pour," Jason spoke calmly as if there was nothing peculiar about the idea of constructing the building in such a short time.

"I already spoke with Ben about the pipes needed to tie the bathroom into the septic, along with the water pipes." Harold placed his nearly empty coffee cup on the desk. "He can place everything he needs concerning the plumbing at the north end. It shouldn't hold us up at all, if we begin from the south."

"We need all the shovels and picks we can find to begin digging." Jason's mind was swirling as he thought about how he could most efficiently begin the framing. "You and I will need to string out the outer walls, so the digging takes place in the correct location."

"I placed stakes last night. But we should measure together to make sure everything is correct."

"What about bolts for the bottom plate of the framed walls?" Jason knew there were not enough to attach the framing.

"We can space the bolts that we have. Since the concrete will have cured for only a day, drilling into it will be easy after the walls are up. We can epoxy rebar, bent at a ninety-degree angle, through the plate."

"What about insulation and siding?" Jason looked at the muscles bulging out in Harold's neck.

"Ben thinks there is enough of both at his lumber yard for the building. He plans to take a trip back to Limon either today or tomorrow."

Jason had always fancied himself to be a problem-solving person. Now, he was in the presence of someone who could think out solutions faster than he thought possible. It was going to be an interesting twelve days.

Neighbor Farm

The neighbor's farmhouse was only about fifty meters off the county road. Although pictures from the drone showed no movement or sign of human activity, Jon still stopped the car on the gravel road in order to assess the situation before rushing in. The farmhouse was much smaller than the one at the Lisco's farm, and the barn was very old and weather-beaten. What caught Jon's eye was the chicken coop on the side of the barn, with several chicken visible in a pen attached to the hut. He stepped from the car and listened to the chicken's cluck. Sheriff Bob climbed out of the passenger side and waited by the open door.

"This is Martha and Lucky Robert's farm," Bob stated loudly. The cackling of the chickens was the only other sound at the eerily quiet farm.

"How long can chickens survive without feed?" Jon asked.

The sheriff looked to the back seat. "Ben, how long can chickens live if they are not fed?"

"They can live for quite a while, but not very long without water." Ben clambered from the back of the car. He moved next to Jon, as Terrance and Irving followed, both carrying rifles. "They won't give any eggs if they go without feed for a couple of days."

"Ben, you stay with the car and wait for a signal to move forward. Irving, you and Terrance go to the back side of the house. Bob and I will check the chicken coop, and then meet you at the front porch." Jon zipped his jacket before pulling the collar tight around his neck.

The chicken coop was built out of redwood, with the chicken run on the side of the main structure being made from electric netting. The whole operation appeared new and modern.

"It's warm inside here." Jon opened the door of the coop, allowing the heat to escape. He stepped inside to a humid and musky smell. Sheriff Bob followed him inside.

"They have water, but it looks to be on an electric timer." Bob moved to a sitting hen who chirped and flapped its wings at him when he touched the comb on top of its head. "It looks like they have been fed."

"Let's check the house." Jon backed out of the coop.

Irving and Terrance were waiting for them at the gate to the front yard. Bob and Jon stepped up a single step and onto the porch, while Irving and Terrance lingered behind.

"Sheriff," a soft voice was barely audible.

"Did you hear that?" Jon moved backwards off the porch and into the yard.

"Who's there," Sheriff Bob yelled. He pushed his hat back on his head and waited for a response.

"It's Martha and Frank," the reply came from beneath a wooden door on the far corner of the farmhouse.

Bob went to the door and tried to lift it. "Unhook the door," he yelled after finding the door wouldn't budge.

The latch clicked, and he flipped the door onto its side with a thud. Martha struggled to make her way up the concrete steps. Jon reached his hand down and helped her out of the cellar.

"Someone is going to have to help Frank. He can barely see nowadays."

"Lucky," Bob yelled into the dark cellar as he climbed half-way down the extremely narrow and steep steps. The locals had always called Frank, Lucky. "Come on Lucky, take my hand and I'll pull you up."

Ben drove the car down the short driveway when he saw the Roberts emerge from the cellar. He parked close to the group and exited.

"How long have you been down there?" Jon figured them to be in their late eighties. Lucky was as thin as a rail with white hair. Martha walked almost sideways, limping terribly because of a broken hip which was never fixed.

"On and off for the past month." Lucky turned toward Jon and blinked his eyes rapidly before squinting, giving his best effort to focus and identify who he was talking too. "We have a hidden door that goes up and into the main house, so Martha could go up and retrieve things."

"I'm Lt. Col. Jon Lisco."

"Oh my gosh. You are one of the Lisco kids." Martha placed her hand on Jon's forearm. "I knew your mother."

"Why don't you two come with us to the Lisco farm? Bob and Judy along with me and Paula are staying there." Ben moved next to Lucky. "There are a lot of people there right now."

"What we really would like is for someone to drive us to Illinois, to be with our daughter." Lucky's lips twitched as he spoke. "Ben, I just can't see well enough anymore to drive us. We tried to let the car drive itself, but the damn thing took off in the wrong direction. Something must have gone haywire with the GPS."

"I know you bought a brand-new pickup last year. Did someone take your vehicles?" asked Bob."

"We hid them," Martha spoke with a slight grin.

"Where in the world did you hide them?"

Martha pointed to two neatly placed haystacks in the field just past the chicken coop. "We covered them with hay."

"Have there been many people come by here and try to take things?" Jon asked.

"Oh yeah. The day all the fighting took place at your farm there were so many strangers in our yard, I was sure they would discover us. From the number of explosions, and the amount of shooting taking place we figured everyone at your farm were dead," Martha sighed. "Just yesterday a group of about fifteen passed through our land. They took all the eggs from the chicken coop but left the chickens alone."

Jon was somewhat taken aback to hear that only the day before the insurgents had come so close to their farm. But he wanted to hear more about the Roberts wanting to go to Illinois.

"Several people arrived at our farm who are looking to travel back east. I'm sure they would be willing to drive you wherever you want to go, if you supply the transportation." Jon hesitated for a moment realizing he had a chance to lessen the number of people at the farm and find a way to help feed the others. "If you decide to go, can we take your chickens and milk cows? Everyone at our farm is tired of eating powdered eggs and drinking powdered milk."

"You can take whatever you damn well please." Martha stepped next to Lucky and placed a hand on his arm. "If we leave, we will never return."

Brown Farm

Two men propelled an electric Polaris auto cycle across the quiet grounds at the Brown's farm. They quieted the engine as they maneuvered through the partially open double doors into the cold and musky barn. They quickly hopped off the three-wheeler and moved to the large doors, where they had a vantage point of the driveway and the farmhouse. Having stolen the vehicle and escaped from the group of insurgents they had been traveling with over the past several days, they were on edge.

There was no sign of life at the farmstead, but they could hear the thumping sound of a tractor coming from the south. Finally, the tractor came into view, pulling a trailer full of hay about eight-hundred meters away. Both men moved out of the barn to the wood railings of the corral where they watched the heavy load of feed travel through a gate before making its way across the pasture toward the Lisco farm.

They hopped on the three-wheeler and drove down the same furrowed tracks through the pasture as the men hauling hay. They crossed a land bridge at a stream where they drove to the north over the rugged landscape full of shrubbery. When about four hundred meters from the western fence of the Lisco property, they parked their vehicle on the backside of a bush. They could hear the chatter of people.

"It sounds like there are a hell of a lot more people than when we were here before." The man with the cap pushed the lower strand of barbed wire down and climbed through the fence.

"Where are you going?" asked the blond-haired man, pulling the collar of his light jacket tight around his neck.

"I'm going to take a closer look."

They made a wide swath around the farm to keep from being noticed by the Jacobys unloading the trailer of hay. The retractable door to the warehouse was open, with several people visible inside, all wearing make-shift masks made from cloth. Many of them were laying on cots, while others gathered in groups. None of them were concerned in the least about the two strangers in their midst. Several strips of cloth sat on a table immediately inside the open door. They each grabbed a strand of cloth, and wrapped it around their face, and tied it at the back of their head.

The area between the garage and farmhouse was full of people, with none of them being recognizable as those who they encountered several days earlier. Only a few were wearing masks. They maneuvered through the people to the location where they were detained the first time they arrived at the farm, by Jon and the others. The blond-haired man instinctively glanced toward the top of the tower, remembering how he looked up and saw Sherry, before being identified as Caroline's attackers. Now, Irving was visible in the window, but was looking down at a group of men working below his location.

"We need to blend in with the group over there." The man in the cap motioned toward a larger crowd standing at the end of the Jacoby's RV.

The sound of children playing could be heard coming from the front yard of the farmhouse. The blond-haired man tapped his cohort on the back of his shoulder. He pointed in the direction of the front yard. Both Sherry and Caroline were laughing and clapping as they played games with the children. They moved nearer the cluster of people, but far enough away to where they could view the two women without the RV blocking their line of sight. They didn't notice Bill and Nicole, walking quickly from the garage across the grounds, until the mother and son were right next to them. They both looked away. Bill hesitated for a moment, as though subconsciously he recognized something was amiss, before continuing past the two intruders.

"We are pressing our luck here," stated the blond-haired man, taking a step toward the warehouse.

"You are right. I recognize more people." He watched as Irene and Breanna stepped out of the RV.

They walked quickly back to the warehouse.

La Cienega, New Mexico

Since arriving at headquarters for 2nd Brigade, situated near the town of La Cienega, New Mexico, Deb had been robustly studying a map of the Sandia Wilderness, paying attention to the most minuscule points of the terrain. Soldiers, in the large tent, were busy behind her setting monitors and electronic lines for the communication center. She looked up from the map and noticed Command Sergeant Major Talfoya, with a Soldier, entering the tent.

"Colonel, this is Private Montoya. She is from this area and has some information pertinent to our mission," stated Command Sergeant Major Talfoya.

The soldier saluted Colonel Deb.

"So, you are familiar with the Sandia area?"

"Yes ma'am. I was born and raised here." The private remained at attention. Her bronze face looked like it was chiseled out of granite, with high cheek bones, a pointed nose and a wide chin. Her dark eyes darted straight forward.

"Relax Private Montoya. Come here and tell us everything you know about the wilderness area." Colonel Deb indicated a location on the map, as the private moved to her side. "What sort of vehicles can we use to traverse the terrain right here."

"We can move vehicles up to this point." The private indicated an area just below where Deb had pointed. Her hand was shaking. "Past that position, in all directions forward, movement with vehicles would be difficult. Now, there are roads in the wilderness area."

"Private, why are you shaking?" Deb stepped back from the map.

"Ma'am, may I speak freely."

"Not only may you, but I expect you to."

"This afternoon, my uncle, who has been a guide in the region for many years, came to our barracks to warn me about the dangers we are facing. He told me that he was near Sandia Peak, much further south of the location you indicated on the map. The place was crawling with enemy soldiers. They are everywhere ma'am."

"Can I speak with your uncle to get a firsthand account of what he saw?"

"Yes ma'am, he wants to meet with you. He is ex-marine, and is very worried about my welfare, should I go into Sandia. He told me some things that you should hear before you send soldiers into the wilderness."

"Can you have him here within the hour?"

"Ma'am, he is waiting outside." Private Montoya rushed a salute, before hurrying past Command Sergeant Major Talfoya, and out of the tent.

"Tommy, come here and look at this. In the scheme of things this area is relatively small. There are just so many ravines and valleys that we are going to need to be very precise in where we concentrate troops." Deb pointed to a location on the map. "If the iron dome over the area is as impenetrable as we are being told, and air support is not possible until we destroy their weaponry, we have to decide the timing and amount of force we send at any one time."

Command Sergeant Major Talfoya stared at the map. "I don't know how 4th Infantry artillery will be able to cover our three Battalions, as well as Stryker Brigade?"

"It is something we will have to work out." Deb looked up as Private Montoya entered the tent with a man who didn't look much older than her. He was dressed in a white shirt with puffy arms, wearing a turquoise necklace, supported by a bright blue lanyard. He wore a silver bracelet on each of his wrists.

"Ma'am, this is my uncle Chet." Private Montoya saluted.

"At ease Private. Chet, would you tell us what you know about the wilderness area?" Deb contemplated asking specific questions concerning the interceptors but thought it best if she let him give her all the information first.

Chet had a noticeable limp as he moved next to the table and leaned over the map.

"I go to Sandia Mountain to try and clear my mind, something I have done for many years, right here." He pointed to a location on the map that showed a peak with an elevation of 3255 meters. "About a month ago I noticed soldiers as far as my eyes could see. They were wearing special cone shaped headgear."

"That is right in the middle of the wilderness area. Did they know you were there?" Deb was intrigued that he was able to observe the area.

"Until two days ago, they never noticed me. I would sit on the cliffs, hurting nobody. When they did see me, no bullets came my way, but a hot wind hit me in the face, and I immediately had a terrible headache, and my nose began to bleed." He looked directly at Deb. "They were using some form of a directed-energy weapon to make me leave."

"Private Montoya told us that you were in the military." Deb wrenched her hands. "I take it that you know about electromagnetic weapons."

"Yes ma'am. I worked with Robotic Combat Vehicles during my time as a Marine. I was briefed thoroughly on high frequency weapons. I didn't see it, or where it was coming from, but the heat from the weapon was extreme."

"Why would you go back to the mountain when you knew it was occupied with the enemy?" Tommy asked.

"It is a place where plants and nature live in harmony." Chet stepped back from the map. His facial features were different from those of Private Montoya. His face was round and chubby, but his deep dark eyes were the same as his niece. "Over the years there have been many high-end homes built in the wilderness, as well as several housing developments established in the small surrounding towns. I want to enjoy the nature before it disappears."

"Did you see jammers or artillery?" Deb asked.

"Nothing that I could identify."

"Do you think you could return safely to Sandia Peak?"

"I don't know about safely, but I plan to go back."

"Colonel, all monitors are functional, and we have communication established with the three Battalions." Captain Dodson waited at the end of the table.

"Thank you, Captain. I want you to contact Colonel McDonald with 4th Infantry Field Artillery Brigade. Let me know when you have him online." Deb returned her attention to Chet. "Could you help guide a squad of our soldiers to the location on the mountain where you were hit with the electromagnetic weapon, without being noticed?"

"No, ma'am, they have advanced technology that would make it far too dangerous for your soldiers to try and go there without force. With all the surveillance they have, they would quickly identify and destroy your soldiers." Chet took in a deep breath and then let it out. "I do have members from both my tribe, and the surrounding tribes who are very familiar with the area. Any one of us could go to the higher locations unnoticed."

Deb glanced in the direction of Tommy. "Can you organize the group of civilians to be used as guides for reconnaissance?"

"Yes, ma'am." Tommy stepped toward the entrance of the tent. Captain Montoya and her uncle followed closely behind as they left.

"Captain Dodson, have you been able to reach Colonel McDonald?" Deb moved toward the monitors in the communication room.

"No ma'am, but I do have Lt. Col. Jacob." The captain motioned in the direction of a large screen.

"Lieutenant Colonel, have you got intelligence and reconnaissance platoons into the wilderness area." Deb sat down in front of the monitor.

"Yes ma'am. We have one platoon just inside state highway 14, and the second platoon about four kilometers to the northeast of their location. They are stationary, waiting for further orders."

Deb thought for a moment, trying to visualize where the platoons were located. She realized they had not even reached the outskirts of the wilderness area.

"Why have they stopped?" she asked.

"There are problems with the communication system."

"Are the glitches on our end, or are they being jammed?"

"There are no problems on our end."

"Okay, keep us informed." Deb rose from the seat in front of the monitor. If the I&R Platoon was only able to reach the outer perimeter of the Sandia region, and nonhuman aerial vehicles were unable to fly over the zone, then Deb had to quickly find a way to get eyes on the enemy. She needed to let Tommy know the urgency in finding out if Chet and his friends would be able to help with reconnaissance.

Colorado Farm

Hank watched the workers, Jason and Harold had amassed, gather around the work area on the south side of the tower. He was scrutinizing the large group from in front of the Jacoby's RV when he saw Gina walking from the farmhouse in his direction. When she was about ten meters from him, she stopped and pointed toward the county road. A pick-up pulling a twenty-meter-long hay trailer was slowly approaching with two SUV's following behind.

Hank stepped away from the RV for a better look. "The back vehicle is ours."

"Jon must have found something at the neighbor's farm."

Terrance maneuvered the pick-up and trailer forward almost all the way to the garage. Ben stopped the SUV right in front of Hank and Gina.

"This is Lucky and Martha Roberts. They are going eastward to Illinois and are willing to take as many people as possible with them. They need someone to drive," Jon introduced the couple, wasting no time in disclosing their reason for being at the farm.

"We want whoever you find to drive us to know that we are going to Springfield, Illinois." Martha stared at Hank's tan face and prominent, chiseled jaw. "You are definitely a Lisco."

"Yes ma'am. I'm Hank Lisco. Jon, Ted and Deb's younger brother. And this is Gina, Jon's wife."

"I knew your mother. I never took time to know your sister very well, but I heard she did some amazing things with this farm." Martha turned to look at the tower and apartment. "It is astonishing what she has done."

"Hank, lets round up the new arrivals so we can decide who will be leaving with the Roberts tomorrow morning," said Jon.

"How many people?" Hank looked at the long trailer.

"We are thinking thirty-five," stated Jon. "It will be crowded but the trip should take only about twenty-four hours, if they drive straight through."

"How do we choose. There are more than thirty-five who want to leave." Hank looked at a large group of people gathering at the garage.

"Have them draw lots."

****

The building process was underway with a massive group of people swinging picks to break loose the frozen ground, with others right behind the groundbreakers with shovels, removing the dirt. Jason Jensen and his large crew of carpenters were working frantically in the field to the east of the tower, nearly finished with the framing for the west wall of the building, which laid in the frozen grass. Harold tamped the ground at the trench of the northern wall of the building, preparing to pour concrete.

Maddy and Scotty convinced Sherry and Caroline to move the game of kickball away from the small front yard to the wide-open pasture, nearly three hundred meters from the north side of the barn. All the children were bundled in coats, keeping them comfortable from the cold wind.

Lurking near the corrals at the barn were Caroline's assailants. The Polaris three-wheeler auto cycle was hidden behind a shrub about four hundred meters to the west of the playing children. The men slowly skirted their way closer and closer in the direction of the two unsuspecting women.

Caroline pulled the collar of her jacket tight around her neck. She was having a hard time convincing the children to keep their coats on, even though the frigid wind was piercing on their exposed skin.

Sherry and Caroline planned on leaving the play area and joining the masonry crew as soon as Harold gave the go ahead to start mixing mortar. They figured they would summon Nicole and Jacqueline to help watch the kids when they left.

"Caroline, can you and Sherry play too?" Maddy's loose fitting stocking cap was perilously close to falling and covering her eyes. The cheeks on her face were bright red.

"You two can pick teams." Scotty's light jacket was unzipped and open at the front. The knees of his pant legs were wet from sliding on the moist grass.

"We have to make the goals," insisted Sherry, noticing a bush about fifty meters west of them. "Maddy, come help me break off a couple branches from that bush."

The light bronzed grass was short enough to run across with ease, but there wasn't even a single broken branch on the treeless prairie. A large bush was about fifty meters north of the play location, next to the barbed wire fence. Sherry hurried to the bush, with Maddy about five meters behind, and began breaking branches off. Out of the corner of her eye she caught the form of the blond-haired man approaching from the side. Before she could react, the man grabbed her from the back of her shirt and tried to pull her to the fence. She twisted out of his grasp, landing hard on her back, knocking the wind from her lungs. Using both hands he began to pull her by her legs. When she kicked him hard in his chest, he viciously attacked her with many of his punches landing squarely on her head. Maddy kicked at the man who was hitting Sherry.

"Caroline, look," yelled Scotty, pointing at Sherry and Maddy, before running in their direction.

Caroline wavered for a moment before running at full speed toward the assault. She saw another man rushing across the pasture.

"Wait Scotty," she yelled, running past him, beating the second man to Maddy just as he came forward with his arm ready to strike. She tackled Maddy and went under the man's punch. She pulled Maddy to her feet and faced the assailant. She knew immediately she was again face to face with the man who brutally attacked her weeks earlier.

"Scotty, run and get help." Caroline stepped between the man and the two children. Her intention was to fight him with everything she had.

The man with the cap realized her resolve would make it impossible to kidnap her. He moved toward the blond-haired man, who continued the assault on Sherry. Scotty ran away, but Maddy remained by Caroline's side.

Irving was in the top room of the tower watching Harold and Jason's crews work on the building below, when he heard the yelling from the children on the far side of the barn. At first, he figured he was hearing sounds of youngsters playing, but when he saw several kids running around the garage, he realized that there was a problem. He jumped down the stairs, leaving his fifty-caliber rifle in the tower, and rushed across the farm grounds, passing the frantic children.

Nicole and Jacqueline were in Ted's office when they heard the children screaming. They both ran out the back door of the garage, just as Irving went flying by.

"Stay here Maddy," Caroline yelled as she ran hard in the direction of the assailant who continued to beat Sherry. She moved past the man in the cap, who was crawling through the barbed wire fence. She leaped at the blond-haired man, grabbing him by the neck, pulling him off her friend. She rolled off his shoulder and immediately jumped to her feet. Sherry attempted to stand up but was disoriented and fell back down. She prepared to fight with all she had when she saw Maddy moving toward her.

"Maddy, stay where you are," Caroline yelled.

The blond-haired assailant saw his accomplice running across the pasture. As bad as he wanted to abduct Sherry, when he heard the screams from the farm grounds, he quickly climbed through the fence. He ran in the direction of the hidden three-wheeler.

Irving rushed to Caroline and Maddy, when he saw they were okay, he leaned down to check on Sherry who was sitting up in the wet grass. She had a purple bump already forming under her right eye, and her nose was bleeding.

Nicole went to where Caroline had her arm around Maddy. She fell to a knee in front of her granddaughter. Bill and Jon came rushing to their side.

"Is she ok?" Bill picked up his daughter. She wrapped her arms around his neck and hugged tightly.

"Maddy wasn't harmed," said Caroline, turning to Jon. "They were the two guys who attacked me and left me to die in the ditch. The ones we let go."

"They headed west across the pasture toward the Brown's farm. They must have used the land bridge to get across the creek." Irving pulled Sherry's hair back to inspect a small laceration on her forehead. He could see the half-moon scar on her cheek from the concrete shrapnel at the tower.

"We have to catch them." Jon pounded his right fist hard into his left hand as he looked at Sherry. She was being lifted to her feet by Irving. "After having mercy, I told them we would shoot first and ask questions later if they ever came near us again. I can't believe they are so brazen that they would come back here."

"Let's go get them." Sherry's right eye was nearly swollen shut, and her lower lip was beginning to swell. Blood from her nose had covered the front of her blouse.

"You need to get some ice on that face. You took a bad beating." Jon clenched his teeth.

"I've been beat up worse." Sherry breathed hard through her mouth as she steadied herself. "I'm going to get that son-of-a-bitch if it's the last thing I ever do."

"I'll bet you will. And I will help you." Jon shook his head up and down and clicked his tongue. "Right now, let's put the drone in the air and see if we can find out where they went."

"I'll take you to the clinic," Jacqueline placed her hand on the side of Sherry's arm. The wellbeing of the baby was on her mind as they made their way to the farmhouse. She couldn't help but wonder if the badly beaten girl's unborn baby might be her grandchild. She would never say out loud to anyone her thoughts about her high school aged son and the beautiful, rugged woman having a child together. She noticed the hidden glances between the two over the past few weeks, which caused her to believe that her notion might be reality.

****

Jacqueline sensed there was something terribly wrong the moment she led Sherry into the clinic. Sue was sitting in a chair with her face in her hands next to the bed where Travis lay on his side, emitting a terrible gurgling noise with every breath. His eyes were closed tightly. Julia, standing with her hand on the bed, turned to acknowledge Sherry and Jacqueline when they entered the door. Seeing her badly beaten face, she pointed to the extra cot at the back of the clinic.

"What happened?" Julia asked, clutching Sherry's chin. She pulled her head to an angle where she could better examine her eye.

"She was assaulted by the same men who attacked Caroline," stated Jacqueline, noticing Julia's subdued reaction to remembering the incident that brought her to the farm with her husband and in-laws.

"Have her sit there." Julia made eye contact with Jacqueline and said somberly, "If Travis is going to have any chance of survival, he must be taken to a hospital immediately."

Jon and Bill both entered the clinic just in time to hear Julia's stark warning. Bill moved next to Travis, where he heard his faltered breathing. Sue looked up at him with pleading eyes.

"Sue, Sheriff Bob told us that there is a hospital in the small town of Hugo. We have no idea if it is still operational or not, but I am willing to take Travis there in order to give him a chance to live." Bill put his hand down, allowing the wife to grasp it. She squeezed tightly. "Most likely he will not survive the journey back if it is no longer there."

"Please, let's try." Sue rose from the chair. The sides of her eyes were bright red, and tears streaked down her cheeks as she looked in the direction of Jacqueline. "Can you watch my girls?"

"Of course. You should pack to prepare to stay for an extended period." Jacqueline smiled at Sue, trying to give her a sense of positivity.

"I'll check with Bob and Ben to see if they will leave immediately." Bill looked at the dark circles under his Uncle Jon's eyes. The stress of having everyone relying on him to make decisions was taking its toll.

"Bill, you can take Terrance and Irving with you. I am going to stay here and see if I can track the two men who attacked Sherry."

"I guess we should take Ben's lumberyard truck, and I can drive our SUV. Travis will have to lay in the back with Sue." Bill stepped into the living room before turning back. "Sue, let's leave within the next thirty minutes."

"Another thing Bill. Why don't you take several packets of meat? You might need something to barter with," said Jon.

Julia stopped working on Sherry and stared at Travis. It was a miracle she had been able to keep the extremely strong man alive. After all the worry and constant attention, she had provided to the pilot, at a time that would otherwise have been given to grieving, it would be a relief for him to be removed from her care.

Sherry slid off the cot.

"Get back up there." Jon moved toward the beaten girl.

"No, it's okay. She needs rest and ice," Julia stated. She stared at the beautiful girl's swollen face. "You need to take it easy for a day or two."

Sherry's head was thumping as she relaxed. Her lower lip was enlarged so much that it affected her speech. "We are going to get them, right?"

"You can bet your bottom dollar on it. They are just like wild animals that have the taste of blood on their lips. They will never stop attacking us." Jon took in a deep breath and released it. He realized he needed to step up security at the farm. With so many new arrivals he had no idea who they were. Identifying the new people would be easier said than done.

La Cienega, New Mexico

Deb called for Lt. Col. Woodworth and Captain Hendersen of F Company from the 2nd Battalion, along with Command Sergeant Major Talfoya, to join her in the communication area of the command tent. By the time they situated in front of the monitors, images from 1st Battalion advancing from the south into the wilderness area were already being transmitted onto the four closest screens.

Company A of 1st Battalion, with Captain Singh in command approached highway 165 just south of the small town of Placitas. Three platoons on foot were nearly a kilometer further south than the main body of the company, which was traveling slowly, maintaining several light tactical vehicles equipped with weaponry to fight off incoming hostile drones. With the compromise of the Global Positioning System satellites, Soldiers carried the quantum positioning, timing, and navigation system inside their backpacks. Theoretically, the cameras as well as the communication system should all be free from enemy jamming.

Captain Singh moved his troops south on highway 165 with a mission to deploy the ten kilometers to where the drones were jammed. He planned to set a perimeter to allow aspects from 4th Infantry Field Artillery to move forward with interceptors and cannons before advancing further into the wilderness area.

"Tommy, can you retrieve Private Montoya and her uncle. I have some questions I would like to ask them as A Company moves deeper." Deb watched the soldiers of the forward platoon move quietly over the cactus infested terrain. She could see the red dots signifying soldiers on the largest video display screen hanging over the top of the smaller monitors.

"Captain Dodson, have Lt. Col. Barnet's transmissions with A Company brought up on speaker so we can listen in, only a one-way radio transmission," Deb glanced at the captain as she spoke.

"Ma'am, we are having some difficulty with verbal communication. We are starting to have intermittent interference," stated a corporal, sitting to the side of the video monitors.

"Watch it the best you can. Keep me informed if you lose communication completely."

"The images from all cameras are clear and vivid." Captain Dodson motioned to one of the screens.

Just as Deb moved next to the captain the screen began to flutter, making the image of rolling hills and cactus barely visible.

"The display that is fluttering is being transmitted from the most forward platoon just to the south and west of the main body of A Company." Captain Dodson looked back and forth between Deb and Lt. Col. Woodworth.

"How much further before they reach the ten-kilometer mark?" Lt. Col. Woodworth asked.

"They are there now," answered Captain Dodson. "Lt. Col. Wilson already has J and M Companies on the move on highway 14, just to the east of Captain Singh."

"Josh, something doesn't seem right here. If there are 20,000 enemy troops in the wilderness area, then we should have encountered some of them by now. I would think they would try and stop us from setting interceptors and artillery at these strategic locations." Deb moved back from the monitors to get a better angle to look at all the screens at the same time. Command Sergeant Major Talfoya entered the tent with Private Montoya and her uncle following closely behind.

"Colonel, Private Montoya and her uncle have more than fifty locals willing to scout the area at the Sandia Peak ski area." Tommy felt the frustration Deb was experiencing as she moved next to him. Colonel Lisco was a master with strategy and tactics, so he knew she wasn't blindly positioning troops. Although everything was moving quickly, he was somewhat surprised she had not discussed her ideas in detail with him.

"How have you come up with so many locals willing to assist us?" Deb shot Chet a grateful look.

"This is our home. Everyone wants to help. We can find many more to assist if you need."

"Can you move immediately? We need as much information about the enemy's numbers and locations as possible."

"We already have eyes at Sandia Peak."

"Tommy, make sure they are equipped with the Quantum Codo," Deb said.

"No, Colonel Lisco. We don't need any type of communication devices. We will get the information quickly to your commanders." Chet glanced at his niece.

"Ma'am, may I speak." Private Montoya remained at attention.

"At ease private. Yes, I want you to speak frankly."

"Ma'am, we are worried that the enemy has the technology to follow the sensors in the backpacks that our troops are using for communication."

"What evidence do you have of this." Deb noticed the hard cheeks on the private's face bulging out. "Relax, Private Montoya. Tell us why."

"Several members from the reservations have traveled to the wilderness area since it was invaded by the enemy. Just like my uncle. Most of the time they go unnoticed. They had their phones with them the times when they were detected. Even one of them who didn't have his phone, but was wearing a sports watch, was discovered."

Deb took in a deep breath and released it. She turned to Lt. Col. Woodworth. "Josh, can you inform Lt. Col. Barnet and Lt. Col. Wilson to be advised of the possibility of the enemy having the capability to track our troops through the sensors. Also, notify them of the information that will be coming their way from the local guides."

"Deb, do you want me to reposition aspects of 2nd Battalion closer?" Josh asked as Private Montoya and her uncle left the room.

"Not yet. Only F Company." Deb looked into Josh's narrowing eyes, where she saw confusion. She turned to Captain Hendersen, "You are to position F Company about five kilometers west of Albuquerque. This enemy will try everything they can to flank us. I want you to make sure that they don't."

"We haven't the luxury of time. We must keep moving forward." Tommy scanned the room as he made the statement to everyone.

"As soon as 4th Infantry Field Artillery is in place, 1st Battalion will continue to advance another five kilometers, and then five more kilometers if need be. One way or another we will eventually engage this enemy."

"Colonel, what is 2nd Battalion's role in this mission?" Lt. Col. Woodworth asked.

"Josh, I want you to remain in reserve, but ready to deploy at the drop of a hat. Until then, you are to stay here and help coordinate the attack. I want to keep General Lauer informed as well as align with Stryker Brigade and artillery."

Deb remembered her father telling her that one of the basics in war is to attack the enemy's strategy. The enemy had entrenched themselves in the area, making use of all the modern technology to ensure that it would be all but impossible to root them out. There was no way that they could sustain the number of troops located in the wilderness without a constant line of supplies being brought forth from Mexico. Their strategy was going to be to fight her Brigade in the roughest of terrain, where they would be content in losing two of their soldiers for one of hers, until the aspects of the Chinese Army found a way to edge further east, past the line of United States Army Divisions to the south of them.

Deb's plan was to have 1st and 3rd Battalions along with Stryker Brigade push up the center of the wilderness area and engage the enemy. After the fighting began, she would have Josh and 2nd Battalion make a wide swath several kilometers west of Captain Hendersen's A Company and flank the enemy, disrupting their communications and supply line. They would be forced to abandon their strong position. She thought about waiting to have A Company position west of Albuquerque, but since she knows the commanders of the Korean forces would suspect something was amiss if she didn't protect her flank, she decided to have them immediately move to the area. The entire plan was accepted by General Lauer, in fact it was him who decided to blast over the communication system the ruse that they did not have enough time to stop the supply chain before attacking the forces at Sandia.

She would divulge her entire plan to Tommy as soon as she could find time alone with him. She needed the Command Sergeant Major to get her securely in contact with General Prost so she could implement another of her plans. Her method was to turn the tables and disrupt all the enemy's schemes, tactics, and strategies. She was born for this moment.

Fowler, Colorado

Sprawl hit the area around the small towns east of Colorado Springs and Pueblo hard with new developments, enveloping many of the ranches, and much of the agriculture land. Shira and Christian's information about meeting Anastasia at a farmhouse in the Colorado Springs area brought Ted to a suspicious location at a ranch west of the small town of Fowler. He had a full-time group of techs at the communication center in Fort Carson constantly scrutinizing video from surveillance drones flying over the farms and ranches. One of the drones captured an extraordinary amount of human traffic at the ranch.

Ted ordered Staff Sergeant Clint Williams to move his 18-man Intelligence and Reconnaissance Platoon to the ranch while he waited in the communication vehicle at the outskirts of the city of Pueblo. The remaining platoons from D Company would remain at the county road approximately eight-hundred meters from the ranch house.

He was concerned that the NAV was able to send back images of the ranch house without any interference. Either the occupants inside were innocent civilians or they were setting a trap by making it seem safe to check the premises. Ted wasn't falling for it.

"Sir, we see no sign of civilians on the premises. Shall we proceed to the house?" Staff Sergeant Williams spoke into the camera attached to his Oshkosh W-ATV assault vehicle.

Ted stared at the images of the ranch. The rails of the fence at the corrals had fallen and the barn doors were missing. The house itself was unpainted with several of the windows broken and boarded up. It was completely unkempt.

"Colonel, what do you want us to do here?"

"Stay put. I want to use the RCV to breach the house." Using the Robotic Combat Vehicle was something he aimed to use whenever there was a smidgen of a question about the safety of a situation where he was sending his troops. This was something he had the luxury to do, unlike other commanders in war like conditions.

Ted watched over the shoulders of the technicians as they transported the pictures from the RCV to the monitors in the communication vehicle. The robot showed white paint peeling away from the wood of the front door as it moved forward, smashing the doorknob, and pushing the door open. The inside showed light fixtures hanging from the ceiling with holes in the walls. The robot stopped at the edge of the living room and waited.

"Why have you stopped?" Ted asked the Specialist controlling the RCV.

"The unit senses something is wrong, and it is not safe to continue. I'll scan the area and see if I can tell what it is seeing. I can override and continue inside," stated the specialist.

"No, bring it back outside." Ted thought for a moment. "Sergeant Williams, you stay in place and have EOD Technicians sweep the house."

If the house was booby trapped it would tell him much about the plans of the people in command of the insurgents. Taking so much effort to deceive and harm his troops, while leading them on a wild goose hunt, meant only one thing, they were planning a major operation. If Shira and Christian's information about an attack on NORAD was correct, his time would be best served sweeping the areas closest to the complex at Cheyenne Mountain, within spitting distance of his office at Fort Carson.

Ted was cognizant to the fact that Deb was less than five-hundred kilometers south of his location preparing for, if not already in battle. The area he was asked to search for the insurgents was so vast that he needed to concentrate and condense his thinking. He decided to return to the task force communication center at the base and try to put it all together.

Hugo, Colorado

The population for the town of Hugo had remained the same since the turn of the century. Although less than a thousand people, the townsfolk were a hardy breed. The type of people who figured they could do anything, and nothing was out of the realm of possibility. The one thing they were wary of was scamming and scheming strangers, who they could identify with pinpoint precision. Thus, having Sheriff Bob and Ben along to try and convince them to admit Travis into their Community Hospital was an absolute necessity.

Sheriff Bob rode in the front seat of the Lisco vehicle, while Bill drove, and Sue held Travis' head in her lap in the back seat. Ben followed behind in his lumberyard truck, with Terrance and Irving as passengers. They stopped about five-hundred meters from a roadblock which consisted of trailers full of hay, tractors and even two bulldozers spanning across the main highway into the town. Sheriff Bob opened the front door of the car and stepped out. He put his cowboy hat on his head.

"I'm going to walk up here and see if I can reason with these folks." He could see several people at the roadblock, holding rifles. "I'm going to take it for granted that none of these yahoos are going to take a shot at me."

Ben pulled his truck up next to the car. He asked Terrance and Irving to get out.

"Hop in Bob. I've delivered a lot of material to these people, I'm sure they will recognize my truck." He reached over and pushed the door open. Bob jumped up and into the truck.

Ben proceeded slowly, allowing the ever-increasing crowd of people gathering on the outside of the roadblock a chance to see his truck insignia. When they were about twenty meters away, several armed guards moved in front of the crowd. Ben stopped the truck and both men exited.

"Is that you Bob?" A voice came from behind the initial group with rifles.

"Yeah, it sure is." He took his hat off and ran his fingers through his hair. "Who's asking?"

"Matt Holden." A short man with bright white hair moved around the people still holding their guns on the two men. "Put your damn rifles down. This is the sheriff from Limon."

Sheriff Bob limped forward. He knew Matt was the mayor. Ben followed him.

"You have this place pretty well fortified up," said Ben.

"Ben Stewart," said a woman standing next to Matt. "What are you two doing out and about, traveling on these dangerous roads?"

"We heard that Limon is almost a ghost town since they moved the FEMA camp east to Quinter," stated Matt.

"I haven't been there for a few days. We relocated out to the Lisco farm," Sheriff Bob sniffled. "It's what brought us here."

"We have a young fella that needs medical attention bad. He is in the car down the road." Ben pointed as he stared at the old lady. Although her face was familiar, he had a real problem remembering her name.

"We can't help you," said a large man in a camouflage jacket.

"If we had a dime for everyone who wants to use our hospital, we would be rich," said a young woman wearing a button-down shirt and jeans, standing next to the man in camouflage. They held hunting rifles, pointed straight up in the air.

Matt narrowed his eyes and glanced at the man and the young woman. He looked at them disapprovingly for several seconds. They both turned their heads and looked away. Although the townsfolk were most likely going to reject the request for medical help, the actions of the two youngsters was not the amiable way the mayor planned to do it.

"Listen Bob, we have denied many travelers over the past days the right to come into our town. If we don't, we will never survive this war. We only have so many resources here. Food is a problem."

"We are talking about the life of a very good, young man here." Bob turned his head and spit on the ground. "But none the less, we understand your need to protect your own. So, we have brought several packs of meat to pay for the medical services."

"If you take him in, we will bring half a beef more when someone comes from the Lisco farm to check on him," stated Ben.

"I think we can agree to those terms," the older lady stated quickly, looking at the mayor. "Just yesterday we sent a couple of trucks to Indianapolis to purchase food."

"Go ahead and bring the car up," Matt instructed as he took in a deep breath. "The truck we sent to Indiana takes about four days, round trip, and they only bring back nonperishable items. If you have extra beef, we can barter with you."

"You say you have the meat with you now." The older lady moved closer to Ben where he could see she had a chaw of tobacco in her lower lip.

"We do. Another thing though, the man's name is Travis, and his wife Sue is with him. She needs to stay too." Bob turned around and signaled to Bill.

"We will take care of them," said the older lady, swallowing loudly.

Both Ben and Sheriff Bob knew that they could take the lady at her word. If it was possible for Travis to survive his injury, he would now have the chance.

"Do you have enough coffee in the town?" Ben wanted to reward the people. It was an understanding, an unwritten rule, that many settlers and old farmers followed throughout the years, where one reciprocates friendliness, with kindness of their own.

"No, we sure don't. Coffee goes quickly around here," the man in the camouflage jacket stated.

"We are going to Limon after we leave here. If my store hasn't been ransacked, I will bring you back a sack."

Bill pulled up next to Bob and rolled down the window. Matt looked in the back seat at Sue.

"We'll pull the trailer out of the way, and you can follow us to the hospital." Matt made eye contact with Bill.

Sue started weeping as Bill drove through the barriers and onto the main street of the small town. The hospital was only a stone's throw away.

Limon, Colorado

The town of Limon was eerily quiet as Ben maneuvered the large truck toward his lumber yard store. There were many cars abandoned on the streets, and trash covered the chain length fence surrounding the abandoned FEMA camp. The wind howled loudly through the streets of the abandoned town.

Sheriff Bob stared at the broken windows and smashed in doors of the businesses along the main street. Since he and Judy relocated to the Lisco farm, he had been experiencing some guilt from having to abandon his post as sheriff. When he saw the looted businesses and ransacked homes in the town, he realized he could have never stopped the destruction, and most likely would have been killed.

Ben pulled the lumberyard truck into the parking lot of his store. The first thing he saw was the front door wide open, flapping in the wind. He drove through the parking lot, past a small shed, to the back of the building. Nearly his entire inventory was still there, neatly placed in the metal bins. All the framing lumber, drywall and roofing materials were untouched. He thought of all the time and energy he had spent over the years considering the different products he wanted to sell from the store. He even had some chicken feed.

"What should we load up?" Bill asked.

"I guess a little bit of everything. Jason told me he needs drywall, insulation, two-by-sixes, plywood, nails. and screws to start." Ben scratched the grey stubble on his chin. "We might as well take a full load, so whatever else you think they might need."

"I'll get the forklift and start loading." Terrance stepped up and into the seat of the large electric forklift.

"Bill, do you want to come with me and see if there is anything worth salvaging inside?"

The inside of the store was ravaged, with so much destruction that it was almost impossible to discern where the aisles once existed. Ben and Paula held major discussions on whether to sell groceries from the lumberyard store. After much debate they decided to sell a minimal number of foodstuffs, but now there wasn't a morsel of food left.

"Looks like they did a number on the inside." Bill glanced at the dejected store owner.

"I kind of expected it would be this way," Ben said softly as he stepped over the broken shelves, making his way toward the back. Bill followed him to a metal door.

"Looks like the thieves were too lazy to try and knock down the door to the cellar." Ben used a key to open the door. They both walked down the steps into the cold and musky smelling basement.

The storage area was much larger than Bill expected it to be, with nearly empty wood shelves covering the concrete walls. At the bottom of one shelf were several twenty-kilogram bags of coffee beans.

"We were two days away from a delivery of groceries when the war broke out. All we have down here is coffee beans."

"We might as well take them." Bill looked at the wrinkled face of the storeowner. He could see the strain in his eyes from witnessing the ruin of many years of sacrifice to his business. He placed a hand on his shoulder. "Sorry about all this Ben."

"Nothing we can do about it now," he sniffled, thinking how heartbroken Paula would be if she saw their life's work destroyed. "We just need to make the best of everything now."

West Colorado Springs

Deep in the basement of a large home, worth well over two million dollars, situated on a two and half acre wooded lot in the southwestern part of Colorado Springs, three large men and two buff women worked frantically to pack pieces of wire, tubes and explosives into three burdensome backpacks. Watching the rebels prepare the weapon, from the location only about five kilometers from the Fort Carson Army Base, were the three most sought-after people in America, Anastasia and Troy Vasilyeva, along with Mike Chen.

Off to the side, situated on the floor of the basement were five bright white Shanpa 1600 climate-controlled climbing suits. Two oddly shaped canisters sat next to the wall. Right next to the canisters were three FIM-92 shoulder launch weapons, with six infrared seeker missiles next to them.

"We will set the jammers on the 23rd." Mike Chen stepped near the canisters. His small frame made it easy for him to bend down. "Then on Christmas Day we fire the weapons."

"We need to have all the local rebels in place by Christmas Eve," stated Anastasia, flipping her hand at an annoying piece of hair that fell over her eyes.

"But not too soon. The rebels need to continue causing chaos in Denver and on the eastern plains." Mike made the statement in a thoughtful manner. He had the appearance of a schoolteacher or a pharmacist, more than that of a terrorist.

"We only have three EMP weapons left in this area. We can have some more transported from Louisiana." Troy ground his teeth and twisted his lip. His legs were thick, like his sisters, but his large, hawklike nose and dark complexion were much different from her smooth face and button nose.

"The phone towers and electrical grid are being replaced in the Denver area." Mike placed the canister back in its spot next to the wall. "Taking them out should be a priority."

"It won't be easy this time. There is no element of surprise," stated Anastasia.

"Do we care if we lose the rebels?" Troy glanced at his sister. His left eye was weaker than the other, a result of a punch when he was eleven years old.

"Yeah, I do care." She gave him an annoyed look. "We may need them to help with our escape back east, after the operation at NORAD."

"That's the only reason?"

"No, I do feel some accountability to them for their loyalty."

"Anastasia, you know as well as I do, when this is all over, things aren't going to end well for the American rebels. Most of them can't see past the end of their noses."

"What about us?" Anastasia turned her focus to Mike. "Are things going to end well for us?"

Mike caught her eyes and looked deeply into them. He blew off her question. He would allow her brother to explain the plan they devised for them to leave the country as very wealthy people.

"By the way. We need to leave Colorado immediately," Troy spoke firmly to his sister. "I mean like right now, this minute."

Anastasia gazed at the expressionless face of Mike Chen. Sensing she was being left out of some information she should be privy to, she decided to not question the need for them to leave. But she did want to know where they would be going.

"Where do you want to go?"

"Atlanta, Georgia." Troy shot a glance at Mike, who remained expressionless. "I want to leave here within the next half hour."

"Are you coming with us Mike?" Anastasia asked.

"No."

"He has business in central New Mexico," Troy said with a sneaky expression on his face.

"What's going on here. Why am I being left out of this?" Anastasia had a feeling the attack on NORAD was only a ruse. Now, she was positive it was. "Is there something bigger planned I don't know about?"

"You need to get going. Your transportation will take you to Aurora, but you must walk from there," Mike stated. He made it obvious he wasn't going to talk any more about his planned operation.

"We have to walk."

"It's the only way out of Colorado for us," Troy said, "so we better get going."

Colorado Farm

The sounds of people busy working on the new building filled the air at the farm. The Jacobys wasted no time in traveling to the Robert's farm to retrieve their two dairy cows. Irene understood the value of having fresh milk available daily. There were still two pallets of dry cereal in the warehouse, and everyone was becoming tired of eating it with powdered milk.

Nicole, Jacqueline, Gina, Irene and Breanna sat at the kitchen table drinking coffee, discussing the best way to feed the multitude of people. Jerry was at the stove watching over four large frying pans full of hamburger, sizzling and crackling. Off to the side, Glenda Hernandez and the new arrival, Odette, worked cutting onions, and opening cans of tomatoes and beans to be placed in the large pots used for cooking chili.

"Deb made it clear, before we arrived, that the food we have could sustain a hundred people for three months," stated Jacqueline.

"Even with the people who left this morning with the Roberts, there are still over a hundred people here," replied Nicole.

"Let's get an inventory of all the food we have stockpiled, so we know exactly where we stand." Gina stared at her two sisters-in-law. Just like her, neither of them wore make-up, and the grey had spread to cover most of their hair. They looked much different than they did six weeks earlier, with sun chaffed skin covering their faces. Especially Nicole, who before, always had a flavor of sophistication to her appearance. They were slowly turning into prototypical country women.

"Everyone working on the building deserves to be fed well," said Irene.

"They really are working hard, and fast," stated Jacqueline.

"There is a group of about twenty-five people who haven't lifted a hand to help around here. Most of them just lay around in the warehouse and sleep all day. I asked them this morning if there was someone willing to help me with cleaning out the horse stalls. They looked at me like I was some sort of leper." Breanna shook her head and looked from woman to woman. "They shouldn't get one bite to eat."

"Breanna, stop being so judgmental, please." Irene glanced at the other women to see how they were reacting to her daughter's disparaging remarks.

"Has anyone checked to see if they are able to help?" asked Gina.

"I don't plan on going back in there. The damn people look like they have every disease known to mankind," Breanna groaned.

"We should check on them," stated Gina, glancing at Nicole and Jacqueline to see their reaction to Breanna's tirade. The glimpse didn't go unnoticed by Irene.

Bobby and Emilee entered the front door and quickly came into the kitchen. They were covered in cement. "Are there some snacks we can get for the workers?" Bobby went straight to Jerry. He sensed there was something bothering the group. "What's going on?"

"We were just talking about those freeloaders in the warehouse." Breanna stood up from her chair. She closed her mouth tightly, making her chinless face seem to have no features at all.

"Come on, Breanna, you need to stop being so nasty," Irene said forcefully, "you have no idea about their circumstance, they might need help."

"Mom, I am who I am. I'm not going to hold back saying what I feel is right."

"Well, sometimes you need to have a filter."

Bobby glanced at Emilee. That morning they witnessed some of the people eating a bag of frozen food from one of the freezers in the warehouse. He figured with Breanna's state of mind he would wait until later to mention it to his mother. He looked toward Jerry.

"Bobby, I don't have anything this morning that would work for a snack, but if Irene will help me, we can make some peanut butter bars for this afternoon." Jerry looked toward Irene.

"Let's get the young kids to help. I told Maddy and Scotty they could help the next time we baked." Irene smiled at Jerry before turning back to Breanna. It bothered her greatly that her daughter was being so insensitive. "Breanna, we need to treat others how we would like them to treat us."

Breanna grunted.

"We'll let everyone know they have to wait until lunchtime to get something to eat." Bobby motioned with his head to Emilee, letting her know he didn't want to partake in the conversation.

Outside, the breeze had picked up, causing the wind chill to be near freezing. Although there was a chance the mortar might freeze, Harold never stopped building. He had help with laying block from two of the new arrivals familiar with masonry. He had them use the trowels to spread the wall with mortar while he lay the block right behind them.

Bobby proceeded from the warm kitchen straight to the mortar mixer where Sherry and Caroline were busy mixing cement. Sherry's swollen lip and large purplish bump under her right eye were now covered with a layer of cement blown from the heavy bags as she lifted them onto the grate of the mixer.

"Take a break Sherry. You still have a concussion." Bobby shouldered her away and picked up a large bag of cement. He tossed it onto the mixer and used the sharp edge of the shovel to cut the bag, creating a cloud of cement dust that propelled high in the air, which was swiftly swept away into the wind. "Me, Caroline, and Emilee can keep up with Harold. If we can't, we will get Dave or some of the football players to help."

Sherry looked at him with irritated, red eyes. She had been experiencing spells of dizziness whenever she lifted a heavy bag of cement, and realized that Bobby was right, she should rest. It was just that her adrenaline was so high, she couldn't relax. The next time she came face to face with the men who attacked her and Caroline, she would be prepared. She was planning on going to search for the tyrants, with or without help. She sat down on a half pallet of cement.

Two concrete mixers were running at the same time, along with the mortar mixer, creating so much noise that it was nearly impossible to hear someone speak. The workers pushing the wheelbarrows never had a chance to rest as they quickly filled the outer trench of the monolithic pour. Harold had begun laying and leveling the concrete block as soon as the northern edge of the building was poured. He had three courses of block laid before nightfall the day before. Now he and his helpers were working on scaffolding, with the idea of having the block wall built well before the end of the day. They left an opening in the wall for the fireplace and hoped to remove the scaffold before nightfall, in order to begin the chimney early in the morning.

Jason Jensen's crew of carpenters had the west and southern walls framed. He himself was designing and laying out the trusses, using the available wood to build them, as others framed the east wall. He was happy to have many experienced carpenters and, for the first time since starting the project, believed that they would have the entire building ready to use by New Year.

Jon walked across the farm grounds, unnoticed by Sherry and tapped her on the shoulder with the back of his hand. When she turned, he motioned for her to follow him, he began walking in the direction of the garage. When they were away from the noise of the cement mixers, he spoke as they walked, "our drone uncovered a group of people about fifteen kilometers southwest of here. We think the two who attacked you might be with them."

"Are we ready to go get them?" The color of her hair was hard to distinguish with so much cement matting it down.

"I have a call in to Ted. This might be something he can help us with."

Jon glanced at her as they strolled toward Ted's office.

Sherry walked quickly in front him. She turned and began walking backward, trying to look directly into his eyes. "I want you to show me how to fire a fifty-caliber rifle."

He didn't give her an answer, just kept on walking. He held a soft spot in his heart for the hardened, young woman. The way she looked at him immediately after being attacked and severely beaten, was imprinted in his mind. After he came running to where she was assaulted, her eyes stayed transfixed on him, even though Jacqueline and others were the ones administering aid, her eyes were on him. She trusted him, and he was not about to abuse her trust. He stopped walking.

"I want you to go get cleaned up first. Then come to Ted's office. I should have a plan formulated on how we are going after these guys."

She took in a deep breath, and paused, as if she had something to say. She released the breath, then turned and walked away.

Sherry's hardnosed attitude of refusing to be knocked down without a fight reminded him of his sister Deb. When they were children, she always refused to lose, but at the same time would look for approval from her two older brothers. He and Ted, often from orders of their father, would never allow her to win undeservedly. When she did defeat one of her brothers at a game, she would look for acknowledgement, with her big eyes transfixed into theirs. It was this same brotherly love he gave to his sister that he planned to show Sherry.

La Cienega, New Mexico

"Ma'am, we lost visual with the forward platoon." Captain Dodson approached Deb.

"Do we have good pictures from the main body?" Deb followed the captain to the monitors.

"Yes ma'am. We are getting some interference, but the pictures are vivid."

Deb looked around the room at the more than thirty different specialists and technicians working in the communication center. The soldiers not in front of a monitor were busy communicating with different aspects of her brigade. Each one of them held a specific task. It was her job to discern the important information from the negligible material and make decisions accordingly.

"We have enemy fire," yelled a specialist from a monitor at the front of the room.

Deb hurried to the monitor.

"Turn up the volume." The sound of gunfire could be heard as the image on the screen displayed an area of rolling hills, cactus, and boulders with no visible signs of the enemy.

"Is this 2nd Platoon?" Command Sergeant Major Talfoya asked.

"Yes," stated the technician at the monitor.

A Light Armored Vehicle sped into the picture and began firing in front of the camera transmitting from the helmet of the soldier from 2nd Platoon.

"We have more fighting with 3rd Platoon just east of 2nd Platoon's location."

"Ma'am, we have visual on a large force of enemy emerging into the area."

For the first time Deb caught a glimpse of the Korean Special Forces. They were dressed in all white, with cone shaped helmets, like something a bike racer would be wearing. In the distance, behind the enemy troops could be seen several vehicles that looked like dune-buggies, moving rapidly over the rough terrain.

All screens were now full of battles. The constant chatter from within the communication center was kept at a consistent volume, where every transmission could be discernable by the soldier receiving the broadcast. Captain Dodson's communication center was professional and efficient, something Deb only expected.

The voices from the commanding officers were intense, and clear, as they ordered the tanks and Light Armored Vehicles forward. Captain Singh's request for an Armored Combat Earthmover to be used at the battle sight seemed unusual, causing Deb to squeeze her lips together, and glance at Command Sergeant Major Talfoya. He shrugged his shoulder.

"Colonel Lisco, I have General Lauer online." stated a specialist.

Deb moved in front of the monitor where the General's face took up most of the screen. He began speaking the moment she moved in front of the monitor.

"Colonel, have 2nd Battalion begin their operation."

"Already, sir." Deb scoffed. The original plan was for Josh to move in the dead of night after the attack was well established.

"Immediately."

"Yes sir. One other thing, General. I want to make a request to have a missile fired into the Sandia Peak area at 2200."

There was silence and Deb could see General Lauer's chin raise into the air as he leaned back.

"Sir, I have eyes on the area and would like to see where the interceptors are located. Also, if we can bring them out into the open, I believe we will be close enough to get a good description of what they look like, and how they are transported." Deb folded her hands and waited for a response from the general.

"At 2200 unless otherwise notified. Now put 2nd Battalion in motion." The image on the screen went blank. She turned to Lt. Col. Woodworth.

"Josh, I thought we had a little more time here."

"We are prepared to deploy."

"Josh, I want you all the way past Interstate 40 by 2200."

"Yes ma'am."

"After you arrive, have Captain Hendersen and F Company position back here."

A glimpse of Command Sergeant Major Talfoya, as Lt. Col. Woodworth left, prompted Deb to the fact that Tommy had been left completely out of her and General Lauer's plans. There was some explaining to do, and he didn't look happy about the situation.

Colorado Farm

Sherry's blonde hair was still wet when she entered the garage office, with the bruises on her face being much more noticeable without the cement coating. The old scar on her cheek she had received in the tower when the bullet hit the concrete block was red and protruding slightly out. Another thing Jon noticed for the first time was a large purple bruise on the inside of her left wrist, which she must have sustained from blocking punches during the attack. The sight of the discoloration made Jon even more adamant about bringing her assailants to justice.

"The lumberyard truck, with the car right behind it, just pulled onto the driveway," Sherry stated as she joined Jon and Gina at the computer on Ted's desk. "It looks like it has a really big load."

"That is good," said Gina. "We were all worried they might run into trouble."

"Come sit by me," Jon patted a chair to the side of the computer. "The lieutenant in Ted's office at the base just told us he will be available to talk in just a moment."

"Are you feeling, okay?" Gina looked closely at the roughness of Sherry's puffed-up lower lip, and her eye that was swollen nearly shut.

"I'm feeling pretty good." She didn't mention her dizzy spells.

"I have some lip balm you can use, if you like. Please let us know if you need anything at all." Gina could see Ted on the screen.

"Ted, I have Gina and Sherry here with me," stated Jon.

"Is everything okay Jon?" Ted looked refreshed. The skin on his face appeared taut, especially around his eyes, making him look young.

"We had a problem with a couple of the rebels coming to the farm. When we put up the drone to follow them, we found a group of insurgents about fifteen kilometers southwest of our location." Jon decided not to go into detail about Sherry being the one they attacked.

"When I came out to the farm a couple weeks ago with Jessica, we were stopped by a band of insurgents on the county road. I wonder if these might be the same ones?"

"Could be," said Jon.

"I have a NAV sending us pictures from a location north of the farm. I can have it make a pass over the area to see if it can capture images of the group to the south. Give me a moment and I will be right back." Ted moved away from the screen.

"I'm going to go out and see if Bill had any luck with getting Travis admitted into the hospital," said Gina.

"Let us know." Jon acknowledged Gina before returning his gaze to the screen.

Just as Gina left through the door, Ted came back online.

"The Nonhuman Aerial Vehicle will take a few minutes to arrive at the site to make the pass over."

"Have you heard from Deb?" Jon asked.

"Not firsthand." There was a tenseness in Ted's voice. "There is major fighting taking place in New Mexico where her brigade is at now."

"Will you let us know whenever you hear any updates."

"Of course, I will. You said that Sherry is there with you."

Sherry moved over in front of the computer's camera. "Hello Colonel Lisco."

"Sherry, I have a question to ask you." Ted could barely see her on his screen. "When you were with the rebels before all this started, how well did you know Christian?"

"Sort of well. He was older but we had somewhat of a bond because we went to the same high school. After I graduated, we spent a lot of time together."

"How about Shira Rosenfeld?"

"About the same, I guess. Christian and her were always arguing over politics. I thought they would hook up, but Shira had her eyes on another guy with more clout in the insurgency than Christian did. It always put Christian in a bad mood when he came around."

"Do you remember any of the names?" Ted noticed the bruises on Sherry's face.

"I don't. Tim was the person I was around most. Probably because we were closer in age."

"I noticed when Christian and Shira were at the farm you hardly spoke to them."

"I suppose I avoided them because I want to wash my hands of all the rebels. I should have never got involved with them in the first place, and I never want to go back."

"Do you remember the name of Shira's boyfriend?"

"Oh, let me think." She narrowed her eyes and looked off to the side, then turned back quickly. "Troy, his name was Troy."

"Do you remember his last name?"

"No."

"What did he look like?"

"Normal, I guess. He had big legs." Sherry gazed into the monitor and her left eye opened wide, with her right eye remaining nearly shut. "Oh yeah, his nose was kind of crooked."

"Did you ever meet his sister Anastasia?"

"I don't remember seeing her, but I know that Christian met with her several times. Troy and his sister were around quite a bit during the last month before the war started, when everything became so secretive. They gave us our orders."

"Thank you, Sherry." Ted looked away to another screen. "It looks like we have pictures coming in from the drone southwest of the farm."

"Is there a group of people traveling on the road."

"They must have left; we aren't picking up anyone on the roads. It looks like we do have a lot of people at a farmhouse about eight kilometers further south."

"I'll bet it is them."

"Jon, I have to go now, I have a meeting with the FBI task force in less than twenty minutes. I'll let you know when I can come your way." Ted left the screen.

Jon looked at Sherry, who was sitting on the edge of the chair with her back perfectly straight. It was a shame that she took the path in life that led her to the insurgency. She held so many redeeming qualities that would have made her successful had she been mentored in the right direction.

****

Hank and Jacqueline sat on the hearth of the fireplace, with a pad and pencil, making notes for a meeting he called for five pm that afternoon. Many more people wanted to leave the farm to go back east with the Robert's group than could fit in their vehicles. After speaking with Bill, when he came back from Limon and Hugo, Hank figured he had a solution to the problem.

George Saxton made it clear that circumstances in the city were very dire. So, either people need to stay put on the farm, or find a way back east. With the food situation approaching a crisis level, maybe both problems could be solved at the same time. If the people of Hugo were sending trucks to Indianapolis for food, then the Liscos could do the same. Load up people who wanted to leave into the lumberyard truck, and drive them to Indiana, and bring back supplies.

"We better make sure Ben and Paula are good with us using the truck," stated Jacqueline.

"This is just an idea. We have a lot of details to hammer out." Hank took in a deep breath as he leaned in next to Jacqueline's neck. "Do you have a new lotion? It smells good."

"I ran out of body lotion and Gina gave me some of hers."

"If we can pull this off, we can get shampoo, toothpaste and all the basic items, besides food." Hank stood up.

"Irene told me that Ed has been out of his heart medication for a couple of days now. They are so considerate of others that they never mentioned it." Jacqueline was happy to see her husband back to being a planner again. He could offer so much to everyone if he could regain the confidence he had when he coached.

"If Ben is good with us using the truck, we will have everyone give us a list of needs."

"Another question, who is going to go on the trip? If we send three people, they all need to be good drivers." Jacqueline looked out the picture window. "I see Bill and Jon with a group already gathering."

"Isn't it odd that we haven't seen Samantha and Bill together for quite some time?" Hank asked.

"That is something we should keep our noses out of." Jacqueline slipped her coat over her shoulder.

Hank and Jacqueline stepped out onto the front porch where they saw a bright red sunset. The sound of hammers pounding slowly dwindled to where there was only one or two, finally stopping, like popping from a bag of popcorn. Hank considered starting the meeting earlier because of cold and darkness, but with the construction taking place at a frantic pace, he decided on five o'clock.

Jon and Bill were just outside the fence surrounding the yard, facing a crowd of people spanning an area almost all the way to the garage. A few of the workers were still making their way to the meeting from the construction site. Ben Stewart and Paula were standing next to Sheriff Bob and his wife Judy next to the fence. Hank strolled across the yard in the direction of the store owner.

"Ben, I have an important request to make of you." Hank leaned over the fence.

"What might that be?" Ben stepped closer. He and Paula were bundled with heavy coats pulled up tight to their necks.

"Can we use your truck to go to Indianapolis for supplies?" Hank hesitated, unable to read the stoic look he was getting back from Ben. "We heard that the people of Hugo were sending a truck to Indianapolis for supplies. I was just thinking it would solve a lot of problems if we did the same."

"Who would drive?"

"We haven't thought that far ahead. I wanted to check with you first before we began planning the trip."

"I guess we don't care," he looked at Paula.

"I certainly don't care," she shook her head.

"I know one thing. I don't want to drive all the way to Indianapolis," stated Ben.

Hank listened in as Bill and Jon tried their best to inform the crowd about food supplies and expectations. The new arrivals were all vocal and disruptive, with many of them upset from not being chosen to leave with the Robert's group. Breanna Jacoby was not about to let the new people disrespect the Lisco family. Much to the chagrin of Irene, she left nothing back in letting the newcomers know how she felt.

"You are a bunch of lazy freeloaders who would rather lay around drinking from your bottle of whiskey than lift a hand to help anyone," Breanna turned to face the assembly, and yelled at the top of her lungs. "If you don't like it, nobody is going to keep you worthless people from leaving."

She was standing next to Patrick and his wife Odette as several insults were thrown her way.

"Hey now, let's not get so bloody personal here," Patrick yelled back at the crowd. Insults were hurled toward him, many disparaging his size.

"Stop with the nasty remarks," Jon yelled to no avail. He turned to Bill. "What shall we do here?"

"I guess let them yell until they get tired of yelling." Bill turned to Hank. "What do you think coach?"

"I just spoke with Ben Stewart and asked him if he was willing to let us use his truck to take a load of people to Indianapolis, and then bring back supplies," Hank spoke loudly. "He agreed to the use of his truck. So, tell them we will transport some of them east."

"Listen everyone, listen!" Jon moved closer to the throng of disgruntled people. Bill, Hank and the Jacoby children, led by Seth, followed him. "We have a truck that is going to go back east, first thing in the morning."

"It is going to be an uncomfortable ride for twenty-four hours, but we want those of you being so vocal tonight on the truck." Bill didn't ask them if they wanted to leave or not. He was fed up with the angry newcomers. It was time to rid the farm of the complainers.

"You people pack. We will load all your belongings on the truck this evening and leave at daybreak," Hank yelled before turning to Bill. "Are we good with that?"

"I'm absolutely good with that timeframe," replied Bill.

"Wonder if we don't want to go to Indianapolis? My family is in Cleveland." A large man yelled.

"You can get off at any time, but the truck itself is going to Indiana," Jon yelled back.

"We can live with leaving the first thing in the morning," yelled another man. "As long as we don't have to listen to that fat cow up there anymore."

Jon knew that all hell was about to break loose when he saw Arthur Jacoby's jaw drop, and he made eye contact with his brother Seth. The flood gates opened as the Jacoby children charged in the direction of the men who had been cursing at their Aunt Breanna. Nothing was held back as the two sides fought.

Jon tipped his head to Bill and Hank, indicating that the fighting was out of their control, and it was time to go inside.

Fort Carson, FBI Central Command Center

Before Ted was even halfway into the large room being used by the FBI Task Force, he was ambushed by Lieutenant Siegman carrying two large envelopes. People were scurrying from one station to another, in what appeared to be total chaos.

"Colonel, these were left for you by Special Agent Elder. He just left." The lieutenant handed him the envelopes.

"Has it stayed this busy in here since I left?"

"Yes sir, it has been nonstop craziness." Lieutenant Siegman smiled at Ted.

"Did Special Agent Elder give you this personally?" Ted held up the envelope.

"Yes sir."

"I'll be in my office for the next couple of hours."

Ted tossed the envelope onto his desk. After the breach of the house where Anastasia was last seen, he wondered why the CIA men wanted to keep Shira with them. They obviously knew about her connection with the Vasilyeva's. He now wanted to do a little more investigating before he discussed the situation with the members of his own task force. Deception and pretense were tools used by the intelligence services. In a time where data driven models were manipulated to make major decisions, having knowledge and information were the only way he could protect his soldier's interests.

He sat down at his desk and opened the envelope and slid the contents out on his desk. Six pages of typing paper filled with addresses fell out onto a map of Colorado. The map was full of red x's. At the top of the first page of addresses was a handwritten note that said, "These might help you narrow the search of agricultural land, ranches, and farms. All are foreign owned with the red x signifying Russian or Chinese entities that were purchased within the last thirty years."

He rose from his chair and leaned over his desk, scanning the map for all locations nearest the Lisco family farm. Three red x's were within a forty-kilometer radius of the farm, with one of them being the farm he just surveilled with the NAV. He folded the map, pushed it to the side, and picked up the second envelope. He cut the top and poured the contents on his desk.

Three pictures fell out, along with a post-it size note. The note stated, "Anastasia and Troy Vasilyeva and Mike Chen."

He stared at the photographs, wondering if the CIA operatives he was working with would tell him about the connection between Shira and the Vasilyeva's. It would be something he would have to get from them, on his own terms.

The last item he examined was a copy of a ripped piece of notebook paper with two sets of numbers, 5220326 and 36144386 with the 6's at the end of both numbers being partially torn, making it likely there were more numbers to follow. He rubbed his chin, figuring the numbers were telephone numbers with area codes 361 and 522. At the very bottom of the paper was the name Marlee Proctor.

La Cienega, New Mexico

Deb stepped outside the communication tent as a cool breeze hit the side of her face. Scattered clouds dotted the sky of bright stars. The sounds filled the air of trucks moving and helicopters flying to the battle over forty kilometers south of her position at 2nd Brigade Headquarters. She took in a breath through her nose as she heard Tommy approaching from the back. She turned when he reached her and gave him a closed mouth smile.

"I'm sorry Tommy that I haven't ran more of this plan by you."

"I am a bit confused why you have left me out on many of the decisions." It was uncharacteristic for the command sergeant major to be so blunt.

"General Lauer has been much more demanding in the tactics we are using than I thought he would be." Deb looked at his deep eyes, and tanned face. "Josh, Loyd and Teresa all want to have a say too. I guess I didn't want to have another voice telling me not to do something."

"I never thought of myself as being another voice." Command Sergeant Major Talfoya stepped in front of her, standing uncomfortably close.

"You're not." She placed her right hand on his shoulder. "I'm really going to need you these next few days. I'll do better with keeping you informed."

"Deb, how are we going to penetrate this enemies' defenses? They are using so many new age weapons and jammers that I can't figure out how to counter them."

"General Lauer has sent three more Special Force teams to try and penetrate their lines. They are moving up on the Albuquerque side of the zone as we speak," Colonel Lisco sighed. "We are hoping they will be able to take out some of their weapons."

"What is the Special Forces objective?"

"Same as ours. To destroy the jammers and interceptors." She pulled the collar of her light jacket tight around her neck.

"Colonel Lisco, Lieutenant Colonel Barnet is online." Captain Dodson yelled from the door of the communication tent. "The fighting has escalated. We are receiving reports of massive casualties."

Captain Dodson directed Colonel Lisco and Command Sergeant Major Talfoya to the monitor displaying Lt. Col. Barnet.

"Colonel, we have encountered a large force, and have two of the forward platoons from E Company trapped in a ravine about three kilometers southwest of the main body of 1st Battalion." Lt. Col. Barnet had his helmet on as he spoke into the screen. "The terrain is so damn rough, with deep gorges, we can't advance our tanks any further."

"Do the North Korean's have tanks of their own?" Command Sergeant Major Talfoya asked.

"None that we have encountered, Tommy. But they have new age tank stoppers that I have never seen before."

"We have Special Forces teams in the area of the forward platoons who might be of assistance," Colonel Lisco stated.

"Any help we can get will be appreciated. They have been able to call in coordinates for us to use the cannons to keep the enemy from swarming them. Captain Singh is trying to fight his way to their location, but with the rough terrain there is no way to reach them tonight. Their ammunition is going to run out quickly."

"Are you able to use the RCV's?" Colonel Lisco asked.

"We tried, but they were jammed. This place has so many types of electromagnetic and directed energy weapons that you can almost feel the electricity in the air. They are using kinetic energy interceptors to protect their forces against our artillery."

"Loyd, where are you at now?" Command Sergeant Major Talfoya stood shoulder to shoulder with Colonel Lisco.

"I am in C Companys communication vehicle approximately 200 meters north of the ten-kilometer mark we established as a stopping point for artillery, just west of highway 165."

"So, you have divisional artillery and cannons in front of you?" Command Sergeant Major Talfoya asked.

"Yes, aspects of E Company are the only parts of 1st Battalion remaining to our rear." Lt. Col. Barnet answered.

"Loyd, I can't emphasize enough to you that you need to protect your flank, you are especially vulnerable from the west."

"We are about to launch a missile to help us locate the interceptors. We anticipate you will witness a major light show." Colonel Lisco raised her jaw as she stared into the monitor.

"Colonel, this is going to be very slow going if we don't figure a way to penetrate their weaponry. Without air support it will be difficult for us to advance."

"Can you step outside and describe what you see when the laser interceptor takes out the missile. It should be happening within the minute."

Images from the Lt. Col. Barnet's helmet camera showed the vapor trail of the probing missile in the night sky several kilometers to the north as it made its way toward Sandia Mountain. The intense, bright light of the lasers struck out like a diamond back rattlesnake, hitting the unarmed missile, blowing it to pieces.

"Oh, my God." Colonel Lisco's mouth was wide open as she turned to Command Sergeant Major Talfoya. "That was even more powerful than the lasers at the warehouse in Montana."

"Colonel, it was as though they shot a large lightning bolt at the missile," said Lt. Col. Barnet. "Now I understand why we can't get air support. I don't know how far away the missile was when it was intercepted, but it was a long way from our position."

"Did you get a location on the laser?" Colonel Lisco was breathing hard and pinched her lower lip.

"Deb, it was so bright that I have no idea, but I'm sure tech has a bearing on it."

"Loyd, let us know what we can do to assist you." Colonel Lisco moved away from the monitor. She rubbed deeply into her right eye, before placing her hand on her chin.

"What are you thinking?" Tommy asked.

"Can you get me in touch with General Prost?"

"It's after midnight back east."

I need to speak with her immediately."

"Okay, I'll wake her." Tommy swallowed hard before approaching Captain Dodson.

Colorado Farm

The living room was packed. Bill wanted only a select few to help him make the decisions pertaining to the farm. His aunts and uncles, along with Bobby were summoned to the kitchen. He allowed everyone to sit at the table, while he remained standing.

"We have a lot of questions we need to have answered." Bill's right eye twitched as he leaned his right arm on the kitchen counter. "First and foremost, we need to figure out who we are going to ask to drive the truck."

"As defiant as these people are, we have to consider that they might try and steal the truck," stated Gina.

"How many drivers do we need?" Jacqueline asked, looking at Jon.

"I'm thinking three. They can trade off driving." Jon tipped his head slightly in the direction of the living room where Patrick's booming voice overflowed into the kitchen.

"As dangerous a drive as this is, not only from the disruptive people we have here, but from strangers on the road, we should have a couple of armed guards following in our car." Nicole looked directly at Bill. "We need Ted involved; he might be able to assist with one of the army convoys traveling east on the Interstate."

"It is kind of risky sending a car, there is a chance we could have it highjacked. But, on the other hand, we should protect the truck the best we can. The supplies they bring back are vitally important to our survival, so I'm good with having a car follow," stated Jon.

"That means more people will need to go." Hank looked from person to person.

"I'll go," said Bobby, seeing his mother's jaw drop. "Me, Von and Emilee can follow in the car."

"That is not going to happen." Jacqueline's chest was noticeably rising and falling. "Bobby, I realize you have matured over the past couple months, but you and Emilee are still high school kids."

"Mom, we have to do our part, the same as everyone else. In a few months we will most likely be drafted into the service."

Bobby avoided his father's eyes and turned to his cousin. "Bill, why don't you ask Terrance, Irving and Seth Jacoby if they will drive the truck? They all have military experience."

"The Jacobys just got done beating the shit out of half the people we are going to be hauling, I don't know if that will be a good idea having Seth travel with them." Jon shook his head.

"Maybe they will think twice about messing with him," said Hank.

Bobby smiled, knowing that his father decided not to argue with his idea of going on the trip. Jacqueline was still glaring at him.

"We need to speak with the three of them to confirm that they are willing to leave on such a short notice." Bill looked at Hank. "Coach, can you take care of it?"

"Since Irving and Terrance are in the living room, I will check with them, if you want to try and find Seth." Jon placed a hand on Hank's shoulder.

"Bobby, you better go and prepare for the trip." Bill placed his lower lip over his upper and nodded to his cousin.

"There is something else we should discuss," interrupted Nicole. "Besides all the new arrivals who were making such a stink tonight, how many of the people who have been here for a long time want to leave. We are taking it for granted that everyone wants to remain here."

"That is such a good point Nicole," stated Gina. "Julia is a good example. When we first met the Hamilton's along the side of the road, taking care of Caroline, they were on their way to be with their son and grandchild at a small town north of St. Louis. We need to check with everyone to see who wants to be here now that we can offer them an option."

"Caroline was on her way to Savanna Georgia." Jon rose from his seat at the table.

"We can let everyone know that they have an option," Hank replied.

"I agree, but let's let them know that we will have a lot more information about the state of affairs and living conditions back east when the truck returns." Bill moved away from the counter, as everyone rose from the table.

"Wait a second. We are missing something important." Nicole held up her hand. "How are we going to pay for all the supplies. If there is a semblance of normalcy in Indiana, then they are not going to just give us the supplies."

"Another good point Nicole," stated Gina, looking from Jon to Bill.

"We have the cash." The lines on Bills face deepened. "No matter the cost, we have enough money."

"I want to speak with Julia." Nicole went to her son's side. "We should give her an opportunity to leave if she wants."

Bill nodded to his mother. She walked out of the kitchen to the closed door of the clinic and knocked. After the death of Fred, Julia began sleeping in the clinic. As Nicole waited for the physician assistant to answer, she noticed several people gawking at her from the living room, including Harold and Becky.

Julia opened the door, wearing a large tee-shirt, and baggy shorts. She shifted back and allowed Nicole to enter. After nearly five minutes the door opened, and Nicole took a step into the living room to try and get the attention of Becky and Harold. When they spotted her waving to them, they went to the clinic and followed her inside.

"The Lisco's are sending a truck back to Indianapolis to try and get more food and supplies. The truck will travel right by Michael's home in Maryville." Julia looked directly at Harold. "They said we can catch a ride on it if we want."

"When are they leaving?" Becky asked.

"At daybreak," answered Nicole, noticing Harold take in a deep breath and release it.

"I understand that I am needed badly here, but I need to know that my son and his family are okay." Julia continued to look directly at Harold. "I was the one who insisted we come here in the first place."

"Julia, we all made the decision. Considering that our car barely made it the forty kilometers from where Jon and Gina met us, we would have been stranded. Finding this place was a Godsend." Harold stared at the smooth skin of his forty-two-year-old sister-in-law's face. He remembered back to when Fred first told him he was going to marry the eighteen-year-old college freshman. His brother was nine years her senior and working as an accountant at the University of Colorado in Boulder.

"This is a time where you need to make the best choice for yourself." Becky glanced at Harold and placed a hand on Julia's shoulder.

"If I go, are you two going to stay?" Julia placed her hand over Becky's hand and looked at Harold.

"Yes," Harold answered quickly, "at least until construction on the building is completed."

"We have settled in here," said Becky, stepping back from her sister-in-law.

"Another option," Nicole interjected, "is for you to wait and find out the situation east of here. If you feel like you want to go, you can catch a ride on the truck when we send for more supplies."

"That could be several months from now."

"It most likely would be."

"Who is going to drive the truck in the morning?" Julia brought her right hand up to pinch the loose skin below her chin.

"Terrance, Irving and Seth Jacoby are going to take turns driving the truck, with Bobby, Emilee and Von following behind in the SUV. They will take close to thirty people with them." Nicole waited for a moment to allow Julia to process the situation before stating, "if you go, you can ride with Bobby and his group."

"I don't know. I want to find out if Michael, Beth Ann and the baby are okay."

"Would Bobby take the time to stop by Michael's home, if we gave him the address and a map?" Harold asked Nicole. He made a great connection with Bobby and Emilee when they worked together on the block walls. "I would trust Bobby to make every effort possible to find Michael."

"How far off the road do they live?" Nicole asked, noticing moistness in Julia's eyes.

"They live right on Interstate 70 just outside St. louis. It's on the way to Indianapolis." Julia flicked a finger over the inside corner of her left eye. "If Bobby will agree to try and convince Michael to come back with him, I'll stay here."

"I'm sure Bobby will do everything in his power to do what you ask," stated Nicole.

"Should we have Bobby tell Michael about the death of Fred?" Harold asked.

"I don't want him traveling all the way here without knowing. So, yes, he should tell him." For the first time since the death of her husband Julia felt a great sense of hope. She smiled with a tear leaking from her brown eye.

La Cienega, New Mexico

"We have contact with General Prost." Tommy motioned Colonel Lisco toward a monitor where Captain Dodson was standing behind a chair.

"She will be on momentarily," stated Captain Dodson, pulling the seat out for the colonel to sit.

"Colonel Lisco, what is going on?" General Prost's eyes were red, and her hair was tied over her head.

"I'm sorry General for waking you, but I have an urgent request that I believe only you can handle."

"Shoot."

"I need some of the REMP weapons that the insurgents have been using to cause havoc in our cities." The Colonel continued to use the term radical which she attached to the Electromagnet Pulse Weapons the first time she met the general.

"Almost all of them that we have in our possession have been discharged. The last I heard research and development were asking for some that had not been fired." The general pushed her top teeth out and crinkled her nose as she stared into the monitor.

"The last time we spoke you mentioned that you uncovered several weapons from the insurgents' warehouses across the country." Deb stared at the mousey little woman who was adjusting her eyes to the bright screen.

"There are three weapons per box, and the ones we have found at various locations have been in unopened containers." General Prost took in a deep breath and released it. "I'll do what I can Colonel to find you some of the weapons."

"Thank you, ma'am. I don't want to be pushy, but time is of the essence. We are in a tough situation, and I need the REMP weapons immediately."

"Okay Colonel." General Prost almost laughed from Colonel Lisco stating she didn't want to be pushy after calling her in the middle of the night. "Give me a few minutes and I will see what I can do. Hang tight and I will be right back."

Colonel Lisco could feel Command Sergeant Major Talfoya's hand on the back of the chair as she leaned back in the seat. She knew it would take some time before she would hear from General Prost, but she didn't want to take her eyes off the screen.

"Colonel, Lt. Col. Wilson is asking for you," Captain Dodson pointed to a monitor to the right of her.

"Tommy, can you check with Teresa?" She twisted her neck to look back.

"Yes ma'am." The command sergeant major followed the captain to the side of the command tent.

Deb could hear the calls being received from the battle raging at the wilderness area. The lights from the screens flickered across the large room as the late-night specialists and technicians worked to keep the three battalions supplied with ammunition, food, water and medical assistance. General Prost popped back up on the screen.

"Colonel, we can get you four boxes," the general stated.

"That is twelve weapons?"

"Yes ma'am, they will be leaving Arlington within the hour. You should have them in approximately five hours."

"That will be 0400 our time. I appreciate all your help at this late hour." Colonel Lisco rose from the chair.

"It's the least I can do. You go get them Colonel." General Prost disappeared from the screen.

"Colonel, the command sergeant major wants you in on the discussion with Lt. Col. Wilson," said Captain Dodson.

"Colonel, Lt. Col. Wilson is requesting to shift 3rd Battalion's eastern edge of their zone five kilometers to the west for support of 1st Battalion." Command Sergeant Major Talfoya remained seated in front of the monitor with the lieutenant colonel on the screen.

"Do you want to move all of 3rd Battalion?" Colonel Lisco leaned over the command sergeant major.

"Yes ma'am.

"We must coordinate with 1st Stryker to your east. We can't leave a five-kilometer gap on the front lines. Especially against this enemy." Deb took in a deep breath and released it. She was surprised that the request would be made at the early beginning of the mission. "Remain in place until daybreak. We will reassess at that time and make decisions on troop movements accordingly."

"Yes ma'am." Lt. Col. Wilson disappeared from the screen.

"Tommy, General Prost has secured us twelve of the REMP weapons. They are being sent from Arlington and should be here by 0400."

Colonel Lisco walked quickly out the door of the command tent with Tommy following close behind. They marched to the mess tent where she stormed inside and went straight to the coffee. They sat down at a table in the coolness of the tent.

"With twelve of the weapons, we have to decide how many to fire at one time." Redness was noticeable in Deb's eyes.

"The first thing — is who is going to fire them?"

"It's going to have to be Infantry Fire Teams. To be effective they will have to get as close as possible to the enemy." Deb took a sip of coffee.

"Are these weapons going to come with operational instructions? I imagine firing them is more complicated than just pulling a trigger," Tommy said.

"I bet our technicians can figure it out."

"What about if we fire one of the weapons from Loyd's location and see how it works?"

"We would lose the element of surprise. These are their weapons, and they might have a way to counter them." Deb's dark eyes were drooping. "I'm thinking we light them up with half the weapons."

"I'll work on finding six fire teams for the mission." Command Sergeant Major Talfoya sat his coffee cup on the table. "Why don't you go to your quarters and get a couple hours of sleep?"

"Wake me no later than 0345." She didn't try to argue.

Deb's father always told her that when difficult times occur, never sacrifice sleep. She pulled her cap off and laid down on the blanket on top of her bed. She wondered what General Song was thinking at that very moment. From her research of the North Korean military tactics, when she was stationed in South Korea, she knew the high command were dedicated, with nothing more important to them than being good soldiers. As she began to fall asleep, she pondered if the North Korean general had a profile of her. She felt as if her head had barely hit the pillow when she heard Tommy yell into her tent.

"I received notice from Fort Carson that the weapons from Arlington arrived there and are on their way here. They will be arriving by helicopter in approximately twenty minutes." Tommy waited outside the tent.

"What time is it?" Deb placed her feet on the floor.

"It's 0345."

"Give me a moment." She took in a couple deep breaths as she felt her heart beating hard in her chest.

A slight breeze hit Colonel Lisco's face as she stepped out of her tent.

"Captain Hendersen just arrived back with F Company." Command Sergeant Major Talfoya walked quickly next to her as she limped in the direction of the command center.

"Have you secured the Infantry Fire Teams?"

"Six teams are ready to be briefed."

Have you given both battalions, as well as Stryker, ample warning to protect the electrical components of their vehicles?"

"They all know."

"Have the fire teams meet us in the command center." Deb looked at Tommy who continued to show no signs of fatigue as he hurried away.

Deb walked past the communication center to the command room. She placed both palms flat on the table and leaned over the map. Taking a deep breath through her nose, she studied the map for a couple minutes, picked up a sharpie and made three x's. Tommy entered the room.

"The helicopter has arrived with the EMP weapons. The fire teams will be here momentarily." The command sergeant major noticed the marks on the map. "What are you thinking?"

"The more I have thought about it, I want to have two fire teams move to each of these spots." She pointed at the x's. "They will be no deeper into the wilderness than the front of our lines.

"Do you want them to fire three weapons?"

"They are to fire a weapon from each of the locations at the same exact time. Ten minutes later fire the next three." Deb stared at Tommy as he rolled his eyes sideways to look at her.

"Why do you want to fire only three at a time? A ten-minute pause for firing the next three weapons might give the Korean's time to respond." Tommy licked his lips.

"They will be too surprised from the blasts to counter quickly. Maybe it's my amateur knowledge of physics that makes me think we might be countering some of the power of the weapons by firing them all at the same time." The colonel could see a smile coming to Tommy's tanned face. "What are you smiling at?"

"Don't you think we might have physicists available to give us scientific answers?"

"Yeah, if we have about six months to have them do their tests." Deb elbowed him in the side. "We don't have time."

"We need to make sure the weapons are fired from a location in front of our troops. I do know that almost all the energy from the weapon goes forward, with very minimal amount of damage occurring on the backside." Tommy knew it was his job to find any flaws that might harm the mission.

"They need to advance forward and fire the weapons and move back quickly," stated Colonel Lisco.

The DARPA officials in Arlington sent detailed directions on the firing of the REMP weapons. Colonel Lisco and Command Sergeant Major Talfoya synchronized the times for the detonation, and the location each weapon would be fired from. Within thirty minutes of the start of the briefing, the fire teams were being trucked to the wilderness area. Lieutenant Morris was now in charge of the communication center as Colonel Lisco and Command Sergeant Major Talfoya entered the room. The lieutenant came quickly to the Colonel's side.

"Ma'am." The Lieutenant saluted as he stood at attention.

"At ease Lieutenant. We need three screens together with Lt. Col. Barnet, Lt. Col. Wilson and Colonel Blake online."

"Just one moment ma'am."

Deb wondered how Tommy's demeanor could be so calm given the seriousness of the situation, when earlier he was a nervous mess while waiting for the chastising from General Lauer for the incident with the FEMA director. The tight lines meandering from the corners of his eyes were deepened as he watched Lieutenant Morris secure three monitors.

All three technicians came out of their seats as Command Sergeant Major Talfoya and Colonel Lisco approached. The two lieutenant colonels and Colonel Blake were on the screens as Deb took the center seat, and Tommy sat next to her. After describing what was about to take place with the detonations of the REMP weapons, Deb ordered Lieutenant Morris to get Lt.

Col. Woodworth online. Although he was several kilometers away from the zone, he would most likely see the flashes.

Chatter from the other areas of the communication center continued, while an eerie quiet fell on the commanders as they sat and waited for the first firing of the weapons. The camera on the screens of the monitor were now displaying the landscape of cactus, boulders, bushes and in the near distance, mountains covered with pine trees.

The bright flashes caused a momentary shadow across the terrain as the bursts of light from the electromagnetic pulse filled the screen. Both Deb and Tommy jerked back slightly from the sudden explosion of light.

Deb clenched her teeth and folded her hands as she listened to Tommy discuss the ferocity of the detonations with the commanders. She waited in deep thought for the next flash of light. She remembered the first time she witnessed the intensity from the EMP when they were at the warehouse in Montana. She wondered how General Song would respond after being on the receiving end of six blasts.

The second volley from the weapons were not as synchronized as the first, with the detonation of the weapons being nearly a second off, causing a wave of light traveling from the east to the west across the wilderness area.

"Now we see what this has done to their jammers and electromagnetic weapons." Deb rose from her chair and looked from monitor to monitor. "This is going to be a long day. We need to advance forward as quickly as possible while we have them on their heels. This is the time to move with all our force."

Colorado Farm

Bobby couldn't get a wink of sleep thinking about the long trip. Adrenaline continued to pump through his body as he watched the construction workers prepare to start work on the buildings. Almost the entire population of the farm was out mulling around the grounds. The Jacobys all gathered at the lumberyard truck to see Seth off, while Irving's parents, Li Na and Shen, watched quietly behind the large family.

Although there was little to load, Hank and Jacqueline were busy helping Bobby and Emilee place the suitcases in the back of the SUV. Bill was about thirty meters away, helping Terrance, Irving and Seth with the loading of the people and their belongings onto the bed of the lumberyard truck.

Von, Tyrone and their father strolled up to the back of the vehicle. Von was carrying a small plastic bag full of clothes.

"That's it?" Bobby stared at his new friend.

"We left all our belongings with those fools we were with before we came here." Von looked at his father.

"You all are going to be careful and not make any stupid decisions, right?" The dark skin on the dad's face sagged at the jowls as he stared at Bobby.

"Yes sir, we won't take any unnecessary chances." Bobby began to feel apprehension as he stared into the worried fathers' smokey eyes.

"I agree, you need to stay on your toes." Hank gazed at Von's powerful shoulders, remembering how remarkable a football player the young man was only a few months ago. A surge of uneasiness fell over him as the thought of his only son leaving on such an uncertain journey.

"You three take turns driving, and don't keep driving if you become drowsy." Jacqueline moved between Bobby and Emilee.

"We won't fall asleep at the wheel." Bobby noticed Emilee looking toward her mother and two sisters standing next to the gate at the front yard. "You better go and say good-bye."

Emilee walked in their direction as Julia and Harold approached Bobby.

"Here's the address and a map for the location of my son. I have a letter for him inside that explains everything that has taken place over the past two months, including the death of his father." Julia handed Bobby a brown envelope with Michael written in large black letters on the outside.

"I'll do everything I possibly can to find him." Bobby reached his arm around the physician assistant and gave her an awkward hug.

"I know you will." She stepped back and patted him on the side of his face. "You really are a good person Bobby."

"Hopefully we will be bringing you a present when we return on Christmas Eve." Bobby's expression showed genuine concern for the widowed physician assistant.

Emilee returned from speaking with her mother and went directly to the back seat of the SUV. When Von saw her enter the car, he took his place in the front seat. Bobby caught Jacqueline's eye and gave a half wave in her direction before slipping into the driver's seat.

Maddy reached to take Bill's hand as he stepped back from the lumberyard truck. Terrance hopped into the driver's seat while Irving and Seth took their position as passengers. The siderails on the bed gave a semblance of safety to the mass of people in the back of the large truck who prepared to depart.

Nicole joined Bill and Maddy to watch the vehicles ease down the driveway to the county road. Nicole placed her arm on the shoulder of her granddaughter.

"Grandma, were those people zombies?" Maddy stared up at Nicole with a bewildered expression on her face.

"Oh my gosh, Maddy where did you get such an idea?" Nicole rolled her eyes to Bill.

"Some of the kids said they were zombies, and we had to get rid of them." Maddy held her mouth open, wondering why her grandmother was so startled by her inquiry.

"Remember when we talked about not believing everything someone tells you. This is a time where you should not have believed it. Zombies are not real." Bill picked her up and smelled the side of her neck. "When was the last time you had a shower, young lady?"

"It's been a while," stated Nicole. "I'll take her in and get her cleaned up if you want."

"That would be great if you would. Jon told me he has been in contact with Dad and there is a chance he will stop by today."

"Maddy, that's a good reason for you to get cleaned up. Grandpa won't like it if you smell like an old towel." Nicole took hold of her hand.

Maddy chuckled as they walked in the direction of the house.

Irene was back in the kitchen, and the rest of the Jacobys were working at the barn. They planned to take the tractor and trailer to the Robert's farm to load the chickens and chicken coop. They already hauled half of the old couple's hay back to the farm.

Bill listened to the sound of the hammers pounding. The construction crews were back to working at full steam, and the fruits of their hard work was visible in the form of a large building with all the roof trusses in place. Almost all the people who didn't want to be at the farm were now being carted eastward.

He glanced toward the greenhouse, wondering about the mindset of Samantha. He figured she was alone. After pondering for a moment, he began walking toward the glass house.

Samantha was sitting at a small table. When she looked up, he could see her swollen and moist eyes. She turned away, twisting her neck as far as it could go.

"Samantha, please let me know what is wrong," Bill sighed. "I'm sorry."

"It's not you or being here that is the problem. I felt this anxiety way before all this mess began."

"Why would you feel anxiety?" He felt some relief when she turned to face him.

"I don't know if I can explain it. I feel like I'm a failure, and at the same time nothing is good enough for me. Everything happens to me so quickly."

Bill waited for a moment to try and process what she was telling him. Communication had been an issue between the two of them from the moment they met. Half the time he didn't understand what the hell she was telling him.

"I chase away everything that could possibly be good for me. And then I wonder why I'm all alone." Her eyes squinted as she looked up at him, while continuing to slump over the table.

He placed his hand on the side of her arm and nodded, hoping she would keep talking so he wouldn't say the wrong thing to her. Her hair was a total mess. He wondered how long she would have to brush it to get rid of all the tangles.

"Right after I got the job with the airlines, I felt like I should have made a different career choice," she sighed and jerked quickly, sat up straight and twisted her body to where she was staring him right in the eyes, with her nose only a few centimeters from his. "I mean right after I got the job, Bill."

He leaned back slightly, moved his face back and forth, then stuck his chin straight out and started moving his head up and down, hoping she would continue speaking. She remained quiet and stared at him. The thought entered his mind that from all she was telling him, maybe her family history was full of mental illness. Thank God, something told him to hold his tongue, that this wasn't the time to tell her she needs to see a psychiatrist.

Knowing when to speak to comfort the women in his life had always been his Achilles heel. He remembered Maddy's mom telling him that he was clueless about her emotions and wondered why he would sit like a lump of coal while she expressed herself to him.

"I'm sorry to lay this all on you." Samantha continued to gaze at him. "It's like Maddy has been saying, I needed to get it off my chest."

"I'm glad you did," Bill whispered. He placed his hand on top of hers. "I am going to spend the day in the tower, since Irving is gone. Why don't you join me? We can continue this conversation."

"I would like that." She smiled. "I think I will get cleaned up first and meet you there."

He was glad he was not the one to mention she should shower.

Eastern Colorado

Ted was at the center of a convoy of Army Stryker and Assault vehicles along highway 15 about thirty kilometers from the Lisco farm, with the sun peaking over the eastern horizon. The farm that the NAV had flown over the night before was immediately ahead.

"Have 2nd Platoon take the lead on this one." Ted climbed out of the MRAP onto the gravel road, followed by Corporal Pint and Corporal Flanigan, who immediately relayed the message forward by way of her pulsnet radio on her wrist.

"Colonel, 3rd Platoon is requesting orders on how far they should advance to the south." A technician yelled out of the door from the communication vehicle.

"How far are they now."

"They are approximately seven klicks to the south on highway 145."

"Tell them to stop and remain in place." Ted turned and looked at Corporal Pint's rosy cheeks as she smiled back at him. "Jesus, I told them to stay no more than five kilometers in front of the main body."

"Colonel, 2nd Platoon is at the house ahead, and are advising that there are a lot of people inside," Corporal Flanigan moved in front of Ted.

"Have them order the civilians to come out."

"Yes sir"

Ted stepped into the ditch where he could better look down the road in the direction of the farm. He heard several pops in rapid succession. There was a pause, before the sound of gunfire became continuous.

"Sir, 2nd Platoon has come under fire. They are reporting casualties." Corporal Flanigan remained on the gravel road.

Ted moved quickly out of the ditch.

By the time the MRAP Ted was traveling in stopped six hundred meters from the farmhouse, the barrage of gunfire had ended.

"Colonel, we have control of the farm," said the corporal.

All the windows were destroyed, and bullet holes speckled the farmhouse. Several people waiting in the yard were detained in handcuffs. Sergeant Kahn waited at the fence line of the front yard for Ted to exit the MRAP. Two soldiers were being attended to just a few meters from the sergeant.

"Sir we have eighteen detained." The sergeant motioned to the yard.

"How many casualties did we suffer?"

"Two, as far as I know, sir. Private Tiger took one in the ass, and Corporal Lewis was nicked in the hand. Neither one of them serious." He pointed to the medic.

Ted went to where Private Tiger was situated over a stretcher with his butt in the air. "Do we need to have him airlifted out of here?" He asked the medic.

"Sir, it's going to be uncomfortable for him if we don't," he answered.

"Make the request for the chopper."

Ted stepped back through the metal gate and into the yard where the prisoners were all on their knees. The people detained looked like they could have been a choir from a church, or a debate team from a high school. They were an ordinary, diverse group. The only thing noticeably common about them was their age. They were all relatively young.

"Sergeant, have you spoke with any of the detainees?"

"Only to tell them to stick their faces in the dirt."

Ted smiled at the sergeant as he entered the gate. G Company's sergeants were all older and experienced veterans of the Army. He had no problem with them being a little caustic. They had earned it.

"You are trespassing here. This is my home," yelled one of ladies at the center of the group. Her dark hair and facial features resembled those of Shira.

"Well, your home is being used as a refuge for enemies of the United States." Ted moved closer.

"We have done nothing."

"Then you won't have any trouble proving your right to be here." He wanted to have the discussion about who owned the property but thought that might be better handled by the FBI interrogators.

"You are the one who is going to be charged with attempted murder." The young lady turned her head to the side as a strong gust of wind blew dust into her eyes.

Ted ignored her threat, surprised that none of the people inside the bullet riddled house died during the battle. "None of the insurgents are KIA?" Ted asked Sergeant Kahn.

"None, sir. I don't believe they suffered any casualties at all."

"With all that damage and no casualties. That is impressive sergeant." The pattern of holes was all at least a meter from the floor level.

"Thank you, sir. What do you want us to do with the prisoners?"

"2nd Platoon has had enough action. Load them up and take them back with you to the brig at Fort Carson."

Ted watched, almost in a trance, from the yard of the farm, with the wind blowing in his face. He waited while the young soldiers from 3rd Platoon loaded the bound prisoners. He watched patiently as they drove down the driveway before turning his focus to the house. He could see parts of old wooden siding under the bullet holes in the newer aluminum siding on what used to be a hard-working farmers home. He estimated the farmhouse was at least ninety years old, maybe older. The records showed that all three of the farms, he planned to visit during the day, showed ownership being changed to a foreign owned corporation, by way of a warranty deed, all within the past fifteen years. He could hear a helicopter approaching in the distance. He walked outside the fence to where the medic was waiting with Private Tiger and Corporal Lewis for their evacuation.

"How in the hell did you get shot in the ass, private?" He could see Private Tiger's upper teeth as he curled his lip up, obviously in some discomfort.

"I was discharging my weapon from over there, behind that shed." He was breathing heavily as he pointed to a small wooden structure. "I guess I stuck my butt out too far, and one of those assholes got in a lucky shot."

"Is it serious?" Ted asked the medic.

"No, but he will have a nice scar on his butt cheek."

As he watched the two soldiers airlifted from the pasture, he remembered having to reprimand the private for cussing in front of Maddy. With G Company having so many green recruits, not ready for combat, he knew he would have to rely on his combat ready sergeants from here on out.

La Cienega, New Mexico

The threat of a new age weapon, that they had not yet encountered, was of great concern for Colonel Lisco. The battalions were in the process of moving forward into rougher, mountainous terrain. Both 1st and 3rd Battalions advanced 2200 meters in four hours. Josh moved 2nd Battalion, minus F Company, closer to the battle on the southwest side of the wilderness area.

With the enemies' jammers and directed energy weapons disabled, Lt. Col. Barnet was able to go to the aid of E Company's two forward platoons. They advanced to where they were now fighting in the mountains.

Chet and the civilian guides were providing invaluable information directly to battalion communications concerning the size of the enemy forces, and their location. The relay system of having scouts situated along the ridge line of the cliffs overlooking Albuquerque made it possible to have important details conveyed to the Army Intelligence within a matter of minutes.

A minor cold front passed over the area bringing the temperatures down to near freezing. None of the commanders brought up the issue of weather, even though the temperature was several degrees colder at the higher elevations. It was a concern for Colonel Lisco. They had the enemy on the run, and she wanted to be prepared for any scenario that could change the tide.

Tommy broke down and retired to his tent to grab a couple hours of sleep, while Deb retreated to her office at the command center where the chatter coming from the communication center was loud and continuous. She considered what General Song's next move might be with the American forces advancing so quickly. The fact that he is a great tactician caused her discomfort, knowing he would never make a battle easy, and if it was, then there was a good chance it was a set-up. The worst thing she could do, while everything seemed to be going her way, was to become overconfident. She already warned Josh, Loyd, and Teresa to keep the troops rested, fed, and remain vigilant.

"Ma'am, General Lauer is online and wants to speak with you." Corporal Miller stuck his head inside the door.

Deb realized that any maneuvers she was planning to use to move 2nd Brigades troops up the mountain could be changed in an instance by the brass at headquarters. She prepared herself for the worst as she entered the communication center.

"I have already spoken with Colonel Blake and Colonel McDonald. Colonel, I want you to push along the ridge line overlooking the city toward the tramline," General Lauer spoke the moment her image came onto his screen. He had already decided the outcome of the next strategic move, without any discussion with her.

"Sir, the mountainous terrain is posing a real problem for equipment and troop movement. I'm afraid we are going to be slowed to a crawl as we try and make our way to the enemy interceptors on Sandia Mountain."

"Colonel, the Chinese Army have strengthened their position at Ruidoso. 1st Infantry is giving them all they want, but if we give the enemy enough time, they will reinforce the North Koreans. If they are reinforced, they could hold out for weeks. We must move now, and we must move swiftly."

"Yes, sir we will move as quick as humanly possible." Colonel Lisco realized the only way to move faster, was to put her brigade at risk. "Also, sir, Lt. Col. Woodworth with 2nd Battalion is south of the wilderness area detached from the rest of the brigade. With Stryker just to his east I request having him attached to Stryker Brigade." Command Sergeant Major Talfoya and Captain Hendersen entered the communication center where they moved to stand behind Colonel Lisco.

"Negative on that Colonel. Colonel Blake is moving to the north of San Antonito where they plan to attack westerly along Sandia Crest Road. This road is vitally important to the North Koreans."

"Sir, if the North Korean Army retreats, 2nd Battalion will be the only force in their way."

"Colonel, this enemy will never retreat."

Deb sat for a moment and stared at the empty monitor after the general abruptly exited the screen. She realized it was a mistake having Josh on the backside of the enemy, where moving over the mountainous terrain was nearly impossible.

"Colonel, we received a message from one of the special forces stating that they have the location of an interceptor but are unable to get close enough to destroy it." stated Lieutenant Morris.

"Can you get them on camera?"

"No, ma'am. The message came via radio, but they wanted to keep it short. I have the coordinates." The lieutenant handed her a handwritten note, before pulling up a map of the wilderness area on the screen. He pointed to a location. "It's right here."

"Our closest forces are still two klicks from that location. And we haven't advanced forward in three hours." Colonel Lisco turned to Command Sergeant Major Talfoya and Captain Hendersen.

"The Special Force Teams are at the top of the tramway. Why don't we move Josh to the bottom of the tramway? If they can hold the area long enough to get a Platoon from 2nd Battalion to the top of the mountain, then we can secure it enough to move the rest of the Company to the top." Tommy tapped the monitor at the Sandia Tramway with the back of his index finger.

"How far is the Special Force Team away from the interceptor?" Captain Hendersen asked.

"My guess is about 800 meters. The weather has turned to light snow showers on top of the mountain." answered Deb. "I'm sure if they stated they can't get to it, then there must be a lot of enemy combatants, and with inclement weather things aren't going to get any easier."

"Ma'am, Specialist Coalman is asking permission to speak with you. She is a Tactical Data System Specialist." The soldier was standing behind Lieutenant Morris. "Also, ma'am, Captain Dodson is about to come back on duty as the communication center commanding officer."

"What is it?" Colonel Lisco motioned for the young, petite specialist to come forward.

"Ma'am, all our forward troops are at a standstill, with the enemy imbedded into the forests and hills, making it nearly impossible to advance. With the laser interceptor more than two kilometers away from both 1st and 3rd Battalion's, I figure it is my duty to make you aware of another option we have in our arsenal for destroying the enemy's laser weapon."

"We are all ears." Colonel Lisco made a fist with her right hand and placed it into the palm of her left.

"We have nine GFR's in the arms warehouse, which we have never used. This weapon is perfect for the scenario we are facing."

"Okay, you are going to have to be very clear here. What in the hell is a GFR?" Colonel Lisco looked at Captain Hendersen and Tommy. Both men shrugged their shoulders.

"It is a Ground Force Robot. It is a robot that stands about a meter high." She held out her small hand with bright pink fingernail polish. "I was involved with the prototype of the android at the International Technology fair in Oslo, nearly six years ago, when I was a sophomore in college. Our robot blew all the other entry's out of the water, and after the Army took over the prototype, it has been improved significantly. This thing is amazing."

"Specialist Coalman, I appreciate your enthusiasm, but you need to be clear on the weapons capabilities. Also, how we can utilize it under these circumstances." Colonel Lisco could see a piercing hole in the side of her nose, and small dots on the outer edge of her eyes.

"The robot can travel at forty kilometers-per-hour over a field of boulders, through a forest or around a building without hitting any obstacles. It looks like it is running, but the bottom is about ten centimeters off the ground. We can program a route we want the robot to take to any destination." The sergeant smiled with her pink lips closed. "The only downfall is that the payload must be detonated remotely. Now that we have disabled the enemies jamming capabilities, and have vivid images from the cameras, I figured I would recommend using the GFR."

"How much explosive can it carry?" Command Sergeant Major Talfoya asked.

"I'm not a demolition expert, but I think we can place enough explosives to blow down a large building. The cargo area on the back of the unit is 45 centimeters by 30 centimeters and 60 centimeters deep."

"What is it's range?" Captain Hendersen asked.

"I can program it to find a target up to eleven kilometers away."

Command Sergeant Major Talfoya raised his eyebrows as he looked to Colonel Lisco.

"Alright, I want you to prepare the GFR to deploy immediately. One way or another we will find a way to get it to the top of the tramway." Deb could see the continuous fighting on all the screens from the monitors around her.

"Ma'am, might I recommend we prepare two of the robots and program them for different routes." The specialist clinched her front teeth, wondering if she might be overstepping her bounds.

"Specialist Coalman, this is your baby. I want your full attention on handling this project." Colonel Lisco turned to Command Sergeant Major Talfoya. "Tommy, will you coordinate and assist with getting the robot into position to launch?"

"Absolutely." Tommy felt confident he could find a way to get the robot close enough to the interceptor. If it worked, then all they needed was to locate the other two interceptors and their mission could be over quickly.

COLORADO FARM

The sights from the top of the tower showed Bill a different perspective of life on the farm. The solar heater and small refrigerator, along with the comfortable chair gave him a better understanding why Irving had no problem with spending entire days at the turret. Viewing the workers busy below in complete synchronization, as they raised the building, was the type of cooperation and unity Deb dreamed about when she began to fund and prepare the farm.

Nicole and Maddy came out of the house and stopped to chat with him, but with the construction taking place it became hard for them to hear him shouting out the window of the tower, they soon departed to Ted's office in the garage.

The whole farm was active and alive. Julia was playing with the two small dogs in the front yard. Jon stood next to Sheriff Bob and Ben in front of the Jacoby RV speaking adamantly about something. Off in the distance the Jacobys were busy at the barn as they repaired the log fencing on the corrals.

The sound of Samantha walking up the steps brought a smile to his face. He hoped that getting clean would bring her to a better mood. The smell of perfume and lotion filled the room as she entered the top floor of the tower.

"Oh my gosh. It looks so much higher from up here than it does down below." She stepped close to the front window and stared at the scenery.

"I sometimes wonder how Aunt Deb came up with the idea for building this tower. The view from here is amazing, so she obviously had a good idea what the landscape would look like from this height before designing it." Bill pulled the chairs close to the center of the room so they could look out of both the front window and the west window where the construction workers toiled on the roof. "What do you want to drink. We have water or diluted juice."

"Water will be fine." Samantha showed her white teeth. Her face was meticulously made, disputing the idea that he held earlier about her running out of make-up. He handed her a cold bottle of water.

"I was thinking, with so many people leaving the farm and reconnecting with family members, that we should make an effort to try and find your mother and father." Bill's knee touched her thigh as he moved close.

Samantha blatantly stared at Bill with a smile on her bright red lips. Looking at him like it was the first time she had ever seen him. Most of his facial features were the same as his fathers, with a chiseled chin and muscular cheeks, but his eyes were deeper and darker, like his mothers.

"I spoke with several of the people who arrived from Denver. They told me that food was a major issue, but it wasn't like people were randomly killing each other." She hesitated and continued staring at him. "I really would appreciate any help you can give me with going back to the city."

"I would like to speak with Dad first. He might be able to give us some protection."

"Have you talked with Ted recently?"

"This morning. There is a good chance he will be at the farm this afternoon." The thought entered his mind that he should be careful not to promise Samantha more than he could deliver.

"I'm sure he will help me." She was making it clear that she had a solid relationship with Ted.

"If he…."

A loud blood curdling scream rushed through the front window, causing Bill to stop in mid-sentence. He rushed to the window and looked down to where he could see Breanna moaning in front of the RV with her face buried in her hands. Ashley Jacoby stepped out of the vehicle and placed her arm around her sisters-in-law's shoulder. Aaron and Adam were just past the garage, walking from the barn with several of the grandkids following behind them.

"Daddy's dead," yelled Breanna, looking up at her brothers as they approached. Her bulging eyes on her round face were soaking wet.

Aaron, wearing a dirty pair of coveralls, didn't say a word as he rushed past his sister and stepped into the RV. The rest of the family, including the ones who were working at the construction site, soon crowded together, waiting to hear from someone inside to verify that their grandfather was indeed dead.

Jacqueline, followed closely behind by Julia, walked through the gate to the front yard and hurried up the step into the

Jacoby's mobile home. There was complete silence until Aaron opened the door, and announced what everyone knew was the fate of Ed.

"Dad has passed," Aaron said in a strong voice, holding his chin high.

Nicole stood at the garage door, holding Maddy in front of her as they watched the Jacobys crying and comforting each other.

"I'm sorry, but I do need to go down." Bill moved back from the window.

"I'll come with you." Samantha grabbed him by his bicep.

"Of course." He nodded and smiled. "Thank you for thinking of me as someone who you can tell your deepest secrets."

Bill realized he was a terrible psychologist. He had no idea why people's behavior was so erratic and unpredictable, especially the women in his life. But he did know that Samantha's anxiety was real.

Albuquerque, New Mexico

Light rain soaked the pavement at the parking area for the tramway. Lt. Col. Woodworth, along with select members of G Company, from 2nd Battalion, prepared to travel up the cloud covered mountain, overlooking Albuquerque.

The Assault Vehicle carrying Command Sergeant Major Talfoya and Specialist Coalman drove past members of G Company, traveling to the place closest to the tram entrance, where Lt. Col. Woodworth was standing in the drizzle. They exited the vehicle and approached the commander who was decked out in full combat gear.

"Josh, this is Tactical Data System Specialist Coalman." Tommy motioned for her to come in front of him.

"Colonel Lisco briefed me on the situation. I will be accompanying you to the top of the mountain," Lt. Col. Woodworth stated to the young specialist. "I figured if this goes the way we all hope, we will save a lot of American soldiers lives."

"We hope so, sir. I have the GFR programmed with the coordinates. After making some adjustments we should be able to launch it within thirty minutes from the time we reach the top."

"If the coordinates are incorrect, can you readjust?" asked Lt. Col. Woodworth.

"Yes sir, I can always go to manual control."

"Alright, let's move to the platform and get ready to load."

Five Infantry Fire Teams carrying electro-optical infrared sensors, to provide high-definition, full motion video of the area above, were the first to take the fifteen-minute ride to the crest of the mountain. They joined the three Special Forces units at the top to help secure the terminal location. The second tram car was at the bottom of the mountain the moment they reached the summit.

The Ground Force Robots, along with Specialist Coalman and her two technicians, loaded on the second tramway, along with 2nd Platoon, G Company. Lt. Col. Woodworth squeezed his way into the crowded car. The threat of the tram car being hit by a shoulder launched surface to air missile was on his mind the moment the cable jerked and began the journey up the rocky mountain. He had confidence that the soldiers above would protect them from such an attack as they cruised into the wet fog. The beautiful bright greys and dark brown colors of the mountain were enhanced by the drizzle hitting the rocks and vegetation. The rain turned to sleet and then to snow, blocking the view to the valley below, as the cable car took them higher to the ridgeline overlooking Albuquerque.

At the top, the rapid popping of gunfire filled the air. The barrage was further away than Josh had anticipated it would be. Four soldiers helped the tech specialists by lifting the robots from the tram car, before rushing to join their unit at the tree line. Specialist Coalman was visibly shaking as she removed her gloves and began punching information into a handheld computer. She calibrated the final bits of information into the GFR for its journey through the forest, and over the rocky terrain to its destination of the laser interceptor. The tight straps on her camera outfitted helmet puffed her red cheeks out as she concentrated on finishing the final adjustment on the first robot. One of the technicians programming the second robot took a step back when she noticed Specialist Coalman had finished the synchronizing process. It took less than five minutes before both weapons were ready to deploy.

"Are these robots going to be able to maneuver over this terrain?" Lt. Col. Woodworth asked the young specialist who continued to quiver. "Coalman, you are making me nervous here with all your shaking. Are you okay with doing this?"

"Yes sir, I'm good. Just a little cold. The GFR can navigate this terrain."

"Will the snow cause problems with the robots?"

"No, sir, right now, less than two centimeters of snow is covering the ground. They are capable of navigating over nine centimeters." She sat down on a wet, stone bench, and placed the computer on her lap. She brought both hands to her mouth and blew a warm breath across her fingers. A whirring sound came from the two robots as she began to type. "The first GFR will travel in a southerly route to the destination. It will take one hundred and eighteen seconds. The next robot will leave fifty-five seconds after the first. It will travel in a mostly straight line, arriving at its target one hundred and two seconds after discharge."

"Let's launch them." Josh was relieved that the specialist was being so precise.

"Sir, can you move to the other side of this bench?" She placed clear safety glasses over her squinting eyes.

Josh moved behind the three young computer technicians. A loud humming sound transmitted from the robot as it lifted ten centimeters off the ground, spraying wet snow in a circular pattern. It shot like a rocket off into the brush and trees, out of sight within a couple of seconds.

Lt. Col. Woodworth jerked back. "Good Lord. That thing isn't going to hit any of our troops, is it?"

"No sir, it won't hit anything at all." Specialist Coalman's face was two shades of red, with her puffed out cheeks being bright red, and the remaining parts a dull rose color. She kept her eyes on the screen watching the first GFR as the whooshing sound of the second robot started. It soon shot straight forward with the same speed and tenacity as the first.

Specialist Coalman gazed at the screen on her computer. The robot was moving so fast that the trees and landscape were a blur. She watched it flying sideways and vertical over the topography before it abruptly stopped. The camera rotated until it located the large interceptor perched on a trailer about five meters away. Enemy soldiers could be seen gawking at the odd-looking contraption that had suddenly shown up at their camp.

Specialist Coalman pushed a button on her computer, and the screen went white. An explosion could be heard in the distance. The screen switched to the second GFR which sped into the cloud of smoke and stopped at the location where the interceptor was verified by the first robot. She pushed another button and the sound of the second explosion echoed across the mountains.

Private Montoya and her Uncle Chet were standing to the side of Lt. Col. Woodworth. When he noticed them, he waved them toward the abandoned restaurant next to the cable car loading zone. They entered the cold building as 4th Platoon rushed off the platform, completing the arrival of the entirety of G Company onto the mountain.

La Cienega, New Mexico

Command Sergeant Major Talfoya could tell something was bothering Colonel Lisco the second he stepped into her office at Brigade Headquarters. He expected her to be ecstatic about the success of the mission of destroying one of the interceptors.

"Okay, what's bothering you, Deb?" Tommy sighed, moving to where he could better see her face.

She didn't answer him. Her eyes were tight, causing several wrinkles to protrude down the side of her face to her cheek. Her thick eyebrows were pushed together as she tapped a finger on the table.

"Are you going to tell me what is bothering you?" He placed a hand on the arm of her chair.

"General Lauer wants us to shift 1st Battalion to the east. He wants 3rd Battalion attached to Stryker and move up to San Antonito."

"It would be best to have 1st Battalion move up the ridgeline. They could connect with Josh at the tramway terminal, while we have the opportunity." Tommy pointed at the map.

"Lauer isn't asking. It's a direct order." Deb folded her fingers. "Teresa and Loyd are already on the move."

"The Sandia Crest Road is the best escape route for the Korean forces." Tommy lifted his hand from the map.

"What the hell Tommy. Let them leave." Deb slammed her fist on the table. "We have images now of the laser interceptor. There is no way they can fire that damn thing while it's being transported. We should pull all the troops from San Antonito and give them a way out. I doubt that General Song is stupid enough to take the bait, knowing the second they begin moving the two remaining interceptors, we level them with missiles. But the whole concept that we should reinforce the rough terrain west of the small town makes no sense at all."

Tommy looked back at the map. "If Stryker and 3rd Battalion advance from that location, then the Korean's will have to move west and attack at the weakest location. That will be Josh and 2nd Battalion."

"Intel from the civilians will give us the location of the two remaining interceptors. We should blast them again with the

REMP. Then send in the Ground Force Robots, instead of fighting them toe to toe."

"We have less than an hour of daylight left," stated Tommy. "3rd Battalion has transported pieces of artillery to the terminal at the top of the tramway. Hopefully they can fortify the area enough to fend off the attacks."

Deb continued staring at the map. She had hoped when she began this mission, she would have more control in the tactics used to fight the Korean Special Force. She understood leadership does not depend on always being right. In the military there is always a bigger picture to consider, and no matter what, the Brass are always correct, even when they are wrong.

Colorado Farm

The day before Christmas Eve.

Jerry whisked a large bowl of pancake batter and listened to the chatter from the ever-increasing crowd of people cramming into the living room. He fashioned a crew of hard-working cooks who were efficient and creative in using the lessening amounts of ingredients to feed the masses. Although he was an accomplished airplane mechanic, cooking was his passion, and being able to command the kitchen where many people relied on him for their meals, was a dream come true. He had known about the Jacoby family for many years, mostly because Terrance would mention the old couple, with the large family, when he went to work on one of Ed's cars. It was over the past couple of months where he learned so much about Irene and her easy-going ways of preparing food and sharing her recipes. She was one of the most caring people he had ever crossed paths with, and he was worried about her wellbeing. He untied the apron from his large belly and tossed it on the kitchen counter.

The smell of pancakes filled the living room, but the people weren't gathering to eat. They were there to console the Jacoby family over the death of Ed.

"I want to go into town and try to find Dad a nice coffin." Breanna's eyes were red with a purple chafed spot under her right eye where she had rubbed the entire night. She slumped on the couch between Adam and Aaron.

"I know there aren't any caskets in Limon," Sheriff Bob tried his best to speak in a soft tone. "Everyone in town was complaining about the lack of coffins about a month into this war."

"We'll have Jason make a nice coffin for Dad." Aaron patted Breanna's hand. He looked at Irene sitting in a lounger with her great granddaughter at her side. Her face was pale white, with her eyes staring straight ahead. "Mom, are you okay with us having the coffin built?"

"There isn't much else we can do." She took in a deep breath and gasped slightly as she let it out.

"Arthur took some of his cousins up on the hill to start digging the grave. He wants to make sure it is deep enough." stated Adam.

"We can't bury Ed until Seth returns." Ashley sat on the edge of the couch next to Adam.

"If they haven't run into trouble, they will be back sometime tomorrow." Jon gazed from each of the Jacobys to the other. "I know I can speak for all the Lisco family, and most likely everyone on the farm, when I say we will do everything possible to help you at this difficult time."

Samantha, with tears in her eyes, leaned down on one knee in front of Irene, and spoke softly, "if it weren't for you and Ed I would most likely be dead. Ed lived a meaningful life, and I can never repay you for what you did."

"Thank you, sweetheart. We all helped each other." Irene's voice sounded much stronger as she watched the flight attendant, who came so unexpectantly to their farm, stand and move back into the crowd.

Maddy pulled away from Nicole and went to Irene's side. She patted her on the arm, before placing the side of her head onto her soft shoulder. Irene reached up and touched her chin.

"Come here Maddy." Bill stepped in to pull his daughter back.

"No, it's okay, Bill. I don't think there is anything in the world that can make me feel better than hugs from these two little girls." The old lady placed the palm of her hand on the side of Maddy's face. She rolled her tired eyes up to look at Bill. "Maddy feels awfully hot."

Bill pulled Maddy back. He placed both hands on the side of her face and looked into her drooping eyes. Her cheeks were pale white with several red blotches scattered on her forehead.

"Do you feel sick Maddy?" Nicole came to the side of her granddaughter and son. She noticed a purple crescent moon under each of her eyes.

"A little." Maddy leaned over and vomited on the carpet.

Bill picked her up and took her into the clinic.

Hank shot Jon a look as he saw Patrick lumbering across the room. The large Englishman pushed a couple people aside so he could stand in front of the Jacobys. He couldn't hold his tongue, even during the most solemn of times.

"Might I add my condolences." Patrick dipped his chin. "Farming is the life blood of a nation. It sounds as if Mr. Jacoby was an agronomist of the highest caliber. It is men such as he who has fed not only this country, but many people of the world."

"Thank you for your kind words." Irene forced a smile.

Hank and Jacqueline slipped into the clinic where Bill and Nicole were watching Julia perched over the top of Maddy, who was in a fetal position on the examination table.

"I don't know what is wrong with her coach," Bill said as Hank came to his side. "She just told us that Scotty is sick too."

"I noticed she had a nasty cough this morning, but she seemed to have a lot of energy," stated Nicole. "Now she can't hardly lift her head."

Jacqueline placed her hand on the back of her sisters-in-law arm. She could sense the tension in Nicole's voice, and the stress in Bill's eyes as they waited to find out the cause of Maddy's illness. All they could do was rely on Julia to render her better.

Indianapolis, Indiana

Farmsteads dotted the landscape with their bright red barns, exhibiting steep gable roofs with icicles falling from the gutters like stalactites in a cave. Large silos rose from the fields surrounding colonial style farmhouses with stone planters, and magnificent entries framing the homes of the middle American families who lived in central Indiana. A slight dusting of snow, kept visible by the near freezing temperature, edged the highway.

The group from the Lisco farm made much better time than anticipated. Late the night before, when they arrived at the FEMA camp at Quinter, Kansas, the disgruntled passengers being transported, decided to take leave from the cold, almost unbearable, ride on the back of the lumberyard truck. All of them decided to stay in the small Kansas community.

The journey over the flat plains of Kansas and Missouri was uneventful, with the only real disappointment occurring when Bobby, Emilee and Von arrived at Julia's son Michaels' modest home at the outskirts of St. Louis. A note written, using a black sharpie, on a piece of cardboard greeted them on the front door. It explained that the family left the St Louis area to be with Michael's wife's' parents in Boston. They were sorry to leave so quickly without saying farewell to friends. At the bottom of the correspondence was a message made directly to Julia and Fred, giving an address in New England, along with a plea for them to continue traveling east. Bobby removed the cardboard to take back to Julia. He hoped it would give her and Harold some relief in knowing the family was safe.

Police vehicles blocked the lanes of traffic as they approached Indianapolis, with motorists allowed to pass through on the shoulder of the highway, after being checked. The process was slow, taking much longer than when they passed through the checkpoint on the western side of St. Louis. It was becoming more and more unlikely they would be able to find supplies in Indianapolis and be able to head back toward the farm before dark.

After Terrance, driving the lumberyard truck, was waved through the checkpoint, Bobby pulled up next to an officer and stopped the car. The older Indiana State Patrolman was more than congenial, he was empathetic, but warned Bobby that the EMP attacks that hit the Denver metro area were now occurring in the Indianapolis area. Finding large quantities of food might be difficult, because over the past week the insurrectionists had caused havoc in the metropolises. The officer gave good directions to a warehouse distribution district he thought might be able to help supply some bulk items. Bobby hurried ahead of the lumberyard truck in order to lead them directly to the dispersal area.

The windows on several of the warehouses were boarded over, and trash covered the chain-link fence that bordered the wide road that passed through the rough neighborhood. A gust of wind blew gravel across the paved road, pelting the side of the vehicles as they pulled into a large parking lot. A small box truck was backed up to a dilapidated concrete dock with a forklift busy filling the vehicle with cargo.

"I don't know Bobby," Von stated, "this doesn't look like a place we can make a legitimate purchase of food."

"It looks like they are taking food from the warehouse." Bobby watched Irving and Terrance exit the truck.

"There is someone standing on the dock who looks like he wants to talk," said Emilee, sliding across her seat in the back of the car to where she could better see out the side window. A man wearing a hoodie stood with his toes at the edge of the dock gazing down at the two vehicles.

"I guess this is as good a place as any to find out where we can find supplies." Bobby opened the door and stepped out. Irving and Terrance waited at the back of the truck, leaving Seth in the driver's seat.

"Good day gentlemen." The man continued to look down from the dock as he took a step back.

"Good afternoon." Bobby placed a hand on the dock. "We are hoping you can help us with finding some supplies."

"Are you wanting to purchase lumber?"

"No, no, the lumberyard truck is the only truck we had available." Bobby gazed up. The man had a purple color to his face, and his snub nose looked as if he were a prize fighter. "We are looking for food."

"I take it you want quite a large amount of food." The man turned as a forklift with a trash container filled with empty boxes, came to park right behind him. A thick man with a square forehead stepped off the forklift and moved to the side of the man wearing the hoodie.

"Yes sir, we want to buy a full truck load."

"Do you have cash?" The thick man asked without introduction.

Bobby hesitated for a moment. He looked at Terrance, and then at Irving, trying to get a feeling as to how he should answer the question. The two burly men seemed innocent enough, but they were in a shady location in a strange city, and broadcasting that he held nearly seventy-five thousand dollars in cash, and another fifty thousand dollars worth of gold and silver bullion in the back of his car, could possibly prove to be a fatal mistake.

"We can get cash," Irving answered confidently.

"Give us a list of what you want, and we will see what we can do." The man in the hoodie turned to look at the thick man. A fresh scar was noticeable at the corner of his mouth.

"I have a list of the food we would like to buy." Bobby went to the passenger side of the car and motioned for Von to open the window. "Can you give me the paper in the console with the list of food?"

"I'm not sure they are on the list, but we can use toothpaste, soap and shampoo." Irving stared at the two men.

Bobby handed the man in the hoodie the piece of paper. He breathed through his nose while reading the inventory of food items, using his left index finger to rub the scar at the corner of his mouth, before turning back toward Irving.

"If you want all of this, it will cost you up to twenty-five thousand dollars." The man tipped his head and furrowed his eyebrows, checking to see how the random amount of money was being perceived by Bobby and Irving. "Also, we will need a deposit."

"How long will it take to have it ready? We want to leave the city before dark," stated Irving.

"We can have it all this afternoon."

"How much deposit do you want?" Bobby asked.

"Half."

"That ain't going to happen," Irving's reply was quick. He looked directly at the man in the hoodie. "We will get you the money in full after we are satisfied with the food, and the truck is loaded."

"Okay, good luck with finding food. All the stores and warehouses are empty." The man in the hoodie turned his back and took two steps up the dock. The thick man grabbed him by the arm and pulled him close. They spoke quietly for a moment before they both moved back to the edge of the dock.

"Give us three hours and we will have your supplies," the man in the hoodie stated.

Although he was sure the men at the dock were aware that the money for payment was in one of the two vehicles, Irving decided it would be best to wait at a different location while the supplies were gathered. They drove nearly three kilometers to a vacant parking lot. All six of them grouped in front of the lumberyard truck.

"Can we trust these guys?" Terrance asked, pulling the collar of his winter coat tight to block the cold breeze.

"My grandpa always told us that you can't trust a harvest until you've seen it sown," said Seth.

"I agree, let's make sure we are prepared if they decide to take advantage of us." Irving moved to where he was standing in front of the other five. "We'll park the truck at the edge of the dock and leave the car at the entrance of the parking lot. I'll go up and check the goods while Terrance and Seth wait with rifles at the ready."

"I wonder if I shouldn't go up first and inspect the supplies?" Bobby interrupted. "It would be much better if you protected us with one of the rifles."

Irving stared at Bobby for a moment. He thought how the young man's facial features were identical to his Uncle Jon's, all the way from his high cheek bones and prominent chin to his muscular shoulders. He spent so many dangerous times in different parts of the world with Lt. Col. Lisco, where young soldiers were put in harm's way, that having Bobby by his side gave him a sense of security. The situations he faced during his time in service made the one they were now facing at the warehouse seem like a walk in the park. But there was something lingering in his mind that triggered a warning about the dangers of the men on the dock.

"Bobby, I would rather have you and Emilee stay with the car. You have access to the cash, and it would be better for you to handle the payment after all the goods have been loaded on the truck." He shot a glance toward Seth and Terrance to see if they wanted to chime in on the plan.

"What about me?" Von asked.

"You wait with Bobby and Emilee. After the food is loaded you can come forward and help strap it down." The retired army captain's sure way of giving directives was explicit, giving everyone a clear role in the mission.

Three pallets wrapped in cellophane sat right outside the large door of the warehouse, with forklifts visible inside moving quickly about. Seth drove the truck into the parking lot and prepared to back up to the dock when a man on the dock yelled at him to stop. They wanted to bring the pallets off the dock to the parking lot and lift it onto the truck.

Bobby stopped the car at the entrance and exited. Sirens could be heard ominously off in the distance as Emilee waited by his side. Von began the two-hundred-meter walk to the truck.

"We will wait until Seth waves us forward." Bobby fumbled with the pistol in the holster hanging on his belt. He held a brown paper bag containing twenty-five thousand dollars.

"Should I come with you when you pay them?" Emilee spoke with the deep Irish brogue he hadn't heard her use in quite some time.

"No, absolutely not. You stay here and bring the car up when I wave." Bobby watched her as she grabbed hold of her long red hair and pulled it into a ponytail. Her beautiful face was flushed pink by the cold wind. She was the type of girl who didn't realize how incredibly beautiful she was, he thought, as he smiled at her."

"Why are you smiling at me?" She tapped him on the stomach with the back of her hand.

"Just thinking how lucky I am." Bobby could see Irving motioning in his direction from the dock.

The first pallet was slid into place on the front of the bed of the truck. As one pallet was moved off the dock another was brought out of the warehouse and took its place. Irving hopped up onto the dock and moved to a pallet with the tops of several boxes visible through the plastic surrounding the food. Boxes of cereal, scalloped potatoes and oatmeal were detectable. He walked over to another pallet and could see through the plastic bags of flour, rice and sugar.

"How many pallets do you have?" Irving asked the man in the hoodie.

"Eight."

"Do you have an invoice?"

The man rolled his eyes, and stated, "I can get you one."

From his perch on the dock, Irving could see Terrance and Seth standing at the front of the truck, but it wasn't apparent if they were holding their AK-47 rifles. Von waited calmly to the side while the truck loaded.

"Go ahead and start strapping the load," Irving said to Von as the final pallet was raised up onto the bed. He waved in the direction of Bobby to have him come up on the dock. It was time to pay and get on the road back to Colorado.

Von watched from the back of the truck while the final pallet was being loaded. The forklift driver left the pallet short of the one already loaded. He brought the forks back and, in his haste, to push the pallet forward he nicked a bag of flour, ripping it open. Sand and bits of foam flowed from the sack onto the pavement of the parking lot.

Irving was on the dock with his back to Von, checking the invoice with the man in the hood looking over his shoulder. A group of tough looking warehouse workers congregated in the large open door next to their forklifts. Bobby was walking up the concrete steps holding the paper bag full of money.

Von used the truck hitch to step onto the bed of the truck, where he leaned over and pulled open the paper sack of flour. A large amount of sand intermingled with small bits of foam fell onto the pavement. He leaned over the pallet with the broken bag and pulled the plastic away from a box of cereal on one of the middle pallets. He ripped open the box, bits of foam blew out of the package. He jumped off the bed of the truck.

"This is a scam," Von said in a voice slightly above a whisper as he approached Terrance. "There's sand coming out of the bags at the back of the truck."

Terrance gazed in the direction of the threatening men amassed at the door on the dock about five meters from where Bobby was standing next to Irving. He tallied eight men at the entrance, making a total of ten. He reached behind the seat of the truck and retrieved two rifles. He handed one to Seth.

Seth maneuvered from the right of the truck as Terrance approached from the left side. They reached the edge of the dock just as Bobby handed the bag of money to the thick man.

"Irving, we have a problem here. Don't give them the money," Terrance yelled, keeping his eyes on the men at the overhead door. He could see several of them were already holding weapons. He raised his rifle.

Irving pulled Bobby back to the concrete block wall on the dock when the first shot exploded from the door of the warehouse. He pulled his pistol from its holster as a barrage of shots were fired. The man in the hoodie, pulled a .45 caliber Smith and Wesson pistol. Irving shot him directly in the chest. The thick man scurried to the far side of the dock, still holding the bag of money, and ran down the steps away from the fracas. Seth and Terrance returned fire over the concrete floor of the dock with their powerful rifles.

Von moved to the side of the truck to get a better vantage to see how he could assist his friends. He just made eye contact with Bobby when a stray bullet caught him high on his forehead. He took one step back before stopping and falling forward, face first onto the cold pavement.

Bobby ran to the edge of the dock and jumped, landing in full stride on the asphalt. He hesitated when he arrived at Von's motionless body. A forty-five-caliber bullet hit him square in the back of his head. He fell to his knees and then headfirst onto the feet of his friend.

Irving could see Emilee standing to the side of the car at the entrance to the parking lot. He moved away from the wall of the warehouse to get a better angle to fire, just as the overhead door came down. Terrance and Seth kept their rifles fixed on the closed door. Irving leaped off the dock and went to Bobby and Von. He stared at the young men for several seconds before Terrance came to his side with two wool blankets. He could see Emilee slowly walking across the parking lot as they finished covering the two bodies.

Irving had heard it said that the death of one man is a tragedy, when the death of thousands in war often becomes a statistic. The twisted face of Emilee, as she came to a halt ten meters from the two covered figures laying on the cold asphalt, fortified this philosophy. Her hands went to her mouth as she fell to her knees in heartbreak.

PART TWO

La Cienega, New Mexico

Flashes of light bouncing off the clouds lit up the early dawn horizon. Deb stopped outside her quarters, on her way to the mess tent, to watch the display of tactical missiles being fired toward the enemy positions nearly forty kilometers to the south. With the second laser interceptor having been destroyed overnight, and the third one in the crosshairs, it should be only a matter of hours before she could pull back all aspects of her brigade. The Air Force could finish the job of defeating the North Koreans, who were embedded deeply into the Sandia Wilderness.

With her eyes transfixed on the light show, her mind wandered to where her next mission might lead her and the 2nd Brigade. There was chatter, through the usual ranks, that the Chinese and Russians were planning an all-out assault that could take place as early as tomorrow, Christmas Day. If the front lines to the southeast of her were broken, the enemy would advance into Louisiana, and possibly to parts of Oklahoma. She hoped that the next assignment would take her straight south into the heart of the Chinese Army, and eventually to the Mexican border.

She grabbed a cup of coffee, before sitting down at a table where Command Sergeant Major Talfoya was convening all alone. His eyes were clear, and he was clean shaven. Having left him only about four hours earlier, she wondered how he could look so good, with so little sleep. She barely had time to sit when a corporal approached the table.

"Colonel, I have Lieutenant Colonel Woodworth on my radio." The corporal handed the colonel a handheld radio.

"Josh, please give me good news," Colonel Lisco yelled into the radio.

"I believe it is as good as it can get. General Song just surrendered."

"Who has he surrendered too?" She smiled at Command Sergeant Talfoya, who could hear Josh screaming into his radio.

"Captain Maltova with I Company. We expect them to arrive at the top of the tramway within the hour. We plan to bring him down to the parking lot on the tram."

"Have you arranged for his transportation?"

"Yes, I just spoke with General Lauer, and he wants us to dispatch him to Fort Carson."

Deb hesitated for a moment and glanced at Tommy. She was surprised Lt. Col Woodworth contacted General Lauer with the news of the capture of the Korean general before telling her.

"We will meet you at the bottom of the mountain," Deb stated with a sharp tone. "I want to speak with General Lauer first, but we should be there before you arrive at the parking area."

"Do you want to use my radio to contact General Lauer, ma'am?" asked the corporal after Colonel Lisco discontinued the call with Lt. Col. Woodworth.

"I'll make the call in the communication tent." Deb chewed on her lower lip as the corporal left the mess tent.

Tommy could tell she was upset that Lt. Col. Woodworth bypassed her in giving the information about the capture of General Song, first to General Lauer. He wasn't going to express to Deb that it was totally appropriate that Josh spoke directly to the general. The new Army was one where it was necessary for smaller regiments and battalions, even companies to be more autonomous, unlike the army of the past. He decided not to breach the subject.

"I'll arrange transportation for us to the Sandia area." Tommy pushed his chair back from the table.

"I'm hoping Lauer will allow us to move brigade headquarters south to the Albuquerque area." Colonel Lisco perked up. "I'm hoping he will tell me where 2nd Brigade fits into our attack strategy."

"I will have a platoon from F Company accompany us," stated Tommy.

"Have Captain Hendersen come too. I will run by the communication tent and will meet you in fifteen minutes.

Albuquerque, New Mexico

The welcoming roar of aircraft flying overhead greeted Colonel Lisco. She waited with Command Sergeant Major Talfoya next to the Armored Multi-Purpose Vehicle that brought them to the cold and muggy parking lot of the Sandia Mountain Tramway. She was dressed in her Army Combat Uniform with a coat that bore her name, rank insignia, combat patches and skill badges, with a full colored U.S. flag on her right shoulder.

The cable for the tramway was visible for five-hundred meters before it disappeared into the clouds covering the mountain above. The sound of helicopters thumping, and the roar of airplanes was nearly deafening as Deb pulled her collar tight around her neck to keep the moist wind at bay.

"Colonel, General Song has been loaded on the tram and is on his way down." Captain Hendersen stepped next to Colonel Lisco.

"Is Lt. Col. Woodworth on the tram with him?"

"Actually, he came down on the last tram and is at the entrance, right above." Captain Hendersen pointed up the hill from the parking lot to a plethora of soldiers congregated outside the buildings where tourists, before the war, would purchase tickets for the ride up the tram. The large tram car could be seen slowly descending.

"They will be evacuating him from down there." The captain motioned toward a parking lot where two helicopters waited.

"Let's walk to the lower parking area. I'd like to look the general in the eye before they take him away." Colonel Deb cocked her head toward Command Sergeant Major Talfoya.

A small group could be seen walking down the hill in formation. General Song marching with Lt. Col. Woodworth and Captain Malkova on his right, were followed by several soldiers from 2nd Battalion's I Company. She took several paces toward the group as they neared the helicopter posed to transport the general.

General Song was bald as a cue ball, and it looked like he had a frown on his head. He drew himself straight when Josh stopped in front of Deb and Staff Sergeant Major Talfoya. His irascible face flushed a bright red when his dark eyes read the name tag on her jacket.

Deb gazed warily at him, knowing he recognized her, but was content in watching him being led to the helicopter without speaking a word. The general had a different idea. He didn't want to let the opportunity to speak with her pass.

"Colonel Lisco, my staff will have to buy me a case of Taeha," General Song spoke perfect English. His smooth face wrinkled. "I told them that you would be the one to figure out that our weaponry could be compromised with the EMPs."

"General, I don't understand how a brilliant soldier such as yourself could be used by the PLA to sacrifice so much." She looked at him intently, directly in his eyes. "Even with the laser interceptors it was always only a matter of time before you lost this battle. You were on a suicide mission."

"Not so fast Colonel. I'm still alive. You are about to be hit with a force that you cannot defeat." He shrugged slightly. "Your leaders all know this. I might have to experience some pain while in your captivity, but I will eventually be released. Most likely very soon."

"You are in the United States now. You will be treated with the utmost respect." Deb turned to Tommy and nodded her head. They walked away, giving the general no satisfaction of an answer to his assertion that the war would be lost quickly. Lt. Col Woodworth led the captive to the waiting helicopter.

Deb stopped and watched as the helicopter disappeared over the horizon. She realized that new age warfare was not only about the new machines, but also about sacrifice, and finding advantages in small battles. Much like all wars from the past. A corporal brought her back from her thoughts. He saluted her.

"What in the hell is wrong with you soldier." Tommy went nose to nose with the corporal. "Don't you ever salute the colonel when she is standing in an exposed location. Haven't you ever heard of a sniper check?"

"Yes sir, I have." He was shaking, and momentarily moved his hand to salute the command sergeant major, but fortunately returned both hands to his side. He looked momentarily at the colonel who was dressed much differently from the other soldiers. Luckily he didn't make note of this to the command sergeant major. "General Lauer wants to speak with the colonel in the communication vehicle."

The corporal turned quickly and led them to the command vehicle.

"Sir." Deb stared into the monitor. She sensed impatience from General Lauer.

"Colonel, you are to take 2nd Battalion to La Junta, Colorado and set up headquarters there. Your orders have been sent."

"What about 1st and 3rd Battalions?" she stared at him in surprise.

"They are now attached with 7th Infantry Division. Right now, colonel I need you to move." General Lauer raised his eyebrow as though he expected to be challenged.

"Yes sir." Deb turned her head away from the screen. It was blank when she looked back.

Colorado Farm

Nicole watched over Maddy's shoulder as she and the other children worked on wrapping everything from a pinecone to a piece of colored wood. The living room floor was covered with torn wrapping paper and small boxes, while Christmas music played quietly in the background.

"What is Maddy making?" Jacqueline came over to stand next to Nicole. Maddy twisted to hide a piece of typing paper with a picture of a bright green Christmas tree.

"I think you just walked up on her while she is wrapping your present."

"That is so nice. Are we going to open them tonight, or are we waiting for Christmas morning tomorrow?" Jacqueline asked.

"It depends on if Bobby and Emilee get back in time this afternoon." Nicole gazed in the direction of Jessica who was sitting on the floor with Avery and Reagan coloring a picture. "I think the plan is if they get back before dark, we will open them tonight."

"Maddy seems to be over her sickness."

"I guess it was a twenty-four-hour bug. With her being an only child, and only grandchild, I think we all overreact with her sometimes. Scotty is feeling better too."

"Believe me I can understand." Jacqueline looked in the direction of Caroline and Sherry sitting in the middle of the children helping with projects. "Have you thought much about who the father of Sherry's baby is?"

"A little, I guess. I just haven't spoken out loud about it." Nicole was surprised by the abruptness of the question. She almost felt guilty while contemplating the different men who might have sired the baby. Although Bobby seemed totally dedicated to Emilee, on several occasions she noticed her nephew staring lustfully at the beautiful young woman, so he had on more than one occasion entered her mind as being the father. Of course, it was the last thing she would mention to her sister-in-law.

"Who do you think it is?" Jacqueline asked.

"I really don't know."

"Come on, you just said you have thought about it." Jacqueline smiled at Nicole.

"Maybe Dave," Nicole said quietly, throwing her hands in the air, looking to make sure that Kori Jensen wasn't in earshot. "Who do you think the father is?"

"I'm thinking it was one of the insurrectionists who she was with before coming to the farm. As tough and independent as Sherry is, something tells me she will never disclose it to anyone." A crooked smile crossed Jacqueline's mouth as she stared at her sister-in-law. A fleeting thought rushed through her mind about mentioning that it possibly could be Bill. She thought better of it.

A cold breeze rushed into the room as Hank entered the front door and came to the two women's side.

"Jon and I just had a nice talk with Ted. He's busy as hell and doesn't know if he will make it here for the holidays. He let us know that the President is planning to speak at four on Christmas Day, and we will be able to hear him on the radio."

"That will be interesting," stated Jacqueline.

"Sheriff Bob and Ben are thinking of going to Hugo and checking on Travis." Hank took a step back as Jessica moved to stand next to Jacqueline.

"Am I correct in assuming Bobby and Emilee are planning on being back this evening?" Jessica stared directly at Jacqueline.

"The plan is for them to be back tonight for Christmas Eve," Jacqueline spoke in a soft tone, noticing the conciliatory nature of Emilee's mother's inquiry.

"I really haven't missed my cell phone until now. I wish I could call Emilee and make sure everything is all right." Jessica smiled, showing her off white teeth.

"I wish we could call them too." Jacqueline smiled back, gazing at her neatly combed red hair. Her heart pounded hard in her chest as her feelings toward the young mother softened.

"I would like to sit down with you some time and talk, if you could find it possible to do so," Jessica spoke with a deep Irish accent. "Bobby and Emilee have gotten closer and closer since we arrived at the farm, and I want to make sure we can be amicable with each other should they take the relationship to the next level."

"I would be up for that," Jacqueline nodded her head, and curled her lip. She felt somewhat slighted that it wasn't her that suggested reconciliation. On the other hand, she still held a deep resentment for the actions of the young mother in leaving her children behind while galivanting away with Christian.

"The car and lumber truck are just coming down the driveway." Bill yelled from the front door.

Jessica followed Hank and Jacqueline out the door, with Nicole lingering behind to help Maddy with a jacket. The constant sound of hammers pounding filled the air while many assembled at the middle of the courtyard. The Jacoby family was already gathering outside their RV as the truck made its way down the driveway to park in front of the garage. Several people made mention of the truck being empty, but nobody noticed the two bodies wrapped in blankets strapped tightly at the front of the bed.

Irving was the only one visible in the car as he parked next to the truck. He twisted his head to look at Emilee laying quietly in a fetal position on the back seat, before exiting the vehicle. He scanned the crowd until he made eye contact with Jon, who was standing next to Nicole, Bill and Maddy. He made a beeline right to the lieutenant colonel.

Jon saw Seth and Terrance step out of the cab of the truck before he caught a glimpse of the blankets strapped on the bed, just as Irving arrived at his side.

"It's Bobby and Von," stated Irving solemnly.

"Oh Lord," Jon gasped, turning to locate Hank and Jacqueline. His brother and sister-in-law looked as if they were walking in slow motion to the edge of the truck. Both Gina and Nicole moved to their side, while Von's father and brother moved closer.

Irving hopped up on the bed where he gaped down at the crowd, unsure how he should proceed. Bill hoisted himself up on the cold, metal bed, to join the captain. Bill's jaw was tight while he stood over the bodies, making it apparent he should be prudent in uncovering his cousin. Hank climbed up, followed by Von's father, where both froze in place, staring at the wrapped bodies.

"Please, let us take them off of the truck, and prepare them to be viewed," Irving pleaded with the two fathers.

"I want to see my son," Von's dad stated adamantly, moving down to one knee, taking hold of the blanket. He looked at Irving to get affirmation that it was Von he was about to unwrap. Irving nodded his head. He pulled the blanket back and gasped loudly.

Hank felt dizzy when he caught a glimpse of the horrific wound to the head of the strong young linebacker. He moved his eyes away from the young man, before reaching down to the blanket covering Bobby.

"Coach, can we wait?" Bill placed his hand on his uncle's bicep. He glanced away from his cousin's body in anticipation of catching a vision of something he really didn't want imprinted in his mind. Off to the side of the truck, next to the car, Emilee was standing in a trance with her hair matted to the side of her face.

"It's okay Bill." Hank pulled the blanket away from Bobby's body. His mind was a tornado of memories and thoughts of his only son. He stared at his lifeless body, realizing he had made a mistake in witnessing the horrific sight of the gunshot wound to the skull. The blood rushed from his head as he closed his eyes tightly, knowing the moment the storm dissipated within his mind, the pain would be unbearable. His dominion had blown into a million different parts, and it could never possibly be put back together. The rest of his life would be living within a fabricated world with stitched hopes and possibilities.

He pushed the cover back and stood up. From his vantage point on the truck the people below all seemed to have their heads bowed. The image of his neighbors, Al and Linda, who had watched Bobby grow from the time he was a baby, appeared blurred as they crowded next to Jacqueline whose face was covered by her hands. He felt Bill's hand firmly on his shoulder as he fell to his knees, trying to rid his mind of the realization that he would never again have a conversation with his son.

Pentagon, Arlington County Virginia

Army Chief of Staff Ron McClinton, along with the heads of the other service branches, mingled around a table in the crowded war room, waiting for Chairman of Joint Chief of Staff Ernie King, to join the strategy session. The chairman entered nearly thirty minutes late. He tossed a packet of papers onto the table and paused momentarily to allow everyone to take a seat, while he remained standing.

"I know many of you helped to draft the report that I found on my desk this morning." His grey eyes were narrow slits on his face, making him seem to be barely awake. Everyone at the table knew that wasn't the case. "I want to be positive that the intentions I am reading in this memorandum are what each of you explicitly believe to be true. The burden for all of you, currently, is to convince me that the use of nuclear weapons is our final option. Then the onus will be upon me to convince the Commander and Chief, as well as the Secretary of Defense and the National Security Council."

"Sir, I think the report was hastily, and quite frankly, poorly worded. It describes a finality that I don't believe was the intent of those of us who contributed it. The report makes our willingness to use nuclear weapons seem to be our only option. Some of us still believe there is an avenue for preemption," stated the Chief of Naval Operations.

"Either we are intending to use nuclear weapons, or we aren't. And from what I am reading in this document," the chairman picked up the paper, "your aim is to stop the enemy by utilizing tactical nuclear weapons at sea, and on our homeland."

"Sir, we want the Chinese and Russians to realize that we will employ the weapons to stop their fleets of ships now approaching our land on both the Pacific and Atlantic oceans, along with the multitude of troops and equipment preparing to invade from the southern edge of Mexico." The Commandant of the Marine Corp shot a glance in the direction of the Chief of Naval Operations. "We want President Weller to understand that the nuclear option is something we are serious about using, and that we are very capable in delivering the payload."

"What was understated in this document is the absolute determination that all of us feel in utilizing all weapons at our disposal. It is important that the President convinces both Beijing and Moscow the seriousness of our intentions to use the nuclear weapons if they continue to advance," Army Chief of Staff McClinton sighed. "If he wavers or falters in any way while expressing our firmness in stopping the advancing forces, to the point where they call his bluff, the possibility of any deterrence will be out the window. We hope that the enemy will understand his resolve and retreat their forces, but if they continue to bear down on us, the intent from the report is that we blow them all to hell."

Fort Carson Army Base

The FBI task force made great strides with squashing the insurgents' efforts to destroy several key locations along the front range of Denver. Although the Cherry Creek reservoir was damaged, it wasn't completely breached. The city was still in turmoil, but strides were being made in creating safety zones for citizens to obtain food and medical assistance.

Ted understood better than anyone that his orders could change on a dime. He was not surprised at all when he met with General Lopez, he was informed that the two companies under his command, being used to thwart the insurgents, were to be redirected to join the rest of the 99th Infantry on the front lines.

The 2nd Platoon would remain at his disposal, and orders were issued to allow the forty-person platoon to station on the eastern plains. The National Security Branch of the FBI took over the brunt of the task of fighting the terrorist in the city. With quieted rumors that the war could escalate into a nuclear crisis, he wanted to stay close to his family.

With only a platoon of soldiers to work with, he decided to focus his attention on solving the whereabouts of Mike Chen and the Vasilyeva's. If they were still in the Colorado Springs area, finding them would be the first step in the prevention of an attack on NORAD. He wasn't totally convinced the threat to NORAD was valid, but he did know that the three characters he was searching for were still a menace to the country.

His mind wandered as he stared blankly at the top of his desk. He was having a hard time considering any scenario where the country could come together at the end of the war, win or lose. The damage done to the citizenry by the homegrown insurrectionists was so atrocious that it would take generations for healing to occur. Wars throughout time were full of carnage and viciousness. Society always found a way to bounce back.

A knock on the door brought him out of his deep thought.

"Your wife is on line one," a private stuck his head inside the door.

"Yes, Nicole," He spoke with a deep voice into the telephone.

"Ted, I have some terrible news to tell you." Nicole's voice was quivering. "Bobby was killed in Indiana trying to buy food for the farm."

"Oh my God. I can't imagine what Hank and Jacqueline are going through." He felt selfish for thinking how devastated he would be had she told him Bill was dead. "Where is his body?"

"It's here." Nicole hesitated while she swallowed. "Jon is taking control of everything. We are planning on having a service for him late tomorrow."

"I will make every effort I can to be there."

"We need you, Ted."

"I'll see you tomorrow."

White House, Washington D.C.

President Weller pinched the top of his nose, trying to relinquish the pain of an insufferable headache. He listened to Secretary of Defense Robert Maes lay out the near apocalyptic situation of the war. The council briefed him about the enemy breaking through the lines in Texas, and moving slowly to the north and east, with the likelihood of actual fighting taking place on the east coast by the middle of January. There was a real possibility that the capital of the United States would have to move from Washington DC inland. But the most daunting of all the information he was hearing, was that all his advisers were now proponents of using nuclear weapons to stop the enemy.

"Bob, you say that we are at DEFCON 1. When did this happen?" The President placed both hands on the table. He was beyond being concerned with sounding stupid by asking questions of which he should already know the answer.

"The moment the commander at North American Aerospace Defense Command went to EMERGCON, all Branches of our Military moved to DEFCON 1."

"Precisely, what does it mean?" Deep in the back corners of his mind he knew what it meant. He never for the life of him thought he would be seriously having this discussion.

"It means that our nuclear weapons are locked and loaded."

"Mr. President, we are to the point where you have to be willing to use all the power at our fingertips or be ready to lose the country." The voice of Barbara Stone, the Director of National Intelligence, was loud and strong. "The enemy has positioned nearly two million additional troops ready to move north through Mexico. If we allow them to replenish troops in Mexico with the purpose of reinforcing the troops already here, we will lose the war within a month."

"You're telling me that we cannot stop them without using nuclear weapons?" The President's right eye twitched as he shot a restless look at the members of his National Security Council.

"According to the Joint Chiefs of Staff, the answer is no, if they continue the assault. All of them have stated that we should immediately let Beijing and Moscow know that we will use the nuclear option if they move forward," stated Secretary of Defense Maes.

"Let me understand. The Joint Chiefs of Staff recommend the United States of America use of nuclear weapons on enemy troops advancing across Mexico." President Weller glanced incredulously at Vice President Trupp, who was seated next to White House Chief of Staff Alexander, with a blank expression on his face.

"The answer to that question is yes." The Director of National Intelligence Stone folded her hands in front of her as she leaned forward with her elbows on the table. "The leaders from China and Russia must understand that we are serious when you tell them we will use every weapon at our disposal, including nuclear. Hopefully they will believe us and stop the invasion."

"Where do we make the red line?" The President continued to stare in disbelief. "Do we make it northern Mexico where we obliterate thousands of people, or after they cross onto our soil where we destroy San Antonio and the small communities of southern Texas? The fall out will not only affect the people of the United States but also the Mexican citizens for years to come."

"We don't make a red line," stated the Secretary of Defense. "We must make it clear that you, Mr. President, are serious about pulling the trigger if they leave us no other option. But sir, it is you who must be willing to use the weapons, and you, who must convince our enemies that you are deadly serious in your resolve to do so."

President Weller felt his heart pounding rapidly as he coughed twice into the sleeve of his shirt. He took in two deep breaths and exhaled before stating, "I want recommendations on where we should strike. Prepare a message, immediately, to inform Beijing and Moscow of our intentions."

"I'll get it out immediately," said the Secretary of State. "It will be ready within the hour for your approval."

"I want a detailed plan as to where and when we should strike."

"Sir, I recommend that you tell the public in your address to the nation of your decision to use our nuclear arsenal if the enemy continues to advance," interjected the Vice President. "By stating publicly, to our citizens, that we are willing to use all weapons at our disposal, the leaders from China and Russia are much more likely to believe that you are serious."

Colorado Farm

Christmas had always been a time to share blessings. The most wonderful time of the year for both the Lisco and Jacoby families, who always found ardor in the presence of family. This Christmas they both shared the bounty of loss as they gathered in the living room of the farmhouse, whilst the rest of the members of the farm congregated inside the newly framed building. Although far from finished, with uncharacteristic warm weather, the structure allotted the non-family members a place to gather, while allowing Bobby and Ed's families privacy.

Large red blotches covered the otherwise pale face of Irene. She rested in a chair, with Breanna perched next to her, grasping her left hand with both of her hands. There was a hush while the remainder of the Jacoby family scattered about the room, all neatly dressed, some standing with hands in their pockets, and others silently staring at each other, waiting for someone to give them direction to proceed to the field to bury Ed and Bobby.

Von's father was adamant that his son be buried at a cemetery in Denver, and not at the farm. After some discussion, in the darkness of the early morning it was determined, by Aaron Jacoby, that they could use Ed's F-250 to transfer Von back to the city.

Maddy sat on Bill's lap in a chair next to the fireplace hearth. The side of her face rested on his chest as she kept her wide eyes on Hank and Jacqueline who were settled into the couch next to Jon, Gina and Nicole. Jason and Kori Jensen, along with George and Toby Saxton watched silently from the side of the room. Dave took a group to the hilltop to finalize the digging of the two graves.

"I don't want Bobby to be dead." Maddy shifted on her father's lap to where she sat more upright. She gazed up at his sagging face, with her dark eyes, trying to hold back the tears.

"I don't either." Bill felt his heart pounding as he patted her shoulder.

Sherry, followed by Caroline, Jessica and Emilee, entered the front door and moved silently past the grieving family members in the direction of the clinic. Emilee was carrying the piece of cardboard that she and Bobby found on the front door of the home of Julia's son. Bill noticed Jacqueline pivot her head to watch Sherry as she led the group through the clinic door and closed it. Jacqueline caught Bill's eyes as she turned back to the family members in the living room. She grimaced before lowering her head.

Bill had no idea about the identity of the father of Sherry's baby. He wondered if his Aunt Jacqueline might be grasping at straws, hoping that Bobby left her a grandchild. Everything he knew about the virtue of his cousin caused him to believe that there was little or no chance that he was the father of the unborn child. He felt terribly sorry for the false hope his aunt was experiencing.

"Everything is going to be okay." Maddy sniffled as she patted her father on his hand. She shook her head up and down and repeated, "It will be okay."

Bill stared into the tiny slits of her eyes, realizing that she was repeating the phrase she had heard many times over during the past couple months. It was heartbreaking for him to have her experience such tragedy but comforting that she would react in such an empathetic manner. The uncertainty and dire danger they were facing, enhanced by the fact that they were only moments away from marching to a field, a remote pasture, to bury his friend and cousin, caused him anxiety that he didn't want to portray to his daughter. He rose from the chair and took hold of Maddy's hand. They moved next to Nicole. He whispered, "I am going to the office and see if I can get ahold of dad."

Nicole wilted as she looked up at her son, sensing his anguish. She understood his desire to take Maddy out of the stressful situation.

Bill nodded before turning and walking out the door. The sun was beating down as they crossed the courtyard. Chatter and the sound of children laughing could be heard from the shell of the new building, as many of the people gathered inside the large structure to celebrate Christmas.

The roar of aircraft in the distance was now so commonplace that it was usually imperceptible, but the clapping of the blades of a helicopter caused Bill to stop and look to the west. He reached down and picked Maddy up as the sound increased. The sight of a low flying helicopter came into view on the horizon.

"It's a Blackhawk," Irving yelled to Bill from the window in the tower. "It looks like they are going to land north of the apartments.

"Is it Grandpa?" Maddy asked, watching the helicopter disappear behind the buildings.

"It's either him or Aunt Deb." Bill let Maddy slip to the ground and turned in the direction of the descending helicopter.

Ted was already walking toward them by the time they were at the end of the apartments. He was smartly arrayed in his dress blue uniform. Maddy ran to him and threw her arms around his waist.

"Bobby's dead." Maddy pushed her chin into Ted's side, keeping her eyes upward toward him.

Ted placed his hand on the side of her face where he could feel moisture near her eyes. He didn't say anything.

"I guess you know that Ed passed away too." Bill stared at his father's tan, clean-shaven face. His salt and pepper hair was neatly combed back.

"No, I didn't hear about Ed." He felt a cool breeze on his face as he gazed at his son. Both sides of Bill's eyes were swollen, and deep lines crossed vertically down his face. He looked as if he hadn't slept in days.

"Mom is in the house." Bill took a small step toward the farmhouse. Maddy relinquished her hold on Ted, and they made their way in the direction of the grieving families.

When Nicole heard the helicopter fly past the house she moved out onto the porch. She waited for the three members of her family to arrive at the gate before stepping away from the doorway and meeting them in the yard.

"It's really bad." Nicole placed her hand on the side of Ted's face. She rubbed her hand in a circular motion over his smooth skin.

"I can only imagine." He leaned down and kissed her on the cheek.

He expected he would be walking into a very solemn, room but was surprised that it was quiet enough to hear a pin drop. Usually at times of grief there were members of the family who found solace in talking, of making noise as a reminder that they were still alive. Everyone seemed to be frozen in place, sitting and standing like mannequins in a department store.

The moment Ted stepped in front of the couch, Jacqueline rose and threw her arms around him. He wrapped his arms around her. He could feel her quivering as she hugged his neck forcefully. Moisture escaped to settle on his chin when she squeezed her eyes tightly shut. Hank stared up at him from his seat on the coach, with glazed eyes and an absent expression.

When Jacqueline relinquished her hold, he leaned down to one knee in front of his youngest brother and placed a hand on the top of his shoulder. He could hear him struggling to breathe, and his jaw was clenched shut.

"Hank, we are all here for you and Jacqueline." He used his powerful left hand to squeeze his upper shoulder.

Hank breathed through his nose and gave a subtle nod. When Ted rose, he caught a glance of Irene sitting near the fireplace. She gave him a closed mouthed smile.

"I'm terribly sorry," Ted moved in front of her. She pulled her hand out of Breanna's and grabbed hold of his right hand. She was shaking as she gripped as hard as she could.

"Ed was an exceptional man. He had a wonderful life, and I'm sure he is in a very good place right now," his voice rang out louder than he intended.

Dave entered through the front door and moved to the middle of the room. "We have the grave sites ready," he directed the statement to Hank, before lowering his eyes.

****

Having a funeral so quickly, located in a pasture, without a service seemed both natural and inappropriate at the same time. The raw splendor from the waves of blowing grasses under the haze of the low December sun subscribed more for the interment of an older man from a farming community in Utah, such as Ed, rather than for a high school student from the city, such as Bobby.

The two wood coffins sat to the side of the holes in the earth, spaced about five meters apart, next to the graves of Carol, Christian and Fred. Inhabitants of the farm covered the hill, with many of the men sporting beards, and all the women's hair blowing in the wind. It could have easily been taken from a scene of travelers from a wagon train, stopping to bury a settler, a couple hundred years earlier.

Two rows of folding chairs sat on the dry grass for the family members to sit and listen as those who wished to do so shared stories and thoughts about Bobby and Ed. When the proceedings seemed to be coming to an end, Jerry and his crew of cooks began to walk back toward the farmhouse to prepare lunch. Patrick Montgomery stomped to the front of the family members. He positioned himself between the two coffins. Members of both families warily glowered at him, unsure of his intentions.

"After listening to the stories of these two fine men, I would like to say a word. I promise I will be short winded." Patrick stood up straight and held the palm of his massive right hand toward the people. *The goal of life is death, something we all face. At this extraordinary time where ordinary life, as we knew it, has vanished, we must realize that living is the best prayer we can offer to God. What would be dreadful for all of us to consider is not to live, not to try, not to help one another. As we eat steaks and stew, we should think of Ed. When we think of possibilities we can think of Bobby, who gave his life trying to make ours better. I just want to say to the families that to live in your minds is not to die. The memory of these two men, much different in station and age, will not be buried for many years."*

There was a collective sigh from the family members, making it clear that they appreciated the Englishman's wonderful tribute to Bobby and Ed. It was a fitting way to end the services.

****

Maddy took hold of Ted's hand as they prepared for the journey back to the farmhouse. The grass crunched under their feet.

"Is Patrick a giant?" Maddy asked animatedly.

"He is a giant-sized man," Ted answered.

"Not like the giant in Jack and the Bean Stalk." Nicole grabbed Maddy's other hand.

"Were you able to inform Aunt Deb about Bobby?" Bill walked with his head hanging low.

"I left a message with General Lauer this morning. I think she is still in the Albuquerque area." Ted looked at the top of Maddy's head, remembering the terrible feelings of helplessness he felt when the two of them were stranded away from home.

"When do you have to return to the base?" Nicole asked.

"I'm going to stay here for a couple of days, and work from the office. There is a lot happening on the front lines, and most of the soldiers from my task force have been called forward."

"So, you might be here longer than a couple days?" Nicole stopped walking with her grey hair blowing in the wind.

"We'll see. Everything is so up in the air right now; I can't say with certainty what will happen this afternoon. 2nd Platoon is scheduled to arrive this evening, with the idea of stationing at the farm for the immediate future. But we could be diverted at any time."

"President Weller is supposed to speak this evening." Bill turned toward Ted. "I guess we will be able to receive the message over the radio."

"We will. I want to spend some time with Hank and Jacqueline before I get caught up in my office. Bobby being gone seems so surreal, and I don't know how much comfort our words will be, but we must be there for them." Ted sighed and shook his head. He squeezed Maddy's hand and started walking again.

La Junta, Colorado

Headquarters for 2nd Battalion was set on the north side of the small city of La Junta, a little over a hundred kilometers east of Pueblo, Colorado. Deb and her staff were able to attain quarters in an abandoned farmhouse on the northern edge of the city. She was in the process of settling in when a corporal entered the premises with a message for her from General Lauer.

Command Sergeant Major Talfoya watched from a distance behind her as she read the dispatch. She sat down in a soft chair as she held the transmit tightly in her hand.

"What is it," He asked hesitantly.

"Bobby's dead."

"Just Bobby." Tommy wondered if the farm suffered another attack.

"I have no details. But I presume it is only him."

"How far is the farm from here?"

"If we drive it's a little over an hour." Deb lowered her head thinking of the time she spent with her nephew and his friends when they were at the farm.

"I'll inform Josh and Captain Hendersen that we will be leaving within the hour. He moved closer to her. "We'll take 2nd Platoon with the idea of working from there for the next couple of days.

She nodded affirmatively to Tommy before he walked out the door. It was always apparent that the war would reach her family, but never in her wildest dreams would have she imagined that Bobby would be the first to die. He was kindhearted and considerate to others as any individual she encountered during her life. She wasn't sure how she could help Hank and Jacqueline, but she felt deep in her stomach the need to be with her family. There was much uncertainty with her situation concerning the next mission, but she knew that life was hardly ever what you expect.

Colorado Farm

Ted was busy at his desk hashing over the files he received from the FBI task force concerning the proposed attack on NORAD. He separated the map with the x's marking the properties owned by the Chinese and Russian entities from the pictures of the Vasilyeva's and Mike Chen. He began to feel some apprehension when he picked up the torn piece of paper with the two numbers 5220326, 3610326. If the digits were telephone numbers, then the 361-area code was in Texas and the 522-area code was from Iowa. Without the missing torn pieces with the remaining numbers, the numbers alone were useless.

He looked hard at the name Marlee printed neatly at the bottom of the paper. He wished he could quiz Shira to see if she was an acquaintance of hers. He looked up from his deep thoughts to see Bill and Samantha walking toward him.

"Dad, your platoon just arrived, and it looks like they are setting up at the same place they were at before." Bill glanced at the papers on the desk.

"I've been in communication with them." Ted turned in the chair as Samantha moved to stand closely at his side. He smiled at her and said, "I'm glad you came."

"I wanted to see how you are feeling. Everything seems to be happening so quickly," Bill stated.

"The conversation I had with Hank and Jacqueline after the funeral went well, but they wanted to spend some time alone, so everyone is going to give them their space."

"I feel almost numb to the fact that Bobby is gone." Bill glanced at Samantha. "It worries me that I am not more emotional."

"You can't fake your feelings, Bill. Everyone knows you cared a lot about Bobby. You need to keep in mind that all this might hit you later." Ted understood the reaction his son was experiencing. Unfortunately, war had found its way to the everyday life of his family, and post-traumatic stress disorder was something they were going to most likely experience along the way.

"What's all this, Ted?" Samantha leaned close enough for him to smell the lotion on her skin. She touched the picture of Mike Chen.

"I'm trying to figure out where these people are hiding out." His eyes remained on his cluttered desk.

"Is there any way we can help?" Bill moved from the back of the chair to Samantha's side.

"I really don't know how." Ted glanced at Samantha. Her bright red lips were the same as the first time he saw her on the airplane. But she looked different than she did a week earlier. She was thinner, and the skin around her cheeks was tanned and rough, giving her a more natural look. It was the area under her eyes that caught his eye. The skin was drooping, causing her to look sad.

"What are the numbers?" Bill noticed the torn piece of paper.

"I'm thinking they are telephone numbers, but without the remaining digits they are useless." He returned his gaze back to the desk.

"I don't think so, Dad. Telephone numbers would have the area code either in parenthesis or a dash after it."

"I suppose so, but I have no idea what else they might be," Ted sighed. "The FBI is working to see if it is a coded message, but I'm not sure they find the piece of paper to be very important. I'm thinking if I could speak with Shira, she might be able to help."

"Why don't you interview her."

"The CIA still have her under wraps."

"Where did the piece of paper come from." Bill placed both hands on the desk.

"That's a good question. The head of the FBI task force gave me the packet, but I have a feeling he received it from the CIA."

"They must think it is important or they wouldn't have given it to you," Bill stated.

"To be honest I'm about ready to toss it. I'm not going to spend much more time contemplating the possibilities." He didn't want to mention to Bill that he was wary of anything the CIA, or for that matter, the FBI gave to him. Anything he received from the deep, administrative state was used with guarded seriousness, because he figured if they found it important, they would have already acted on the information.

"They are MLS numbers," Samantha blurted out.

"They are what?" Ted was taken back by the ease of Samantha in solving the riddle.

"It looks like pieces of paper I had on my desk when I was searching to buy a house. The numbers are from the multiple listing service used to identify homes for sale, and I bet Marlee was the realtor."

Ted turned in his chair toward her. His mind was in turmoil as he gazed straight into the belly of the flight attendant. Could the FBI have let something so obvious get by them. He swung back around and picked up the telephone.

Bill moved away from the desk and placed his hand around Samantha's waist. Jon and Gina entered, and soon were followed by others until the room was filled, waiting for the President to speak. Nearly half the people living at the farm swarmed into the garage. Nicole and Maddy shuffled through the crowd to stand by his side as Ted finished his call.

The monitor on the desk showed the President walking to the podium. Ted turned up the volume so those who couldn't see the screen would be able to hear.

White House, Washington D.C.

President Weller's face was flushed red, as he marched toward the podium. There was no returning from his commitment. Messages were delivered warning Beijing and Moscow that if they did not withdraw, nuclear weapons would be utilized against their forces. Allies were notified of the United States intentions to use all weapons at its disposal. Now, the President needed to make it completely clear to the Chinese and Russian governments that he had the tenacity to follow through.

The President was a great orator, with a thunderous voice. The moment he reached the lectern, his heart slowed as he prepared to speak. His choice to address the people from the podium, rather than sitting at his desk in the oval office, was the correct one. He felt comfortable with his hands on the side of the stand.

"My fellow Americans, during this of the darkest of times, where our homeland is under attack, I come to you to state that America, even under the direst of circumstances, is still the brightest beacon for freedom, opportunity and hope in the world. We look into the future knowing that democracy must survive, we fight for the freedom of humankind, and understand we must win through absolute victory."

"To our allies, the time of neutrality is gone, and out of the question. We together, are the world's greatest bastion of freedom. We call for you to give us your full support to help us preserve ourselves for future generations. America is facing the grimmest circumstances, where some scholars are suggesting we surrender, and negotiate our own existence. My reply to them is to quote Churchill, nations that go down fighting rise again, and those that surrender tamely are finished."

"Tonight, I will be to the point, frank and forthright with you, the people of our great nation. We are facing a prodigious evil, not only from abroad, but from within. I ask all those who have fallen, and decided to fight against your fellow citizens, to come back into the fold. It will never be too late to rejoin us because tyranny cannot prevail. It takes all of us to fight for a common cause. We can and we will triumph together."

"As I speak to you, the United States southern border remains breached, and the enemy looms to move to the north, and to the east, threatening the entirety of our country. Our brave soldiers are fighting valiantly, but tonight, enemy ships are crossing both the Atlantic and Pacific

Oceans. While these great fleets of ships near, millions of enemy forces are posed to move to our southern border from southern Mexico. A massive buildup of forces that we cannot defeat without taking drastic steps."

"We did not ask for this fight, and we must defend ourselves to the utmost. The fear we have faced for the past one hundred years of atomic military build-up has finally come to fruition. We are taking immediate and resolute action. Therefore, I have sent a message to the Chinese and Russian governments that if they continue to move troops in the direction of the United States, and the armada does not return to their home countries, we will use nuclear weapons to protect our homeland. I repeat, we will use nuclear weapons to stop them."

President Weller hesitated and took in a deep breath. The teleprompter showed the words "use all weapons at our disposal" He changed it to "use nuclear weapons", so there would be no confusion on the part of the American people.

"I know there are many who wonder about my steadfastness to use our nuclear arsenal if the enemy persists. I want to be perfectly clear to everyone listening tonight that my determination and resolve to protect this country is beyond difference. Those who think differently will soon find themselves to be greatly lacking. Our government of the people, by the people, for the people shall never perish from this world.

God Bless America."

The President turned and walked off the stage without answering any questions from the media. There was much more to say to the American people, but he wanted to make it crystal clear to the Russian's and Chinese officials that he was going to use nuclear weapons if they continued to advance. He didn't want to temper his message with any fluff.

Colorado Farm

Ted sat with his hands clasped in front of him, staring at his desk. The loud conversations, inside the small space, with people shouting over one another, made it difficult to understand what any one person was saying.

"I guess we should have seen this coming," Jon shouted, standing right next to Ted.

"Let's go outside," Ted yelled.

Jon, Gina, Bill, Samantha, Nicole and Maddy followed him out the side door of the garage. They could smell the smoke coming from the fireplace in the new addition. It was cold with the bright stars producing a natural glow that created shadows across the landscape. A few colored light bulbs placed on the fence around the front yard flickered, along with the muffled sound of children laughing, coming from the addition, were the only indicators of it being Christmas. There was a sense of confusion as others moved out of the garage to scatter on the farm grounds. They gathered into groups to discuss the Presidents message.

"Do you think we are on the eve of nuclear war?" Bill pulled Maddy's face tight to his leg as he asked his father the dreadful question.

"If the Chinese and Russians don't believe him, and continue to advance, then yes I believe the President will use the nuclear weapons." Ted put his arm around Nicole and looked warily at Jon. "We are barely holding the enemy at bay as it is."

"The President means everything he said, and if he does utilize them, then there will most certainly be a response in kind from the Chinese and Russians," said Jon sternly. He stopped speaking when he noticed the lights from a convoy of trucks moving down the county road, turning onto the driveway. He turned toward Ted. "Are you expecting more troops tonight?"

"It's Deb," Ted said forcefully.

They all watched as the lead vehicle in the convoy stopped in front of the farmhouse, and Deb jumped out. She walked quickly inside the house. The convoy then continued to drive further onto the property.

"I'm glad she is going in to see Aunt Jacqueline and coach first," said Bill with a sad expression on his face.

Ted took a step forward to intercept the convoy. The large Tactical Command Communication Vehicle stopped, and Command Sergeant Major Talfoya stepped out.

"Good to see you, Tommy," Ted greeted the Command Sergeant Major.

"You must be going to stay a while since you brought the communication vehicle," Jon stated quickly.

"Deb is pretty upset about the loss of Bobby, so I'm sure we will be here as long as we can."

"Are you still headquartered in Albuquerque?" Ted always felt a sense of security when in the presence of the command sergeant major.

"No, we've been deployed back to southern Colorado, near La Junta. Deb and I both thought we would advance to the south after securing the wilderness area in New Mexico. The brass obviously has different plans."

"Were you listening to the President's address?" Jon joined into the conversation.

"We were listening," Tommy's voice strained. "I believe he plans to use the nukes if they continue forward. I pray to God that the leaders in Beijing and Moscow believe him."

"Any idea why you were deployed to La Junta?" Ted sensed the answer to his question was already answered in the Presidents message.

"Us moving north is the biggest reason I believe the President is serious about using the nuclear weapons if the enemy continues to advance." Tommy noticed Deb, along with Hank and Jacqueline walking in their direction across the courtyard.

Deb's jaw was clenched tight as she went directly to Bill. She grasped the back of his arm and squeezed tightly, while looking him directly in the eyes. "I would have never guessed in a million years we would be standing out here under these circumstances," she said grimly.

Bill nodded understandingly, staring into her deep eyes. Over the years, in preparing the farm, they had discussed many scenarios, but never ones that involved the death of a family member, or for that matter, the looming threat of nuclear war.

With an expression of benevolence, he gazed at his Aunt Jacqueline whose natural exuberance had disappeared and was replaced with a woeful face that looked like she was frozen in place. And Uncle Hank was no longer the strong and confident coach who had always inspired him. He was a defeated man with an unrecognizable expression on his face. He felt guilty that his grief for his cousin had already begun to evaporate. He vowed to make a conscious effort to stay alert in respecting everyone else's anguish.

"Maddy, you should be with the other children for Christmas," Jacqueline used an appeasing tone as she leaned toward Bill to speak. The door to the new building came open in the far distance as Patrick and Al stood in the doorway. The sounds of merriment escaped from inside.

"I want to stay here," Maddy said softly, burying her face deeper into Bill's side.

"We were going to join the others shortly," Bill stated more enthusiastically than he intended. The tension of the situation felt like it could be cut with a knife. He had already given all the condolences he could think of and was now at an utter loss for words.

"I would like to go up to the grave site tonight," Deb said warily.

Hank shot Jacqueline a look with a guarded expression on his face.

"We will walk with you so you can say goodbye to Bobby," Jacqueline said with a low, quivering voice.

Sherry, Emilee and Jessica exited the garage and made their way toward the apartments. Jacqueline twisted her head and watched the three women until they were out of sight. Bill took in a deep breath and released it, realizing he needed to help his Aunt Jacqueline in realizing that Bobby was not the father of Sherry's baby. He planned to pull Sherry aside and ask her point blank, hoping she would disclose who the father was.

"I think I will take Maddy to the celebration," Bill said softly, glancing toward Nicole and Ted.

"We'll go with you." Nicole looked up at Ted for affirmation. He nodded.

Jacqueline leaned down and placed her hand on Maddy's shoulder. Maddy moved slightly away from the comfort of Bill's grasp toward her father's aunt. "I know you made all of us Christmas presents." There was a glimmer of light in her eyes. "I can't think of anything more I would like than to have you give them to everyone tonight."

Maddy looked to Nicole.

"We can get them and have them when you get back," stated Nicole animatedly.

****

Flames from a large fire reflected off the face of Harold. He stood proudly in front of his pride and joy, a large field stone fireplace, which he finished just in time for the Christmas celebration. Nearly all the people from the farm were inside the partially finished, uninsulated building, except for the Jacobys who were gathered around their RV. Warmth from the fireplace along with the body heat of everyone made it comfortable to mingle without wearing burdensome winter coats.

Bill was surprised that several of the inhabitants in the room seemed like people he had never seen before. A red-haired man with a matted beard and a freckled face nodded to him as they made eye contact. He finally remembered him to be a carpenter who came to the farm in the group with Patrick.

"Colonel, are we on the eve of destruction tonight?" A man with chestnut hair and a sharp nose moved to stand only a couple feet in front of Jon, vociferously asking the question.

Jon puffed his chest out as he acknowledged the man. He never tried to tell him that he was a lieutenant colonel, retired, and not a colonel, before answering the question. "Sir, if we are, there isn't a damn thing we can do about it now."

"I don't believe one word this President or anyone in his administration tells us. All these leaders, and all their lies, have led us to this point in time." Al positioned himself solidly in front of the Liscos. He slighted Jon to look directly at Ted. "If our military uses nuclear weapons, and the Russian's and Chinese launch their own weapons, where will they likely target first?"

Ted leaned down and brushed a smudge of dust off his pant leg before standing up straight. He glanced at Nicole. She quickly sensed he wanted her to take Maddy away to play with the other children. A crowd gathered around as Ted prepared to answer the dentist's inquiry.

"I imagine they will hit our largest cities first." Ted hoped everyone would accept his answer without question, and he and his family could simply watch Maddy, and the other children celebrate Christmas.

"Don't you imagine that one of their primary targets would be Cheyenne Mountain Air Force Station in Colorado Springs?" Al asked abruptly, with a smug expression on his face. "If I'm correct and the wind blows easterly, we will be directly affected by a nuclear explosion."

Blood rushed to Ted's face as he stared at the little man, something that didn't go unnoticed by Jon.

"Brilliant Al. Who would have ever considered they might attack NORAD?" Jon stepped up to stand next to Ted.

"Don't get short with me Jon." Al shot Patrick a look as the big man nudged closer to join in the conversation. "We have a right to know everything that might ensue during a nuclear war."

"Shoot away," Ted said assertively. "I'll answer your questions to the best of my knowledge."

Jon examined the expressions of everyone within ear shot as he pointed at Al. "You best do it in a respectful manner."

"I believe cordiality is certainly called for at this time," Patrick stated genially.

"Are there super bunkers provided for the elites of this country?" Al asked bluntly with a cocky expression on his face.

"Yes." It was a fact he couldn't deny. Ted's face was taut as he gazed across the large room to Nicole and Samantha who were conversing, while watching Maddy play with the other children.

"Can we stop the enemies' intercontinental ballistic missiles from hitting our land?" Al asked, using the same quarrelsome tone.

"Although some of the missiles they launched a month ago were able to hit our soil, we are better prepared at this time to stop them. All I can say is I hope so." Ted's eyes narrowed. He knew that new interceptors were being placed at secure locations as they spoke, but even as benign as the situation was at the farm, he wasn't going to give any information that might be a security breach. "We still have to consider the insurgents as a threat to sabotage our nuclear storage depots and command centers."

"Even if they did destroy the ICBM bases and nuclear storage depots, don't we still have bombers and submarines that could attack them with nuclear weapons?" Patrick's voice boomed off the walls.

"Yes, we do." Ted acknowledged him with a shrug. The whereabouts of the submarines was top secret and very few military leaders knew of their location. Without a doubt they existed, but he had no idea where they were positioned. "We can only pray that the leaders of China and Russia understand that a nuclear war would be a no-win scenario and will withdraw the attacking troops."

"If they don't?" Al gave a hard look to Ted.

"We will have a nuclear war," Jon jumped into the conversation. "God only knows what the final result might be."

"Here's Aunt Deb." Bill tapped Ted on the shoulder and pointed in the direction of the entrance where Deb, Jacqueline and Hank entered through the door.

Off to the side of the room Jessica was sitting on a metal folding chair next to Emilee, Caroline and Sherry, watching Reagan and Avery play. She cocked her neck and watched intently as Jacqueline followed Deb and Hank toward Ted and Bill. She shuffled in her seat, conflicted as to how to approach the grieving mother. Emilee noticed her discomfort and reached over and took hold of her hand.

Bill felt a sense of relief when he noticed that Jacqueline and Hank were more relaxed after spending time at the grave site with Deb. Out of the corner of his eye, he could see Sherry staring at the group, but before he could break away to speak to her, Jessica moved to the back side of his aunt and placed her hand on her elbow.

"Jacqueline, can we speak with you and Hank, in private?" Jessica asked softly. Emilee was standing right beside her.

The brashness of the woman who left her children to run off with Christian caught Jacqueline by surprise. For a fleeting moment she endeavored to conjure a way to deny the request, but deep in her mind there was a twinge of empathy from remembering how Bobby always went to the rescue of Emilee and the O'Brian family. Losing Bobby must be heartbreaking for them also.

She glanced at Hank with a caring expression on her face. He had heard the request and nodded affirmatively.

"I know it's getting cold outside, but it might be easier to talk if we go out."

The bright sky was now half filled with drab grey clouds, and the cool breeze had turned into a cold wind. Jacqueline pulled the collar to her coat tight around her neck.

"It looks like a storm might be coming," said Jessica with the wind raising the back side of her bright red hair.

"Maybe we should talk inside," Hank stated firmly.

"No," said Emilee quickly. "I really want to be alone with you when I tell you this."

Jacqueline felt her hair blowing in the breeze as she watched the distressed young woman struggle to speak.

"I loved Bobby more than anything in the world." Emilee sniffled and dabbed her right eye with the back of her hand. She began to sob. Jessica placed her arm over her shoulder.

"Tell them," she whispered.

"I'm pregnant," Emilee blurted out. Her face was bright red, and her eyes filled with water.

Hank was in a state of dazed shock. It was only a few months earlier that he and Bobby were working through the football season, trying to win a state championship, where all the pressure and difficulties were artificially made up to create an environment to learn life lessons. Now, in such a brief time Bobby was gone, and he left a child behind. He wasn't sure if he should rejoice or be more sorrowful to the fact that Bobby would never be able to enjoy his child.

"I thought I might be pregnant before we went on the trip. But I didn't confirm it until this morning."

"Did you tell Bobby when you were in Indiana that you thought you were pregnant?" Hank asked.

"Yes, I think it is why he made me wait at the entrance while he delivered the money for the food." She clenched her teeth and sniffled. "He always did everything he could to protect me."

Jacqueline's joyous eyes rested on the glowing Emilee, whose eyes transfixed on hers, crafting a bond between the two of them, signifying that they would support one another through the difficult period. She would be the one to protect the mother of her grandchild, just like Bobby would want her to do. She sighed and smiled before cocking her head and moving her gaze to Jessica. She hoped it was simply her imagination, but she sensed the expression on the soon to be other grandmother was one of spite, a face that loathed her with a passion. Her piercing eyes communicated that she was in a superior position in terms of the nurturing of their grandchild, as she pulled her daughter tighter to her chest. There could now be major consequences for anyone who might feel required to tell her she was a bad mother or a bad grandmother.

Pentagon, Arlington, Virginia

All twenty monitors on the wall in the war room were filled with scenarios from around the world, with none more important than the two largest screens in the middle of the half-moon room. The left monitor displayed an image of hundreds of ships scattered across the Pacific Ocean approximately 180 kilometers west of Hawaii. The second screen showed an even larger fleet, approximately 310 kilometers east of Nassau in the Atlantic Ocean.

"Are they staying course?" Secretary of Defense Maes asked the Chairman of the Joint Chiefs of Staff.

"They made only minor adjustments," he answered with a raised eyebrow.

"My God, how many ships do they have?"

"There are 420, with 120 of them being destroyers, in the Pacific and nearly 500 in the Atlantic, with 140 destroyers" stated the Chief of Naval Operations warily. "For years we have underestimated the size of their naval power. As we speak their shipyards are working around the clock producing more."

"We are about to go online with the President." Secretary of Defense Maes expression hardened. "Keep the chatter down and speak only if you are asked a direct question."

Two large monitors showed the image of President Weller sitting at a large table surrounded with his council. The President leaned back in the chair with his legs crossed.

"Sir, can you see and hear us?"

"Yes, we have a perfect visual." The President stared at the different monitors showing the enemy fleets and graphics from the Pentagon. "Tell us what we are seeing."

"The image on your right shows the feed from the Pacific Ocean, and the one on the left is the Atlantic Ocean."

"Have we seen any indication they might alter course?"

"No, sir."

"Sir, both fleets have slowed slightly in the past ten minutes." The Chief of Naval Operations clenched his teeth, wondering if he should have requested permission to speak. The sharp look he received from the Secretary of Defense told him he should have done so.

"If our Navy were to engage the enemy, can our forces stop them from advancing?" President Weller asked.

"No, sir." Secretary of Defense Maes stated ominously. "We cannot win that battle."

"If it comes down to it." The President's voice cracked with uncertainty as he prepared to ask the question, "can we successfully deliver nuclear weapons?"

The Secretary of Defense recognized the doubt in the President's voice. He glanced at the Chairman of the Joint Chiefs of Staff. "Ernie, do we feel confident we can deliver the payloads?"

"One hundred percent confident."

"What will the environmental impact be?" The Secretary of State's tone was aggressive as she interrupted.

"Significant," Chairman of Joint Chiefs of Staff King said sharply.

"Can you elaborate?"

"No ma'am, I cannot at this time." He sensed there was going to be reluctance on the part of the President and his Cabinet with using the weapons at their disposal. The enemy would certainly take any sign of weakness as a green light to continue forward.

"How many tactical nukes will it take to destroy the armada?" Having never served in the military President Weller was trying his hardest to understand the situation. "With the enemy ships spread so far apart it seems like it will take several."

"Sir, you are correct. We are prepared to deploy however many devices needed at each location to eliminate the threat." Chairman of Joint Chiefs of Staff King stared blankly into the monitor.

"Explain to me why we cannot stop them with our air power?" The President asked with a perplexed tone.

"They have directed energy anti-aircraft weapons and laser interceptors on board the ships that keep our air power at bay."

"Can we destroy, or jam them?" President Weller asked, wanting to make sure everything was being done to avoid a nuclear conflict. He couldn't care less if he sounded uninformed about the basics of war in front of his war council.

"No sir, we don't have the capability. We previously found out when we countered their missile attack on our soil, by hitting them at sea, that their interceptors are far superior to what we anticipated them to be." Chairman of Joint Chiefs of Staff King coughed into his hand. He never once considered the question from the President to be ill-informed. Not long ago he was under the impression that we had the technology to defend against any type of attack, and that our missile defense was the best in the world. The events of the previous months changed all his perceptions.

"What are their headings?" The President decided not to press the issue as to why our missiles and air might were unable to penetrate the enemies' defenses.

"Sir, on the Pacific side, unless they change course, or we stop them, they will arrive on the western shore of Baja California about sixty kilometers from the United States Border." The Chief of Naval Operations crossed his arms. "On the Atlantic side, the direction taken has changed slightly to the north. They are going to end up in the Gulf of Mexico."

"Sir, some of our models are showing them hitting land in the New Orleans vicinity if they continue unimpeded," Chairman of the Joint Chiefs of Staff King interrupted. "All models indicate they will adjust course and turn in the direction of southern Mexico.

"We cannot, nor will we allow them to move forward unchecked." President Weller's combative tone was welcomed by everyone in the command center.

"Sir, the enemy ships in the Atlantic have come to a complete halt," yelled a lieutenant.

"How about in the Pacific?" The President sat forward in his chair.

"They are slowing too."

"Here is where I draw the red line." The President stood up and pounded his fist on the table. "I want the tactical nuclear weapons in place and ready to utilize. I will send a message to Beijing and Moscow stating that this is the moment of truth. God help us, but if they continue forward with the aggression, we will wipe them off the face of the earth."

A thought flickered through the mind of the Chairman of the Joint Chiefs of Staff. Nothing in this war is random, there is always a purpose to every action taken.

"Sir, I don't think you should send a message," he stated abruptly.

"Why not?" The glitter in the President's eyes turned dark with disappointment.

"They stopped a good hundred kilometers from our fleets. They have a reason for doing so."

"Give me some reasons they might have."

"Sir, they want to know when and where we plan to utilize the tactical weapons, so they can disable them."

"How do we plan to deliver the payloads?" The President asked the question that only a few members of his military knew the answer too.

"Sir, can we speak to you in a more private setting?" Secretary of Defense Maes spoke with desperation in his voice, realizing he was slighting several people in the room with the President.

The President rose from his chair and was escorted to a closed office. The Secretary of Defense and the Chairman of the Joint Chiefs of Staff also exited the war room to a secure location. They explained to the President that nonhuman underwater vehicles would deliver the nuclear payload. The new submarines used a water propulsion system for movement with stealth capabilities. The main issue was that the enemy armada was protected by nonhuman underwater minesweepers scouring the ocean floor below their ships. It would be necessary to eliminate the minesweepers for the nuclear payload to be delivered. But if given enough time and a general knowledge of the whereabouts of the underwater vessels used to destroy the minesweepers, the enemy could find, and either disable or destroy them.

"So, we first have to eliminate their minesweepers before our nuclear weapons can be used?" The Presidents frown deepened. "And we have the capability to do this?"

"Yes sir," the Chairman of the Joint Chiefs of Staff said in a sturdy voice.

"Let's take out their minesweepers on both fronts." The President sucked in a breath through his closed teeth. "I understand why it would be wrong at this time to give them a warning, much less a time frame."

"Sir, you have already warned them." The Secretary of Defense ran his thumb over the stubble on the front of his chin. "We should proceed on our own time, and at our own bidding. You are correct in your plan Mr. President. If we blind them by taking out their minesweepers, and they continue to advance, they will be playing Russian Roulette with their entire fleet."

Colorado Farm

Deb sat on a metal chair with a wool blanket wrapped around her shoulder, looking out the large window in the tower, with Command Sergeant Major Talfoya, Bill and Samantha sitting at her side. The cold breeze cleared the air, making it possible to see lights flickering in the far distance on the deep dark horizon. It was nearly midnight, but her adrenaline was still too high to allow her to sleep. She felt relaxed for the first time in quite a while.

"What do you two think is going to happen." Bill glanced back and forth between both Aunt Deb and Tommy. "Is there going to be a nuclear war?"

"I don't think so." Tommy's tone was so placid that it gave a ring of comfort to his answer. He was the type of man who was always taken seriously.

"That was quick," Deb said flippantly, staring at the command sergeant majors tan and rugged face. Cavernous crowfeet crept from the corners of his eyes, seeming to be deeper by the dim light.

"Although I never would have believed this war to have escalated to this point, I don't believe our leaders will continue to the mutual destruction of the world." He tipped his head toward Deb.

Noticing the interaction between Deb and Tommy created a warm feeling in Bill's heart. He placed his right hand, palm up on Samantha's leg. She hesitated for a moment before reaching with her hand and taking hold. She squeezed tightly and gave him a quick smile before letting go.

Deb sensed the tension between the two of them.

"The next two days will be critical in deciding the progression of this war." Deb noticed Samantha looking off to the side, detached from everything being said. "All we can do is wait and see what happens."

"Even if there isn't a nuclear war, how will this country ever come back together? We have a civil war taking place," Bill used a frustrated tone.

"It will take generations to overcome," Samantha's face tightened as the faraway look escaped her eyes. "I don't see how people whose lives were ruined will ever be able to forgive the insurgents. I know I won't"

"We built this farm as a sanctuary for people who want to work together. To create an existence where everyone can live and thrive together. It's far from perfect, but we will still have it after we chase the enemy from our soil." Deb all but ignored Samantha's declaration.

"To your point Samantha." Tommy looked at her with a furrowed brow. "You are probably correct that it will take generations to heal, but we did recover from a civil war once before."

"That was two hundred years ago, and I'm not sure that we really did recover." Samantha's face had a withered look.

"When this is all over, we will be stronger because those who took everything for granted will realize that nothing comes free." stated Tommy.

Samantha shrugged her shoulders and subtly nodded her head back and forth.

"I know this isn't the best time to bring this up, but we are going to have food issues if we don't find a way to resupply." Bill brought up the subject of food, partially to change the topic, but mostly because it was the most pressing issue facing the people on the farm. "I wonder if you have any pull with FEMA. It would be nice to be able to get some supplies on a regular basis."

"Ha, ha." Tommy leaned back in his chair.

Deb shot him an annoyed glance, with a slight smile on her face. "We will figure a way to get some basic supplies."

Bill prepared to ask Tommy why he thought it was funny to have his aunt ask FEMA for food, but before he could do so he noticed headlights on the county road. He gazed out the window as the lumberyard truck entered the courtyard.

"I wonder why Sheriff Bob and Ben would be traveling so late at night?" Bill looked out the window. Travis stepped down from the high truck door and reached up to help Sue exit. He turned to look at Samantha's reaction.

"Where are they coming from?" Deb asked.

"They went to the hospital at the little town of Hugo to check on Travis."

"Let's go down and see what's going on." Deb moved quickly down the stairs.

Sheriff Bob looked stiff as a board while trying to unlatch Travis and Sue's suitcases from the bed of the lumberyard truck. Ben Stewart's shoulders were hunched over as he watched.

"Here, let me help." Bill hopped up onto the back of the truck, and easily unhooked the straps. He noticed Samantha linger at the tower as he asked, "why did you take a chance of traveling so late at night?"

Tommy reached up to lift the suitcases off the bed as Sheriff Bob hobbled to stand next to Deb.

"The damn town is being attacked, and we got out of there as quick as we could." He cleared his throat before spitting on the ground.

"Who attacked them?" Deb asked.

"I have no idea who they were, but there was a hell of a lot of them." Sheriff Bob pulled on the crotch of his pants to loosen his stiff jeans.

"They destroyed the blockade the citizens put up around the town," Ben said sourly. "We were lucky we saw it coming and left by the back roads."

"How are you, Travis?" Bill gazed at Travis who was gingerly standing with his arm pressed to his side.

"I'm doing good now. But I'll tell you what, I was ready to leave that place." He stared furtively at Sue.

"We can send up the NAV to get surveillance." Deb turned to Tommy. "I don't know if it is a threat to us, but it wouldn't' hurt to check."

Bill could see Sue looking in the direction of Samantha with a protected look on her face. Samantha turned and walked toward her apartment.

"We need to get you settled in." Bill picked up the suitcases.

Pentagon, Arlington, Virginia

"Sir, the mission is underway." Secretary of Defense Maes stared at the screen showing the President, along with his senior leaders, sitting silently around a table gazing at the monitors on the wall.

"How long do you estimate it will take?" The President's voice was strong and loud. He just finished briefing his council on the operation he and the Secretary of Defense had discussed earlier.

"Once we begin, it shouldn't take more than thirty minutes." The Secretary of Defense's face was expressionless. "The mission must be precise and well timed. All the minesweepers will be taken out at the same time, so the enemy won't have time to retaliate."

"We are seeing some adjustments with the enemy fleet." The President watched the monitor showing the enemy ships in the Atlantic. "Is this something that should concern us."

"Sir, they are repositioning, attempting to identify the threats." The Chief of Naval Operations stated with a guarded voice.

"What happens if they do locate our submarines?" Vice President Trupp asked.

"It's too late. If not already, all their minesweepers will soon be destroyed."

"What do we do now?" President Weller's voice was strained, and his face looked drained. He knew immediately after asking the question it made him seem weak.

"Sir, we have to wait and see how they respond." Secretary of Defense Maes answered steadily.

The room at the Pentagon was silent.

"If we wait too long, they can bring in more minesweepers," the President's voice had a ring of desperation to it. "How long does it take for our nuclear weapons to be in position?"

"Sir, we can deploy them right now."

"I am going to open communication with Moscow and Beijing. The sun is just on the horizon in the Atlantic. If they do not turn their fleets around by noon Pacific time, we will use the nuclear weapons."

Colorado Farm

The sound of the chickens clucking was soothing to Ted as he opened his eyes to find Nicole perched on a pillow staring at him through her penetrating dark eyes. She reached over and placed her fingers on his rough chin.

"I haven't seen you sleep in this late in many years," she said.

"What time is it?" He turned to face her.

"It's 0730, Colonel Lisco." She dropped the top of her nightgown from her breasts and settled the side of her face on his chest.

"I was exhausted. It's nice being here with you." He smiled and placed his hand on the side of her face.

The door to their bedroom burst open, and Maddy rushed in. Nicole quickly sat up as their granddaughter jumped up on the bed landing squarely on Ted's stomach.

"Maddy, what are you doing?" Nicole pulled the bedspread over her breasts, holding it under her chin. "You know you are supposed to knock before coming into this bedroom."

"Ah, Grandpa don't care. Do you Grandpa?" She placed her hands on both sides of Ted's cheeks and twisted his head toward her.

"Maddy, this is not okay. You know better than to come in here like that," Nicole continued scolding, just as Bill came to the door. He knocked with the backside of his hand on the mostly opened door.

"Sorry, she was supposed to be eating breakfast. She took off in a sprint when I told her dad was still here." Bill gazed uncomfortably at his parents. "Come on Maddy, let's go, now!"

"Grandpa, can we go exploring today?" She continued to sit heavily on his stomach, ignoring her father.

Bill went to the side of the bed and grabbed ahold of her around the stomach and lifted her off the bed. He carried her to the door, turning momentarily to smile. "Sorry, you two go back to sleep."

"Maddy," Ted yelled as they left the room, "I'll find some time for us to spend together."

Corporal Pint came to the door before Bill had a chance to close it. She hesitated unsure how to approach, before entering. "Colonel, we just received a message that there has been an attack on NORAD."

Ted sat up exposing his muscular chest. He glanced at Nicole whose intense expression turned to a smile, before he replied, "I'll be right there."

He wanted to be in the presence of his soldiers when he found out about the severity of the assault on the North American Defense Command, so he bypassed going to his office in the garage and went directly to the communication center. The idea that the attack could be a prelude to nuclear war entered his mind, as he climbed into the large communication vehicle.

"What do we know so far." Ted sat down in front of the largest of two monitors. The monitor showed a hazy view of Cheyenne Mountain.

"They used a high energy weapon to penetrate the electrical cables from the top of the mountain," Lieutenant Graves stated as he pointed at the screen. "We are not sure of the totality of the damage inside the base."

"I want you to get me in touch with General Lauer at Fort Carson." Ted knew General Lopez was on the front lines in central Texas. It was General Lauer he needed to warn about the threat from the insurgents who gathered near Fort Carson. "Can I get a broader view of the area?"

"Sir, we have General Lauer." Lieutenant Graves stepped out of his seat.

Ted leaned over to investigate the small monitor. General Lauer's face took up most of the screen.

"General, a large force of insurgents is positioned in the Colorado Springs area, who could pose a danger to the base at Fort Carson."

"Ted, the FBI informed us of the threat last night when they discovered the location of the rebels planning the attack on NORAD. We have it fully under control." General Lauer's demeanor made it clear he was in a hurry to finish the call.

"How bad was the damage at Cheyenne Mountain?"

"It was minimal. Anything more?" General Lauer hesitated. When Ted didn't respond he disappeared from the screen.

Ted looked mystified. Why in the world was he not informed about the discovery of the rebel's hideout who were planning the attack on NORAD. Obviously, his information about the numbers from an MLS played a big part in the unearthing of their location. Even more troublesome was the fact that he didn't have any pending orders. He and his platoon were on their own. He wasn't about to shake the apple cart by requesting directive.

He was trying to make sense of everything taking place so quickly when Corporal Pint said, "Agent Elder with the FBI task force is online, requesting to speak with you sir."

"Yes, what can I help you with?" Ted looked at the diminutive man staring back at him on the screen.

"Colonel, with the news the President delivered last night about the possibility of a nuclear war, we have a massive exodus of people from the cities." The agent spoke in a robotic manner. "I have been informed that Anastasia and Troy Vasilyeva, along with Mike Chen, escaped the house they were using in Colorado Springs. We assume they are trying to blend in with those evacuating from Denver."

"Do you have any more information that you can share with me at this time?" Ted spoke sternly, trying to make it clear to the FBI man that he was fully aware that he had been left out of the loop when they went over his head to give information concerning the insurgents to General Lauer.

"Only that we are doing everything in our power to find these three."

"What would you like for me to do?" Ted realized he was still only receiving partial intelligence, otherwise the agent would have been specific in telling him details of everything they were doing to find the three terrorists.

"We want you to be prepared at moment's notice to deploy to any location should we have a sighting."

"You know I am stationed at my family's farm on the eastern plains."

"Of course, I know."

"I would say we are as prepared as possible to move at any time." Ted stared keenly at the screen.

"Let's keep a good line of communication." Agent Elder's face was frozen in an awkwardly neutral expression.

"I will definitely do so," Ted stated in an annoyed tone, before watching the monitor go blank.

He was being used by the members of the Justice Department as a tool who could be blamed when anything went wrong and ignored when things went well. It would be nobody's fault but his own if he allowed the manipulation to continue.

****

Ted leaned back in his chair in front of his desk in the garage, sipping on a hot cup of coffee when the side door opened, allowing a cold gust of wind to enter the warm room. Deb, followed closely by Tommy, entered. Corporal Pint and Sergeant Harris sat at smaller desks in the far corner of the office.

"My God, that wind is cold." Deb continued to pull her warm coat tight around her neck as she neared Ted.

"I just saw the Jacobys walking toward the barn. They are certainly a hardy group." Tommy motioned out the window where the early morning sun was glaring off the glass.

"Grab a cup of coffee." Ted pointed to the coffee pot as the sound of the howling wind continued.

"I love the smell of coffee early in the morning." Deb dropped her hands from the collar of the coat.

"Here ma'am." Corporal Pint came forward with a cup of coffee in each hand.

"Thank you, Corporal." Deb stared at the rosy face of the smiling corporal, thinking how young she appeared, before turning back to Ted. "Our surveillance is showing a ton of people migrating from the Denver area."

"Yeah, we are seeing the same. Most of the activity is still along Interstate 70, but there are large pockets of people taking the back roads." Ted looked in the direction of Sergeant Harris who was staring at a flickering screen on the desk in front of him.

"The NAV we have up is showing a considerable amount of activity on the dirt roads to the south." Tommy took a sip of coffee and looked over the shoulder of Sergeant Harris at a group of people walking slowly down a county road.

"Any which way we look at it, at some point, we are bound to have an influx of people stumble across our location here at the farm," said Deb animatedly.

"Sir, we have a large faction of people moving down county road 12, about eight klicks to the west. If they don't divert, the group will arrive at our location in approximately two and a half hours," Sergeant Harris stated, using a professional tone.

"We need to contact Homeland Security to see if we can find a source for food before we become inundated with people we can't accommodate," Ted said warily.

"Can you ask the task force you are working with for help?" Deb asked.

"I can ask."

"It would be good if they can offer transportation for the people moving to the east." Tommy gazed at Deb with a crooked grin. "Maybe a couple of the buses we used to move civilians out of Utah."

"There are three cars approaching fast from the east," Sergeant Harris yelled, looking at Ted. "Sir, they are civilian vehicles."

"Have 1st Squad meet them at the foot of our driveway. Tell them not to engage if they continue by our location." Ted rose from his seat. "If they do turn into our drive, detain them until we know who they are.

Pentagon, Arlington, Virginia

Beads of sweat covered Secretary of Defense Maes's forehead. He lowered and closed his tired eyes from the monitors showing the enemy ships still stationary in the calm waters of the Pacific and Atlantic oceans. When he gazed at the screen of the President in the situation room in Washington DC, he was surprised to see his Commander in Chief, along with his senior leaders eating donuts, brought to them by a lower staff member.

"Sir, the ships in the Atlantic are moving." The Chief of Naval Operations rose from his seat and stared at the large armada.

President Weller leaned forward, placing his hands flat on the table as he watched the ships move forward. He felt nauseous with fear of having to make the decision to launch the nuclear weapons when he heard the Secretary of Defense yell out, "they are turning around."

A gasp came from the President's mouth, as others around him screamed loudly. He felt lightheaded as Vice President Trupp slapped him hard on his upper left shoulder.

"They are retreating in the Pacific too."

The President took in two deep breaths and released them as his council continued to celebrate the withdrawal. His face was a picture of confusion. As much as he wanted to revel in the triumph of the withdrawing enemy, he knew that success of winning the battle could soon be fleeting.

The visual of the white wake of the ships moving in the blue waters mesmerized the President as the celebrating came to an end. Everyone watched quietly as the armada gained speed away from the danger of the robotic nuclear hoagies precariously remaining behind in the backwash.

"Sir, we are moving our ships forward to the location where we positioned the nuclear weapons," Secretary of Defense Maes said.

The President understood that he was not being asked permission for the advance of the forces, so he remained silent. His face was roused by curiosity while contemplating the situation. Were the Chinese and Russians conceding their position, signaling to him that they understood he was serious in his resolve to use the weapons?

"The ships in the Atlantic are slowing again," the Chief of Naval Operations voice rang out. "They are about to come to a complete stop."

"The fleet in the Pacific is still moving," stated the Secretary of Defense.

"Sir, they are also reducing speed," a technician to the side of the room replied loudly.

"So, they are just repositioning away from our nuclear weapons," the President said crisply. "Playing a game of chess with us. I'm sure their models are showing that we will forego using our most extreme weapons if they are withdrawing, even if it is only ten kilometers."

"The Pacific fleet just came to a complete standstill," the Chief of Naval Operations said with some apprehension.

"Okay, let's hash this out. I want some ideas what our next step should be." The President felt a twinge of relief as he brought his right hand to his upper chest, using his thumb to rub a button on his shirt, staring blankly at his council. His heart was pumping hard. Deep down in his core, he realized that he would have given the go ahead to use the nuclear weapons. He could only pray that the enemies' leaders retreated because they realized that had they stayed in place, their navy would have been annihilated.

The President's war room remained eerily quiet, no one wanted to give the wrong guidance that could start a nuclear war. At the Pentagon, everyone gathered around the Secretary of Defense.

"Mr. President, we feel we should sit tight, leaving everything as is," Secretary of Defense Maes stated brusquely. "Let's see how long they want to play this game."

The President hesitated for a moment of thoughtful silence, before asking, "Has there been any movement of enemy troops in southern Mexico?"

"None, sir."

"Then let's wait them out. But I do want to know the second there is activity of advancing troops."

"Sir, another thing, for the past couple of hours we have been receiving an influx of strange messages that are originating from behind the enemy lines in northern Mexico." Stone, the Director of National Intelligence, raised an eyebrow as she gazed at the President.

"Go ahead."

"Much of what they are sending seems to be gibberish, which the analysts are working to decrypt. Each message closes with 'Jornada del Muerto' and 'Father, Son and Holy Spirit'." The Director of National Intelligence gave the President a sour look.

"You lost me here." President Weller held his hands up with an exasperated look on his face. "Please explain what you are getting at."

"Father, Son and Holy Spirit is the trinity. In July of 1945, at the end of the Manhattan Project where the atomic bomb was developed, the first nuclear explosion occurred in New Mexico. Robert Oppenheimer, the Director of the Manhattan Project, named it the 'Trinity' test. It occurred south of Albuquerque on the Alamogordo Bombing Range known as 'Jornada del Muerto' or journey of death," she spoke sternly. "We must take these messages as a serious threat for a nuclear strike."

"What do you think Bob? Can you take anything from these messages? Could it be a warning?"

"Sir, one of our greatest fears is that the enemy have tactical nuclear weapons on our soil," stated the Secretary of Defense.

"Are you telling me we don't have enough intelligence to detect whether they do or don't?"

"Sir, I cannot tell you with certainty, either way," the Secretary of Defense stated with a sigh.

"We do have a series of Nonhuman Aerial Vehicles that can detect nuclear and chemical weapons. But they have limitations." Secretary of Homeland Security Nygaard squinted, unsure if the President was listening. "Do you want me to continue?"

"Please do."

"A neutron drone will irradiate the area with neutrons, activating nitrogen in a likely explosive. The resulting gamma rays are then picked up by the sensor drones. The problem is that none of this works with a device using Plutonium or Highly Enriched Uranium. The type of bomb a terrorist would most likely use."

"Can our Navy utilize this technology?" The President gazed at the Chairman for the Joint Chiefs of Staff.

"Apparently, the hydrogen in water slows down the neutrons, making it impossible to detect an explosive, unless it is within a meter of the water surface," the Chairman stated with a grimace.

President Weller released his breath loud enough that the members of his assembly recoiled. His face became doleful as he thought how close he came to making a grave mistake with ordering the nuclear strike. His head seemed to clear as he made a conscious decision that under no circumstances would he authorize the use of the weapons. How could he have forgotten the statement he had uttered many times before that, "a nuclear war cannot be won, and must never be fought."

Colorado Farm

"Colonel, the three civilian cars turned into the driveway. 1st Squad has them detained," Sergeant Harris cradled his right arm, lowering the pulsnet radio on his wrist, as he spoke to Ted.

"Ask them to identify themselves." Ted moved to the window and looked out in the direction of the driveway.

"They said they are from the town of Hugo." Sergeant Harris walked away from his desk and quickened his pace toward Ted. "They know Sheriff Bob and Ben Stewart."

Ted shot Deb a curious glance.

"They say they are the doctors from the hospital that took care of Travis." The sergeant stopped next to Ted.

"Allow them to pass and then have 1st Squad proceed west on county road 12 to the location of the group moving our way. Have them engage and find out who they are." He reached for his coat.

Deb and Tommy were out the door by the time Ted had his coat on. Before he could make it to the door, Corporal Pint yelled out from the corner of the room, "Agent Elder from the task force is online for you, sir."

"Go ahead, I'll take this and meet you out there." Ted motioned to Deb before he removed his coat. He sat back down in front of the monitor.

The cars stopped in front of the farmhouse. Both passengers of the front two cars exited, while the drivers waited inside. The back seats of the cars were all filled to the brink with boxes and suitcases.

"I'm Colonel Deb Lisco. This is my farm." Deb placed her hand on the hood of the front car.

An older, grey-haired woman with a pale complexion and penetrating blue eyes stepped forward. A younger man with dark hair and a neatly trimmed beard advanced to stand next to the woman.

"Colonel Lisco, I am Doctor Nancy Kinney and this is Doctor Jay Stees." The older lady nodded in the direction of the younger doctor. "Travis and his wife Sue told us about your farm, and how it has become a place for many families to find a sanctuary during this war."

"Unfortunately, we are in need of refuge." Dr. Stees noticed people gathering behind Deb and Tommy. Others gathered at the front yard of the farmhouse.

Sheriff Bob limped forward to stand between Tommy and Deb. "When we left with Travis and Sue the townspeople had stopped fighting and were fleeing the town. Why didn't you go east with the others?"

"It's too dangerous to travel," stated Dr. Kinney. "Most of the people moving away from the city are civilians getting out of the Denver area, but there are a group of criminals like the ones who attacked our town, still ambushing people on the roads."

"Before, or maybe I should say while, they destroyed our hospital we loaded up as much medicine and supplies as we could, with the idea of traveling east to Kansas City. We encountered a large group of armed rebels on Interstate 70. After making it out by the skin of our teeth, we decided to come here."

"Matt Holden?" Sheriff Bob yelled to the short man with grey hair who stepped out of the driver's seat of the back car. He turned in the direction of Deb. "He's the mayor of Hugo."

"I'll be honest. We couldn't be happier having more doctors. It looks like there will be an influx of people arriving at this location, most likely sooner than later," Deb said with an excited voice.

"The physician's assistant you have working here did an excellent job with taking care of Travis. It's amazing he survived without immediate surgery," stated Dr. Stees.

"Let's go inside the house and get out of the cold. We can introduce you to her, and have you check out our clinic." Deb hesitated as Bill approached from the front yard, and Corporal Pint stepped next to Tommy. She glanced at the private before introducing Bill, "This is Bill, my nephew and partner at the farm."

"Ma'am, Colonel Lisco would like to speak with you in his office," Corporal Pint said.

"Did he say what it is about?"

"No ma'am, not really." She stood at attention. "I do know that there is a large group of civilians approaching the farm."

"Tell him I will be there in a moment."

"I will take them inside." Bill motioned for the new arrivals to follow him.

Ted swiveled his seat around as Deb and Tommy entered his office.

"FBI Agent Elder is going to coordinate with Homeland Security to get us food and transportation for the travelers who come by the farm," Ted's voice stiffened. "Since the camp at Limon has been moved east to central Kansas, they are willing to help us with the migrants as they move past the farm. They plan to send an official from FEMA to evaluate our situation, either this evening or first thing tomorrow morning."

"Did they tell you the name of the official they are sending?" Deb's voice cracked.

Tommy chuckled to himself. He remembered FEMA Deputy Assistant Theodore Sutherland's startled face when she told him to shut up or she would knock the hell out of him.

"No idea. It'll be someone from region eight." Ted sensed his sisters concern, but let it pass. "1st Squad is about to engage the group of civilians approaching from the west. Having more people here when the official comes by will be a positive thing for receiving assistance."

"Hopefully they will supply transportation for those who want to keep moving east."

Nicole, Maddy and Scotty entered the office.

"Grandpa, we have some things we need to talk with you about," Maddy yelled as she rushed past Deb and Tommy and jumped onto Ted's lap. "Scotty and I really, really, really need you to help us find our moms."

"Maddy, I can't…."

"No, Grandpa, you told us you would help us. I don't think Samantha is going to marry Dad, and we need a mom."

Ted was caught off guard and was surprised Nicole didn't chastise Maddy for the aggressive behavior. He suspected that Deb and Tommy wondered why he would let her behave in such a manner. Quite frankly, she had him wrapped around his finger. Having gone through so many years of rigorous discipline with the military, the carefree actions of his granddaughter caused him to reflect on what was important in life. Her happy-go-lucky attitude was a breath of fresh air, and he loved her energetic personality.

Scotty's round and freckled face held an expression of great concern as he watched Maddy with her nose only a couple centimeters from Teds. He stepped closer and placed his hand on the desk.

"I'll tell you what I will do." He lifted Maddy off his lap and set her down next to Scotty. "I will ask the FEMA representatives who are coming to the farm if they can assist us with getting a message to the Los Angeles offices to let your mothers know you are safe."

"You have to find them and tell them to come here and be with us." She nodded to Scotty.

"Yes, I want to see my mom and dad." Scotty swallowed hard, trying to keep the tears from coming to his eyes.

Although Ted understood the chances of finding the mothers was going to be all but impossible, he figured he would at least try to contact the authorities in Los Angeles to see if they could convey the message that the two children were safe. Scotty's grandmother, Carol, left in his possession, when she died, the address of Scotty's parents. After thinking about it for a moment, maybe he wouldn't need the help of homeland security. With having Scotty's information and Maddy's mom, Cindy's address, it all seemed like a perfect mission for Corporal Pint.

"Corporal, we need your assistance." Ted shot her a firm glance. It was obvious the young soldier was listening in on the conversation.

"Yes sir."

"I am going to get you the addresses in the Los Angeles area for the two families. I want you to do your best to track them down." The expression on Ted's face was one of eagerness.

"I can do this." Corporal Pint smiled hard enough at Maddy to show all her teeth.

"That settles it, we are now officially looking for your mom's." Ted was surprised at how confident the soldier sounded in handling the assignment that would be likened to finding a needle in a haystack.

"Sir, the large group of civilians is following 1st Squad toward our location. They are less than a klick out. I'm also receiving pictures of two other large groups to the west, moving this way," Sergeant Harris said exuberantly.

"Let's check it out." Ted made eye contact with Nicole.

Most of the inhabitants of the farm were already gathered at the Jacoby RV by the time the group of over fifty refugees made it down the driveway to the courtyard. Bill was the first to approach the tired travelers.

It was a slovenly looking group of wanderers. Many of them wore ragged clothes and were wild haired as they took a seat on the cold gravel.

"Could we possibly have something to drink," said a man with a large, curved nose, making his request using a quiet, mannerly tone.

A stocky, muscular man, holding a baby, followed closely by a young woman with a small child clutching her side, stepped directly in front of Bill. "We need help for our baby," he said with an expression of utter terror.

Before Bill could react to him, Nicole came to the families aid and ushered them inside to the clinic. The residents of the farm went to work comforting and assisting the motley group.

"There are more coming. Two more factions that just met up with each other less than an hour away." Ted stood between Bill and Jon, with Tommy and Deb right behind them.

A sound caused them to turn and look. A large Westland CW 301 Transport Helicopter landed in the pasture north of the barn.

Eastern Colorado

Two kilometers west of Lisco farm
Anastasia Vasilyeva adjusted the ski cap to cover all her hair. Although the group of migrants escaping from the city was quite large, it was a stroke of good luck to hook up with an even larger group of migrants. From the moment they began the journey east, Troy separated from her, making it difficult for anyone to connect the two. She attached herself to a band of six single women, all close in age, who bonded through the hardship of making the long journey on foot.

Although there was transportation easterly out of Denver, the wait to attain such a ride was nearly a month long. With an all-point bulletin out for her and Troy's capture, there was only one way out of the city, and that was to walk.

She focused on keeping track of her brother as the two groups merged. He was sticking close to two couples, and two single women. He was becoming cozy enough with them that the outward appearance was that he was attached to one of the very petite women.

With Troy securely situated, she thought that she could better her situation. Her traveling companions were all quite attractive, and in extremely good shape. With them, she stuck out like a sore thumb. Quite frankly, her large ass ached from rambling across the desert plains of eastern Colorado. Her salvation came in the form of three women from the new group, all with extremely large thighs, who greeted her as though she was a long-lost sister. All she had to do was make an introduction of the latest arrivals to the beautiful friends, and her ability to hide in plain sight increased by tenfold.

The constant roar of unseen aircraft flying above the grey clouds, in the distance, was a reminder of the real havoc her insurrectionists created. She and Troy, along with Mike Chen were responsible for the disorder across the country that allowed the foreign forces to attack America, without worrying about the citizenry fighting back. She and Troy only need make it to Atlanta, Georgia for the final act of treachery to take place, that would allow them to escape from the country. Now, as dust filled her nose and the cold wind blew her hair, she would be happy with an indoor bathroom.

The sound of a helicopter brought her eyes to the eastern horizon where she saw a puff of dust rise about two kilometers away as the chopper landed. An Army Stryker vehicle approached and stopped at the front of the large group. After the self-proclaimed leaders of the two factions spoke with the soldiers, everyone began walking eastward down the frozen road in the direction of the Lisco farm.

Colorado Farm

Bill and Maddy fled to inside the fence at the front yard of the house as the farm grounds became inundated with strangers. Jon and Gina were taking charge of trying to administer to the needs of the travelers by delegating tasks to the original inhabitants of the farm. The sound of hammers pounding, conspicuously filled the air from Harold and the construction workers placing drywall in the new building. Unfortunately, they ran out of drywall screws, and they had to attach the wallboard with nails. Off in the distance Ted, Deb and Tommy conversed with the group from FEMA. He made a conscious decision to allow his father and aunt to deal with the government officials.

"It looks like we are going to need the large building tonight." Julia moved to Bill's side next to the fence. "It might start snowing at any time."

"My gosh, I hope it doesn't snow until we get everyone settled." Bill was startled by the presence of the physician's assistant. He shifted his position to better look at her. There was a twinkle in her eyes, and her facial muscles were relaxed.

"Bill, you really do a good job with managing this farm." She smiled at him fondly. "Thank God for you and Colonel Lisco."

He recoiled slightly, somewhat taken back by her compliment. She was the one who came through during the greatest of hardship.

"Well, thank you for the compliment, but you are the one we all should be grateful for." He felt Maddy take hold of his arm.

"Just like in every war, there are going to be heroes and villains." Julia pulled the collar of her dark jacket tight to her neck. The color of the coat heightened her chocolate brown eyes.

"How are you doing?" Bill asked guardedly.

"Every day gets better." She looked up at him, showing the whites of her eyes. "Having the new doctors here will allow me some time for myself."

"I am really glad for that," he said, noticing his heart pounding harder. For the first time he noticed how beautiful she was. The skin around her eyes was taut, giving her cheek bones an Egyptian princess appearance. Her natural red lips accentuated her beauty.

"It's all a new start for me." She noticed his intense stare and dropped her gaze.

Irene entered the gate to the yard. She was limping slightly.

"Maddy, do you want to come inside and help me with some baking? Jerry and I are going to need all the help we can get to feed everybody," Irene said.

"Is it okay Dad? I'll go in and help cook." She gave Bill a hard penetrating stare before whispering, "you can stay here and talk to Julia."

"Nope, I'm going inside too." Julia took a step forward.

"I better go and check on how everything is going with handling the new arrivals." Bill opened the gate, before turning to look back. He watched until they were inside, wishing he would have had more time to speak with the physician assistant.

The FEMA officials were infatuated with the damage to the farm caused by the mortars when the rebels attacked a few weeks earlier. The destruction was a testament to the steadfastness of the residents of the homestead for staying and creating a place where people could survive during the war. Having everyone crowded onto the farm grounds, created a clear need for help from the government administrators.

"We'll have a truckload of food here by nightfall," said one of the officials.

"And port-a-potties," another said tetchily. "In fact, I need to find a restroom now."

Bill left Ted and Deb with the handling of the bureaucrats. He noticed Samantha and Sherry standing off to the side of a table with buckets of drinking water. He received a cold shoulder from Samantha when he moved between the two women.

He was about to make meaningless, casual conversation when he heard someone yell from about ten meters away, "Samantha, is that you?"

A plump, red-faced woman waddled toward them. "Oh, my God, you are alive."

"Madison," Samantha threw her hands to her mouth. She could barely catch her breath.

"Your mom and dad thought you perished in a plane crash."

"Are they okay?" Samantha asked excitedly.

"They were when I left on Christmas Eve. There was no way they could walk all this way, so they stayed in the shelter at the recreation center."

"I have to go and see them." Samantha shuffled her feet, barely able to stand in one spot. She turned toward Bill. "I have to see if Ted will take me to the city."

She sprinted in the direction of the garage before Bill could respond. He glanced at Madison.

"I was her neighbor. I grew up in the house right next to hers."

"I'm glad you found her."

Bill stared at the people waiting patiently for guidance. Jon was busy administering to them, making sure those with children were handled first. After processing, people were taken to the new building. The large bathroom was now functional, and it was only a matter of time before the place would be crammed full of people.

"How are things going with you?" Bill asked Sherry, inconspicuously looking at her stomach to see if the pregnancy was showing yet. The heavy coat she was wearing covered her front, making it impossible to see any bulge.

"I'm sort of treading water here, just passing time, trying to keep everyone hydrated." She moved slightly to the side to allow Patrick and Odette a chance to set two more heavy buckets of water on the table.

"We are back to having an influx of people. I hope this lot is better behaved than the others." Patrick forced his large body between Sherry and Bill.

Anastasia Vasilyeva along with a group of women stepped up to the table. They began filling their water bottles from the buckets of water. She had a black, military tactical backpack strapped to her back.

"How are you ladies?" Bill noted that Anastasia had a faraway look in her eyes, completely different from the other women with her, who looked tired and beaten down. Although she was dressed in very casual clothes with a ski cap, her mannerisms indicated the demeanor from a high-level executive of a large corporation.

Anastasia stopped filling her bottle, and took a step to the side, when she became aware of his intense gaze. She lowered her eyes and moved even further back when she caught a glimpse of Sherry.

Sherry observed the odd behavior of the woman trying to escape their attention. Although her hair was covered, her button nose looked familiar. "Do I know you?"

"I don't believe so." Anastasia turned and quickly walked away. She had never been introduced to Sherry or even spoke to her before, so she was unaware of her name. But she remembered vividly when she last saw her dressed in a cheerleading outfit, while the young woman was still in high school. Christian and Shira placed all the new rebel recruits on display for Troy to observe. She was in the background during this occurrence and was less conspicuous than Troy. Now, her brother's identity was in grave danger of being disclosed. She hurried to locate and warn him.

"It seems like I've seen her before. Do you know who she is?" Bill asked Sherry.

"No idea."

"Maybe she is one of them ladies with a common face," Patrick said fleetingly.

The abruptness of her departure made Bill suspicious of her identity. He tried to watch where she scurried off to, but she had already dissolved into the crowd. He had much more on his mind than to worry about a skittish woman who most likely wasn't interested in giving out her life story. It was beginning to snow and all the new people would need some sort of shelter.

White House, Washington D.C.

"Bob, do you have any thoughts on what they plan to do next." President Weller stood with one hand on the edge of the table in the situation room, looking at the large monitor projecting the image of the Secretary of Defense from the Pentagon.

"The model showing the highest probability of their movement is for them to alter course and try to accomplish their objectives." Secretary of Defense Maes just finished going over the scenarios with the Chairman of the Joint Chiefs of Staff.

"If they do, what should our response be?" President Weller wanted, more than ever, to be briefed on any military actions. He didn't want anyone, including the Secretary of Defense to consider his willingness in using all weapons, to mean that he had already given the go ahead to use them."

"We are working on that sir."

"I want any decisions from here on out to come from my office," the President used a cross tone.

"Yes, sir."

"Mr. President, can I speak with you in private?" The Director of National Intelligence stood close to the President.

"We can go to the outer office." He motioned the way, before following her out the door.

"Our agents have uncovered more information concerning the messages from northern Mexico. They feel that the threat of a rogue element utilizing a nuclear device is highly probable, if not imminent," the Secretary sighed.

"Who's making the threats? Do they have ties to any of our enemy's military?"

"We are not entirely sure if they have ties, sir. I want to give you what we have now, to give you an opportunity to get a message to the Chinese and Russian governments as a warning."

"Why would anyone outside the military want to explode a nuclear bomb?" The President raised up his left hand and squeezed the temples on his forehead. His head was throbbing.

"I can't answer that question with any certainty at this time, sir."

"Well, you better damn well find me the answer to it."

She swallowed hard and nodded, as he turned and walked out of the room. She had never seen the President so upset.

Everyone was standing when he entered the war room. All eyes were on the monitor from the Pentagon.

Vice President Trupp's face was white as a sheet as he stated, "there has been a nuclear explosion in New Mexico."

"A what?" The President's face showed utter disbelief.

"Mr. President, a low yield nuclear weapon was deployed near the White Sands National Monument in southern New Mexico just moments ago. We will have pictures of the area briefly. It was…," the Chairman of the Joint Chiefs of Staff faltered while looking at a computer over the shoulder of a staff member. He continued speaking, "it was a two and a half-kiloton bomb."

"Did we have troops at the site of the explosion?" President Weller's face continued to hold an expression of astonishment.

"There were both American and Chinese troops in the vicinity of the detonation," he answered gloomily. "We don't know the extent of casualties, if any.

"Get me a direct line to Beijing. Right now. I need to know the degree of damage, and who is responsible." The President slammed his hand hard on the table before rushing out of the room, with his entire staff in pursuit.

Colorado Farm

Snow was beginning to fall, and the light breeze turned in to a heavy wind. People crammed into the garage, warehouse, and the new, unfinished building. Bill caught up to Deb, Ted, and Jon as they approached the porch of the farmhouse. The sounds of people arguing inside was ever apparent as they reached the front door.

Jacqueline was standing over Jessica with both fists clinched, screaming at the young woman. Emilee was sitting right next to her mother, with Gina and Nicole trying to calm their sister-in-law. The screaming stopped when the rush of cold air entered the room.

"Oooh, you have no soul," Jacqueline wailed while shaking her fist, before stepping back to stand next to Hank, who was sitting on the hearth of the fireplace.

"What's going on?" Jon directed his question to Gina.

"They are having a disagreement about the baby's name," Gina said.

"All I said was that I want to name the baby after my grandfather," Jessica stated with a deep Irish brogue.

"Why, why would you say such a thing to me right now, after losing my son?" Jacqueline screamed. "Wouldn't you imagine I would want the baby to be named Bobby?"

"Wonder if it's a girl?" Jessica held her hands out.

"Bobby could be a girl's name too," Emilee said softly.

Jessica gave her daughter an annoyed glance.

"Since the first time I met you, you have done nothing but look down your nose at me." Jessica wiped her pasty forehead with the fingers of her left hand.

"That is so untrue." Jacqueline's eyes flashed with anger. "I always respected you, at least I did before you took off on a fling and left your children to survive on their own."

"You can judge me all you want, but remember this, people in glass houses shouldn't throw stones."

"Please, can everyone take a deep breath," Jon decided to intervene.

"We'll leave." Jessica rose from her chair and looked at her daughter. Emilee stood up and gave Jacqueline a sad look. Both women made their way to their rooms in the basement.

"I'm sorry. I'm having a hard time navigating all of this." Jacqueline sat down next to Hank on the hearth.

"We understand," Nicole remained next to Ted as she spoke.

Corporal Pint entered the front door and stood at attention in front of Ted. "Colonel, General Lauer is going to have an urgent conference call in fifteen minutes."

"What's it about?" Ted glanced at Deb.

"Unsure, sir. He requested you be on it."

"I'll meet you in the office."

Deb noticed a soldier from her platoon walking up the sidewalk, as Corporal Pint opened the door. She put her coat on and waited at the door for him to enter.

"Ma'am, Command Sergeant Major Talfoya wants you to come to the communication center." The soldier stood at attention as Deb rushed by him, with Ted right behind her.

"I will listen in the communication vehicle," Deb stated, turning to gaze at Ted. "I assume you will take it from your office in the garage."

"Yes, I want my staff there with me."

White House, Washington D.C.

President Weller's face was flush red as he sat at the head of the table next to Vice President Trupp. He was able to contact and have a brief discussion with the CCP officials about the origin of the nuclear device in New Mexico. The Chinese Communist Party representatives appeared to be genuinely surprised by the blast. They were just as concerned that the United States would blame them for the explosion as he was with them blaming the United States. His gut reaction was that they did not have anything to do with deploying the bomb.

"Who is responsible?" the President stared a hole through Director of National Defense Stone as she sat with five staff members right behind her.

"Sir, all we can do is speculate," Director Stone stated.

"Then speculate," President Weller yelled. He examined the expressions on the faces of her staff, sitting on the edge of their seats. The man with hollow facial features who spoke at a meeting of his council, about a month earlier, rose from his chair.

"Mr. President, it was a crude nuclear device that was designed and built by someone outside any of the nuclear countries."

"Again, I will ask — who is responsible?"

"At this point, we are not one hundred percent sure."

Director of National Security Stone jerked her head to look at the operative before fixing her gaze back on the President. "Sir, our best guess is a terrorist group associated with the insurgents that have destroyed the infrastructure in preparation for the enemy invasion."

"Specifically, who are we talking about?"

"The three people at the top of the list are Mike Chen, Troy Vasilyeva and his sister Anastasia Vasilyeva," the Director's voice became cautious. "We have information linking supporters of theirs with purchasing bomb making materials from suppliers in Kazakhstan."

"Are you telling me that anybody can buy nuclear products off the black market?" the President asked incredulously.

"No sir, this is where we are speculating. There would be catastrophic consequences for any nuclear state to sell to a terrorist. But there have been instances over the years where Highly Enriched Uranium became available for purchase. Where the HEU came from is a mystery." The Director held her left hand up and sighed. "Because there has been a nuclear explosion, and we know that someone was able to purchase the Uranium, our best guess is that it was Mike Chen and the Vasilyeva's because of their past attempts to purchase the elements to build a nuclear device."

"Okay, I want answers here. What was the extent of the explosion?" The Presidents demeanor calmed considerably.

"The kill radius of the device was a little over one and a half kilometers. The shockwaves and electromagnetic pulse extended further." The operative's face showed little emotion as all eyes fixed on him. "We are confident that no troops on either side were KIA, but I must emphasize that it has not been confirmed."

"There is a reason this bomb was detonated in the remote area and not in one of our cities. I want these three suspects caught immediately. If they have more devices, then God help us if we don't find them."

Colorado Farm

The living room was jam-packed full of people with the smell of fresh baked cinnamon bread filling the farmhouse. Bill sat on the couch with Maddy, cuddling next to him, as they watched the fire burning in the fireplace. There was a lingering worry in his mind while he waited to hear from Ted as to the reason for the urgent meeting called by the brass from Fort Carson, which caused Aunt Deb and him to hurry away to their prospective communication centers. The administrators from FEMA also rushed off, leaving the promised food and supplies all up in the air.

Heavy snow covered the farm grounds. All the new travelers who were posed to spend their first night at the unfamiliar location crammed into any building available to get reprieve from the harsh conditions. The front door opened, and Jon stepped inside, and shook the snow off his shoulder, before removing his coat.

The tightness in his jaw, and the way he diverted his eyes from looking directly at anyone, while walking to the center of the living room, made it clear to Bill that there was something greatly bothering his uncle.

"There has been a nuclear explosion in New Mexico." Jon listened to several people gasp.

"Lt. Colonel Lisco, can you give us more details?" Patrick asked, lumbering forward to tower over Jon.

"I only know that a small nuclear bomb was detonated somewhere in New Mexico earlier today."

"Is it the beginning of nuclear war?" Al shouted, using a hostile tone.

"I'm pretty sure Ted and Deb will come inside and let us know what is happening before they depart." Jon glanced at Nicole to see her reaction to the news that Ted was about to leave.

"We have the right to know if we are about to be involved with an all-out nuclear war," Al stated vehemently.

"Al, I think it's time you sat down and let this play out," Hank said tersely, standing shoulder to shoulder with his brother.

"You complaining about everything is only making the situation worse.

A large smile came to Jon's face as he reached over and patted his little brother on the shoulder. Al snorted and took a step back. The front door opened, and Ted stepped inside. He marched straight to where Nicole was sitting in a chair to the side of the fireplace, with everyone's eyes following him.

"What can you tell us Ted?" Jon asked.

"This afternoon a small nuclear bomb was detonated in a remote part of New Mexico." Ted's eyes diverted in the direction of Maddy. "Everything indicates it was a terrorist act by a rogue element. I am going to Denver tonight to meet with the FBI task force."

Nicole reached over and squeezed his hand.

"Do you expect them to have more bombs?" Al looked hard at Ted.

"I don't know Al," Ted said harshly.

"We should be thankful that we are here during this time of distress," said Jason Jensen. "We could be in a large city where the threat has to be much greater."

"Yeah Jason, we are all blessed as all hell to be crammed tightly together within miles of NORAD, waiting our fate," Al groaned sarcastically.

"If you don't like where you are Al, I'm sure Ted can give you a ride back to the city this evening." Jon stared a hole through the dentist.

Al cowered back to stand next to Linda, without replying.

Having heard Jon indicate the possibility of catching a ride to Denver, Samantha crossed the room to stand next to Ted.

"Would it be possible for you to give me a ride to Littleton?" she asked quietly.

Ted remembered when he stopped at the Wadsworth location in the western suburb as they made their way from Utah to the family farm. His meeting with the FBI was being held at the Federal building, maybe fifteen minutes from her parents' home.

"You have to be ready in thirty minutes." Ted glanced at Bill and Maddy before focusing on Nicole. "There is a chance I will return late tonight, but it will most likely be sometime tomorrow morning."

Samantha never bothered to look toward Bill and Maddy as she rushed out the front door.

"Are you taking your entire platoon with you?" Jon asked, noticing Deb enter the front door left open by Samantha's hurried departure.

"Yes, they are going with me."

"What about you Deb? Have your orders changed?" Jon asked as Deb stepped between Hank and Ted.

"They have. Tommy is preparing our platoon to leave immediately." Deb didn't want to state in a public setting anything about 2nd Battalion's orders.

"Colonel, La Junta ain't very far from here." Sheriff Bob limped forward. "Is there a chance that the war is going to end up here, right in our lap?"

"Bob, we should prepare for anything," Deb said tartly. "I will be back as soon as I can."

****

Troy Vasilyeva spotted Anastasia sitting next to a pallet of cement, all alone, with an anxious frown on her face. Although there were many people in the large warehouse, none of them seemed to be concerned with anything but finding a warm place to sleep for the night. He decided it was safe to speak with his sister in the dimly lit storeroom.

Unbeknownst to the two of them, a frail man of about thirty furtively watched from a spot at the side of the room. The moment he saw Troy, once the large group left the city, he thought he recognized the large man with a hooked nose as the leader who spearheaded the revolt which caused so much havoc for the country. Three years earlier he had fallen for the ruse of creating a better society and joined the insurrection. He became one of the leaders of a small group of rebels, something that now greatly haunted him. He knew that Troy had a sister who was his partner at the top of the chain of command, so once he saw the two of them collaborating, he realized he found the heads of the terrorist organization. He remained hidden as he listened.

"We just went to the next level of this insurrection," Troy stood to the side of Anastasia with his hand on a bag of cement. "Mike successfully initiated the explosion."

"I knew it was him the moment I heard the whisperings of a nuclear attack." Anastasia's face showed disappointment. "You and Mike should have discussed all this with me."

"If I could go back in time, I would have told you. Mike convinced me to keep you out of the loop." Troy's expression showed his concern. "We are involved with all this up to our necks now. When we get to Atlanta there is a chance, we will have to make a decision that could kill a lot of people."

"We still have choices here. We need to start leveraging things for our own benefit, not for Mike's. I just want to be involved with any decisions from here on out."

"That you will be."

"Right now, we have a more immediate concern. The FEMA people are going to bring in buses to haul people back east, and they are going to want to check the identity of everyone here." Anastasia's face sagged with worry. "You know the CIA already have our pictures plastered across the board."

"Is there a safe house anywhere close for us to walk to?"

"The little town of Eads is east of here. They have motor bikes we can use."

"Let's lay low and try to blend in with the people here while stockpiling some food." Troy glanced around the room to make sure nobody was listening in on the conversation.

"There is a problem," Anastasia said with a strained voice. "The blonde girl at the water table today was one of the recruits who worked with Christian and Shira. She seemed a little startled when she noticed me, but I don't think she placed who I am. That's why I decided to separate from the ladies I arrived with when they went to the garage to spend the night."

"Okay, we fill our back packs with food and leave tomorrow. The only chance we have is to walk to Eads and use the motorbikes to take us to Kansas. If we can make it to the farm outside Liberal, Kansas, we will have transportation to Atlanta."

"What happens if we don't make it to Atlanta?"

Troy jerked his head to the side without answering. A spindly man, all hunched over, was walking directly toward him. "I think we have been recognized," he said with a muffled voice.

"Is your name Troy?" the man asked loud enough to cause the people closest to take notice.

"No, you have me mixed up with someone else," Troy stated with a low, even voice. "My name is Frank James."

"Yeah right, and my name is Jesse James." The man's eyes were hard and calculating.

"Ha, no, it is. Why don't we step outside, so we can talk in private?" Troy motioned with his head to a side door, noticing that the disturbed people were no longer paying attention.

Troy stepped into the cold, with the man following right behind, and Anastasia exiting last. They were on the west side, facing the barn, allowing the warehouse building to block most of the easterly wind. It took a moment for the pungent, wet smell from the corrals to hit their nostrils, while the snow continued to fall to the ground.

"Okay, I am Troy, and this is my sister Anastasia." He hoped that the man was an ally.

"I heard you talking about having a part in the nuclear explosion. I knew you were bad, but that is unimaginable." The man's face twisted. "Do you realize that you bastards ruined the whole fucking country."

Troy's mouth fell open as his heartbeat quickened. His eyes went to his sister, as the man took a step in the direction of the door.

"I hope you are satisfied with all the destruction you caused, because your time is finished," he said bitterly.

"Just one moment. Can we talk about this?" Anastasia blocked the door.

"There is nothing to talk about. What you did to this nation is pure evil. I can't even sleep at night because of my involvement with you. I'm going to make sure you pay for it." He threw an elbow up toward Anastasia. "Now get out of my way."

Troy reached around the man's neck and placed him in a death lock. The slender man kicked and struggled but Troy was much too strong for him to escape. He finally hung in Troy's grasp like a half empty bag of potatoes.

"What are we going to do with him?" Anastasia fixed her gaze on the flickering lights of the barn.

"Over there," Troy pointed in the direction of the haystack at the side of the barn.

Anastasia picked up his legs as Troy held most of the weight. They carried him about fifty meters to the large haystack where they heard voices coming from the barn. In their haste they positioned him to the side of the rick of hay and placed two large bales over the top of him.

"Let's find another location to sleep tonight." Wet snow covered the top of his head, with a heavy fog coming from his mouth.

"If this guy was traveling with others, they most likely were part of the revolution. Hopefully they are worried about their involvement, and will hesitate to speak up," Anastasia's voice quavered.

"Let's not take the chance of them remaining quiet. You said the women you were traveling with went to the garage to sleep?"

"Yes."

"That is where we should go. We get our bags from the warehouse, and then straight to the garage." He began to walk away from the crime scene, tightening the grasp on the collar of his coat. "Once inside, don't go immediately to your friends, just stay off to the side, and later on make yourself noticeable to them."

The inside of the garage was wall to wall people. Troy removed his coat and wiped the wetness from his hair, trying to adjust his eyes to the darkness. There was no way he would be able to recognize Anastasia amongst the mass of bodies. He made out the form of an older man going through a door that he surmised must be a way to the bathroom.

After stepping around several people, he made his way to the door that led into a small office. The man was exiting the bathroom when he entered the room.

"They told us not to linger in here, but it's okay to use the bathroom." The man's sleepy eyes were barely open.

"Thank you," Troy whispered.

The outside light reflected through the large window onto the desk at the center of the office. Troy cautiously looked over his shoulder to the closed door which led back into the garage, before moving to the desk. There was a picture of Colonel Lisco with his arm around Nicole in a frame at the corner. He pulled open the center drawer. He recoiled when he saw the pictures of Mike Chen, Anastasia, and himself.

****

Irene and Jerry finished the herculean effort of spearheading the cooks with making hundreds of silver dollar sized pancakes, that were used to feed the multitude of people. Irene sat at the kitchen table with Nicole, Maddy and Bill, while Jerry swabbed the kitchen counters.

"Maddy did you like the pancakes?" Irene noticed the tousled hair and droopy eyes of her young friend.

"I really liked them," Maddy replied with a distant voice.

"I noticed you haven't been spending much time with Scotty lately," Irene stated.

"He's found some boys he wants to play with more than me." Maddy sighed. She stared blankly at the tabletop.

"What are you thinking about so seriously?" Nicole noticed the distracted nature of her granddaughter.

"I was wondering if Samantha will ever come back here?" She leveled her head and stared across the table.

"I suppose it depends. If her parents are in a secure place, she will probably stay with them," Bill said calmly.

"Does that mean she is not going to marry you?" Maddy rose from her chair and stood next to Bill. She placed a finger at his temple. "Dad, you are getting grey hair."

"You need to get that out of your mind. Samantha and I are not going to get married." He subconsciously brushed the side of his head.

"How about Julia? You should marry her."

Irene chuckled.

"Maddy, what would make you say such a thing?" Nicole asked in a hushed voice, glancing in the direction of the clinic.

"You like each other. Don't you Dad?" She poked her father in his side with a finger.

"Maddy, stop," Bill said with a smile. He pulled her around into a bear hug.

"You like her, don't you?" She twisted her neck to look back over her shoulder at her grinning dad.

"Maddy, you need to stop," Nicole said curtly. "Julia recently lost her husband, and it is very disrespectful for you to say such a thing."

Maddy continued to look at Bill with a sly smile on her face.

"Okay, I'm going to go out and see if I can help organize things." Bill relinquished his hold on Maddy.

There were only a few lingering clouds remaining in the otherwise bright blue sky. Terrance finished clearing the snow from the courtyard as a large bus, followed by two box trucks, rumbled down the driveway. The air brakes hissed as the bus came to a halt about ten meters from the garage.

The FEMA crew used a donkey forklift to unload six bright orange portable toilets, and a portable shower, off the first truck. Jon and Bill directed them to the best locations to utilize the units. A crowd of people gathered to watch the proceedings.

"We have eight pallets of food," the FEMA official stated to Bill. "Everything is non-perishable."

"I suppose we should place them in the warehouse." Bill glanced at Jon to see if he agreed.

"Looks like you brought a little bit of everything," Jon said to the administrator.

"Sugar, flour, cereals and all sorts of canned vegetables."

"Let's take one pallet of canned items to the kitchen. The pantry has plenty of room."

"Let the forklift driver know where you want the pallets." The FEMA man was short and stocky with a deep brown, bulldog face. "There is something else that I can offer you. If more people arrive over the next couple of days, we can provide a food tent which we can staff with cooks to help feed everyone."

Bill sighed and hesitated for a moment. He needed to discuss the idea with Aunt Deb about the bureaucrats taking over part of the farm. "Let us discuss that."

"We should begin vetting the people for the bus ride east." The FEMA official wasn't bothered in the least with Bill not jumping at his offer. "We would like to depart before noon. There are already bagged lunches on board, so there is no reason to worry about lunch."

"How many can fit on the bus?" Jon asked as several of the people came closer to listen to the conversation.

"Fifty."

"We have a lot more than fifty who want to leave." Bill held his jaw out. "When will the next bus arrive?"

"At least two days out."

"How about if we allow families with children to get the first choice of leaving?" Jon demanded. "After that we can have a drawing to see who leaves."

After finding the fifty people for the first trip away from the farm, there were still nearly a hundred new arrivals left to wait for the next bus. With the prospect that there was another large group of people approaching from the west, the task of handling the refugees was going to be a full-time job.

Security in knowing who was arriving at the farm was still a great concern, especially for Jon. He realized he didn't have enough people at the farm to handle the vetting of so many people. After experiencing the attack from the insurgents that killed Christian and Fred, not knowing who was in their midst was beginning to worry him sick.

"Absolutely no weapons are allowed on the bus." The FEMA man stood uncomfortably close to Jon. "I understand that some of the people left their homes quickly and don't have identification. Those without a picture ID should step to the front, so we can take a photograph. We will run it through the FBI FACE service unit."

Troy Vasilyeva crouched behind several people, away from the departure proceedings, keeping an eye on Anastasia who waited patiently with her new friends. He figured there would be an identification process to get on the bus, so nothing changed from the night before. He and his sister would have to walk in order to escape the farm.

"It looks like Ted's platoon is returning," Terrance yelled from the top window of the tower.

The large crowd parted as the platoon passed through. Bill took a discreet glance at the front vehicle, with his father sitting in a passenger seat, to see if Samantha might have returned with the soldiers. There was no sign of her. The vehicle stopped and Ted jumped down.

"Looks like Homeland Security came through." Ted appeared clean shaven and well rested.

"They sure did," said Jon. "How was your trip?"

"Since the nuclear explosion, things are a lot more intense. Everything I have been working on with the task force has become even more important than it was when we began."

"Are you going to be able to work from here?" Bill asked hopefully.

"A lot of my work can be taken care of remotely. I have to be ready to move at a moment's notice."

"What about Samantha, were you able to find her parents?" Bill asked eagerly.

"We dropped her off with a group of people from the neighborhood that she grew up in, who knew right where her parents were. She seemed happy to be with them, but I never saw her mother or father." A sound from the bus engine whining caused Ted to stop and watch as the large transport vehicle made its way down the driveway. "Did they bring only one bus?"

"The next one is due to arrive in a couple of days," Jon stated.

A loud scream erupted from the barn area. Breanna came running around the garage with her breasts and stomach rising and falling with each step. She was yelling bloody murder, "there is a body by the haystack. There is a dead person…" She tried catching her breath. Her face was pale white as she approached Ted, pointing to the north.

"Are you sure he is dead?" Jon asked skeptically.

"Believe me, he's deader than a doorknob." She dejectedly looked back in the direction of the barn.

"I'll find Sheriff Bob and meet there." Bill was on the move before anyone could respond.

White House, Washington D.C.

The Secretary of Defense along with the Chairman of the Joint Chiefs of Staff left the Pentagon. Their intention was to sit face to face with the President and his war council. Over the past twenty-four hours nothing changed with the stalemate at the Pacific and Atlantic fronts. Neither navy had budged an inch.

President Weller's eyes showed strain, but he was clean shaven, and wore casual clothing. He sat at the head of the table intently staring at the staff sitting behind the members of his National Security Council. He hoped they all had been busy through the night coming up with intelligence on the nuclear explosion. He wanted solid answers on why such a bold statement was made in the middle of nowhere.

So far, he was disappointed in the information he previously received from the assembly. Everything was speculative, offering theories, all the way from an innocent accident caused by a left-over explosive from a century ago, to the possibility a rogue military member had something to do with it in order to show the world the extent of damage that could be caused by such a small device.

"I am going to start with the premise that the nuclear device was not disseminated by any actors associated with the Chinese or the Russian Governments." The Presidents voice boomed, and his tone was stern. "I want answers on who brought this device to our soil. No more questions, just answers."

"Sir, your supposition about the Chinese and Russians being directly linked to the device is correct. But there is an indirect connection," Director of National Intelligence Barbara Stone stated unequivocally. "We have received a message from a group taking responsibility for the explosion. The faction is attached to the hip of the two governments."

"I take it you find the message to be viable?"

"Very much so, sir."

"The million-dollar questions are who are they and why did they do it?" The President felt a loathing in his stomach.

"Believe it or not Mr. President, the primary reason is money." Director Stone raised an assured eyebrow.

"For money? Someone is blackmailing the United States Government during a time of war." The President's face showed a doleful expression.

"For five billion dollars, sir."

The first thing that entered the President's mind was that five billion dollars was nothing in the scheme of things. He would give ten times that amount of money if there was a guarantee the danger to the American people would go away. He knew that the only way to be certain the threat was diminished would be to find those responsible and eliminate them.

"Who is trying to extract this money." President Weller asked shortly.

"Just as we suspected, the main perpetrator is Mike Chen, the leader of all the insurrectionists. We are not sure if the others in his organization are culpable, but we assume that they are." Director Stone stated. "I have a dossier on the profiles of the three main actors for you to review, Mr. President."

"Do they have more nuclear devices?" the President asked forcefully.

"They claim to. We must believe them. The threat for the next explosion, if we do not go along with their demands, will occur in a large American city, which they did not identify."

"Barbara, how are they communicating with you?" Secretary of Homeland Security Peg Nygaard asked.

"We received two handwritten notes, both delivered to our home office in Virginia, by an unsuspecting courier."

"How can you be certain Chen is involved?" the President asked.

"He signed the messages, sir."

"Why would he do that?" Vice President Trupp asked disbelievingly.

"He is at the top of the priority list of criminals wanted by the FBI and CIA. He knows there is no way for him to sneak out of the country. Having the nuclear bomb threat is his ticket back to China, or wherever he wants to go. Why not take a few billion dollars on the way out." Director Stone said flippantly. "For the past month we have been hot on his trail, along with his abettors Troy and Anastasia Vasilyeva. Many of their confederates in Colorado have turned on them, making it likely they are, or have, fled the Denver metropolitan area."

"Is Chen part of the Chinese Intelligence Services," Secretary of State Mahorn asked.

"No, we don't believe he is part of CIS. It is our opinion he has gone rogue with this act. But to be totally transparent here, we have no idea who is with the CIS, there is not one singular representational name known to us from the Chinese Intelligence Service." Director of National Intelligence Stone folded her arms.

If nothing else, the nuclear explosion froze all the enemy forces in place. Officials from neither Beijing nor Moscow are willing to give orders to advance their troops. Considering the volatile situation, it is a wise decision. As far as they know, the United States Military is ready to utilize tactical nuclear weapons. Something that President Weller desperately hopes they believe.

Colorado Farm

The weather had warmed to the point where much of the snow melted. Sheriff Bob stared down at the deceased man with wet pieces of hay sticking to his hair and forehead. He leaned over and pushed the chin of the middle-aged man up to examine his neck. He used his three middle fingers to rub along the jawbone all the way down to his clavicle.

"This man was strangled," the sheriff stated confidently, turning the body over. "He doesn't have a damn thing in his pockets."

"He had to have someone traveling with him." Jon looked inquiringly at the victim. "Let's check to see if there is anyone missing a traveling companion."

"It needs to be taken care of quickly. There is another group of people about to converge on the farm. It will be less complicated to manage the situation without more people," Bill said.

"Do we have a megaphone?" Sheriff Bob asked.

"No, but Ted does on the Stryker Combat Vehicle. Believe me, he can make an announcement everyone on the farm will hear," Jon said readily, gazing at Bill. "Can you go and ask him?"

Bill hurried to the garage. The smell inside was almost gagging. He sidestepped several people lounging on the floor and tried to open the door to his father's office. It was locked. He knocked lightly. Corporal Pint opened the door and allowed him in.

"We forgot that this office might have sensitive information. I should have locked it last night when we allowed all the people to crash in the garage." Bill had an apologetic expression on his face.

"I don't think anything is missing." Ted smiled. "We should lock it tonight."

"Can we use the loudspeaker on one of your vehicles to ask the people if there is anybody who knows the dead guy Breanna found by the haystack. Sheriff Bob thinks he was murdered."

"Corporal Pint, have Private Johns move the Stryker vehicle to the center of the courtyard by the RV."

"Yes, Sir." The corporal rushed out the door.

Sherry, Caroline and Emilee moved to Bill's side as Jon's voice exploded over the loudspeaker, asking for help with identifying the unknown dead man. Sherry's head was on a swivel, looking closely at all the people while Jon made his plea.

"Have you seen anyone you recognize?" Bill asked Sherry probingly.

"Not that I know for sure. There are a few people who sort of look familiar. The only reason a person would be killed here is if they knew too much that someone didn't want known. I am positive we have some rebels in our midst." The edges of Sherry's eyes tightened as she thought back to her time as a member of the insurrection.

"I'm sure you will let us know if you recognize anyone." Bill glanced at the bulge from the pistol in her waist band. It went without saying that she was not only checking for rebels, but, also, the two men who attacked her and Caroline.

She took a breath through her nose and nodded.

Troy Vasilyeva watched from the far westerly edge of the crowd, glancing back and forth from his sister, who was surrounded by her traveling companions, to Sherry, who he could see clearly. She was staunchly examining everyone closely. With her frazzled blonde hair and chiseled features, it was uncanny how much she looked the same as when he first saw her during her senior year of high school. The combination of her beauty and tempestuousness made her very memorable. He was sure she could easily identify him if given the chance.

Anastasia also kept her eyes on her brother. She identified a few rebels hidden in the crowd, who at one time were sympathetic to their cause. After dealing with the former insurrectionist the night before, she kept the loyalists at a distance, trying to figure the best way to approach them to see if they were still dedicated followers.

Jon gave a description of the dead man and offered his final plea for anyone to come forth with information on his identity. He stepped down to join Bill, still standing next to the three ladies.

A red-faced man with a big pot belly approached, but stopped a couple meters in front of Jon. His face was a picture of frustration. He waited without speaking, looking as though he might bolt at any moment.

"Do you have something to tell us?" Bill gazed at Sherry to see if she might recognize him as a rebel. Her face told him she did not.

"The dead man you found is my friend." He looked cornered, jerking his head side to side, checking to see if he was being watched.

"Will you take a look at the body and verify for sure that it is the man you know?" Jon asked calmly, taking a step toward him.

"His name is Earl. I saw him last night outside in the snow by the haystack." He threw a worried look at Bill. "He left the warehouse with a big guy and a woman. He never came back in, so I went looking for him."

"Why didn't you let someone know after you found him?" Bill asked carefully.

"It seems like the entire world has flip-flopped on me. I don't have any idea who to trust. Besides that, I didn't want to end up dead right alongside of him, so I went back to the warehouse and fretted about it all night long." The man's left hand was shaking. He continued to gaze over his shoulder at the crowd.

"Can you identify the man and woman who you saw leave with him?" Bill looked the man directly in the eyes. "We can protect you."

"It was so dark inside the warehouse; I didn't get a good enough look at them to be able to make a positive identification."

The expressions on both Bill and Jon's faces told each other that they didn't believe him.

"We want you to tell your story to the sheriff." Jon turned in the direction of Caroline. "Caroline, would you take him to Sheriff Bob. He is still at the haystack on the east side of the barn."

"I'll go with you," said Emilee.

"Right this way." Caroline flung her arm out almost hitting Ted as he approached.

"Looks like you have some results from your announcement." Ted stood next to Sherry in front of Bill and Jon.

"The guy we just spoke with said he saw the man leave with two people. He then claims that when the man didn't come back in, he went out to the haystack, where he found him dead. He just let him lay there all night long." Jon looked annoyed. "It all doesn't add up."

"Since we bussed off most of the families, I wouldn't be a bit surprised if half the new people aren't rebels or former rebels." Bill gave an awkward glance at Sherry.

"There is another group of a hundred and twenty that is going to arrive here in about an hour and a half. Homeland Security is having FEMA set up five satellite stations on the eastern plains to feed, and at the same time check the identities of the people leaving the cities. We are the closest location to Denver, so as information circulates about our camp, we will have a lot more people arriving here," Ted announced. "Sherry you should try and get a good look at everyone already here, as well as all the new group when they arrive. I am going to get a hold of the FBI task force and see if they will transport Shira to the farm to help identify any of the insurgents who might be passing through. I'll request a processing team to help us identify the people who arrive."

"This is a dangerous situation we have right now." Jon inadvertently looked up to the window of the tower where Irving was sitting. "I think we should rope off the area around the farmhouse as well as the apartments and make them off limits to the new arrivals."

"We better place guards at the gun safe in the basement," Bill said. "With rebels in our midst, it would be disastrous for all of us here if they armed themselves with our arsenal."

La Junta, Colorado

Headquarters for 2nd Battalion was situated in a large warehouse behind a Quality Inn motel on the outskirts of the small town of La Junta. The motel itself was used to quarter the officers. Colonel Lisco, Command Sergeant Major Talfoya and Lt. Col. Woodworth were waiting in the communication center, at the center of the warehouse, for General Lauer to come online.

They hoped to receive more information concerning the nuclear bomb explosion. But more pressing to them was information on the next mission that would be given to 2nd Battalion. It was difficult for any of them to understand why they had been asked to stand down, while battles raged on several fronts to the south of their location. Colonel Lisco was especially eager to find out if 1st and 3rd Battalions would stay attached to other Divisions or if they would be reattached to her command under 2nd Brigade.

General Lauer sat at his desk in his office at Fort Carson. His demeanor was calm, and he appeared relaxed.

"For the past twenty-four hours the enemy at the front outside San Antonio have made moderate, but constant, withdrawals of troops back to northern Mexico. 1st and 3rd Battalions will reattach to 4th Division and are to join you in La Junta to wait in reserve. 2nd Battalion will immediately reposition back to base in Fort Carson." General Lauer crossed his arms on his desk.

"Sir, do we have any sort of timetable here?" Colonel Lisco asked.

"I want 2nd Battalion back on base tonight." He scratched his forehead before looking off to the side of the room. He gazed back into the monitor. "1st and 3rd Battalions should be prepared to move at a moment's notice."

"Sir, why La Junta. Wouldn't it be better for the entirety of 2nd Brigade to return to Fort Carson?" Deb knew her question would be interpreted as bold.

"Colonel, with the nuclear threat, we are trying not to congregate troops. We will keep personnel at a minimum on site until the danger is terminated." General Lauer expected Deb to be forward with any questions concerning her troops. "As far as being at La Junta, all I can say is you won't be there long."

"Is there any more information concerning those who deployed the bomb?"

"We know it was the head of the insurrectionists who masterminded the explosion. Ted probably knows more about the three rebels than anyone else."

"As you know, I spent a couple of days at my farm a little over an hour north of here. On the drive across the plains, we noticed an extraordinary number of civilians walking easterly." Deb glanced at Tommy. "It seems to me that there must be a lot of bad actors amongst the good people escaping a bad situation. Something tells me, sir, they are planning on going to new cities to cause chaos."

"Again, Ted's work with the FBI task force makes him a more reliable source of information on the rebels than I am," General Lauer stated amicably.

Deb was stunned at how agreeable the general was being. Never had she seen him so amenable. Her mind was racing, trying to think of something to ask him for, before he went back to his dogged, stubborn self. She couldn't think of one favor to ask for.

"Thank you, sir. If that is all, we will begin the preparation for the arrival of 1st and 3rd Battalions and the departure of 2nd Battalion."

General Lauer watched the screen go blank. He felt a twinge in his stomach from the fact that he had to withhold information from one of his most tenacious commanders. New orders for 2nd Brigade were being formulated. If all the models predicting the flow of the war on our soil proved correct, it would be only a matter of days before Colonel Lisco and her brigade would be shipped off to the Horn of Africa.

Colorado Farm

After seeing the next influx of migrants arrive at the farm, Bill made the decision to ask the government officials for help with staffing the new mess hall. They were overly agreeable to transform the farm into a FEMA satellite camp. With people completely covering the farm grounds, the FEMA team began setting up tents in the pasture on the west edge of the property to help house the travelers before busses could arrive to ship them east. The chaos was slowly coming under control, with Troy and Anastasia Vasilyeva being the only one's hoping for the bedlam to continue.

As the long line of new arrivals finished trudging down the long driveway, Troy Vasilyeva watched patiently as they made their way to the table to register at the camp. He recognized nearly thirty of the migrants as members of his insurrection. Only one of them noticed him. She was a plump woman with a bright red face, who he recognized as a cohort of the rebels from the north side of the Denver metro area. A smile showed on her face when she detected him.

Ted joined Jon and Irving at the top of the tower to observe the government officials, who took over the entire administrative duties of handling the new arrivals. The sound of helicopters coming and going from the farm was becoming common place. The one helicopter with an FBI logo on the side of it stuck out from the rest.

"I take it you are expecting them?" Jon asked, watching the helicopter land in the distance.

"The FBI are sending two agents, along with Shira, to investigate the death of the man we found." Ted watched the assembly of people below as he stood between Jon and Irving, gazing out the top window. "Others will be arriving later today."

"I know Bill is concerned with allowing the farm to be turned over to the FEMA officials. He's worried how Deb is going to react," Jon stated.

"There is no way we could have fed and managed this many people without help." Ted stared intently out the window, in the direction of where Anastasia and her circle of friends were innocently conversing.

"I don't understand how they can have busses come here, when there is such a short supply of them in the city?" Jon held a frustrated expression. "Why not intercede before the people walk all this way? Hell, if a blizzard occurred, a lot of these people would die. They have no idea how dangerous it can be on the eastern plains in the wintertime."

"We spoke about that at the task force meeting. There are stringent requirements to board a bus in the city, along with a long waiting list. Some people are impatient and decide to walk. Others are avoiding being identified." Ted turned to Irving. "Can I use your binoculars?"

Anastasia was standing at the southwest edge of the garage, with her back to the tower, amongst a group of about ten other women. Ted focused in on her heavy thighs, before moving the sight of the binoculars to a couple of other women with equally big thighs. He shifted his position to rest his elbows on the sill of the window to try and get a better angle to see the women's faces. Of the ones he could see, none of them looked like the picture he had of Anastasia Vasilyeva.

Troy, observing from his position nearly thirty meters west of his sister, kept his eye on Ted, leaning out the window of the tower. He turned to face west when he saw the red-faced woman, he noticed earlier, approaching.

"Are we safe here?" She remained at arm's length from him as she spoke.

"No," Troy answered bluntly. He remembered the woman's name was Kathy.

"Do you have a plan?"

"I'm working on it." He glanced over his shoulder to see if Ted was still watching. He was no longer looking out the window of the tower. "Kathy, I need you to get a message to Anastasia. She is at the corner of the garage with a group of women.

Kathy's round face was overly cloaked with curiosity. Her mouth hung open as she blatantly scanned the farm grounds, and finally spotted Anastasia.

"Tell her to meet in the barn in ten minutes," Troy whispered, "and don't be so damn obvious."

He slowly made his way to the barn. As he waited for his sister, the sound of the horses snorting had him constantly turning to look in the direction of the stalls, to make sure nobody was sneaking up. He stepped back in the shadow of the large barn door, watching the FEMA crew assemble tents for housing off in the distant pasture. Just outside the barn entrance, Anastasia and Kathy walked shoulder to shoulder, much faster than he would have liked for them to be. When they were within a couple meters of the garage door, Kathy slowed down as she approached a mud puddle. Her feet slipped out from under her, and she landed hard on her plump butt in the gooey mud.

Troy guided the two women into a vacant horse stall, next to another stall with a horse that continued to snort noisily. Kathy sat down in the straw and tried to wipe the mud off her hands and lower legs.

"We have to leave here tonight," said Troy, watching the big woman try to clean off the sticky muck. Anastasia tried her best to assist with wiping away some of the mud from her backside.

"We can't leave without food, water and directions to the town of Eads." Anastasia had bits of straw stuck to her hands, and some in her hair. She jerked her head when the gate to the horse stall swung open. Breanna was standing in the opening with two oversized work gloves on her hands. The lower part of her jeans was coated with mud and manure.

Troy took a step deeper into the stall.

"What in the hell are you doing in my barn?" Breanna's eye's deepened when she saw Kathy laying on the floor of the stall covered in mud and straw.

"We just tried to find a place to get away from all the confusion." Anastasia held out her muddy hands, startled by the quick appearance of the older lady.

Breanna looked forcefully at Troy. His lazy eye and crooked nose gave him a menacing look.

"We are sorry if we intruded here. It's such a shock for us having to leave our homes to travel east." Troy said politely, noticing her intense stare.

"I'm very protective of my animals. I want to make damn sure they are not disturbed."

"We were just trying to find a place for some privacy away from the crowd," Troy stated conciliatorily.

"Obviously, you can tell this isn't a good place to come to socialize." Breanna's large belly jiggled as she chuckled from the sight of the plump woman covered in mud. She reached her hand down in the direction of Kathy. "Now, let me help you up."

"We really are sorry," Anastasia stated. Troy moved threateningly toward the backside of Breanna. One of the horses neighed loudly.

"Oh, be quiet Harry Potter." Breanna yelled in the direction of the adjacent stall, before turning toward Troy. "Do you like horses?"

"We love horses." Anastasia clutched Breanna's arm and pulled her closer, shooting Troy a questioning look. "But I haven't been on a horse in many years."

"Well, if ya'll are here for a couple of days, I can take you out riding." Breanna decided to heed her mother's advice to look at people from their perspective. Being away from their homes had to be hard on them too.

"That would be wonderful." Anastasia's thought process went into overdrive. Maybe a ticket out of the situation just fell into their laps. "I have a question. Do you know how to get to the town of Eads?"

"I'm from Utah, so I really couldn't tell you." Breanna pinched her heavy jowl. "I will find out for you."

"Aunt Breanna," Arthur yelled from the front of the barn.

"I'm here, in the stall," she yelled so loud that the skin on her pudgy face waggled.

Arthur stuck his head past the metal gate. He stared animatedly at the four people crammed inside the horse stall. His long stringy hair was snarled.

"What's going on?" He crinkled his face, causing the ring hanging from his nose to move straight out.

"Nothing you need to concern yourself with."

"Don't look like nothing to me." Arthur sensed there was something wrong from the guarded look he was getting from Troy. "With a murderer on the loose, we should all be concerned."

"I suppose so," Breanna's eyes flashed a glint of fear as she gazed back at Troy. "I suppose you heard about the dead man. I was the one who found him."

"That had to be awful," Troy stated with his most sympathetic voice.

"A person can't possibly realize how scary it was. I was paralyzed with fear," Breanna sighed, shaking the fist of her left hand.

"I can't even imagine." Troy gave her a supportive frown.

"We probably should go and check to see when the next bus will arrive here," Anastasia stated with a hardened face. She looked directly into Breanna's grey eyes. They were standing so close in the tight quarters that she almost gaged by the musky smell of the older lady. "Thank you so much for giving us a moments reprieve from all the people. If it's alright, we might check back with you about a horse ride."

"You need to do that. There is nothing better than getting out in the fresh air to change your perspective on life." Breanna stepped back, allowing the rebels to move past her.

Troy stopped in his tracks when he walked around the corner of the garage. Shira was standing next to two men, talking with Ted. He was able to stop Anastasia and Kathy before they made it around the edge into the courtyard. The three of them leaned against the brick wall on the west side of Ted's office.

"Shira is around the corner. I think the guys she's talking with are FBI." Troy stated astonishingly.

"How in the world did she end up here?" Anastasia's face was vibrant with curiosity. "She can identify a lot of the people, including us."

"They already have pictures of you and me. We need to leave immediately," Troy spoke frankly, gazing back at the barn.

"Kathy, do you know Shira?" Anastasia could see the trepidation in the portly woman's eyes.

"No, I never ran across her."

"Would you go into the garage and get our backpacks?"

"What are you planning on doing?" Kathy asked with a baffled voice.

"Take a horse ride out of here." Troy stared at her unmercifully.

"Don't worry, you aren't going with us." Anastasia noticed the startled look on Kathy's face. "You can stay here and try to organize the rebels. We need you to get our bags, so we don't have to expose ourselves."

White House, Washington D.C.

The situation remained the same with the two enemy fleets in the Atlantic and the Pacific oceans. Neither of them had budged an inch. An unofficial cease fire ensued after the nuclear explosion in New Mexico. President Weller was unsure if the break in fighting might be long lasting, or if it was a way to give the enemy a chance to reorganize. No matter how he looked at it, he was thankful to have a moment to think.

There were several unconfirmed reports on sightings of the three terrorists responsible for the nuclear explosion. All ended up as false, with the intelligence officers only chasing shadows. The President was finished with becoming excited when hearing about the possible capture of the criminals, and he made it clear to his Security Council that he did not want to hear any more speculation or conjecture. The next report he received needed to be positive confirmation that the three evil doers were apprehended.

The Presidents belief, before he became president, that any war in the modern world would take place between two countries, and never heighten to worldwide warfare, was now being challenged. There were flare ups in combat across the world. Most of them were minor, but the fight for strategic position in the Horn of Africa was escalating. The enemies' focus on eastern Africa was something the United States could not ignore, even with the grave dangers faced at home.

Vice President Trupp took it upon himself to be the lead man for relaying information to the President from the State Department Security Services, and other intelligence agencies, concerning the affairs in Africa, in particular, Camp Lemonnier in Djibouti. Camp Lemonnier was the only United States Military Base on the African continent.

The Vice President thought back to before the war began, where having an abundance of troops in Africa would have been looked upon as a threat. A geopolitical presence supported by even the most modest number of troops in Africa was considered a confront to peace from both Russia and China. Of course, both strengthened their positions in the area while chastising the United States for the most minor of escalation of troops on the continent. He now wanted to make sure we went to the Horn of Africa with full forces. Movement on the monitor from the Pentagon brought him back to the present.

"Mr. President, we are getting confirmed reports that enemy forces in southern Texas are moving back into Mexico." The Secretary of Defense's voice was calm, but his hardened face showed how excited he was in relaying the news.

"Are you telling us, Bob, that they are retreating?" President Weller asked enthusiastically.

"Yes sir. For the past twenty-four hours. We received intelligence that they were having difficulty supplying their forces. There is no mistaking it, they are moving back." Secretary of Defense Maes shook his fist. "This is huge for us. It will give us a chance to strengthen our defenses along the border. They are going to have a hell of a time getting on our soil, ever again."

In a contrary sort of way, having the nuclear explosion was proving to be a Godsend.

Colorado Farm

The living room of the farmhouse was packed to the brim. Space was becoming a premium with more and more travelers arriving and taking over much of the farm grounds. Ted made it clear to his family and friends, especially the children, that although there were many good people trying to find a way to safety, also lingering among them was a threatening presence.

Jon insisted that armed members guard the perimeter around the house. He also talked Ted into moving an Oshkosh R-ATV with the machine gun on the turret next to the Jacoby RV. Without finding the perpetrator of the murdered man, he was taking no chance of harm coming to his family and friends.

"Listen everybody," Jon yelled from his perch standing on the fireplace hearth. "I want to update everyone on what's taking place around us now."

"Why is there an army vehicle with a machine gun on top of it, sitting in front of the house?" Al asked indignantly. "What are we going to do, shoot these people who just arrived?"

"No Al, we are not going to shoot them." Jon stuck his prominent chin out and grimaced.

"Then why is it there? It's not a very welcoming thing for us to have in front of the farmhouse. It looks like an accident ready to happen." He turned and raised his hands, looking for support from others in the room.

"It is kind of intimidating," said Jessica guardedly. She stood at the side of the room with Emilee, Sherry and Caroline.

"It's because we have killers in our midst." Jacqueline looked incredulously at Jessica.

"Okay, listen everyone. Colonel Lisco, Ted, is working along with the FBI task force to keep us safe," Jon said in a firm voice. "We need to all do our parts in allowing the FBI and FEMA personnel do their work for the next couple of days. I promise you, if we stay out of their way, things will quickly get back to normal."

"Normal," Al yelled mockingly. "Tell us lieutenant colonel, what is normal about any of this?"

"Shut the hell up Al," Jason Jensen said furiously. "We've all had enough of your negativity."

"I agree." Harold the bricklayer stepped next to Jason. "It is time for all of us to think positive."

Bill sat on the sofa next to Irene, with Maddy, Scotty and Bella, Irene's great granddaughter playing at their feet. Maddy rose from the floor and crawled up on her father's lap.

"I'm not feeling very good," she whispered in his ear.

"What's wrong?"

"I hurt all over. I need to have Julia look at me."

"Are you really sick."

"Yes," she gazed at him sleepily.

Bill glanced in the direction of the clinic. Julia was standing in front of the doorway with the new doctors on each side of her. Bill held Maddy in one arm as he carried her to the physician assistant. By the time they were standing in front of her, Maddy was hugging him with her arms tight around his neck.

"What's wrong?" Julia asked.

"She's not feeling good," Bill said lightheartedly, towering over the petite lady.

"You not feeling good." Julia rubbed Maddy's back lightly.

Maddy cocked her head and stared at Julia. She nodded up and down.

"Okay, bring her in and set her on the table."

Bill positioned his daughter on the examination table. She squinted her eyes and looked up at the ceiling with a solemn expression on her face as she lay flat on the hard slab.

Julia held the little girl's eyelids open and peered into them. She probed her neck and tapped on her stomach. "Does any of this hurt?"

"A little, when you tapped on my stomach," Maddy said babyishly.

Nicole opened the door and stepped into the clinic. "Is everything okay," she asked with a concerned tone.

"She might have eaten something bad. She has a little stomachache." Julia placed her hand on the back of Maddy's neck and raised her to a sitting position.

"You smell good," Maddy said in a low voice as she let her legs dangle off the table.

"It's a special lotion I use," Julia whispered, with a playful grin.

"Looks like we need to watch what you eat." Bill took hold of Maddy's hand and helped her off the table.

"Bill, can I speak with you." Julia glanced at Nicole, hoping the grandmother would take the hint that she wanted to speak with him alone.

"Come on Maddy, let's go." Nicole checked back with a curious glance as they exited.

"I have to tell you this." Julia smiled, showing her beautiful white teeth. Her head was tilted up to look at him with dark eyes wide open. "Maddy came into the clinic and spoke with me earlier this morning."

"Oh Lord," Bill said with a deep voice.

"She told me that she was going to get right to the point." The physician assistant's eyes showed a flash of humor. "She asked me to marry you. And, after I became her stepmother, we would have to adopt Scotty."

"Julia, I apologize." He squared up with her, and inadvertently brushed her shoulder with his right hand. "This came up the other day. I should have stopped it at that time."

"So, she told you the same thing?"

"Yes, the exact same thing."

"Also, that I would be the queen of the farm."

"Well, no," Bill chuckled. "I never considered myself to be the king here, but that does sound like something she would come up with."

Julia gazed at him inquisitively. The skin around her eyes was smooth, and her face was glowing. She continued to rigorously stare without speaking.

"I guess that is how an eight-year-old mind works. I hope she didn't offend you." Bill clenched his teeth.

"I'm not offended at all," she said softly, continuing to hold the mystified expression.

They looked at each other for a moment, a period that should have been considered awkward, yet in an uncanny way, having the beautiful woman completely focused on him was a time that Bill relished. His terrible understanding of women was coming back into play. He couldn't tell if it was passion in her eyes, or if she was conflicted about Maddy asking her to marry him only a short time after the death of Fred. One thing he knew without a doubt, it was desire that was flickering in his eyes. A fleeting thought entered his mind that both Samantha and Jessica were correct in their evaluation of him. He did have some sort of affliction, a debilitating sickness, that caused him to fall in love with every beautiful woman he crossed paths with. He rationalized that his condition in falling for Julia was warranted, because she was not only beautiful, but also brilliant. As he tried to grasp the situation, his mother opened the clinic door and stuck her head inside.

"Bill, Corporal Pint is out here and wants to speak with you," Nicole said excitedly. "She wants you to take Maddy and Scotty to Ted's office."

****

Breanna just finished cleaning the tack room, off to the side of the horse's stalls, when Troy entered the barn. Her muddy pant legs were now covered with a mixture of grain dust and hay chaff. She flinched slightly when the large man approached, sensing something was not quite right. He had a scowl on his rugged face that frightened her.

"Can we get that horseback ride, now?" Troy asked demandingly.

"That won't be possible. I just have a lot of work to do." The unfriendly tone used by the brutish man made it clear to her that she was in danger. Her heavy breathing increased as she took a step in the direction of the door.

"Okay, listen. I don't have time to mess with you. You are going to saddle up three horses." He pulled out a pistol from his waist band and pointed it at her head. He roughly grabbed the fabric on the back of her shirt. "Then, you are going to come with me and my sister on a long ride."

Breanna knew that several members of the Jacoby family were working on the fence at the pasture, far enough away that they would not hear her if she screamed. Having the firearm pointed at her head was unnerving, but she realized that if he shot her, he and his city slicker sister would never figure out how to saddle the horses.

She relaxed, knowing that once she had them on the mounts, they would be in her element. He wouldn't be so brazen when the two stallions, she was preparing to saddle, tossed him and his sister ten feet into the air, landing them upon their big asses onto the cold, hard ground.

She tried to control her breathing as she finished bridling the three horses. Anastasia rushed into the barn carrying two back packs. While she drew near, Breanna unhooked the bridle from her horse and tossed it into the dirt on the side of the stall. She stated musingly to Troy, "I have to put a different one on. The bit isn't fitting right."

"Just hurry," Troy said angrily.

"Kathy's warning everyone about the FBI's presence. She heard there are a group of over a hundred foreign insurrectionists in the area. Several of the rebels here expect them to attack this farm." Anastasia's face went taut. "She has no problem with staying here."

"I wish they would attack this place now," Troy said with a strained voice, moving aggressively closer to Breanna. "What is taking you so long?"

"You don't want me to put the saddle on incorrectly." She pulled the cinch tight on the first horse. For the briefest moment, she thought about leaving the back strap, or bucking strap, loose, but she thought better of it, and tightened them.

"We can't go out the front door. Can we get out the back?" Troy's hand holding the gun was shaking.

"Yes, there is a back door." Breanna didn't want to take the chance of someone from her family getting shot by approaching the dangerous man. She wrapped the reins for her horse around a hitching post and handed the reins to the other two horses to Anastasia. Both horses neighed and stomped their hoofs. "Hold these for a second while I get some grain."

"You get back here," Troy yelled.

"Don't worry, I'm just going over here. If we are going to be gone for a long time, the horses are going to need to eat."

Troy watched anxiously as she filled the saddle bags with grain. When she finished, she took hold of the reins to her horse.

"I told you before that I'm not familiar with any of the towns around here." Breanna glared at Anastasia.

"We know it's to the east. Just get us away from this farm." Troy took the reins to his powerful horse.

She led them to the back of the barn and out the door into the open pasture. It took several attempts for the greenhorns to get into their saddles, but when they finally did, they all began to trot off to the east.

****

Ted stared out the window inside his office at the garage with the two FBI men. Shira and Jon stood next to him. There was no question that the crowd outside, consuming the entire courtyard of the farm, contained elements of both the homegrown rebels and the foreign anarchists. Deep down he knew that there were rebels who wanted out of the insurrection, who only needed a solid way to return to being citizens of the United States again. All that would have to be figured out by people with a higher pay grade than his, after he had them in custody.

His plan was for Shira to ascertain known rebels and persuade them to identify other rebels. The last thing he wanted to do was cause a battle to occur on the farm grounds, so he brought Deb into the fold. He figured his platoon could handle the insurgents should they decide to fight, but for the welfare of all the innocent civilians at the farm, he wanted to make sure the force was overwhelming to quash any uprising. Deb informed him that she and Tommy would be back at the farm within an hour with troops. Shira and Sherry were taken to the top of the tower to cautiously search the crowd for those they could identify as members of the rebels.

In the meantime, Ted waited for Corporal Pint to arrive with Maddy. He remembered the concerned look on Cindy's face when she said goodbye to them at the airport in Los Angeles, for what should have been a routine trip on the airplane to Colorado. He was proud of the young corporal for using all resources at her fingertips to find the young mother. She also went beyond the call of duty in finding Scotty's parents.

Bill, Nicole, Maddy and Scotty entered the office. Maddy had her hair neatly pulled back into a ponytail. Scotty's hair was combed, but the hair covered half of his ears.

"Come over here." Corporal Pint waved enthusiastically. "I was getting worried you weren't going to make it. We should have them online at any time."

"Did you find our moms?" Maddy asked excitedly.

"Yes," Corporal Pint's round face held a huge smile. "My brother is a marine stationed in the Los Angeles area. He has all sorts of connections. They found your families."

"Where are they now?" Bill asked enthusiastically.

"They are at the Marine base in Montebello, California." Corporal Pint was so happy she was almost laughing. "Maddy, are you about ready to talk with your mom?"

"Yes," she rushed over and hugged the corporal. She glanced at the monitor where people were beginning to move around.

Cindy's image popped on the screen. Her face was tan, and her blonde hair was brushed to set on her shoulders.

"Mom," Maddy yelled.

"Oh God thank you." Cindy slumped in her chair. She placed her hand to her forehead. "I was so worried about you. I miss you so much."

"I miss you too." Maddy said with tears in her eyes.

"I was told that the plane you were on went down, but that was all the information we could get. I couldn't believe it when we received news yesterday that you are alive." Cindy could hardly catch her breath as the tears flowed. She looked past Maddy to Bill. "What happened Bill?"

"The plane her and Dad were on landed in Utah about an hour after they left you at the airport in Los Angeles. They had quite an adventure getting back to Colorado," Bill's voice tempered with nostalgia. He couldn't believe how vibrant and beautiful his ex-wife looked. "We were worried about you too. Maddy has been constantly asking about you."

"Everything has been total chaos here. Things seem to be improving somewhat," Cindy sighed.

Maddy glanced at Scotty. "Is Scotty's mom there?"

"Yes, both his mother and father. I just met them." Cindy moved back, allowing Scotty's parents to fill the screen.

Scotty's mother and father were bawling so hard that he could hardly understand them. They both took turns making it clear to him how much they missed him, and how blessed they felt for knowing he was safe. Finally, they stopped talking, and took noticeably loud, deep breaths. Scotty's dad moved his bright red face closer to the monitor. "Where's Grandma?" he asked animatedly.

Scotty grimaced. He closed his eyes tightly and began crying. "She died," he gasped.

"What, she died? How?" Scotty's dad held his mouth wide open.

"She got shot." Scotty began to sob.

Bill stepped closer to the monitor. Scotty's dad looked nauseous as he contemplated the bittersweet reunion with his son.

"Carol was severely injured on the trip here from Utah. She did pass after arriving at our farm." Bill gazed into the screen, unsure of how much detail he should give about the death of Carol. "I'm terribly sorry for your loss."

"How long ago did she die?" His frown deepened.

"A little over six weeks ago."

"Where is she buried?"

"On the hill north of our farmhouse," Bill answered.

"I want to have her body brought back here." Scotty's father continued looking into the monitor dejectedly.

"That will have to wait until the war is over." Bill did his best to be straightforward with the parent, trying to be comforting and realistic at the same time. "Right now, we need to find a way to reunite you with Scotty. There are FEMA officials helping us on the farm. I will check to see if they have a way to transport him to California."

Eastern Colorado

The terrain in the pastures to the east of the Lisco farm was made up of sagebrush and rolling hills. On several occasions small gullies, too deep to ride across, caused the three riders to alter course. A cold wind hit their backsides as Breanna led the way across the unrelenting countryside.

After a little more than an hour into the journey, Troy fidgeted in his saddle, trying to find a comfortable position to ride. He jerked back tight on the reins, causing his horse to rear. He continued to hold the pistol in one hand as he tugged on the straps.

"You need to loosen the reins, or he is going to buck you off." Breanna worried that the ruthless man would accidentally shoot her, or one of the horses on his way down to the ground.

"We need to take a break. My ass is killing me." He slackened the reins and the horse stopped fighting.

"It won't hurt for us to walk for a while." Breanna slid off her horse.

Anastasia's padded backside seemed to adapt better to the saddle than that of her brother. After getting off her horse she was able to walk normally. Troy took a couple of minutes of walking bowlegged before gaining his normal stride. They insisted that Breanna always walk in front of them.

"It's going to get dark pretty soon." Anastasia glanced over her shoulder to the sun low in the southwest sky.

"We have to travel through the night," said Troy determinedly. He glanced at Anastasia. "Once we get away from this God forsaken area, we can sleep on the trip to Atlanta."

"Is Mike planning on meeting us at Piedmont Park?"

"He might be there now." Troy's voice held a tone of excitement. "He made sure the bomb at White Sands was prepared correctly, but I'm sure he left before the explosion."

Anastasia stubbed the front of her right foot into a cactus. "Dammit, this place is nothing but a desert."

"You have to watch your step." Breanna turned in the direction of the brother and sister. Her round face was taut. "We might want to ride for a while, since it is still light outside. It is kind of stupid to be out here in the dark."

Troy gave her a menacing look. Her confident demeanor worried him.

"We know the town is east. Once we come across a road, we are bound to find someone who can give us exact directions," Anastasia stated logically, nodding toward Breanna. "I agree with her. We should ride."

Breanna helped Anastasia climb aboard, while Troy muscled his way onto his mount. She grabbed a leather strap out of her saddle bag before mounting her horse. She could see, far off in the distance, on the northern horizon, a line of barely visible telephone poles, signifying to her that there was a road. She veered slightly to the south to keep the posts sticking out of the flat panorama out of sight. Hearing the two terrorists speak freely about their destination of Atlanta, and involvement with the atomic explosion, made it clear that she was in grave danger. If she continued to cooperate fully with the evil brother and sister, there is no way she would be left alive when she was no longer useful.

Colorado Farm

Ted realized something was wrong the moment Irene rushed inside his office, followed closely by Aaron and Adam Jacoby. Irene was breathing hard as she walked past the FBI men and Jon to place her right hand onto his shoulder.

"Something has happened to Breanna," she stated anxiously. "We can't find her anywhere."

"She can't be far." Ted was caught completely off guard.

"Three horses are missing too. There is no way she would take the horses out this late." Aaron glanced at the FBI men. "We found one of the new bridles laying in the dirt outside a stall. She would never treat her equipment so badly unless there was something wrong."

"We think she was telling us she is in danger," Adam stated.

"This all has to be connected with the dead man we found at the haystack." Jon moved next to Irene.

"Oh my God, who would do such a thing?" Irene placed her hand over her mouth.

"Sergeant Harris," Ted yelled across the room to the soldier sitting at the desk in the corner of the room. "Prepare our drone to immediately surveille in a fifteen-kilometer radius of the farm. Contact Petersen and have them launch a NAV. I want pictures on our screens of any human movement within a fifty-kilometer radius of our location."

Irene lowered her hand and started to breathe easier. She could see the determination in Ted's face.

"We are thinking of saddling up and going out to see if we can find her." Aaron wore dirty bib overalls. The sagging wrinkles on his face gave him the appearance of a basset hound preparing for a hunt.

"We have all-terrain vehicles that we can use." Ted turned to Irene. He took hold of her fragile hand and gazed straight into her eyes. "You all go inside the house out of the cold. I will do everything I can to find Breanna."

Irene smiled at him. "I know you will Ted." She slowly exited the door with her two sons.

"Deb just pulled into the driveway," Jon said loudly, looking out the window. "She brought more than just a platoon with her."

"Yeah, I spoke with her about an hour ago. 2nd Brigade is stationing at Fort Carson. She wanted Lt. Col. Woodworth to check out the farm on the way through." Ted moved to the window.

"This couldn't have come at a better time," Jon said. "There is no way the rebels will cause problems with so many soldiers here."

"We better get things underway because Lt. Col. Woodworth is going to want to get his soldiers to Fort Carson."

Eastern Colorado

Breanna pulled the collar of her coat tight to her neck. Cold and blackness shrouded the unremitting grassland. The harsh land would be inhospitable to even the most seasoned farmer and rancher. If she had anything to say about it, the soft city dwellers were about to find out how forbidding the territory could be.

The three horses snorted and fidgeted to a greater degree the further they moved into the darkness, away from the warm barn at the farm. Troy and Anastasia remained riding a couple meters behind Breanna. Each time they stopped for a moment to change directions in order to miss a gully or small chasm, the brother and sister would move quickly forward to sit alongside her on their horses. On each occasion, she made note in the back of her mind of their impatience.

"Are you sure we are going east?" Troy held the pistol on the horn of the saddle.

"I'm positive. There is the north star." Breanna pointed assuredly into the sky at a random star. "I just want to be careful that we don't hurt the horses by having them step into a crevice or hole."

"I could give a shit about these horses. This place can't be so isolated that we don't come across a road somewhere," Troy said angrily. He waved his pistol at Breanna. "I'm starting to think you are leading us in circles. Besides that, it is getting cold as hell out here."

"There is nothing I can do. I have never been here either," Breanna stated exasperatedly. She pulled the hood of the coat over her head and tightened the strings.

"How far do you think we have traveled?" Anastasia threw out the question, turning her horse so the wind was at her back.

"Maybe twenty kilometers," Breanna said. "Maybe a little more."

Troy in frustration pulled the reins tight on his stallion and the horse reared back. He struck the animal hard on the side of its neck.

"Knock it off," Breanna yelled angrily, hopping off her steed. She held on to the straps of her horse as she grabbed the metal on the side of the bridle of Troy's horse. The horse stomped before quieting. She placed her forehead on its wet, cold nose.

"Better I smack this horse than you." Troy's distorted face held an expression of animosity. "You can take it to the bank that I'm going to slap you across your head if we don't come across a road pretty damn soon."

"You don't have to be a bully with me."

"Lady, you don't know what I'm capable of."

"I think I do." Breanna's lips quivered as she stared at him loathingly. "You killed that man I found back at the farm. Didn't you?"

"Yeah, I did. If you don't get back on your horse, I'm going to do the same to you." He pointed his gun at her.

Breanna turned in the direction of Anastasia to see if she might find some hope of sympathy from the sister. There was none, only coldness in her eyes.

She placed her foot into the stirrup, and quickly mounted her horse. As she rose high in the saddle, a dim light flickered on the eastern horizon. Troy glanced quickly in the same direction the moment he noticed her looking.

"I see lights." She pointed to the finding, realizing she should be quick to make note of the lights before he accused her of hiding the discovery. "It might be a farm."

"How far away do you think it is?" Anastasia asked excitedly.

"Closer than we think," Breanna feigned eagerness in her voice.

"Get going," Troy motioned to Breanna, "you first."

It took only thirty minutes of riding before the outline of a barn became visible. The roar of military planes off in the far distance was the only noticeable sound, until they came close enough to the farmstead to hear people talking.

Breanna's heart sank the moment they rode into the courtyard of the farm. A single light at the front of the decrepit farmhouse was the only form of illumination for the entire farm grounds. People holding weapons, dressed in heavy black coats were everywhere. It was obviously a stronghold for the insurrectionists. For the briefest of moments, she thought about racing her horse back into the darkness of the pasture.

"Troy is that you?" A woman with slit eyes and thick dark hair watched from a couple meters away as Troy tried to control the horse.

Troy yanked hard on the reins, causing his steed to pull its head back and snort loudly. The excitable horse stumbled backwards as he jerked the reins tighter. Everyone nearby scattered as he dismounted.

"Seeing you ride up on a horse is the last thing I would have expected." The woman continued to stand back as he tried to control the horse. He slapped the tall stallion on the side of its head.

Breanna slid off her mount and hit Troy hard on his shoulder with a round house punch. She roughly snatched the reins from his hand. His face flashed raging anger as he raised his right hand threateningly.

"You can't treat my horse like that," she sneered at him with her chin thrust forward. She turned her back to him, and looked into the horse's large eyes, waiting for a blow.

Troy grabbed Breanna by the collar of her shirt and tossed her to the ground. She bumped the back side of her head as she hit the cold gravel. She gazed up at the abnormal face of the monstrous man posed to strike again. He kicked hard, catching her on the forehead with the heel of his right boot. She looked straight up in the air with blurred vision. Flying high in the night sky was a large drone with blinking lights. Even in her semi-conscious state she could hear the humming of the nonhuman aerial vehicle as it rushed over top of the insurrectionist's stronghold.

"We can't stay here." Troy looked at Anastasia while glancing in the direction where the NAV disappeared into the darkness.

"Do you know how to get to the town of Eads?" Anastasia asked the insurrectionist leader.

"I do," said a man wearing a cap with a long skinny nose and an oblong face.

Breanna struggled to pull herself off the ground. She was still dazed, but able to recognize the man with the cap, and his blond-haired friend standing next to him. They were the two who attacked Caroline, and most recently Sherry.

"If you go down the driveway to the county road and head east, this road will dead end. Just go right, and you will hit the town."

"How far is it?" Troy asked.

"I would guess about forty kilometers." The man in the cap wore the same arrogant expression as when he was caught by the men back at the farm.

"Get on the horse." Troy latched hold of Breanna's shoulder and pushed her toward her horse.

She placed her foot in the stirrup and climbed aboard. She stared at him with an expression that showed utter distain. It would be only a matter of time before he killed her.

Colorado Farm

Colonel Deb, Command Sergeant Major Talfoya and Lt. Col. Woodworth entered Ted's office after walking through the crowd of people being processed into the FEMA tents. A large number of FEMA personnel worked to quarter the civilians for the night.

Ted sensed that there was more to Breanna's disappearance than met the eye. The more he thought about the murdered man, the more he realized the desperate nature of the perpetrator. They were searching for a person with a lot to lose. He noticed Sergeant Harris motioning to him.

"Colonel, Agent Elder with the FBI task force wants a moment with you."

Ted moved to the sergeant's desk in the far corner of the room. Agent Elder appeared on the screen of the monitor with an expression of exuberance.

"We caught Mike Chen," he spoke the moment Ted's image appeared. "His rebel counterparts rolled on him."

"Where did you find him?"

"Just outside Springfield, Missouri."

"Have you any leads on the Vasilyeva's?" Ted's face was taut. Deb and Tommy moved over to stand next to him.

"We haven't, but we hope to get some information from Chen." A look of annoyance came over Agent Elder's face. "Apparently, he has made threats of another nuclear device. He wants passage to China for information of its whereabouts."

"Agents Maloney and Edwards are here now. We are about to weed out the insurrectionists from the civilians. Hopefully, we will be able to glean something from them."

"Colonel, I'm sorry to interrupt," said Corporal Pint, holding her position at the monitor at her desk. "The NAV has discovered a large group of people at a farmhouse about 25 kilometers southeast of our location. Three horseback riders are among them."

Ted glanced at Deb with a questioning look on his face. She understood without any words being spoken that he was asking her if she would use aspects of 2nd Battalion to investigate the situation. Before she could answer, the door to the office opened and Theodore Sutherland, Deputy Assistant of response for FEMA region eight stepped into the office.

Deb candidly looked at the man with an expression that radiated confidence. He still had the same stoic face, and drooping eyes as when she told him in Utah that she would beat the hell out of him. Command Sergeant Major Talfoya recoiled back, unsure of what might come from the two leaders meeting face to face.

"I have four buses scheduled to arrive here by 0800 tomorrow morning. That is, if everything is okay with you Colonel?" The Deputy spoke seriously. His face was expressionless as he gazed directly at Deb.

"Sir, that is fine with me," Deb stated with an appeasing voice. "I do appreciate the professionalism and help we have received from your agency."

"We will work well together and get everyone off your farm in no time." The Deputy cracked a smile.

Deb took a breath through her nose and smiled back at him.

"How about if we send Captain Hendersen and F Company to investigate the insurgents?" Tommy felt a surge of relief in how Deb and the FEMA official made amends. He turned in the direction of Lt. Col. Woodworth. "Josh you can continue with G, H and I Companies to Fort Carson."

"Are you good with that Ted?" Deb glanced at her brother.

"It works for me. We can begin the process of separating the rebels from the citizens here at the farm," Ted said.

Everyone turned to acknowledge a soldier enter the office. He saluted and stood at attention in front of Deb. His deep voice echoed in the room, "Colonel Lisco, you are wanted at the communication vehicle. General Prost is online waiting to speak with you."

"Tell her I am on my way." Deb quickly saluted and turned toward Lt. Col. Woodworth. "Josh, have Captain Hendersen move immediately to the location of the insurgents. You are going to be traveling in the dark, so you might as well remain here for a couple more hours before departing to base."

"You can communicate with Captain Hendersen from this location." Ted turned toward the command sergeant major. "Tommy, can you stay here and assist?"

"Of course." Tommy's eyes were full of concern as he watched Deb leave the room. He couldn't think of any good reasons why General Prost would be contacting her.

Deb walked quickly to the battalion communication vehicle. The technician seated in front of the monitor displaying General Prost on the screen, rose from her chair, allowing the colonel to sit.

"Colonel, I have some sensitive, more personal, information I want to pass to you. You might want to secure the communication area before we speak," the general stated.

"Give me some privacy here." Deb glanced at the three soldiers. She felt some remorsefulness in having the technicians leave the warm vehicle to saunter out into the cold. "I will only be a moment."

"Colonel, I wanted to tell you personally that you have been recommended to be promoted to Brigadier General." General Prost's front teeth protruded out as she smiled. "The process for the promotion is already with the Secretary of Defense and only needs the President's approval. It is a mere formality now."

Debs face was a picture of astonishment. "I'm speechless."

"This is an endorsement of your bravery and outstanding ability to lead. As a fellow woman warrior, I want to tell you this advancement is well warranted."

"Thank you so much General Prost." Deb realized the significance of being the first Lisco general in the long line of her military ancestors. A tear came to her eyes when she thought of her father. He would surely remind her that success comes to those who are too busy to be looking for it. Now, she wanted to bring her three brothers together to let them know they would have to address her as General Lisco. This promotion was for them as much as for her.

Eastern Colorado

Breanna's head ached, and she felt nauseous from the brutal attack she endured from the terrorist. They were riding on the dark pastureland about a hundred meters to the south of the county road, in the direction of the tiny town of Eads. She kept looking into the night sky, hoping to get another glimpse of the NAV. The horses were tired. She groaned inwardly from the realization that should one of her animal's flounder, the vicious man would certainly shoot it, along with her.

She stopped her horse at the top of a small chasm that crossed the path ahead. The crevice was about five meters deep. Troy slapped the neck of his steed with the loose rein, and moved up next to her, with Anastasia pulling up on the other side.

"Why are you stopping?" Troy asked nastily. "This is no deeper than the gullies we went down before."

"The horses are tired. I want to make sure they don't stumble." Breanna gazed reflexively at Anastasia. "Let's ride them down slowly."

Troy's expression showed that he was skeptical, but when Anastasia moved forward on her horse, he followed. The second the front legs of Troy's horse hit the downslope; Breanna slapped it hard in the flank with a leather strap. She reached across and hit Anastasia's mount hard on the rump. Both horses bucked hard, sending the riders airborne. The brother and sister landed firmly on their backs and rolled toward the bottom of the chasm.

Breanna turned her horse and rode hard in the opposite direction, rotating in the saddle to whistle loudly. Both horses followed behind her as she raced away. She was a good three hundred meters away, and riding fast, by the time Troy was able to climb out of the gulley and fire his pistol. He shot into thin air.

After riding for nearly a kilometer the bright lights of army vehicles appeared in the distance. She stopped and took hold of the reins of the two horses following behind. Although her head ached, she clicked her teeth commanding her horse to trot forward. The form of soldiers in the headlights appeared on the county road.

"The terrorists are about two kilometers down the road, and approximately a hundred meters to the south." Breanna slid out of the saddle and leaned over in pain. Soldiers came to her aid, taking the straps of the three horses.

"Are there only two?" Captain Hendersen asked.

"Yes." Breanna was breathing hard.

"What weapons do they have?"

"They both have handguns."

"Have 2nd Squad get them," the captain barked the order to the sergeant standing at his side.

"Yes sir, right away."

The all-terrain vehicle carrying the squad drove around the captain and Breanna. It shot down the road toward Anastasia and Troy.

"I take it for granted that you are the lady who went missing from Colonel Lisco's farm." Captain Hendersen held his arm around the weakened lady.

"Yes, I am Breanna Jacoby. I came to the farm from Utah with Ted."

"Were you part of the group at Monticello with Colonel Lisco and his granddaughter when we found them a couple months ago?"

"Yes, I was in the RV with my mother and father." Breanna felt a twinge of pain when she remembered Ed.

"We will call ahead and inform them that you have been found."

"What about the other terrorists? Did you capture them?" Breanna asked tensely. "There was a hell of a lot of them."

"They are all apprehended." Captain Hendersen showed no emotion at all in sharing something that most people would find to be a great accomplishment. "G Company is processing them as we speak."

"I need to talk with Ted, right now." Breanna's face twisted with concern. "I have information I overheard from the two you just sent the squad to capture. They are part of the group responsible for the nuclear explosion."

"We can contact him on the radio." He motioned to a soldier. "Corporal, connect us to Lt. Col. Woodworth and have him dispatch us through to Colonel Lisco."

The soldier spoke for less than thirty seconds into his pulsnet radio. "Captain, I have Colonel Lisco."

Captain Hendersen wasn't sure which Colonel Lisco the corporal was speaking with when he stepped closer and spoke into the radio, "Colonel, I have Breanna Jacoby who has some pertinent information she wants to share with you."

"Breanna," Ted's voice reflected the happiness he felt from her being found. "Are you okay?"

"They beat the hell out of me Ted, but I'll live. The two who took me are dangerous. They had a part in the nuclear explosion." She moved closer to the corporal to better hear Ted.

"Do you know what their names are?"

"Anastasia and Troy."

"Captain Hendersen, do you have them in custody?" Ted's voice indicated the importance of catching the two terrorists.

A sergeant situated next to the captain nodded his head up and down when he heard Colonel Lisco's question.

"We have them, and they should be here within a couple minutes."

"I overheard them talking about another nuclear weapon at Piedmont Park in Atlanta, Georgia," Breanna stated briskly.

"Bring them here as quickly as you can." Ted clenched his fist and slammed it on his desk.

"Another thing Ted," Breanna said. "The terrorists captured at the farm have the two guys who attacked Caroline and Sherry. You might want to let Jon know."

Ted stared at Deb and Tommy in utter astonishment. He wished he could see the faces of the CIA operatives when they heard the news that, not only were the Vasilyeva's captured, but he also had information on the whereabouts of the nuclear device.

White House, Washington D.C.

President Weller spent the day meeting with his cabinet in the large conference room adjacent to the Oval Office. Never had he seen such a positive group. Secretary of Defense Maes was overly confident that the enemy would not be able to move across the border of Mexico. Having the enemies' fleets retreat from both the Atlantic and Pacific locations supported his certitudes. Everyone was cautiously optimistic that it signified the beginning of the end of war on American soil.

Mike Chen and the Vasilyevas were going to be held accountable for their part in the insurrection. Without the threat of the nuclear bomb to blackmail their way out of the country, justice would be served.

The President was completely relaxed as he sat in his favorite recliner with his feet raised, sipping on a glass half filled with Glenlivet 18-year-old single malt scotch. First Lady Elizabeth sat right next to him on a hard chair, while Chief of Staff Alexander took a seat in front of the President and First Lady in the piece of furniture he considered to be the most uncomfortable chair on the face of the planet.

"This is all far from over," President Weller sighed, "but with the withdrawal of enemy forces, and receiving the news that the terrorists responsible for the nuclear explosion have been captured, we took a huge step in bringing this conflict to an end."

"We need to preserve all documents and make sure your true legacy is safeguarded for history." Chief of Staff Alexander shifted in his chair. "I can't think of any President in history who could have handled the war better."

"Thank you for saying that." President Weller was aware that his Chief of Staff was a true historian, and a loyalist. "I'll be honest with you Tom, there were times where I was completely lost when our military leaders described the capabilities of our armed forces."

"It would be impossible for you to be an expert in all phases of our very complicated military. FDR concentrated on strategic matters while delegating tactical aspects to his commanders during World War 2. You led sir, just like he did, sometimes making decisions against the advice of military advisers when you needed to."

"I should have never let the idea that we could lose the war enter my mind." The President scrutinized the faces of both his wife and his Chief of Staff.

"President Lincoln, during his campaign, wrote of his belief that the Union could lose the civil war," the Chief of Staff stated knowingly. "During the heat of battle everything must come to mind. Lincoln probably never truly realized the Union would win the Civil War until Sherman took Atlanta, and the war turned favorable."

"I'm not so sure historians are going to be very kind to me. There are so many things we missed with the country being deeply divided, before this war started." The President took a miniscule drink of scotch. The leathery bags under his eyes seemed to darken.

"Paul, the country has been split for many, many decades." Chief of Staff Alexander held his glass of scotch in both hands as he sat on the edge of his seat. "Presidents Johnson and Nixon faced the polarization of the nation during the Vietnam War. Nixon withdrew our troops while speaking of ending the war and winning the peace. So much of what is perceived by a country divided is ascribable to phraseology. He was able to navigate the divided citizenry by retreating and winning at the same time."

"Tom, I can't tell you how fortunate I am to have you as an adviser, and friend." The President glanced at his wife. "You too Elizabeth. I don't know what I would have done without our times of discussion."

"We have to figure out now how to bring the country together and, at the same time, create a world where we will never again be invaded," Elizabeth spoke with an exasperated tone. "Disagreements we have with other countries must be solved in a peaceful manner. I guess we can imagine a world without nuclear weapons."

"I always said that if the nuclear bomb never existed, somebody would eventually invent it," Tom stated categorically.

"I wish this war occurred because of disagreements, or some form of dispute. Misunderstandings can be resolved." President Weller shook his head and gazed at the last couple of swallows of scotch at the bottom of his glass. "This war occurred because our enemies wanted to conquer us. They attacked only because they believed they could do so."

"Now we go back to the geopolitical fights."

"The war is not over. It just hit a fork in the road." The President placed his glass on the side table and folded his arms over his chest. "I do have complete faith in our military to defeat our enemies. The biggest obstacle I will face in the future is bringing the country together."

"Pauley, that has been the task of every president since George Washington," Elizabeth stated supportively.

"Over the years we allowed the wonder, the marvel, and the incredulity of America to be destroyed. We lost our liberty, freedom, and self-determination. I know it sounds cliché, like a campaign slogan. But I truly mean it from the bottom of my heart that I will do everything humanly possible to make America a place of truth and justice. Bring back a spirit of conquest, where people live with principle, purpose, and idealism. Everyone needs to have a sense of dignity, united as one, with freedom being important again."

"I do believe you will do it." Elizabeth's expression showed utter adoration for her husband.

Colorado Farm

Over two hundred travelers were removed by the FEMA buses, during the final day of 2051. The homegrown rebels who surrendered to the FBI without a fight were separated from the citizens journeying to the east and placed on a special bus to be taken back to the city for processing.

A sense of hope encompassed everyone as they assembled in the new building, finally finished by Jason Jensen and Harold. The temperature was below freezing, and the fireplace roared inside, allowing everyone to remain comfortable as they waited for the final couple hours of 2051 to disappear. Most people in the large room congregated around Deb and Ted.

Deb gazed at Command Sergeant Major Talfoya, and latched ahold of his right arm, pulling him tight to her side.

"We need to make a requisition for some more scotch." Jon held up a bottle in front of Deb's face. "There are only five bottles left."

"I imagine we can do that." Deb smiled. "If there has ever been a time to celebrate, this is it."

Jon began pouring the liquor into plastic cups. Patrick was the first to partake.

"Where do we go from here?" Al moved into the circle of Liscos. His face was rigid, seeming bewildered.

"What are you getting at Al?" Jon asked exasperatedly.

"Don't get so snippy with me Jon. We all have a right to understand what is happening," Al stated testily. "Everything has been moving quickly. Are people going to start leaving here to go back to the city?"

"Oh mate, I don't think so." Patrick towered over the back of the small dentist. "There is no way the city could have restored itself yet. It was a total mess when we left."

"I agree with Patrick," George Saxton moved closer. "It will take months for the electric grid alone to become reliable. We learned a hard lesson before by leaving here too soon."

"I would like to at least see what shape our house is in," Al spoke, using a more amicable tone.

"There have been some positive developments over the past week," Ted interrupted. "I can tell you for a fact that there are still rebels in the city who plan to disrupt. They won't stop until they are captured."

"I would like to get back and make sure our belongings we left behind are safe." Hank gazed at his neighbor with an empathetic expression. "Let's give it a little more time Al."

"Going home will be wonderful," Irene said, surrounded by her family. "Us Jacobys have lived in south-central Utah for nearly a century and a half. We miss our homes, but all I can say is thank God that the Liscos created this haven for of us here on the eastern plains of Colorado."

"Here, here, jolly well said." Patrick downed his liquor in one quick swoop to his mouth. He took a step in the direction of Jon with the small plastic goblet held out in his massive hand.

"Thank God it is almost midnight," Jon said under his breath, yet he poured the spirits into the waiting Englishman's cup.

"Might I take a moment to make a toast." Patrick held his cup up next to his ear. *We are lucky to be in the presence of soldiers who have not only sacrificed for our safety and wellbeing, but for our comfort. Tonight, we should remember those who made the ultimate sacrifice for us. We should not mourn the dead soldiers but praise them. We should thank them for our opportunities. If we find ourselves feeling sorry for all we have lost, we should make ourselves feel rich by counting all the things we have that money cannot buy."*

"Well said," said George Saxton, placing a hand on the shoulder of Hank. "We should all take care of those that take care of us. We truly thank the Liscos for their forethought and caring."

Bill picked up Maddy and held her in his arms. Patrick's thoughts on cherishing things money cannot buy resonated well with him. He moved closer to the fireplace, away from those celebrating loudly. "You are going to miss Scotty, aren't you?" he said softly.

"Yeah," Maddy said quietly.

"The good thing is your mom will be able to come here, probably within the next couple of weeks." Bill noticed both Sherry and Emilee staring at him. When he brought his gaze back toward Maddy, his eyes caught those of Julia standing off to the side. He gave her a quick smile.

"You like her, don't you?" Maddy stated loudly.

"Not so loud," Bill said through clenched teeth.

"You like her don't you," she said softly, twisting her head so she could smile at Julia.

"Oh, gosh." Bill turned and gave the physician assistant a quick look.

"Bill, can I speak with you for a moment?" Sherry moved next to him. "If possible, I would like to have Colonel Deb in on the conversation."

"I'll go get her," Bill said timidly. "Come on Maddy, you can hang with Grandma for a couple of minutes."

Jacqueline enthrallingly watched as Deb followed Bill to the back of the room where Sherry was standing.

"I have something extremely important that I want to discuss with you two." The red scars on Sherry's chiseled face were prominent in the light from the yellow flames in the fireplace. "I have decided to bring all of this out in the open, because I want my baby to have the Lisco name."

Deb opened her mouth and stared a hole through Bill, with an astonished look on her face.

"It's not me." Bill tossed his arms in the air and leaned back.

"It's Bobby's baby," Sherry said abruptly.

"It's Bobby's baby?" Bill inadvertently shot a glance in the direction of his Aunt Jacqueline. She still had her eyes on him.

"You are sure of this?" Deb thought of mentioning that if she was trying to scam them it would be impossible because of DNA. She decided not to insult the young lady.

"I'm positive. Bobby knew about it before he left for Indiana." She pulled her hair to the side of her head, and held onto her blonde locks as she spoke, "he told Emilee during the trip that he was the father."

"I'm surprised Emilee didn't tell Hank and Jacqueline," Deb stated.

"Even as terrible as the last few days have been for her with the loss of Bobby, she agreed to my decision not to tell anyone. I understand now Bobby's parents need to know." Sherry let go of her hair and took in a deep breath. "After Emilee told me that Bobby was going to be partners in this property, I came to the conclusion that his child should be a part of it."

Deb stared at Bill with a questioning expression. If both young women were okay with the other having a baby sired by Bobby, who was she to question the morality of the situation.

Bill turned his head just in time to see Jacqueline and Hank approaching. Emilee and Jessica also came to Sherry's side just as the count down to the end of 2051 began. "ten, nine, eight, seven…"

"Is everything okay," Jacqueline asked.

"three, two, one. Happy 2052." Patrick's loud voice boomed off the walls.

About the Author

Dan Peavler grew up on the eastern plains of Colorado in the small town of Bennett. He graduated with a BA in Psychology from the University of Colorado in 1975. He has worked as a counselor, a coach, a real estate broker and a bricklayer.

Family has always been the most important part of his life. Having found a lifelong partner in his wife Helen, raising two incredible sons, Jon and Travis and being a grandpa to Reagan are the greatest and most fulfilling parts of his life.

The central theme in the novel 2051 is the love of family. At the same time, the kindness in people's hearts, allow them to help strangers in the time of devastation.

It is not a story of darkness, but one of hope, love and friendship. It is written with the expectation that the people of America will find a way to unite and collaborate to conquer the problems plaquing our nation before an enemy finds a way to use the divisiveness to end our way of life.

Dan began writing the first novel the summer of 2019 and finished the final one during the summer of 2022. Much happened during this time period. Covid, the death of George Floyd with ensuing riots and the storming of the nation's capital on January 6th, 2020. While writing the novel Dan still remained optimistic the scenario of destruction and betrayal will never actually happen. The idea that it could take place is a warning to everyone of how important it is to work to make the country a place where everyone can live together in peace.

You can see Dan's other books and reach him through his website danpeavler.com.

Henry E. Peavler

Henry Peavler enlisted into the Army the Spring of 1943 at Camp Van Dorn Mississippi and trained at Camp Maxie, outside Paris, Texas, during the summer of 1944. He and the other soldiers of the 99th Infantry Division, the Checkerboarders, sailed for England the fall of 1944 from Camp Miles Standfish near Boston. He and his unit trained for a short period near Dorchester, England before shipping toward France where they landed at Le Havre, five months after D-Day.

Henry was with the 371st field artillery Battery C. After arriving in France. the 99th Infantry immediately sped across France to Belgium, they were entering the war. It was early December as they made their way through the Ardennes Forest with little resistance, only a few German snipers and pill boxes. One of the perks of being in an artillery unit was staying in houses, rather than foxholes, during the terrible cold Belgium winter. He first stayed in the basement of a house in Hunnigen, Belgium before the brass had them move the artillery to a field just outside of Murringen, Belgium. His notes say he stayed at an old farmer's house.

At 5:30 on the morning of December 16th, 1944, he and others of his unit woke to the thunderous sound of shells exploding all around them. The German Panzer Armies sent 200,000 soldiers and a thousand tanks towards the Americans along a seventy-mile front. It was the beginning of the Battle of the Bulge. The 371st was forced to retreat toward Krenkelt, Belgium but first had to destroy all their artillery and vehicles, leaving them on foot, because muddy roads and disabled machinery made it impossible to drive forward. They fought with all their might before being ordered north to Elsenborn where Henry helped defend the Elsenborn ridge.

Early March of 1945 the 99th moved quickly to the Rhine River at Remagen. The 371st gave cover to the brave members of the infantry as they crossed the Ludendorff bridge, before crossing into Germany themselves on March 13, 1945. The picture above has written on the back, **Peavler, Dattenburg Germany, March 1945** – we wonder if it was taken on his 21st birthday. The 99th fought further into Germany at the Ruhr Pocket before joining General Patton's Third Army.

The 99th Infantry distinguished itself defending the "Northern shoulder of the Battle of the Bulge." It was the first full Infantry division to cross the Rhine River at Remagen. They collapsed the Ruhr Pocket, captured more than 100,000 prisoners, and conquered more than 1000 miles of territory. They are recognized as a "liberating unit" by the United States Center of Military History and the United States Holocaust Memorial Museum for liberating concentration camps near the town of Muhldorf, Germany.

After returning from the war, Henry was first and foremost a farmer and family man. In 1946, He met my mother, Betty Harvey, after securing a job on her brother's farm in central Kansas. It was love at first sight, and they were married, three weeks after they met. They moved to Ava, Missouri, and had their first child. Figuring out very quickly that it would be hard to make a living farming in Missouri, they moved to a farm on the eastern plains of Colorado. On the farm in Strasburg, he and Betty had three more children and during the fall of 1953 found they were going to have another. Henry was living his dream of being a farmer and having a large family, but in October of that year, he died in an automobile accident on his way to a parttime job on an oil rig.

The people who knew Henry said he was a kind, gentle, hardworking man. A cousin who knew my dad once said, it seemed he was always in a hurry - as if he knew his time on earth would be short and he needed to move quickly to get everything done. **This book is dedicated to my father, Henry E. Peavler.**

John Millet

John Millet Joined the Military service at Minneapolis, Minnesota on September 17, 1940. President Franklin Roosevelt signed a secret executive order on April 1, 1941, approving recruitment of volunteers from active-duty United States Military personnel to help with the defense of the Yunnan Province on the southwestern edge of China from Japanese bomber squadrons. One hundred pilots and two hundred ground crew, with support personnel, became known as the American Volunteer Group. On December 20, 1941, less than two weeks after Pearl Harbor, the AVG shot down four of ten Japanese bombers in the first Allied victory in Asia, for World War II. The P-40 aircraft noses were painted with a wide grin, flashing teeth and the evil eye of a tiger shark. Time magazine heralded the success of the "Flying Tigers", a nickname which stuck.

John Millet volunteered for the AVG and became one of the initial "Flying Tigers". He spent five years in China where he adopted a pet monkey named Riggs. For nineteen months he was a prime target for Japanese fighter planes while he worked in a fighter control station about three miles from the main base in Kweilin. The station consisted of a power generator and radio transmitter hidden in a cave, with the receiver in a separate cave about a hundred feet away. Forward observers sustained a lookout for approaching Japanese bombers and would pass the information to his location. He shared duties with another soldier working twenty-four-hour shifts, before being relieved by the other. When warned of a threat they would telephone the base via three miles of wire run through the jungle. A warning system, using large balls, was utilized to communicate the degree of alert. One large ball raised meant the Japanese planes were approximately 180 miles out; two balls meant 120 miles away. Three balls alert warned to take cover immediately. The fighter pilots scrambled and received further information from the fighter control station.

He received, from the Chinese people, a red silk scarf with his name embroidered on it, presented to him by Madame Chiang Kai-shek. Another of his prized possessions was an additional beautiful silk scarf, he won in a raffle at a banquet honoring the "Flying Tigers" during the war.

On completion of his service, he graduated from St. Thomas College in St. Paul, Minnesota with a degree in English. He taught High School English and Drama for three years before beginning his career in social work. He married his lifelong partner, Margaret Riley in 1947, and they raised ten children together. His fifth child, Helen, became my wife in 1978. Of all the times I had the opportunity to speak with him, very few occasions did we speak of his war experiences. When the subject was raised, he expressed how much he enjoyed the people of China. When asked specifically of his experiences during the war, he always answered, "war is hell". He was a renaissance man who enjoyed painting, reading, music, his church and his family.

This book is dedicated to my father-in-law John Millet.